I0779711

THE *Complete* COLLECTION

Fighting SERIES

Fighting for a Second Chance
Copyright © 2015 Nikki Ash
All rights reserved

Fighting for a Second Chance
Copyright © 2015 Nikki Ash
All rights reserved

Fighting for Your Touch
Copyright © 2017 Nikki Ash
All rights reserved

Fighting for Your Love
Copyright © 2017 Nikki Ash
All rights reserved

Cover and interior formatting by Juliana Cabrera, *Jersey Girl Design*

This book is a work of fiction. Names, characters, places, and incidents are the product of the author's imagination or are used fictitiously. Any resemblance to actual events, locales, or persons, living or dead, is coincidental.

In accordance with the U.S. Copyright Act of 1976, the scanning, uploading, and electronic sharing of any part of this book without the permission of the publisher constitute unlawful piracy and theft of the author's intellectual property. If you would like to use material from the book (other than for review purposes), prior written permission must be obtained by contacting the publisher at AuthorNikkiAsh@gmail.com. Thank you for your support of the author's rights.

Never stop fighting for love.

FIGHTING *for a* SECOND CHANCE

One

LIZ

Graduation Day

AS I SIT IN THE AUDITORIUM OF MY HIGH SCHOOL SURROUNDED by three hundred of my fellow classmates I've gone to school with my entire life, I look through the sea of maroon and white caps and gowns in search of her. I finally lock eyes with Kayla, the best friend a girl could ever ask for.

How we became best friends is anybody's guess since we're polar opposites in every way. While she has naturally blond hair that is long and pin straight, I have mousy-brown, wavy hair that spirals halfway down my back. She has striking blue eyes to my boring light brown. Her pale skin looks like she has never stepped foot on a beach despite living in Florida and surfing the waves her entire life. My skin is naturally a caramel brown even though I can't stand the beach in spite of living so close to it all my life.

Where Kayla is outgoing and always the life of the party, I'm soft spoken and reserved. We've both been cheerleaders for our local high school for the last four years, but I'm only one because Kayla begged me to try out and I gave in, afraid of losing my best friend to the popular crowd. She made team captain, so it was a given I would be on the squad as well.

I truly enjoy school, and while reading is my favorite pastime, Kayla spends her evenings partying it up and the mornings copying my notes.

When our eyes lock, I smile at her and she smirks back. Words don't have to be spoken to know what we're thinking. After being inseparable for the last thirteen years, we can practically read each other's minds without saying a word.

In about four more hours we'll be on our way to Miami Beach to party it up for the next seven days, courtesy of my parents as a graduation gift. Now, I'm far from a partier, but even I'm excited to spend a week in South Beach. I might be a bookworm, but I'm still a teenager.

The principal begins to call us up by last name and I'm one of the first people to step across the stage since my last name is Browning. As I walk across the stage, I hear Kayla holler my name at the top of her lungs. "Go Liz!" she yells. I also hear my parents and brother cheering me on.

I smile wide and stop at the end of the stage, so the photographer can snap my picture. I'm extremely excited to finally be done with high school and ready to begin my journey as a college student in a few short weeks at the University of Las Vegas. Kayla and I will be going to the same college and living together just off campus. I was accepted to ULV on a full academic scholarship to major in business and accounting. Yep, not only am I a book nerd, but I also love math and I'm really good with numbers. I have no idea what I want to do with the numbers yet, but I know I want to spend my days with them and my nights with a good book.

Kayla's parents are just so happy she's actually going to college, they've insisted on paying her tuition as well as our rent while we're there. She has no idea what she plans to study, but I don't think they care as long as she goes. Since my parents are so thankful to Kayla's for paying the rent since my scholarship doesn't cover room and board, they're paying for Kayla and me to go away for a week before we head to college.

I'm excited to do some shopping and lounge by the pool with my latest romance novel on my iPad. Kayla has bookmarked and sent me every hot spot imaginable she insists we must check out. That girl would seriously have us partying twenty-four hours a day if it were possible. I'm hoping she'll get completely partied out and pass out, allowing me to sneak out and do some serious reading by the pool. With the stress of finals behind me, I have too many books calling my name.

The principal announces Kayla's name and just about the entire auditorium of students cheer. I wasn't kidding when I said she is the life of the party. I don't think there's a single person here who isn't friends with her.

She walks across the stage and when she gets to the end, where the photographer is waiting, she raises her fist and yells, "Yeah, baby!"

Everybody can't help but laugh at her enthusiasm. When Kayla smiles and laughs, you have no choice but to join in.

What feels like several hours later, everybody's names have been called and the principal congratulates the graduating class. Throwing our caps high into the air, we all celebrate our freedom. We are officially high school graduates. I find Kayla, and we make our way to our parents who are waiting just outside the auditorium. After taking several pictures by ourselves, with each other, with our parents, and with our brothers, who are good friends and will be sophomores next year, we make our way to the exit to go out to dinner to celebrate.

"I can't believe my baby is all grown up! It feels like yesterday you girls were coming home from kindergarten and begging to go on your first playdate." My mom can't stop crying while we enjoy our Crème brûlée at our favorite Parisian restaurant downtown.

"Oh, Mom, stop," I mumble back. I swear she's cried more this week than I've ever seen her cry my entire life.

"But it's true! You're going to be so far away in Nevada. Promise me you'll come home and visit often. I'm so afraid you'll get over there and never come back."

I love my mom to death, but I think moving away will help me spread my wings. We're extremely close, but because of that, I always live in fear of not wanting to do anything to disappoint her, not that she would judge me in any way if I screwed up. My mom isn't like that—she has always been more of a friend than a mother. She had me at eighteen years old after my dad and her had been dating for four years. They met their freshman year in high school and it was instant love. I've personally never been in love, but I find it hard to believe one can fall in love with somebody they just met; however, I would never tell her that.

As soon as she found out she was pregnant with me, she decided to stay home and be a full-time mom instead of going to college. My dad worked nights delivering pizzas and went to college so he could get his degree in business. Immediately after graduating, he started his own business and still to this day runs a successful window cleaning company here in South Florida. We aren't rich by any means, but we have always had everything we could ever want or need.

After the business took off, my parents bought their first house in Jupiter, Florida right across from the beach, and that is where I met Kayla on our first day of kindergarten. Kayla, on the other hand, comes from an extremely wealthy family, but they're also the least loving family you'll ever meet. Kayla and her brother aren't really close. He is always getting into trouble, and Kayla's parents are rarely ever home.

Kayla and her brother have both practically grown up at my house and she's always saying she wishes her mom was more like mine. It seems like while Kayla's mom chose the career, my mom chose the family. I just don't understand why people feel like they have to choose one or the other.

I know my mom loves being home with my brother and me, but I also know she wishes she would have attended college before having us. She was so focused on raising us and helping my dad run his business, she never went to school. She always tells me to make sure I follow my dreams and passions. I think it's because she never got to follow her own.

Which leads me back to not wanting to disappoint my mom. I've been so focused on school these last four years to make sure I follow my dreams and passions, I haven't even so much as dated. I am looking forward to finally going out on some dates once we're up at ULV.

"I can't wait to leave tonight to Miami," Kayla whispers in my ear. "It's going to be so lit down there. So many clubs and parties going on. You better be ready to get your groove on, girly." I laugh as she shakes her ass in her seat. Kayla is forever looking forward to the next party.

"Yeah, yeah," is all I can come up with as a response. I have no idea how I'm going to make it seven days with Kayla in Miami partying it up. At least here in Jupiter she has to keep it tame since the town is small and boring to say the least.

We decide to drive Kayla's Volvo SUV down to Miami. It's a graduation gift from her parents and is really comfy. We get to the Miami Beach Resort, valet park the car, and check-in to our room. Looking around, Kayla and I grin at each other, thinking the same thing. *My parents did well.* The resort is literally right on the beach. I inhale deeply and can smell the ocean breeze coming off the waves. I may not like the sand between my toes or between other places, but I still appreciate the beautiful scenery. We walk to the back of the resort and see a beautiful pool surrounded by lounge chairs. Right behind the pool is a cute tiki-bar that separates the resort from the beach.

Once we get to the room, I slide the key card in and open the door. Immediately, we start squealing while throwing ourselves on to the white plush mattresses of our queen beds. Looking around, I notice our room is overlooking the ocean. The balcony hangs directly over the sand, and since we're ten floors up, I can see everything down below. The sun is starting to set and it's a gorgeous pinkish-orange. There hasn't been much rain the last few days and I hope it stays that way, but you just never know in Florida.

"Oh. My. God!" Kayla is still bouncing on her bed as I walk back in from the terrace and lie down next to her on her bed.

"Liz, your parents booked us an amazing room. I can't believe we get to spend seven days here, on the beach, at the pool, and it is literally right near every freaking club we're going to be checking out. Thank goodness I got us those fake IDs that say we're twenty-one. We're going to seriously have the best time before we have to go back to boring books and classes."

I stifle my laugh. Since when has Kayla ever let books and classes bring her down? Never. There is no stopping this girl and I'm sure once we're in Las Vegas, she'll be right back to being the life of the school. Although, if we get arrested for the fake IDs she had made, we may never make it to school.

"Ugh, Kayla. Do you really think it's wise to go to clubs that we shouldn't be in, right before our parents let us fly across the country to go to college? What if the bouncer realizes the IDs are fake and we get arrested? We will be so screwed. My mom will be so disappointed."

"Liz, stop! It's all good. They totally look like the real deal. Trust me, the guy I got them from assured me nobody would be able to tell the difference. Stop stressing over nothing. We're going to have an amazing time this week, then you can go back to your book-loving self next week once we're at ULV. I can't believe you decided to start classes this summer. There is no way I am stepping foot in a classroom until August."

Yes, I'm starting school this summer. I don't know what the big deal is. I can take three classes and get a head start. It's the smart thing to do. I didn't bust my butt the last four years in high school to screw up now.

"Okay, okay. So, Miss Miami, where to first?"

Giving me a look that says she's up to no good, Kayla says, "First we get changed. Then we part-ay!"

Two

LIZ

AS WE WALK UP TO ONE OF THE HOTTEST CLUBS IN MIAMI—according to Kayla—we immediately see the line going down the street and around the corner. There is no way we're going to get in there. Not even as hot as Kayla says we look. I look down at my dress, remembering earlier today when she surprised me with this outfit.

As we opened up our suitcases, I realized Kayla had been shopping without me. I should have expected this, as none of my clothes are up to club standards as she puts it. Of course, she had us both completely taken care of and wasn't taking no for an answer. When she pulled out the dress, I thought for sure it couldn't be for me because that dress didn't have enough material to be something I would wear. I was wrong. Between the dress, heels, makeup, and hair, I prayed we would both pass for twenty-one.

Once we make it to the end of the line, I look down at myself wondering what the heck I was thinking letting Kayla play dress up with me. Remember when I said Kayla and I are complete opposites? Well that extends to our body types as well. Kayla is wearing a silver sequin dress that is way too low up top and way too short below, but of course she looks hot. She's skinny but toned in all the right places thanks to her many years of surfing, and she has perfect size breasts that are spilling out of the top of her dress, which is completely formfitting and shows off her amazingly long legs that go on for days. She has topped off her outfit with matching silver fuck-me heels that have got to be at least five inches tall. I have no idea how she is even walking in them.

I, on the other hand, am curvy all over with large breasts, and while I'm not fat, I'm definitely on the thick side with an ass and hips. Kayla surprised me with a simple spaghetti strap black dress, telling me every woman needs a LBD (little black dress) for her first time in the club—it's apparently a rite-of-passage. Thankfully, she provided me with a pair of cute heels that aren't nearly the height of hers. My feet will definitely be thanking her later. Still looking down at myself, I must be frowning because Kayla immediately snaps me out of my own head.

"Stop overthinking the dress, Liz." She looks at me with one brow raised, giving me the *I know what I'm talking about* look that she always gives when I begin to doubt something she thinks is amazing.

"You look hot as hell! Every guy in here is going to want to dance with you. Maybe tonight you'll finally live a little and do the dirty-dirty with someone." She waggles her brows, and I can't help but laugh at her silly facial expression and the fact that she's referring to having sex as the dirty-dirty.

"I'm not going to lose my virginity to some strange guy here in Miami," I whisper-yell while looking around to make sure nobody overhears me in line. Yes, I'm still a virgin. I know, how cliché. The nerdy girl graduates from high school with a four-point-five grade-point-average and has never even been kissed by a guy.

While I spent the last several years focusing on school, Kayla spent them being a social butterfly, and that includes having plenty of casual sex she has no problem describing to me in full detail. Let's just say I've been living vicariously through Kayla the last few years.

Don't get me wrong, she isn't a slut by any means, but she's definitely had her fair share of guys in her bed when her parents are away on business. She has mentioned numerous times she doesn't want a relationship and makes sure to keep it strictly casual.

Unlike my stay-at-home mom, Kayla's parents are both attorneys for a large firm. According to Kayla, her parents' relationship is more of a business partnership than an actual marriage. Because of their demanding careers, they're rarely ever home, which means Kayla has plenty of time and opportunity to have fun. You know what they say, when the parents are away the kids will play. Hell, if it were possible, Kayla would major in playing.

Just as I begin to think we're going to be stuck in line all night, the bouncer comes walking up to us. He's huge. I'm talking muscles on top of muscles, and he's wearing shades even though it's dark outside. I'm going to assume it's a scare tactic, because otherwise, why would someone wear shades when there's no sun?

In a bored, flat tone he tells us one of the VIPs has invited us to join him. Looking around to make sure he's speaking to us, I begin to ask if he has the right girls, when Kayla immediately jumps in.

"Sounds fabulous!"

He walks us to the podium and puts wristbands on us after barely checking our IDs. He notifies somebody over his walkie-talkie to escort us to VIP, and Kayla is practically jumping out of her skin with excitement. Before we go in, she asks the bouncer to please thank whoever invited us in for the invitation.

"His name is Cooper and you can thank him yourself once you

get up to the VIP area." With that, he points us in the direction of the hallway and goes back to manning his post.

We're immediately hit with the pounding bass of David Guetta and Akon singing the lyrics to *Sexy Bitch*, and I can't help but sway my hips to the music as we walk toward the dance floor. Dancing is my guilty pleasure. We dance at the house parties our friends throw, but I love nothing more than to turn the music up in my room and get lost in the lyrics and rhythm.

The hostess attempts to show us where the VIP area is, but Kayla and I head right toward the gyrating bodies. On our way toward the center of the club, I take a second to look around and am enamored with the scene in front of me. To the left is a huge bar that wraps around the corner with the entire back wall full of mirrors, stacked with at least three levels of liquor. *I wonder how the bartenders get the liquor down.* Up ahead on the second floor is a huge deejay booth with a young guy spinning a turntable. Surrounding the dance floor are high-top tables for people to stand at with their drinks.

I look up and spot what must be the VIP section. My eyes trail to the ceiling to find strobe lights everywhere in various shades pulsing over all the bodies. It's all so mesmerizing. I can easily see how people can get addicted to the clubbing scene. This is nothing like the house parties we've been to throughout high school.

Watching the sweaty bodies rubbing up on one another has me getting this tingly feeling in my stomach. I know we should go thank whomever this Cooper guy is, but all I want to do is dance.

Kayla takes my hand and we move through the sea of hot bodies that are grinding one another to the center of the dance floor. She begins swaying her arms above her head to the rhythm of the song while moving her ass back and forth as I do the same. Locking her eyes with mine, she gives me her signature wink. We both turn around, facing away from each other, and as Akon sings about the girl's booty and not being able to take no more, she grinds her ass against mine while we continue to sway our hips and dance like nobody is watching. She turns back around and grinds her pelvis into my ass with one hand in the air and the other resting on my hip. I grind back while swaying both my arms above my head.

The song ends and the next one begins. The sound of Snoop Dog fills the club, along with The Pussycat Dolls as they begin to sing *Bottle Pop*. I crouch lower and begin to pop my ass out, loving this song. I feel Kayla's hand move from my waist, but I don't bother to turn around—I'm in my zone.

Suddenly, I feel hands on my hips once again. I'd assume they're Kayla's except the hands feel too large and too strong, holding me too tight to be her tiny hands. I feel the front of this person's body up against my ass and it confirms it's definitely not Kayla, as this body has a bulge in the front. As it rubs up on my ass, I can't help but softly moan at the feeling of this man's body rubbing up against mine. It just feels so good.

Angling my face, I see the most beautiful bright green eyes staring down at me while still holding his hands tightly on my waist. He's also sporting one hell of a smirk, as if he knows exactly what he's doing to my body. *I would bet my life this man is no virgin.* Because of how far I have to look up, I would say he has to be a good six foot three at least. Once he lets go of this pull he has on me, I'm able to look at his entire face, and it feels like my heart stops, then begins to beat again at a rapid pace.

His piercing green eyes aren't the only beautiful part of him. This man is downright gorgeous. He has golden-brown hair that is styled like he just got out of bed and ran his fingers through it, but it works. His skin is golden-brown like he's been in the sun recently. His nose is crooked, like it's been broken and wasn't set right, but it fits him and for some reason it makes him even hotter.

As I move my head down, I notice how big he is. Not big like fat, but big like built. He's not overly muscular like the bouncer, but fit. It's pure perfection. His shirt isn't tight, but it still accentuates his muscles. He's wearing a light blue button-down collared shirt with the sleeves rolled up, and as I run my eyes down his body, I can see the muscles in his forearms. I'm not a tiny girl, yet it feels like he dominates me as he stands over me, continuing to check me out.

His top teeth pull at his lower lip, releasing it, and his smirk gets even bigger while he raises a single brow. Oh yeah, he definitely knows what he's doing to me, and it doesn't help that he just watched me totally check him out while my ass is still rubbing against him.

I attempt to step forward, out of the line of his dick, but before I can, his hands grip my waist tighter as he pulls my ass closer to him. I don't know what it is about this guy, but I let it happen. Turning my head to face forward, I raise my arms up and continue to dance against him. We dance together for some time, our bodies rubbing against one another. I'm getting sweaty from the warm contact and the lights hitting down on us, and it feels good.

After a little while, his fingertips glide from the top of my arms, slowly trailing a path down the inside, toward the side of my body, stopping just under the curve of my breasts. His face is so close to my ear I can feel his breath on me. It smells like whiskey, making me want to suck on his tongue to see if I can taste it.

He whispers the lyrics into my ear, asking if it's true that I'm wet, and that is all it takes. My nipples pebble through my bra and dress, and I swear my panties are instantly soaked. This man is a walking billboard for sex. He continues to dance slowly and sensually against me, until the song ends and the next one transitions into the mix.

Once again, he whispers into my ear, calling my 'baby girl' and telling me he could dance with me all night. I know he's only repeating the lyrics, but it doesn't stop the butterflies from fluttering in my belly.

Taking me by my hand, he leads us off the dance floor. I look around for Kayla and see she's still dancing her ass off with a couple of cuties. She makes eye contact with me, grins, and gives me two thumbs up. I smile and look back at this sexy creature who's holding my hand and pulling me toward a set of steps.

The guard standing in front of them gives him a small nod and he raises his chin in response. As we begin to ascend the steps, I realize this must be the VIP area. I glance back at Kayla to make sure she sees where I am heading. We once again lock eyes, and I know she knows where I'm going, which makes me feel a lot better. I am completely out of my comfort zone right now. While this guy is sexy and makes my body tingle all over, I have no idea who he is. He can be an axe murderer for all I know.

Once we get up to the VIP area, I look around and take it all in. It's similar to the bottom floor, but definitely not as packed. There is a small dance floor in the main area with several booths surrounding the outside perimeter that are roped off so people can sit and relax.

As he drags me along the outside of the dance floor toward the booths, I'm able to check him out from the back, and let me tell you, his backside is as sexy as his front. He's wearing jeans that fit perfectly across his nice ass and has on dress shoes, which are clearly expensive. He's wearing a silver watch with a logo I've seen before but could never afford. Looking at his rolled-up sleeves, I spot a bit of tattoos peeking out. *What I would give to take a closer look at those tattoos.* He's dressed nice, yet still casual, as if he takes pride in how he dresses but isn't out to impress anybody.

When we finally come to a stop, there are several people hanging out. I count three large men similar to him—all of them good looking, dressed up, and full of tats as well. With each guy, there are at least two women—that I can tell right off the bat are out of my league—hanging on to each of them. These women are dressed to the nines in tight, sexy dresses, and have the sex appeal I could only dream about. My little black dress looks like something a nun would wear compared to what these women have on.

Spotting a couple of the women giving the guys lap dances, I wonder if they're getting paid, but then I really look at these guys and see how hot they are—there's no way they would need to pay any woman to dance for them. There are several bottles of liquor covering the table with tumblers and shot glasses all over. One of the guys—who has only one woman dancing on his lap while he grabs her ass with one hand and drinks something that looks like vodka from his other hand—sees us walking over and nods his head to the guy I'm with.

We approach the booth and one of the other guys pats the girls on their asses to move them out of the way so he can let my guy sit down. *Hmm…my guy? That has a nice sound to it.* What the heck am I thinking? I'm only here for seven days and this guy is way out of my league. I have college to focus on for the next four years. Sure, I would like to date, but something tells me this guy is nothing like the college guys I'll be meeting at ULV.

He wraps his arms around my waist and settles into the booth pulling me into his lap with him. I fall willingly and cuddle up close, crossing my legs the best I can so nobody gets a peak up my dress. He begins to nuzzle his face into my neck, and a shiver goes down my spine. He must feel it because he laughs softly. Moving my hair off of my neck, he presses his mouth against my sensitive skin where my shoulder meets my neck. I feel the soft brush of his cool lips against my warm skin, and I sigh outwardly. If my panties get any more drenched, I'm going to need to excuse myself to go remove them in the bathroom.

"Yo, Coop. How's it going?"

The guy who's lap I'm in pauses what he's doing to me to look up at the guy speaking to him. *Coop? Is that short for Cooper? Where have I heard that name before?* Holy Cow! This is the VIP guy… the special guest who invited us in.

Looking around at the women once again, I wonder why in the world he'd invite us up here when he already has women like them surrounding him. Maybe he invited Kayla up. She's pretty hot, but even she isn't at the same level as these girls, though I would never tell her that. As he goes to respond to his friend, I cut in, giving voice to my thoughts.

"Did you invite my friend Kayla up here?"

"Whose Kayla?" He looks at me with genuine confusion. God, he's so beautiful. A girl could easily get lost in this man.

"The girl the bouncer invited in by a VIP guy named Cooper."

"I don't know who Kayla is, but I did ask the bouncer to invite you, and whoever was with you, in. As I was getting out of my car, I saw you walking to the end of the line."

"Did you see my friend Kayla? She was in the silver dress. Are you sure you didn't mean to invite her in?"

He chuckles and moves his hand to my chin to bring my face closer. He smiles slightly and stares deep into my eyes. God, his eyes are hypnotizing. *Focus, Liz!*

"No, baby girl. I meant to invite you in. To be honest, I didn't even notice your friend, but she's more than welcome to join us up here. I thought you would come up here when you walked in, but when I saw you head straight for the dance floor, I realized if I wanted you with me, I'd have to come get you myself and I'm damn glad I did."

He situates me closer on his lap and pulls my legs up and over his thighs while keeping his arms around my waist, and then looks back at his friend.

"What's up, Kaden? Didn't see you here a little bit ago. Did you just get in?"

His friend nods, and they start talking about some fight they went to a few days ago. I attempt to listen to their conversation, but it's hard to concentrate, because while Cooper is talking, his fingers are rubbing across my stomach in a way that's giving me butterflies. He moves his other hand up to my face and pushes my hair from out of my eyes like it's the most natural thing in the world.

They stop talking and he looks back to me like he has something to say. His mouth opens then closes, and then he makes a face that has me falling into a fit of laughter.

"You're looking kind of confused. Are you trying to think hard about something?" I can't stop laughing. How is it possible that a man so sexy can also be absolutely adorable at the same time?

"I just realized I know your friend's name, but I don't know yours." His brows are furrowed and he's giving me the cutest pout with his bottom lip jutting out just a little bit. With this look alone, I bet he could a woman to do anything he wants.

"My name is Lizbeth, but everybody calls me Liz," I say, still grinning at his facial expression.

"Are you from around here, Liz?"

"Um, kind of. I live a little farther north, about two hours from here." I decide not to tell him exactly where in case he is an axe murderer after all, and I also don't mention the fact that after this week I'll be living in Las Vegas. It doesn't really matter at this point since I won't see him again after tonight.

"How long are you in Miami for?"

"My friend Kayla and I are here for week. We're staying right up the road at the Miami Beach Resort. It's a graduation present from my parents." I don't mention it's my high school graduation since I'm supposed to be twenty-one to be in this club, and if he knew I was only eighteen he might be completely turned off. I'm already in shock that he would want me when he could easily have his pick of women in this club.

While we continue to make conversation, the entire time he's touching me in some way—his hands caressing my arms, massaging circles into my thighs. They aren't meant to be sexual touches, but they still cause the same reaction from my body. He looks past me at somebody walking over and tells me that I have company. I look behind me and see Kayla is walking over and sporting a huge knowing grin across her face.

"Well, hello there handsome. I take it you're the nice gentleman that invited us up here."

"That would be me," he confirms. He moves his hand off my stomach to shake her hand, and I immediately miss his warmth.

"My name is Cooper and my friends here are Kaden…" He points over at a guy sitting nearby who he gives her a chin nod.

"Bentley." He points over to the guy who no longer has the two women giving him a lap dance, but is sitting by himself and staring right at my best friend like he wants to devour her.

"And the guy over there is Caleb." He points to the other guy who had gotten up to give Cooper his seat earlier.

He glances over at Kayla and back to me with a smile. "Guys, this is Liz and her friend Kayla. They're down here for the next week celebrating their graduation."

"Nice," Kaden shouts over the music since the song that is now playing has serious bass going on.

Bentley walks over to Kayla and asks her to dance and of course she says yes. As she is walking away with him, she turns around and gives me a huge, over exaggerated wink. I wouldn't be surprised if they're having sex by the end of the night. Hopefully they make it out of the club first.

"Would you like something to drink?" Cooper asks, pointing to all the bottles on the table. I probably shouldn't drink since I'm technically not twenty-one, but how ridiculous will I look not drinking at a club? After saying yes, he grabs the bottle to pour us each a shot then shoots his back. I follow his lead and shoot mine down quickly. It burns like a bitch the whole way down, and it takes everything in me not to cough.

Four shots later, and I'm definitely feeling more than good. Kayla has come back over with Bentley and is drinking right along with us.

We're currently dancing our asses off on the table to Beyoncé's remix of *Single Ladies* while taking another shot of whatever this yummy vodka stuff is. The other women are dancing with Kaden and a couple of other guys who have shown up during the last couple hours. Bentley and Cooper are sitting in the booth below us laughing while they continue to drink.

Every time I look down at him, I catch him staring at me with what I think is lust in his eyes. The song ends and Cooper stands to help me off the table while Bentley helps Kayla. I realize just how drunk I am, when the room starts to spin.

When everybody decides to head out, I know I have a decision to make. Do I have sex with Cooper tonight? Kayla has clearly made her decision but still asks me if it is okay since it means I'll be going back to the room by myself. I am not about to pussy-block my best friend, so of course I tell her to go. We're eighteen and heading off to college. We're not babies anymore, and if she wants to hook up with Bentley that's up to her. Since she's going back to Bentley's room, they tell me they can drop me back off at our room on their way.

Cooper texts somebody, and it must've been to let his driver know he's ready to go, because when we walk out to the front his expensive and shiny SUV is waiting for us. We all pile in and he gives the driver the name of the resort I'm staying at.

The entire car ride he sits with his hand in my lap, his fingers rubbing over my knuckles. When I look at him, his lips curl into a small smile. He takes my chin in his hand and places soft kisses all over my face. I try to focus, but his lips brushing across my temple, my cheek, the corner of my mouth are distracting me.

I'm still attempting to debate whether I should invite him up, when the SUV pulls up. He tells his driver he's going to walk me to my room and helps me out of the vehicle. Kayla gives me a smile when I turn around and hug her goodbye, whispering in her ear to be careful.

We get to my room and I twirl around, coming face to face with Cooper. I'm now up against the door and he's using his palms to hold himself up and over me. I glance up at him, wanting to invite him in, but knowing I'm too drunk to want to sleep with him. I really want my first time to be memorable and I can't imagine remembering any of this after all of those vodka shots.

Cooper looks into my eyes and, with the next words he speaks, makes the decision for me. "If I come in, it would only be to sleep next to you. You have drunk too much for us to do anything else. When I take you, I want you to be clear headed and remember everything my body makes yours feel."

Unsure of how to even respond, I simply nod. He pulls out his cell phone and texts something to someone, probably to his driver, letting him know to go ahead.

We enter the room and I excuse myself to rinse off and change into my pajamas. I brush my teeth and blow dry my hair so it's not soaking wet. As I exit the bathroom, I see him lying in my bed in nothing but his boxers and holy Jesus does he look hot. For a second, I'm frozen in my place, but I quickly gather myself and walk toward the bed to join him.

"Hope this is okay. I didn't plan to spend the night out, so I don't have any clothes to change into."

"No, I mean, yeah, that's cool," I say, trying not to sound like the inexperienced teenager I am and pray he doesn't notice.

I walk around to the empty side of the bed and climb in, wondering if he can tell this will be my first time sleeping with a guy. I can only imagine how many women he has slept with. I shake off the thought because it really doesn't matter.

Not quite sure how I am supposed to lie down, I awkwardly roll onto my side away from him. He doesn't seem to notice how nervous I am as he pulls me closer, spooning me from behind.

"Are you tired?" he asks softly.

Being wrapped tightly in this man's arms makes me feel protected. I can feel his bulge again through our clothes and I know he's turned on. I feel my cheeks heat up. Thank goodness, it's dark in here and I'm facing away from him or my blush would give away just how inexperienced I am.

"I'm exhausted but feel energized at the same time. I want to go to sleep but feel like I could stay awake all night. It must be the alcohol."

He laughs softly into my hair. "What do you usually do when you can't fall asleep?"

"Okay, don't laugh at me. I usually count."

"Count?"

"You know…sheep or pigs or some other farm animal until I pass out."

He closes his arms around me, kisses me softly on my temple, and begins to count.

"One sheep, two sheep, three sheep, four sheep…"

I can't help but laugh at this man counting sheep to help me fall asleep. My body relaxes and eventually I hear Cooper whisper in my ear, "Goodnight, Liz."

Falling asleep in this man's arms feels better than I could have ever imagined. I never thought I could feel so safe and wanted by a man to the point I feel choked up and can't even respond. With his soft breathing in my ear, I let sleep overtake me.

Three

COOPER

I WAKE UP AND LOOK AROUND, TRYING TO REMEMBER WHERE I am. I feel warm skin under me and I look down at her. I can't help but smile at her rare innocence. She was so adorable last night when we got back to her room. I doubt at her age she's a virgin, but she's definitely inexperienced. I'm not a manwhore by any means, but I've definitely had my fair share of women in my bed. What red-blooded twenty-two-year-old male hasn't?

My mind goes back to when I first saw her walking to the end of the line at the club. I knew I had to have her in my arms. The way she smiled shyly made me want her to smile like that at me. I didn't even notice who she was smiling at because I couldn't take my eyes off her. The way her beautiful curves shown through the tight yet modest little black number she had on, leaving everything yet nothing to the imagination. It was a tug-of-war between sexy and innocent. She doesn't even realize how banging her body is.

When I watched her dance—the way she moved like she has no idea how fucking sexy everything about her is—was a complete turn on. And when I got closer and her brown eyes connected with mine, I knew I was done for. I would give this girl anything she wanted. I wasn't looking for love. Only here for a UFC conference for a few more days, I was just looking for a hook-up, someone to help me forget about all the stress of my real life, but this girl could never be a simple fuck. She's meant to be cherished, adored, and loved completely, something I'm not capable of. It isn't in my DNA.

I glance back down at her and she's still snoring softly with her backside rubbing up against my dick. I groan at the feel of her perfect ass up against me and reluctantly get up to take a piss.

While in the bathroom, I decide a quick shower is necessary. Afterward I put back on my clothes from last night because I don't have any other clothes with me, and if I don't put something more on

I'm going to be tempted to take hers off. The truth is I never stay the night with a female. Staying leads to commitment, and commitment isn't something I'll ever be able to give a woman, and I don't want to lead anyone on.

Since she's still sleeping, I order room service for breakfast. Unsure of what she eats, I order a little of everything and give them my credit card to cover the bill.

I pull out my phone and check for any messages. There are a few texts from Kaden reminding me of when our flight leaves and asking if I got laid. I ignore those. There's one from my mom congratulating me on my win. *A little late mom, that was almost a week ago.* She's probably drinking again. The last text is from my dad, asking if we need anyone to come by to help with the move. I text him back to let him know it's all taken care of and I'll see him in a couple days at the new training center. Just thinking about my dad puts me in a foul mood.

I shake off the aggravation I feel brewing from just the little contact I had with him and put my phone back into my pocket. I notice Liz starting to stir awake as she begins to stretch her legs and pull her arms over her head. The sheet that was wrapped around her entire body starts to move downward.

By the way, she's totally a bed and sheet hogger.

Under the sheets, she's wearing a cute, light pink tank top with her nipples poking through the thin material and tiny, cotton polka dotted matching shorts. Everything about her screams innocence. Her eyes come into focus and after a second, a small, shy smile spreads across her face. I'd like to think she's remembering last night.

"I ordered us breakfast. It should be here any minute."

"Oh, thank you."

She gets up to use the bathroom and, while she's in there, the food arrives. After the guy wheels it inside, and I give him a tip, I grab the various plates and move it all onto the outside terrace so we can eat and enjoy the Miami ocean breeze.

We enjoy breakfast in companionable silence. It's insane how comfortable I am around this girl, like I could just stay here in this fake cocoon forever with her. I can't remember a time I felt like this around a woman. Usually, I'm out the door before the sun comes up. I only have until tomorrow, but I think I would really enjoy spending some more time with her. I decide to bring it up, figuring the worst she says is no.

"I was wondering..." At the same time, she says, "Do you think..."

We both look at each other and laugh.

Like I said, it's just so damn comfortable with her.

"Go ahead, you first," she says, the corner of her lips quirking into a half-smile.

"I was wondering if you might want to spend the day with me. My flight leaves early tomorrow morning, but I'd love to spend what time I have left here with you."

Her face falters for a split second, and if I weren't staring at her, I wouldn't have even noticed. She immediately catches it, though, and gives me a wide smile.

"Yes, I'd love to spend today with you."

I'm not sure if her fallen smile was because she's unsure about wanting to spend the day with me, or because I said I'm leaving tomorrow. I'm obviously hoping for the latter, but either way she's on board for spending the day with me, so I'll take it.

In another lifetime, this would be the start of something new and beautiful, but this girl is just starting out in life. Having just graduated, she has her whole life ahead of her, and she definitely doesn't need to be bogged down by the drama that is my life. From the little I know of her, I can already tell she's the whole package and deserves the whole *happily ever after* bullshit all women want.

I can't give her the happily ever after, but I can give her today. When we part ways, I'll be moving forward toward advancing my pro career as a UFC fighter in Vegas, and Liz will have the entire world at her fingertips. With the grueling training days ahead, there's no room for anything but fighting. I have worked my entire life to get here and, with all these recent wins under my belt, I can finally see the light.

Fighting is all I have.

When I leave here, I'll be going back into the devil's lair. I spent the last four years away, but in order to advance my career, I've finally come to my senses and made a deal with the devil himself. My dad might as well not even be my dad. He's the owner of one of the most elite UFC training facilities and has decided to open one up in Las Vegas. I've been training at a smaller facility in Colorado for the last few years, but now, with my recent wins, my current trainer isn't pushing me the way I need him to, and that's where my dad comes in. Kaden is a huge trainer at one of my dad's gyms and my best friend.

My dad has transferred Kaden to the Las Vegas location and I will be moving to Vegas to train at my dad's facility with him. Bentley and Caleb have decided to make the move as well. I know it is the right move but the thought of being this close to my parents again is making me sick to my stomach.

In my dad's eyes, I am just a fighter that can potentially make money now that I have proven myself. My mom has been drunk since my dad caught her cheating and left her ten years ago. My dad was a fighter back in the day and rarely ever home. Since the day, he caught my mom cheating, he has drilled it into my head that fighters shouldn't be in relationships and they definitely shouldn't be married.

According to him, you can't have both and be successful. Fighting isn't a nine-to-five job. Some days I'm in the gym for thirteen to fourteen hours, whether it's to workout, train, or just to watch fights and learn about my opponent. I go home to eat and sleep, and then I'm back at it again the next day. Watching what my parents went through years ago, I'll never put a woman or myself in that position.

"So, what are you in Miami for?"

Her question breaks me out of my thoughts. I look at her and realize she has no idea who I am. I'm not in the top ranking in my weight class yet, but since my wins recently and the fact that I'm undefeated, people are starting to notice me when I'm out in public. Women are definitely starting to notice me. It's nice to be around a girl who doesn't just want me because I'm a fighter.

"I'm here for work." I tell her vaguely in hope that she won't ask any more questions. She seems content with that answer, so I quickly change the subject.

"You mentioned you graduated. What's next for you?"

She thinks for a moment and replies just as vaguely.

"Kayla and I are moving in together."

We finish up our breakfast and decide to start our day at the pool. While she's changing into her suit, I run downstairs to the resort shop to purchase one.

When I get to the resort shop, I notice the cutest stuffed animals for sale that remind me of her counting sheep. None of them are farm animals, but there are a few I think Liz might like. I grab one, along with a swimsuit, and head to check out.

When I get back up to the room, I knock since I don't have a key and she answers the door in her bright blue two-piece polka dotted bikini that instantly has me hard. *What is with this girl and polka dots and why the hell do they turn me on so much?* I knew she had a hot body in that dress last night, but now that it's all on display I'm speechless.

After running my eyes over her body for the second time, I finally speak up so she doesn't think I'm nuts just standing here staring at her.

"God damn, Liz. Are you sure you want to go to the pool in that? I hear skin cancer is on the rise. Maybe we should stay inside. I can think of a better use of our time in this room where the UV rays won't kill us," I choke out, while trying to adjust myself without making it look obvious.

It takes her a second to catch the meaning behind my words and then she starts to laugh, and not just any laugh. No, she's practically doubled over with tears rolling down her cheeks.

I didn't think it was that funny. I was just trying to save her life… and my dick from remaining painfully hard all day.

"You're silly. Go get changed and we'll head down to the pool. I hate the beach." See. Fucking innocent.

"Wait a second." I hand her the stuffed animal. "I saw this and thought of you. Something to remember our time together by."

She stares at the flamingo. "Um, okay, you're going to have to explain."

"It's a flamingo. You said you count animals. So, the next time you can't sleep, you can count flamingos and think of me."

Her smile widens as she hugs the flamingo close to her and proceeds to give me a kiss on the cheek.

"Thank you, Coop."

As I get changed in the bathroom, I almost consider taking a quick cold shower, but she knows I already took one earlier, and I really don't want to have to explain that.

Four

LIZ

WE GET DOWN TO THE POOL AREA AND LUCKILY IT'S NOT TOO packed. We find two lounge chairs side by side and lie down next to each other. I didn't even think I would see Cooper after last night and now I'm spending the entire day with him. He didn't mention anything about tonight but, I'm hoping he'll spend the night again.

Last night I had way too much to drink and he was so sweet not to take advantage, but today I have no intention of getting drunk, and I'm not planning on leaving here a virgin. I know Cooper isn't my forever, but like Kayla says, *There is nothing wrong with having a damn good for-now.*

We spend the day lounging by the pool, and I can't get over how delicious Cooper is in his bathing suit. He is amazingly fit. The way his suit hangs down just right, exposing that perfect V in a way I thought was only found on guys in my romance books, makes me want to attack him right here. Whatever he does for a living must involve him staying in shape which makes sense because he did mention he works an obscene number of hours leaving him barely any time for a social life.

We order drinks by the pool: he orders Jack and coke and I order those cute fruity frozen drinks with the umbrellas in them to keep me hydrated. They're so yummy, I doubt they have much alcohol in them.

I'm watching Cooper swim laps in the pool while I'm reading my latest romance novel, when he comes over to the edge and splashes me just a little.

"Hey! Watch out for my iPad. If it gets ruined, it will be the death of you as well," I say jokingly as I turn it off and put it back into my beach bag.

My phone goes off and I check it to see if it's Kayla. It is, and she's confirming that she's spending the day with Kaden and Bentley and will see me later. I type back a quick okay and then join Cooper in the pool.

Putting one foot into the water, a chill runs up my leg from the water being freezing cold. I thought it would be warm in Miami in the middle of May. This is exactly why I stay away from the water. Cooper laughs and explains a huge rainstorm came through recently, which caused the pools and oceans to get colder.

He grabs a hold of me by my waist and pulls me into the water, holding me close. I use him as my human buoy to hold myself up. My legs are wrapped around him as we float lazily in the water. His hands gently massage circles on my ass as he holds me close to him, nuzzling his face into my neck. I'm so relaxed in his arms I almost start to drift off when I can feel the same bulge from last night push between my legs.

Needing a distraction, I ask, "What's your favorite color?"

He looks at me like I'm crazy but then responds. "Um, if I had to pick I would say black, I guess."

"Black isn't a color, silly. It's a shade."

He chuckles at my fact. "Well, then black is my favorite shade."

I let him keep his answer and ask another question.

"What's your favorite food?"

He thinks for a moment and responds with a bit of a frown. "Definitely my mom's lasagna when she used to cook."

I get stuck on the part about his mom but choose to leave it alone. I've noticed he doesn't like to talk about his parents or his life outside of right here and now.

"Yum, lasagna is good. What's your favorite movie?"

He stills his hands from rubbing on my ass and gives me a smirk. "Are we playing twenty questions? Because if we are, I'm pretty sure it's supposed to work both ways."

"I'm just trying to get to know you. My favorite color is pink and my favorite food is Crème brûlée. Now what's your favorite movie?"

He gives me a soft kiss to my lips, one that I hope will continue but ends too quickly. "*Batman.* My favorite movie is *Batman.* I could watch it every day."

I laugh at that.

"What's so funny?"

"Nothing." I shrug. "Just imagining a grown man watching *Batman.*"

"Hey, now! Have you seen *Batman*? *Batman* is not just for kids. He's a grown man himself who saves Gotham from all the bad guys."

I laugh even harder. "Okay, okay. It's a grown man movie, and no, I haven't seen it."

"You've never seen it? Then you don't get to judge."

"Ha ha! Okay, Coop. I'll take your word for it. What do you like to do in your free time?"

"Wait, first, tell me what your favorite movie is."

"Okay, don't make fun of me, but *Love and Basketball.*"

"So, you like basketball?"

Oh boy, he's totally going to make fun of me. "No, I just love how the girl is so strong, and how over years, through all their crap, they love each other. And in the end, even though the ends were against them, they end up together. Okay, now tell me what you do in your free time."

He doesn't even think about it when he says, "Work out. I love to work out and do MMA."

"What's MMA?"

"Mixed Martial Arts."

"Oh! Like *The Karate Kid*?"

He bursts out laughing. "So, you've seen *The Karate Kid* but not *Batman*? Yes, like that movie, I guess. What do you enjoy doing?"

I have to think about this because I don't want him to realize I'm an eighteen-year-old, recent high school graduate, with no job. I decide to just be honest but vague. "I enjoy reading, but books can be expensive, so when I find a book I really like, I usually read it several times."

"That's commitment right there," he says with mock seriousness.

"Oh hush!" I move out of his arms, getting just far enough away to splash him with the water. His face is drenched and the water is dripping down his hair. Cooper's gaze heats with intensity, causing me to back up a little more. I'm not sure what he's going to do, so I wait in anticipation. As soon as the words "*it's on*" leave his mouth, I take off, but before I can even swim two feet away, he jumps at me and grabs me by the waist, spinning me around. I close my eyes tight so when the chlorine hits me it won't burn my eyes, but no water comes.

Suddenly, I feel his lips on mine, but once again, he pulls away quickly, leaving me with nothing more than a tease. It can barely count as a kiss, but it makes me want more.

Several hours, questions, and drinks later, and I'm beat to death by the sun and ready to go back up to the room. Cooper agrees, and we head back up. When we get inside, I start to head to the bathroom to change out of my bathing suit and rinse the greasy sunscreen off my body when Cooper stops me. He rubs his hand down my arm and looks into my eyes like he's dehydrated and needs me to personally rehydrate him. He moves toward me, closing the distance between us as his lips crash into mine. I gasp softly into his mouth because *holy shit!* I'm finally going to experience my first real kiss.

First softly, then more roughly, our mouths move against each other. His tongue glides across my lips seeking entrance and I willingly open them to allow him access. His mouth tastes similar to what it did last night, sweet with a hint of spice. It must be the Jack he keeps ordering. His hands rub up and down my arms smoothly causing goose bumps to rise across my skin. My hands wrap around his neck and then move further up to grab ahold of his hair as I continue to kiss him back. He groans softly and tugs my body closer to his but stops the kiss way too soon.

"Let's take a shower," he whispers into my ear. Before I can answer, he's grabbing my hand and pulling me into the bathroom. He turns the handle for the water and gets in with his bathing suit still on. I know he is doing this for my benefit, not sure where I stand in this situation, and that makes me want him that much more. He puts his hand out to take mine and I follow him in, still in my bathing suit as well.

The water is warm and feels good against my sun-kissed skin. I turn around to face away from the water and allow it to massage my body. When I open my eyes, Cooper is towering over me, giving me a heated look that tells me exactly what he wants from me.

He grabs the soap from the sidebar and squirts some into his hand, turns me around, and begins to rub it onto my shoulders and down my arms, untying the top string around my neck. It causes me to shiver and he stops, turning my head to face him. He gives me a look with one brow up, silently asking *is this okay?* Unable to find my voice, I nod eagerly.

He continues to rub the body wash all over my body. When he gets to my back, I can feel him untie my last bathing suit string, causing my top to fall to the floor of the shower.

He moves his hands toward my front and begins to rub circles around my nipples, palming my breasts. The stimulating sense I feel from his touch causes me to let out a whimper.

He takes my noises as a cue to continue, slowly sliding my bikini bottom down my thighs as I lift each foot up just enough for him to remove it as it joins my top on the floor.

His hands go back to massaging my breasts and it feels unbelievable. He squeezes more soap out of the bottle and begins to soap up my entire body, moving to my stomach and then to my mound. *Thank god Kayla made me get a full Brazilian before we left.* I think he's going to stop there, but he keeps going.

He soaps up my thighs, and when he gets to my feet, he lifts my foot up and kisses the insole. If he's trying to drive me crazy with want, it's working. He moves back up the inside of my thigh until he reaches the apex between my legs. I can't take my eyes off him as he pulls my pussy lips apart with his fingers, then inserts one into me. I moan quietly at the fullness I feel. *Why in the world did I ever wait so long to be touched by a guy?*

"Damn, baby, you're so tight," he says, pushing his finger in and out of me.

I should tell him I'm a virgin, but I don't want him to stop. Kayla told me she barely bled her first time, so if we have sex in the shower hopefully he'll never know. Plus, I got on the pill a few days before we left, so I'm covered.

He inserts another digit into me, and even in the shower, I can feel how wet I am around his fingers. He pumps in and out of me, causing my body to tremble at his touch. His other hand reaches up and starts pulling and tugging on my nipples. His fingers are bringing me to the edge of insanity and I don't know what to do.

His fingers begin to move faster, delving deeper, and suddenly they hit a spot deep inside of me that causes me to clench. My climax is building, and my body is shaking with the need to release. "Let go, baby girl. Come for me." When I hear those words from him, I have no choice but to let go as the most intense orgasm I've ever felt overtakes me. The ones I've given myself are nothing in comparison to what I'm feeling now.

With a beautiful smile on his lips, Cooper moves the sopping wet hair from my face. His list filled eyes lock with mine and then his mouth crashes against mine. This kiss is different from the first one. This one screams of want and desire. His tongue finds mine, and they move in a rhythmic motion, swirling around each other. It reminds me of how close we danced together last night. Every part of me just fits with every part of him.

As I come down from my orgasm, he removes his fingers and I immediately want them back in me. He sees my face turn to a pout and he kisses it away before he takes the fingers he just had in me and puts them into his mouth. *Holy shit!* My vagina pulses as I watch him lick my essence from his fingers.

"You taste damn good. I'm going to need to taste some more of this soon."

When he removes his fingers, my eyes stay glued to his mouth. It's then I realize he's removing his bathing suit. I watch as he unties the drawstring that holds them up and pushes his shorts down, exposing his long thick dick. He continues to push the shorts farther down and then steps out of them, dropping them on to the floor on top of my bathing suit pieces.

My eyes move back to his hard length as he takes it in his hand and begins to stroke it a few times, never losing eye contact with me. I know it sounds crazy, but I'm seriously wondering how in the world that thing is going to fit inside me.

He must sense my nervousness because he lets go of his dick and moves closer to me, gripping my chin so I'm looking right into his beautiful green eyes. Keeping eye contact with me, he whispers, "Wrap your arms around my neck, baby."

I do as he says. Then he grabs my ass in his hands and lifts me against the shower wall. It's cool against my back but feels good against my overheated flesh.

"I plan to take you in the bed, but right now I can't wait to have you. Are you on birth control? I'm clean."

He continues to look into my eyes, searching for what, I don't know. This is where I should tell him I'm a virgin, but instead I simply murmur, "I'm clean and on the pill."

As soon as he hears those words, without any barriers between us, he presses the head of his dick to my entrance and, in one fluid motion, buries himself inside me. At first, I feel a burning sensation as he rips through my virginity, but after a few minutes, it begins to feel good. *Damn good.*

I hold onto his hair with my arms around his neck as he moves in and out of me. His hands are holding my ass cheeks tightly as he pulls his dick out slowly, then pushes it back in with more force.

"Fuck, Liz. You're so tight. It's like you're choking my cock." He pulls out and then thrusts back in. "Fuck, I don't know how long I'm going to last. It's never felt this way."

My orgasm builds higher, until it's teetering on the edge, as Cooper fucks me with abandon.

"C'mon, baby, give it to me one more time," he growls.

All too soon, my orgasm slams into me. My walls clench around his dick, and he pumps into me relentlessly, chasing his own release. My head smacks against the shower wall, but I don't even care. If I die from a concussion from this, I'll die a very happy girl.

His mouth moves to my neck, sucking hard like he needs an outlet to release all his built-up tension. His thrusts get choppier and his cock begins to swell inside of me as his hands and legs shake from the intensity of his orgasm.

He comes to a complete stop, breathing heavily, and moves his face from out of my neck, giving me a small smile as he carefully sets me on my feet. I'm pretty sure this man just ruined me for every guy whose to come in the future. After we finish washing ourselves, we venture out of the bathroom in our plush towels.

After we get comfy in my bed, he orders room service for dinner, and we watch some television. As we lie together, he rubs up and down my arms absentmindedly. I don't even think he realizes he's doing it. It's like he has to be touching me in some way at all times. As he watches some sports game, I take the opportunity to try to burn every beautiful feature of him into my brain for later, which makes me want him all over again. If tonight is all I get, I need to make it count.

When I start moving down the bed, Cooper looks over at me with a confused expression across his face, but I don't say anything, letting my actions speak for themselves. I get down to the bottom of the bed and pull the sheets off him and staring right at me is his big beautiful dick.

I'm not sure if a dick is supposed to be called beautiful, and I've never seen one until today, but looking at it up close, I have to say Cooper has one mighty fine looking dick.

He stares down at me, wondering what I am doing, probably wondering why I'm staring at his dick. Taking his hard length into my hands, I stroke it up and down. It feels soft like velvet yet rough. I can't believe this was in me a little while ago. I kiss the tip of the crown, feeling the smoothness of it across my lips. I look back up, and his brows are raised, but he still hasn't moved a muscle. I wonder if he realizes this is my first time touching one.

I lick my lips in anticipation before putting the head of his dick between my lips once again. I swirl my tongue over the tip, tasting the little bit of precum that surfaces. I do it once again and Cooper groans out loud. Knowing that I'm causing this reaction from him spurs me on.

I go up higher onto my knees and place my mouth over the entire length and slide it down to the back of my throat, coating it with my saliva. I begin to bob my head up and down, stopping at the top to swirl my tongue around the head.

Cooper takes my hair and moves it out of my way, gripping hold of it tightly, while I continue to deep throat him. Down, up, swirl. Down, up, swirl. I can feel his body begin to tense and feel his grip on my hair go even tighter. The way his dick swells, tells me he's getting close to his release, so I start going faster, taking him as deep as I can go.

He tries to pull my head off him, but I figure if I'm going to do this I might as well fully commit. I keep going, and if it's even possible his dick gets harder and thicker, and within a few seconds I can feel the warm, salty, liquid shoot into my mouth and coat my throat. He groans my name as I continue to suck and lick him through his orgasm, swallowing it all down.

When he's done, I look up at him, hoping it was good for him. His wide smile is confirmation enough that my first blowjob was a success. I get up to wash my mouth out and come back to bed to cuddle with him. I hate that when tomorrow comes this will be the ending, when in another lifetime this would be the beginning.

The food arrives, and after Cooper takes the cart from the guy, he brings it all into the bed.

"I want some of your burger." Cooper goes to grab a piece and I give him a look that says he's crazy. He pouts and I laugh, figuring it will be funny to tease him with my juicy burger.

"Mmm…I bet it's going to be delicious. Maybe you shouldn't have ordered a salad."

I take a huge bite of my double bacon cheeseburger, all the condiments packed inside of it dripping down my face. Of course, he starts laughing at me.

"I don't think your mouth can handle all that. You need to share with me." He swipes his finger up the side of my mouth, removing the mess I've created and puts it into his mouth.

"I handled you just fine, didn't I?"

"Damn right you did. Now share some of that burger with me." I give in and bring the burger to his mouth, allowing him to take a bite.

Once we're finished eating—and Cooper has finished eating almost half my burger—he grabs the empty trays, puts them on the cart, and rolls it outside the door before climbing back into bed. As he gets situated, I'm able to sneak a closer look at his tattoos since he isn't wearing a shirt.

I notice the tattoo on his arm is of a huge dragon that begins at the top of his shoulder and covers his entire arm with the tail extending to his forearm. There's writing in the tail, but I can't make out what it says.

Cooper notices me staring and gives me a wink, moving closer to me. "The dragon symbolizes strength." He points to the dragon. "And him breathing fire symbolizes me breaking free from my parents' constraints. I got it a few years after my parents split up and shit got bad. I was working with my dad and ended up leaving to go work on my own. I'm heading back home to work with him again and have no idea how I'm going to deal with him. In the tail, it says, 'I breathe in my courage and exhale my fear.' It's to remind myself that I'm strong enough to stand up to him and be my own person."

"It's beautiful," I whisper without realizing I'm running my fingertips along the words of the quote he just read to me. I can feel goose bumps rise up, and I look at him and see he's staring at me like he's about to devour me. His look of want causes my lady parts to tingle and I instinctively tighten my thighs to seek relief. He leans forward and begins to kiss me with such passion it's as if he's making love to my mouth. His lips mold to mine, his tongue battling with my own, and it's official, Cooper has ruined me.

We make love a few more times throughout the night, until I once again fall sleep with his body wrapped around mine, wishing tonight would never have to end.

I wake up to the door unlocking and then opening and realize the space next to me is empty. The clock reads five in the morning. Kayla is tiptoeing into the room in a shirt and cotton shorts that reads Miami, Florida. She must've bought them from one of the tourist shops. She has her dress and heels in her arms, and I can tell she's trying not to wake me.

When she looks over at me and sees I'm awake, she giggles and lies down in her bed, patting the spot next to her for me to join her. I get up to crawl across the bed when I feel the crinkling sound of paper. I look down at it and see my name scribbled along the top. The only person it could be from is Cooper, and my stomach falls at the realization that it's a goodbye note. I knew this was coming, but I didn't realize how much it would hurt.

> Liz, I had to catch an early fight and I didn't want to wake you. You looked so peaceful lying in bed wrapped up in my arms. I wish I could hold you like that forever. Thank you for the most amazing thirty hours of my life. I will never forget them and will probably fantasize about them for years to come ;) Stay sweet, baby girl.
>
> - Coop

I take the note with me over to Kayla's bed so she can read it. "Do you regret sleeping with him?" she asks after reading the letter.

"No, it was perfect. I knew going into this it would be a one-night stand, or a thirty-hour stand as he put it. We're just starting college and I'm not about to try to start a relationship with somebody right now. Did you get Bentley's number?"

"Nope, we had fun but agreed what happens in Miami, stays in Miami. Let's get some sleep and enjoy the rest of our week. And don't think I'm letting you off the hook. After I get some shut-eye, you'll be giving me all the details."

"Yeah, yeah." I laugh, and we curl back up into the sheets and fall asleep. My thirty hours with Cooper were amazing and I'll never forget our short time together.

My first day without Cooper is a bit depressing. I can't stop thinking about him and Kayla seems a bit down as well. She hasn't really said what happened with Bentley, but I think—like Cooper did to me—he took with him a little piece of her heart.

Kayla and I spend the day lounging by the pool. She's listening to music while I'm reading my book. Then, by the late afternoon, we decide to go back up to our room to shower before getting a bite to eat. When we walk inside our room, I see a thin white rectangular box wrapped in pink ribbon on my bed.

Kayla gets excited and tells me to hurry up and open it. When I pick it up, there's no card stating who it's from. I pull the ribbon off, and when I open the box, I don't know whether to laugh or cry.

"What is it? I'm dying over here," Kayla says, coming closer to see what I'm looking at.

"It's gift cards to Barnes and Noble, Amazon, and iTunes."

Kayla cocks her head to the side, her eyebrows shooting up. "Um, okay. Am I missing something here? Why do you look like you're about to cry over them? And who sent them?"

I take the gift cards out and find a small piece of paper with typed words.

I wasn't sure where you get your books. Whenever you buy a new book, think of me. - coop

"I made him play twenty questions to get to know him and told him I love to read but that I don't always have the money to buy new books, so I reread my favorites."

Kayla's eyes go glossy at my explanation. "Oh, Liz. That is so romantic."

"Yeah, it is. Too bad I can never thank him."

The next day Kayla and I check out some of the sites in Miami. We take a taxi to the art district and check out the graffiti walls while having lunch at a delicious Cuban restaurant. When we get back there's another box on my bed.

"Get the hell out of here!" Kayla shouts when she spots it at the same time I do.

I open the box and this time inside is the entire collection of *Batman* movies. I burst out laughing and look for a note. Sure enough, there's another one.

For your viewing pleasure. Only once you watch all of these can you judge Batman. - coop

Kayla reads it silently over my shoulder. "Another twenty questions fact?"

"Yeah, it's his favorite movie."

"Did you by any chance tell him you love huge houses and expensive cars?" Kayla jokes and we both burst into a fit of giggles.

Day three post-Cooper and I haven't received a package yet. I wonder how he is doing all this. If he is sending them daily or if he did all this before he left. To be honest, I don't even want to know. It feels magical and I don't want to lose that feeling.

Kayla and I decide to go down to the restaurant in the resort for dinner. When we're done eating and ready to get the bill, the waiter brings me out a Crème brûlée. Before he walks too far away I call him back over.

"Excuse me. I didn't order this."

"Yes, I know. It was supposed to be delivered to your room this evening, but since you're dining with us, I thought you might like it now."

It hits me that I told Cooper this was my favorite dessert.

"By any chance is there a note to go with it?"

"Yes, ma'am. I was supposed to attach it to the receipt. I can go get it now."

A few minutes later he comes back with the note and hands it to me.

I wish I were there with you sharing this dessert. I bet it tastes delicious but not half as delicious as you. – Coop

Kayla slowly shakes her head after I hand her the note to read. "Geez Liz, this guy clearly has it bad for you. Maybe one of these will include his number."

I don't want to get my hopes up, but in the back of my mind I've been thinking the same thing.

The last two days of our trip pass by quickly. The day after I got the dessert, a huge blanket for the beach is delivered to our room with a note that says *To keep the sand away.* No phone number.

The last day of our trip I wonder if there'll be a gift. We're checking out at ten to head home and say bye to our families before we head to Las Vegas, so it would have to be delivered before we leave. At ten, nothing has arrived yet, so we go to the front desk to check-out and that's when the woman asks which one of us is Liz.

"Um, I am."

"This is for you."

I grab the box and pray there'll be a number inside. Removing the top, I find a beautiful white gold necklace and charm. I look closer at the charm and it's a pair of boxing gloves. I lift them up to look for a note and find it, only there isn't a phone number.

To always remember me xo – Coop

"Boxing gloves?" Kayla asks. "Another question?"

"It must be. He said he likes mixed-martial-arts."

I hand it to Kayla and ask her to put it on me. Once it's on, I grab the boxing gloves, bring them up to my lips, and think to myself, *I will never forget you, Coop. I don't even think that's possible.*

Five

LIZ

FOR THE THIRD DAY IN A ROW I'M BENT OVER THE TOILET throwing up everything in my stomach while Kayla holds my hair back and earns her best friend title.

"Ugh! Do you think it was something we ate at the Chinese restaurant last night?"

"Liz, if it were food poisoning, you wouldn't be throwing up for days. I really think you need to go see a doctor. It could be the flu."

I know she's right. It's time to make a doctor's appointment. I stop throwing up long enough to go to my room to find my insurance card and locate a doctor in our area.

Our apartment is so cute and bigger than we expected. Kayla's parents went all out renting us a three-bedroom apartment walking distance from campus. We both have our own room and the third bedroom is used as an office to do our schoolwork. It has a computer desk and a super cute futon that can turn into a bed if we have somebody stay over.

It has been over a month since we've left Miami and I'm not going to lie, Cooper has been on my mind. But it doesn't matter because only knowing his first name means I have no way of finding him, and since he doesn't know my last name, he isn't going to be locating me any time soon either. As much as I wish things had ended differently, there's no point in regretting something I can't change. All I can do at this point is just chalk it up to an awesome experience and move forward.

Kayla made me dish out the details and said I'm lucky I was with a guy who actually knew what he was doing. Orgasming the first couple times she had sex didn't happen for her and she was in shock at how many times he got me there. Any guy who comes after Cooper will definitely have a lot to live up to.

I've started my classes at ULV and Kayla has found a part-time job at a cute bistro right down the street from our place. Her parents are covering all her expenses, but Kayla is too much of a social butterfly to sit at home all summer while I'm in class. She's already met several people there and has attended a few parties.

I make an appointment for this afternoon, hoping the doctor can shed some light on why I've been throwing up for the last few days. When I get inside the room, the nurse has me give a urine sample and asks me to explain what's been going on. Then I change into a gown and wait for the doctor to come in.

"Hello, Lizbeth. It's nice to meet you. My name is Dr. Lee. If you don't mind me asking, other than throwing up, have you had any other symptoms?" I think about it for a second and conclude that other than throwing up, I haven't felt all that bad.

"Not really. Nothing else feels wrong except I keep throwing up. I'm thinking food poisoning, but would it go on for days? My friend Kayla said it might be the flu."

She looks down at her notes and gives me a small smile. I feel like she's preparing me for something bad. "Lizbeth, your urine test shows high HCG levels. In other words, you're pregnant, which explains why you're throwing up every day. Unfortunately, those symptoms can vary depending on the pregnancy. I take it you didn't know you're pregnant."

Every part of me begins to shake, and I suddenly feel like I need to throw up again. I jump off the medical bed, making it to the trashcan, just in time to empty the contents of my lunch into it. Dr. Lee hands me a wet paper towel and I dab my mouth. It doesn't make any sense.

"Doctor, there has to be a mistake. I started taking the pills over a month ago, and I only had sex a couple of times after I started the pill."

"How soon after you started taking the pill did you have sex? The pills should be taken with another form of protection for the first seven to ten days to be on the safe side."

I do the calculations in my head. I started the pills four days before we left for Miami and we had sex a couple of days later. *Shit. Shit. Shit. It had been less than a week.*

Dr. Lee gives me a sympathetic smile. "Judging by your reaction I'm taking it this was unplanned."

"Yes, it is. I didn't realize it hadn't been a week since I began taking the pills."

"You know, Liz. Some of the best parts of life are unexpected miracles." She smiles and continues on. "I'm going to write you a referral to see an obstetrician and they can tell you how the baby is and how far along you are."

She types up the referral and hands it to me. "There are many options these days. Until you decide how you wish to proceed, make sure you stay hydrated and start on prenatal vitamins. Make an appointment to see the obstetrician as soon as possible."

I thank her and walk out feeling like I'm in some crazy dream, until another bout of nausea hits, reminding me I'm not in a dream at all. This is my reality. I'm pregnant with a baby from a guy I lost my virginity to, and I wouldn't know how to get ahold of him if I tried. When I said I would always remember him, I thought it would be from memories, not from a baby growing in my belly.

I get home and Kayla's in the living room watching some ridiculous reality show while munching on popcorn. She looks up at me and immediately knows something is wrong.

"Hey, sweetie. How did the doctor go? Do you have the flu?"

"Yeah, I have the flu all right and it'll be over in about eight months."

Her eyes widen as she soaks in what I'm implying. She grabs my hands and sits me down next to her, closing her arms around me tightly. The tears begin trickling down my cheeks as she hugs me close. We don't need words to say what we both know. My life is about to change. Apparently for me, what happened in Miami, didn't stay in Miami.

Six

LIZ

Five years later

HE GRABS HOLD OF MY HIPS AND PULLS ME ONTO HIM, PUSHING his massive cock deep into my core. I feel so full. I grip his chest with my hands and begin to move up and down as his hands palm my breasts. "C'mon, baby girl. Yeah, that's it. Come for me." I'm so close, just a few more thrusts and I'll...

"Mom...Mommy...Wake up, please. Auntie Kay is making us yummy pancakes."

Slowly, I open one eye, recognizing I was once again dreaming. Five years of no sex will do that to a woman. I open both my eyes to find my four-year-old daughter sitting on my stomach, smashing my cheeks together with her tiny hands while trying to wake me up. I can't help but smile when I see her bright green eyes looking at me like I hold the golden ticket to the chocolate factory. It's then I remember what today is.

"Mom, I see your eyeballs. I know you're awake."

I laugh as I grab hold of her waist and throw her onto my bed, tickling her. Her giggles bounce off the walls and hit me straight in my heart. As I look down at her, she's smiling from ear to ear and the same butterflies that always take over my stomach when I see that smile invade me once again.

She'll never know her daddy or what he looks like, but when I look at her, he is all I see. Same green eyes, same beautiful smile, same golden-brown hair, and the same naturally sun-kissed skin. She's a spitting image of the man who gave me the best memories I could ever ask for, my daughter. If I didn't have the stretch marks to prove it, I would swear Isabella Faith wasn't even carried by me but by her father instead.

I continue to tickle her belly as she begs me to stop. "Mom, I'm gonna pee myself! You better stop." I'm definitely not taking a chance of that happening. It's too early in the morning to be washing sheets, so I stop tickling her. In return, she huffs and rolls over to sit across from me in my bed.

"And to what do I owe this pleasure of you waking me up at…" I glance at the clock. "Seven o'clock?" I know why she's up and ready to go, but her excitement is so infectious I want to hear her tell me herself.

"Mommy, how could you forget? Today is the bestest day ever! I start preschool today. Duh!" She glares at me with such seriousness I have to hold in my smile.

"Oh my goodness." I pretend to suddenly remember. "How could I forget the most important day of Bella's life?"

She stares at me without blinking, trying to figure out how in the world I could ever forget something so important. As funny as it is to watch her reaction, I know in a few seconds she's really going to believe I forgot. One thing I often wonder is if her father has a temper, because I have no idea where she could've gotten hers from, but my sweet angel can go from zero to sixty in the blink of an eye.

"Of course I didn't forget what today is. You're so silly, Bella. Look at you all dressed up and ready for your first day of preschool. Okay, let me get up, jump in the shower, and get dressed, and I'll meet Auntie Kay and you for pancakes before we head out to take you to school. Tell Auntie Kay to save me at least two pancakes!"

Bella beams at me, shaking her head up and down excitedly. I smack her bottom as she jumps off the bed and runs down the hall to the kitchen, yelling to Kayla to save me two pancakes.

I can't even begin to imagine what I would have done without Kayla in my life these last five years. When I found out I was pregnant, I lost it. How in the world was I going to go to school and raise a baby? Kayla was amazing from day one. She held my hand through my entire pregnancy and delivery. We transformed the third bedroom into a nursery, and Kayla became Auntie Kay. Although, she's more like a second mom to Bella.

The first year was the hardest. After Bella was born, I thought about Cooper constantly. It was almost scary how much she looked like her father. I cried for weeks after I found out I was pregnant and then for weeks after Bella was born. Kayla tried to look up Bentley and Kaden's name while I tried to look up Cooper's, but it was pointless. We didn't even know where to begin. We didn't know where any of them lived, their last names, or any of their personal information. I did look up MMA and Cooper but wasn't able to find anything.

Kayla was the glue that held all my pieces together. She made sure we took classes at opposite times and on different days so somebody could always be home with Bella. We both also worked part-time shifts at the Bistro to pay for her necessities. So many times, I felt weak and

Kayla was there to be my strength.

It took a little longer than planned, but a few months ago we both graduated from ULV. I received my bachelor's in business and accounting and Kayla received hers in physical therapy. Luckily, the sports complex where Kayla did her internship had a spot available and hired her the day she graduated. I was able to take the summer off to spend time with Bella before she starts preschool, but now I need to find a job.

After showering and getting dressed, I make my way to the kitchen, following the delicious aroma of Kayla's homemade chocolate chip pancakes. She doesn't make them often but when she does, I eat them until I'm so full I can barely button my pants.

As I sit at the table and begin buttering my pancakes, I notice my daughter is scarfing hers down. "Whoa there, Angel. You're going to get a tummy ache if you don't slow down. What's the rush?"

She stops chewing and looks at me, her eyebrows furrowing in the same way I can still remember her father doing. "I don't want to be late," she says matter-of-factly through her mouthful of food.

"Bella, school starts at nine o'clock. You're not going to be late. Please slow down. You won't be going to school if your belly hurts."

She must agree with my reasoning because she immediately slows down eating her food.

I start eating my pancakes, when I look over at Kayla, who is giving me her *I'm up to something* look. The last time she gave me this look I ended up meeting Cooper and got knocked up, so this look seriously scares me.

"I haven't seen that look in a very long time. What are you up to?" I raise my brows in hope that she'll see I'm serious and back down.

"I'm not up to anything. How dare you jump to conclusions?"

"Kayla, let's not beat around the bush. What's going on? I need to get Bella to school and I have a couple potential jobs I want to check out."

"Okay, hear me out before you say no." I go to cut her off, knowing where this is going, but she doesn't allow me to break in as she continues speaking a hundred miles an hour.

"We did it, Liz! We graduated college. We got our degrees. I think we have done a pretty good job with Bella so far. She isn't completely traumatized and she's alive and in one piece. One night with a sitter isn't going to kill you or her. You deserve this. You've focused on school and Bella for the last five years. Please come out with us Friday night. Hayley has tickets to this cool UFC fight and also has an open invitation to the after-party. It's supposed to be off the hook. Please!"

Kayla and I met Hayley while working at the Bistro. She was also going to ULV but a few years ahead of us and majoring in sports medicine. We all instantly became friends and she is over here so often

Bella calls her Auntie Hayley. She got a job a few months back at a UFC training center and is always begging us to come to the fights.

"Kayla, you don't even watch UFC. Why do you want to go to a fight so badly?" I shake my head, trying to figure out her motive. With Kayla, there is always a motive behind her madness.

"Um, hello! Have you seen their hot bodies? I don't care what's going on with the fight. I just want to see their sweaty bodies and maybe do the dirty-dirty with one of those hot guys I'll meet at the after-party," she says, waggling her eyebrows up and down.

Well, that makes more sense. Where there are hot guys, you can you bet Kayla will find them.

I try to keep a straight face, but when Bella cuts in and asks, "Auntie Kay, what's a dirty-dirty?" I can't help but laugh.

Raising my brows, I join in the fun. "Yeah, Auntie Kay, What's a dirty-dirty?"

Kayla's eyes go wide when she realizes what she just said in front of my very impressionable four-year-old and attempts to back slide by telling her it's when people play in the mud together.

Now, I'm laughing so hard tears streaming down my face. Kayla isn't laughing, though. When I look at her through my blurry eyes she's glaring at me.

When my precious daughter responds, I completely lose it.

"That sounds like fun! I wanna go play in the mud! Can Tristan come play with me in the mud? He loves to jump in the puddles and get all dirty!"

Kayla's eyes completely bug out as she looks to me for help. I give her a look that says, *Nope, ain't gonna happen. You got yourself into this mess, now get yourself out.* Now she is full on shooting daggers my way, which is making me laugh even harder.

She looks at Bella and says very calmly, "No, you may not play in the mud with Tristan. Not until you've graduated from college, have a good job, and are married."

Bella looks at her completely confused and begins arguing when I decide to help Kayla out and change the subject. "Oh, Bella, look at the time. If you don't want to be late we better get you washed up so you can be on your way to preschool."

Hearing the word preschool, she immediately forgets all about playing in the mud and getting dirty with boys. Kayla shoots me a look of gratitude and begins to clean up the dishes from breakfast. I mouth to her, *"you owe me."*

After dropping Bella off at preschool—and crying my eyes out at the fact that my baby is growing up—I head to a couple places to apply for an accounting position. I love numbers so it was a given I would major in business and accounting, but I never imagined it would be so hard to find a job in this field.

After filling out several applications, I make my way to the coffee shop on the corner near our apartment to get a cup of coffee and continue looking for a job. Right after getting my coffee and pulling out my laptop, I get a text message. I check it and sigh. I should've known she wouldn't drop this.

Kayla: Please, Liz. Friday night 7 p.m. UFC fight

Me: Not happening

Kayla: One night out isn't going to make you a bad mom. Pleeeeaaasssseeeee!

Me: I don't even have a sitter.

Kayla: I already spoke to Tristan's mom and she said she'd watch Bella for the night. No excuses!

Me: All night? You know how I feel about leaving her with someone overnight. I barely even let my mom take her.

Kayla: Your mom lives in Florida! You can't compare the two. One night. Bella will love staying up and watching movies with Tristan. You've known Ashley for three years and she's a mom just like you! Plus, she's a teacher! C'mon...do this for me!

Me: Fine.

Kayla: Seriously? You're really going to go?

Me: Yes

Kayla: Your one-word answers are scaring me...

Me: Good, you should be scared. I'm not happy about this.

Kayla: Yay!! I'm so excited. I will be home around 3 so we can go buy new dresses for Friday. C-ya later!

It's Friday night and I seriously can't believe she's talked me into this. I should be immune to the craziness that is Kayla, but I'm clearly not. For starters, I haven't worn a little black dress since before I got pregnant with Bella, and if I remember correctly, it was that damn LBD that got me into that position in the first place. Although, I can't really be upset about it because it got me Bella, and I wouldn't trade her for anything in the world. But that's not the point.

The point is, I don't want to be wearing this dress and going to this fight when I can be home hanging out with Bella until she goes to bed, and then reading one of my romance novels that I live vicariously through since my own sex life is non-existent. *Well, except for in my dreams.*

After our mini-shopping trip, we pick Bella up from preschool, where she explains to us the entire way home in detail every second of every minute of every hour of her first day at school.

"Mommy, I love preschool so much I I've decided I'm going back tomorrow." *Well, that's good because she doesn't really have a choice.*

I do my best to stifle the laugh I have building up because she's being dead serious right now. I guess it's good she's decided she's going to continue her education on her own because trying to force Bella to do something she doesn't want to do is like pulling teeth.

After dropping Bella off at Tristan's house with my friend Ashley, we head over to the stadium. I met Ashley through a mommy-and-me class we attended with our kids and she's probably the only person outside of my family I trust to watch Bella. As luck would have it our kids also ended up in the same preschool class.

Since Hayley had to get there early, since she's working the event, she left us tickets at will-call. We take our tickets and head to our assigned seats.

As I sit here, in my little black dress and heels, looking around at this madhouse of an event, I wonder why I'm so gullible that I let Kayla talk me into this shit. The entire place is packed. Music is pounding through the speakers, women are everywhere dressed to kill, and everybody is clearly pumped for the event. I never realized how popular the UFC is.

It appears Hayley has hooked us up with decent seats. We're sitting pretty close to the front—or the middle I guess? In the center of the arena is a huge stage looking thing with a fence that runs around the perimeter. From where we're sitting, the guys can practically sweat on us when they're fighting. To our left is a black carpet that leads from what looks like the dressing rooms or is it fitting rooms? Shit, I don't even know. It's some type of room where the guys will come out of and walk down the carpet to get to the stage.

One by one the fighters get announced, along with their opponents, to fight. They each have their own song and they walk out almost in a trance. Most of them have an entourage accompanying them, and many of them are wearing headphones.

Each fight goes a few rounds, until one guy either gets knocked out or they both last and the judges tally up the points, and then a winner is announced. I have no idea what they're fighting for, but it must be something major because these fighters are taking this entire thing extremely personal.

Fortunately for Kayla, every guy who comes out of the…locker room (Oh! Maybe that's what it's called.) has to walk by us and she's definitely taking advantage of the situation by snapping pictures left and right.

The fights are crazy to watch. These guys are seriously no joke. I wouldn't last a second in that ring. At the end of every fight they both walk away beat to shit—bleeding everywhere—several parts of their body bruised and broken.

I'm starting to wonder how many of these fights are going to take place tonight—*there's only so much blood and gore a girl can take*—when the lights dim down and it's announced that coming up is the main event of the evening.

The first guy enters to Imagine Dragon's *Radioactive*. He has a hoodie on and is surrounded by a bunch of guys. He is shaking hands and smiling wide for everybody to see, like he knows he's got this shit in the bag. *And hot damn he's a big guy.* I don't know who the other guy is, but I can't imagine anybody beating this guy. Heads are going to roll, and I doubt it'll be this guy's head. He walks to his corner of the ring and his entourage starts getting him ready for the fight.

The music ends and the next song begins. This time, the guy is walking out to Eminem's, *'Til I Collapse*. Like the first guy, he's wearing a hoodie, but unlike the first guy, he keeps his head down and doesn't shake anybody's hand. It's not that he isn't sure of himself…it's more like he doesn't feel the need to be cocky about it like the other guy. He's focused and his song matches his mood perfectly. His entourage following him acts the same way. They walk out determined like they're here to do a job. I take it back, this guy will be the winner. There's no doubt about it. He's about to fuck this guy up.

"Oh. My. God, Liz! Is that Kaden? Wait, is that Bentley?" Kayla starts tapping on my arm, while jumping up and down, trying to get a closer look.

Everything in my world goes still as I finally catch a good glimpse of the guys surrounding the fighter. A loud gasps escapes my lips—not loud enough for anyone to hear over the music and cheering, but loud enough I can hear it. That's when I take a look at the fighter, like really look at him, and I see it, on his right arm is the dragon tattoo I'll never forget.

Holy mother of God, it can't be. There's no way.

My fingers go up to my necklace. The boxing gloves he gave me. He told me he practiced MMA.

Well isn't that an understatement of the year.

Kayla continues to shout at me, but my mind is all foggy and I can't focus on anything but the man walking away from me toward the ring. It feels like the boxing gloves resting on my neck are suddenly burning a hole through my skin. The music stops and the guy on the loudspeaker introduces the two fighters.

"And now three rounds in the UFC Middleweight division. Introducing first, fighting out of the blue corner, this man is a valid judo fighter holding a professional record of twelve wins and zero losses, standing at six feet two inches, weighing in at 165 pounds fighting out of Los Angeles, California. He is The Ultimate Fighter season winner, Damian The Massive Garcia. And now introducing his opponent, fighting out of the red corner with a record of eight wins and zero losses, he stands at six feet three inches, weighing 170 pounds, fighting out of Las Vegas, Nevada, he is Liam The Raaaaaage Cooper."

Holy hell. I can't believe it. A few things come to mind when I hear his introduction. First, Cooper is his freaking last name, not his first name. And that makes me wonder if maybe I did come across him online but didn't realize it.

Second, he's a famous fighter. That explains why he has to stay in shape.

And third, *Rage?* Well, goddamn that explains our daughter's temper.

Kayla and I lock eyes, having an entire conversation without having to say a single a word. What the hell are the chances of running into my daughter's father here?

Seven

COOPER

I STEP INTO THE OCTAGON AND TUNE EVERYTHING OUT around me. I need this win. Not only will it keep me undefeated, but it'll also ensure me a place in the title fight in a few months at the MGM Grand. This is what I've been working my ass off for for the last ten plus years. This is why, after five years of hell from being around my father, I'm still in Las Vegas.

I look around and see my dad in the corner, along with Kaden, who's still my trainer, and Bentley, who hasn't left my side all these years. I know Caleb is out there watching. I don't know what I would do without these guys. They're my fucking rock. I'd never have been able to deal with my dad all these years without them pushing me.

Three rounds. Three. Fucking. Rounds. If I can beat this guy, I'm one step closer to the title fight and everything I've been through will be worth it.

I look out into the crowd like I do before every fight. Watching them scream my name is a complete ego boost, not to mention their enthusiasm helps to get me pumped up. I hear someone shouting Cooper, which isn't something I normally hear. Normally, the fans are yelling Rage. I look toward where the voice is coming from and my eyes lock with hers. I realize it isn't her voice screaming my name but her best friend's.

It takes me a second to make sure I'm not hallucinating. This girl has been in every fantasy of mine for the last five years. The guys have a bet as to when I'll mention her name again. *She's my girl who got away.* There have been times when I was walking down the street and could've sworn I saw her, only to come face to face with a stranger who has a similar skin tone or hair color or the same curvy body. Well, not the exact same, because everything about Liz is one of a kind.

For five long years, I've lived with the regret of walking away and not taking her number or giving her mine. When we first got back and

I couldn't stop thinking about her, I asked Bentley if maybe he had gotten her friend's number, but when he said he hadn't, I knew there was no way I would ever find her again.

Kaden screaming my name knocks me out of my fog and our connection is lost. I want to try to find her, but right now I need to focus on this damn fight.

"Bro, what the fuck is wrong with you? Focus," Kaden says, while wiping Vaseline on my face to prevent too much bleeding.

I look over at my dad and see him scowling at me. He can tell I've lost my focus and is wondering what the hell just happened. The few times he overheard the guys and I talking about Liz ended with us arguing. If he knew she was here, he would definitely lose it. I can't even imagine the lengths he would go to ensure my focus remains on fighting.

I know better than to mention anything about a woman to my dad, not if I want to remain on his good side. So, I shake it off for the moment and get my head back into the fight.

Three rounds. Three. Fucking. Rounds. I just need to get through this fight and afterward I'll find her. There is no way I'm letting this girl go again.

Eight

LIZ

SOMEBODY PINCH ME BECAUSE I MUST BE DREAMING. I REMAIN standing, staring at this guy that looks even more like my daughter than I've imagined over the last four years.

I look over at Kayla and she's in just as much shock as I am. No words are spoken. We just watch in silence while the majority of the crowd chants, "Rage, Rage, Rage." Some of the women are holding up signs that say things like "Marry me, Rage" and "I love you, Rage". *Eww!* One sign even says, "You can take your Rage out on me." *I think I just threw up in my mouth a little.*

I'm in shock. I don't even know what to think right now. The many sleepless nights when Bella was first born and would wake up with Colic, I would hold her in my arms and rock her back and forth while I imagined what it would be like to have Cooper by my side. I'd make up scenes in my head where I'm out with Bella and we run into him. I tell him about his daughter and we ride off into the sunset. Okay, not really ride off into the sunset, but you get the drift. Not in any of those scenes did I ever imagine I would run into him at a UFC fight where he's fighting in the main event.

In all reality, does it really matter how I found him? The fact is, we're both here, and I'll finally be able to tell him our short but amazing time together created the most perfect, beautiful, little miracle.

The bell rings, and the fight begins, and Cooper owns up to his name. He goes after the other guy in pure rage. They both go back and forth swinging punches. I wince several times at the hits they're each getting in. The other guy gets him good in the eye, causing it to bleed, but Cooper doesn't even seem affected by it. It's like he's in a zone.

The fight can't be more than a couple minutes in when Cooper throws a punch straight to the guy's chin that knocks the guy to the ground. The referee jumps in front of Cooper to stop him from continuing his attack on the guy who is now motionlessly lying on the ground. The medics run over to the guy to check him out. *Holy shit!* Cooper must've knocked him out cold because the guy still isn't moving. The crowd goes wild. They're screaming and chanting his name. The arena is a damn nut house.

The announcer declares Cooper the winner and raises his arm in the air. He doesn't even crack a smile, but I notice he's scanning the crowd, and when his eyes meet mine once again, he raises his two fingers to his eyes and points at me. Kayla nudges me, a grin spreading across her face. I'm in such shock I can't even move or respond. I try to make my head shake up and down, but I have no idea if it's working.

The other guy finally gets up with the help of the medic and walks out of the fighting ring, leaving Cooper there with his entourage.

I recognize his three friends from the club that night. Time has definitely been good to all of them. Also with them is an older gentleman who looks to be in his late forties, built like Cooper, with the same color hair and eyes. If I had to guess, I would say that has to be his dad or somebody related to him. He doesn't smile like Cooper's friends do. While his friends are patting him on the back and shoulder and giving him hugs to congratulate him, the guy just stands there and stares, the look on his face sending chills up my spine.

Once Cooper is done with his interviews, they all head out of the fighting ring back toward the room they came from. He whispers something into Bentley's ear and Bentley's head shoots up, looking around until he spots me. He smirks and nods his head. While they all head to the back, Bentley stops right in front of us.

"Well, God damn. If it isn't the girl who got away."

His grin gets wider as he looks me up and down, clearly checking me out. Then he turns his head to Kayla and his face morphs from humorous to full-on lust. Kayla never admitted to what happened between them, only that they had sex and moved on, but looking at his expression, I swear he's reliving it all over again, and I'd bet there was more to them than just a wham-bam-thank you-ma'am.

"And her best friend," he adds. "Never thought we'd ever see you two again."

Because I'm still stuck on *the girl who got away* part, I don't hear anything Kayla and Bentley are saying. *The girl who got away? Could that mean he's thought about me?* It doesn't make any sense because he's the one who left that morning without leaving his phone number.

I catch what must be the tail end of the conversation—Kayla telling Bentley we will be there. *Be where? Where are we going?* Oh! She must be referring to the after party. That would make sense since it's for the fighters and Cooper is a fighter.

Bentley nods at Kayla, then at me, and then walks away. This is too much to take in. To think, if I wouldn't have come tonight, I would've missed running into Cooper. This whole time we've been living in the same city. What are the odds?

Nine

COOPER

HOLY. SHIT. MY WORLD FEELS LIKE IT'S JUST BEEN TURNED ON its axis. No, more like picked up, shaken every which way, and flipped the hell all over the place. I've spent the last five years imagining what Liz would feel like beneath me again, but I never thought it could become a reality.

I just won my fight. I should be focusing on the fact that I've ensured myself a spot for the title fight. I've worked my ass off to get here. Thinking about this girl is not going to help me get ready for this fight, that's for damn sure. She would be nothing but a distraction if I let her in. Plus, I'd never be able to devote the time to her that she deserves and where would that leave us? All I have to do is take a look at my drunken, cheating mother to remind myself what women are capable of when they don't get enough attention. But damn, when I think about Liz and our short time together in Miami, it feels so different, like the connection we shared could possibly mean more.

Out of nowhere a wet rag smacks me right in my face and I'm brought back to the present.

"What the fuck was that for?" I ask, looking around to see who threw that shit at me.

"Get your fucking head in the game, boy!" my dad shouts. His face is beet red and a couple veins in his forehead look like they're about to bust open.

"My head is in the game," I tell him, dropping the rag on the ground. "I just won my damn fight, didn't I?"

"No, it's not! I can hear that shit running through your head about that girl. I heard Kaden mention to Bentley that she's here. You want a championship or do you want a piece of pussy?"

I just shake my head—there's no point in arguing with him. I've learned the hard way to just let him say his peace and walk away. He's never going to change his way of thinking and he definitely doesn't care what I think or how I feel.

"I asked you a fucking question, son. You gonna answer or just stare at me?" And at this simple question, I lose it. All the years of keeping it all in finally rises to the surface and boils over.

"Of course I want a championship. Haven't I made it clear over the last five damn years that I've been working my ass off at the gym every goddamn day? Will anything ever be good enough for you? I'm twenty-seven years old and other than having a very rare one-night stand or a drink with the guys, I've spent every waking moment at this gym. I get that mom cheated on you. I've listened to you tell me for the last fifteen years that women are no good. Ever think maybe she cheated because she couldn't stand the way you treat her or your family? And that maybe not every woman is like mom? I've chosen this career over everything. What more do you want from me?"

He stares at me in silence like he is contemplating how to respond to my outburst. For a second I think maybe he gets it, but then he says, "I'll ask you again. Do you want a championship or do you want that piece of pussy out there in the crowd? You can't have both. If you want her, then go—go after her, but don't bother showing up at the gym tomorrow."

I can't even respond. I just simply look at him and laugh humorlessly to myself while I walk away. It feels like for the first time I'm seeing him in a whole different light. I've always known he doesn't see me how a loving father should see his kid, but I never realized how truly unhappy and bitter he is.

Ten

COOPER

I JUMP IN THE SHOWER BACK AT MY HOUSE AND GET DRESSED. Normally I'd shower at the arena, but I left so quickly I forgot about needing to get ready for the after-party. Bentley and Caleb are meeting me back here and then we're going to ride over to the Kaden's for the party. I head downstairs to see Caleb and Bentley already in my living room waiting on me.

"Are Liz and Kayla coming to the party?"

Bentley is the first to speak up. "Yeah, apparently, they're friends with Hayley, the chick that works as the on-site doctor at the gym. Hayley invited them to the fight and after party. When I went to go invite them, Kayla told me they were already planning to go. What are the odds, man?"

"Seriously, this whole situation is surreal. Get this shit, my dad told me if I go to the party tonight to see Liz, not to show up at the gym tomorrow. I'm done with him running my life. I get I can't be in a committed relationship. Between the fucked up crazy DNA running through me and the insane hours I put in at the gym, I know it'd never work, but I'm not going to just *not* see her. I've thought about this girl for years. I'm twenty-seven years old and he's still trying to run my life."

"I'm going to say this for the millionth damn time, Coop. The shit your parents put each other through and continue to put you through has nothing to do with you. You're just the collateral damage. You deserve to be happy. You don't realize it now, but one day you're going to wake up and wish you would've went after more than just a title. I'm not saying you shouldn't work hard, but find a balance and let someone in. Just because your parents are both unhappy doesn't mean you have to be as well. Fuck them both."

"Bentley, I get you come from a home with two loving parents and all, so you honestly believe what you're saying, but me and you aren't the same. You're okay with where you stand in your career. You fight and enjoy it, but you don't care whether you win or lose. On top of that, cheating isn't in your DNA. I'm already set up to fail in any relationship, and that's without adding my fighting to the mix."

He slowly shakes his head with a sad smile that tells me this conversation clearly isn't going anywhere so he's giving up. And it's for the best, because yeah, Bentley is one of my best friends, but the truth of the matter is we come from two completely different worlds.

I look at Caleb to see if he's got anything to add and he just shrugs. That's one of the things I like about Caleb. He doesn't throw in his input. He does his thing and let's everyone else do theirs. I grab my keys from the bowl near the garage and we head out in my SUV.

The entire ride none of us says a word. I know for me, I have a lot to think about. Liz's going to be there tonight, and judging by the way she looked at me, I think she might have missed me as much as I missed her. But is it right to be with her again, knowing I can't give her anything more? Maybe if I explain it to her, she'll accept me the way I am. I know it's wrong to ask this from her, and I know she deserves more, but I am a greedy fucking bastard and I want her.

We pull up to Kaden's house and can hear the music thumping from the road. He has some nice ass neighbors to ignore all this, that's for damn sure. If I so much as sneeze too loudly in my community, somebody is all over me hitting me up with fines and citations. I've thought about moving to somewhere with more land, but I don't really see the point. It's just me and most likely will always be just me.

For about four years, when we all lived in Colorado, Kaden, Bentley, and I were roommates while Caleb was living elsewhere. When we all moved out here to Vegas, Kaden and I decided to get our own places, and Bentley and Caleb decided to rent an apartment together. I'm actually shocked Caleb agreed, because while he's one of my best friends, he's definitely more of a loner. Nobody really knows much about his life except that when he fights it's like he's chasing off some demons.

I moved into a four-bedroom townhouse in a gated community only a couple miles from the gym while Kaden decided to move a little further out of the city and into a more rural area where the houses are a bit more spread out, which is why the parties always end up taking place at his house.

I park my vehicle along the road but away a little bit so I don't get blocked in, in case I want to leave early. Walking around back to where the bonfire is going, I immediately start looking for Liz. I look over at Bentley and I can swear he's looking for Kayla as well.

After we left Miami, I asked him about her, and he said she was a cool chick but wasn't the girlfriend type. When I asked him what he meant by that, he just shook his head and changed the subject.

There are people scattered everywhere. I walk around the fire pit, over by the patio, and around the side of the house, getting stopped every five seconds by another person congratulating me on my win. I don't want to be rude, so I force a smile and say thanks but try to keep moving along to find her.

When I don't see Liz anywhere outside, I head inside to look for her. Generally, Kaden tries to keep the party outside. He even has people use the bathroom in the guesthouse near the pool instead of in his house. I'm hoping he's made an exception for her because if she isn't inside that means she might not be here. The thought of not seeing her again makes me feel ill. *How did a girl I only spent thirty hours with manage to turn me into such a damn pussy?*

I get inside and go straight to the living room, where I find her sitting on the couch with Kayla and Kaden. I watch her for a second as she throws her head back in laughter, her thick head of curls flying around her face as she continues to laugh with abandon and all I can think is that I want to be the one to make her laugh like that. *C'mon Coop, get that shit out of your head.*

I make my way over to her and it as if she can sense me getting closer. Her back goes straight and she stops laughing. Maybe she hasn't missed me after all. But then I crack a smile and her face completely lights up, telling me she feels something of what I'm feeling.

She stands from the couch and brushes down her dress. It reminds me of the one she wore that night at the club. I take a minute to check her out and notice that time has been good to her. Her looks have matured. While she still has the same beautiful curly hair and amazing tan, her face appears to be less girlish and more woman, her body is still curvy but again womanlier. She's filled out more in all the right places. Don't get me wrong, she isn't by any means fat. She's still fucking perfect. It's just that something is different about her.

Realizing I'm checking her out, she blushes the most adorable shade of pink while covering her front by wrapping her arms around her stomach. I close the distance between us and pull her into me for a kiss. She must be shocked by my actions because she tenses up as I wrap my arms around her waist and seek entrance into her mouth with my tongue.

She finally gives in and gives me access, and in this moment, it feels like all is right in the world. I want this reunion to be soft and sweet, but the moment she exhales into my mouth and relaxes into my arms, I can't hold back. I attack her mouth with mine, nipping at her bottom lip and then the top one. I move my tongue back into her mouth to taste her.

Her hands come up to my head and tighten around my short hair. *God, I've missed this woman.* I run my hands down her back and over her perfect ass, to her thighs, grabbing hold of the back of them and lifting her up. She can feel it happening and immediately wraps her legs around my waist, locking her ankles together.

She pulls her head back and looks into my eyes, smiling, and I know I would do anything to keep that smile on her face. I vaguely hear our friends in the background chuckling and somebody says to get a room. I can't help but laugh at that. This girl could easily become my entire world.

"Kaden, guestroom?" I can't stop looking into her beautiful brown eyes as I ask him for permission to get this girl alone.

"Yeah, yeah," he replies through laughter.

Not taking my eyes off Liz, I walk her down the hallway and kick open the guestroom door. Once inside, I make my way to the bed and sit on the edge with her still wrapped around me.

"Baby girl, do you have any idea how often I've thought about you over these past five years? How many times I wished I had gotten your number? Too many times to count."

She smiles brightly. "I feel the same way, Cooper…or is it Liam? Or Rage? I thought Cooper was your damn name! What the hell do I call you?"

I chuckle at that. "Baby, you can call me any name you want as long as you are naked and in my arms." I wink at her and she shakes with laughter. *I could never get tired of hearing this girl laugh.*

I bring my lips to hers again and kiss her. It starts out soft and slow. I can smell her vanilla shampoo. It's the same smell from five years ago. She continues to kiss me back and then begins to move her body closer, like she is trying to climb up me. It's then I realize she's tightening her thighs and trying to grind herself against me for relief. My girl wants this as much as I do.

Without stopping the kiss, I grip her thighs and flip us over, so she's lying under me. As our kiss becomes ravenous, I take one of my hands and move it down her side to the bottom of the dress and roughly lift it up. When I get it right above her panty line, she puts her hand over mine to stop me from going any further, and I still my movements, wondering if I read this all wrong.

Eleven

LIZ

A few minutes earlier

I'M SITTING IN THE LIVING ROOM OF KADEN'S HOME, TALKING to Kaden and Kayla. Hayley is around here somewhere, chatting with everyone she knows since she works with a lot of these people. I'm not really paying attention to the conversation because I'm too busy looking around for Cooper. I hear Kayla tell Kaden that he needs to introduce her to some of his hot UFC friends because sharing is caring and I can't help but laugh at my crazy best friend.

And then I feel him before I even see him. When I look over, he's standing ten feet away from me just staring. I don't know what to do, so I stand and look at him. He's checking me out and it makes me uncomfortable. Not because it's him who's checking me out, but because I know my body isn't the same as it was five years ago. I worked hard to get back in shape after I had Bella, but I'm not delusional about my post-baby body. My breasts got larger during the pregnancy and never went back to my original size. My stomach is much softer now and there's a permanent little pooch from the emergency caesarean I had to have when Bella's heart rate decreased during labor.

Luckily, he can't see the stretch marks that, if after four years haven't completely faded, will probably never fade. Thinking about all the hot women who were chanting his name today, begging him to marry them, and wanting the chance to sleep with him, I can't imagine why in the world he would want me now. Instinctively I wrap my arms around my stomach as if that's going to hide anything. Before I can say anything, Cooper's right in front of me, his lips on mine.

At first I'm in shock, but when I feel the way his lips move against mine, I can't help but give in to him. It just feels right. After a few seconds, he lifts me into his arms and I wrap my ankles around the back of him. Words might be being spoken, but I can't hear a damn thing that is being said. The only thing I can focus on are Cooper's hands on my ass and the delicious smell of his cologne invading my nostrils and hitting me right between my legs.

The next thing I know, we're moving down the hallway and into a bedroom. Cooper sits on the bed with me still in his arms and tells me he's thought about me often and regrets not getting my number. Hearing this from him sends my heart soaring. It gives me hope that when I tell him about our daughter, he'll be accepting of her. Not a day has gone by that I haven't thought about this man. I know I haven't spent enough time with him, but when I'm with him it feels like all the pieces of the puzzle are put together.

When I tell him I've thought about him as well and make a joke about not knowing what the hell to call him since he has so many names, he laughs and then tells me I can call him whatever I want as long as I'm naked and in his arms.

Watching him go from the intense fighter in the ring to this sweet, funny guy makes me laugh. I love the many sides of Cooper. He graces me with the most beautiful smile before we go back to kissing. The need between my legs is getting so intense I can't help but try to relieve some of the tension by rubbing up against him. Jesus, I'm like a damn dog in heat! He must realize what I'm trying to do because he flips us both over and pins my body under his.

While continuing to kiss me, Cooper moves his hand down my body and grabs the material of my dress to pull it up. Once it makes it almost to my stomach, I remember that if he looks at my stomach he'll see the scar from my cesarean as well as my stretch marks. As much as I know I need to tell him about Bella, I just want a few minutes for whatever is happening to be just about Cooper and me. Once he finds out about our daughter everything will change.

Afraid of him seeing what's under my dress, I grab his hand to stop him and he stills. I must've sent him mixed signals by doing this because he completely freezes and drops his gaze to mine. Needing to save this without explaining, I do the only thing I can think of and take control.

I slide out from under him and push him down onto his back. He looks confused, but once I move my hands down his shirt and to his pants, his expression goes from confused to pure want.

I move his shirt up enough so I can undo his belt and unbutton his jeans. I unzip his pants and look up at him, silently asking him to lift up so I can pull his pants down. He understands what I want and lifts up while I grab the top of his jeans and yank them down, taking his boxers with them.

Once his cock is free it springs up hard as steel. So many times, I got myself off remembering the taste of this perfect cock in my mouth.

Taking his shaft in my hand, I wrap my lips around it, taking the entire member into my mouth until it hits the back of my throat, causing me to gag for a second.

He goes to stop me when he hears me gag, but I shake my head and go back down again. I start bobbing my head up and down, getting it soaking wet with my saliva. His dick is hard as granite, and I know he must be close because I can taste the precum on my tongue.

Entwining his fingers into my hair tightly, he pulls my face up to his. "Slow and easy, baby. I've been fantasizing about this very moment for too damn long for this to end so soon. I need to take my time and get to know your body all over again."

When he says shit like this, my body comes alive.

"I need to be inside you, baby girl. Please."

His words have me dripping wet. I remove my panties and get on top of him, bunching my dress up so it isn't in the way, but is still covering my belly and scar.

Since I haven't been with anybody but Cooper I know I'm clean, and although I don't consider Bella a mistake, I decided that getting on the shot would ensure I never get pregnant until I'm ready to again.

I hover above his dick, waiting to see if he wants to use protection, when he grabs hold of my waist and slams me down onto him. My core expands and stretches, taking me a few seconds to adjust to his size.

"Fuck, Liz! You're so tight. It is like you were made for me."

If he only knew that he's the only guy who has ever been inside me.

I lean forward, putting my hands on his shoulders to steady myself, when Cooper stills and then raises his hand up from around my waist to my neck.

"You're wearing it. You're wearing the necklace I gave you five years ago." He says this with such amazement in his tone.

"Yes," I choke out. "I've worn it every day since the day I received it."

Pulling my face down to his, he kisses me with such passion that when he pulls away I swear my lips are bruised.

He moves his hands back to my waist and uses his ass to lift up, pumping into me from underneath. The feeling of him in me is amazing. I don't know how I went five years without this.

"Baby girl, you're too tight and too wet on my cock. I'm not going to last. I need you to rub on your clit. I need you to come for me."

I move my thumb to my pussy and gather up the wetness he's created and move it to my sensitive nub. I begin rubbing it in circles while he hits some crazy spot deep within me with the tip of his cock.

"Oh, my God. Right there. Please don't stop." Between the friction of my finger to my clit and his cock filling me so completely, I know I'm about to have a huge orgasm. It keeps building, and what feels like seconds later, I lose it. My body tightens before it releases, and it feels like I'm going to blackout from sensory overload. I scream out

Cooper's name over and over again, clearly forgetting where we are.

He must suddenly remember because all too quickly, he's pulling my face down to him and swallowing my cries with his mouth.

Cooper waits for me to ride out my orgasm then flips me over onto my back, his hands on either side of my face, as he starts drilling his cock into me with a punishing rhythm. Within minutes, he finds his own release, pulling out, and coming in his hand.

I look down at him and he chuckles. "We didn't have the whole protection conversation so I didn't want to assume you're covered. I wouldn't be much of a gentleman to knock you up the first time I get back between your legs."

He gives me that damn wink and stalks off to the bathroom that's attached to the room. A few minutes later he comes back with a small, wet washcloth and wipes between my legs to clean me up. I feel myself blush at this action, as if him doing this is even more intimate than what we just did.

"C'mon baby, don't get shy on me now."

I smile at him and then get up to go use the bathroom. I grab my panties and put them back on while I go pee. I flush the toilet and wash my hands. Looking in the mirror I see my reflection. My face is flushed, my hair is a mess, and my eyeliner is smudged, but I can honestly say I can't remember the last time I looked and felt this content and satisfied and…taken care of. I know what, or I should say who, caused this look and this feeling in me. Cooper. He invokes these feelings inside me that nobody else ever has.

I just want to cuddle up in his arms and never lose the way I feel in this moment. Now I just have to pray when I tell him about Bella he won't run the other way.

I walk out of the room and find him sitting on the end of the bed dressed again. I take a second to watch him and notice his head is in his hands and he's slumped over. My initial thought is, *did I do something wrong? Does he regret this?*

He must sense my presence because he looks up and tries to play it off by smiling way too big, but it's too late because I already saw. I wait for him to explain, and when he doesn't, I go over and sit next to him. I want so badly to put my arms around him or take his hand, but I have no idea where his head's at so I sit close but refrain from touching him.

I swallow the thick lump in my throat and summon up the courage to ask what I'm thinking. "Cooper, did I do something wrong? I mean, do you regret what we just did?"

His head flies, and his eyes meet mine, his expression softening. "Why would you even think that? Of course, you didn't do anything wrong. I could never regret being with you. It was perfect. You're perfect."

I hear the words he's saying, but the thickness of his voice tells me something's wrong regardless of him trying to convince me otherwise. Now my mind is running all over the place. *Does he have a girlfriend? Did he just cheat on her? Oh, God. Am I a homewrecker?*

Going against my initial instincts, I take his hand and put it into mine, needing to touch him in some way. He looks at our joined hands and gives me a small smile.

"Liz, there's something…"

"Cooper, I need to…"

We both laugh, but I can feel the uneasiness between us. It's like a wall is being put up and I can't get over it fast enough to get to his side.

"You go first." He's clearly upset and I think I'll explode if I don't find out why he's done a complete one-eighty.

He sucks in a deep breath and releases it with a sigh. *This can't be good.* My heart feels as though it's going to implode in my chest while I wait impatiently for him to speak.

"Liz, when we met five years ago I wasn't looking for love. As you can see now, I'm a fighter. It's my entire world. I told you a little bit about my dad during our time together, but there's so much more to it. I won't get into all the details, but what you need to understand is, I can't give you what you deserve."

My hands begin to shake and the lump in my throat is back. I can see where this is going, and it's clear we're not on the same page at all. Even if he doesn't want me, all I can hope for is he'll at least want our daughter. I hope he doesn't think I was trying to trap him. What if he doesn't want her? How will I tell her that her father doesn't want her? I need to calm down. I'm getting ahead of myself. He hasn't said anything yet.

"I never thought in a million years I would ever see you again. The connection we shared in Miami ruined me, baby girl. You ruined me. If I was looking for love, I'm pretty damn sure you would be it. No, I am damn sure you would be it. You're beautiful and sweet and so damn innocent. How you're still single is crazy. Some guy is going to figure out how amazing you are one day, and when he does, he'll grab hold of you and never let go. The problem is I'm not looking for love and I'm not the guy for you. I don't do commitment and I'm not husband or father material. I don't plan to ever be in a relationship where the girl requires either of those roles from me."

The entire time he's saying all this, his head is down like he's ashamed of himself and can't look me in my eyes. Finally, he looks up and gives me the saddest smile I've ever witnessed, and my heart plummets into the pit of my stomach. My heart beats erratically, making me feel as if I'm having a mini heart attack. He doesn't stop there though, so I try to remain calm to hear him out.

"When we hooked up in Miami, we both knew it was a one-time thing, but then when I saw you tonight at the fight, my head started to spin. I never thought about what I would do if I saw you again. I reacted without thinking. What we did tonight was wrong. The fact is you deserve the entire world. You deserve the husband and kids and goddamned white picket fence and the happily ever after, and I can't give you any of that. I never should've touched you knowing I have no intention of being with you in any way but physical."

"Why can't you?" That's the only thing that comes out of my mouth in response to what he just said. Is it that he doesn't want any of that or is there something stopping him from being able to have it all?

He lets out long sigh and says the words I was praying he wouldn't say. "I don't want any of that." I can feel a panic attack coming on, my heart shattering into a million pieces. The air is leaving my lungs, and it's hard to breathe. I need to get out of here before he sees me lose it.

He doesn't want it.

He doesn't want me.

He doesn't want our little girl.

He doesn't want to be a part of our lives.

I get up slowly from the bed and will my body to hold back the tears that are forming. "I understand."

As I head out of the door, I pray he doesn't try to stop me because I don't think I can hold my emotions in much longer.

As I run out the door, I hear him calling my name, but I don't stop. I can't stop. I don't know how I read this all wrong. I'm definitely no expert in the love department, but I was way off. We aren't just on different pages…we aren't even reading the same book. I don't think we're even browsing the same genre at this point. It's like I'm in fantasy and he's in non-fiction.

I walk quickly through the house looking for Kayla. I need her and I need to get out of here now. I need to go pick up my daughter and hold her.

I find Kayla standing outside with Bentley by the bonfire. She's laughing and touching his chest while he rubs his hand up and down her arm. Are they on the same page? They're both smiling and laughing but apparently that doesn't mean anything because Cooper and I were laughing and smiling and now my heart is breaking. At least he was honest with me and didn't lead me on, but maybe he should've told me all this before we had sex. At the same time, I'm glad I had this time with him. I refuse to regret it.

The truth is I'm not even mad, I'm just sad. I really just need to get out of here. Only a few more minutes. I need to hold it together for a few more minutes and then I can let go.

Bentley spots me coming over and nods my way. Kayla looks behind her and I know she can see the pained look in my face because she drops her hand from Bentley and runs over to me.

"What the hell happened, Liz? What did he do to you?"

"I can't talk about this here. Please. I need to leave. If you want to stay, it's fine. I don't want to ruin your..."

Kayla doesn't even let me finish the sentence before she cuts me off. "Stop! Stop it right now. You know damn well I have your back and there's no way I would *ever* stay at this party or anywhere else for that matter when you need me. Let's go."

She takes my hand and pulls me alongside of her to the car in silence.

As we're walking down the driveway, I hear Cooper scream my name once again. I attempt to run, but he catches up quickly. I get to the car and turn around to see him standing right in front of me. I can't say anything. I'm choking back the tears, and if I say a single word, the tears are going to release.

Cooper looks at me like I'm the one who just broke his heart as he lifts his hand up to my face to touch it. It's then I feel it, the wetness he's wiping off my cheek. *Damn traitor tears.* He wipes one on the other cheek away and chokes out, "I'm sorry." No sooner are the words out of his mouth, his back is turned to me as he walks away.

I want to scream at him, run up behind him and pound on his back. I want him to take back every word he said in the last ten minutes. I can handle him not wanting me. I can handle not having him. Yes, it hurts like hell, but I can handle it. I'm strong and know I can make it through anything, but the fact he doesn't want our daughter drives a sword right through my heart.

However, I don't go over to him, and I don't scream at him. I accept his decision because I would rather know now how he feels than take a chance of him hurting our daughter. It's for the best that it's over before it even began.

I get into the car and wait until Kayla is out of the driveway to cry. I cry for my little girl. I cry for the fact that she has a father who doesn't want her. I cry for my innocent, sweet angel who'll never know a father's love. For years, I wished to run into him so I could tell him he has a daughter. Well, you know what they say, *be careful what you wish for...*

While we're driving, Kayla tells me it's probably best to leave Bella with Ashley for the night. It's already after two in the morning and picking her up would mean waking everybody up in the house. As much as I want Bella in my arms, I agree with her, so we head to our apartment.

We get home and I'm surprised Kayla hasn't jumped on me to tell her what's happened yet. I get in the shower and let the hot water burn my skin. I grab my loofa and squirt some soap onto it, scrubbing down my body and wishing I could scrub away all the hurt I feel inside me right now.

When I can't take the pain in my chest anymore, I sink down to the floor of the shower, letting the water beat into the back of my skull. I close my eyes and let the tears fall as I make a new wish—to go back five hours and not see Cooper because then I can have it in my head that my daughter's father doesn't see her because he doesn't know about her, not because he doesn't want her. I make a deal with myself. When I get out of the shower, I'm going to start fresh. Looking back it's almost like I put my life on hold in hope one day Cooper would come back. Now that I know how he feels, it's time to move forward. I refuse to be some pathetic woman who wants a man who doesn't want her back.

Kayla knocks on the door and I realize the water's gone cold. I stand, turn the water off, and get out. I look in the mirror and promise myself I'll never cry over Cooper again.

Hearing the knocking still coming through the door, I yell out that I'll be out in a second, then grab a towel, dry myself off, and put on some comfy pajamas.

I take several deep breaths, then head out to the living room where I find my best friend sitting on the sofa with two pints of our favorite Sorbet ice cream and a bottle of sweet white wine. She hands me a spoon and pours us each a glass. Ice cream and white wine is our thing. For a second, the urge to cry again hits me, but when I look at Kayla, I remember that while Cooper may not want us, I'm surrounded by people who do.

We sit in comfortable silence, eating our ice cream and sipping our wine, when she finally brings the subject up. "So, what happened? You guys were practically dry humping in the living room before you went to the bedroom. You come out and it's like somebody just told you there's no Santa Claus."

I have to laugh at that, and then I look at her and scowl, which makes her laugh. When we were nine years old, I spent hours writing my letter to Santa. When Kayla came over to play one day, she saw it on my desk. I asked her if she wrote her letter yet and when she said no and she isn't going to, I asked her if she believed in Santa. Kayla told me flat out she didn't believe and that he was fake. It was the first and only fight we ever got into. I told her she was a liar and that I couldn't be friends with somebody who lies. Santa was real. She told me I was acting like a baby and kept insisting there wasn't a Santa. I went to my mom and demanded to know the truth. She admitted there was no Santa and I swear I cried for like three days.

"Remember after my mom admitted there was no Santa, what you said to me?"

She thinks for a minute. "Yeah, I told you I wish I would've lied and said Santa was real because I hated to see you cry."

"Well, right now I'm wishing I could've been lied to."

She waits for me to continue, but when I don't, she prompts me. "Lied to about what?"

I start from the beginning when we went into the room. I tell Kayla how he said he missed me and wished so many times he would've gotten my information. I tell her about us making love and how attentive and sweet he was the entire time. She laughs when I tell her how he pulled out and came in his hand because he said it wouldn't be gentlemanly of him to knock me up.

"Boy, if he only knew that ship has already sailed. Wait, does he know about Bella?"

I breathe in, and let out a cleansing breath, as I prepare to get to the hard part.

"I never got a chance to tell him. After we got cleaned up and dressed, he got all weird on me. It's like a switch flipped in him, and he went from sweet and flirty to depressed and sad. Before I could tell him about her, he flat out told me he can't...no, he told me he doesn't *want* to offer me any type of future. He said I deserve everything he can't give me. When I asked him why, he said he doesn't want to be a husband or a father. I didn't even know what to say. My heart just broke thinking about one day having to tell Bella her dad isn't around because he doesn't want her, so I decided not to tell him. At least then I can be honest and say he doesn't know about her. After he said all this, I got up and left, and that's when I found you and you know the rest."

"So, he doesn't know that Bella exists?"

"That's what I just said. What was I supposed to say? 'Oh, that sucks you don't want to ever get married or have kids because surprise, you have a daughter.' Um, no. I wasn't about to open myself or Bella up for him to tell me flat out he doesn't want our daughter."

Kayla stays silent for a minute thinking. "Maybe he only said that because he doesn't know he has a daughter. Sometimes we don't know what we want until it's right in front of us. Maybe if you tell him he has a daughter he'll change his mind. When he said all this to you, it was strictly hypothetical, right? He wasn't actually saying he doesn't want Bella. It's like when you send me to the grocery store with a list and I end up picking up a ton more junk food than you told me to. You don't even know you want it and you don't miss it because you don't have it, but once I get home and put those yummy brownies on the counter, you can't help but eat one. No, you didn't put the brownies on the list, but once it's right in front of you, you still want it, right? Maybe right now Cooper doesn't think he wants a kid, but once you show him Bella, I bet he'll totally want her."

I stare at her for a second thinking about what she just said then bellow out a laugh so hard, my stomach cramps up. "Did you seriously just compare my daughter to a brownie? We're talking about a living, breathing, innocent tiny human being. Not a piece of chocolate."

Kayla laughs and then gets serious. "Well, she is as sweet as a brownie, and once you get to know her, you're addicted."

And this is why Kayla's my best friend. She knows just what to say.

Twelve

COOPER

IT'S TWO IN THE AFTERNOON AND I'M PRETTY SURE DEATH IS knocking on my door. After Liz left last night, I tried my hardest to forget about her, but I should've known by now, that girl is unforgettable. As proof, several hours and a bottle of Jack later, not only did I not forget about her, but I couldn't take my mind off her.

At one point my drunken ass wanted to go after her, but Bentley told me to leave it be until I was sober. Being drunk and trying to talk to her wouldn't help the matter. I finally passed out in Kaden's guestroom to the smell of Liz's sweet scent all over the bed.

Now I'm in the gym fighting against Bentley and I'm pretty sure I'm sweating out the entire bottle of Jack through my pores. My head is pounding and I'm close to throwing everything in my stomach up.

"So now that you're sober, what do you plan to do about Liz?" Bentley asks while throwing a punch to my stomach.

I dodge it, and sigh in relief, almost positive if he'd connected, I would've thrown up all over the ring. I stop fighting and bend over panting like I haven't worked out in years. He walks over and punches me in the arm, while chuckling at my pain. *Asshole.*

"There's nothing to do. For one, nothing has changed from last night to today. She deserves to be with a man who can one day marry her and gives her kids. I can't be that man. I would never want her to go through what my parents have gone through. And two, even if I wanted to take back what I said, it wouldn't matter because I didn't get any of her information. I wouldn't even know how to contact her."

Bentley looks like he's going to give me another one of his lectures but changes his mind. "You're aware her best friend works at this gym, right? And even if she didn't, I got Kayla's number last night."

I shoot my head up. *Shit, this is a game changer.* How will I ever be able to stay away from her knowing I have access to her? It was easier when I thought by not having her information, the choice was made for me. Now, knowing I can get ahold of her, makes me second-guess everything.

Of course, my dad decides to come over at this moment, and by the look on his face, I can tell he overheard our conversation.

"Bentley, if you want to stay training at this facility, I suggest you make choices that help Liam and not hurt him. I would recommend you throw that number away and both of you focus on what's important." First, he points to me. "You have a title fight in six months you need to be training for."

Then he points to Bentley. "And you need to stop fucking around and take this shit seriously. Any more losses and you're going to be removed from this team. I can't have you tainting my gym's reputation. I signed you up to fight against Dante Cobalt. The fight is in two months. You need to win this. Understand me?"

Bentley looks like he's about to rip my dad's throat out, so I jump in and tell him we understand so he'll walk away. Bentley turns to me, fuming. "Bro, why the hell do you let him talk to you like that? If it wasn't for your reputation, this gym wouldn't be doing half as popular as it is. It's you that brings the people in. Fuck him."

I get what he's saying, but it's pointless to argue with either of them, so I just shrug my shoulders and head to the locker room to try and wash away some of this hangover. I need my mind clear if I'm going to figure out my next move.

Thirteen

LIZ

KAYLA AND I ENDED UP TALKING THROUGH THE NIGHT WHILE enjoying our ice cream and wine. On my way to Ashley's to pick up Bella, I can't stop thinking about what Kayla said to me about Cooper. She's right in a sense. He doesn't know he has a daughter. I think I need to tell him about Bella and leave the ball in his court. If he still doesn't want anything to do with her then at least I can say I tried. I don't want Bella to grow up one day and think I purposely kept her father from her.

I pull up to Ashley's house and am barely out of the car, when Bella barrels out of the door, leaving it wide open. She throws herself into my arms, and I pick her up, holding her tight as she pulls her head back and gives me the most adorable toothy grin. "I missed you sooooo much, Mommy! Did you miss me?"

"You bet I did. I missed you to the farthest, brightest star and back."

Her eyes go wide before she starts to giggle. "Mommy, you're so silly. You can't miss me that much. The stars are like infinity miles away!"

"Well, that's how much I missed you. Did you have a good time with Tristan?"

"Yes! We played Uno like a gazillion times and I won more times than him." Her voice goes lower like she's telling me a secret. "But I saw he was getting sad, so I let him win so he would be happy again."

I look at my little girl and feel so proud to call myself her mother. She's so caring and has such a huge heart. I can't imagine not having this beautiful little miracle in my life. If Cooper doesn't want her in his life, he's the one losing out.

She hugs me again and thanks me for letting her spend the night here. I tell her she's welcome and decide for sure I'm going to tell Cooper about Bella. Whether he wants her in his life or not, he deserves the chance to make the decision.

Then it hits me…I left the party without getting his information again.

After having coffee and chatting with Ashley, we head back home to find Kayla passed out on the couch, limbs sprawled out, looking like she's barely breathing. This is what happens when she drinks too much.

Bella walks up to her slowly, placing her fingers under Kayla's nose, and smiles at me.

"Whew! Don't worry, Mommy, I can feel her tickling my finger. She's okay."

I try not to laugh at the fact that my daughter just confirmed Kayla's not dead.

"Bella, you're silly. Of course, she's okay. She just fell asleep on the couch watching TV. Why don't you bring your backpack to your room and empty it out and I'll make you some cereal?"

"Ooo-kay, Mom!" She drags her backpack full of toys and clothes she brought to Tristan's last night down the hallway to her bedroom.

"Hey sleepy-head, wake up!" I yell into Kayla's ear, causing her to jump a half a mile into the air and grab her chest like it's about to explode. She looks around and then glares at me.

"Was that necessary? After I stayed up all night comforting you with ice cream and wine, that's how you repay me?"

I ignore her question and ask the one that's been on my mind since I left Ashley's. "You don't by any chance have any of the guys' numbers from last night, do you? I made the decision to tell Cooper about Bella and then realized I, once again, didn't get his damn number."

"You're in luck. I just so happened to get Bentley's number last night."

"Oh, awesome. Wait a second, you, miss no commitment, miss one-night stand, miss no strings attached, miss never get a guy's number or give him yours, actually got a guy's number?"

"Trust me, I didn't ask for or want it. When I set my phone down on the counter to pour myself a drink, he stole my phone and wouldn't give it back without calling himself from my number so he could have mine. I was seriously pissed, but it looks like it was for the best, because now I can look in my call log and we can get Cooper's number from him."

She gets out her phone and pulls up the number from the recent calls list and hits call. She waits a beat and gets the voicemail. After a few seconds, she hangs up and starts typing on her phone.

"What are you doing?"

"I got his voicemail, so I'm texting Hayley to find out the name of the gym. Okay, here we go. She said it's called Cooper's Fight Club and it's only ten minutes from here. Here's the address. This should be something you do in person." She sends the address to my phone and it beeps with the text from her.

"Isn't it crazy that for the last few months Hayley has been working with these guys and we had no idea?"

"Seriously! To think Cooper was so close this whole time is mind blowing."

"Okay, just pull the address up on your GPS and head over there."

I don't think I can do this in person. It's one thing to tell him about Bella over the phone where I can't see his looks, but to tell him in person feels like I'm making myself too vulnerable to him.

Kayla must sense what I'm thinking because she doesn't give me a chance to protest. She is literally pushing me out the door as she yells for Bella to get her cute butt to the kitchen to help make pancakes.

"Go. Go tell Cooper about Bella and we'll be here when you get back. I got her. Everything's going to be fine." *I really hope she's right.*

I follow the directions on my GPS and pull up to what looks like a state of the art gym. The building is huge and looks like it is three stories high. It's all by itself in its' own complex. The entire front of the building is made of mirrored glass and there's a huge sign that reads:

COOPER'S FIGHT CLUB

HOME OF UFC'S OWN 'THE RAGE'

Directly underneath it, is a life size *Cooper* in a fighting stance in gym shorts and nothing else. He has his hands up in fists and he's glaring in the photo. It looks so real, it's scary. I would seriously hate to get on his bad side.

I stand outside of the door for a few minutes, staring at his picture and trying to muster up enough courage to tell the man who told me less than twenty-four hours ago he doesn't want a wife or kids that he does, in fact, have a kid.

Just when I finally decide to put on my imaginary big girl panties and go inside, the door swings open and almost smacks me in the face. I jump back, immediately recognizing the person holding the door open. It's the older guy from the other night, no wait, from last night. *Jeez has it only been less than a day since the fight? This has seriously been the longest twenty-four hours, ever.*

He clears his throat to get my attention and I smile at him. If I'm right, this man could be Bella's grandfather. He doesn't smile back, though. In fact, the glare Cooper has on that poster on the wall has nothing on the daggers this man is shooting me with right now. Instinctively, I back up a little and get control of myself.

"Hi, my name is—" I'm not even able to get out my name before this guy cuts me off.

"I know who you are and I know who you're looking for. You're wasting your time. He doesn't want anything to do with you."

Well, okay then. I try my best to keep a smile on my face. "That may be true, but I need to speak to him, nonetheless. It's very important."

"Well, he's not here, and even if he was, he made it clear he doesn't want to speak to you."

The way he says it leaves no room for argument, so I simply say okay and walk back to my car. I'm not about to get into a fight with this man. Something about him feels off.

Fourteen

LIZ

THE REST OF THE WEEKEND'S SPENT LAZILY LOUNGING ON the couch while watching movies with Bella. Of course, her latest favorite is Disney's *Maleficent* so we have to watch it twice.

The second time we're watching it, when the mom dies, Bella turns to me with a sad look on her adorable face. "Mommy, if you die, who will take care of me since I don't have a daddy?"

I look at Kayla and she gives me a small encouraging smile. I really need to tell Cooper about her. This isn't about anybody but Bella.

"Angel, first of all, I'm not going anywhere. However, if something did happen to me, Auntie Kayla would still be here and so would Grammy and Papa and Uncle Mattie even though they live in Florida. You would never be alone."

I hope this will satisfy her, but of course it doesn't. She's way too inquisitive to accept that answer.

"Okay, Mommy, but where's my daddy?"

I've always known this question was coming, but nothing prepared me for the pleading look in her eyes when she asks it. I'm her mother, which means it's my job to protect and love her. It's my job to make sure she always feels wanted and never hurts, especially when I can help it.

"Umm…" I'm totally stalling, having no clue how I'm going to explain any of this to her. Thank God for Kayla's quick thinking.

"Oh, my goodness! Bella, I just remembered I have all the ingredients to make a batch of fudge brownies. Want to help me?"

Bella's eyes light up and she jumps up and down cheering, "Yes. Yes. Yes," forgetting all about the Daddy question for now.

Of course, when Kayla blurted out that she has the ingredients what she really meant was she has no ingredients. So now we're on our way to the grocery store to pick up the stuff to make the brownies. I want to be annoyed, but I can't be because she totally saved me. I have no idea what I would've said to Bella about her daddy. There's so much going on in my head, but I know that the first thing I need to do is corner Cooper and tell him he has a daughter, even if he wants nothing to do with me. Once I know whether or not he wants Bella in his life, I can figure out my next move to ensure my daughter doesn't get hurt.

We walk up and down the baking aisle, gathering all the ingredients to make my mom's famous fudge brownies. Once we have everything we need, we're heading to the checkout line, when I hear, "Excuse me Miss, I think your daughter dropped this."

I turn around to the familiar voice and stare into the same beautiful green eyes my daughter has.

I'm stuck frozen in place as I catch the recognition in his eyes. First, that it's me he's speaking to, then at the fact he just referred to Bella as my daughter. His eyes turn cold and hard, his body visibly tensing, as he places all the pieces together in his head.

Slowly, I take the raggedy pink stuffed flamingo from him. "Thank you."

Luckily, Bella breaks the uncomfortable moment with her sweet little self. "Mommy, my flamingo! I didn't even see it drop." She turns to Cooper. "Thank you. I love my flamingo. Mommy gave me it when I was a little, little, tiny baby, and she said it's very special to her because somebody special gave it to her. You know what else I love?" She doesn't even wait for him to answer. She just keeps on going in typical Bella fashion.

"I love *Maleficent*. It's my most favorite movie ever. And there's a dragon in the movie. I want the dragon so he can be friends with my flamingo. I asked my Mommy to buy me the dragon, but she said I have to ask Santa. Do you know how far away Christmas is? Like a gazillion trillion days away. I will die before I get my *Maleficent* dragon."

I laugh quietly at her ranting away to Cooper. It's her favorite movie right now, but by next month it'll be something entirely different. I must be smiling outwardly because Cooper cocks his head to the side like he's waiting for me to fill him in.

"She has a different favorite movie every month."

One of his brows quirks up, and I realize that's not what he was referring to. *Oh, shit.* He wants me to address the elephant in the room, or in our case the adorable four-year old standing next to me.

"Mommy, let's go! You promised we would make Grammy's brownies. Auntie Kay is waiting for us."

She grabs my hand to pull me away, ignorant to the silent conversation currently taking place. When I don't move, she looks up at me with a questioning stare.

Of course, this is the moment when Kayla decides to end her phone call outside and comes walking over oblivious to what's happening. How she doesn't see Cooper standing there boggles my mind. The guy is like a damn wall. He takes up so much space, it's impossible not to notice him.

"Hey Liz, what's taking so long? I thought for sure you would be done before I got off the phone with my boss. Now I'm craving some vanilla ice cream to go with the brownies." She laughs but stops when she takes in the intense situation in front of her.

"Oh, fuck," she spouts out before covering her mouth, remembering there's a little person right here.

"Ooooohhhhh, Auntie Kay! You said a bad word." Bella starts wagging her finger at Kayla like I do to her when I'm upset with her. Even though she's so damn adorable, this does nothing to break the awkwardness surrounding us. Cooper is watching all of this probably thinking we're nuts.

"Yes, I did. I'm sorry. I shouldn't have said that. Bella, why don't you come help me find the vanilla ice cream to go with our yummy brownies?"

She doesn't wait for her answer as she grabs Bella's hand and drags her along, giving us both one last glance before disappearing down the aisle.

"Is she mine?" *Well, damn, I guess we're going to dive right in.* There's no reason to deny it at this point.

"Yes, she's yours."

"Did you plan to ever tell me about her?" Is this guy serious right now? Judging by the look on his face, I think he's dead serious. If looks could kill, I would be in a puddle of blood on the ground right now. Well screw that and screw him. He has no right to be mad at me. I didn't do anything wrong.

"When would you have liked me to tell you, Cooper? When I found out I was eighteen and pregnant with no way to contact you since you never gave me any information on you? Or how about the other night when you made it clear you wanted nothing to do with ever being a husband or father? Or maybe I should have screamed it from outside your gym when your asshole bodyguard told me that, according to you, I'm not welcome there, and you want nothing to do with me. When should I have told you that we have a daughter? Huh, Cooper?"

His face softens for a second and then goes hard again. "What fucking bodyguard? You came to the gym? When?"

"I showed up yesterday morning, determined to tell you about Bella, and before I could make it in, some asshole guy, who looks a lot like you, stopped me and said he knew who I was and that you want nothing to do with me, leaving me no choice but to leave. I was planning to try again, but I needed to figure it out in my head how to handle it. None of this is going how I spent the last five years imagining it would. I'd never keep your daughter away from you even if you don't want anything to do with either of us."

He looks so pissed I swear smoke is about to come out of his ears. That rage better not be aimed at me. "I can't believe him. I told him to mind his own business." I tilt my head to the side confused. Is he talking to me or to himself?

"That must have been my father. He makes it a point to get into my business when it can possibly take my full attention away from fighting. God forbid I do anything that messes with his potential income."

It's clear there's huge animosity between Cooper and his dad and that saddens me. I can't imagine not having my dad as part of my support system. It doesn't matter that he lives across the country. He's there for me in every way that matters, same as my mom. They've always been my two biggest cheerleaders supporting me, even from afar.

When I found out I was pregnant with Bella they begged me to move home so they could help me, but I knew if I did, I'd never graduate from college. Bella and I try to visit them a few times a year and they come up to Las Vegas to visit us as often as possible as well. Since we're long distance, Bella video chats with them on the computer often.

I hear Bella's excited voice coming back down the aisle and remember we're having this conversation in the middle of the grocery store.

"Look," I say quickly before she gets within hearing distance, "I tried to find you when I found out I was pregnant, but I had nothing to go on. When we had sex, I was on the pill. I just didn't know it wasn't effective yet. I've tried to tell you a few times since I found you, and I'm sorry it never actually came out, but I never intentionally kept this from you. When your dad insisted you wanted nothing to do with me, I thought you told him to say that. I was still going to find you to tell you, though. I get you don't want to be with me..."

He attempts to interrupt me, but I don't have time to argue, so I shake my head and continue talking faster.

"...but I would never keep a child from her father. If you want her in your life, we can figure it out, and if you don't then that's on you. I get you don't want kids and a wife and I respect that. I know I should be sorry I messed up with my birth control but I'm not because Bella is my beautiful little miracle. You need to decide what you want and either way I won't hold it against you. I just don't want her to know anything until you decide. It would break her heart if she knew you knew about her and didn't want her. So, think about what you want. None of this is Bella's fault."

I grab his phone and dial my number into it and hear the ringing on my phone.

"Here's my number. Call me when you decide. But Cooper, think hard because she deserves more than a guy to claim her as his just because he thinks it's what he is supposed to do, and then change his mind later because he doesn't really want her. You can hurt me all you want, but you will not hurt our daughter."

And with that, I hand him back his phone and head into the checkout line. He grabs me by my wrist, looks deep into my eyes, and says, "You gave her the flamingo I gave you." He doesn't ask. He states it. He remembers.

I nod my head quickly and then he nods back before walking away as Kayla and Bella walk over to join me.

"You okay?" Kayla whispers.

"Yeah, let's go make some yummy brownies and ice cream."

"Finally," Bella huffs out, and we laugh at her impatience.

Fifteen

COOPER

TOTAL. MIND. FUCK. THAT'S WHAT I FEEL RIGHT NOW AS I watch Liz walk out of the store holding hands with my daughter. *Our daughter. Liz and I have a daughter.* We created that precious little girl five years ago. I have a daughter that I had no idea about and it's my own fault for walking away that day and leaving her no way to contact me.

She looks like a perfect, beautiful mixture of Liz and me. She has my green eyes and light brown hair, but it is curly like Liz's. She has tanned skin just like the both of us, and when she smiles I can see a piece of my mom in her from her happier days.

For the last fifteen years, I've told myself a wife and kids will never be in my future. After watching my parents destroy each other and our home, I never want to put anyone I care for in that position, which means there has never been any room for love in my life. But looking at that precious little girl and her mother walk away from me makes me want to run after them. I can't believe my dad actually told her I wanted nothing to do with her. He and I are definitely going to get a few things straight.

I jump in my car and head back to the gym and go straight to his office. He's finishing up a phone call, so I wait. He looks up at me without a smile and I'm once again reminded of how miserable this guy really is. I don't think he's smiled in years. He has no real friends and he hasn't dated that I know of since my mom. I can't imagine living my life like this.

"To what do I owe this pleasure, Son? Are you planning on training at all today or are you taking a page from Bentley's book and are simply here to take up space?"

To think for a second I almost felt sorry for him. The truth is he's chosen to live this way. He's chosen to push everyone away, including his own son, and now, without even realizing it, he tried to push away the mother of his granddaughter. I've had enough.

"I'm so sick of the way you treat everyone around you. We all bust our ass at this gym yet nothing is ever good enough. You walk around here all high and mighty, putting everybody down. I get Mom cheated on you, but did that make it okay to destroy her? And what the fuck did I ever do to you? I have tried to love you and be a good son to you, but you don't want love and you sure as hell don't want me as a son."

He leans back in his chair, annoyed that I am ranting to him. "What's got your panties in a twist now, *Liam*? I don't have time for this. Get to the point, please." I hate when he calls me Liam. It's why all my friends call me Cooper. Since I was little, he would only use my first name when he was upset with me.

"All right, I'll get to the point. Did you tell Liz I want nothing to do with her and then send her away?"

"Yeah, I did. You don't need that distraction and she definitely doesn't need to be coming in this gym looking for you. Keep your pussy where it belongs, in the bedroom!"

It takes everything I have not to punch him in his face. I only refrain myself because I know if I do punch him I'll be falling into his trap. He's always looking for a fight.

I do and say the only thing I can, because at the end of the day the only person I can control is myself. "I'm done here. I'm done with you and this fucking gym and I doubt that you even care, but I'm done being your son. Find a new moneymaking machine for this gym. I. Am. Fucking. Done."

I turn to walk out the door and he calls my name. For a second, I hope he'll apologize, tell me to come back in, and want to make this right, but I know deep down that's not his style.

He lifts his chin and says, "Don't bother coming back when you destroy your entire career over a piece of trashy pussy. You're a disgrace to this gym and to the UFC. Close the door on your way out."

I don't even bother to respond. Instead, I simply shake my head and walk out. He'll never change and I'm done living my life like this. If his advice is to stay away from Liz, maybe I should do the opposite because I'll do anything to not end up like him.

I head to the locker room to gather my shit. Once I have it all and am about to leave, Bentley and Kaden come walking in. Seeing all my stuff in my hands, they look from me, to my now open, empty, locker, and back to me again.

"Are you seriously leaving? Where are you going to go?" Kaden asks. I know he's concerned because he's under contract with this gym. He can't train me if I'm not training here.

"I have no idea. I just found out my dad sent Liz away when she came here yesterday to tell me that…get this shit, I have a daughter."

"Oh, shit."

"What the fuck."

"Yeah, I ran into Liz and Bella—that's her name—at the grocery store. She looks just like me. It's crazy. Apparently, she was scared to tell me because I pushed her away by telling her I didn't want a wife or kids the other night. She got the guts to come here to tell me anyway, feeling I should know about my daughter, but my dad decided to be my personal secretary and tell her I didn't want to see her. He actually sent her away. I went to his office to confront him and not only did he admit to it but he defended his actions. I told him I'm done here. I just can't do this shit with him anymore."

Both of them are looking at me with sympathy in their eyes. They've seen the shit I've gone through with my parents for the last several years.

"So, what are you going to do?" Bentley finally asks.

"I don't know. I just need some time to think. I'm going to head home and take a few days to figure this all out. Liz told me I'm either all in or all out as far as our daughter goes, and I don't blame her. Bella deserves to have stability in her life. I need to think about all this. You guys should have seen her. She's so adorable and so freaking smart, and she has my attitude."

The guys laugh at that.

I take a deep breath, then release it and continue. "I just don't know if I can be the dad she deserves. Look at the example I had growing up. A dad barely home, who put his career above his family, then when his wife cheats on him, he lashes out and destroys her entire world, turning her into a drunk. And where does that leave Liz and me? She's been doing this on her own for four damn years because I walked away without giving her my number. She doesn't need this shit in her life. She had this image in her head of what it would be like when I found out and I fucked it all up before she could even tell me. I just need to wrap my head around all of this. I don't want to make their life worse."

Kaden and Bentley both nod in understanding. I'm sure they want to say something, but they can sense I just can't deal with it right now.

"I'm gonna head home. I'll let you guys know what I decide."

"Bro, you know I got your back. If you're sure about leaving this gym, I am too."

I nod and give Bentley a small smile to thank him.

Kaden adds, "You know I can't leave here, but whatever you need from me, I got you. We'll figure this out."

I pat him on this shoulder and thank him, then I walk out of the locker room and out of the gym for what I believe will be the last time.

Sixteen

COOPER

IT'S BEEN FIVE DAYS SINCE I WALKED OUT OF THE GYM. I haven't spoken to anybody during that time. I've started going for a run in the morning and in the evening down by the lake in my neighborhood. Years of training for hours a day keeps me from being able to just sit at home and do nothing. I've had some time to think about what I want to do now that I'm away from my dad and the gym. I'm thinking about joining another training center to get me through this title fight and then taking some time off.

Between all the wins I've had over the last ten years, my contract with the UFC, and the several endorsements and sponsorship deals I have, I have a nice cushion in the bank.

It sucks that Kaden won't be able to train me anymore, but I just can't be around my dad. His latest stunt was the last straw. I've been thinking a lot about Bella and Liz and where I want things to go with them. I need to spend some time getting to know my little girl and her mother. Now that I know I have a daughter, I need to step it up as a dad and make sure I'm nothing like mine. Then there's Liz and me…there was definitely a connection there between us both times we hooked up, but I don't know if I fucked it all up beyond repair when I said all that shit to her. When she was going on and on at the store she made a comment about me not wanting to be with her, but she never actually said she doesn't want to be with me, so maybe there's still a chance for us to get to know each other.

I glance at my phone ringing and check the caller ID hoping it's Liz, but it's just my mom. I send it to voicemail, having too much going on in my head to deal with her right now. I'm not surprised Liz hasn't reached out to me since the day at the grocery store, but I was still hoping she would. She obviously meant it when she said she was leaving the ball in my court so I'm going to need to call her soon so we can talk.

My phone rings again, and I see it's my mom, again. I haven't had a real conversation with her in almost two years. She calls and leaves voicemails occasionally, and I text her back that I'm busy. She doesn't usually call back to back, so I answer it in case it's important.

"Hey, Mom, sorry, I was just out running. Everything okay?"

I can hear her sniffling into the phone but she hasn't said anything yet.

"Mom, are you drunk?"

She starts crying harder. "No, I'm not drunk. If you could ever stand to speak to me for more than five seconds you would know that."

I cut her off, not having the patience to deal with her right now on top of everything.

"Okay, Mom. If you aren't drunk then what's going on? I'm kind of busy right now."

I can hear her sigh into the phone. "Liam, it's your father. He had a heart attack."

"Is he okay?"

"No, sweetie, he's not. I'm sorry but he didn't make it. I guess he never updated his emergency contact information, so they called me."

I sit in the grass and stare out at the lake. I don't know whether to be happy or sad about this. For years, I wished he would just disappear, but I never wished him dead. He was so damn unhappy all the time. I just wish he could've found a way to be happy before passing away. He never even knew he had a granddaughter. Shit, my mom doesn't even know she has a grandmother.

"How did it happen?"

"The doctor said he was feeling chest pains, so he went to the ER. While running tests he had a heart attack and they couldn't revive him. The tests they ran afterward said he showed signs of smoke inhalation, which is weird because he doesn't smoke. They said they found traces of soot in his lungs as well as fluid. They think he might've been in a fire and the fluid in his lungs most likely lead to the shortness of breath, which caused him to have respiratory failure. I'm here at the hospital now. Can you come down?"

"Yeah, I'm heading back to the house now. I'll be there as soon as I can."

"Okay, sweetie. I'll see you when you get here."

I hit end on the phone and begin jogging back to the house. Respiratory failure from smoke inhalation? It doesn't make any sense. *Where the hell was he that he was inhaling smoke?*

Seventeen

LIZ

Three Hours Earlier

"BELLA, IF YOU DON'T GET OUT OF BED RIGHT THIS INSTANT I'm going to hide *Maleficent* from you!" I yell down the hall to my sleepyhead daughter as I finish getting dressed.

I have an interview at an accounting firm and, if we don't get moving, I'll never make it across town in time. I don't know what I was thinking agreeing to an interview so close to when I have to drop Bella off at school.

The first week of school went great. She was so excited to be going, she was up and ready before the crack of dawn. Now, the newness has worn off and she's back to wanting to sleep until noon. Not happening, especially not today. I finish putting on my heels and run back to her room to make sure she's up and getting ready. The fact that she didn't respond to my threat of taking away her favorite movie isn't a good sign.

I walk inside her room and sure enough she's still curled up in her sheets with her little head poking out softly snoring away.

"Bella Faith! You've got to get up. Did you hear me? I'm going to take away *Maleficent* for a week."

She pushes her covers down just enough, so I can see her attitude peeking through. "Oh, Mommy, you can have it because it's not my favorite no more. Dolphin Tale is my new favorite." See? Didn't I tell you? New movie every month!

She starts to contemplate something, and if I wasn't running so late, I might find it funny. Then she actually has the nerve to say, "Mommy, if I get out of bed, can we go buy a dolphin? I want a *Winter!* Pleeeease!"

And with those words, I draw the conclusion my daughter could be a professional hostage negotiator, and to be honest, at this point, I probably would buy her her own dolphin just to get her out of bed, but I'm definitely not going to tell her that. Parenting rule number one: You don't give in to the battle. You give in once and it's all downhill. At this rate, by next week, I'll have to buy her a car to get her out of bed.

"Bella Faith Browning." I'm trying hard to keep my composure because you can't let the enemy know you're sweating. "No, I will not buy you a dolphin, and I'm not negotiating with you. They belong in the ocean! Get up now."

She starts giggling. Yup, actual full-on giggling. I have no clue what she thinks is funny, but in a second I'm going to send her butt to the ocean to play with the dolphins!

"Bella what is so funny? Please get out of bed."

"Mom," she says between giggles. "I don't want to buy a real dolphin! I want to buy a cute squishy one at the toy store. One that is grey and smooth just like Winter the dolphin. Duh! Where would we even put a real dolphin? Wait a second, can it fit in the bathtub? How big is a real dolphin?"

Once again, Kayla, my savior, comes to the rescue.

"How about you go to your interview and I'll take Bella to school? I have the morning off. They're cutting back hours at the sports center." She's sporting a sad smile, which tells me her loss of hours is really upsetting her even though she doesn't want me to worry.

God, I'm such a crappy friend. Kayla works so hard and she's stressing out since she's the sole provider in this house. I really need to get this job. She's done so much for us over the years. I need to pull my weight around here as well.

"Okay, thank you," I say, as I glare at my darling daughter who's back to snuggling under the sheets. I'll deal with her later, hopefully after I'm gainfully employed.

"Wish me luck." I kiss Bella on the forehead and give Kayla a one-armed hug before I rush out the door, hoping I'll be coming home employed.

I'M AT THE INTERVIEW AND IT'S NOT GOING WELL. FIRST OF all, my phone keeps vibrating in my purse, which keeps distracting me. On top of that, the gentleman, Bernard, who's running the interview is speaking in a monotone voice and looks like he's bored out of his mind to be here. I know. I know. Do I really expect a job that involves crunching numbers to be fun? I guess not, but I think he should at least look somewhat happy to be here. If this is how I'm going to look if I get a job here... No, thank you.

My phone vibrates in my purse again, and he looks at me with a brow raised, daring me to answer it. What the hell, I'm not going to take this job anyway. What if it's an emergency?

I excuse myself for a moment to take the call. "Liz, thank God you answered." I glance at the screen, but it doesn't have a name on the caller ID.

"Um, yes, it's me. May I ask who's calling?"

"Liz, it's Bentley. Listen, there has been an accident. Kayla and Bella are both in the hospital. I was here getting my hand checked out and saw them come in the ambulance. You need to get here right away."

Without bothering to explain anything to Bernard, I grab my purse and, with the phone still to my ear, run out the door with a million horrible thoughts going through my head. "Okay, I'm on my way. Bentley, are they okay? What happened?"

"I don't know. I'm not family so they won't tell me anything. Apparently, you're Kayla and Bella's only emergency contact and they've been trying to reach you. I would get down here now."

After telling him once again, I'm on my way, we hang up.

As I drive down the highway, I feel like I'm having a panic attack. Not having any idea what's wrong causes me to consider every worst-case scenario possible, and as a mom, those scenarios are really freaking scary.

After going at least twenty over the speed limit, and running every light and stop sign on the way, I make it to the hospital and run up to the front desk in a panic.

"Hi, I need to find out what's happened to Kayla Peterson and Bella, I mean Isabella Browning. I was told they were brought in by ambulance. Do you know where I can find them?"

The nurse gives me a small smile and types on her computer. "Isabella Browning is the children's wing, room 245C, and…Kayla Peterson is in the patient recovery wing around the corner, room 156R. It says here they were brought in for smoke inhalation."

My heart starts beating even faster, my lungs feeling like they're having trouble working. It's suddenly hard to breathe. *Oh God, my poor baby and Kayla.* "Smoke inhalation? What happened? Are they okay?"

"I'm sorry, ma'am. Unfortunately, I can't answer either of those questions. It does say both are stable. If you want to head to the children's wing, the nurse there can fill you in."

I thank her and head to the children's wing first. I hate that I can't go to both of them, but I know Kayla would understand the need to get to my precious baby first.

When I reach the second floor, the sound of a child crying causes goose bumps to prickly my skin. Every mother knows her child's cries. Not only is it the sound of child's cry, but it's a cry of pain. I pick up my pace and rush into her room, and what I see, breaks my heart. There are what looks like two nurses and a doctor standing over Bella while trying to hold a mask over her face. She has an IV in her arm and she's thrashing around crying. The nurse is trying to soothe her, but isn't having any luck.

I make my way to her bed and lock eyes with my little angel. Her eyes are red and blotchy and filled with tears. Her cheeks are stained pink, telling me she's been crying for a while. The doctor and nurses try to speak to me, but the only thing I can focus on is getting to my baby and hugging her. I wrap her into my arms, holding her close, and attempt to inhale her shampoo, but it doesn't smell right. I can't think at the moment what it smells like, though. She's okay and that's all that matters right now. I can feel her pulse and her heart beating, and that means she's okay.

Bella sobs against my chest, her hot tears spilling onto my skin. I pull my face back a little, trying to kiss away those tears as I rock her back and forth the best I can from next to her bed, murmuring softly into her ear, "It's okay, baby. It's okay. Mommy's here."

She finally calms down and the doctor begins to explain what's going on. "I can't give you the specifics of what happened since the police and firemen haven't come in yet, but according to the EMT's that brought your daughter in, she was in a fire."

I gasp and look down at Bella to reassess her. She looks okay. I do a mental inventory of her body parts, looking for any indication she was in a fire. Her arms look okay and her face is perfect aside from the tearstains. I pull the bedding down to check her legs and everything looks okay. When I get a closer look, though, I notice she has soot all over her hair. I sniff her again, recognizing what I smelt is smoke, like what you smell when you sit around a campfire too long.

I bring my attention back to the doctor and he continues. "When she came in, she was coughing very badly. We hooked her up with a saline drip to make sure she's hydrated and when you walked in, we were trying to get her to put an oxygen mask on to help the oxygen flow. We did a scan and her lungs are clear. She's very lucky, ma'am. The man who saved her covered her face with a wet washcloth, which kept the smoke from entering her lungs."

I feel like I'm in a nightmare. I have no idea where Kayla and Bella were or why they were with a man who needed to save Bella. "Thank you, doctor…"

"Dr. Maven. Please let me know if you have any questions. I'd like for your daughter to breathe into the oxygen mask as much as possible and we're going to keep her overnight to monitor her to be on the safe side."

He gives me a smile, and I shake his hand. I sit next to Bella and thank God she's okay, and that's when I remember Kayla.

"Um, nurse…" I look at her nametag. "Nurse Holly. Is there any way you can stay with my daughter for a few minutes? My best friend was brought in with my daughter at the same time and I have no idea how she's doing."

"Absolutely. I'll be happy to keep Bella company while you go check on your friend." She turns to Bella and bribes her with an iPad to play with if she can put on her oxygen mask for a few minutes. Bella gives in, of course, because, really, what child would turn down the chance to play electronic games? I give Bella a kiss on her cheek and tell her I'll be back soon.

I head down the hall to the adult recovery wing and press the button on the elevator to go down. I need to call Bentley to thank him for getting ahold of me and to let him know where Kayla's room is. As I'm getting on the elevator, I'm staring down at my phone, and without realizing it, I run straight into the wall. Only, it's not actually a wall, but a beautifully fit man, and that man is Cooper standing in front of me. My breath catches and he looks just as confused to see me.

"Did you come here to see Bella?"

"Um, no. I came here to see my dad…well, not see him…Wait, Bella is here in the hospital? Is she okay?"

He visibly begins to panic, so I grab his hand to calm him down. "Yes, she's here, but she's okay. I don't really know what happened. I was actually just heading to see Kayla. This is all so crazy. Both of them were brought in by ambulance. Bella inhaled smoke, but the doctor said she's okay. However, they're keeping her overnight to be on the safe side. I haven't had a chance to see Kayla yet, so I don't know how she's doing or what the heck happened. I guess some guy was there and saved Bella. I really need to find out who he is and thank him. The doctor said he saved her life."

When I notice that Cooper has visibly paled, I stop rambling. "Cooper…are you okay?"

Eighteen

COOPER

I CAN FEEL MY HEART SHATTER. I MEAN, I CAN ACTUALLY FEEL the pieces falling apart as Liz tells me our daughter was brought to the hospital. I don't even know this little girl, but I can feel it in my heart and in my bones when she tells me about what happened. To think I could have lost her before I even got to know her. What was I thinking taking time to consider whether I should be in her life? I'm her father. It's not her damn fault I was raised in a shitty situation. That little girl deserves the world and she deserves for her father to be in her life. I have so much to make up for.

"…I guess some guy was there and saved Bella. I really need to find out who he is and thank him. The doctor said he saved her life."

I suddenly feel sick when I hear Liz speak these words. What are the odds that my dad's cause of death is the same reason my daughter was brought into the hospital? Something is definitely off. It's all way too much of a coincidence. She stops talking and looks at me closely, then asks if I'm okay.

I clear my throat. "Yeah. Yeah, I'm okay. If you're going to see Kayla, who's with Bella?"

Liz straightens up, and it hits me I just asked that too harshly. She probably thinks I'm judging her. I quickly back track before she flips out. "I'm just asking because I can go stay with her if you want. I mean, if it's okay…you know, while you go make sure Kayla's okay."

Her body relaxes and she gives me a small smile, but it isn't her usual happy one. It's got a sad tilt to it.

"I would like that Cooper, but…" She stops for a second to consider what she's going to say next and then sighs loudly. I can tell she's exhausted, so I don't give her a chance to explain. I get it. I might be Bella's dad, but she doesn't even know me.

"You don't have to finish your sentence. I completely get it. She doesn't know me and seeing me would only confuse her. It's okay. I'm really glad she's okay. I was actually meaning to call you. I've thought about everything the last few days and I'd really like to be a part of your and Bella's life, if it's still on the table, that is."

She gives me a soft smile and then wraps her arms around my waist. As she hugs me, her body shakes with soft sobs. I can't even begin to imagine how emotional she must be, and I have no words to comfort her, so I put my arms around her back and rub circles to try to soothe her, just letting her cry it out.

After a few minutes, she calms down, then backs up and gives me a shy smile. "I'm sorry. I don't know what came over me. I'm glad you want to be a part of our life. That makes me very happy. I better go check on Kayla."

Her phone rings from her back pocket, and after looking to see who it is, she answers the call. "Hey, Hayley, I'm so glad you called…Yes, we're at the hospital now, but Bella and Kayla are in different wards… Great, thank you so much…Okay, bye."

She turns to me and looks a little calmer. "That was Hayley. Bentley called her and told her we're here. She's going to come and stay with Kayla tonight, so I can be with Bella."

"That's good. I've only known Hayley for a few months from the gym, but she seems really nice. She's a good asset to the gym."

"I can't believe she's been working with you the last few months and I had no idea you were working with her." She laughs softly.

"Yeah, it's crazy. Do you mind if I join you in visiting Kayla? I think Bentley is in there with her."

I need to get to the bottom of all this, and since Kayla was there, I'm hoping she'll help me get some answers. Luckily, Liz agrees to me joining.

We get to Kayla's room and Bentley's sitting by the side of her bed, holding her hand. Kayla's eyes are closed, and I can't help but think the worst. She must hear us approach because she opens her eyes and starts crying, and although she looks devastated, at least she's alive and okay enough to cry. Liz runs over to Kayla and gives her a hug. They both cry for a few minutes and then calm down.

"Oh, God, Liz. I'm so sorry. I don't even know what happened. After you left, Bella asked for ten minutes more in bed so of course I gave in because I'm a softy. I went back to my room to browse the online classifieds to see if there's anybody looking to hire a physical therapist. I must have dozed off because the next thing I know the fire alarm was going off. I immediately ran to Bella's room to check on her and to see what was going on, but when I stepped into the hallway the whole apartment was filled with smoke. I ran to Bella's room, but it was empty. I started freaking out. I checked her closet, under her bed. I screamed her name several times.

"That was when I started to choke on the smoke, but I swear to you, I kept looking. I went to the bathroom to see if she was in there and I couldn't find her anywhere. By then I heard the fire sirens so I knew they would be there soon, but I kept looking." At this point, Kayla is crying hysterically, tears pouring down her cheeks.

"I started to panic and ran to the kitchen. The smoke was just too much and I blacked out. She could've died and it would've been my fault. I'll completely understand if you hate me. I hate myself. I just don't know what happened. Nothing was on. It doesn't make any sense. Anyway, the next thing I knew I was in the ambulance and they were giving me oxygen. I told them there was a little girl in there and they said she was already out. I thought maybe she got herself out, but the EMT said some guy got her out. I don't know who, though, maybe a neighbor. I'm just so thankful she got out."

"It's okay," Liz says. "I could never be mad at you. Yes, things could've ended badly, but thankfully they didn't. I know you would give your life for Bella. I'm just so glad you're both okay."

As they're talking, there's a knock on the door and in walks a police officer with two firemen. Hopefully we'll get some answers from them because right now I have some crazy thoughts going through my head.

"Hello, ma'am. I'm officer Jim Kelley and these two gentlemen are the ones who showed up to your home to put out the fire. This gentleman, here"—he points to the guy on the right—"pulled you from the fire." They both give a small nod and smile. "I'm glad to see you're okay. Is it okay to speak to you in front of everyone?"

Kayla says yes and informs the officer that Liz is Bella's mom and they all live together.

"Unfortunately, everything in the home was destroyed from the fire. After assessing the situation, we've determined the cause of the fire was intentionally started from arson. We were able to pull up the footage of the security cameras and we have a shot of a guy entering your apartment and leaving, and then entering again. The first time he enters he's carrying a small can of gasoline. What's odd, though, is that he's also the man who saved your daughter."

As he says this, he glances over at Liz, hoping she can help him figure out the confusion. He hands her a grainy-looking picture and she gasps loudly, dropping to her knees. She looks up at me with such confusion in her eyes and I already know who she's looking at in that photo. I can feel it in my bones.

She puts her hand out and I take the photo, looking at it closely. I can tell right away it's my father, and there's no reason for him to be anywhere near where Liz lives.

"The man in this photo is Marc Cooper. This is my father."

The police officer must know what Liz, Kayla, and Bentley don't know yet, that my dad is dead, because he looks at me with a look of sympathy and simply nods his head.

Liz stands and I can see the fire in her eyes. Mama bear is pulling out her claws. The problem is the man she plans to go after for answers is in the morgue.

"Cooper," she spits out. "Where is your dad at? I want to know what the hell happened. Why was he at my apartment? Why did he torch it and then save my daughter? I don't even know what to think right now. I need to find him."

She takes a deep breath before she continues. "If you don't want to tell me, fine! You want to save the man who could've killed Kayla and *our* daughter? Fine! I'll find him my damn self."

As she goes to leave, I grab her arm and spin her around to face me. "He's dead, Liz. My dad is dead."

Nineteen

LIZ

DEAD. HIS DAD IS DEAD. THE MAN WHO TORCHED MY HOME, destroyed everything in it, and nearly killed my daughter and best friend, only to turn around and save my daughter, is dead.

I back up against the bed and sit on the edge in shock. I don't even know what to think or how to feel at this point. This is just one big cluster-fuck. He looks at me with tears in his eyes and I don't know whether they're in mourning over his father or the fact that his father almost killed his daughter.

"Did your dad know about Bella?"

He shakes his head. "After I found out you came to see me, I confronted him and we got into a huge fight. I told him I was disowning him and I quit the gym. He blamed you for me leaving the gym. The only thing I can think of is when you left to go to your interview he went in to torch your place. He must not have known you lived with Kayla and have a daughter. Once he realized somebody was in there he must have gone back to save her. Only he didn't realize Kayla was in there or maybe he couldn't make it back in. He died from a heart attack caused by smoke inhalation. I'm so sorry, Liz. This is exactly why I didn't want to be in a relationship or create a family. My life is so fucked up. This is why I told you that you deserve more."

Bentley walks over to Cooper and gives him a hug, telling him he's sorry for his loss. "I know you two didn't get along, but I never thought he was capable of this."

Cooper doesn't say anything. I can't even imagine how he feels right now knowing his father is the one who put our daughter in danger and then saved her.

I walk over, wanting to comfort him. I place my hands on his forearms, but he flinches at my touch. "I'm sorry for your loss. Your father shouldn't have done what he did, but I'm grateful he made the right choice in the end to save Bella."

He takes a step back and looks at me with a resigned face. "It's probably for the best we didn't tell Bella I'm her father. Neither of you need this in your life. I'm not good for you. I'm sorry."

As he walks out the door without looking back, I repeat the words he said in my head.

I'm not good for you. I'm sorry.

Those words hit me like a dagger to my heart. I've waited for five years for this man, hoping to one day find him, and without even discussing it with me, he makes the decision for both of us to walk out of my life once again. I clutch my hands to my heart in a pointless attempt to ease the pain as I close my eyes, trying to keep the tears that are threatening to release at bay.

The police officer and firemen let us know the report will be available later today to pick up for the renter's insurance and then excuse themselves.

I look over at Kayla and Bentley and start to cry. Kayla waves me over, and I climb into bed with her. I cry for Cooper and the loss of his father. For Kayla and what she went through, worried sick about my daughter and almost dying while trying to save her. I cry for my daughter who was almost killed by her grandfather, who she'll never meet. I cry for the man I care about, who doesn't think he's worthy of love. When I'm all cried out, I wipe my eyes and sit up, moving back to the bottom of the bed.

"Now what?" I ask Kayla.

She sighs heavily. "It'll be okay, Liz. We'll figure it out. We always do." And I know deep down, she's right. With Kayla by my side, we can get through anything.

Bentley clears his throat, and we both look over at him. I completely forgot he was even in the room. He gives us a small smile and says, "Why don't you go back to Bella, and I'll stay here with Kayla. When they're both ready to be discharged tomorrow, you girls can come stay at my place. You've met Caleb. He lives there with me, but he's usually working or at the gym. We have a guest bedroom and, although it isn't huge, we can get a small bed for Bella and it'll give you a place to sleep until you figure things out."

I'm so choked up by his generosity, I just nod.

Luckily, Kayla speaks up and thanks Bentley for the both of us. I give Kayla and Bentley a hug and then head back to Bella's room for the night. I run into Hayley on my way out, but I have a feeling she won't be needed after all.

WHEN BELLA AND KAYLA ARE DISCHARGED THE FOLLOWING

morning, we head over to Bentley and Caleb's place. It's a decent sized condo in the heart of downtown Las Vegas.

We walk in and I'm thankful Bella's old enough to know better than to touch stuff because this apartment is definitely not kid friendly. Bella goes to the couch to find the controller while pouting that there probably won't be anything good to watch, when Bentley points her in the direction of a stack of movies that's almost as tall as she is. She squeals in delight as she starts naming every Disney movie known to man. I smile at Bentley and thank him.

"Don't thank me. Coop came by last night after you left. When he found out you guys were going to be staying here, he went out and bought all that. There are also clothes for you, Kayla, and Bella in the room. He wasn't sure of your sizes, so he had to guess. He said the receipts are in the bags in case you have to exchange anything. There are some toiletries in the bathroom, and he also bought toys and a bed and sheets for Bella. It's all in the guest room as well. He bought all types of groceries, which are in the fridge and pantry, since all we had was water and beer. He said if you need anything else to let me know and he'll make sure to handle it."

I'm awestruck. For him to go out of his way to make sure we're taken care of is so thoughtful, yet it's also saddening because he's made it clear he doesn't want to be part of our lives. He most likely bought all this stuff out of guilt for what his father did even though it's not his fault.

"How is Cooper doing?"

"Not good. He and his mom decided to just hold a small funeral instead of something big. He told his mom that his dad didn't deserve a funeral after what he did, but she insisted they needed to do something. She probably wants Cooper to have some kind of closure. The funeral is in a couple of days. I despise his old man, but I'm gonna go to support Coop. If you need anything, just let me know. I'll have keys made up while I'm out tomorrow. If you hear somebody coming in late at night it's probably Caleb. He works security at a club and casino on the strip, so he gets in late."

With that, he pats Kayla on the shoulder and kisses her cheek then excuses himself to his room.

I know Cooper made it clear he doesn't want to be part of our lives, but I can't just let him bury his father and not be there for him. I decide then that I'll be at that funeral. Not for his dad, but for Cooper. He needs to see that his father's choices aren't his own. I don't blame him, and he shouldn't blame himself either.

Twenty

COOPER

AFTER GETTING EVERYTHING SITUATED WITH THE FUNERAL director, my mom asks me to go to dinner with her. We head out in my vehicle to the local steakhouse I know she loves. Once we're seated, she looks at me softly and says, "We need to talk." I nod, indicating for her to go first.

"When I met your father, I fell in love immediately. Things progressed so quickly that he soon became my entire world. We were inseparable and within a year we were married and a year after that you were born. At first, your dad was so sweet. He was completely devoted to us. He was boxing, but he never allowed it to take over his life. Once he started winning and felt that sense of accomplishment, he clung to it. I was home with you and we were close. In some ways, I think your father resented that my world no longer revolved around his. He would go away for boxing matches, and where I would've gone with him before, I chose to stay home with you. Please understand I'm not in any way blaming you. I just think we had different priorities and we grew apart. There were times when he would be gone for weeks and I became very lonely. Sure, I had you, but it's not the same thing as being with another adult. I tried to fix us, but when I realized we were just going through the motions, I sought comfort elsewhere.

"I know I was wrong. I just felt like he didn't even notice we were there anymore. I didn't want to disrupt our house. My affair went on for five years. When you were twelve, he threw out his back while training and had to come home. He was so miserable, abusing the drugs, and drinking. He missed fighting. I told him I wanted a divorce and when he refused, I admitted to having an affair. He threatened to take me to court if I didn't give him primary custody. Losing you was the worst thing that ever happened to me. I didn't care about him. You cried several times that you wanted to stay with me, but every time, he would tell me that he would destroy me if I tried to get custody. Then, when I had to watch him put all his effort into training you because he wasn't able to fight, I just lost it. I started to drink. But here's the thing. I stopped drinking five years ago."

I open my mouth to say something, but she holds up her hand, motioning to let her finish.

"It's true, I have not had a sip of alcohol in five years. I wanted to be a part of your life so badly, but when you told me you were moving back to Vegas to work with your dad, I knew the best thing I could do was keep my distance. Your father was a miserable, spiteful person, and if he knew you and I were close, I was afraid he was going to take it out on you and your career. I just couldn't do that to you. I don't know if it's too late, but I'd really like to be in your life."

I feel like everything I thought I knew is wrong and I don't really know anything. My parents weren't fucked up. My dad was. My mom made choices she felt were best to save me from him, just as he made choices that led to the life he lived.

I reach over and take my mom's hand. "Of course you can be a part of my life and there's something you should know. I recently found out that I have a daughter, which means you are a grandmother. It's a long story, but her name is Bella and she's four years old. She is the most perfect little princess I've ever seen."

She cups her hands over her mouth and silent tears pour down her face. "Oh, sweetheart, I can't wait to meet her. Thank you!"

"It's time for a fresh start, Mom."

And it really is. I need to get through this funeral tomorrow and then I need to go over to Bentley's to get my family. They don't belong with him. They belong with me. Hopefully I can convince Liz to give me a second chance.

THE FUNERAL IS FILLED WITH PEOPLE WHO'VE ASSOCIATED with my dad in some way the last several years. He may not have been liked, but I have to hand it to everyone who showed up to pay his or her respects.

I feel a hand on my shoulder and when I turn around I see Liz. "What are you doing here?"

"I came to support you. Whether you like it or not, you're the father of my daughter and he was her grandfather."

This woman's selflessness knows no bounds. I pull her into a hug and thank her. As we're breaking apart, my mom comes walking over and introduces herself to Liz.

"Mom, this is Liz. She's Bella's mother."

Liz looks at me bewildered. The last she heard I wanted nothing to do with our daughter or her.

"Oh, sweetie! It's a pleasure to meet you. My son told me all about Bella. I'd love to meet her."

"Of course. She's at home with my friend Kayla right now, but I'm sure we can arrange something soon."

My mom gives her a hug and excuses herself to speak to other people who are here to pay their respects. When she leaves, I look at Liz and give her a soft smile. "I know you just settled in at Bentley's, but I would really like for you and Bella to come and stay with me."

She looks dumbstruck for a second, but it quickly morphs into anger. She pulls me by my hand into a private room away from everyone else and closes the door behind us.

"What changed from the other day to today? You do remember telling me you wanted nothing to do with our daughter or me, right? And that was after you said you did. You are giving me whiplash, Cooper. You've changed your mind like five times. How do I know you won't change your mind, again? Sorry, but Bella and I are just fine where we are. As soon as I find a job, we'll move out. If you want to get to know your daughter, fine, I won't stop you, but you can't expect us to just move in with you after you've played ping-pong with my emotions. I already gave you one chance and you threw it out the window the second shit got rough."

I know she's right, but shit, I've lost enough time with them. I need to take a step back and take things slow, so she doesn't freak out on me anymore.

"Okay, I understand," I say, as I close the space between us.

Needing to touch her in some way, I run the back of my hand down her cheeks. She freezes, unsure of what my motives are, and I hate that I've created this awkwardness between. Leaning down, I kiss the side of her mouth and whisper into her ear, "For now, I understand. I get I have to earn your trust, and I will. And once I do, you'll be in my bed, and in my arms, that's a promise." I leave her to think about everything I just said because I'm not playing around. I'm going to get my family back.

Now, I just need to get this damn funeral over with.

A FEW DAYS AFTER THE FUNERAL, MY MOM AND I MEET WITH the attorney who's in charge of my dad's will. The attorney lets me know I've inherited all the training centers, as well as his life insurance policy, his house, and cars. Of course he didn't leave shit to my mom, but since I have more than enough money, I insist that she gets the money I make off the house when it sells. I make the decision to take the insurance money and put it away in an account for Bella. After what he did, she deserves the money. There's enough that she'll be able to go to any college of her choosing and have a nice nest egg when she decides to start a family or pursue whatever dream she wants.

After our meeting, I go to the gym to let everyone know I'm the new owner. I ask for everyone who works here to join me quickly in the office, and once it looks like most people are here, I begin informing everybody of the change in ownership. Thankfully everyone seems okay with it. Some of the guys give their condolences, but most of them know my dad was a prick, and instead congratulate me on the inheritance.

After they all file out, Kaden lets me know that right before my dad died, the physical therapist on staff quit to move across the country to be closer to family, and that sparks the perfect idea. I just need a little time to form a plan.

I show up to Bentley's place around ten o'clock, hoping to talk to Kayla and Liz, and walk in like I always do without knocking. I have a key and I've never knocked before.

Bentley and Kayla are at each other's throats arguing about something. They stop when they see me and Kayla looks pissed while Bentley looks exhausted.

"What's going on?"

Kayla is the first to respond. "Oh, you know, Bentley thought it would be okay to bring some whore around here last night, and when she went to leave after he was done with her, she walked out half-naked and Bella saw!"

"Look, I said I was sorry fifty damn times! Liz is being understanding about this. I forgot there's a child here. You act like I purposely brought her here and told her to leave, knowing Bella was out there. Damn it, woman! We both know you're just mad because you said you wanted nothing to do with me, so I went out and found someone who does."

Kayla huffs, and as she's about to start in on him again, Liz comes walking down the hall and gives me a smile that turns into a frown. I chuckle at that. She must've forgotten for a second that she's mad at me. Figuring now is the perfect time to throw my plan into motion, I say, "Okay, well, first of all. Before we get into all that, Kayla, I have a job opening at the training facility and was wondering if you'd like to come work there. You would be working with Hayley and the fighters—"

I don't even finish my sentence before she runs over to give me a hug as she chants, "Yes, yes, yes. You are a life saver!"

"You don't even know the specifics. Don't you want to know your hours and pay?"

"Yes, of course, but the job I am at now just let me go today, so whatever you're offering I'll take. The sooner I have an income, the sooner we'll be out of here," she says while glaring at Bentley.

I move on to the next part of my plan directing myself to Kayla still. "Also, about the living arrangements…After what I just walked into, I'm thinking that while you guys start saving for a new place, you girls can come stay with me. I have three extra bedrooms and I promise I won't bring any other women home." I look over at Liz and give her a wink. She just rolls her eyes and crosses her arms over her chest. She looks so damn cute when she's mad.

Kayla looks between Liz and me, then smirks. "Actually, I think all of us there would be too much. How about Liz and Bella stay with you, that way you can spend time with Bella, and I can stay here. It's just temporary. I can handle the whorehouse." Bentley scoffs under his breath at that.

I look over at Liz and she's shooting daggers at Kayla. I also notice Kayla is making it a point not to look at Liz. I already like this woman. Bentley jumps in and says he agrees it's a good idea, and I know Liz can't say no, not when everybody else is saying yes.

She throws her arms in the air, huffs, and says, "Fine. We'll move in with you tomorrow after Bella gets home from school." Then she moves toward me and gets right into my face. She's so close I can smell the vanilla on her, and it's taking every ounce of restraint I have not to grab her and kiss her right now.

She leans in close and says, "But know this, Cooper. I'm only there temporarily, and I'm only there for my daughter, so she's not traumatized from the half-naked women wandering around this place. You and me, not happening. My mom taught me a long time ago that if you share your toy with someone and they break it, it's their fault. If you share it with them again, and they break it again, it's your fault. You have already broke my heart once, Liam Cooper, and you aren't going to get the chance to play with and break it again."

She turns to make a grand exit, but she's crazy if she thinks I'm going to let her have the last word. I trail down the hallway after her, until we get just outside her door. Of course she turns around, raising her eyebrows, daring me to continue this fight.

But I don't need to say shit. I just need to show her. So, I take her face in my hands and kiss her. She tries to pull away, but I hold on to her. When I finish kissing her, I trace my lips to the corner of her mouth and give her another soft kiss, then I move to the spot just under her ear and kiss her again. I know she's affected. I can feel her trembling under my touch, trying to remain calm. I give her one more kiss on her collarbone, and then I turn and walk away. Before I get to the end of the hallway, I look back and see she's staring at me, so I give her that wink that drives her crazy.

"See you tomorrow, baby girl."

Twenty-One

LIZ

WE DON'T HAVE MUCH STUFF SINCE WE LOST EVERYTHING IN the fire. The only items we have are the ones Cooper purchased for us the other night, so it's easy to pack everything up quickly. I drop Bella off at preschool and then attempt to scour the classifieds for a job. Living with Cooper is not a good idea. Sure, it's the lesser of the two evils, but at least living with Bentley meant my heart was safe. I seriously need to find a job so we can move out as soon as possible.

And what the heck was Kayla thinking? Staying with Bentley instead of coming with Bella and me? What ever happened to bros before hoes or I guess for us it would be hoes before bros? Okay, that doesn't exactly work in our favor either, but you get what I mean.

I know she has a thing for Bentley but I didn't think it was enough to make her stay living with him, especially since he's clearly hooking up with other chicks. She and I will definitely be sharing some words.

My phone pings with a text from Cooper. What more could he possibly want?

Cooper: What time does Bella get out of school?

Me: 2 p.m. Why?

Cooper: So, I know what time to get you guys.

Me: I have my own car, and we only have the stuff you bought. Just give me your address and we'll head over after she gets out of school.

After a few minutes, he sends me a text with his address. I go back to looking for jobs, copying down the information of a few possible leads.

After picking up Bella, we head back to the apartment to get our stuff. Before heading over to Cooper's, I need to explain to her what's happening. I'm sure she's confused about moving so many times.

"Angel, do you have any questions about what's going on with us moving?"

"No. I'm just sad all my stuff is gone away and I can't get any of it back," she says with the most heartbreaking look on her face. I make a promise to myself that as soon as I'm gainfully employed, I'm going to buy her as many new toys as I can.

"Do you remember the gentleman we ran into at the grocery store a while back? You dropped your flamingo and he picked it up?" Her eyes go bright at this and then dim down.

"Yes, he was so nice to find my flamingo. My poor flamingo didn't make it in the fire."

"I know, and I'm so sorry." I give her a hug. "But you're right, he was nice. His name is Cooper, and we're going to live with him until we can get a new home. Kayla is going to stay here, though."

Bella takes a minute to think about what I'm saying. "Can he be my daddy since I don't have one? Tristan said Daddies live with you."

This would be the perfect opportunity to tell her that he is in fact already her daddy, but I think it would be best to talk to Cooper first, just to make sure we're on the same page. Then we can tell her together if that's what he wants.

"That is true. Daddy's do live with kids, but how about we focus on moving there first, and then we'll figure it all out." Thankfully, she accepts this answer and starts to gather up the few toys Cooper had purchased for her.

When we finish packing all our stuff, we head to Cooper's house. For some reason, this feels like a new chapter of our life is starting, and I'm not sure how I feel about it.

We arrive at Cooper's neighborhood and I press the button on the call box, so he can let us in. He hits the buzzer and I drive until I see the address he gave me. This neighborhood is absolutely gorgeous. I would never imagine somebody like him living here. I shouldn't be surprised because Bentley and Caleb's place is really nice, but looking around, their complex has nothing on this one.

I pull up into the driveway and park next to his slick, black Range Rover, which puts my old Nissan to shame. We get out and look up at the townhouse in front of us, if you can even call it that.

"Mommy, is this my new house?" Bella asks, awestruck.

"Yes, baby. For a little bit."

We both stand there checking out the home. She's standing by my side, and in one hand, she's holding the replica of the flamingo she lost in the fire that Cooper replaced. She reaches up and grabs my hand with her other one.

The house might be called a townhouse, but it's really more like a miniature mansion. It's got to be three stories high. The only difference between a mansion and this place is that all the homes are connected and all are identical. It looks like there's four homes connected in each set. The outside of each home is white with cute black shutters and a set of stairs that lead to a dark red front door. Directly under the stairs appears to be a garage door. The garage must be the first floor and the next two floors are the home.

I'm no stranger to a nice home. The home I grew up in was very nice but modest, built in the 1960s. It was a typical family-style home. For the last five years, Kayla and I have lived in an apartment made for college students. It did what it needed to do and allowed us to live close to campus and gave Bella her own room, but I think my entire apartment could fit in Cooper's driveway.

We must be admiring his home for a while because he walks out of the red door with a quizzical look on his face and says, "It's not going to bite you. Get in here you two." I nod quickly and go back to the trunk to grab our stuff as Bella runs up to the door. Cooper meets me at the trunk and helps me grab everything.

"This car isn't suitable for driving Bella around. We need to do something about that soon."

He says this so nonchalantly I almost think he's just thinking out loud, until he looks at me and raises one brow.

"Let's just focus on one issue at a time. I can't afford a new car, and once I find a job, my money needs to go toward a new place for Bella and me, and hopefully Kayla, too."

His jaw ticks like he wants to protest, but he decides to let it go. Good thinking on his part, that's for sure. We get inside and the first thing I do is introduce Cooper to Bella. Although she's seen him a couple times, they haven't formally met.

"Bella, this is Cooper. We're going to be staying here in his home for a little bit. Cooper, this is Bella."

They both suddenly look so shy. "Hi, I'm Bella. You found my flamingo when it fell at the store. I have a new one now because it went away in the fire."

"Actually, Bella, Cooper is the one who bought you the new one and…he's the one who bought me the one you had before."

Bella's eyes bug out with this new information. "You're the special person who gave my mom the flamingo?"

Cooper nods. "Yes, I gave it to your mom five years ago when I met her. She said she liked to count animals when she couldn't sleep."

Bella laughs. "She still does! When I can't sleep, she always counts the flamingos for me until I fall asleep." Cooper appears to be so overcome with emotions, I quickly change the subject before it gets too deep.

"Yep, I count flamingos. Anyway, how about you give us a quick tour of this beautiful house and show us to our rooms?"

I hope Bella's room is near mine since I've never been too far from her. Bella must just now notice the stairs because she starts squealing and jumping up and down. "Yay! Stairs! I love stairs. Is my room up the stairs? Huh, is it? Please? I will be so happy and I promise to walk so slowly up and down the stairs. Please!"

Cooper starts chuckling at her rambling, and I can already see the love in his eyes. Bella is easy to love. I just hope it's enough to keep him around, for her sake.

"There are four bedrooms. The master is on this floor with its own bathroom, along with the library-slash-office and a half bath in the laundry room. Upstairs are two more bedrooms. One is your bedroom."

He stops for a second because she starts jumping up and down again, saying, "Thank you" over and over.

Once she calms down, he continues. "There's a bathroom connected to your bedroom and the third bedroom was converted into a small gym. There's another guest bathroom up there as well."

Bella doesn't even wait for him to tell her it's okay to head upstairs before she's flying up the stairs. *So much for taking them slow.*

We both follow her up and when we catch up, she's standing outside her room with her hands over her mouth. "Is this my room?" she whispers with such hope in her voice.

I walk closer to see what the big deal is, and when I look inside, I see the most beautiful little girl's room I've ever laid my eyes on. The room is light pink with a white chair rail running along the length of the walls. On the walls are huge hangings of all the different Disney princess characters including a huge hanging of Cinderella's Castle.

In the center is a huge bed fit for a princess with pink and white polka dotted bedding and in front of the pillows is the dragon from Maleficent she's been asking for. Bella spots it and hugs it to her chest then continues to look around the room.

There's a delicate, light pink, silk canopy spread out over the top of the bed. White wood dresser and nightstands are placed against the walls, and since the floors are all hardwood, there's a cute pink princess rug spread out in the center of the room. Near the bathroom, there's a sitting room that's about half the size of the bedroom. Against one wall is the most adorable pink chair that looks like it's from Pottery Barn kids, and on the other wall is a flat screen television with a DVD player. I walk into the bathroom and the princess theme continues. I look back at Cooper and he looks uneasy like he's suddenly unsure of himself. He's staring down, and his feet are shifting from one to the other.

Bella run around the room, checking it all out, and then stops right in front of Cooper, making him look up. "Is this all mine? Like really mine? Like black-black no trade back, mine?"

"Um, I'm not sure what black-black no trade back means, but yes, this is your room. I hope you like it. I wasn't really sure what you're into," he says, his lips curling into a slight frown.

He's second-guessing all of this, and he shouldn't be. He just made Bella's entire year and he doesn't even know it. "What you did here is amazing," I tell him. "I don't even know how to thank you. Any chance my room looks half as good as this?" I ask jokingly to lighten up the mood.

He starts laughing, and I get to see his beautiful smile return. I can't help but smile back.

"Well, I haven't done anything to the master bedroom since I moved in, but you're welcome to add or change anything you like," he says with a huge knowing smirk across his face.

It takes a second, but then I remember when he named all the rooms he didn't mention a room for me. *Motherfucker. He thinks he's slick. Two can play this game.*

"Oh, that's okay. I'm sure this bed is big enough for Bella and me to share."

Liz: 1 Cooper: 0

Bella glances back and forth from the bed to me, and with hands on her hips, says, "Mommy, I'm almost five years old. I don't want to share a bed with you. Remember when I tried to sneak in your bed and you told me big girls sleep in their own beds." *Well damn it, she has me there.*

I swivel around to give Cooper the evil eye and almost run right into his chest. He must've moved closer to me while Bella was giving me her mom speech.

His eyes are dancing with laughter as he sucks in his bottom lip to keep from laughing. When my eyes lock with his, he says, "Don't worry, baby girl. My bed is big enough for both of us." Then the cocky bastard winks. He actually winks. He's so lucky our daughter is in the room or I'd choke him with my bare hands.

Cooper: 1 Liz: 1

I rub my hands over my face in frustration then walk out of the room. I walk toward the room he said holds the gym and open the door to see if I can put a bed in here. Unfortunately, the room is filled with tons of gym equipment, and a bed, no matter the size, would never fit. I continue down the stairs opening each door along the way. I open the door to the master bedroom and close it immediately. I can feel Cooper on my heels. but I ignore him.

When I open the door to the library-slash-office, I notice there's a comfy oversized reading chair in one corner and a chaise lounge in the other. *Well, this will have to do.*

"I'll just sleep in here. Hopefully, I'll find a job soon and then we'll be out of your hair. Until then I can just sleep on this couch. It looks super comfy." *Ha! Another point for me.*

Cooper walks up to me slowly like he's afraid I might attack him, and I almost laugh at how nervous he looks. He grips the curves of my hips, and before I realize what he's doing, he kisses me softly. I can't help the sigh that escapes my lips as I get lost in his touch. When the kiss ends, I assume he's going to pull back, so I'm shocked when he places another kiss to the corner of my mouth. When nipples tighten and my lady parts tingle, I back up before I completely embarrass myself.

"Look, I know I've messed up," Cooper says. "But I'm here now and I'm fighting. Just give me a second chance to fight for us. Let me at least have one more shot. I have a proposition for you, if you'll hear me out."

There's now a huge lump in my throat. This is all I ever wanted, all I ever prayed and wished and hoped for. I nod my head for him to continue.

"I have a job opening at the gym. My dad ran all the books. I have no clue what I'm doing and I'm too busy training to focus on the money aspect of the business. Come to work for me and live here. Give me this last chance to fight for my family. If, after a while you don't want this, you can move out and we can figure out the custody arrangement for Bella. But I really hope it doesn't come to that. I want both of you. Please."

I want to say no because I feel like he's offering me a job I didn't earn, but I need the money and it would be great to work in the same place as Hayley and Kayla, plus Cooper would be there often. The problem is, can I give him another chance? He's already broken my heart once, and I honestly don't think I would survive a second time.

He takes my chin between his fingers and kisses me once again, letting it linger for a few seconds, when we both hear little feet padding into the room and a shriek coming from Bella.

"Ewww, you guys are kissing like Cinderella and the Prince! Does this mean Cooper can be my daddy? He gave me the most bestest room ever and I love him now."

I laugh at that. It clearly doesn't take much to win over my daughter. Cooper looks scared shitless and that makes me nervous, so I elbow him and tilt my head to the side, silently asking if he's okay.

He snaps out of it and whispers, "She wants me to be her daddy and she loves me." It must all be hitting him at once.

"Bella, why don't you go pick a movie for us to watch in your new room." Yep! Parent of the year award goes to me for once again ignoring her daddy question. She says okay and runs out to pick a movie. I wait until I hear her feet thumping up the stairs, then I turn and look at Cooper, who's sporting a mixture of emotions on his face.

He backs up and sits in the reading chair. Without saying a word, he scrubs his hands up and down his stubble. Figuring he just needs a moment to catch up, I stay where I am.

Finally, after a good minute, he glances up at me and says, "I never thought anybody would ever call me Daddy. And when she asked if I could be her daddy, I thought it would scare me to death, but it didn't. I just wanted to grab her and hug her and never let her go. I barely even know her and I already love her more than life itself. I felt it in the hospital when you said she was brought in, but hearing her calling me Daddy, my heart feels like it just grew ten times bigger. I just want to give her the world."

"I know what you mean. When she was born, I held her in my arms and stared at her, refusing to believe she was mine. I guess it's a parent's love. You don't have to know everything about her to feel that connection."

His gaze locks with mine, and a single tear falls down his cheek. "I missed it all. I missed you being pregnant. I bet you were so beautiful carrying our little girl. I missed her birth, her first steps, and her first words. Damn it, Liz. I missed everything. All because I was a fucking idiot who thought I didn't deserve any of this so I pushed you away. For four years, I had a daughter who had no father all because of the choices I made. I will never be able to get any of that back."

I move closer to Cooper and put my hands into his. "You didn't know, Coop. It wasn't your fault. You had a crappy childhood and you made the choices you thought were best at the time. I was just going off to college. I didn't try to give you my number either."

"Yeah, that was cute the way you got into a twenty-one and older club and acted like you just graduated college," he says with a smirk. "Any younger and you'd have been jail-bait."

I smile big and stick my tongue out at him. Wait until he hears the other half of it. "Oh, well, you also didn't realize that I was a virgin when we hooked up."

His eyes bug out and he goes serious. "Liz, what the fuck. I took you in the shower our first time. Why didn't you tell me? I would have been gentler or caring…"

"No." I shake my head. "You were perfect. My first time, and second time, and third time were all perfect. I don't regret anything we did. I wasn't lying when I said I was on the pill. The problem was I had only just started it a couple days before. I didn't plan to have sex so I didn't look into when it becomes effective. I had no clue birth control pills take a week to work. I was eighteen and stupid. I got to Las Vegas and four weeks later, after throwing up for days, went to the doctor where she confirmed I was pregnant."

"I can't even imagine how scared you were. I wish I could've been there for you. I'm so sorry, Liz."

"It's okay," I say honestly. "Kayla was there every step of the way. We worked part time and took classes and graduated together. It wasn't easy, but we did it."

He lets out a loud sigh, shaking his head. Before he can respond, Bella comes running back into the room. "I got the movie!" She waves it in the air.

"Perfect! Go pick out a couple of stuffed animals and we'll be there in two minutes to watch it." She nods excitedly and runs back out.

"You're the strongest woman I know," Cooper says once she's gone. "You're raising a beautiful, sweet, little girl. Thank you for taking such good care of her. But I'm here now. Please give me the chance to take care of you."

"I want to, Coop. I want to so badly. But you're the one who told me several times you don't want to be a father or a husband. I know I owe it to you to let you get to know Bella, but I'm scared for her and for me. I don't know if I can handle you breaking my heart again. What if you wake up one day and decide you don't really want a family after all? Then what? What would I say to Bella? How would I explain to her that her daddy doesn't want her? You heard her. She's been on this daddy kick for weeks. She hears at school from all the kids who have a daddy. In her movies and shows there's a mommy and daddy, or in many cases like the Disney movies, there's only a dad and no mom. She wants one so badly. What if I tell her you're her daddy and then you change your mind…it'll devastate her. And I'll be left to pick up the pieces."

I wipe away a traitor tear and Cooper frowns. "Baby girl, I know my words don't hold any weight and I've confused the shit out of you with everything I've said. But I promise you, I'm not going anywhere. The fact is, you don't owe me anything, but please just give me a chance to prove I'm in this for the long haul with you and Bella."

It suddenly occurs to me that he isn't playing a game. He isn't keeping points and it doesn't do any good for me to play games. Bella deserves for us to try. We deserve for us to try. This is what I wanted for so long and I'll always regret it, if I don't give us a shot. Sure, there's a chance Bella and I end up hurt, but I want so badly for the other option, the one where we end up together as a family.

So, I give in and say, "Okay, one more chance. We'll see how good of a fighter you really are."

Cooper leans forward and, grabbing my waist, pulls me up into his lap so I'm straddling him, one leg on either side of him. "Thank you, baby," he whispers. Then he kisses me like I just told him he's won the lottery, his lips attacking mine. His hands roam all over my body—up my arms, over my breasts, down my back. I can feel him getting excited between my legs.

Instinctively, I grind against his hardness while lacing my fingers into his hair that's just long enough to grab ahold of. We continue to kiss and his fingers tweak my nipples over my clothes. I need him. I need his body on mine without any clothes…and then suddenly I'm flying through the air, my butt hitting the couch. *What the heck?*

I shoot him a look that conveys he's damn near lost his mind, but he shakes his head, quickly looking toward the doorway, and in the next second, in walks Bella. *Holy. Shit. What kind of mother forgets her daughter is in the other damn room while trying to get laid?*

"C'mon! Movie time!" Bella bounces up and down and then grabs one of my hands to pull me up.

Cooper starts to chuckle. Guessing what's going on in my head, he leans over and whispers, "Tonight, baby girl. You're all mine tonight." And with that, my panties dampen.

Damn this man and his way with words.

Twenty-Two

COOPER

AFTER BELLA DETERMINES HER BED ISN'T BIG ENOUGH FOR all of us, we get situated in the living room, instead, to watch some movie called *Frozen* as Bella explains why she wants to watch this movie even though it came out a long time ago. It's so hard to keep a straight face listening to my four-year-old explain why it's okay to watch an old movie even though she has a lot of new ones.

"It's not that I don't want to watch Dolphin Tale. It's still my favoritest ever. It's just that I love Anna and Elsa and I want to be Elsa for Halloween. I can't be a dolphin for Halloween because that would be so silly!" She says all this as she explodes into a fit of giggles at her own comment. I have no idea what she's talking about, but she's the cutest damn thing.

Liz obviously understands completely as they go back and forth about her Halloween costume.

"Mom, it's so important to get my costume now. If I wait too long and they have no Elsa, I will die." Holy shit. Apparently, costume shopping is a life or death situation to a kid.

"Bella, why don't you wait to decide what you want to be for Halloween? We still have six weeks and you might change your mind."

Bella huffs, clearly not happy with her mother's answer, but chooses not to argue either. *Oh man, I haven't lived with a woman in years, and now I'm living with two. This should be interesting.*

After popping some popcorn and ordering a pizza, we all get comfortable. Liz is snuggled up to me with her head resting just under my chin and Bella is spread out on the floor using the pillows from the couches as a makeshift bed. She looks so adorable lying on her belly with her hands under her chin. I should probably be focusing on the movie, but I can't stop watching my girls. *My girls.* I had no idea I even wanted any of this, and now, sitting here with them, my heart feels so full.

The pizza arrives and we eat in front of the television still watching the movie. Bella gets up every time a song comes on and dances across the room belting out all the words. She has an awesome personality. When the guy kisses the girl, Bella looks back and gives her mom and me a knowing look. I laugh softly at that and give Liz a kiss on her forehead. She looks up at me and smiles contently.

The movie ends and Liz announces to Bella it's time for bed. She groans and begs for ten more minutes, but Liz isn't having it. I wonder if she's thinking about what I mentioned earlier.

Bella says, "Fine," then stomps up the stairs to her room, Liz following behind her. I'm not sure what my role in all this is, since we still haven't told her I'm her dad, so I hang back and wait to see what Liz wants me to do. A few minutes later I hear Bella scream my name from upstairs and I head up there to make sure everything is okay.

"Hey princess, you okay?" I ask as I walk into her room. She's wearing one of the nightgowns I picked out. It's pink with ruffles and has a picture of a princess on the front. She's rummaging through her bag, until she finds what she's looking for.

"A-ha! Got it. I found my favorite book. Will you read it to me?" She hands me the book and climbs into bed.

I look at Liz to make sure it's okay and she nods her head that it is. I walk over to the bed unsure of where to sit when Bella looks up at me smiling and pats her hand on the bed next to her. *Damn, this little girl has officially stolen my heart.*

Sitting awkwardly on the bed next to her, I read the title. "The Giving Tree by Shel Silverstein." I open to the first page and begin reading. At first, Bella is sitting up, her body not touching mine, but eventually she snuggles up next to me to see the pictures while I continue to read. The pages and images are in black and white but that doesn't stop her from enjoying this book. Several times I hear her recite the words along with me. I don't think she can read yet, but she must have heard this book so many times she has the words memorized.

About fifteen minutes later I hear a light snore and glance down to find her fast asleep. I look over at Liz smiling. "She sounds just like you the nights we spent together five years ago. You snore the same."

She narrows her eyes at me, clearly not taking my comment as a compliment. I laugh as I set the book down and gently move Bella's head off my side, slowly moving off the bed.

Liz kisses Bella on her forehead, then turns the light off. The night-light spreads a soft glow over the room, and I take a moment to watch my little girl sleep.

"C'mon, Coop," Liz whispers. "It's bedtime."

Once we're in my room, I jump in the shower to wash the day off me. Definitely not expecting her to join, I'm pleasantly surprised when she enters the bathroom right after me.

Twenty-Three

LIZ

I SWEAR MY OVARIES JUST ABOUT BURST AS I WATCHED COOPER read our daughter a bedtime story. After she falls asleep and we head to our room. He goes straight to the bathroom and a few minutes later the water turns on. Flashbacks of our first time at the resort in Miami, up against the shower wall, surface, sending shivers down my spine.

I don't know what's come over me, but without even thinking, I brazenly enter the bathroom, remove my clothes, and join him in the shower. He turns around, his eyes slowly running down my body, assessing me. Feeling suddenly shy, I cast my eyes down, only to find his erection growing.

He grabs my hand and tugs me into him, putting us both under the water. His hands come up to my face, and with a soft smile, he wipes the wet tendrils of hair out of my eyes. "Baby girl, I want you so bad," he says, his voice thick with emotion. "If you aren't ready, you need to tell me now because having you in this shower, naked and wet…you're making it hard as hell to control myself."

I don't respond. Instead, I squat down so that I'm face to face with his hard erection. Glancing up at him, I find his chest is rising and falling heavily, and his eyes are hooded over with lust. I love that I haven't even touched him, yet he's already completely turned on. He doesn't say anything, so I take his dick in my hand and start stroking it from the root to tip. It's thick with a few veins popping out as it points straight at me, only centimeters from my mouth. I can't be this close to it and not taste it, so placing my hands on his thighs, I steady myself then take his full length into my mouth until it hits the back of my throat.

"Oh, fuck. Liz, that feels incredible," he groans.

His words spur me on as I continue to lick and suck his dick like it's a lollipop, before going deeper and taking more of him. I gaze upward and notice his back is against the wall and his fists are tightened at his sides. I don't want him controlled, though. I want him to let go.

Steadying myself by putting my hands on his thighs, my head bobs up and down sucking his dick forcefully, swirling my tongue around the head every time my head comes up. This seems to do him in and, a few seconds later, his legs are trembling and he's warning me that he's about to come. I don't stop, though. I want to taste him. I want him to come undone because of me.

If I'm honest with myself, remembering all those girls shouting his name at the UFC fight makes me feel like I need to remind him why he wants me and not them.

A few seconds later, his dick swells and he lets out a loud grunt. Then he's coming down my throat. I taste his seed on my tongue before it coats the back of my throat. I take it all, every drop, until his dick starts to go soft in my mouth. His lips lazily stretch into a smile as he looks at me with awe and maybe something else. Could it be love? No, he's just received good head, that's all it is. But I can't deny that it makes me happy I'm the one to put that look on his face.

We finish showering and make our way back into the bedroom to get dressed in comfortable silence. Before I can grab my clothes from the luggage, Cooper pulls me against him, my back hitting his front. Every time he touches me, I swear my body comes alive.

I glance up and can see him in the dresser mirror staring at me with lust-filled eyes. Taking both my breasts in his hands, he begins to massage them. I should be embarrassed that we're both watching him touch me like this, but I'm not. Instead, I simply feel wanted...and seriously turned on. I squeeze my thighs together, failing to quell the ache, needing more.

He continues to palm my breast with one hand, but moves the other straight down to the area between my legs. *Thank God!*

"Spread your legs, baby," he murmurs, and I do. He separates my pussy lips with his two fingers and then push one deep inside me. Simultaneously, he leans down and starts planting kisses along my neck, trailing his way up to the sensitive spot below my ear. He moves his lips up to my ear and gently bites down on my lobe, causing my body to shudder and tighten from sensory overload.

"Oh my God, Cooper. Please." I can see him through his reflection in the mirror, silently laughing at my neediness, but my body is wound too tight to focus on anything but him giving me an orgasm.

"Please what, baby girl? What do you need?"

"I need you. Now. More. Now." I know I'm not making any sense, but surely, he gets the damn point. Of course, his ass laughs at my incoherence, but at least while he's laughing, he obeys by sticking another digit into me. He stops palming my breast and instead begins to tweak the nipple between his fingers. My head goes back against his chest, my eyes closing, as the pleasure from his fingers and mouth shoot straight to my core causing me to moan embarrassingly loud.

And then the feeling stops. My eyes fly open in time to see Cooper walk around to face me until he's sandwiched between me and the dresser. Before I can ask what the heck he's doing, he places my hands against the dresser on either side of him then drops to his knees. I have no idea where he's going with this, but I'll trust he knows.

With him no longer standing in front of me, I see my reflection in the mirror. My hair is a mess and my cheeks are a light pink from being worked up and turned on. I look crazy, but at the same time, happy, carefree.

Something soft and wet hits my clit, and I jump slightly. Looking down, I have a bird's eye view of Cooper's tongue lapping at my pussy. *Holy. Shit. That feels good.* He taps my thigh to spread them wider, then puts two fingers back inside me while he gives my clit plenty of attention. Hot damn, this guy is an amazing multitasker.

While fucking me with his fingers, his mouth is feasting on my pussy. At first, he licks his way up my slit, then he sucks on my clit before he bits down on it, only to lick away the pain. I can hear the slurping sound coming from my pussy while he drinks up all my juices. I can't stop watching him. I've never witnessed something so intimate and erotic in my life.

He continues to suck and lick while fingering me deep. His fingers start to hit that spot, the one that will have me coming in no time. Then his tongue hits my clit in just the right way and I know I'm about to experience the biggest orgasm to date.

He takes his mouth off me just long enough to say, "Look in the mirror. Watch yourself as you come all over my tongue and fingers." And then his mouth is back on my clit. My body, wound up too tight, begins to spasm and shake, as waves of pleasure course through my body as I ride out my orgasm. His tongue and fingers never stop until I've completely come down from what I can only imagine heaven on earth feels like.

"Damn, baby, that was fucking hot, the way you just came all over my tongue. You taste damn good." He stands and licks his fingers clean, leaving me wanting him all over again.

We both clean up in the bathroom then get dressed. As much as I want to lay naked with him, I can't chance our four-year old running in here in the middle of the night or in the morning and seeing us without clothes on. He flicks the light off on the nightstand and spoons me from behind.

No words are spoken for a few minutes, so I assume he's fallen asleep, when he says, "I want Bella to know I'm her dad, Liz."

I know it's only been a few hours, but I'm all in. Watching him tonight with her, I can't deny him this chance. All I can do is hope and pray he doesn't break either of our hearts.

"I know, Coop. We'll tell her tomorrow. I promise."
I feel him relax against me as we both allow sleep to overtake us.

Twenty-Four

COOPER

I WAKE UP TO THE SMELL OF VANILLA AND IT MAKES ME SMILE. I look down and my beautiful girl is next to me, wrapped up in our blankets. I can't help but laugh at the fact she's still a damn sheet-hogger. I don't know how I got this lucky to be given this second chance, but I'm going to do everything in my power to make sure Liz never regrets it. I start to stretch and remember today is Sunday, which is my day off from training. I'm hoping we can tell Bella about me being her dad and do something as a family. *What do families do?*

Not knowing the answer to that simple question reminds me that my parents never did any family stuff. My dad was either traveling for fights or at the gym training. My mom was always home with me, but we didn't really go anywhere as a family. She always seemed upset that my dad was gone. Eventually she'd leave me with a sitter and go out by herself.

And those thoughts start to make me panic. I'm home right now, but soon I'm going to have to be away from home training long hours. I'll have to start traveling again to promote the upcoming title fight. There'll be press releases and conferences and then the fight itself. Bella is in school, so Liz will have to stay home. Will she regret giving me this chance? Will she turn to someone else who can give her more attention? I feel my anxiety rising, my chest tightening at the image of another man comforting Liz. I need to calm myself down. Liz is not my mom and I am not my dad. We will get through this.

"Mommy, Cooper, can I come in?"

Lifting my head, I see my little princess poking her head around the corner. I look back at Liz and she's still sleeping, so I place my fingers over my lips so Bella doesn't wake her mom up.

Carefully, I get out of bed, making sure not to jostle Liz. Then, taking Bella's small hand, I give her a smile and whisper, "Why don't we make your mom breakfast in bed?"

She lights up at the idea and starts skipping down the hallway, pulling me along.

"Yes, please! Can we make chocolate chip pancakes? Oh! And bacon? And can we make cupcakes and cookies, too. Mommy loves all that."

"Bella, you sure it's your mom who loves cupcakes and cookies for breakfast?" I ask, chuckling. The fact my daughter is already trying to get one over on me has me grinning like a Cheshire cat. This girl already has me wrapped around her cute little finger and I'm absolutely okay with that.

"Maybe it's me that likes all that stuff, but I bet my mom would eat it all. She likes junk food too. Her and Auntie Kay always buy it and say junk food makes every woman happy."

"I'm sure they're right. Why don't we start with pancakes and bacon, and we'll see about maybe going out for lunch and dessert later."

"Okay." She stops abruptly and turns around, pointing her crooked pinky out at me. *Damn, kids still do this shit?* I give her my pinky and we hook them together for a good ol' pinky promise. I hope Liz is okay with going out later because there's no way I'm breaking our first pinky promise.

We get to the kitchen and I'm glad I bought groceries once Liz agreed to move in. I grab the griddle and plug it in, then set about grabbing all the ingredients to make pancakes. Bella grabs a chair and drags it to the counter to stand on. Even on a chair she's still so tiny.

"Can I put all the stuff in and mix it all up, please?" She looks at me while batting her eyelashes.

Fuck! Are all women born with the ability to make a man do whatever they want through their damn eyelashes?

"Of course, you can, Princess."

I place all the stuff within her reach, and she begins pouring it all into the bowl carefully, then mixes it all together. While she's doing that, I throw the bacon in the oven. I have to wonder if all kids are this cute and helpful. One thing is for sure, Liz has done a damn good job raising her. At eighteen, I was fighting and fucking. Liz was going to college and taking care of a baby. I wish I could do something to show her how amazing she is, but I can't think of anything that's anywhere near equivalent to this amazing woman caring for our daughter for the last four years.

I spoon the pancake mix onto the hot griddle as I listen to Bella rattle on about preschool and the mean boys who have cooties.

"...And then I told Tristan if he touches me one more time and gives me the cooties, I'll punch him in the face." Hmm…I don't like this Tristan. I'll have to ask Liz about this kid. I can't have some little shit giving my princess any cooties.

"Good for you, Princess. Don't take anyone's crap."

"Ahem. I don't think it's a good idea to encourage our daughter to punch anybody."

Bella and I both turn around to find Liz standing against the island giving us what I imagine is the *mom look.*

"Mom, you're supposed to be in bed. I can't bring you food in bed if you aren't in bed." Bella's standing there looking all cute and mad with her hands on her hips just like her mom does, when she switches gears.

"Wait, Mommy. I'm Cooper's daughter too?"

Liz's eyes open as wide as saucers when she realizes what she just implied, and I grin. Now's the perfect time to tell Bella she is in fact my daughter.

I take the pancakes off the griddle and pull the bacon out of the oven, setting it all on the center of the table. I pour everyone some orange juice and we all sit at the table, Bella and I both looking at Liz.

"Bella, how would you feel if Cooper was your daddy?"

I tense up, waiting for her answer, as Bella nonchalantly grabs a pancake from the platter and says, "I would feel happy. Duh!"

And…my entire body relaxes.

"Well, yes. Cooper is your daddy," Liz says.

I'm wondering if she's going to go into all the specifics. I mean, how do you explain to a four-year-old a *thirty-hour stand?* Yep, I'm still sticking to that. Liz was so much more than a one-night stand.

Apparently, that's all the explanation she needs, though. "Cooper, can I call you Daddy?"

And there goes half my heart…gone. It's now been handed over to the four-year-old sitting across from me, and I pray she never gives it back.

I have to take a second to control my breathing. I'm suddenly choked up and there's a lump in my throat. I'm afraid if I speak, I'll start to cry. Bella's looking at me shyly and I know I need to answer her before she thinks I don't want that. Screw it. *If I cry, I cry.* If that makes me a pussy then so be it.

Sure, enough as the words come out so do the tears. I get up and walk around the table to kneel next to Bella, turning her little legs to face me.

"Oh, Princess. I would love it more than anything in the world if you would call me Daddy."

Bella reaches her hand out and swipes at my face to get rid of the tears.

"Then why are you crying?" she asks in a sad voice.

"These are happy tears. I know it doesn't make much sense, but I promise you, I am so happy right now."

I pull her into a tight hug, never wanting to let her go. She's mine. This precious little girl is mine.

"Daddy, you're squeezing me so tightly my head is going to pop off!"

I let go of her and we all laugh. I go back to my seat, looking around, as we all grab our food and begin to eat. This is my family and I'm the luckiest damn guy in the world.

Twenty-Five

LIZ

AFTER BREAKFAST COOPER ANNOUNCES TODAY IS SUNDAY-Funday Family Day. What that entails I have no clue. When Bella and I ask him, he tells us to go get dressed and be ready to head out in fifteen minutes. *Ha! That's funny.* He clearly hasn't spent enough time with women to know we don't get ready in fifteen minutes. That's okay, though. He'll learn.

An hour later we're piling into his Range Rover to head out. I go to grab Bella's booster seat from my car, but he tells me he already has one. *Is there anything this man hasn't thought of?*

The entire drive Bella keeps guessing where we're going. Cooper keeps laughing and saying he's not telling her. About twenty minutes later we pull up to a grocery store, where he insists we wait in the vehicle for him. When he gets back, he's carrying several bags and a wicker picnic basket. He loads the shopping bags and the basket into the trunk and then we're back on the road.

A few minutes later we pull up to the Town Square. Bella is trying to figure out where we are, but she can't see beyond the parking lot.

"We've never been here. What's there to do?" I ask as we get out.

"You'll see." He grabs the basket, which must be filled with the stuff from the bags, slams the trunk closed, and we all head toward the buildings. As we walk down the sidewalk, in the distance, it looks like there are a bunch of playhouses. Bella starts walking faster, wanting to see what's going on. When we get closer, sure enough there's a huge park filled with sidewalks and playhouses everywhere. To one side, there's a huge Oak tree, and connected to it is a tree house with a rock wall and a fort. Just past that there, is a cool fountain that's shooting water up in the air. On the other side, is the most adorable princess tower playhouse with slides coming out of the sides.

"Oh, my God! Mommy. Daddy. Can I go play?" Bella squeals in delight. She's looking every which way, not even sure where to begin. I see a couple benches nearby and Cooper must notice them too because he heads straight for them. I think he's going to sit and watch her play, but he shocks me once again when he sets the basket down on the bench and says to Bella, "C'mon, Princess! Let's go play."

She's so excited he's joining her, she jumps up and down, grabs his hand, and then pulls him along. *Mom who?*

We follow Bella through the playground. She runs from playhouse to playhouse and Cooper keeps up with her every step of the way. It's hilarious to watch this six-foot-three man try to go where the barely three-foot little girl goes. I have to give him credit, though. Cooper can barely fit in some of the tunnels and slides, but it doesn't stop him from trying. Where Bella goes, Cooper goes.

I pull out my phone and snap a bunch of pictures of them running around, climbing up the rock wall, and going down the slides. I'm sure he'll love to see these later.

After a while of playing, Bella spots the water fountains from earlier and asks if she can go play in them even though she didn't bring a suit.

"Um, Bella, we don't have a change of clothes. You can't get back in the car wet."

Of course she pouts and looks right at Cooper. *Little girl is smart.* Cooper gives her pout one glance and of course comes up with a solution.

"Sure, Princess. You go play and when you're done, we'll buy you a towel and a new outfit at a store."

After squealing her thanks, she takes off like a bat out of hell, racing toward the fountains while we sit on the bench and watch her.

"Coop, you can't just give in to everything she wants. I can't afford to just buy her a new outfit whenever she wants. I'm going to take the job you're offering, but I need to save for a place."

Cooper's jaw begins to tick and then his face softens. "I'm glad you're taking the job because I know you want to work, but Bella and you aren't going anywhere. I make more than enough money to support both of you, and I have four years of her life to make up for that I missed out on, on top of four years of making up to do with all the time you and I missed. You don't want to work, you don't have to. You want to stay home and take care of Bella, I'm more than fine with that. Whatever money you make is yours. I don't care what you do as long as you both are under the same roof as me."

I want to get angry with him because I don't appreciate him going all alpha-male on me, but I can see it in his eyes. *Guilt.* He thinks he owes us because he wasn't there.

While still watching Bella, I tell Cooper, "This whole situation, you not getting to see Bella, wasn't either of our faults. It was a crappy situation, but we're here now and you don't need to make up for anything. I don't want you to take care of us. I want us to be equal."

He looks over at me and takes my hand in his. "Baby girl, I own several training facilities left to me by my dad. I have endorsements and contracts, and I make decent money fighting. I make more than enough to take care of you, and that's my job. Your job is to take care of our princess. My dad's life insurance policy was several hundred thousand dollars and I didn't even touch it. I put it in a trust account for Bella. She can use it to go to college, get a car, buy a house, whatever she needs or wants to make sure all her dreams in life are within her reach. If we have more kids one day, we'll make sure they have one as well. Please, just let me do this. Let me take care of my girls." I glance over at him and see the need in his eyes. It's obvious this is important to him.

"Okay, but don't spoil her, Coop. She needs to learn that getting handed everything isn't reality. You, of all people, know it takes hard work to accomplish your dreams."

"Okay, I'll try my best," he says, and for some reason, I think he's full of it, but I let it go for now.

We sit and watch Bella for a while until Cooper gets up and walks over to a woman and gives her a big hug. She turns to face me and I see it's his mom. What a nice surprise.

He calls Bella over to make introductions. "Mom, this is my daughter, Bella Faith. Bella, this is my mom, your grandma."

"Oh, Liam! She is absolutely beautiful! And she looks so much like you."

Bella looks confused and asks, "Are you my grandma like my mom's mom? I call her Grammy, and who's Liam?"

Ms. Cooper laughs. "Liam is your daddy's real name. All his friends call him by his last name, which is Cooper. And yes, I'm your daddy's mom, so that makes me your grandma as well. You can call me Grandma if you like."

"Okay! Cool! Now I have two grandmas! Do I get another grandpa, too? I call mommy's daddy Papa. I can call daddy's daddy…uhhh… Grandpa."

Everybody goes quiet, clearly at a loss on how to handle this, so I step in and explain the situation to Bella the best I can. Fortunately, we haven't had any deaths in our family, so I haven't had to explain death to her.

"Angel, remember the fire that happened in our apartment?"

"Yes, all my toys and clothes and bed went away."

I hear Cooper suck in a loud breath at the same time his mom puts her hand to her heart. They can't possibly think I would tell my daughter the whole story of that day. I rush out the words before they freak out on me.

"That's right. Well, your grandpa was the one who saved you that day."

"Wow, that was really nice of him. Can I say thank you? I was really scared and the smoke was choking my throat really badly."

"He knows you're thankful, but he had to go to heaven. Heaven is where people go when they die."

Bella's bottom lip juts out. "Like Carl in the movie *Up*? When he takes the balloons, and goes into the sky?"

Leave it to my daughter to compare her grandfather's death to a Disney Movie, but she's nailed it right on the head. "Yes, Angel, like Carl. Grandpa went to heaven so we can't see him or thank him, but he knows we're thankful he saved you."

"Okay, I'm hungry. Can we eat?"

Cooper and his mother release an audible sigh, most likely thankful the conversation is over.

Cooper jumps in and says yes, but first we have to get Bella a dry outfit. In and out of a small children's clothing store and Bella's dry and starving.

We find a spot in the grass and Cooper pulls out a large blanket, shaking it open and laying it across the ground. We all find a place to sit and he dishes out the food. Subs, cookies, some fruit, and bottles of water for everybody.

"Ms. Cooper, I'm so glad you were able to join us today," I tell her, trying to make conversation.

"Oh dear, please call me Lauren. We're family."

"Okay." I feel so blessed that Bella and I have another family member close by. I always miss my parents and brother since they live so far away.

After we have lunch, Bella is rearing to go once again. We spend the rest of the afternoon checking out a cool hedge maze, and then head to a sweet little bakery that looks like one of the playhouses. Cooper let's Bella pick out a treat and then we walk around some of the shops until Bella is so exhausted she has Cooper carry her while she sleeps with her head resting on his shoulder.

I can't help but snap another photo. It's just too darn precious not to. His mom sees me snap the picture and gives me a wink in agreement.

We walk back to the car and say bye to his mom, promising to have her over for dinner soon. Cooper puts Bella in her booster seat and she doesn't even attempt to stir. Precious little thing is knocked out from all that playing.

We drive home in a comfortable silence and as we're getting out, Cooper comes around to my side of the vehicle and blocks me in before I can get out.

"Thank you."

I have no idea what I even did. "For what?"

"For today. It was one of the most amazing days of my life."

"Um, Coop. I didn't do or pay for anything. I was just along for the ride."

"No, Liz. You aren't just along for the ride. You gave me a second chance, even though I didn't deserve it. You gave me that miracle sleeping in the back seat. You helped create priceless memories today. You gave me a family. Thank you."

Damn this man. I frame his face with my hands and give him a soft kiss on his mouth. "I love you," I say without meaning to.

Cooper's entire body stills and I want to back track. I want to take it back before he shuts me out. It's not that I don't mean it. I do. I love Cooper. I think I always have. I know realistically people don't fall in love when they first meet, but between the time we shared years ago, watching Bella grow up with his beautiful features, and listening to and watching him these past few days, I can feel it. I love this man.

Just when I think he's going to leave me hanging, he kisses me. It's not a soft kiss like the one I gave him, but it's not rough either. It's a beautiful, sensual combination of both. His lips move over mine with ease, his tongue smoothly slipping in, and I swear this man is making love to me with his mouth. When he ends the kiss, he pulls back and smiles at me with a big cheesy grin.

"Baby girl, I love you, too. I love you so damn much."

I can't see myself, but I'm almost positive I'm mirroring the same cheesy-ass grin on my face that he's still sporting on his.

After Bella's nap, we spend the rest of the afternoon lounging around, playing Uno. Bella beats us every game. We order Chinese for dinner, and then I give Bella a bath while Cooper excuses himself back downstairs.

After Bella's in bed, Cooper tells me to get changed into my pajamas and then meet him in the living room. When I ask him why, he tells me he has a surprise for me.

After getting changed I enter the living room to find a ton of candy, popcorn, and drinks spread out across the coffee table.

"What's all this?" I ask.

"It's an adult movie night," he says as he grabs a DVD from inside the entertainment center, puts it in, and comes to sit next to me. I grab the throw blanket from the back of the couch and spread it across our laps as I snuggle into his side.

After skipping through the previews, the title screen comes on and I squeal in excitement like my daughter. "You remembered?" I slap him on the chest, and he laughs.

"*Love and Basketball* is my favorite movie!"

"I know! I remember everything you tell me, Liz. You and that girl upstairs are my world. You mean everything to me." *And swoon...*

"We might be now, but I wasn't five years ago. I told you this was my favorite back when it was just a one-night stand."

Looking anger at what I just said, he says, "First of all, it wasn't a one-night stand. It was a thirty-hour stand." *He is so damn adorable.*

"Second of all, I knew you were my world back then. I was just too stupid to do anything about it. I've never even spent the night with another woman. You were the first and you will be the last. Got it?"

"Yeah, I got it," I say as he presses play on the movie. He may not know it yet, but he's quickly becoming my entire world as well.

Twenty-Six

COOPER

I'M AT THE GYM TRAINING WITH KADEN, BUT INSTEAD OF training it's more like I'm getting the shit kicked out of me. I can't focus and it's not my fault.

"Coop! Put your fucking hands up. How are you supposed to beat this guy if you can't even remember how to block a simple punch?" I hate to admit it but Kaden is right. I'm off my game and I blame the sexy woman who's invading my every thought. My mind goes back to that first Sunday we spent together as a family when we got home from the Town Square, after we both declared our love for each other.

After Bella went to sleep, we watched *Love and Basketball* while cuddling on the couch, and when it was over, I had to make a few calls for the gym, so Liz went to take a shower and then read one of her trashy novels on her iPad she loves so much.

Once I was done with my calls, I went into the room to shower as well, but when I walked in, I found Liz lying on the bed in a black silk negligee looking sexy as fuck. Her legs were spread wide open and I could see her bare pussy peeking out through the silk crotch-less panties.

I walked over to the bed and crawled across it, until I was nose to nose with my woman, with a hand on either side of her head, kneeling between her sexy thighs. Leaning on my forearms, I began to kiss her neck as I trailed my lips down her collarbone, stopping at each breast. I sucked on each nipple through the silk material leaving wet spots where my tongue was. She arched her back, begging for me.

I moved down to her stomach and lifted up the silk top with only my teeth. Liz froze and tried to move my mouth away, but I wasn't having it. I knocked her hand away with my head and continued on. I could feel her tense as her stomach became exposed. "Relax, baby."

That's when I saw what she was trying to hide—stretch marks. They were left over from her pregnancy with Bella and for some crazy reason she was ashamed for me to see them. Shaking my head, I thought to myself, *This beautiful woman has nothing to be ashamed of.* She has a banging body and a few stretch marks aren't going to turn me off. Plus, these aren't just stretch marks. These are proof this beautiful woman carried our baby in her belly for nine months, keeping her safe. She should get a fucking medal for that. However, I knew if I said that to her, she'd just shoo me off. So, instead, I showed her exactly what her stretch marks did to me.

As I trailed my tongue down her stomach, I stopped at the first stretch mark and gave it a soft kiss, causing her to tense up. I moved to the next stretch mark and once again gave it a kiss. This time she didn't tense. I continued kissing every stretch mark, until I had kissed them all. From there, I moved lower, stopping at the scar from when they had to take our baby out of her. Starting on the left side, I trailed kisses from one side to the other. Her body started squirming, her legs tightening, trying to seek relief, and I knew she was starting to get turned on.

It was time to take care of my girl. I moved my mouth lower and placed a wet kiss on the top of her pussy. She jerked her hips upward in response, and I chuckled at her impatience as I took one finger and pushed it inside her.

"Fuck, Liz, you're soaked." And she was…dripping fucking wet.

"I know. Please. I need you inside me. Now."

"I will, baby, but first I want to make you come with my fingers."

I pushed my fingers back inside her, pumping them in and out. With my other hand, I massaged her clit with my thumb. She continued to writhe all over the bed until finally her body began to shake and I knew she was about to orgasm. Moving my thumb off her clit, I latched onto it with my teeth and tongue, sucking hard. She completely lost it, calling out my name as she came all over my mouth and fingers.

That will never get old.

When she came down from her orgasm, I crawled up her body and kissed her on her mouth.

"Can you taste me on you, baby? You taste so fucking good."

She whimpered and attempted to reach for my cock, but before she could, I took both her hands in mine and lifted them up over her head, holding them there. My cock was hard as steel and she was slick to the touch as I slid my cock right into her warm, wet pussy and almost came right then and there. We'd had sex a few time, but tonight was different because we didn't just have sex, we made love. Slowly, never breaking our kiss, Liz and I became one with each other until we both found our release.

And every night since then, I've been inside my woman making sweet, sweet love to her, confirming over and over again, there'll never be another woman for me. Liz, is it.

"Cooper! Earth to Cooper! You gonna focus or do you want to just call Griffin and let him know he can keep the title because you forfeit?"

"Yeah, sorry. Give me a few minutes. I'm just going to go check on Liz before she heads out to get Bella."

"C'mon, man. We all know that's code for you going to get a quickie in the office on the damn desk."

Okay, so maybe I've been inside her during the day as well. Hey, like I said, I blame my sexy-as-sin woman. This isn't my fault. I repeat this is *not* my fault. Her sexual appetite is insane. She's clearly trying to make up for lost time and I'm just trying to be the dutiful boyfriend and make sure she's satisfied.

Boyfriend. The word sounds so insignificant compared to how we feel about each other. She's the mother of my child, the love of my life. I wonder what she would say if I proposed. I could become her fiancé and eventually her husband. Fuck, what the hell am I thinking? It's only been a few weeks. She'd probably freak the hell out.

Kaden calls my name, but I ignore him as I make my way out of the ring and head to check on Liz in the office. We originally agreed we would keep our personal life separate from our professional one while at the gym, but so far I've yet to keep to that agreement and it won't be happening today either.

"Knock, knock," I say as I walk into what was once my dad's office. The feeling I get when I enter now, is warmth compared to the coolness I used to feel. Liz hasn't changed much in the office except adding a few pictures on the walls and a couple on the desk. She even blew up a few from our family day at the park. The truth is, she could've made zero changes and the vibe would still be completely different because wherever Liz is, she emits a warm feeling into those around her. You can't help but gravitate toward her—she's just good. Even guys who come in to pay their monthly dues can't help but hang around her. I swear I'm going to have to kick some ass soon to remind them whose woman she is.

I frown when I see, sitting at the desk with Liz, is Hayley and Kayla, and they all appear to be having lunch together. Liz glances over at me and gives me a knowing smirk, while I pout at her like a child. So much for getting into her sweet pussy today. Looks like I'll have to wait until tonight.

She mouths, *"I'm sorry"* as the other girls turn to say hi.

"Hello, ladies. How's everyone doing today?"

All of them answer various responses of good, then Kayla adds, "I was just telling Liz, how Hayley and I are traveling with you and the other guys to Boulder at the end of October since you and Caleb will be training while shooting promo photos for the fight in February, and Bentley is fighting at UFC Fight Night. I told her she should join us, but she isn't having it. Tell her she should go."

Oh, hell… I haven't discussed this trip with Liz yet. I'll be gone for four days at the end of October doing some press shit for the title fight that's taking place in February, and I need to be there to support Bentley at his fight. Ever since I took over the gym, he's been working hard to get ready for this fight.

"Kayla, I can't just up and leave. Bella's in school and she needs stability, plus it's going to be around Halloween and she will die if she can't wear her Elsa costume and go trick-or-treating in the same neighborhood we take her to every year."

Kayla pouts when she hears this. "Oh, no! I forgot about Halloween. I've never missed a single one of Bella's Halloweens. This seriously sucks."

Damn it, it does suck. My first holiday with my daughter and I won't even be here with her.

Liz gives Kayla a sad smile. "Things have changed." She shrugs. "Jobs have changed, living arrangements have changed, nothing can stay the same forever. I'm sad that you guys won't be here, but I need to stay here and make sure Bella's schedule is stable. I don't want her to get confused. It'll suck going trick-or-treating without you guys, but I'll send pictures. I promise."

Of course she won't drop everything, take Bella out of school, and travel to Boulder with us. Why not? It's simple. Liz is a damn good mother and puts our daughter first, always. Just like my mom tried to do every time my dad traveled, but look how that ended. The question is, how long will she put up with me being gone and missing important family moments like taking our daughter trick-or-treating? How long until she feels lonely like my mom did and she seeks comfort in another guy who can be at all those events?

Twenty-Seven

LIZ

I CAN TELL SOMETHING IS BOTHERING COOPER, BUT I DON'T want to ask him in front of Kayla and Hayley, so I let it go for now. I check the time, seeing I need to leave soon to pick up Bella from school. I promised her we'd go get her costume today, so, we'll find out soon if she sticks to the Elsa one.

"All right everyone, I need to go pick up my daughter and take her costume shopping. I just spoke with my mom and they're about to board their flight, and should be in tonight around dinner, so don't forget about the barbeque Sunday." I walk over to Cooper and give him a quick kiss. "And I will see you tonight."

He grabs me by my arm, looking conflicted. Something is clearly bothering him and I need to make sure we get time alone later to talk about it after Bella's sleeping, so I can find out what's going on.

"Can I go with you to get Bella? It's bad enough I'm going to miss her trick-or-treating. I'd like to at least be there to help her pick out her costume."

Oh, this man. My heart swells every time he says stuff like this.

"Well, I don't know how much helping you're going to be doing since our sweet child has a mind of her own when it comes to all important decisions such as which costume to get, but you can always join us, Cooper. You never have to ask."

I run my hand down his cheek and a hint of a smile graces his face. "Give me a few minutes to shower and change."

"Sure."

After he exits I notice both my friends are staring at me.

"What?"

Hayley is the first to comment. "Nothing, he's just so sweet. I want a man like that."

Kayla nods. "I don't want a man like that because we both know I don't want a man at all, but I'm glad you have a man like that. You deserve to be happy."

I debate on how to reply to Kayla's comment because it drives me nuts that she never wants to be in a relationship just because her parents' marriage isn't one based on love.

"Hayley, you'll find your man. I didn't think it would ever happen to me, but I'm glad I waited, and you"—I mock glare at Kayla—"need to stop. Just because your parents chose to have a marriage of convenience doesn't mean all couples choose that. If you never let a guy in, you'll never see how different it can be, and trust me, it can be amazing."

Both girls wave me off and we all exit the office and head to the front. Hayley goes to her office and Kayla stands with me in the front as we discuss our plans for the weekend. I'd like to take my parents and brother out to dinner tomorrow night. I hate they are only here for a short time, but I'm so excited to just see them. Kayla mentions us going to get manis and pedis in the morning with my mom.

Cooper and Bentley walk up, overhearing our conversation. "Why don't you guys schedule a full spa day and I'll watch Bella and hang out with your dad and brother? Bentley can even come over and chill. We can invite Caleb and Kaden as well."

Kayla gets excited at the mention of a full day at the spa, but there's no way I'm spending that kind of money. Yes, I'm working and I'm pretty sure Cooper is paying me more than he should be, and yes, I do have a home to live in and I don't plan to move out, but I need to start saving just in case. I'm never going to be in the position I was in when our apartment caught fire with no money in the bank and nowhere to go.

But before I can say anything, Cooper gives me a raised brow indicating he isn't going to let me argue. "And it's all on me. I've been meaning to add your name to the account so I'll do that today when we get done at the costume store. Kayla, I know Liz, and I'm willing to bet she won't book it. So, you're going to need to book it. Make sure you include whatever you ladies want and I got it covered."

And with that, he grabs my hand and stalks off, dragging me behind him and not leaving any room for argument, as the sounds of Bentley and Kayla's laughter ring through the building. *Damn this man. This is just another example of why I can't help but love him.*

We leave my car at the gym and take Cooper's Rover. He refuses to take my car anywhere we don't have to and he keeps complaining my car needs to be thrown into a junkyard, but I continue to ignore him. I'm hoping to save up enough in the next year to buy a newer used car.

We get to Bella's preschool, and when she sees her dad, she comes running over to him, jumping straight into his arms. After she shows him her cubby and desk, we say good-bye to her teacher and head out.

"Daddy! Are you here to go with Mommy and me to pick out my costume?"

Cooper smiles wide and gives her a big kiss on her cheek. "You betcha, Princess."

"Mommy never gets a costume. Do you want to get a costume so you can go trick-or-treating with me?"

Cooper's smile fades instantly, and I think I'm starting to understand why he was upset earlier. He's going to be missing his first holiday because of work. It's part of his job and I won't let him feel guilty over something out of his control. He works hard and without even blinking an eye has offered everything he has to Bella and me, and the last thing he needs is to feel like he's done something wrong by making a living.

"Bella, unfortunately, Daddy is going to be working on Halloween. He has to go away for a few days and one of the days he'll be gone will be on Halloween. But we'll take a lot of pictures and I'll text them all to him, and when he gets home, we can show him all the candy you got. Does that sound good?"

Bella's look of disappointment mirrors her father's, both of them looking adorable with matching pouting faces. "No, that doesn't sound good. That doesn't sound good at all. That sounds bad, really bad."

Whoa! I knew she was disappointed, but I didn't expect her to get so angry over him not going trick-or-treating with her. I take her out of her father's arms and set her on her feet, then I kneel down so I can make eye contact with her.

"Well, I'm sorry that doesn't sound good, but that's the way it has to be. I'll be with you and you'll have lots of fun."

She pouts some more. "Will Auntie Kay be with us?"

Oh Lord, this conversation is going downhill fast. "No, you know how Mommy and Auntie Kay work with daddy now? Well, when Daddy travels, sometimes Auntie Kay has to travel too, so she'll be gone with Daddy. It will just be us this year."

Bella stomps her foot and crosses her arms over her chest in full-blown temper tantrum mode. "Then I don't want to go trick-or-treating. This is stupid. Can we go with Daddy and Auntie Kay where they're going?"

"First of all, Bella," I say in my mom voice that seems to just make her even more mad. "We don't say stupid. That isn't nice, and no, we can't go away with them. They're working and you have school. I'm sorry you're upset, but that's the answer. Would you like to go get your costume, or go home and take a nap? Because if you keep up this attitude, you will not be going trick-or-treating."

She huffs and puffs but finally relents. "Okay, I guess I'll go get my costume." My poor baby looks so defeated, it breaks my heart.

I look over at Cooper and he looks just as defeated as our little girl. These two are going to be the death of me. I can't have them ganging up on me.

When we get home from the costume shop, Bella takes her costume up to her room to put in her closet. Luckily once we got there her mood improved and after almost an hour of debating, she decided on the Elsa costume. Of course, Cooper bought her every matching accessory to go with the costume, most likely out of guilt, but I didn't stop him. He tried to be upbeat for Bella, but I could still see the sadness in his eyes.

Glancing at the clock and seeing it's almost time for my parents and brother to arrive, I do a sweep through of the house, making sure everything is clean. Because we don't have any guestrooms, they'll be staying at a hotel nearby, but they'll be coming here after they check-in to have dinner with us and meet Cooper.

I look around for Cooper and notice he's disappeared. I search the house for him and find him in the office.

"Hey, handsome. What are you up to?"

He looks up and with sadness in his eyes. "Nothing, just looking at a couple of work emails. What time will your family be here?"

Wanting to speak to him about his sour mood, but knowing we don't have time since my family is due to arrive any minute, I move in front of him to sit on the desk, wrapping my legs around his body and my arms around his neck. I pull his face toward mine. He knows what I'm after, and as always, he doesn't disappoint.

His lips meet mine in a punishing kiss as his hands move to my ass. He pulls me closer to him until my body is almost one with his. We kiss for several minutes, our tongues swirling around one another until Cooper backs up.

"Fuck, baby girl, I needed that. I'm sorry I'm being a cranky ass. I'll try to shake it off before your parents get here. I don't want them to think I'm an ogre."

Laughing at his comment, I lean in for another kiss, my tongue swiping across his lips, seeking entrance. When my tongue enters, he sucks on it before backing away leaving me unsatisfied and frowning.

"Hey, now who's the one pouting? We both can't be cranky." He runs his thumb along my lips to straighten out the frown on my face.

"Cooper, there's no reason to feel guilty. You have to work. There'll be plenty of holidays in the future. Don't let this get to you and ruin your day."

"Liz, did you see how upset Bella was? Of course I'm going to be upset and feel guilty. I don't want to miss important shit in her life. This is exactly why I said…"

I cut him off, knowing exactly where he is going, refusing to let him go there.

"Oh no, you don't. Don't start. Missing a holiday doesn't make you a crappy dad or boyfriend and it doesn't mean you don't deserve to have us in your life. So just get those thoughts out of your head. You hear me?"

"Yeah, baby," he says, the sad undertone still residing in his voice. I'm going to need to come up with a way to make this right. I can't have him beating himself up every time he has to go away for work.

I hear a knock on the front door as Bella starts yelling my parents are here.

Letting her open the door, she squeals in glee as my mom and dad both take her in their arms for a hug and then move on to me. My brother lifts Bella into his arms and gives her a huge hug as he carries her into the living room.

"Mom, Dad, Mathew, this is my boyfriend, Cooper. Cooper, this is my mom, Macy, my dad, Randy, and my brother, Mathew."

Cooper shakes everyone's hands and says it's nice to meet them. Bella watches the entire exchange and then has to join in the conversation.

"Umm, you forgot to tell them the best news ever. Cooper is also my daddy! And the bestest daddy ever."

Everybody laughs. My family might live long distance, but we talk almost every day and they know all about Cooper. Bella runs right into Cooper and latches on to his legs, giving him the cutest leg hug.

My mom looks at me, her eyes glossy like she's about to cry from the sweet exchange. I understand completely. We agree on Chinese food to keep it easy, and Bella drags everyone upstairs to show off her room. She spends the entire time explaining every toy and movie her dad has bought her until the food arrives.

I nudge Cooper and nod toward our daughter. "See, one holiday isn't going to change how she feels about you. She loves you."

The weekend passes by way too fast. On Saturday, Kayla, Hayley, my mom, and I all spend a wonderfully relaxing day at the spa. I invite Ashley to go as well, but she's heading out with Tristan to visit her parents. When we get there, it's clear Kayla has booked us for everything. An hour massage, facial, mud wrap, and of course manis and pedis. I didn't realize how much I really needed this kind of pampering. Saturday night we all go out to dinner at a yummy Italian place, and Sunday everybody comes over for a backyard barbeque. I've noticed that while Bentley joins us for dinner and the barbeque, he and Kayla are completely avoiding each other. I really need to ask her how her living arrangements are working out.

Now it's Monday, and Cooper is dropping Bella off at school on his way to the gym, so I can see my parents and brother off on their flight back home.

I pull my parents into a loving embrace, sad their trip is already over. I love where I live, but I also wish I could be close to my family. "Oh, Mom, Dad. I'm so glad you guys came. I miss you so much."

"Sweetheart, I'm going to miss you, too. But I'm so happy for the love that Bella and you have found. Cooper is a great man and father, and I feel so much better leaving, knowing he's here taking care of my girls," my dad says through glossy eyes.

Next, I give Mathew a hug goodbye. "Don't be a stranger."

"You never know. Maybe after I finish my two years, I'll decide to transfer to ULV," he says with a wink.

"Don't even tease me!" I shout, and people walking by stare at me. We get to the security entrance, and since I don't have a ticket, I can't go any further. We exchange a few more hugs and then they're gone.

Twenty-Eight

LIZ

AFTER SEEING MY FAMILY OFF, I HEAD STRAIGHT TO THE GYM to get caught up on some bookkeeping. Cooper is already there, training with Kaden, and when he catches my eye, he gives me a wink. *God, I love that man.*

I'm not even in my chair yet when Kayla comes bounding into my office, her face red and hands in the air.

"Aghhh!!! I swear that man is trying to drive me insane!"

I have a feeling I am about to hear all about Bentley. "Who?"

"Oh, give me a break, Liz. You know who I'm talking about... Bentley!"

And as if she's beckoned him over, the man of the hour comes walking into my office. *So much for getting any work done.*

"Hey, Liz." Bentley addresses me when he walks in, and it doesn't go unnoticed he just completely ignored Kayla. I look over at her and she's shooting daggers at the poor man.

"Hey Bentley, what can I do for you?"

Kayla huffs, and when nobody acknowledges her, she does it again louder.

"I just wanted to see if there's anything else I need to do before the fight next week." I do everything in my power to contain my laughter. It's blatantly obvious he's going out of his way to ignore Kayla, yet he looks so uneasy doing it. I just want to hide him under my desk to get him out of her line of attack. It's only a matter of time until Kayla boils over, burning everyone in her line of sight.

"Let me check for you." I pull up his file, but before I can get another word in, Kayla loses her shit.

"Excuse me, mister. I know you think the world revolves around you, but Liz and I were talking first. So, you're going to need to get in line. As a matter of fact, you can go wait outside." She's practically shouting by the time she makes it to the end of her sentence, and then she's up, out of her seat, and pushing him out the door.

Bentley looks terrified. Seriously? This is a grown ass man and a fighter. What the hell is he afraid of Kayla for? She weighs like one twenty dripping wet.

Before the door shuts, I yell, "It's all covered, Bentley. I handled everything."

And he may have responded, but the door slams shut, blocking out all outside noise. Kayla sits back down and takes a few deep breaths, trying to calm herself.

"Care to explain why you just lost it on your roommate?"

"Liz, he is so maddening. I seriously need to find a new place to live. The problem is I actually like living there. Caleb is awesome. He's barely home and when he is, he's totally chill. Bentley on the other hand is driving me up a damn wall."

"Driving you up a wall because you like him?"

Kayla sputters out a, "No!" But her face turns a deep shade of pink, telling me she's full of crap.

"Anyway," she continues. I'm here, not to talk about Bentley, but to tell you we were supposed to go get our shot almost two weeks ago. You always make the appointment. Can you make it for us, please?"

"Yeah, I'll call tomorrow. I completely forgot. Ever since the fire, it's been crazy."

"Yes, it's definitely been crazy lately. I better get back to work. Don't want the boss to fire me," she says with laughter in her voice as she gets up and walks to the door.

"You know, eventually, you'll talk to me about Bentley."

"Yeah, yeah." She waves me off before leaving my office.

Two o'clock rolls around and I head out to get Bella. Cooper texts me he'll be working late at the gym and to please save him dinner. I smile at that. Before I moved in with Cooper, I didn't do a whole lot of cooking and it definitely wasn't healthy. Because Cooper's a fighter, he's a health freak and has to eat a certain way. He's been teaching me about eating healthy and we've been cooking together. With him at the gym so often, I've started to find recipes and surprise him with dinner when he gets home. He seems to really love my cooking and it makes me want to cook for him more often. It also doesn't hurt that I'm shedding the few pounds left after having Bella.

Eight o'clock comes around and I'm tucking Bella in bed after I finish up reading her a bedtime story. She's eaten, completed her daily reading, watched some television, and is freshly bathed, in her pajamas.

"Mommy, can I please stay up and wait for Daddy? Please!" She begs like she does most nights when Cooper isn't here to tuck her in. We're lucky he has a flexible schedule, so if needed, he can be home any time. With the fight coming up and him the owner of the gym, he's been staying late to help with Bentley's training and such. Bella and I both miss him, but I try to bring her by the gym as much as possible to see him if I know he'll be working late.

However, today Bella had a playdate so we weren't able to stop by. I want to let her stay up, knowing it's important to her to say goodnight to him, but Cooper can be there extremely late and she needs to get her rest. Plus, if I say yes once, she'll continue to ask, so I never let her wait up. The problem is my consistency doesn't deter her from continuing to ask every single time Cooper isn't home on time. I make it a point not to tell Cooper since he has this crazy notion he must spend every waking moment making up for lost time or he'll receive the award for worst father of the year. If he knew Bella begs for him on the nights he's not here he'd feel even worse.

"No, Angel. We're not going to discuss this again. When Daddy isn't home you go to bed on time. You'll see him in the morning."

And cue my four-year-old's tantrum. Tears pour down her face instantly—I swear they're crocodile tears because really? How does one produce real tears that quickly? But she still looks absolutely heartbroken and pitiful, and as a mother, that's hard to deal with, especially when it's because of how much she adores her father and not over something materialistic.

"Mommy, it's not fair! I miss him when he's not home and he misses me. I have to go to school all day. I want to drop out of school and be a fighter like Daddy."

And now I'm about to cry right along with her.

Twenty-Nine

COOPER

I TRY SO HARD TO GET HOME BY EIGHT ON THE NIGHTS I DON'T see Bella at the gym, never wanting to go a day without spending time with my little princess. Our time together is so precious and I never want to take it for granted.

Tonight, Bentley and I were working on some grappling techniques for his upcoming fight and I completely lost track of time. When I realized how late it was, I ran out the door without even showering and rushed home determined to kiss my sweet little girl goodnight.

Growing up, my dad barely ever made it home, nor did he care to. My mom was the only one who tucked me in at night and the unhappier she became, and the more she went out, the more often a babysitter tucked me in. I don't ever want to become my dad and I never want to drive Liz to become my mom.

There are moments in life when one small thing happens that shouldn't be a big deal but it is, and it changes everything. It changes the way you see yourself, it changes the way you see those around you, and it changes the way you view the situation. I would define this moment as just that, a life-changing moment.

I run up the stairs to Bella's room, hoping to catch her still awake, and hear my princess sobbing. I'm about to enter the room when I hear her hiccup out, "Mommy, it's not fair! I miss him when he's not home and he misses me. I have to go to school all day. I want to drop out of school and be a fighter like Daddy."

Remember when I said my heart shattered the day she was in the hospital for smoke inhalation? I take that back. It must have been a mere fracture. What's the difference? A fracture isn't broken. It hurts like a bitch, but it's still intact. A shatter on the other hand is a full-on break. Pieces are everywhere and there's no way they're ever being put back together again. I clutch my chest and try to stop the pain from radiating inside of me. If I never hear my daughter sobbing and crying out like that again, it'll be too soon.

And what's worse is that I'm the cause. I listen for a second to hear Liz's reply. "Bella Faith, you need to calm down. I can't continue to do this with you several times a week. I understand you miss Daddy, and I miss him too, but you are not dropping out of preschool. If you want to work with Daddy one day then you'll go to school and graduate and get a job when you're older. Your job right now is to go to school. Becoming a fighter like your dad is a great goal, but you still have to go to school."

Liz sounds completely exhausted and aggravated. Judging by her response, this isn't the first or even third time Bella has thrown a fit about missing me at night. If Bella is upset then there's a good chance so is Liz. She gave me this second chance and I can't screw it up. If she isn't happy, she'll leave, which means Bella and Liz won't be living under my roof anymore. I can't imagine having to live without these two girls. They've turned this house into a home with just their presence alone.

I've heard guys complain about the messes their kids leave all over the house, or that their wife or girlfriend bought new furniture that's too girly. I don't know why they're complaining. Seeing the pictures Liz has put up, or the new pillows she bought to add color to the living room, or when I walk in and almost trip on Bella's cute princess shoes, it all makes my day. It's evidence that I'm living with the two most precious girls, and the day I don't see any of that is the day my life will no longer have meaning.

I hear Bella sobbing still, but she doesn't respond, which means she must be giving up. When she knows she's going to lose the battle, she shuts down. I absolutely love how bright her passion burns, and I hope it never burns out.

I knock softly on the door to let them know of my arrival then walk in. Bella tries to quickly wipe her tears and Liz freezes in place, probably wondering how much I heard.

I pretend like I didn't hear anything and ignore Bella's tears. "Hey princess, I was hoping you weren't asleep. Has Mommy read you a book yet?" I can see it in her eyes that her mom already read her a book and she doesn't want to lie, but she wants this time with me, shit, she *needs* this time with me, and I need it with her.

"I read her *The Giving Tree*," Liz replies softly, trying to gage my reaction to Bella's tears, but I make sure not to give anything away.

"Nice. Is it too late to pick one more book to read to Bella before she goes to bed?" I direct the question to Liz to make sure it's okay. I know it's after Bella's bedtime, so I don't want to step on her toes, but I really don't want her to tell me no. Bella waits for Liz's answer and when she says okay, Bella jumps out of bed to grab a book.

I mouth *"thank you"* to Liz and she gives me a small smile before walking out to give Bella and me some alone time.

"How's it going, Princess?" My daughter is a smart girl so she knows exactly what I'm asking, but she just lifts her shoulders up like she's not sure what I'm asking about.

"Are you giving your mom a hard time?"

The tears well back up in her eyes and she leans over to hug me tightly, sniffling back the cry that's threatening to breaking out. "I just wanted to see you before I went to bed, but she said I had to go to sleep. I just miss you so much sometimes. I'm sorry. It's just not fair. Bedtimes are dumb."

"I know it's not fair, Princess. Sometimes we have to do things we don't want to do because it's what's best for us. Your mommy loves you so much and she has you go to bed at eight o'clock because you need your sleep. You want to be a fighter, right?" She nods.

"Well, if you want to be a fighter, you have to get plenty of sleep so you can grow. Did you know we grow in our sleep? So, you need your sleep."

I know she gets it, but she wouldn't be my Bella if she didn't still state her case. That's where her passion comes in. When she believes in something, she fights for it. I can't even imagine what she'll be like when she hits her teenage years.

"Okay, Daddy, but I still miss you and want to say good night to you."

It hits me then that we have technology, and as annoying as it can be, it can also be very convenient. "How about we compromise? Any time I'm not home by bedtime, you can use your mom's phone to Face Time me on my phone so we can see each other and say good night?"

Her entire face lights up and she sits up straighter like I just gave her free reign at a toy store. "Okay, deal! Just make sure you answer."

I give her a kiss on her forehead and say with absolute conviction, "I will always answer your phone calls. No matter where I am or what I'm doing, I will also make sure I'm here for you, I promise. Now, let's read you that book."

When I finish reading the book, Bella is passed out, holding onto my arm like she needs it to breathe. It doesn't matter what I have going on, I need to make sure the only time I'm not here to tuck her into bed is if I'm away. Fuck, I can't believe in a couple weeks I have to leave. It'll be the first time I've been away from Bella and Liz since they moved in here. Sometimes it feels like I need them to breathe.

I walk downstairs to the living room to find Liz curled up on the couch reading, and I almost feel bad taking her away from her book but I need some quality time with my woman. She sees me coming toward her and puts the iPad away.

"Hey baby, I thought you were going to be gone longer. Is everything okay?"

I sit next to Liz's feet, dragging her body to me until she's sitting on my lap. Then I wrap my arms around her body and drink in her scent. This right here is home, yet looking at this woman, I feel like I barely know her. Yes, I know the person she was when we met five years ago and the person she is today. She was and still is fun, and sexy, and so damn smart. She's an amazing mother and friend, and she has the biggest, kindest heart. I mean, what woman goes to the man's funeral who almost killed her daughter?

She cooks dinner for us every night even though I know it isn't her cup of tea, and she works hard at the gym even though she knows how much money I have. Liz could easily stay home all day and let me take care of her, but she wants to earn her own way and be equal. What I don't know is the person I missed out on for the last five years, the woman who was forced to grow up at eighteen because she was pregnant so young but still determined to make it through college. I want to know all about that woman.

"Tell me about the last five years."

She seems a bit confused at my request. "What do you want to know?"

"I want to know everything. I want to know all about your pregnancy and Bella, every age, every milestone, and every detail. I hate that I missed out on so much, and I feel like no matter how much I try to catch up, I'm too damn far behind."

"Um, okay. Well, after I found out I was pregnant, Kayla started coming with me to all my appointments. From the minute she found out, she never missed one. We would make sure they were on a day neither of us had school. I think the nurses and doctors thought we were lesbians. I had morning sickness for the first trimester, which totally sucked, but then it went away and the rest of my pregnancy was smooth sailing, thank God. At twenty weeks, I could've found out the sex, but Kayla wanted to know so badly I decided to wait. It was so much fun driving her crazy. She couldn't even shop like she wanted to because everything had to be in neutral colors."

She laughs through all of this and I'm glad she had Kayla and has good memories, but I hate those memories don't include me. I cuddle her harder, needing her closer to me. "I wish I could have been there. I would've held your hair back when you were sick, and we definitely would've found out the sex of the baby. I would've gone crazy not knowing how to prepare. I know Kayla was there, but I hate that it wasn't me."

"I know, baby, but you can't think like that or you will go crazy from guilt about something you can't change. Okay, let's see…At forty-two weeks pregnant, they induced me because Bella didn't want to come out, and after forty-seven hours in labor they had to do an emergency caesarean because her heart rate dropped. When they took her out, at first, I couldn't hear her crying. I kept asking Kayla if she was okay and

I could tell by Kayla's answers something was wrong, but they had a sheet put up, so I couldn't see.

"When Bella came out she wasn't breathing so they had to pump oxygen into her lungs. Finally, she took her first breath and started to cry, and it felt like my world was complete. They brought her over to me and announced she was a girl. After a few days, we both went home and then the fun began."

I know she's trying to make light of the situation by joking, but I can't even imagine how hard it was for her and Kayla to raise a baby on their own at eighteen. I don't say anything though, because I like listening to her talk. Instead I give her a kiss and she continues.

"The first year was exhausting. Bella had Colic, which is like acid reflux, kind of. So, she had to get put on a special formula, and I wanted to breastfeed, but I couldn't pump, and I had to go back to school. I had her in the middle of the semester, so I only took off the days I was in the hospital. I couldn't afford daycare and I didn't want her to be with strangers so Kayla and I made sure our schedules were opposite, so one of us was always home with Bella.

"My mom came to visit for a few weeks after Bella came home. She slept in my room, and I slept in the third bedroom with Bella." She smiles absently like she is reliving those memories. What I would give to be in her head and heart, and see all of her memories firsthand.

She pulls out her phone and opens a photo app. "I lost all our photos and such in the fire, but luckily, I have all Bella's pictures saved digitally."

She begins flipping through them showing me Bella as a newborn, Bella at one, two, three years old, Halloweens, Christmases, and birthdays. Most are of just Bella, but once in a while I see a picture of Kayla and Liz as well—it's like watching them all grow up together. When she gets to the last one, she has silent tears falling down her face.

I swipe them away and turn her to face me. "Why the tears, baby girl?"

"I love looking at pictures of Bella, but looking at them with you feels bittersweet. I have such mixed emotions because I feel like I should feel bad I messed up with the birth control but at the same time I don't want to feel bad because my screw up got me Bella and I would never wish to not have her. Then I feel bad that you didn't get to experience any of those memories, but at the same time I wouldn't trade those memories for the world because I created them with Bella. Does that make sense?"

"Yes, it makes perfect sense, and I'm thankful for your screw up. I can't imagine not having Bella in our lives." I kiss her forehead and we sit together for a few minutes just enjoying each other's company. I don't know what comes over me but suddenly I blurt out, "I want to have a baby."

She looks at me like I'm crazy so I continue. "I missed so much with Bella and she's already almost five years old. I want to experience all of that with you. I know we aren't married, but we're living together and we'll be together for the rest of our lives. I'm an only child and would have loved to have a sibling. I bet Bella would love having a little brother or sister, plus we have plenty of rooms here. I can move the gym to the garage or we can move. We can buy a bigger house with a bigger yard…"

"Whoa, whoa. Slow down, there. Are you sure, Cooper? I mean… you went from not wanting a family to having an insta-family. Are you sure you want to add another baby to the mix?"

My heart sinks. "You don't want to have another baby with me?"

"Of course, I do! I just want you to be sure. With Bella, you didn't have a choice. You've accepted her from day one and you two have an amazing relationship already. I know you'll be an amazing father to any other babies we have. I just want you to be sure. I actually have to go get my shot this week because I forgot after the whole fire situation. If this is what you really want I can skip the shot, or I can get it and we can think more about it."

"No, don't get the shot. Let's let nature take its course."

She smiles and turns to straddle my lap, wrapping her arms around my neck. "Okay, baby. We'll let nature take its course."

I lift her up by her ass and begin walking her to our bedroom. "I say we go practice baby-making right now."

"I agree," she says through her giggles as I slam the door behind us.

Thirty

LIZ

IT'S MONDAY MORNING AND EVERYBODY LEAVES TOMORROW night to go to Boulder. Well, everybody besides me that is. I'll be here running the gym even though it pretty much runs itself. I walk into my office and see a huge bouquet of pink roses. The note on the front reads:

Pack an overnight bag and be ready to go at 6 p.m. —Coop

Hmm…Well, okay then. The rest of the day I attempt to crunch numbers, pay bills, and print receipts, but I can't focus because I'm too intrigued about tonight. At one thirty, just as I'm about to give up and head out to get Bella, Kayla comes walking in shaking her head.

"Where do you think you're going? Home I hope, to get ready for your romantic night with Cooper."

"How did you know about that? I'm going to get Bella and then going home."

"Nope, not happening. I already have her stuff Cooper packed and snuck out this morning. She's coming to my place for a sleepover. I'm getting her from school and you're going home to get ready. I'll see you tomorrow." And with an over-exaggerated wink that reminds me of Marilyn Monroe, she exits as quickly as she came in.

Cooper gets home around five o'clock and runs up to jump in the shower while I finish getting ready. When he's done, we walk outside and waiting for us is a cab.

When I go to ask him a question, he raises two fingers to my mouth to shush me. We get in and he gives the driver an address to go to. When we pull up to a BMW dealership I'm confused. "I know you weren't big on relationships, but surely you know that a car dealership isn't considered romantic."

He laughs and shakes his head, while grabbing my hand, kissing it, and then pulling me along.

The gentleman manning the door asks how he can help us and Cooper tells him he's picking up a purchase. He gives him his name and the gentleman directs us to the pick-up area. Cooper signs a few papers and then is handed the keys and pointed in the direction we need to go.

When we get to the vehicle, it's a beautiful midnight blue SUV. I'm not sure why he's getting another SUV, but it's his money so who am I to judge. I go to get in the passenger seat, but he cuts me off before I can get in.

"Would you mind driving?"

Okay, I never drive. I mean, I *can* drive, but Cooper is one of those guys who insists the man drives everywhere.

"Sure," I say, taking the keys. We get in and I inhale the new car scent.

"Do you like it?" he asks, sounding almost nervous like whether I like it's important to him. I look around taking the vehicle in. It has pretty grey leather seats and touch screen everything. It has a built-in DVD player and TV in the back seat. It's a dream car. What's not to like?

"Yeah, it's a beautiful car. Are you getting rid of the Rover?"

He bites his bottom lip then pulls it out from between his teeth slowly. I'm kind of worried he's going to draw blood.

"No…this car is for you."

"What? For me? Cooper. No, you didn't." I should have seen this coming!

Damn, this thoughtful man.

"I did, but hear me out. I have to go away and I get you're okay with your car, but I'm not. I let it go because I've been around and if I'm not, one of the other guys usually are. So, if your piece-of-shit car breaks down we can handle it. However, we're all leaving and I need to know my girls are safe. It even has roadside assistance so you can get a tow truck or with one press of a button call someone to come fix your flat tire for you. You can even call to get gas delivered in case you run out."

I want to be upset, but when he looks at me with those cute puppy dog eyes begging me to understand, I don't have the heart to hurt him. I know his heart is in the right place and he genuinely cares about our safety.

I take his hand in mine, bringing it up to my lips, and kiss his knuckles. "Thank you, Coop. This was very sweet of you. I love the car and I love you."

I think I just put him in shock. He was obviously gearing up for a fight, because he doesn't even know how to respond.

"Well, good. I'm glad you like it. I love you, too."

He gives me directions to where we're going and we end up at the Venetian hotel on the strip. We pull up and valet park. Is it weird that I totally don't want to hand over my new baby to this stranger? Cooper sees my reluctance and whispers, "It's insured." *Whatever.*

We enjoy a great Mexican dinner at the restaurant and then we stroll over to one of the bakeries and share my favorite dessert, Crème brûlée. When we're both stuffed, we make our way to the counter where Cooper checks us into a room.

"You didn't have to do this. We could have gone home. Bella is at Kayla's you know."

"Please don't argue about this, baby girl. I'm leaving for four days and I want to give my woman a romantic night away from the house." *How can I argue with that?*

Once we're in the room, the door barely shuts before he's on me. He pushes me against the wall and begins to kiss me. God, I will never get tired of how remarkable this man can kiss. His hand lifts my chin and then his mouth is on me. He sucks lightly on my bottom lip and then on my top, asking for access. I open up for him and his tongue swirls in my mouth, his kisses feeling like the most potent drug. I honestly think it's possible to get high off Cooper's touch.

He moves his body closer, if that's even possible, and within seconds I'm shamelessly writhing against him, begging for him. He grinds his erection into me, and I moan loudly into his mouth. The need gets stronger, and suddenly we're all mouths and teeth and hands, and it's just too much.

I pull his shirt up and he yanks it off the rest of the way. He pulls down my dress and I kick it off. His hands grip my panties and I feel him rip them off me. I grab his belt to unbuckle it and his jeans fall to his feet, exposing his incredible erection.

The growing need for each other exceeds our ability to make it to the bed. I wrap my leg around his waist and he lifts me up, wrapping my legs around either side of him. Once he has me steady, he thrusts his hard cock up into me. There's no foreplay. There's no need. I'm wet, he's hard, and I need this man more than air.

My back hits the wall hard as he continues to pump into me. I lower my head to kiss and suck on the side of his neck and he tastes delectable, better than any dessert.

He hits deep inside me over and over again, the pleasure inside me increasing with every thrust. "Fucking hell, Coop. Right there. Don't stop," I pant. My pussy is clenching tight and I know I'm getting close.

A few more thrusts and I'm flying high, my orgasm exploding around his cock. Cooper picks up the pace and with a grunt he comes inside me. As he comes to a stop, both of us breathing heavy, he looks at me, beaming, and I melt inside. This man is my entire world.

We shower together and then get into bed with him spooning me from behind. He plays with my hair for a few minutes, combing it with his fingers, then stops. I think he's asleep until he lets out a heavy sigh. "I hate leaving you guys tomorrow."

"Cooper, it's going to be fine."

"I hope so, baby girl. I hope so." A few minutes later, I hear his soft snores, but I can't sleep. I just don't understand why he's so worried about leaving us. I have a feeling this all stems back to his parents, with his dad being away often and his mom cheating. At some point, he's going to have to believe in us, that we're not his parents and we aren't going to go down the road they did. I guess all I can do until he does, is believe in us enough for the both of us.

Thirty-One

COOPER

I WAKE UP IN THE MIDDLE OF THE NIGHT TO FEEL LIZ'S BODY rubbing up against mine as she moves a bit in her sleep. I don't know why it is, but I have this incessant need to show her she's mine and ruin her for any other man. No, that's a lie, I know why it is. I have it in my head that if I ruin her for other man she'll never leave me. My goal is to leave her with her feeling me between her legs for the next four days so she won't forget about me and seek comfort elsewhere.

Gently moving the sheets off her body, I move my hand to her pussy and slide one finger in and then another. She's still half asleep, but she's starting to move. I spread open her lips just enough to wrap my mine around her clit and pull it. Her body begins to writhe against my fingers and mouth, wanting more.

"Fuck, baby, you taste so good," I whisper as I go back for more. With my fingers still pumping slowly deep inside her warmth, I start to suck hard on her clit then soothe it with my tongue. Her legs tense, telling me it's going to be a quick but strong orgasm. Her body shakes and then her legs tremble around me as she softly moans my name.

"Well, that's one way to wake up," she says, and even though, it's dark and I can't see her, I can hear the laughter in her words. I give the top of her pussy one last kiss then I drag my body up hers until I'm face-to-face with her. I give her a kiss that begins soft, but quickly turns rough, all my emotions trying to convey what my words can't say, begging her to love me enough, to want me enough—for me to be enough— so she'll never leave me.

When I end the kiss, she licks her lips, tasting herself. "Does that taste good?"

She nods shyly and I laugh. Even with her own pussy juices on her mouth, she's still adorably shy.

We wake up around nine and order room service. I feel like the clock is counting down and it's making me sick. I want to beg her to come with me, but I know it would be for the wrong reasons. Of course, I'm going to miss her and Bella, but the real issue is, I'm scared shitless she's going to stray away from me. I know it's crazy because she loves me, and I know, deep down, she wouldn't cheat, but if you saw what I saw growing up you would understand. *Fuck, maybe I need to see a therapist.*

After breakfast, we pack up and head home to meet Kayla and Bella. As soon as she's through the door, she's in my arms. "Daddy, I missed you so much. I had so much fun with Auntie Kay and Uncle Bentley."

She started to call Bentley, Uncle Bentley, a few days ago and I swear the man almost handed over his life savings to her when he heard her say it for the first time.

"I'm happy to hear that, Princess. Why don't you go get dressed and we'll go out for the day before I leave tonight?"

Bella smiles wide at going out, but as soon as she hears that I'm leaving tonight her sadness mutes her smile. She says okay and runs upstairs to get ready.

The three of us spend the day at the park. Bella insists I push her on the swings even though she can do it herself, we make castles in the sand area, and we watch her play tag with other kids. I find myself mentally soaking it all in before I leave.

Eight o'clock comes around and we're all gathered in my house ready to go. Liz and Bella wanted to say goodbye at the airport, but with so many people going, we decided to take one vehicle to the airport. Plus, there's no reason for her to drive all the way there and have to drive back late at night with Bella.

"I love you so much," I tell Liz. "I'll call and text you. Please send me pictures of Bella on Halloween." I give her a chaste kiss because anything more and I just might not leave her.

"I love you, too, and I promise I will. Have a safe flight." She peppers several kisses on my face and neck before she hugs me goodbye.

We're taking a chartered jet over to Boulder because it's easier than dealing with a public flight. Bentley, Kaden, Caleb, and I are sitting in the chairs bullshitting while Hayley and Kayla are sleeping in the one bedroom the plane has.

I know my phone doesn't have service up here, but it doesn't stop me from checking it every five minutes.

"Bro, you're seriously pussy whipped. Chill out." Bentley laughs, nodding at my phone burning a hole in my hand.

"Yeah, whatever. I will gladly accept that name if it means I can be inside my woman's pussy for the rest of our lives."

Kaden jumps in. "Well, shit. Those are some big words. Are we talking marriage here?"

"Well for starters, I told her I want another baby, and she said okay.

So, I would say marriage is definitely coming soon."

All the guys look at me like I've grown a third head and I chuckle, changing the subject. "So, Bent, what's going on with you and Kayla? Bella said she had a great time with both of you last night. I'm pretty sure we only asked Kayla to watch our daughter."

Caleb, who barely ever speaks, cuts in. "He's just as pussy whipped as you are except he isn't getting any of Kayla's pussy."

"Shut the hell up, man," Bentley retorts. "She wants me, but she wants it to just be all fucking and I'm not having it. She's either all in or not at all. She'll come around, it's just a matter of time. I told her the next time we fuck, she's mine."

Kaden throws his head back with a laugh. "So now you guys aren't fucking at all. How's that working out for you?"

Caleb adds, "It sounds like Bentley has the pussy in this relationship."

We all start laughing and the girls come out. Kayla looks around and asks, "What's so funny?" We all go quiet and both girls are glaring at us. Hayley says, "Hmm…Sounds like the guys were just caught gossiping like a bunch of chicks."

She's definitely not off base with that observation.

Thirty-Two

COOPER

IT'S THURSDAY NIGHT AND IT'S BEEN TWO DAYS WITHOUT MY girls. I've been busy with interviews, press conferences, and photo ops. Between my title fight coming up in February, Caleb fighting that night as well, and Bentley fighting in two days, it's been crazy. People don't realize how much more goes into being a part of the UFC aside from the fight they see on the television. And now with me being the owner of several of the training facilities, I have even more responsibility.

It's nine o'clock here in Boulder, so it's eight o'clock where we live. Knowing Bella will be going to bed soon, I break away from the craziness and call my girls to say good night. Liz's phone rings but goes to voicemail. I try again and it does it again, so I send her a text asking her to please call me as soon as she can.

I spoke with Liz and Bella a couple times yesterday and was able to say good night to Bella. I would like to say good night to her tonight as well, so I can keep my promise to her. I hate that I'll be missing Halloween with her, so I take a look at the schedule to see if I can find a way to fly home tomorrow to be there for the trick-or-treating and be back by Saturday morning. It would mean a lot of flying but getting to see my princess in her Elsa costume trick-or-treating would be worth it. I find a large enough gap in my schedule, only having to reschedule one meeting, so I pull up the flights to book one.

A few hours later, there's still no call back from Liz, and we're finishing up at the training center. Everybody agrees to grab dinner at a local pub on the way back to the hotel. I'm nursing my second beer when I see Caleb and Bentley looking down at one of their phones, looking nervous. I don't know why, but I get a bad feeling deep in my gut.

"What the hell are you guys looking at? Don't be rude. Share."

This gets Kayla's attention. "It's probably one of the whores Bentley brought home. Did she let you take pictures?"

His eyes turn murderous and he growls out, "That was one time! One time, woman! I didn't even sleep with her! I haven't brought anyone else home since then, and I said I was sorry a million damn times. I don't know why you even care because you sure as hell don't want me. And for your information, the picture we're looking at is of a woman, of your best friend actually, who appears to be cheating on my best friend. So, before you talk shit, get your facts straight."

He turns to look at me, realizing he just threw up at the mouth. "I'm sorry, man. It's probably nothing. Alex is at club Surrender. He just sent me a picture of Liz and some other guy there…together."

Kayla and Hayley both yell, "Bullshit," and stalk over to Bentley, yanking his phone out of his hand. It must not be good because one look at the photo and both women are trying to make excuses. "It has to be a mistake because Liz would never cheat. For God sakes, you are the only guy she's ever been with."

Hayley chimes in her opinion. "Yeah, plus, she went five years without getting any. There's no way she would cheat now, so there has to be a reason for this."

I get up and slowly take the phone from Kayla. Staring at me is my woman and she's absolutely stunning in a dark purple strapless dress with black fuck-me heels on. Her hair is down and curly, and I want to touch her through the screen. The issue isn't her, though. The issue is that with her, is a guy probably in his late twenties, with his arms around my woman, his front to her back, while she throws her head back against him. And it looks like they're fucking through their clothes.

I throw the phone on the table and stalk out. I can hear everybody around me shouting my name but I need to be alone. This is what I get for thinking for even a second I could have a career and a family. My dad warned me over and over again. He said I couldn't have both, but I thought he was wrong. I thought if I just tried harder, gave more, loved them enough, I would be able to prove him wrong. The man might have been a complete asshole, but according to that picture, it seems he knew what he was talking about. I guess the joke's on me.

Thirty-Three

LIZ

Four Hours Ago

"BELLA, GO HELP TRISTAN CLEAN UP THE TOYS AND GAMES YOU guys took out and played with, please. We need to go soon."

I'm sitting in Ashley's kitchen, having a glass of wine while gossiping over my sex life and her nonexistent one. We spent the afternoon shopping with the kids, and then took them to a cute trunk-or-treat event at the local church. They got a bunch of candy and are currently running around completely hopped up on sugar. I have no idea how I'm going to get Bella to sleep, but I'm glad her mind is off her daddy being gone. It was a rough night last night. After she spoke to Cooper, she threw another one of her tantrums and I ended up letting her sleep with me. I know, shitty parenting move, but I was exhausted and, to be honest, I hated the thought of sleeping in my bed alone.

"You know, my parents are coming over to watch Tristan tonight so a few friends of mine and I can go to Club Surrender. They wouldn't mind watching Bella as well. They would actually love it because Bella would keep Tristan busy."

"Oh, I don't know. I know Bella would be fine here but going out to a club without Cooper feels wrong."

"Sweetie, you are going out for some drinks and maybe some dancing. That's it."

I remember the first and last time I was at a club. It was the night I met Cooper. I fell in love with the music and ambiance. It would be fun to have a drink and let loose a little.

"Okay, I'm in. Drinking and dancing."

"Yay! Okay, let's find us something to wear."

Four hours later and I'm at the club, on my sixth, maybe seventh shot of tequila…I'm not exactly sure, but what I do know is Ashley's friends are drinkers. It's a good thing we cabbed it here because I'm definitely not fit to drive anywhere on my own.

I down another shot and it goes down my throat like water. I know I'm definitely drunk when I no longer feel the burn of the alcohol in my throat. I hear *Talk Dirty* by Jason Derulo come on and Ashley shouts this is her jam, so we make our way to the dance floor. We're having a blast, grinding up against each other and laughing at some of our drunken moves, when the room begins to spin. I tell myself after this song I'm done for the night. *2 Chainz* pops on the surround sound and I can't help but lower my ass and pop it out to his solo. Dancing can be so freeing. I should ask Cooper to come out with me to the club, again.

Out of nowhere, I feel a strong pair of hands wrap around my waist and it's like Déjà vu to the night in the club with Cooper. In my drunken state, I tilt my head back, but when I see the horrific look in Ashley's eyes, I jump forward, realizing it can't be Cooper because Cooper is in Boulder. *Shit.*

I make my way back to Ashley, a bit shaken up at the thought of another man's hands on my body. I know it isn't his fault. He didn't do anything inappropriate. I stopped it immediately, but I still feel guilty.

"I'm going to head back to your place," I tell Ashley when I get over to her.

"No way, I'm ready to go as well. What happened with that guy over there?"

"He came up behind me the same way Cooper did all those years ago at the club when I first met him, and for a second I thought it was Cooper. It wasn't until I saw your face I remembered Cooper's out of the damn state."

Ashley laughs and says, "Yup! We're definitely drunk. It is time to go home. Our rugrats will be up before we know it."

We make it back to Ashley's place and both pass out in her bed. Tomorrow is going to seriously suck. Hangover plus trick-or-treating equals…I don't even know what the hell it equals, but it sure as hell can't be anything good.

We wake up to the kids running around and playing. I grab my phone to see what time it is and it's dead. *Shit.* "Hey, Ash, I'm going to head out with Bella. My phone is dead, so I need to charge it." She mumbles what I think is a reply and goes back to sleep. Luckily for her, her parents spent the night and are hanging out all day with Tristan.

We get home and I jump in the shower to rinse off last night then swallow a few pain relievers hoping to get rid of this massive headache I have going on. Once my phone charges enough to turn it on, I check it and see my phone is overflowing with what looks like a million texts.

Coop: Hey baby girl. I tried to call you to say good night to you guys. Call me. Love you.

Coop: Baby, everything okay? You haven't called me back.

Coop: Bella must be in bed by now. I tried to call to keep my promise to her. Just let me know you guys are okay.

Coop: Liz, are you mad at me?

Damn, I should have told him I was going out, but I didn't even think to. I've spent so many years coming and going as I please, I didn't even think about that fact that Cooper would be worried if I didn't answer his calls or texts, and on top of that, he didn't get a chance to say good night to Bella. I keep scrolling through my texts.

This is where it gets weird…

Kayla: Liz, you need to call me ASAP

Hayley: Where are you?

Hayley: Liz, please call someone as soon as you get this.

Kayla: Liz, I know you wouldn't cheat on Cooper. Please just call so we can get this whole thing figured out.

Cheat. On. Cooper. What the fuck?

I immediately try to call Cooper, but his phone goes straight to voicemail. I try again and again and nothing. I feel sick to my stomach with worry. Why would they think I was cheating on Cooper? I try his phone a few more times and just as I'm about to try Kayla, I hear the front door open and close, and then Bella screams, "Daddy!"

I walk into the living room and see Cooper standing in the doorway with Bella in his arms holding her tight to his chest. His gaze turns to me, and my stomach drops when I see the exhausted and defeated look in his eyes.

He swallows loudly, composes himself, and gives his attention back to Bella. "Hey, sweetie. Did I make it in time to go trick-or-treating with you?"

"Yes! Yes! Yes, you did. Thank you, Daddy!" Bella gives him a huge wet kiss on his cheek.

"Good. Why don't you run upstairs and get your costume ready and then we'll all go to lunch and trick-or-treating."

"Okay, Daddy!"

Cooper waits until Bella is upstairs before he turns his attention to me. I open my mouth to say something but close it again. I'm not sure what happened, but for him to be here when he should be in Boulder says a lot. It should be a good thing that he's here, but after reading the texts Kayla and Hayley sent me, I have a feeling he's here for another reason.

"What's the matter? Not sure how to explain what happened last night? If you want, you can call up my mom and ask her how it's done. I'm sure she can help you explain and justify what happened."

I flinch at his words, like I was just slapped in the face. I don't know what's going on, but it must be bad because Cooper doesn't speak to me like this, ever.

He moves a step closer, and I finally speak up. "I don't know what you think I did, but you're wrong."

He moves a bit closer. "You didn't go to Club Surrender last night?"

"Yes, I did. Ashley and I went with a couple of her friends."

He moves closer with his eyes never leaving mine. "Did you dance with anyone?"

What. The. Fuck! "Yeah, Coop. I did. I danced with Ashley and a few other people. What's going on?"

He takes one more step and he's right in my face. If I didn't know Cooper would never hurt me, I would be terrified of the expression on his face. I can see why other fighters fear this man. When he's pissed, he's not someone you want to mess with.

He pulls out his phone and lifts it up to my face. It's so close I have to pull my head back a bit and squint to see what he's showing me. My stomach drops when I see the grainy photo of me and some guy, who isn't Cooper, extremely close to each another. I'm sweaty from all the dancing and shots, and I have my head thrown back up against the guy's chest while his hands are around my waist. *Fuck. Not good.*

"How did you get that?" I spit out more harshly than intended. I should feel bad about the picture but the truth is nothing happened, and I'm pissed that someone is sending photos to him. I'm even more pissed that he doesn't trust me.

"Does it matter how I got it? What fucking matters is why *my* woman is grinding all over another man's dick while he has his hands wrapped around her."

Wow, it's not even a question, just straight up accusation. Apparently, I'm guilty without even a trial.

"So, let me get this straight? You get some picture, taken by God knows who, and you jump on a plane, not to take my daughter trick-or-treating, but to accuse me of cheating on you."

He lets it sink in for a second before he responds. "No, I was already coming here to take *our* daughter trick-or-treating. I just figured while I was here I would find out why I was only gone for less than two days and the woman who supposedly loves me is already all over another man.

Taking a closer look at Cooper, I notice his eyes are dark with black circles under them like he hasn't had a decent night's sleep in a few days, his shoulders are slumped over a little, and while his words sound so sure, I can see he's sad and scared and confused. I could argue with him. I could scream and curse and be pissed about his accusations, but it wouldn't do any good. Cooper needs to feel secure about us and arguing isn't going to help anything. He might be a badass fighter on the outside, but on the inside, he's an insecure little boy who's been traumatized by the choices his parents made.

So, I wrap my arms around his torso and look up at him. He tenses under my touch, so I bring my hand to the back of his head to lower it, giving him a small kiss, and after a few seconds, I feel him melt into me. The kiss goes deeper and he sighs into my mouth. We kiss for a short time and when we separate he closes his arms around my body tightly, nuzzling his head into my hair. I hear a sob, so soft I almost wouldn't have caught it if it wasn't so quiet, and when he looks up, there's a tear falling down his cheek. I stand on my tip-toes and gently kiss it away.

"I love you, Cooper, and I'd never cheat on you. What you saw was a shitty picture and I'm sorry you saw that. While I was dancing, a guy came up behind me, and for a second I thought it was you. I was drunk and it reminded me of our time together five years ago, but as soon as I realized it wasn't you, I freaked out and decided to go home. Ashley was there and saw the whole thing play out."

He squeezes his eyes closed and then opens them again. "I'm sorry, baby girl. I know you'd never cheat. I just freaked out. I saw the picture and I lost it."

"It's okay." I give him another kiss to calm him down.

"Kayla said I'm the only guy you have ever been with. Is that true?"

"Yeah, it is. I just couldn't stop hoping that maybe one day you'd come back to me. I focused on school and Bella, and I just had no desire to be with anybody but you."

Just then Bella comes prancing down the steps looking like a princess in her Elsa costume.

"I'm ready to go!" she squeals.

We head out to eat lunch and then take Bella trick-or-treating around the neighborhood Kayla and I take her every year. We've never lived in this neighborhood, but we found it years ago. It has nice houses that are close together and the people who live there all sit outside at the end of their driveways giving out candy.

After going up and down several streets, Bella is candied out and Cooper is carrying her back to the car. Every time she asked for a piece with her cute little voice while batting her eyelashes, he would give in. The day started off rough, but it ended up being an amazing Halloween.

We get back home and after Cooper takes Bella to bed he finds me in our room. I'm changing into my pajamas when he comes up behind me and wraps his strong arms around my torso. Remembering this is why he accused me of cheating, I freeze. He must sense what happened, because while nuzzling my neck he says, "I'm sorry, baby. I just want to be the only man to ever touch you like this. Please forgive me."

I turn around to face him. "And you are the only man who will ever touch me this way. You own me, Cooper, Mind, body, heart, and soul. There's nothing to forgive. I love you."

We make love several times throughout the night before we pass out with our bodies entangled in one another.

Thirty-Four

LIZ

IT'S BEEN ALMOST A MONTH SINCE COOPER WENT AWAY AND received that stupid picture. Thankfully we've moved passed it, for the most part. There are times when I still see Cooper's insecurities come out, like when he texts me and I don't answer or if I go somewhere and don't mention it. He isn't an asshole about it. He doesn't yell or get mad. It's more like he gets sad and worried like I'm going to leave one day and never come back.

He's been busy at the gym training for his fight. Bentley won his fight in Boulder, so he's been helping Caleb and Cooper train for theirs. Cooper has been insisting Bella visit every day and is home by her bedtime every night.

Thanksgiving is almost here and we've decided to fly to Florida to have Thanksgiving with my parents and brother. Kayla is flying with us, but will be spending the day with her family. Cooper's mom has decided to join us tomorrow as well so it will be nice.

I've been feeling kind of queasy lately so I'm hoping I'm not catching something before Thanksgiving. That will surely ruin our trip to Florida.

We arrive at the Palm Beach Airport on Wednesday afternoon to find my brother waiting for us.

"Hey you! We could have taken a cab."

He just scoffs at me and gives Bella a big hug, then shakes Cooper's hand. We grab our luggage and head home. I'm excited to show Cooper where I grew up. Kayla catches a ride with us since she only lives down the street. Matt drops her off first and then we head to our house. Bella spots the beach across the street and asks if we can go swimming.

"It might be a little chilly, Angel, but we can head down later to at least walk along the sand."

When we pull up, my mom and dad come out to give us all hugs and kisses before we make our way inside. As soon as I walk in, the smell of pumpkin and stuffing makes me stumble back. I put my hand over my nose and excuse myself to the bathroom. After throwing up everything in my stomach, it hits me that I've been feeling queasy a lot lately. I have also been extremely exhausted, and now I'm throwing up. I thought maybe I was catching the flu, but when I was pregnant with Bella certain smells made me feel the same way. *Could I be pregnant?* Before I tell Cooper, I want to get it confirmed. I don't want to get his hopes up if it's just a coincidence.

I give Cooper a tour around my house, including my bedroom where he laughs at the fact my parents have kept it the same since I left, and wants to know if I still have my cheerleading uniform from high school. *Damn perv.* Needing to get away from the smells that are making my stomach churn, I suggest we take Bella for a walk on the beach.

It's beautiful outside here in the fall. Florida doesn't really have different seasons and it barely even gets cold, but it drops enough in the fall and winter occasionally for it to feel nice. Today, it's in the low seventies so it's too chilly to go swimming but perfect for walking along the beach.

Cooper is walking between Bella and me, holding our hands, as Bella stops every couple feet to pick up a new shell. They all look the same but Cooper shows the same amount of excitement every time she shows him a new one. It makes me sad to think this time last year we were here without Cooper. This Thanksgiving I'm so thankful for Kayla making me go to that UFC fight. I can't imagine Cooper not being part of our lives.

We decide to sit in the sand while Bella plays at the edge of the water. Cooper sits first then pulls me down in between his legs, wrapping his arms around my waist.

"Thank you, baby girl," he says, giving me a soft kiss on my cheek.

I twist my neck to look at him. "For what?"

"For everything…for giving me a second chance, giving me Bella, turning my house into a home. I've never felt so at peace."

I don't say anything. I feel the same way, but I'm suddenly so emotional. *Pregnancy hormones?*

"I've been thinking…After this title fight, win or lose, I'm going to take time off from fighting."

"Cooper, you love fighting. Why would you do that?"

"I'm still going to run the gym, but I just want to focus on Bella and you. I've spent the last fifteen years fighting, and I want to take a break and spend some time with my girls."

I want to ask if it's because of the picture, but I'm afraid it'll upset him. So, I just say, "Well, if that's what you really want to do I'm not going to complain. But make sure it's for the right reasons. Are you actually retiring?"

"I'm not saying I'll never go back, but it won't be any time in the near future."

THANKSGIVING IS AMAZING. COOPER'S MOM GOT IN EARLY this morning, and Kayla ended up getting into a fight with her parents so she's here as well. Bella is chowing down on cookies and biscuits in the living room sitting on Cooper's lap while the guys all watch football.

"Dinner's ready," my mom announces. Everybody makes their way through the lines of food spread out across the countertops and gather around the table. Sadly, my plate is a bit bare. Food I'd normally eat doesn't seem to be appetizing at all, and I'm struggling not to throw up.

"Liz, don't you want some sweet potatoes? They're your favorite," my mom asks innocently. I haven't told anybody I suspect I might be pregnant so it doesn't make sense why I'm not grabbing all my favorites. I take a scoop of sweet potatoes and plop them onto my plate, making sure they don't touch my other food. *Please Lord, don't let me throw up all over my plate of food.*

Before we dig in, it's a tradition for everyone to say what he or she is thankful for. Bella begs to begin, so of course we let her.

"I am soooooo thankful for my mommy because I love her because she gave me my daddy." Everybody *oohs* and *ahhs* around her, but she keeps going naming everybody around the table. "I'm thankful for my auntie Kay because she is the best at painting my nails. I'm thankful for all my grandmas because they let me eat cookies. I'm thankful for my grandpa because he gives me a dollar every time he sees me. I'm thankful for my uncle Matty because he always sneaks me bubblegum even though my mommy says I'm too little to eat bubble gum."

Matt laughs out loud and says, "Kid, you aren't supposed to tell people that!" She looks genuinely confused, not realizing she's telling on everyone around her while saying thank you. Finally, she gets around the table to Cooper and says, "And I'm thankful for my daddy because he is the bestest daddy ever because he's going to get me a puppy and a baby brother or sister. I really want a sister, but a brother will still be good."

Cooper turns white as the entire table goes quiet, looking at him, and then we all burst out laughing.

"I squeeze his hand and whisper loudly, "Sounds like someone has been making secret promises to our daughter."

He just nervously laughs. Everyone takes turns going around the table, saying what they're thankful for, and after the final person goes, it's time to eat. Of course, within twenty minutes, the food is completely gone.

Friday morning Cooper offers to keep Bella with him and the guys while the women check out the crazy Black Friday sales. While I'm out, I put a call into my doctor so I can make an appointment for next week to confirm if I'm pregnant. Nobody is in the office, so I leave a message with the answering service for someone to call me back with an appointment.

Thirty-Five

COOPER

WE HAD A GREAT WEEKEND WITH LIZ'S PARENTS IN FLORIDA. We'll definitely need to plan another trip back soon, especially once it's warmer and we can take Bella swimming in the ocean. It's Monday morning and we're at the airport with Kayla and my mom since we're all flying back together. Liz's phone rings and she glances at it nervously. Before it goes to the voicemail, she answers the call and excuses herself to speak to whoever it is on the other end away from us. Kayla raises her brows at me, telling me to chill out. Fuck, I'm not that guy. I don't do jealousy and I sure as fuck don't monitor who my girlfriend talks to.

Liz comes back over and doesn't say who it was, but she looks guilty as hell. I know I have my issues, but I'm not seeing shit. My woman looks like she needs to tell me something but decides not to, so I let it go because I need to trust her and trust us.

We make it home and we're all completely jet-lagged. The five-hour flight to and from Florida was no joke. On top of that, add an energetic four-year-old to the mix, and a three-hour time difference, and we're done for.

Liz and I cuddle up in our bed with Bella between us and sleep for hours. I'm sure we'll regret this tonight when Bella is wide-awake, but right now it feels damn good.

I groggily wake up and reach for Liz when I feel Bella beside me laughing softly to something on her iPad. I look over her to see if Liz is in bed, but she's not.

"Hey, Princess, where's your mommy?"

"She said she had to run out."

"Do you know where she went?"

"Nope, she just kissed me goodbye and left."

I grab my phone off the nightstand and see we've only been asleep for a couple hours. I look to see if there are any texts from Liz, but there isn't, so I shoot her a text asking what time she'll be back and what she wants to do for lunch.

She replies back almost instantly letting me know she'll be home soon and we can order something in. I repeat the mantra in my head, *I will not assume shit.* I trust her and we're not my parents.

She gets back a couple hours later and joins Bella and me on the couch. We're watching some crazy movie where everything is made out of Legos and they run around singing some weird ass song about everything being awesome.

"Hey baby," Liz says. "I was thinking we could take Bella to see Santa today since he's at the mall."

Bella jumps up like she wasn't just in a trance watching these weird fuckers building and tearing shit down Lego-style. "Yes, please! I want to go see Santa. I know what I want for Christmas."

She runs to her room to get dressed, leaving Liz and me alone. "Everything okay?"

"Yeah." She gives me nothing more except a kiss on the cheek, before she heads upstairs to help Bella get dressed. *I will not assume shit.*

We get to the mall and you can tell Christmas is around the corner. The mall is packed with people and Christmas music is playing through the speakers. We head straight for Santa, and once we get through the line, Bella sits right on his lap, telling him exactly what she wants. "My daddy already said he's going to give me a baby and a puppy, so from you, all I want is a swing set for the back yard. I would like for it to be pink and purple please. I would also like for it to have benches with a table where I can have tea and cookies with my daddy and mommy and my dolls. I've been really good, well…except for when I don't want to go to bed, but I'm trying really, really hard."

Damn, this girl is so sweet, and honest to a fault. She'll be getting that swing-set and puppy. Now, the baby on the other hand, that's going to take a little bit of work. I smirk at Liz and she hits my arm. "Are you thinking about sex?" she whisper-yells.

"What? No! I was thinking we needed to work on Bella's Christmas gifts." She laughs at me and when she's done, her smile still lingers. I love her smile and will do anything in my power to keep it there.

"And what do you want for Christmas?" she teases.

"Not a damn thing. I have everything I could want right here." Her smile widens and I can't help but kiss it.

We join Bella for pictures with Santa and I insist on buying them all, including the frames, so we can put them out around the house. We decide to do a little shopping, but when Bella sees the giant Christmas tree in the department store she begs for us to go get ours.

After picking one out for the living room and a mini tree for Bella's bedroom, we head to Target to get the decorations. Liz lost all hers in the fire, and I've never had a tree since living on my own, so we're buying all new stuff. I think the last time my mom got us a tree I was twelve and it was right before my parents split up.

"I think this one is perfect." Bella holds up a cute pink princess crown ornament. When I nod my okay, she places it into the basket.

"How about this one?" Liz holds up an ornament that reads *First Family Christmas.*

"That one is absolutely perfect."

This goes on for the next hour. The girls pick out ornaments, while I push the cart through the store. We eventually move on to lights, and while we're in that section they convince me to get lights for the outside along with some huge blowup snowman. I don't know why they even ask. We all know I have a problem with saying no to anything they ask for.

On our way home, I call my mom to join us for dinner and to help decorate the tree. Liz insists on getting break-n-bake cookies and eggnog on the way home as well.

And that's how we spend the night. Sipping eggnog, eating cookies, listening to Christmas music, and decorating our first family tree. Today will definitely go down as one of the best days of my life.

Thirty-Six

LIZ

IT'S BEEN TWO WEEKS SINCE FINDING OUT I AM INDEED pregnant. Hiding it from Cooper is killing me, but I decided since Christmas is so close I could give him—and Bella—the gift of a new baby. The first couple days I felt like I was betraying him by not telling him right away. I think he even noticed how guilty I felt, but since then it's been smooth sailing.

Christmas is in two weeks and I need to think of a cool way to tell him. Simply putting a box under a tree and saying, *Surprise you're going to be a daddy again* isn't fun enough. So, I've gathered my girls together to help me figure it out. I know, I admit them knowing first probably isn't the best idea, but hell, how do I plan without telling them why I'm planning?

Cooper has been gracious enough to watch Bella and Tristan at our place. Caleb, Bentley, Kaden, and Alex are all joining him to watch a UFC fight on pay-per-view. I don't really know much about Alex except that he goes to the gym and he's the one who took the picture of me at the club. You know, the one that almost blew my relationship up in smoke.

He did apologize and explain that he was just looking out for Cooper. I forgave him, but it still stings. He should've come to me before sending that picture to him. However, I'm not about to hold a grudge. That brings us back to the present.

Hayley, Kayla, Ashley, and I are all sitting at Hayley's place, giving each other homemade facials, manis, and pedis while listening to Iggy Azalea's *Fancy*. That girl can seriously rock those lyrics.

Hayley gets up and dances to the kitchen, bringing back a bottle of Jack in one hand and Coke in the other. Now is probably a good time to let them know I'm preggers.

She passes out the glasses and dishes out ice into all our cups, and then begins to pour the Jack.

"Just coke for me," I say.

"Excuse me?" Kayla cuts in. "Since when are you going sober?"

"Since I'm pregnant and I'm not sure how much the baby will enjoy Jack Daniels."

Everybody goes silent and then cheers erupt. They all take turns congratulating and hugging me.

Ashley finishes pouring everyone's drinks, but Kayla says she'll remain sober with me.

Ashley raises her glass and we all follow suit. "A toast. To the new precious little miracle."

"Here, here," all the girls say.

"So, does Cooper know? How far along are you?" Hayley asks.

"Not far at all, only six weeks, and no, Cooper doesn't know yet."

"How is he going to feel?" Kayla asks. She almost seems despondent about my news. I give her a quick look, silently asking if she's okay and she nods.

"I'm hoping he's going to be ecstatic since it was his idea. Back in October, he told me he wants another baby and we decided I wouldn't get the shot. I didn't think it would happen so soon, but I'm excited. Speaking of the shot, we never ended up going together. Did you go get yours done?" Kayla nods, but something is off with her.

"So, anyway, I want to come up with a cool way to tell him. Whenever I ask him what he wants for Christmas he says he has everything he could want."

"I got it! You can plan a family weekend away, like to Disney and say it's the last trip before you're a family of four."

"Oh, I like it, Hayley! Yes, that's what I'll do, and it'll be a Christmas present to Bella as well. Yay! I'm so excited! You guys can't say anything to anybody. It would break Cooper's heart if he found out he wasn't the first to know."

All the girls vow to keep silent and I'm ready to plan our trip.

Thirty-Seven

COOPER

ALL THE GUYS ARE HERE, WE'VE ORDERED PIZZA AND WINGS, the pay-per-view fight is on, and Bella and her friend Tristan are running around playing. I'm thinking tonight is the night I'm going to let the guys know I'm going to be taking a break from fighting.

"So, I've decided something…" The guys all turn to me, but when I see Bentley, he looks like he's a hundred miles away.

"Yo, Bentley! What's up with you?" I ask.

"Women, bro. No, not women. One woman. One stubborn damn woman that is going to be the death of me."

We all laugh and nod because we've been there.

"Kayla?" Kaden asks.

Bentley just shakes his head and we wait to see if he's going to explain. Finally, with a deep sigh, he says, "We had sex in Boulder."

We all congratulate him. Because really, that's what men do…A guy gets laid and you say, *Congratulations.* Yep, we suck.

"So, does this mean you two are together now?" I ask, remembering he said the next time they have sex would mean they're together.

"No, we aren't. Not only are we not together, but she's barely talking to me. She knew if we had sex it meant we would be together, but once it happened she said she made a mistake and left. I really care about this girl, but I don't know what to do anymore. I think it's time to move on. I'm already almost thirty years old. I want a family one day. I want a wife and kids, and I don't want to wait until I am too old to enjoy all of that. There's a girl I've been talking to, so we'll see…"

Because he hasn't been kicked down enough, Caleb adds, "She actually mentioned she might be moving out soon. I'm sorry, Bentley."

"Well, screw her then." And with that he gets up to clear his head.

I decide to hold off on my news for now.

A few hours later, and I can hear loud screeches and yelling from outside the house. When I look outside, I see Liz and her friends walking up the steps to the front door.

Ashley and Hayley appear to be drunk ,while Liz and Kayla are both sober.

"Hey, baby." She gives me a soft peck on the cheek and walks in with Kayla, while everybody else stumbles in loudly. It's actually quite amusing.

"What's with only half of you being drunk?" Bentley asks. Kayla turns her attention to him, and if looks could kill, he would be dead and buried six feet under.

"Not that it's your business, but I wasn't in the mood to drink and either was Liz. Is that okay with you?"

Bentley puts his hands up in surrender and turns back to the fight.

"Sorry to ruin your little fight party," Hayley says as she plops down next to Caleb and pats him on his leg. He blushes. The fool actually fucking blushes. Then he gets up immediately, like her hand set his leg on fire, and Hayley frowns at his reaction.

"I have to get to work," he says, and without saying goodbye to anybody, he's out the door.

Tristan and Bella come running down to say hi to their moms and tell them about all the Halloween candy they've been eating. *Damn traitors.*

We all find a seat and watch the fight. Liz is in my lap with Bella passed out next to us. Eventually everyone heads out. Kaden gives Ashley and Tristan a ride since her car isn't here and she's been drinking, and Kayla gives Hayley a ride home. Liz and I put Bella to bed and then head back to finish watching the main event.

"Are you going to miss this?" Liz asks as we sit back down on the couch.

"Miss what? The fighting?" I ask, stalling before I answer the question I know she's really asking. She wants to know if a few years from now I'm going to resent her and Bella. I've thought long and hard about this and I know this is what's right for my family and me. I would never turn around and blame Liz for my choices, but she needs to hear it so she doesn't feel like I'm making a rash decision.

"No, baby girl. I'm not going to miss it. I'll still be fighting. I'll fight at the gym every day. The only difference is I won't be fighting professionally. My contract ends in February and I'm okay with that. It's time to move forward."

Liz climbs into my lap, placing a leg on either side of me. I look up at the stairs out of habit and she slowly shakes her head. "She's fast asleep."

Taking the bottom of my shirt in her hands, she raises it over my head and throws it on the floor.

"Do you know how beautiful you are, Cooper?" *Maybe she is drunk after all.*

"Um, Liz, I'm not sure you should be calling a man beautiful. Do you want to emasculate me?"

She ignores my question and starts to kiss me. First, she kisses me on my lips but pulls away quickly. "You have beautiful lips. They were made for me. They kiss me with such passion and emotion, and the words that come out of them are just as beautiful."

Next, she kisses the tops of my eyelids. "You have the most amazing eyes. When you're happy, they are bright green, full of life, like the grass after it's been raining for days. And when you're angry, they go dark. I don't like it when they go dark. Bella has the same eyes as you. Every time I would look into her eyes, it gave me butterflies because it brought back the brief time we shared together."

She trails her lips down my neck, over to my chest, and stops right over my heart, placing multiple tender kisses there. "And your heart. It's so full of love. Whether it was for thirty-hours in Miami or every day since we reconnected, you give me your entire heart and trust me with it. The way you instantly fell in love with Bella. Many guys might have thought I got pregnant on purpose or they might have accepted her but they wouldn't have gone out of their way to make her feel so loved and cherished. You didn't just give us a place to live, you made sure we felt at home."

A lump in my throat forms. This girl is my entire fucking world. I'm going to marry her some day and she's going to have more of my babies, and we're going to live happily ever after.

She doesn't stop at my heart, though. She kisses her way down to my stomach and stops at the center of my abs. She's now kneeling on the floor between my legs. "Mmm…and this body. Cooper, do you have any idea how beautiful your body is? You treat it with such care only putting healthy foods in it. It's such a turn on, and I love that this body is all mine."

She moves on from my abs and unbuttons my jeans. Thank God because my dick is so hard it needs to be released from its confined space. I lift my ass and she pulls down my jeans, taking my boxers with her. I go to touch her and she shakes her head.

She gives my dick a kiss on the top of the crown, sucking on it lightly with her lips and then pulls back. *Holy Shit, this woman is going to be the death of me.*

"This is probably one of my favorites parts of your body." I lift one of my brows up. I mean, I know it's one of my favorite parts of my body, especially since it's the part that goes inside of her, but I wasn't expecting a woman to think it's her favorite. She giggles under her breath at my reaction. "Not for the reasons you probably think…Well, actually, kind of. I remember the first time I saw your dick. I thought it was crazy to think it was beautiful. I haven't seen any others to compare it to."

I growl at that. "And you never fucking will."

She giggles again, but continues. "It was so hard and thick, and when I felt it, it was smooth. Then when I tasted it, I thought it would be gross but it wasn't. It tasted like you." She puts her mouth back on my dick to give it another wet kiss, then she starts stroking it up and down slowly.

"But aside from its physical appearance, the reason it's one of my favorite parts is for a few reasons." She kisses it again, and it takes every ounce of restraint not to take her by her hair and push her beautiful mouth onto my erection.

"One, is what I feel when it's inside of me. I feel so close to you, like we're connected. When our bodies are skin to skin and you're pushing it inside of me, hitting me so deep, I feel like we become one."

This time she takes her entire mouth and covers my dick from root to tip with it then drags her mouth back up slowly. "The other reason it's my favorite body part is because of what it's capable of. Not only does it bring me an extreme amount of pleasure, but it's how we created Bella."

"That's really fucking sweet, baby girl, but you can't be bringing Bella up while your hands are stroking my dick."

She laughs at that and then puts her mouth back on me. This time she doesn't remove her mouth. Her tongue slides down with her mouth wrapped around it and she begins to move it up and down, fucking my shaft with her greedy mouth, and I can't take it anymore. I need to touch her. It's like she senses what I need because while keeping her mouth wrapped tightly around me, she grabs my hands with her own and moves them to her hair, giving me permission to touch her.

What started out slow and sensual, turns into rough and crazed. Her mouth starts to move faster as I entwine my fingers into her hair. I don't push her head down, though. She doesn't need me to. She's deep throating me like a champion and within minutes I'm tapping her to let her know I'm about to come. Of course, it only spurs her on, and within seconds, I'm shooting my seed down her throat. She slows down but keeps licking until my dick is licked clean.

"Damn, baby. I've changed my mind. You can emasculate me any time you want."

Thirty-Eight

LIZ

IT'S LESS THAN A WEEK UNTIL CHRISTMAS, AND I CAN'T BELIEVE I haven't told Cooper that I'm pregnant yet. My next appointment isn't until December 30th, so I'll be able to wait until Christmas to tell him when I give him and Bella their gift together, and he'll be able to go to my appointment with me.

Normally I keep the office door open, but I shut it today so I can finish planning our trip to California to Disneyland. I've figured out that we'll go in March during Bella's spring break, so she doesn't miss any school. We're going to go to all the parks and stay at a resort near Disney.

I'm making sure to put it on my personal credit card just in case Cooper decides to look at our joint account. I'm researching online the best hotels to stay at when a site pops up for the cheapest motels in the area. I go to click out of it, but of course the stupid ad opens up. *So freaking annoying.*

I hear a commotion outside the office, so I run out to see what's going on. When I get out there Kayla and Bentley are in the middle of a screaming match.

"I don't give a shit what you think. I'm moving out and you can do whatever you want," Kayla screams at the top of her lungs. Cooper looks at me to do something. This might be a gym, but it's still a place of business.

Bentley looks pissed as hell. His fists are at his sides, knuckles white like he has to hold himself back.

"Okay, I don't know what is going on here, but you guys need to take this to a private area. This is a place of business."

They both look over at me. I place my hand on Kayla to silently calm her down, and Bentley shouts, "Fuck this!" as he storms out of the room.

When I look at Kayla ,she has tears in her eyes. I brush her hair back out of her eyes and suggest we get out of here. Cooper hears me and nods his head slightly, letting me know he heard me.

We get to one of our favorite coffee shops and order ourselves each a hot peppermint mocha. It's only a few days until Christmas and then the delicious taste of peppermint will disappear until next year.

Kayla hasn't said a word since we left and it's killing me inside. "Kayla, I feel like we've grown apart." She attempts to argue, but I raise my hand for her to let me finish.

"I know this isn't about us, but at the same time it is because it's about you, and for the last eighteen years we've had each other's back. So, when you have something going on, so do I."

She slumps over and puts her hands in her hair and shakes her head. I think she's going to tell me what's going on, but when she raises her head, all she says is, "I've decided to move back to Florida. I've been thinking about it for a little while now, but I've decided for sure."

That takes me for a loop because Kayla knows I can't move anywhere. Bella and my home is here with Cooper, and if she moves to Florida we'll be a long ass plane ride apart.

I choke up and try to hold it in because this isn't about me. "Are you serious? Like your mind is made up for sure? I mean, your parents and brother are there, but you aren't really close to them. Bella and I'll miss you like crazy. We've never been apart since the day we met in Kindergarten."

She sighs and looks absolutely defeated. "Is it something I did, Kay?" I don't think it is, but I need to make sure.

"No, Liz. It's nothing you did. I'm just going through some shit and feel like I need a break from it all."

"So, take a vacation, but please don't leave me. I need you. You know I'm pregnant. I can't do this without you." I know it's selfish to say this to her, but it's the truth. I need her so much. I can't imagine going through this pregnancy without her.

"Liz, we aren't eighteen anymore, and you won't be alone this time around. You have Cooper now."

I don't even know what to say. "Can you at least wait until after Christmas? I'd like to have one last holiday together." She nods, and I get up and hug my best friend. I can feel her sobbing and in turn I'm crying. I can't help but feel like this is the end of our friendship. She wouldn't do this unless she really felt like she needed to leave, though. All I can do is respect her decision and be there for her.

"Do me a favor, Liz. Please don't tell anybody yet, including Cooper." Even though I'm not okay with any of this, I agree.

"C'mon, chick, let's go pick up Bella and have a girls' afternoon," I say as we walk out the door with our arms around each other.

Thirty-Nine

COOPER

AFTER BENTLEY WALKS OUT OF THE GYM AND LIZ TAKES KAYLA out to let shit cool down, I take advantage of the fact that Liz's computer is free. I've found Bella's puppy on a local animal rescue shelter website. The mom is a German Shepherd-Lab mix who was found pregnant under a bridge after giving birth to several puppies. The puppies are now eight weeks and can be adopted out. I put in a request to adopt one and was approved several weeks ago. I'm supposed to be getting an email from the shelter today letting me know when I can pick the puppy up. Since it's only a week until Christmas, I'm having Kaden keep the pup at his place until Christmas Eve. He's agreed to bring the little mutt over late at night after Bella and Liz have gone to bed.

I walk around to her desk, sit, and shake the mouse to wake the computer up. There are several webpages open, but the one that catches my eye is the top page. It's an ad for some sleazy motels in the area. I look on the desk and find Liz's personal credit card sitting atop it. Why the hell would she be booking one of these motels? And to top it off, she's using the credit card she keeps for emergencies. It's the only card that we don't have a joint account on. The only reason she would do something like this is if she doesn't want me to know.

My mind starts wandering to the last few weeks. She's been nervous, but nothing that would make me believe she's cheating or wants out. When we got back from Florida, she went out that one time and never told me where she was going, but she's been happy since then.

The last time I assumed the worst, I made her believe I didn't trust her. I sure as hell won't be doing that again. This time I'm going to just come out and ask her. Liz doesn't lie, and if something is going on, she'll tell me.

Quickly exiting out of all the windows, I pull up my email. The shelter says I can pick up the pup today, so I shut down her computer and leave to go pick up our new puppy. Once that's taken care of, Liz and I will talk.

I get home to Bella watching a movie in the living room and Liz in the kitchen making dinner. She doesn't make eye contact with me so I walk over to her and turn her around to face me. When I look at her, I can tell she's been crying.

"Baby girl, what's wrong?"

She just shakes her head. Well, that shit isn't going to fly.

"I can see the dried-up tears. Please tell me what's wrong. Does it have something to do with you booking a sleazy motel with your card?" Okay, well that wasn't how I planned to broach the subject, but now that it's out there...

Her eyes go wide for a second, but she quickly reins her shock in. "Were you seriously going through my computer, Cooper?" Damn it, leave it to a woman to turn it around on the guy like it's his damn fault.

"No, Liz, I wasn't. I got on to pull up my email and it was on the front screen."

"Oh, well no, I'm not booking a motel. It was just an ad that popped up."

"So, why was your credit card out? The one you only use for emergencies?" I force the issue because she isn't giving me much and something isn't adding up.

She looks at me and then loses it. She starts bawling her eyes out. I'm talking full- on crying. I don't even know what to think. Is she leaving me? What the fuck happened to make her cry like this?

I do the only thing I can do and move closer to hold her. She wraps her arms around me and bawls her eyes out. I can feel the snot dripping off her onto my shirt but I'm not about to say anything right now. It's breaking my heart to see her this emotional, especially since I don't know what's going on or how to fix it.

Bella walks in at this moment and I can tell from her soft voice she heard her mom crying. "Mommy, Daddy. Are you okay?"

Liz sucks in her snot and picks her head up to wipe her nose, trying to get herself together. "Nothing is wrong, Angel, I promise. I'm just really tired."

Bella looks from me to her mom and says, "When I'm so tired that I cry you always tell me to go to bed. Maybe you should go to bed." God bless our sweet daughter. May she always stay this innocent.

Liz nods her head in agreement and says to me, "I think I'm going to go lie down. Dinner is done. Can you take it out of the oven in fifteen minutes and give some to Bella?"

One, I don't like how she never acknowledged the issue of the credit card, and two, I definitely don't like that my girl looks like the world has beaten her up and thrown her out into the cold. However, now is not the time to get to the bottom of this, especially with our four-year-old in front of us. So, I agree and let her walk away from me.

When the food is ready, I dish it out, and Bella and I eat together in front of the television, finishing up her movie. It's something her mother barely ever allows, so I know it'll keep her entertained because she feels like she's getting away with something.

After the movie's over, I give her a bath, read her a story, and put her to bed. Liz still hasn't come out of her room, so I tell Bella I'm giving her two kisses, one from me and one from her mom. This makes her think. "Wait, if you can give me kisses from Mommy, can you give me kisses from other people?"

You'd think after living with a four-year old the last few months I would see what's coming, but I don't, and I fall right into her trap. "I guess."

"Great! I want a kiss from grandma. Oh, and a kiss from grandpa. Then I want a kiss from Auntie Kay…"

Twenty minutes and fifty kisses later—from everybody my four-year old knows to some people she doesn't know like Cinderella—and she's down for the night.

I walk into our dark bedroom to find Liz sound asleep. I want to ask her what's going on, but I don't have the heart to wake her up. So instead I strip down to my boxers and wrap my girl up in my arms, praying whatever's wrong doesn't involve her leaving me.

Forty

LIZ

HOW I HAVE MANAGED TO AVOID THE CONVERSATION WITH Cooper the last four days I have no clue. When he said he saw the motels webpage and credit card I thought for sure I was screwed. Luckily, when he mentioned them, it reminded me that I'm hiding my pregnancy from him, which reminded me that Kayla won't be there for me because she's moving, and then I remembered I'm not allowed to tell Cooper, and so I lost it. Poor guy had no clue what to do. He definitely handled it like a trooper though, accepting my snot all over his shirt like it wasn't even a big deal.

I can see it in his face that he wants answers, but dammit, I've made it to Christmas Eve, and I'm not going to give in now. After he gave me back my credit card, I was able to book the flights and hotel, and purchase the Disney theme park tickets. I even had matching shirts overnighted that have our names on them: Mommy, Daddy, and Bella, and for the surprise, I had put on mine below my name an arrow pointing down that reads, "Plus baby".

Everybody came over for Christmas Eve dinner and I have to say it was a bit awkward. I don't know what has happened between Bentley and Kayla, since neither of them are talking, but man their emotions are flying high. It probably doesn't help that Bentley brought a guest.

After everyone left, Bella set out cookies for Santa and carrots for the reindeer, along with a note telling Santa to fly safe. Now the three of us are sitting in Bella's room while Cooper reads *The Grinch That Stole Christmas* to her. I had asked Cooper about the swing-set she wants and he said he has it covered. I haven't seen anything in the backyard, but if he says he has it covered, I trust him. When he's finished reading the book, we both give her kisses and tell her we'll see her in the morning.

We go downstairs and begin setting out all the presents we've kept hidden in the gym. I'm pretty sure there's double the number of gifts here than I bought. It's Cooper's first Christmas with Bella, so I let it go.

I'm kind of shocked about one thing, so I decide to bring it up. "You know, I thought for sure you would have had that puppy under this tree, but I'm pretty sure I don't hear any barking."

He just chuckles and shakes his head. *What is he up to?*

Forty-One

COOPER

OH BOY, IF ONLY THIS WOMAN KNEW WHAT I HAVE BEEN UP TO these last few days. She's not the only one who can keep secrets. When she decided she wasn't going to talk to me, I had two options: Freak the fuck out and assume the worst or go all in. I chose the latter. If she has any intention of leaving me, I'm going to make it hard as hell for her. I meant it when I said I'm going to fight for this second chance, and if I go down, at least I'll go down swinging, knowing I've done everything in my power to show her how much I love her. So, this is the part where I should tell you everything but…Nah. You'll have to wait to find out like the rest of them.

Forty-Two

LIZ

"MOMMY! DADDY! SANTA CAME!"

Cooper and I finished putting the presents out at almost two in the morning. Of course, I never learned where the swing-set or puppy is, or if there is even one. *Sneaky bastard.*

"What time is it? I don't even think the sun is up." Cooper moans and places a pillow over his face before throwing it to the side and getting up.

"It doesn't matter what time a child normally wakes up. On Christmas, their brain wakes them up before five, always."

We make our way down the stairs and Cooper puts some coffee on and makes Bella a hot chocolate. We sit on the couch, while she opens up her stocking first, and she's in heaven! There are new nail polishes, and candy, and tons of Barbie accessories.

Once she's done with her stocking, she moves on to her presents. She gets excited about every single one and thanks us for the ones that have our names on them. I don't think there is a single toy this child didn't get for Christmas, thanks to Cooper.

When she gets to her last present, her smile falters for a second. I don't care how good of a kid you have, when they realize they didn't get the couple items they asked for they're going to be sad. It doesn't make them spoiled…it makes them human. She opens the present and says thank you to the both of us.

Cooper looks way too happy with himself when he asks if she had a good Christmas. Bella says yes, and then he tells her he has one more gift, but it's for all of us and it's not here. I can see she gets her hopes up, but she doesn't mention it or ask.

"Before we get to your gift for all of us, I have one for all of us as well," I say.

I pull a box from the back of the tree and hand it to Cooper and Bella to open. Bella smiles as she tears apart the wrapping paper and shakes the top off. Nestled inside are the three shirts I ordered. I made sure to put mine on the bottom.

Bella pulls them out and attempts to read them. She's not a great reader yet, but she's definitely improving. "Bella," she reads the first one. It has a picture of a Minnie mouse with a crown under her name. She doesn't understand it yet, but I think Cooper does because his lips curl into a huge grin.

Next, she reads Cooper's shirt. "Daddy." This one has a mickey mouse on the front as well.

And finally, she reads mine. "Mommy. And there's an arrow pointing down. It says pl…us plus b.a.by. Plus, baby?"

Cooper whips his head around to me, and with wide eyes, asks, "Are you pregnant?"

Forty-Three

COOPER

IT KILLED ME TO WATCH BELLA OPEN ALL HER GIFTS, KNOWING the only three she asked for aren't under the tree. I was able to take care of two of them, but the baby part is unfortunately out of my control.

Liz telling us she has a gift for us definitely peaks my curiosity. This is the happiest I've seen her so it must be good. Bella opens the box and begins reading the name on the shirts. I see Bella's shirt with her name on it and Minnie Mouse, and I know right away we're going to Disney. Not only am I excited to experience this with my two girls, but it also makes sense why she was using her credit card and looking up hotels. Although, hopefully she has better sense than to book one of those nasty motels that were up on her page. She pulls out my shirt next which has *Daddy* written on it with a mickey mouse under it.

Bella gets to her mom's shirt and she's struggling to read it, but we both let her sound it out. "…plus, baby?"

Putting all the pieces together, I go into shock. "Are you pregnant?"

Excitedly, Liz nods, and Bella starts going nuts, singing that she's going to have a baby brother or sister.

Grabbing her by her waist, I give her a kiss then move down to her belly and lift her shirt. It's too soon for there to be a bump, but I still have to kiss it. I look up with blurry eyes from the unshed tears and say thank you. This woman has just made me the happiest man in the world.

I stand and ask how far along she is. She laughs and says, "I'll be nine weeks on the thirtieth. I suspected I was pregnant on Thanksgiving and had it confirmed the day we returned. I thought it would be fun to surprise you for Christmas along with a family trip for just the three of us, but I didn't realize keeping a secret from you for a month would be so difficult."

Damn, now it all makes sense. The secret phone call and outing by herself, the way she's been up and down with her emotions, and going out of her way not to talk to me about her credit card. I'm so glad I chose to have trust in us instead of flipping out. Now it's my turn to give them my present, and with a baby coming, it makes the present even better.

"Okay, you two get dressed. We're leaving in fifteen minutes." They both look at me like I am stupid. Yeah, I know they will never get out the door in fifteen minutes but I still keep saying it in hopes they will one day get ready in under an hour. *Please let this baby be a boy.*

An hour later we're in my SUV driving towards the surprise and I text everybody to meet me there. This is more like four surprises in one. We pull up to the gated community and I pull my resident card out to swipe so I can be let in. It's a temporary one until we get our barcode decals. I look over at Liz, and she looks utterly confused.

Forty-Four

LIZ

WHEN WE PULL UP TO A BEAUTIFUL GATED COMMUNITY I think maybe we're going to visit someone, but then Cooper pulls out what looks like a resident pass and I'm back to square one. We drive down a few roads until we get to a massive house on the left and Cooper turns into the driveway. Parked along the road are our friends' vehicles. *Maybe there's a Christmas party going on here?*

We all get out and Cooper takes a key out of his pocket to unlock the door. When he opens the door, the cutest brown and black little puppy comes barreling down the hall and straight into Bella's arms. She scoops her up and looks at her father with hope in her eyes. "Is she mine?"

"Yes, Princess, she's yours. Merry Christmas." He kisses her on her forehead.

"Does she have a name?"

"She's yours, so you can pick the name."

She thinks about it, and when she figures out the name she wants, her entire faces lights up. "I know! I want to name her Princess!"

"But that's what I call you."

Bella pouts, but thinks of another name. "Okay, how about Elsa?"

We both laugh. "Elsa, it is!"

"Can I bring her home with me? Why wasn't she at my home?"

"This is her home, Bella. Do you like this house?" Bella looks around, and I do as well. The home is gorgeous. We're only standing in the foyer, but even from here I can see the spacious living room and the beautiful staircase that leads to the upstairs. Off to the side is what looks like a beautiful kitchen with a separate dining room. The floors are all hardwood, and the home is empty, but it's still stunning.

"Yes, I like this house. But why does she have to stay here? I want her with me."

Cooper looks at me as he answers Bella's question. "I bought this home for all of us. I was hoping we could all live here together as a family. I didn't know about the baby, but now it's even more perfect. I figured it would give us more room to grow as a family. It's empty so we can furnish it together."

He gets down on one knee and my breath hitches. I look around, realizing we aren't alone, which makes sense because all of our friends' cars were parked along the road when we pulled up. But now that I'm looking, I see that my parents and brother are also here, as well as Lauren, Cooper's mom.

Turning my attention back to Cooper, I see he's holding up a tiny box with a sparkly ring nestled inside of it.

"Lizbeth, when we met five years ago in Miami at that club it was lust at first sight." Everybody laughs, and I can feel the tears coming. "When I walked away from you, it was the hardest thing I ever chose to do. The only thing I can think of is that everything happens for a reason and maybe it just wasn't our time yet. Seeing you that night at my fight, I knew we were meant to be together. It took me a couple tries, but I finally came around. You have been so patient with me. Even when I didn't deserve a second chance you still gave it to me, and when I didn't have enough trust and belief in us, you did for the both of us. When I felt weak in this relationship, you held me up with your strength. You are an amazing mother to Bella and you're going to be just as amazing to this new baby. I want to spend the rest of our life reminding you why you will never regret giving me that second chance. Will you marry me?"

"Yes!" is all I can say before he's back on his feet, putting the beautiful ring on my finger. I don't know much about rings, but it has one big princess cut diamond in the center with smaller clusters of diamonds around the edges, and it fits me perfectly.

Cooper cups my chin and kisses me softly. "Thank you, baby girl."

Everyone watching takes that as their cue to come over and congratulate us. "Oh, sweetheart. I am so happy for you. A new home, an engagement, and a baby on the way! This is quite the Christmas for you. Congratulations," my mom says as she hugs me.

Everybody takes turns hugging us and when Kayla gets over to me we hug extra hard. "Please tell me you've changed your mind," I say quietly, so only she can hear.

She pulls away, but stays looking into my eyes. I already know the answer before she gives it. "No, Liz. I'm still leaving tomorrow, but I'll visit often, and I'll definitely be back before the baby's here. I just need to go. Please understand that."

"Okay, but please know I'm only a phone call and a plane ride away. Does Cooper know you're quitting?"

"Yes, I told him yesterday. He said he doesn't need two weeks' notice, so I'm flying out tomorrow night."

We hug again and then I watch Kayla slip out the door. I look over at Bentley and see him watching her leave as well. He's showing no emotions, but I know he cares. And if I'm honest, I hate him a little bit right now because I believe whatever is going on with them is the reason she's leaving me.

Cooper announces there is one more present and asks for everybody to join us in the backyard. When we walk out the backdoors, Bella goes running straight to the swing set. I don't even think you can call it that, though. The word swing set doesn't even begin to do this thing justice. It's an enormous pink and purple princess castle with a rock wall, swings, a slide, and of course attached to the end is the cutest little picnic table and benches.

"Look Mommy, Daddy. Santa brought me my swing set just like I asked! He must have known this was going to be our new house."

Cooper holds me in his arms and nuzzles his face into my hair. We just stand like this for a while, just letting it all soak in. It may have taken a little longer to get here, but I wouldn't trade our journey for anything, because every step we took led us to this moment right here, right now, with our friends and family. And these people mean everything to me.

<h1 style="text-align:center">Epilogue</h1>

<h2 style="text-align:center">COOPER</h2>

Two Months Later

I'M STANDING IN THE CENTER OF THE OCTAGON AT THE MGM Grand Garden Arena in my hometown city of Las Vegas. My eye is swollen so it's hard to see, and I'm pretty sure I have at least two fractured ribs, but it's all worth it because at this very moment the referee has my hand in the air, announcing me the new UFC Champion. They hand me my belt and it feels damn good to know I've finally made it to where I wanted to be.

The crowd is going crazy, chanting my name. I've worked my entire life for this moment, but more importantly, it signifies the end of one chapter and the beginning of a new one.

"Tell us, Rage, now that you're the new UFC Middleweight Champion, what's next?"

I knew this question was coming. There have been rumors flying and tons of speculation as to what I'm going to do next. People want to know if I'm going to fight to defend the title, or if I'm going to retire as the champion. The UFC has offered me a healthy contract to stay on board and nobody knows what my decision is except my fiancée.

Looking out at the crowd, I see my entire world sitting in the first row closest to the octagon. Liz wasn't thrilled about letting Bella come to the fight, but our daughter is less like a princess and more like a warrior than Liz cares to admit. She loves watching these fights, and I would bet money that one day she becomes the UFC Champion in the Women's Bantamweight Division. Liz is looking at me through shiny eyes, clapping, and Bella is screaming at the top of her lungs for me.

I crook my fingers for them to come up and join me. When they get up to me, Liz gives me a soft kiss on my lips, afraid to hurt me as Bella grabs the microphone.

"My daddy is retiring," she says clearly, so everybody can hear. The crowd boos and she gets mad. "That's not nice. My mommy is having a baby and my daddy is going to work at the gym and train me to be a UFC Champion just like him." And…the crowd goes nuts.

I throw my head back in laughter at my crazy daughter and then take the microphone from her. "My little girl is correct. I'm honored to be the new UFC Champion. I want to thank everybody who has supported me over the last fifteen years…" I go on to name my friends and family, my trainer, the gym, the UFC, and when I'm finally done, I walk hand in hand with my fiancée and daughter out of the octagon for the last time.

Today isn't just a great day because of my win—today is also my daughter's fifth birthday. Earlier in the week we had a huge party for her. She wanted a doghouse built for her puppy and we all know whatever Bella wants, Bella gets. Sitting in the backyard in matching colors to her princess play set is a doghouse fit for a puppy princess.

It's also Valentine's Day, so this morning when the girls woke up I made sure to have lots of chocolates and stuffed toys for them, along with breakfast in bed. I bought Liz a charm bracelet that has the same boxing gloves as the one on her necklace. It also contains a heart charm with Bella's birthstone. She cried her eyes out when I put in on, not that it surprised me. The woman cries over everything these days. She's sixteen weeks pregnant and is due July eighteenth. I've been going to her doctor appointments with her and even got to hear the heartbeat and see the baby in an ultrasound. A-maz-ing. One thing I've noticed is the farther along she gets, the hornier she gets. I might just have to keep her knocked up the next few years.

"Everybody ready to party?" Bentley yells as we get off the plane in Palm Beach. Everybody gives a, "Hell yeah." We decided there was no better way to celebrate Caleb and my win than to go to the place where Bella and I first met: Miami.

We drop Bella off with her parents and head south. Liz is a bit upset because Kayla is in Florida, but is refusing to join us. I'm definitely not getting into the middle of all that drama. I'm about to spend the weekend with my woman at the resort we spent together five-and-a-half years ago. Life can't get much better than this.

LIZ

WE GET TO THE RESORT, CHECK IN, AND HEAD RIGHT TO OUR room. Everybody wanted to go out, but Cooper wasn't having it, so he told them all they can go without us.

We walk into the room that looks identical to the one from five years ago and Cooper leads me straight to the bed. He takes my shirt off and reaches behind me to take my bra off, so I'm lying in the center of the bed with only shorts on. Of course, those don't stay on for long. He removes my shorts and panties and, leaning over me, runs his eyes down my body.

"Like what you see?" I tease.

He takes his hands and rubs them over my belly. It's not big yet, but there's definitely a visible bump that you can see. If you didn't know me, you might think I was just bloated, but those who know I'm pregnant can tell it's from the baby growing in me.

"Yes, I do like what I see, very, very much."

"And what do you see, Mr. Cooper?"

He continues to rub his hands over my belly then bends down to give it a kiss. "I see the most beautiful woman carrying and protecting our baby."

He lifts his hands up from my belly and moves them to my breasts, gently palming them. "I see beautiful, voluptuous tits. They're preparing to one day nurse our baby." I squirm at his touch. Pregnancy has definitely made my body more sensitive.

He moves up to my face, putting his arms on either side of my head and kisses my eyelids. "I see the most amazing brown eyes that look at our daughter and me with such love."

He kisses my lips softly. "I see the most kissable lips. These lips are mine." And with that, he presses his lips back to mine, pushing his tongue through and sucking on my tongue. Our lips move together like they're puzzle pieces that fit together just right.

Too quickly, he pulls away and moves back down my body. "Mmm…and this sweet pussy. I'm definitely looking at this." I can feel my cheeks blush. I don't know how, after all this time, this man can still make me blush but he does.

He licks up my center from bottom to top. "I want to taste you, baby girl. I want to make you come on my face." And who in their right mind would argue with that? *Not me.*

Cooper continues to lick and suck, devouring my pussy until I'm at the brink of an orgasm. My legs tighten and my muscles clamp down on him, and I moan loudly as my climax barrels down on me.

He pulls his body back up mine, and places his arms on either side of my head with his fingers threading through my hair. His hard length is pushing into me as he slowly enters me. Looking into my eyes with so much love that I want to pocket it all and store it away, he says, "I'm looking at my entire world. Thank you for giving me a second chance. I love you so much."

"I love you, too." And for the rest of the night, Cooper makes love to me, showing me why giving him a second chance was the best decision I ever made.

FIGHTING *with* FAITH

Prologue

KAYLA

Nine Years Ago

"I THINK I SHOULD BE ALLOWED TO DATE. I'M FOURTEEN YEARS old and will be fifteen in May, which is only three months away. I'm a freshman in high school and plenty of girls are dating. I get good grades and I wouldn't let dating affect my schoolwork in any way. May I please go to the movies?"

Both of my parents are sitting on the couch—backs straight, chins up in the air, in the same stuck up way they always sit, like they're better than everyone else. Nancy and David Peterson are big time divorce attorneys in South Florida and treat everything and everyone like it's a business deal, including parenting. I learned a long time ago that when I want something it's best to approach it like one would in business. I called their secretary and scheduled a time to meet, and after them only rescheduling three times—which I don't think is good business practice—here we are in our living room where I'm attempting to state my case as to why I should be allowed to date.

If I had to bet, I would say my parents never even dated. They probably sat down and negotiated their entire relationship. I've never even seen them hug or kiss my entire life.

"Who is this boy you would like to go on a date with?" my mom asks, keeping a straight face.

"His name is Jake. His dad works at the accounting firm you guys do your taxes at."

"Is Jake your boyfriend?" my mom questions me further, and I can already see the trial beginning. We might be in our living room, but my mom is no stranger to bringing her work home. She lives and breathes law. There's a reason why my brother, Zach, and I practically live at Liz's house. We can't get away with anything here unless we're extremely careful.

I think about this for a second, trying to figure out which answer will allow me to win the argument. I'd imagine a parent would want their daughter to be in a relationship if she's going to go on a date, and while Jake isn't technically my boyfriend, I'm hoping that will change after we get to go out.

"Yes, he's my boyfriend." I dart my eyes back and forth between my parents, gaging their reaction.

They quickly glance at each other but give nothing away. This is why they're such good attorneys. They can keep a straight face better than the poker players my dad occasionally watches on television. Zach and I could get in the worst trouble ever at school and my parents would approach the situation calmer than anybody I've ever seen. They stick to the facts and never let their emotions show—I'm not even sure if they have any.

"Do you love him?" My mom's question throws me off, and before I answer, I need to get myself together. Does she even know what love is? I didn't think those words were even part of her vocabulary. She sure as hell has never said those words to anybody in this home that I know of.

"Not yet, but I think I could over time," I say honestly, hoping this will work in my favor, showing my parents I'm taking this whole thing seriously. She may not say the words, but I can't imagine her daughter loving someone would hurt the situation. It's not like I'm trying to go on random dates. I'm interested in one person specifically. That must get me some points.

"Sweetie, I think it's time we have a talk." My mom smiles, but it almost looks like she's in pain, as if having to spread her lips up to form the smile is actually painful for her. She looks at my dad and he nods, then excuses himself. Oh, great, she's about to give me the birds and the bees talk. Fabulous! Do my parents even have sex? I mean I know they must've done something because they had my brother and me, but still…Unlike the noises we hear at my best friend Liz's house coming through the walls of her parents' room at night when I sleep over, I've never heard noises coming through the walls of my parents' room—thank God!

"Kayla, I know at fourteen you want to believe in love, but the truth is love doesn't exist. Love was created by Hallmark to get people to spend money on each other for all sorts of holidays like Valentine's Day and Anniversaries. If you go back hundreds, if not thousands, of years ago, marriages were arranged. The original contracts were made to preserve power, forge alliances, acquire land, and to produce legitimate heirs. The churches eventually got involved ,which again helped to preserve the power in the churches."

What the hell! This is definitely not the type of talk I was expecting…

"The truth of the matter is, up until the nineteenth century, marriage and love didn't even go hand in hand. Don't get me wrong, I'm not against love, because without the loss of it, your father and I wouldn't make a living, and you and your brother wouldn't be living as comfortably as you are. But as your mother, I'm going to tell you what all my clients should've been told before they made the decision to get married for all the wrong reasons. You do not fall in love. It's a fake emotion that people are lead to believe is real. It's okay to have fun: Date, go to the movies, and enjoy being a teenager. Get good grades and go to college to make something of yourself. Of course, I would love for you to go to law school, but to be honest, I'm not sure you'd be up for the challenge. My point is, make sure you pick a career where you can bring something to the table in a marriage one day. Make sure you're completely independent, and more importantly, make sure the man you pick is financially stable."

Oh. My. God!

She continues her speech…

"What I'm trying to say is that when the time comes for you to be in a relationship, you don't do it based on love. Love isn't concrete. You do it based on mutual respect and on what you both can bring to the table. Every day in court I hear the same excuse, 'I fell out of love', but what people don't understand is that love is in your head. Money, education, goals, values, religion, political affiliates are all concrete reasons to base a relationship on. Love, on the other hand, is abstract. It changes constantly. Do you understand what I'm saying?"

I open my mouth and then close it. I don't even know how to respond to this. I decide to go with the first question that pops into my head. "Do you and Dad love each other?"

"I care about your father and he cares about me. We have mutual respect for each other. We met in law school and knew we would be compatible. We both had the same goals, came from the same upbringing, and vote for the same political party. We work well together. That's why, after over twenty years, we're still married. At fourteen years old, you can't possibly know where this boy is going in life. Anything you know about him is simply based on abstract thoughts and feelings that can and will change over time, and I can assure you, Kayla, those feelings will be your downfall."

I always suspected my mom felt this way, but it didn't feel real until she verbally confirmed it. Now I can no longer pretend because she put it all out there. My mother doesn't believe in love.

"I just don't understand. I know you see people divorce a lot, but what about all the people who are still married? The couples who kiss and hug and love each other. Why wouldn't you at least try to feel that way?"

I probably shouldn't push it, but I just don't understand why she'd keep herself from love. I see it on the television and I see Liz's parents, and it seems like something everybody would want in their life.

"Kayla, building a relationship based on emotions doesn't create a solid foundation. Like I said, emotions change. Would you build a home on the ocean? No, because the waves change. They get bigger and smaller. The tide can be high or low. You never know what you're getting. It's what you enjoy about surfing. You build a home on a concrete slab on the ground because you know it will be stable.

"You're too young to understand, but seventy percent of marriages end in divorce. It's why people have to hire your father and me, and why they end up having to split up the house and kids and assets. They base their foundation on an emotion that changes instead of thinking logically about the issues that matter like if he's able to balance his checkbook. Does he plan to have a 401K? What type of investments will he consider? What kind of family does he come from? None of those things have anything to do with love."

I want to tell her that none of that makes sense, but I know she'll just argue with facts like she always does. It's pointless to argue with either of my parents. I know how I feel about Jake. He's sweet and popular, and to be honest, I don't care who he's going to vote for in the next election or whether he can balance a checkbook. I think my mom is wrong, and I'll prove her wrong. When she sees that love is real, she'll understand not everybody is like her clients or herself for that matter.

So instead of arguing, I nod. "I understand. So, can I go out on a date with Jake?"

She releases a heavy sigh. "Yes, Kayla. Just please remember this conversation. I don't ever want to have to say, 'I told you so.' I would rather you be smart and not make stupid, reckless decisions in the first place so that I won't have to clean up whatever mess you make, just like I have to do with my clients."

Three Months Later

"I'M GOING TO DO IT."

"Are you sure?"

"Yes, I'm totally sure. I love Jake, and I know he loves me too."

I've been dating Jake for three months now and things are going good. Clearly my mother had no idea what she was talking about because I'm falling in love with him and I don't see it changing any time soon.

"Okay, Kayla. If that's what you want to do, I'll support you. Not that there's much I can really do to support you in this."

I'm sitting on the beach with my best friend, Liz. I just finished surfing while she sat on the edge of the water on her blanket, reading her latest romance novel. We both recently turned fifteen and are about to be sophomores. Liz is the ultimate best friend. We met in Kindergarten and have been inseparable ever since. Most people who don't know us question our friendship because we're the definition of opposites attracting. While Liz is the shy, quiet, book-obsessed type, I, on the other hand, am more outgoing. I love life. I love to have fun, and if it wasn't for my book-loving best friend, I probably wouldn't even pass my classes. This year I was made cheer captain and I got Liz to join. I know it really isn't her thing, but I love that we get to see each other after school and at games. What I love most about Liz is that she accepts me for who I am and allows me to make my own choices without ever judging. Which is exactly what she's doing right now.

"Just make sure you're safe, okay?" she says softly, clearly embarrassed to even be talking about this subject.

"I will. I promise."

"And make sure you use protection." Her cheeks turn pink.

"I know." I try not to laugh.

"You don't want to get an STD."

"I know."

"And you're sure you're ready? I heard it really hurts."

"I'll be okay. I'm sure Jake knows what he's doing."

The summer is about to begin, and my boyfriend of three months, Jake, is about to go away for the summer. He's been begging me to have sex with him, and I'm going to do it. I love him and I believe he loves me. No, we haven't said the words to each other, but tonight I'm going to tell him. We'll have something to remember each other by and when he comes back from vacation we'll pick back up where we left off.

"This is going to be great. I'll call you as soon as he leaves. My parents are working late tonight on a case and my brother is spending the night at your house with your brother."

We get up and head back to our neighborhood, which is right across from the beach. Liz's house is before mine, so when we approach her house, we hug goodbye and then I walk a little farther down the street to my house. I throw my surfboard onto the sidewalk and use the outside shower to rinse the sand and salt off my body before I go inside. Today was a great surfing day.

Once inside, I call Jake to let him know he can come over in an hour. I jump in the shower, shave my legs, and throw on a cute navy blue halter-top and white shorts. I blow dry my naturally blonde hair quickly. It's naturally straight so I don't have to do anything else with it.

At exactly five o'clock, Jake knocks on the door and I let him in. I'm not going to lie. I'm nervous about tonight. While we've made out like a million times and he's felt me up plenty of times, we haven't gone any further. I'm a virgin, and I'm okay with this, because unlike my parent's beliefs, I believe in love. And Jake is the one.

"Hey, babe. You look hot." Jake reaches for my waist and pulls me into a kiss. Once the kiss is over, we walk over to the couch and sit.

"So, I've been thinking and I'm ready." He looks confused at first about what I'm referring to, but then his eyes go wide when he realizes what I mean. He doesn't say anything. He just nods and takes me by my hand, leading me up to my bedroom, clearly not wanting to waste any time. Unlike me, Jake isn't a virgin. We haven't really talked about it, but I know he's been with a couple girls at school. I do know I'm the longest relationship he's had, which should say something about us.

After he closes the door behind us, he pulls out a condom from his wallet and places it on the bed, giving me a huge smile. He takes his shirt off and then his pants and boxers, while I just stand where I am, staring at him. I'm suddenly completely freaking out on the inside, but I mimic his moves and remove my clothes as well. He takes me by the hand and moves us to the bed.

"DAMN, BABE. THAT WAS GOOD." I'M LYING ON THE BED, NAKED and in pain, next to Jake. I'm not sure why people are so big on sex because *Ouch!* That shit hurt. Jake clearly enjoyed it based off his noises and grunts and calling out my name at the end, but as for me, no, that was not enjoyable. It felt like it lasted hours, but in reality, it couldn't have been more than a couple minutes. In my head, I imagined kissing and holding and words of love being whispered, but none of that happened.

I roll over to face Jake, pulling the covers up my body. He smiles at me like he just won the jackpot. It might've not been the best sexual experience, but the look on his face is worth it. It must be love. I'm sure over time it will get better.

"Kayla…"

"Jake…"

We both say each other's names at the same time and laugh.

He tells me to go first, so I do.

"I love you, Jake."

"Kayla." He says my name, and I'm waiting for *I love you, too* to follow but it doesn't, so I wait for him to say something. He stares at me for a few seconds and then his lips curve down into a frown.

"Kayla, babe. It's been fun these last few months, but it's about to be summer. I'm about to go away and you'll be here."

"I know, but you'll be back." I get this tightening feeling in my stomach, and it feels like I'm going to throw up.

"Look, Kayla, I like you, but we're young. I'm sorry, but I don't love you. To be honest, I don't even want to date anybody this summer. I just want to be single and have fun. You get that, right?"

I can feel the tears welling up, threatening to spill over. If I didn't know it's scientifically impossible for the human heart to physically break from somebody's words, I'd be scared my heart is literally shattering into pieces.

Jake gets up from the bed and puts back on his clothes. He goes to the bathroom to throw the condom away and then comes back into the room. I'm still lying in bed, frozen, unsure of what to do. I just gave this guy my virginity, but more than that, I gave him my heart. I told him I love him and was so sure he felt the same way, when all along he never felt any love toward me at all. Suddenly, my mom's words come back to slap me right in the face.

He gives me a chaste kiss on my cheek and, before walking away, says, "No hard feelings, Kayla. Seriously, it's been fun." And before I can even respond, he's out the door. I don't see him out. I don't lock up the house. I curl up in the fetal position and cry myself to sleep.

I hear my phone going off, and when I look at the clock, I see it's morning. My body is sore from last night and it reminds me of Jake using me for sex before dumping me. When I glance at the caller ID, I see it's Liz.

"Hello."

"Are you okay?"

"Yeah, why wouldn't I be?" I'm not ready to share how bad Jake hurt me, even with my best friend. I know I will eventually, but right now I'm too embarrassed.

"Have you been on Myspace? Jake is telling everybody he had sex with you and dumped you."

"What?" I get out of bed and then remember I fell asleep after crying and never got dressed. I quickly throw on some clothes and then run over to my computer and log into my account. I click on Jake's name and scroll down his wall, where all the comments are, and sure enough, he's bragging to his friends that he got in my pants and won a bet.

She finally gave it up.
About time! Took longer than I thought it would.
Was she any good?
Damn, I knew you would get it in before the summer.

"I'll call you back!" I say before I hang up.

I continue to scroll down the comments and read every nasty thing he wrote about me for everybody on social media to see. I think about everything I thought I felt and everything I thought he felt. It was all a lie. My heart hurts so damn bad. I don't ever want to feel this way again. If this is love, then I don't want it. My parents might not hug and kiss all the time, and they're not exactly what one would call nurturing, but I've never seen them cry or get upset. I've never seen them in pain or hurt each other the way I'm hurting right now.

While I'm looking over the comments, there's a quick knock on the door and then my mom walks in.

"Kayla, your dad and I are going to head out…"

I look up at her, and she stops speaking.

"Kayla, what's the matter?" She comes to my side and kneels next to me, so we're at eye level. I don't want to tell her what happened, but I need my mom right now, so I decide to tell her a shortened version of what happened.

"Jake and I broke up and he's talking crap about me to his friends. Everybody is going to be talking about me at school."

My mom's face turns into what looks like a sympathetic frown and I think maybe she'll comfort me and give me some mom wisdom, but instead she says what I knew all along she would say.

"Kayla, I told you this would happen. I hope you take this as a lesson learned. When you open your heart, you're going to get heartbroken. Instead, open your mind and be smart about your decisions. At least it happened now instead of years from now when you would've had the opportunity to make even worse decisions."

She looks at my computer screen before I can hide it and she stands straight up, glaring down at me.

"Did you sleep with him, Kayla?"

"Yes, and he's telling the whole school."

Of course my mom doesn't even attempt to sympathize with me in any way.

"That's great. So, not only did you not listen to me, but you also allowed your ridiculous emotions to tarnish your reputation, as well as your father's and mine. You know we do business with Jake's father. Hopefully in the future you'll think about what happened when you make decisions based on emotions. I swear, Kayla, sometimes you can be so obtuse. It's why you'll never go to law school. You have to think with your brain and not your fickle emotions."

"I'm sorry. I thought he loved me," I say as tears prick my eyes. I have no idea why I'm even trying to defend myself. I hate that I've let my mom down and disappointed her once again. I hate that I'm an embarrassment to our family. But what's even worse is that I hate she was right about love. I wanted so badly to prove her wrong.

"Well now you know the truth. There's no point in crying over this. Learn from it." As she turns to walk out of my room, she says, "Your father and I are heading out to get lunch. Would you like anything?"

I shake my head and then she closes the door behind her.

And in this moment, I make a promise to myself to never disappoint my parents again. I'll never give my mom another reason to say, "I told you so." The fact is, my mother was right. Love only causes heartbreak and it hurts like a bitch. It's not concrete. You can't use it as a stepping stone. I did and look where it got me, tumbling down the stairs headfirst with no one at the bottom to catch me. Fuck that! And fuck love.

I vow to never fall in love again.

One

KAYLA

Present Day

LIVING IN FLORIDA HAS ITS PERKS. FOR ONE, THE SUNSHINE IS amazing. It's February, and in many other states the snow is still coming down, while here in sunny South Florida it's a beautiful eighty-five degrees. I'm lying on the lounge chair in my bikini, soaking in the sun by the pool. I can smell the ocean breeze in the air, and it's such a tease. I'm only a few yards away from the beach and that beautiful ocean water, yet I can't even do what I love, which is surf. I mean I guess I could, but I'm not sure how well that will go over. Surfing requires balance, and now that my belly is beginning to swell, my balance is definitely not what it was before. I look down at my stomach and smile to myself. At only sixteen weeks pregnant, if you didn't know my condition you'd think I had a few too many beers and fries, but that's not the case. I rub my belly and take a sip of my orange juice that's sitting on the deck table next to me.

I'm excited to become a mom. When my best friend, Liz, got pregnant right before our freshman year of college, she couldn't find the father, and so we worked as a team to raise her daughter, Bella. Because of that, I'm not ignorant to the fact that having a baby isn't going to be easy, especially since I'll most likely be raising the baby on my own most of the time. However, unlike the situation Liz was in all those years ago, I've since graduated from college and have a degree in physical therapy.

"Kayla, I'm leaving for work. Have you thought more about what you plan to do?"

I look over and see my mom standing just outside the back door.

"I haven't made any decisions yet."

"Well, I hope you've thought about what we've talked about. You can live here as long as you need to, but do you really want to once again raise a baby without a father? There's nothing wrong with giving the baby up for adoption. Successful men don't want to be with a woman who has an illegitimate kid in tow."

"Mom, I want this baby, and I'm not looking for a man anyway, so it doesn't matter. Plus, Bella does have a father, and Liz and I did just fine before he came back into the picture."

"You're never going to learn, Kayla" She sighs. "How many times will you make horrible decisions which require your father and me to help clean up the mess while embarrassing this family?"

"What are you cleaning up? I'm staying here temporarily. You don't have to do anything."

"Not yet! Wait until you have to deal with custody and child support. A child is forever, Kayla. Once again you made poor choices out of lust and supposed love, and look where it got you! When will it stop? How many times must we have this conversation? I swear sometimes I don't even think you are my kid."

Without waiting for a response, she huffs and walks back inside, closing the sliding glass door behind her, clearly ending the conversation.

I've only been living back in Florida for about six weeks, but I know I need to focus on getting a job. I'm fortunate that as a physical therapist there's quite a few options and I have some amazing references, but I'm not sure what I want to do yet. I liked my old job, but moving was something I had to do. If I'm honest with myself, I haven't put forth the effort into finding a job because somewhere in the back of my mind I know this isn't really where I want to live. It's simply the only option I could think of at the time.

I'm what you would call a runner. Life is good, too good to be true…I run. Life turns to shit, I feel like I can't handle it…I run. Life gets confusing, I have to make a decision…I run. I'm way better at handling other people's lives than my own. For the last five years, I've focused on Liz and Bella. We both went to school and both took turns caring for her daughter. I used the two of them as an excuse to never date. Don't get me wrong, I've had my fair share of one-night stands, but I never allowed it to turn into more. I'm not interested in love and it's not interested in me either.

I'm currently living in my parents' pool house and it's okay. I could have gone back to my old room but decided the pool house would give me space from my parents, especially my mom. If I hear her say *I told you* so one more time I just might kill her. Yes, she was right about Jake all those years ago. Yes, she was right about my current situation. I get it. Everything I do is wrong. I'm a continuing disappointment in my mother's eyes. Luckily, my parents work a lot and are rarely home, but I still need to get my own place soon. Time is running out and unfortunately, I have nowhere else to run to, so I'm going to have to make a decision. I look out at the crystal-clear pool water and think to myself *tomorrow*. Tomorrow I'll attempt to get a job. Tomorrow I'll figure out my living situation. Tomorrow I'll deal with the reality that I'm pregnant and haven't told anybody other than my parents. Today, I'll swim a few laps in the pool. It may not be the ocean or surfing, but at least it's in the water.

After spending the next thirty minutes swimming laps, I realize it's lunchtime and decide to go inside the main house and make myself a sandwich. I grab my towel and dry myself off, throw it back on the lounge chair, and then walk inside. I'm thinking a peanut butter and jelly sandwich is sounding really yummy right about now. Ooh! Maybe a peanut butter and jelly with banana…Pregnancy cravings are the weirdest. I watched Liz go through it, but experiencing it firsthand is something else.

I pull all the ingredients out of the cabinets, when I hear the doorbell ring. It's only noon here, and with my parents at work and my brother at school, I can't imagine who'd be at the door. As I walk over to answer it, I don't bother covering myself up. I left my towel outside and whoever is at the door will just have to deal with seeing me in my bikini. Without checking the peephole, I swing the door open and come face-to-face with none other than my best friend, Liz. I don't know why I didn't think about this. She told me she was going to be in Miami and begged me to join. I should've known she would make a stop to see me. Damn pregnancy brain!

"Holy shit, Kayla! Are you pregnant?" She looks down, and I attempt to cover my protruding belly, but it's too late. My bikini is as tiny as it gets. Only then do I realize she isn't alone. The whole damn gang is with her, standing in my parents' doorway and staring right at my stomach. Liz's fiancé, Cooper, who owns the gym I used to work at, their daughter, Bella, our friend Hayley, who is the medic at Cooper's Fight Club, Kaden, the guys' trainer and friend, and Caleb, who fights for the UFC and is my ex-roommate. But more importantly, who is also standing on my doorstep is Bentley, and on his arm is the bitch he's dating, Sophia.

For a beat, nobody says anything, and then I remember she asked me a question. Apparently, they're all waiting for my answer. Although, I'm pretty sure it's meant as a rhetorical question because anybody who knows me knows my stomach pre-pregnancy was as flat as a board. Not that I do so much to work out other than surfing, but I'm naturally a tiny woman with amazing genetics and a fast metabolism, standard-sized breasts, small stomach with toned legs and arms from my years of surfing. The only feature of me that contradicts my many years of surfing is my naturally pale skin that never tans. I look at Liz and notice her golden brown tan I've always been envious of. The girl doesn't even like the beach and has beautiful caramel skin. Oh! Did I mention Liz is pregnant too? She looks so adorable with her little belly, and she's so happy…

The sound of a deep throat clearing causes me to snap out of my internal thoughts, and when I see the look on his face, my skin goose bumps, and not in a good way—more like in a *Oh damn, shit is about to get real* way.

Bentley steps forward, clearly done with waiting for my verbal confirmation that I am indeed pregnant, and asks the question he wants to know. "Am I the father?"

Don't worry, it's not about to get Jerry Springer up in here—hopefully.

Two

KAYLA

Six Years Ago

ONE WEEK IN MIAMI. NEED I SAY MORE? LIZ AND I GET ONE week in the hottest, sexiest city in the world to party it up before we're thrown back into jail, and by jail, I mean school. We have finally graduated high school and do we get a break? Of course not. After our week in Miami, we'll be moving to Las Vegas, Nevada to attend college at the University of Las Vegas. I know what you're thinking. How can I complain when I'll be spending the next four years in Sin City? I get it, I do. But how can I fully experience what Las Vegas has to offer when in two short months I'll be stuck sitting in college classes, writing essays, and studying for test after test?

On the bright side, I have two months before school begins. Unlike my bookworm best friend who is insisting on taking summer classes, I won't be starting until the fall, which means parties, guys, and more parties with guys. I'm not sure how many I'll convince her to go to with me, but the fact that we're sitting in a resort in Miami, she's wearing the cute little black dress I bought her without her knowledge, and has agreed to go to a club with me tonight, gives me hope that once we're in Las Vegas she'll continue to submit to my best friend charm.

We get to the club and walk to the back of the line. Liz is completely self-conscious about her dress, even though she looks beyond beautiful. She has the most amazing body that goes to waste because she dedicates her entire life to school. She's thick and curvy in all the right places and her little black dress accentuates all those curves. Her gorgeous curly brown hair is flowing down her back and she doesn't even need to have an ounce of makeup on her face because her skin is naturally flawless.

On the other hand, I'm in a super cute silver dress that helps push up my breasts, giving me a little more cleavage. I'm not a member of the itty-bitty-titty-committee, but they definitely aren't naturally voluptuous like Liz's breasts are. I have on light makeup, just some smoky eye shadow and lipstick. I'm in matching silver fuck-me heels, and I'm ready to show my fake ID to the bouncer and do some serious partying.

Just as Liz is getting restless and I'm afraid I might have to tie her up and drag her inside, the oversized bouncer comes over and tells us a VIP guest has invited us in. VIP? You sure as hell don't have to tell me twice! We show our IDs and head into the club.

The music is pumping, the lights are pulsating throughout the club, and I'm in heaven right now. I've been to more than my fair share of high school parties, but this is nothing like those. I look over at Liz and she's just as mesmerized by the scene in front of us as I am. This is our first time in a club, and if I can make a prediction, it won't be our last.

We head to the dance floor immediately and begin dancing our asses off, grinding on each other, on other people. The music has me in a trance, and when I look over to check on Liz, I see some hot guy all over her After a couple songs I notice he's leading her away. We lock eyes and she confirms all is good. That's all I need to know. Liz is probably the smartest damn person I know. I continue to watch her and see she's heading up to VIP. That definitely makes me feel better knowing she's just going to be a few feet away from me. I decide I'll dance some more with these hot guys down here and join her in a few.

After quite a few songs, my body is covered in a light sheen of sweat, so I head upstairs to find Liz and rehydrate. The bodyguard stops me, and I explain I'm with people who're in the VIP area. In order to be up here, I have to confirm who I'm with, so, with him trailing behind, I go in search of Liz. After walking past a few booths, I find Liz sitting on the same guy's lap from earlier.

But my eyes don't stop on them, because just past them is the sexiest guy I've ever laid eyes on. He has blond hair, shaved short but still long enough to grab ahold of in bed and navy blue eyes, like the color of the water when you paddle out to a deep area of the ocean. His intense eyes lock with mine for a second and it feels like the wind has been knocked out of me. I can't stop looking at him. His arms look strong and he's built but not too built. He's perfect. He must sense me ogling the shit out of him because he looks at me again, but this time he gives me a knowing smirk, then begins to trail his eyes down my body. *That's right, baby. Eat your heart out.* Liz's guy confirms I'm with them, and the bodyguard makes a grunting noise and then walks away.

I approach Liz and her new man friend, and he gives introductions. His name is Cooper, and his friends are Kaden, Caleb, and Bentley. The only name I'm concerned with is Bentley. He's my target, and judging by the way his eyes are intently stuck on me, I would say I got this shit in the bag. One thing I learned from Jake is, if I use the guy, I can't be used, and I'll be damned if I'm ever used again. I also learned

Jake sucks in bed (as well as the other high school guys I've been with) and I'm glad to be done with high school, so I can hopefully find a guy who actually knows what he's doing. After my one shitty time with Jake I hoped it was him and not me that was the problem, but the truth is most guys I've slept with have no idea what they're doing, so I'm beginning to wonder if maybe it's me.

I've learned a few things the last couple of years.

One: Guys are nothing like the characters in the movies and books. They're selfish as hell and are only out to pleasure themselves.

Two: Guys have no idea if a girl orgasms during sex. Trust me, I've faked it enough to know this.

Three: It's easier to give myself an orgasm than to rely on a guy to do it for me.

Don't get me wrong, I've had orgasms with the guys I've been with, but I've had to walk them through it and it hasn't been anything worth applauding over. The foreplay has been decent, at least good enough that if the guy can't handle finishing the job, I'm primed and ready to get myself off. But looking at Bentley, I wonder if maybe I've been with all the wrong guys—the man drips sex.

Once the introductions are done, Bentley comes over and asks me to dance. I follow behind him to the small dance floor in the VIP section. The music is pumping to the fast rhythm of The Black Eyed Peas *Boom Boom Pow.* I turn away from Bentley and back my ass up against him at the same time he brings his hands to my waist and rubs his dick against by ass in a pulsating motion to the music. This guy definitely has some moves. I once read a man that can dance is good in bed. Let's hope it's true.

The mix morphs into Mariah Carey's *Obsessed* and I twirl around to face Bentley, whose eyes are glossed over with lust. We dance so close it's as if we're fucking with our clothes on. His knee comes up the middle of my thighs to separate my legs, causing my dress to rise. He rubs back and forth against my pussy through my panties, creating a friction that has me salivating with want. It has never felt like this before and we haven't even done anything. I wrap my arms around his neck and he nuzzles his face into my hair while he slowly continues to grind that sensitive area between my legs.

The song ends and I need a breather. I'm so hot and if I don't back up I might end up making him take me in the bathroom and that would be an absolute travesty because a quickie against a sink would not do this man justice at all. I'm pretty sure I'm going to need hours with him before I'm ready to move on. And I'll move on, because I always do. You can think what you want about me, but the fact is while you are getting your heart broken time and again, my heart is perfectly intact, and it's going to damn well stay that way.

The rest of the night is spent with Liz and me doing shots of top shelf vodka and dancing on top of the table while Bentley and Cooper watch us from below. Eventually everybody is ready to go and I'm seriously praying Bentley is having the same thoughts as me. While I'm definitely feeling good, we have danced more than we have drank so I know I won't have a hangover in the morning.

My prayers are answered when Bentley comes over and whispers into my ear, "I want you in my bed tonight—naked, legs spread, and wet just for me." Chills run down my spine and he chuckles knowingly at what he's doing to me. He doesn't ask, he demands. I need to be careful with this guy. I always keep the ball in my court. The minute the guy is in control, he will use you and leave you high and dry. I've learned my lesson and won't ever let that happen again. I make sure to remain calm, cool, and collected at all times.

"I have to make sure it's okay with my friend first. You know how it is…sisters before misters." I give him a saucy wink and walk away from him to speak to Liz, swaying my hips just a little more knowing he's watching me walk away.

When I get over to her, she's cuddling up with Cooper and I'm genuinely happy for her. She never lets loose like this. "Hey sexy," I say to get her attention. She laughs at my flirting.

"Would it be okay if I went back to Bentley's hotel with him? I'll completely understand if you don't want me to. I don't want to leave you hanging."

She sighs and says, "No, it's okay. You can go…"

"But?" The thing about being best friends for more than half our lives is that we know what each other is thinking.

"No, buts…I just don't want you to do anything you might regret."

"Like what? Fall in love?" I snort out the last part.

"No, I know you won't fall in love, Kayla. It's just that it's one thing to sleep with the guys from high school, but this guy is older and way more experienced. I just want you to be safe." And that's why she's my best friend. No judgment at all. She just cares.

"I promise I'll be careful." She nods and we all head down to the awaiting SUV.

Bentley and I both get into the third row and I whisper to him that I'm down to go back with him. His face lights up with a bright smile that makes my stomach get butterflies. *What the hell? I don't do butterflies.* I need to get my shit in check, and fast. This is a one-night stand. I've done this several times. This is no different.

After dropping off Liz—and Cooper, because he ended up staying with her, which is a conversation we'll definitely be having tomorrow— we head to the hotel the guys are staying at. It's down the street from our resort but even nicer. We get to the top floor, which is the penthouse, and Kaden and Caleb go to their rooms leaving us alone.

"Would you like a drink?" Bentley points to the mini fridge full of bottles of liquor.

"No, thank you."

He closes the gap between us, and twisting his fingers into my hair, brings my face up to his. He leans in close, and in a soft voice says, "I've never done this before. What are you doing to me?"

Before I can even process what he means, his mouth connects with mine and my mind goes blank. His tongue hits my lips and they automatically part for him. At the same time, his other hand comes down around me to grab my ass, pulling my body into his. I let out a small groan and it spurs him on.

Never taking his mouth off mine, he moves his hand from my hair, and with both hands now on my ass, lifts me up, continuing to lay soft kisses to my collarbone. My thighs close around his waist and my ankles lock around his back. I feel a bit dizzy, but I'm nowhere near drunk, at least not from the alcohol—maybe off this man and his touch. I've never felt like this before, and I'm not quite sure if this is a good thing. As he walks us to his room, Kaden comes back out of his, and gives us a smile of approval. I lock eyes with Bentley and my heartbeat quickens. I need to stop these feelings. I don't do feelings.

I'm suddenly nervous. The lust brewing between Bentley and me is stifling and I don't know if my heart can handle spending the night with him. As a last ditch effort to protect myself, I turn my head to Kaden and ask, "Wanna join us?"

Bentley's whole body goes rigid and he growls out a "I don't fucking think so!"

Before Kaden can even respond, the door is slammed closed and all I can hear is loud laughter coming from the main room.

Bentley drops me onto the bed on my back and looks at me like I just committed a murder. I try to hide my smile by biting down on my lower lip, but I don't think I do a good enough job because he raises his eyebrows and says, "Woman, you think that shit is funny? You think I won't be enough that you need two men to please you? Fuck that! When I'm done with you, you won't even be able to walk straight for a week."

Without giving me a chance to answer his question, he lowers his body down to mine and kisses me with what seems like every ounce of built up passion in him. My tongue enters his mouth and he sucks on it, tasting me. His hand moves to my breast and he attempts to tweak my nipple through my clothes. When he sees how thick my dress and bra are, he puts our kiss on hold, gets up on his knees, and slides my dress over my shoulders and down my body. I lift to help him out and he slides the dress, as well as my panties, the rest of the way down.

My strapless bra opens from the front and with two fingers he expertly pops the clasp open. The two cups separate, falling on each side, leaving my breasts open for him. I'm completely naked under him. His eyes rake down my body slowly. He swallows hard and then his eyes lock with mine.

"You're fucking gorgeous." It isn't the words but the way he says them that sends chills down my spine. It suddenly feels extremely hot in here to the point I feel like I can't even breathe. Nobody has ever looked at me like he's doing in this moment. It is almost as if I'm everything to him. But that can't be possible because we just met.

"It seems like there's a bit of an imbalance," I say, trying to play it cool. I haven't felt this vulnerable in front of a guy since Jake, and we all know how that turned out.

He chuckles and then with one hand pulls his shirt over his head. And hot damn, he's a sight to see. While he looked sexy as hell dressed in his blue and yellow plaid collared shirt and jeans that hugged the curves of his ass just right, Bentley without a shirt on is a whole different ball game. His pecks look like they are carved from stone, and as I lower my eyes to his abs, I begin to count: two, four, six, eight. Eight goddamn pack of abs. I quickly do a recount to make sure I'm not seeing things, and I'm not. This man is definitely sporting an eight freaking pack of abs. I look over him again and notice his body is clean. Not a single tattoo on him. His skin is a beautiful golden brown and I get this overwhelming need to lick down his body starting from his neck all the way to that gorgeous V that meets the top of his white boxers which are partially hidden by his jeans.

"Take off the rest," I say and nod towards the rest of the clothes I want him to remove. He sits back and unbuttons his jeans and then maneuvers them and his boxers off him, throwing them to the side of the bed.

He gets back up to a kneeling position and his dick springs up with him. I can't take it any longer. I need to touch him. I sit up and grab hold of his cock, forcing him to move closer to me. He realizes what I'm about to do and tries to stop me.

"Wait, baby. Let me please you first."

He doesn't realize what his words do to me. They chisel away at the ice chunks covering my heart, scaring the shit out of me. Nobody has ever put me first, and this guy can't be the one to do it now. This is a fucking one-night stand.

With my legs straight out in front of me, I pull him toward me, not giving him a choice. He looks confused but moves over me like I want, setting one knee on either side of me. I grab his hard length and begin to stroke it. I lick my lips readying myself to take him, and then place my mouth right around his hardness taking him all the way down my throat.

"Oh, fuck. Kayla." He moans my name over and over again as I rotate between licking and sucking his hard length. Please don't judge what I'm about to admit. Well...actually...fuck it, judge all you want.

What the hell do I care? There is nothing better tasting than a cock. I love it in my mouth, on my tongue, down my throat. The taste of the precum alone gets me wet. I love the feel of figuratively holding a guy by his balls. I hold all the power and it feels damn good.

While I continue to fuck him with my mouth, he takes my nipples between his fingers and pulls and tugs and pinches them so hard it's almost painful, but damn, it feels so good. I moan around his cock and he must feel the vibration because the precum on my tongue multiplies, telling me he's getting close.

"You like that?" He continues to pinch and pull my nipples, causing my core to drip wet. I squeeze my thighs together, hoping to find some relief, but it's not doing anything. I have a feeling the only relief I'll find is from this man's cock inside me.

I'm torn, though. I want it in me, yet I really want him to come in my mouth. *Decisions. Decisions.*

Bentley looks into my eyes and says, "Fuck, Kayla, your mouth feels so good." And the decision has been made.

I work him harder and faster. The saliva that his dick and my mouth has created allows me to slide him in and out smoothly. I take one hand and cup his balls with enough force that it massages him but not too much that it would hurt him. This is his undoing. He twists my hair into his fingers and begins relentlessly fucking my mouth.

"Kayla, baby, I'm going to come in your mouth," Bentley warns. I don't stop, though. "Holy shit, I'm…" He finishes his sentence incoherently as he shakes and groans out his release. His seed shoots straight down my throat and I swallow it all. When it stops, so does Bentley. He attempts to back up and remove his dick from my mouth, but I grab ahold of his ass to keep him in me. I lock eyes with him while I gently suck him clean until I feel him going soft, and then I release him from my mouth.

He doesn't wait before he lies down on his stomach and sticks his tongue right between my legs. It happens so quickly, I startle. I can feel the vibration from him laughing at my reaction, but he doesn't say a word. His tongue never moves from my clit.

Out of habit I go to tell him what to do to get me off, but before I can say a word he takes a finger and puts it into me, hitting a spot I never knew existed—this must be the infamous G-spot I've heard of but never experienced firsthand—causing my body to almost convulse on the spot.

Remember when Liz warned me he's not like the high school guys? Well, she was right about that. This guy is not at all like the high school boys at home that I've wasted my time on. He actually knows what he's doing, and at this rate I won't have to lock myself in the bathroom to finish my orgasm off myself like I've had to do half the time with the other guys I've been with.

He continues to finger me while his tongue massages my clit. He adds another digit and within a few seconds an overload of sensations hits me all at once, and the next thing I know I'm going dizzy, experiencing the biggest orgasm I've ever felt to date. I swear I almost black out. Bentley doesn't let up until I come down, and with one last lick, he moves his lips to the top of my pussy and gives it a wet kiss.

He looks up at me and gives me the most adorable boyish grin, and in this moment, if I believed in love, I could see myself easily falling for him. It almost be too easy. But I don't believe in love, so it doesn't matter. This was just sex, technically oral sex but just sex, nonetheless. And that's how it will stay. Just sex.

He licks my wetness off his lips and says, "Woman, you taste unbelievable. I'm going to need another taste of that later. But for now, let's shower, and by the time we're done I should be ready to go another round."

He doesn't have to tell me twice. I jump up from the bed and follow his tight sexy ass to the shower.

He turns it on and once it's warm enough we both get in. I reach for the soap as he grabs my hand and brings it up to his lips to give it a soft kiss.

"You're beautiful, Kayla."

"You already got me in bed. No need for the compliments." I laugh it off, but his expression looks serious and it's making me nervous. I don't do feelings.

"You. Are. Beautiful." He takes my face in his hands and bends slightly to kiss me softly. The water is spraying on us, but because of his height, it's mostly just hitting his back.

I wrap my arms around his neck and he grabs me by my ass and pushes me against the wall of the shower. He continues to kiss me with such vigor I feels as though he's devouring my mouth with his. My body ignites from his touch, making me want more. I've never wanted more before. I try to reach down with one hand to find his dick, but he stops kissing me.

"Woman, you're going to be the death of me. I've never wanted someone like I want you. I don't ever do one-night stands. What are you doing to me?"

I don't answer him. I ignore what he's insinuating. This conversation has the prospect of getting deep and I'm not about to let that happen. Instead, I tap his hands to let me down. I grab the soap and begin to wash his body, starting from his neck and moving my way down. While I'm washing him, he grabs my nipples and pinches.

"Hey!" I shriek.

"Sorry, I thought I was losing my balance. I grabbed hold of the first thing I could to keep me upright."

I laugh at his comment, thankful he's letting the serious shit go.

Once I'm done washing him I take the soap to wash myself. He takes the bottle from my hands and then turns me around to face the wall. He massages my neck, and after a few minutes moves down to my arms. It feels so relaxing I let out a soft moan.

When he gets to my ass, he rubs circles on my ass cheeks and then steps closer, so he can wash between my legs. He brushes his fingers over my clit, causing me to tense up. With his dick poking my back, I know he's ready. I rub my ass against it to tease him and he groans into my ear, sending shivers down my spine.

Finding his dick with my hand, I stroke it while he keeps one hand on my clit and the other holds me tight against him.

"I want you right now," I whisper.

He tenses up. "I can't use a condom in here. Let's move this to the bed."

What the fuck was I thinking? Was I seriously about to let this guy fuck me in the shower without a condom on? Yeah, I'm on birth control, but still. He's making me crazy. I need to get my emotions in check. This is not like me at all.

We wash off our bodies, step out of the shower, and before I can even grab a towel, I'm over Bentley's shoulder being carried to the bed. He drops me on the soft mattress and I get a good look at his wet, sexy-as-fuck body. He sees me checking him out, but instead of calling me out, he climbs up my body and hovers over me.

He stares at me for a beat and then says, "I don't know if I'll ever get enough of you. I might just need to keep you a while longer."

"Uh-uh, handsome. Tonight is all we have," I say, pulling him to him.

His jaw clenches for a second. "We'll see about that."

Before I can say another word, his lips are on mine. I can feel his hard cock pressing against me and I lose the fight inside me to argue.

WHEN BENTLEY SAID, I WOULDN'T BE ABLE TO WALK STRAIGHT for a week, he wasn't kidding. I wake up to the sound of huffing and puffing causing me to sit straight up, wondering what the heck is going on. My body is stiff and sore like I worked out for hours. Well, technically I did. After the first time Bentley and I made lo—had *sex*, we both fell asleep, and then he woke me up in the early morning to go another round. The man is insatiable. I've never met anybody who can keep up with my sexual appetite, yet he's given me a run for my money.

This is the first time I've ever spent the night with a guy and I'm hoping he doesn't regret it. After what happened with Jake, I've made sure to never put myself in a vulnerable position again. I choose when and where to have sex and I always make sure I'm the first one to leave. I'll never be made a fool of again.

I scan the room to find none other than Mr. Insatiable himself doing pushups in front of the bed. He's dripping in sweat with his muscles bulging out from the workout.

"Morning, he huffs out through his pushup.

"Morning," I say, stretching my arms and legs. I can't believe how sore my body is, meanwhile it's like he wasn't even affected.

"Are you feeling okay?" he asks with a small laugh, jumping onto his feet like it's nothing. Damn him. He must have seen me wince when I stretched.

"I'm just fine. Thank you very much." I glare at him and it just causes him to laugh harder.

He bridges the gap between us and kisses me softly on my lips. This kiss is simple and sweet and it makes my heart thaw a little bit more. I lean in, wanting the kiss to continue, but he pulls away. I give him a small pout, making it clear what I want, but it only causes him to smile brightly.

"Woman, didn't you get enough last night and this morning? I don't want to break you. So, what are we doing today?" His question makes my heart soar and that scares the ever-loving shit out of me. I haven't even known Bentley for twenty-four hours and he's already tearing down every wall I've worked so hard to build up. The wall that keeps my heart safe. That keeps guys from getting in and hurting me. The same wall that needs to remain erect to keep me safe.

"Whoa there, buddy. Who said anything about us continuing this today?" I give him a smirk and wrap the sheet around me to use the bathroom. He might have seen all of me last night, but it's a bit different once everyone is sober and the sun has come up.

He follows me to the bathroom, but I close the door before he can make it in. I don't care how close we got last night, we're never going to be close enough that I'm comfortable going pee in front of him—or any man for that matter.

Through the door, I hear him say, "I heard you and your friend say you're here for the next week. My boys and I are only here until tomorrow, but I was thinking we could chill until then. My boy Coop is staying with your friend anyway." Hmm…speaking of my friend, I need to text her and make sure all is well. I definitely don't want to rain on her hopefully no longer virginal parade, so I decide it won't hurt to chill with Bentley until he leaves. It's not my usual M.O., but I can take one for the team—or in this case for Liz's vagina. I just need to make sure to keep him at a distance.

I flush the toilet, wash my hands, and open the door to see Bentley standing right in my face. I already know I'm going to hang out with him, but I decide to mess with him a little. I love getting him all riled up.

"Um, well, I'm going to first go and see what your friend Kaden is up to, and if he isn't available, I might consider chilling with you." I shoot him a playful wink as I walk past him to get dressed. It's then I remember I only have my dress from the club. I find his shirt still on the floor, so I throw it on with my underwear and head out the bedroom door.

Before I know it, I'm in the air over his shoulder. "Woman, don't test me," he says as he playfully smacks my ass. I yelp and tell him to put me down, but he ignores me as he carries me like a sack of potatoes out to the main room.

Kaden is in the kitchen making some coffee. When he sees me he starts laughing. Luckily Bentley's shirt is so big on me my ass isn't showing. He puts me down when we reach the coffee pot and Kaden offers me a cup of coffee. I take it with a smile and pour some cream and sugar into it. I imagined the morning after would be awkward, but with Bentley it's not awkward at all. It's like we just click.

"So, what are we doing today?" Kaden asks nobody in particular.

"Have you talked to Cooper?" Bentley asks as he takes a bottle of water from the fridge and downs it all in one long gulp.

"Yeah," he says, smiling at me. "He said he's staying with Liz until we have to go. I've never seen him like this before. You would almost think the guy wants something other than—"

Bentley quickly cuts him off before he can finish his sentence. "Yeah, well, let him enjoy it because in twenty-four hours he'll be on lock down."

Lock down?

"What kind of lock down are we talking here? Is my best friend his last screw before he gets married? Is he about to go to prison?"

Yeah, yeah, I know we should have thought about this before leaving with guys we don't know, but c'mon…we're young and dumb.

They both laugh and Bentley says, "No, is that how you view marriage? Being on lock down? He's going to be working for his dad when we're done here. His dad is a dick. He might as well be going to prison."

I nod, but don't ask any more questions. As long as Liz is safe then it's not my business, and the fact is in six days Liz and I will be on our way across the country to the kickass apartment my parents are paying for in exchange of me going to college like a good little girl. I have no idea what I plan to major in other than partying, but if my parents are going to foot the bill and it means four more years of no responsibilities, I'll take it.

"So, fellas, who here is going to go downstairs to the gift shop and get me some shorts and a shirt so we can go get some grub?"

Kaden puts his hands up in protest and laughs. "I'm not the one getting laid, so I sure as hell am not playing errand boy."

Bentley smacks him on his chest and says, "I'll go down and get you an outfit while you jump in the shower. I was thinking of going surfing today. If you want, I can grab you a suit and you can chill on a blanket under an umbrella and watch."

Chill on a blanket and watch? Oh, boy, does he have another thing coming to him. He's got this girl here all wrong. I'll let him think what he wants, though, and when I tear him apart in the water later it'll be that much more satisfying.

"Sure," I say in a sweet voice, knowing he's going to be shocked to learn there's more to me than a blond chick in a tight silver dress. "I'll jump in the shower and then we can go grab something to eat and then head to the beach, but would it be okay if I joined you in the water?"

He looks over at Kaden and furrows his eyebrows unsure of how to respond. Clearly, he's used to girls like Liz who would rather watch with a book in her hand then get in the water and have fun.

Kaden gives him a shrug and says, "We can get you a board so you can paddle around. If it gets to be too much you can always go back to the shore." It's taking everything in me not to laugh at these guys. It'll just be that much funnier when they realize I'm not that girl.

After we finish eating breakfast, we walk down to the beach and head to the hut that rents and sells surf gear. I send a quick text to Liz to make sure she's okay, and when she says she is, I let her know I'm going to chill with Kaden and Bentley until tomorrow. She texts back a happy face. *Yeah, I bet she's happy.*

Bentley picked me out a blue and white bikini, which is cute but totally not doable if I'm going to be surfing, so I grab a wetsuit to throw over my bikini and rent a board. Bentley offers to pay for my stuff, but I'm not having it. I don't like to owe anybody anything. That goes right along with my feelings on love. The guys are looking kind of confused and it just makes me laugh even harder to myself.

We grab our boards and walk down to the area where people are allowed to surf. Because of the crazy weather lately off the coast, the waves are rolling in, not as high as I'd like, but anybody who surfs knows even the small waves can be amazing. Kaden and Bentley stick their boards in the sand and I can tell they're gaging the surf, trying to decide what the sets look like in front of us.

While they're doing that, I stretch to loosen up my muscles. Surfing can be hard on the body. Paddling out really works the upper body, so I make it a point to focus on my arms, shoulders, and back. I look a little over to the left and see some of the guys I've surfed with several times. I don't want them to see me yet because they'll give away my secret.

"C'mon, boys! There's no time like the present. Let's get out there and surf."

They both look at me and laugh, but I don't wait for their response.

I grab my board and head to the water.

"Kayla, wait up. Why don't you watch us first and then we can walk you through the basics?" Bentley suggests, looking a little worried. I can tell he isn't at all trying to be condescending because the fact is he has no idea of my surfing capabilities. However, there is no way I'm going to sit on the sidelines and watch them surf.

"I'm just going to paddle out with you guys so I can observe from up close."

I drop my board into the water, lie down on the deck, and begin paddling out. I look over at Kaden and Bentley and they're right behind me. When we get to the back, I sit on the deck, spreading my legs out around the board, and check out the sets.

Being out here feels freeing. If you've never surfed, it's hard to understand. Surfing is an experience. It's about the next wave you're going to catch because you always want more, always crave more. It becomes an addiction, and at the end of the day, you might be tired and sore as hell, but it still feels amazing.

I see the guys from earlier paddling out and know if I don't catch a wave soon they're going to out me. Without saying a word to Kaden and Bentley, I wait for the next set of waves, and when they come, I charge for the wave and begin paddling my ass off, pop up, and take the drop. It's hard to describe what my mind goes through while I'm riding the wave. Beforehand, my mind is all over the place. Once I paddle out, my mind only thinks of a few things, but once I'm riding the wave, my mind is clear, and the only thing I can think of is contentment. Before I experienced love, I would have described it as such, but once I experienced the toxicity of love, I would never again associate surfing with love. Surfing isn't like pathetic ever-changing emotions. It's concrete and it's life.

I get to the shoreline and wait for the guys to meet me back here. Bentley goes first and he's decent. He pops up and rides the wave to the shore without wiping out. Kaden is clearly not as good. He tries to take a larger wave and completely wipes out. Bentley gets to the shore while I'm still laughing at Kaden.

"Well, aren't you just full of secrets?" he says through his laughter.

"You didn't ask."

He saunters up to me, grips my wetsuit in his hands, and he pulls me close to him until our bodies are flush against one another. His mouth attacks mine with such force it's just not painful. I'm learning that Bentley is an extremely passionate individual. He doesn't seem to do anything half-ass. Every time he kisses me he gives me all of him. His tongue slips between my lips without asking for permission. He just takes what he wants. My hands go up to his neck and I hold on to the back of it while he continues to assault me in the best way possible.

I don't see Kaden and the guys approach, but when I hear one of the guys yell out, "What's up, *Wahine*!" I push Bentley away. His brows furrow in confusion like he isn't even aware that we were just making out in front of an entire audience. I never do shit like this. This guy is totally getting under my skin.

When Kaden and Bentley realize the guys are referring to me, they both raise their eyebrows. I don't give them an explanation though. I just nod to the guy. "What's up?"

"Nothing much…chilling and surfing. What are you doing with these *Bennies*?"

Before I can answer, Bentley asks, "How do you guys know each other?"

"*Wahine* is a local and a bitchin' surfer in case you haven't noticed. We all see her at different events and competitions. She's a cool ass chick."

Bentley and Kaden look at me in shock and I bite my lip to stifle my laugh.

"All right, well, it looks like the sets are picking up so we're gonna get back out there."

The guys all say their goodbyes and then take off, leaving Bentley, Kaden, and me alone.

Kaden asks first. "What the hell is a *Wahine*? And why did he just call us *Bennies*?"

I smile big. "A *Wahine* is a female surfer. I've been surfing most of my life. I live across from the beach. Liz and I have been friends since we were five years old, and she's spent her life watching me surf while reading a book from the shoreline. A *Benny* is someone who's not from around here. When you live on the beach you know who's local and who's not. I'm not from Miami, but I surf all over."

"Will you marry me?" Kaden asks with a straight face, and for a second I feel like I'm going to hyperventilate until Bentley punches him in the arm causing Kaden to bark out his laughter. *Oh, thank God, he was kidding!*

"If she's going to marry anyone, it will be me." And now I really am about to hyperventilate because for a second I can imagine myself spending my life with this man. I haven't known him long but the little I do know of him already has me addicted. This isn't good. Addiction is need and need leads to commitment and commitment leads to marriage, and you don't base a marriage off any of those things because they're all emotional, and emotions change, leaving you heartbroken. I know all of this already, but for some reason when I'm with Bentley, all my sensible thinking goes flying out the window.

Bentley wraps his body around mine. I feel so protected and…I'm not going to use the L word because it's not possible, but I feel something and it scares me. I move out of his arms to get myself together.

"All right, boys. The tides won't stay like this forever. Let's do some more surfing."

And that's what we spend the day doing. We surf and talk and surf some more. We paddle out together, talking about nothing of consequence, but it's nice. We agree to keep it light. Well, I request to keep it light, but Bentley and Kaden go along with it. Bentley tells me about his friends and how he loves to work out and fight. I tell him about being a cheerleader in high school and about all the trouble I've gotten Liz and me into over the years. Kaden doesn't really say much. He just laughs and joins in occasionally.

Our competitive sides show as we playfully banter back and forth throughout the day over who can surf better. However, when I hit the last wave just right and ride that bitch like I own it, they both agree I'm the better out of the three of us. In another life, Bentley and I could effortlessly be friends. It's just so easy with him, and if I'm truthful with myself, if given the chance we could probably be more than friends. Last night was about sex, but today has been about so much more than that. I've never just hung out with a guy since Jake—and if we're being honest, his immature ass doesn't compare to Bentley—and it's rather refreshing.

Dusk approaches and Kaden takes off to meet up with a couple of friends including their friend Caleb. Bentley tells him we aren't going to join, and then comes up with the idea for us to sleep under the stars on the beach. Bentley mentioned where they live has no beach nearby and where they're about to move to doesn't either. His love of surfing came from his trips with his parents over the years.

We go to a local store and pick up a large sleeping bag, some blankets, snacks, and a bottle of vodka. We make our way down and find a secluded spot to build a small bonfire.

We spread a blanket out and use another one to wrap ourselves up with me between Bentley's legs. It's spring in Florida, but the ocean breeze adds a bit of a chill so we're snuggling close. We don't say anything, just watch the small fire crackle and the waves crash. It's a comfortable silence, though. I've never felt so at ease with anybody except Liz before. Being in Bentley's arms feels so natural like he was made with the sole purpose to hold me.

He moves my hair off my neck and begins to trail open mouth kisses from my earlobe working his way down to my collarbone. His soft kisses give me goose bumps and cause me to visibly shiver. He moves his hands underneath the blanket to my tank top and pulls my top down, releasing my breasts. His mouth goes from kissing to sucking and nipping. Using his thumbs and middle fingers he pinches my nipples making them peak, and using his forefingers he rubs them over the top of my nipples causing them to get hard. The sensation hits my core instantly and I can't help but moan as he continues his sexual assault on me.

I take my hand and move it to the back of his head, pushing his mouth into my neck to show him I need more. He sucks harder, then bites the side of my neck, moving back up to my earlobe to bite it as well. He removes one hand from my breast and taps my legs for me to spread them open. I like him behind me, but I want to see him.

I turn around on my knees—keeping the blanket around us in case anybody wanders by—and go up high enough so his face is right in front of my breasts. I grab him by the back of his head and pull his face to me. He knows exactly what I want because his lips wrap right around my nipple and he sucks hard, tugging on it until it pops out, and then he moves to the other one to give it the same attention.

His hand goes into my shorts and under my bikini bottoms, straight toward my clit. He rubs it for a few seconds and then moves his hand lower to gather up the juices that are already flowing down there.

"Jesus woman, you're dripping wet." I push his head back to my breasts and he chuckles, but immediately goes back to sucking and licking each one. I need to be in control tonight. I feel like I'm losing all control and that doesn't sit well with me at all.

His fingers, full of my wetness, move back to my clit and he starts rubbing it up and down and in circles causing me to squirm a little. It's insane how he knows exactly how to get me off. He should give classes on how to give a woman an orgasm. I know quite a few guys who would benefit from this.

"C'mon baby, let go for me," he murmurs. I want to, but I want him in me when I do. Taking his swim shorts in my hands, I pull them down and then push him onto his back.

"Do you have a condom?" I ask.

He nods and takes it out of his pocket. He must have grabbed it when we stopped by the hotel earlier to grab our stuff. Knowing we would be sleeping here and he would be leaving early, we took our stuff from the room so we wouldn't have to go back there in the morning.

I take it from him, rip it open, and roll it onto his hard length. I lift and then sink down onto him in one fluid motion, both of us moaning as he fills me. He looks into my eyes as he takes my hands in his, holding me steady, and I begin to ride him up and down. His dick hits the inside of me just right causing an unbelievable amount of pleasure. After a few minutes, he places my hands on his chest and I start to pick up speed. He's in me so deep it feels like we're one. He moves his finger back to my clit and rubs circles against the sensitive nub.

Between his dick hitting the inside of me and the friction of his finger on my clit, I know I'm about to lose it, and he knows it too.

"C'mon, woman. Give it to me. Come for me. I want to feel you come all over my dick."

His words throw me over the edge. My body spasms and my legs shake, and at one point I'm not even sure I'll be able to keep riding him so he can find his own release. But the one thing I've learned about Bentley is even though he's only known me for twenty-four hours he still knows me. Once I've ridden out my orgasm, he grabs my hips, holding me down, and begins to pump up into me from the bottom. His thrusts get faster and deeper and I feel another orgasm coming on.

"Oh, my God, Bentley. Please don't stop," I beg. And this time we find our release together.

WE'RE LYING WRAPPED UP IN THE SLEEPING BAG WITH BENTLEY spooning me from behind when he quietly says, "I don't want to let you go."

My entire body stills. I don't even know how to respond to that. I would be lying if I said I wasn't thinking the same thing, but at the same time I already know how this type of story ends. Boy meets girl, boy makes girl fall for him, girl falls, and boy doesn't catch her. Girl hits the ground face first. Splat! The End.

"I just want a chance to get to know you more," he continues. "I've never done anything like this before. I know you feel what I'm feeling."

I take a second to get control of my emotions and then I say, "I'm not at a place in my life to give you anything more. I don't do more. I'm sorry."

He grabs my hips and rolls me over to face him. I keep my eyes down, but he lifts my chin so I'm forced to look at him.

"Kayla, do you believe in soulmates?" Oh, boy, here we go. Why did I have to pick the guy who doesn't want a one-night stand?

Figuring it's probably best to put him out of his misery, I tell him the truth. "No, I don't. I don't believe in love, or soulmates, or happily ever after."

He makes a pained expression like I just ran over his puppy, and it makes me want to take it all back just to see him smile again, but I'm doing what I have to do. I don't want to lead him on and I need to protect myself.

"Who hurt you, baby?" he asks, trailing his knuckles down the side of my cheek softly.

"It doesn't matter. The only thing that does matter is that my mom warned me love wasn't real, but like any teenager I had to experience it for myself, and I learned the hard way she was right."

He thinks about what I said for a few seconds then asks, "Are your parents still married?"

"Yeah, they have a business relationship. They are both divorce attorneys who watch people destroy their lives as well as their children's lives every day. They have been married for over twenty years, though.

When my mom gave me advice on relationships, at first I thought she was a cynic. She told me love is an emotion and emotions aren't concrete so they don't last. It took me having my heart broken to realize she was right. And on top of that, I disappointed her and embarrassed myself."

I don't ask him to give me his opinions because I don't want to know how he feels. Feelings only hurt. He waits a beat and when he sees I'm not going to say anything else he decides to give me his opinion anyway.

"Well, my parents married for love, and they have been married for over twenty years as well. They spent so much time all over each other while I was growing up I thought that's how all parents were, until I got old enough to go to other kids houses and saw that not every parental unit is like mine. I believe in love and soulmates"—he pulls me closer to him until he's so close I could kiss him without moving—'and I believe you very well could be my soulmate. I just want a chance, Kayla. One chance to prove to you that love is real."

I hate how determined he looks and I can't stand to hurt him, so I say, "I'll think about it."

He accepts that answer and we fall asleep with my head on his chest as he rubs circles on my back.

I wake up and it's still dark outside. The small fire has gone out and Bentley is still fast asleep. He looks so peaceful with just a hint of a smile on his face. I would like to think I put that smile there. I check my phone and see it's only three in the morning. I gather up my stuff and carefully slip out of the sleeping bag leaving Bentley sleeping by himself. It's just easier this way.

Three

BENTLEY

Present Day

SOMETIMES THERE ARE PEOPLE AND SITUATIONS IN LIFE THAT we just can't control. No matter how much we try, it's out of our hands and we have to learn to accept that it's out of our hands. Kayla is the person in my life and her refusing to allow me to show her what love is, is the situation that is completely out of my control. I've loved this girl from the day I met her six years ago at the club in Miami. I know what you're thinking, so for argument's sake, let's just agree to disagree. I know what I felt and I know how I feel. Unfortunately, the woman I fell in love with is incapable of letting somebody in, so none of it really matters at this point.

However, what does matter is that at this moment I'm standing in front of said girl staring at her adorable pregnant belly while she's rocking a tiny string bikini that makes me want to devour her while I'm currently holding hands with my girlfriend, and the only thing I can think of is, *is the baby mine?*

Everybody around us goes silent and I realize I just asked the question out loud. Kayla opens her mouth to respond, but Sophia, my girlfriend of three months, cuts in. "Are you fucking kidding me?" Jesus, when did her voice get so damn whiny?

"Isn't this the bitch from your apartment?" she asks. "Why the fuck would she be carrying your baby? We have been together for months, Bentley." She draws out my name and it sounds like nails to a chalkboard.

I go to respond, but Kayla beats me to it. "Bitch? Who are you calling a bitch? Just because I'm pregnant doesn't mean I can't kick your ass back to wherever you came from. You don't know shit about what Bentley and I have done."

Sophia turns to me, glaring. "Bentley, what the hell is she talking

about? Is it possible this baby is yours?"
Ah, hell. Shit just got real.

Six Months Ago

THE CROWD IS CHANTING "RAGE. RAGE. RAGE. RAGE." I'M standing in the corner, watching the announcer declare Cooper the winner of the fight, which means that in February he'll be going head-to-head for the title at the MGM Grand arena. I'm so fucking proud of him. He busts his ass every day at the gym and has been putting up with his dad for the last several years just to get to where he is. I honestly don't know how the hell he does it. Yeah, I work out at the same training facility as him, but I don't have his piece-of-shit father breathing down my neck like he does. If I did, I would have quit years ago.

Before Cooper leaves the octagon to head back to the changing area, he nods for me to come over to him. "Look straight out, four rows back."

I do what he tells me to do and then I spot them. More importantly, I spot her, the girl who left me on the beach all those years ago. The girl I knew was my soulmate but wouldn't let her guard down long enough to give me a real chance. *Well I'll be damned.*

"I need you to make sure Liz is at the after-party."

I give them a smirk when I see they're both looking my way, and nod. I know Cooper feels the same way about Liz that I do about Kayla.

Once Cooper and everyone with him make their way out of the octagon, I approach the girls.

"Well, God damn. If it isn't the girl who got away…And her best friend." I direct my statement at Liz so Kayla doesn't know how much that shit hurt to wake up on the beach by myself in Miami five years ago after she told me she would think about giving us a chance. When I get done looking at Liz, I turn to Kayla and fuck if she doesn't look even more beautiful than she did all those years ago. She still has the same long blonde hair with captivating blue eyes. Her body is still thin and toned, but she's matured. "Never thought we would see you two again."

I wait for Kayla to respond. Most girls would look remorseful when approached after dipping out on a guy after spending the weekend with him, but not Kayla. She puts her hands on her hips, lifts her chin and makes it clear where she stands. Well, we'll just have to see about that.

"Looks like you were wrong because here we are."

"So, I take it you two are UFC fans?"

She laughs at my question. "Ummm…No. I'm a fan of hot guys in no shirts fighting and getting all sweaty, and Liz is along for the ride. Our best friend Hayley got us tickets to the fight and invited us to the party that is going on afterward."

I'll have to thank Hayley when I see her. She's our on-site medic at the gym. I lean in close to Kayla, just enough to invade her personal space but without touching her. "Well, you're in luck because I'm one of those fighters and I'll gladly take my shirt off and get sweaty with you any day."

Kayla's laugh deepens, like she isn't affected at all by me, but I can see her thighs rubbing together—she's putting on a front. I'm going to let it go…for now.

"So, that means we'll see you at Kaden's for the after-party?"

"I didn't know it's at Kaden's. Hayley just sent me an address, but yes, we'll be there. Whether you see us is up in the air."

If it's possible, I swear that woman has gotten even sassier since the last time I saw her, and if I'm honest, I love it. What I would give to kiss the fuck out of that girl just to shut her up, but I need to formulate a plan. I never imagined seeing her again, but now that I have another chance, I need to do this right. I nod to both of them and head to the back to meet up with the guys.

Cooper, Caleb, and I arrive to Kaden's house and the party is already in full swing. I take a look at Kaden's home and the land he's sitting on and I can't help but feel a little nostalgic. I miss the days when we were all roommates. Don't get me wrong, I'm happy for Kaden and Cooper each getting his own place. Kaden has worked his ass off as a trainer to purchase this home on his own. It's a decent-sized house on probably a half-acre of land. Nothing huge, but he's put his heart and soul into making it a home. Back in Boulder we were all roommates minus Caleb. I can afford my own place, but I hate living on my own. It gets lonely. Growing up, my parents and I were very close and when I moved out of their home I moved right in with Cooper and Kaden. I like having my own space but I enjoy the company of others as well.

It's a little different living with Caleb. He's more of a loner. He's an amazing friend and will have your back without question, but something fucked up happened to him. I can see it in his eyes. The problem is, he doesn't talk about it. He has a passion for fighting like the rest of us, but for him it's more like he's fighting something within him. He also works a lot of hours as a bouncer at a club on the strip. I might as well be living on my own, to be honest.

As soon as I see the overflow of people everywhere I immediately start looking for my little firecracker. I don't see her, but I do see a couple friends from the gym, so I bullshit with them for a few minutes before continuing my search. When I finally find her she's making herself a drink in the kitchen. Her phone is on the counter and before she sees me coming I snatch it up. Luckily, it's not locked.

"Hey! What the hell do you think you're doing?" she screams, thinking her phone is being stolen. When she sees me, she simmers down, but then her face morphs into the cutest glare I've ever seen. Before I answer her, I type in my number and call myself. She realizes what I'm doing and tries to snatch her phone back.

I turn around so my back is facing her and she jumps onto my back to try to get to it. I hear my phone ring and know I got her number. Her ass isn't getting away a second time.

I grab her body off my back and put her onto the counter, spreading her legs and positioning myself between them. I think she's in shock at how easily I could fling her around because for the first time she's speechless.

I hand her back her phone. "Now I have your number. There'll be no getting away from me this time," I say with a wink.

She snatches her phone back and huffs out in annoyance. I must be a sick guy because the more pissed she gets, the more turned on I get. She shoves me back and jumps off the counter, grabbing her drink and walking away without saying a word. I follow her outside to the bonfire, and once we're away from the loud noise, I grab her by her arm and spin her around.

"Woman, please stop walking away from me."

She lifts one brow in defiance, and I tug her over to me. For a brief second, she melts into my touch, lowering that impenetrable wall. But before I can jump across, she realizes what she's done, and it shoots back up, blocking me on my side.

"I'm pretty sure I can walk wherever I want, including away from you, and I'm not particularly fond of guys who take my number without asking."

I try to contain my smile. I learned quickly with Kayla when she doesn't think I'm taking her seriously it only fuels her fire.

"Look, I'm sorry. But can you blame me? We had an amazing couple days together in Miami and when I asked you for your number, you said you would think about it, then I wake up to you gone without so much as a goodbye. I searched the beach that morning hoping to find those surfers who knew you, but none of them were around. I've been back to that beach several times over the years hoping to see you surfing and now you're here. I can't take the chance of you disappearing again. I believed you were my soulmate all those years ago, but now that I've run into you again, I know you are."

"Well, obviously, I did think about it and decided not to give you my number," she sasses. "And I'm pretty sure in order to be soulmates, two people have to agree." She crosses her arms over her chest, pushing her amazing tits up, and before I can stop myself, my eyes dart down to appreciate them. Her eyes follow mine and then she lets go of her arms.

"Are you seriously staring at my chest right now?"

I chuckle and then bite my lip to contain my laughter and smile. She's so fucking adorable.

"I'm sorry. They're just there." I shrug. "The memory of you in that hot bikini, and then naked, wrapped around me on the beach is seared into my mind. I've spent five years thinking about you."

Her face softens and she gives me a small smile. "You just remembered me because I'm probably the only girl to ever out surf your ass."

"Hey, now! I let you out surf me!"

She playfully slaps my chest and we both laugh. Finally, I feel like I'm getting somewhere with her, but then her friend Liz walks toward us looking really upset, and I have a sinking suspicion my time with Kayla is up…at least for now. I nod to Kayla to let her know that her friend is walking over. When she sees Liz, her hand drops from my chest and she runs over to her. I can't hear what's being said, but within seconds both girls are walking away.

I follow them out to their car and see Cooper screaming for Liz. I don't know what just happened, but it can't be good. The next thing I know Cooper is walking away and Kayla is peeling out of the driveway.

A little while later, I find Cooper sitting by the bonfire with a whiskey in his hand. "Bro, what the hell happened?"

"It doesn't even fucking matter. She's gone and it's for the best."

I want to talk to him, but I know when he gets like this he just wants me there without my lectures, so I do what he wants and drink with him. At one point in the night Cooper is so drunk he decides he's going to find Liz.

"I never should have let her leave," he says through slurred words. The problem with being drunk is you're always the last person to realize you are in fact drunk.

"Just chill out. You need to get some sleep, sober up, and then you can talk to her in the morning."

He nods in agreement and then takes another swig of his drink. At this rate, he'll probably be sober next week.

The next morning, we're at the training center and I'm totally fucking with Cooper. His ass is so hung over, I don't even know how he's fighting back, but it makes it that much more fun. At one point, I throw a punch to his stomach and he looks like he's going to upchuck all over the ring. I can't help but laugh at his ass. Serves him right for drinking so damn much last night.

While he's catching his breath, I ask him if he's going to contact Liz and he tells me he can't because he has no way to get ahold of her. This guy gives up way too easily, but as much as I want to let him know that, I decide to give him a break.

"You are aware her best friend works at this gym, right? And even if she didn't, I got Kayla's number last night." I must admit, I'm still damn proud of the way I stole her number. Hopefully her stubborn ass doesn't change it just to spite me. I wouldn't put it past her.

I shake myself out of my inner thoughts to hear Marc, Cooper's dad and owner of this training facility, bitching at him and apparently, me.

"…And you need to stop fucking around and take this shit seriously. Any more losses and you're going to be removed from this team…" He goes on and on about my upcoming fight, but all I can focus on is not decking this asshole in his face. He doesn't know shit about me, and if he did, he'd know I fight for fun and I don't give a fuck if I win or lose. I do it because I love it. Sure, I want to win. I'm a guy. I'm competitive. But I do it more to spend time with my friends and have fun, and this asshole isn't going to suck my love for fighting out of me like he's done to his son. Fuck him and the horse he rode in on.

Four

BENTLEY

IT'S BEEN EIGHT DAYS SINCE THE UFC FIGHT AND PARTY, AND I never imagined so much shit could change in that short amount of time. I'm sitting at the hospital with Kayla holding her hand to comfort her as they treat her for smoke inhalation while praying for Liz and Cooper's daughter Bella, who's in the children's wing with the same diagnosis. If you had told me that I would end up here with Kayla, I would have told you you were crazy. If you had told me Cooper has a four-year-old daughter, I would have laughed in your face.

After Cooper and his dad got into it the other day, Liz showed up at the gym shortly after to let Cooper know she got pregnant all those years ago in Miami. Unfortunately, Cooper's ass of a dad stopped her and sent her away. Cooper ended up finding out about his long lost daughter when he ran into them at the grocery store. When he confronted his dad, the asshole made it clear he didn't give a shit about anything but Cooper fighting, so Cooper ended up quitting.

Nobody has seen him in the last several days and since he refused to go back to the gym, so did I. Kaden's ass is stuck there because he's under contract with the gym as a trainer, but Caleb and I aren't. So, until we hear from Cooper about what he wants to do, we're using guest passes at another local gym. I have a fight coming up, so I can't just stop training. Luckily, Caleb is helping me train, so it works out well.

I sent Kayla a few texts, but she only replied with single word responses. I had been working up the courage to ask Hayley for her address so I could confront her in person, but after today it won't matter what her address is since her apartment caught fire with her and Bella in it. Thankfully both of them are okay.

All my life my parents have said we can't control who we love. We're destined to be with one person, and when we meet that person we will know it. It's called fate, and we don't stand a chance against it.

I believe that Kayla is my soulmate. The problem is my parents never explained what would happen if you met your soulmate and they don't believe in love. If I didn't already believe in fate, I would be a believer after today.

While I was training with Caleb, I hit my hand the wrong way on the punching bag, something I never do, and decided to go to the ER to have it checked out to make sure there wasn't any huge damage. Imagine my surprise when I saw Kayla and a small little girl being wheeled in by ambulance. Kayla asked me to call Liz to let her know what's going on—that their apartment caught on fire and both Bella and her are at the hospital—and of course she came immediately. I tried to contact Cooper, but he didn't answer.

That leads me to the present time. While Liz is in the children's wing with her and Cooper's daughter, I'm currently sitting in the recovery wing with Kayla. Her eyes are closed and she has on an oxygen mask so she can't really talk. I just hold her hand and massage my thumb into her palm to let her know I'm here.

Finding her today in the hospital only strengthens my argument that we're meant to be together. Now if I could just convince Kayla of this, we would be golden. Easier said than done, though.

The door swings open and Liz and Cooper walk in. Liz looks terrified, but as soon as Kayla opens her eyes and lifts her oxygen mask, she calms down and runs right to Kayla. They exchange hugs and Kayla explains that she fell asleep with Bella and woke up to a fire in the apartment. She's so upset and heartbroken that something could have happened to Bella. It's clear she loves that little girl like her own.

Of course, Liz tells her it's not her fault and calms her down by telling her it's okay. Those two are more like sisters than best friends. A few minutes later a police officer and a couple firemen come into the room to explain what happened. I'm trying to pay attention, but all I can think about is that Kayla almost died. Whoever set that fire should be dead, and if I ever come across him or her I'll probably kill 'em myself.

I look over to the officer handing Liz a photo of the guy who set the apartment on fire and Liz begins to freak out and then hands the photo to Cooper.

"The man in this photo is Marc Cooper. This is my father."

What. In. The. Actual. Fuck. I know Marc is a first-rate asshole, but to burn down their home to keep Liz away from Cooper is fucking crazy. That man belongs in the loony bin.

Liz and Cooper are exchanging words and their conversation is getting heated, but then what he says next shocks the shit out of all of us.

"He's dead, Liz. My dad is dead."

I walk over to Cooper to give him a hug and tell him I'm sorry. "I know you two didn't get along, but I never thought he was capable of this."

Cooper doesn't say anything. He looks fucking defeated and I don't blame him. I have no clue how I would react if I found out my dad almost killed his granddaughter and then saved her. I'm pissed as hell that he didn't save Kayla, but Cooper doesn't need my anger on top of what he's already dealing with.

I look around and realize the officer and firemen must have left at some point. Liz tries to comfort Cooper but he ends up spouting out some shit about them being better off without him and then storms out. Once he's gone Liz loses it. Kayla is laying in the hospital bed after almost dying from being caught in a fire and she's comforting Liz. She doesn't cry or even look upset. She's the strongest fucking woman I know.

Finally, Liz calms down and asks the question of the hour. "Now what?"

Kayla sighs and says, "It will be okay, Liz. We'll figure it out. We always do."

The love these two women have for each other is undeniable. I think back to that night on the beach when Kayla told me love isn't real. Doesn't she see how much Liz loves and needs her? No, it's not the same as a relationship, but love is love, and Kayla is surrounded by love.

Kayla looks like she has the world sitting on her shoulders and I vow to do whatever I can to show her that it's okay to love and accept love from a man. She doesn't always have to be so strong.

I clear my throat to get their attention and when they both look at me I tell Liz to go focus on Bella and suggest they move in with me. I don't know what I was thinking except that I want Kayla near me and if she's living with me maybe she'll give us a chance. I also don't want any of them being homeless. Hopefully Cooper will come to his senses and figure his shit out, but until then I figure I can make sure they're all safe.

After getting emotional, Liz goes back to her daughter. I can't even begin to imagine what she's going through. Being a single parent and at such a young age can't be easy. That gets me thinking about Kayla and how she fits into all this.

Once she's gone, Kayla says, "You didn't have to do that but thank you. Apparently, Cooper isn't going to man up right now."

"That's not fair and you know it," I tell her. "He just lost his dad. He has struggled for years dealing with that man. Marc has Cooper so fucked up he can't see straight. Just give him some time."

"I get that, but he has a woman and a daughter who need his support."

"And he will come around. Have you and Liz been close the entire time she's been raising Bella?"

I see the adoration in Kayla's eyes when I say Bella's name. "Yeah, that little girl is amazing. When we got back from Miami, Liz found out she didn't wait long enough to have unprotected sex after starting her birth control pills and was pregnant. We tried to look up your names but got nothing. We lived together and made it work. We went to school, worked part time, and raised Bella the best we could. I love that little girl like she's my own."

"Do you want to have your own kids one day?" I ask, hoping she'll open up to me.

"I do. I want to find a man that wants the same things as me so we can have kids and raise them."

"What things are those?"

She thinks for a second before she answers. "Somebody with a career and his own money who wants to partner up to have a family. Somebody who is looking for an equal and is willing to share the responsibilities, bills, etcetera."

Her response tells me she still feels the same way she did all those years ago. I can give her all that, but I can do it with love if she would just let me.

"Sounds like the perfect business relationship, just like your parents."

She just nods and closes her eyes.

"That's all I can give anyone," she mutters before falling back asleep and ending the conversation.

I use this time to text Cooper, and when he doesn't respond, I send out a text to Kaden and Caleb. I get a text back from Caleb letting me know Cooper is there. I let him know the girls are coming to stay with us in our spare room until they figure shit out, and for him to let Cooper know as well.

A few hours later Kayla is still sleeping, but I can hear her whimpering like she's scared. She must be having a bad dream. I decide to lie in the bed with her to comfort her. She tries to be so strong, but sometimes we just need to let someone else hold us up. Carefully, I kneel onto the bed and gently move her over, and once I'm situated, I wrap my body around hers, pulling her close to me. She instantly calms and continues to sleep. She may not want to admit it, but this woman is my forever and I'm hers.

I MUST HAVE FALLEN ASLEEP BECAUSE WHEN I OPEN MY EYES the sun is shining and s staring at me with a smirk on her face.

"Well, good morning, sunshine. First, you take my number without asking, and now you take half my bed without asking? Have you no manners?"

I attempt to stretch, but with the bed being so small and me being so big, it doesn't work out well. I just end up cuddling closer to Kayla, which is absolutely okay with me.

"You haven't seen anything yet, sweetheart. Now that you'll be living at my place I plan to take much more from you. Although, if you would just give it all to me willingly, it would make everything go a whole lot smoother."

She laughs and shakes her head, then attempts to push me off the bed. Good thing the rails are there or my ass would be on the floor right now.

"Let's go, big boy. Out of my bed. You won't be taking anything else from me, and I definitely won't be giving you anything."

The nurse walks in and eyes me in her bed not looking too thrilled, so I get up but not before whispering in Kayla's ear, "Oh, I will, and you will, and the sooner you accept you are mine, the sooner we can get to the fun stuff."

She tries to look like what I said doesn't affect her, but I can see the blush appear on her beautiful alabaster skin. I decide not to point it out though. I don't need her realizing she's giving her true feelings away.

Kayla and Bella finally get discharged from the hospital. Liz came to the hospital in her car, so she takes Kayla to get hers from the apartment complex, and then they meet me at my place.

When the girls walk in, Kayla seems to be impressed at our place, but Liz looks nervous. It must be frightening to suddenly be homeless and have a kid in tow. I had Caleb clean up the night before, but there wasn't much to clean up. We're actually pretty clean guys. I give them a quick tour of the place and they see all the stuff Cooper bought the night before. I knew he was picking up some clothes for them since they lost everything in the fire, but he definitely went above and beyond. There are toys and dolls, and a bunch of girly crap for Bella. He picked up a bed for her as well and a bunch of movies. I don't want to overwhelm them, so after I let Liz know when the funeral will be, I give Kayla a kiss on the cheek and give them their space.

IT'S BEEN A FEW DAYS SINCE THE GIRLS MOVED IN AND everything is going fine. We have had a few meals together and Bella is absolutely adorable. I've watched more Disney movies than I care to admit, but I can't help it. That little girl knows exactly what she's doing with her cute little pouty face and the way she bats her eyelashes. She even got Caleb to watch one with us. Every night Kayla makes sure to go to bed when Liz and Bella do to avoid me, but I think I'm wearing her down. She still won't answer my texts, but I catch her staring at me quite often. I'm not giving up.

It's a little after eleven at night when I hear a banging noise. I know Caleb is working and everybody else should be asleep so I walk out from my room to check it out.

I realize the banging is coming from the front door and I rush to answer it before it wakes anybody up. When I swing the door open, Chelsea, a girl I was dating up until a couple weeks ago, is standing at my door, looking drunk as hell.

"Hey, baby!" She slurs out the words as she wraps her arms around me.

"Chelsea, what are you doing here?"

"I miss you, baby. Can I come in?" Oh lord. This isn't going to be good. After getting to know Chelsea for a few weeks, I learned that she has a drinking problem. I backed away from her after that, but clearly she didn't get the message.

"Chelsea, you can't be here. How did you get here anyway?" I ask, looking out toward the parking lot to see if there is a cab waiting for her. Maybe I can catch it before it leaves.

"My friend dropped me off." I walk her into my room so she doesn't wake up the entire house while I try to figure out how to handle this. She plops down on my bed, so I take her phone and try to call a couple of people I know she's friends with. Of course, nobody answers.

"Chelsea, I'm going to call you a cab so you can go home." When she doesn't answer me, I look up and find her passed the fuck out in my bed. It's late and I'm tired, so I decide to let her sleep it off. I'll just take her home in the morning once she's coherent. I grab a blanket from my bed and lay across the futon I have in my room. I sure as hell am not going to sleep in the bed with her. I don't need to give her any more reason to think she has a chance with me.

I wake up with a kink in my neck and for a second wonder why the hell I'm sleeping on my futon, when I remember what happened last night. I take a second to stretch when I hear screaming coming from the living room. I look at my bed and it's empty. *Oh shit!* I haul ass out to the living room to find Chelsea is in my fucking shirt, going toe-to-toe with Kayla. Then I look around and see Liz, who looks like she's trying to be pissed, but is also attempting to hold in her laughter. And of course the scene wouldn't be complete without Bella mimicking Kayla's stance with her hands on her hips.

"Okay, I can explain." All three and half women look over at me and I put my hands up, metaphorically waving a white flag while praying they don't all team up and kill me.

The first one to speak is Bella. "Bentley, your friend is wearing no shorts, and Mommy says it's rude to not be dressed when you have company over. You should tell your friend to put on some more clothes." She scrunches her nose up, and if I wasn't scared for my life right now, I would laugh at her cuteness.

Liz snorts and Kayla shoots me a death glare. Chelsea looks like the sight of a child revolts her. What was I ever thinking when I decided to go out with her? I don't like to waste my time with women I don't see a future with.

Before I can explain the situation, Chelsea lets out a sound of disgust and retreats to my bedroom.

"Let me explain," I say again to the women left standing in the living room.

Liz speaks up this time. "There's no need to explain. This is your apartment. I'm just thankful for you letting us stay here." Damn, Cooper is one lucky guy. He better get his shit straight before he loses her for good.

"Excuse me? No, Liz! It is not okay…" Kayla begins to yell, but Liz cuts her off.

"Can we please continue this later? I really need to get Bella to school."

Kayla and I both nod, and I get the hell out of there before Kayla finds something to stab me with.

After I drop Chelsea off at her place and make it clear to her we are over, I head over to the gym. Cooper sent everyone a text requesting a meeting.

Once we all gather, he announces that his father left him the training facilities in the will so he's officially the new owner. I'm extremely happy for him. He deserves it.

After telling him congratulations, Caleb and I head to the ring to get a workout in. I'm going to be fighting in less than two months and now that Cooper's shitty dad isn't breathing down my throat, I find myself wanting to win. With Cooper's name on the line, I want to make him proud.

"Holy shit, man! I haven't seen you fight like that in years!" Caleb is bending over panting like a little bitch after I just whooped his ass.

I smile widely and laugh. I have to admit, it feels good to give it my all again.

"So, what's up with you and Kayla?" he asks as we head to the juice bar to get a drink.

"I don't know. She comes from a home where they apparently don't believe in love. I just don't get it. What mom tells her daughter that love isn't real and to never marry because of it?"

"Not every family is perfect like yours, Bent. And to be honest, maybe you're dodging a bullet. In my experience, women are fake as hell and just want one thing from a man. Money."

Caleb looks sad when he says this and it's probably the most he's ever said about relationships.

"From your experience?" I ask, trying to get him to continue, but he shuts down.

"Doesn't even matter. I like Kayla. She's a cool chick, but I don't trust any women. Let's practice."

I spend the rest of the afternoon working out, then shower at the gym, and when I can't put off the inevitable anymore, I head home.

It's almost ten o'clock when I arrive, so I'm hoping everybody will be asleep. I open the door quietly and attempt to tip toe to my room. No such luck.

"Oh, well, look who it is? Sneaking any more whores into your room tonight so Bella can wake up and see them half naked? Maybe this time you can give her your boxers to wear to go along with your shirt."

There is so much shit I could say, but I'm a man and I'm not stupid, so I decide to just beg for forgiveness. "I'm sorry. It's not what you were thinking. You know I've been texting you every day asking you to give me a chance. Do you really think I would bring some woman home and sleep with her while you are here?"

For a second her face softens, but then it hardens into a stoic expression and she no longer shows any emotion. And I know that infamous wall is going up. "I don't give a shit who you bring home. I don't want you. What we had was a one-time thing. I'm not your soulmate or your forever. So just give it a rest. We both know you just wanted in my pants again, and when I wouldn't give it up, you found someone who would. The only problem is you got caught."

"You know what, Kayla? I've tried so damn hard, but you just won't listen. She was drunk and needed somewhere to stay and I let her sleep on my bed while I took the futon. It was late and I forgot about Bella being here. If I would have remembered I would have made sure she was gone before she woke up. I didn't do this to hurt you."

Suddenly the door opens and Cooper comes walking in, assessing the situation.

"What's going on?"

Of course, Kayla is the first to respond. "Oh, you know. Bentley thought it would be okay to bring some whore around here last night and when she went to leave after he was done with her, she walked out half naked and Bella saw!"

Oh my God! This woman is not going to give it a rest. She doesn't listen to a damn word I say. The next words I say rush out—and immediately I wish I could take them back.

"Look, I said I was sorry fifty damn times! Liz is being understanding about this. Why can't you be? I forgot there is a child here. You act like I purposely brought her here and told her to walk out of my room half naked knowing Bella was out here. Damn it, woman! We both know you're just mad because you said you wanted nothing to do with me, so I went out and found someone who does!"

Yep, I just fucking lied and it is going to totally come back to bite me in the dick later. But, fuck! That woman could test the patience of a damn saint.

Kayla lets out a huff in frustration. She honestly looks like her head is about to explode. Luckily, Liz walks down the hall at this moment and joins us, and then Cooper decides to alleviate the situation.

"Kayla, I have a job opening at the training facility…"

Is this guy serious right now? I don't even know what the hell else he's saying because all I can imagine right now is chopping his head off and stringing it on a light pole. If I have to work with this woman every damn day I might kill her or myself.

"…you girls can stay with me. I have three extra rooms and I promise I won't bring any other women home." Well, isn't he the smart one? I'll have to pat him on the back later for using my shitty situation to his advantage.

Then Kayla shocks the shit out of everyone. "Actually, I think all of us would be too much. How about Liz and Bella stay with you, that way you can spend time with Bella, and I can stay here. It's just temporary. I can handle the whorehouse."

Fucking woman. Of course she has to add that in. However, I must give her credit. She's totally taking one for the team right now, and by team, I mean team Cooper and Liz, because she isn't batting for my team. Although, her staying here means I'll have more time to convince her to let down that cement wall and maybe even get her to thaw out her icy heart.

"I agree with Kayla. It's a good idea."

And it's settled, tomorrow Liz and Bella will be moving in with Cooper, and Kayla will be staying here. Now, I just need to formulate a plan to convince her that love is real.

<h1 style="text-align:center">Five</h1>

<h2 style="text-align:center">BENTLEY</h2>

Me: Dinner tonight...you and me.

Kayla: NO

Me: Please...just one dinner.

Kayla: Still no.

Me: What time will you be home?

Kayla: None of your business

JESUS, THIS CHICK IS CLEARLY NOT GOING TO MAKE THIS EASY. It's been a few days since Liz and Bella moved out, and Kayla is still insisting on giving me the silent treatment.

"What's up?" Caleb comes out of his room dressed in jeans and a shirt with the club logo on it that he works for. He must be heading out to work.

"Nothing, man. Just trying to convince Kayla to go to dinner with me, but of course she isn't having it."

He chuckles at my situation...*fucker.* "So, bring dinner to her. Pick up food and wait for her to get home, and then make her sit with you and eat."

Hmm...Not a bad idea.

He pats me on the shoulder as he walks out. Caleb isn't a man of many words but when he does speak he makes it count. I also noticed him and Kayla have been getting closer. He never hangs out with women so maybe whatever they've both been through has helped him to open up and trust her.

I run out to the store to pick up sushi, some flowers, and candles. If I'm going to bring the dinner to Kayla, I'm going to go all out. I may only have one shot to convince her to give us a chance.

I get home and set it all up. Flowers and candles are spread all over the living room, the food is set out, and now I just have to hope she comes home soon.

As luck—or fate—might have it, Kayla comes strolling through the door not even fifteen minutes later. She closes the door and then stops in her tracks, glancing around the room. After assessing the situation, she looks like she's ready to bolt.

"Please, just one dinner. I got your favorite. California rolls, shrimp tempura, and fried rice, and for dessert, I got mango mocha ice cream."

I hold my breath praying she'll give me a little bit. Standing here right now reminds me of Will Smith in the movie *Hitch.*

'One dance, one look, one kiss, that's all we get…Just one shot to make the difference between happily-ever-after, and oh-he's-just-some-guy-I went-to-something-with.'

This is my one shot. Five years ago, we were younger and she had been recently hurt, but now this is our moment. If I can just get her to see this could be the beginning of our story, we could have that happily-ever-after.

I'm staring at Kayla as she closes her eyes. It's as if she's afraid to see what's right in front of her, but luck is on my side today because when she opens her eyes, she bites down on her bottom lip and nods slightly. She clearly afraid and I need to handle her with care.

I give her a small encouraging smile and pull her chair out for her. She has a seat and I push it in. I pour us both a glass of white wine to go with our sushi.

"How was your day?" I ask, trying to start up conversation without scaring her away.

"It was good. I started at the gym today. I didn't see you there. Cooper was showing me around and I met a bunch of the guys. I think I'm going to like it there. Everybody seems really nice."

"That's good. I was in the weight room and ring for most of the day. I saw you but wanted to give you some space."

"How is your training going? Are you ready for the upcoming fight?"

I roll my neck and shoulders, remembering the weight training I did today. Getting ready for this fight is putting a lot of strain on my muscles.

"Up until now I haven't taken fighting as seriously as I should so my body is in shock. I know I have a natural talent for fighting because when I fight and try, I win, but the issue is my motivation for it. Unlike a lot of these guys I don't have to win so I do it because I love it."

She nods, showing me she's listening.

"When I moved here to support Cooper, I think being away from my parents and being around his dad pushed me away, but lately I've been feeling that motivation again. Problem is, my body isn't exactly feeling the same way."

We continue to talk while we eat and the conversation flows smoothly. It probably helps that she has several glasses of wine, which appears to loosen her up.

"So, you moved here to go to college?" I ask, hoping she'll open up a little.

"Yeah, when we left you guys in Miami, we came here for college. Liz found out she was pregnant and we could've moved back home, but made the decision to stay here instead."

"I'm glad you stayed. I hate that it took this long for us all to cross paths again, but if you would've moved back it probably never would have happened."

She blushes slightly and shakes her head a little before going back to eating.

Once we're done and have eaten dessert I pour us one last glass of wine and move them to the coffee table in the living room.

"Sorry, I'm sore. I need the comfort of my couch."

She laughs and joins me in the living room. I expect her to sit next to me but instead she pushes me forward and sits behind me, pushing me onto the ground.

"I wouldn't exactly call the floor comfortable," I joke.

She ignores me, so I stay seated on the floor. And then a second later he hands begin to massage my neck and shoulder muscles.

"Holy shit woman, are you trying to kill me?" I say, groaning in pain.

"Physical therapists don't massage for pleasure. We massage to help loosen up the trouble areas. No pain, no gain."

She continues to massage my upper areas, and after a few minutes I can feel my muscles loosening, and it feels good. I think I let out a couple small moans because she chuckles behind me.

"What are you laughing at? This shit feels good."

She moves her hands over my shoulders and over my pecks and I shiver. Suddenly this massage feels a little less medical and a little more sexual. She rubs my pecks up and down and then I feel her breath against my ear.

Before I can turn around she's laying kisses on the side of my neck. My dick stands at attention, realizing where this is going. I mentally tell it to stand down. I'm not about to have another one-night stand with this woman. I want it all.

"Kayla, what are you doing?" Probably a dumb question to ask, but I don't know how else to word it.

"I thought it was obvious…"

I swivel around to face her. Her legs are spread from giving me a massage, so I kneel between her thighs. Like this we're almost at eye-level.

"I know what you're doing. What I mean to ask is where is this going?"

"Um, again, I thought that was obvious."

Okay, I'm going to have to explain myself better.

"Kayla, when I'm with a woman my intentions are to get to know her in hope that something more will come about. I don't sleep around just to sleep around. If we get together I don't want it to just be a one-night thing. I want more. I meant what I said to you five years ago. I believe in love, and I believe you are my forever."

She removes her hands from my body and frowns. I know this isn't going to be good. I grab ahold of her tiny hands and hold them in mine, not wanting our connection to be lost.

"Bentley, you know I don't believe in love or forever, but that doesn't mean we can't have some fun. What we had all those years ago was hot and we can have that again."

I know my dick is going to disown me for this, but…

"No, when we hooked up I felt something." I stop to give her a kiss on her lips. They're so soft, especially when she pouts like she's doing right now. "I still feel something and I think you do, too. I think you're too scared to admit it because you were hurt. The next time we're together physically it will be because you're giving us a real chance." I give her another soft kiss on her lips and then stand.

"Are you seriously going to walk away from having sex with me over some bullshit obsession with love?"

"I'm not walking away and I don't think it's bullshit nor is it an obsession. I believe that you and I could have something real. It would be fucking magical. I care about you and respect you too much to just have sex with you for fun. What we did back in Miami shouldn't have happened. We should have gotten to know each other more first."

I walk over to the entertainment center and glance back at her. She looks pissed, but once I turn on the music from my iPod, her anger morphs into confusion.

"Dance with me," I ask, taking her hands in mine.

She doesn't answer, but she doesn't pull away either. I wrap her up in my arms and begin to sway to lyrics that couldn't be more fitting. Having Kayla in my arms feels like home. I could spend the rest of my life dancing with this woman and be completely content.

After a few minutes, I whisper the lyrics to certain parts of Brad Paisley's *Perfect Storm* in her ear. It's about a man loving a woman so much, it hurts. She's his *perfect storm*. Kayla doesn't say anything, but she puts her head on my chest and lets me sing to her. When the song ends, I tilt my head to meet hers, and holding her chin, I slip my tongue into her mouth for just a second, just long enough to taste her. Then I kiss her with a little more force before pulling back.

"Good night, Kayla."

I don't turn back to see her facial expression and she doesn't say a word. I don't know if I'm doing the right thing here, but I would rather give up the for-now if it means I can have the forever.

I'm in bed, flipping through the channels, when there's a light knock on my door.

"Come in."

Kayla walks into the room and closes the door behind her.

"Can I lay with you?" she asks nervously.

I'm not sure where she's going with this, but I can't say no to her. I'm not sure why, but I get the feeling it took a lot for her to come here.

"Sure," I say, pulling my covers up so she can lie down next to me. I continue flipping through the channels until I come across *Titanic.*

"Wanna watch this?"

"Sure, gotta love a movie that at least portrays the truth about love." She laughs at her own joke. I look at her quizzically not understanding, so she explains.

"You know…Rose chose to love Jack… She chose love and what did it get her? Heartbroken."

"Maybe so, but during the short amount of time together she got to experience a powerful, unconditional love. It was worth the heartache in my opinion."

Kayla yawns and lays her head on my shoulder. "No amount of love is worth getting your heartbroken. Plus, she completely disappointed and alienated her family. What she did was selfish."

I put my arm around her and stroke her hair. Within a minute, I can hear her softly snoring. The more I get to know Kayla the more I realize her anti-love feelings go hand-in-hand with her relationship with her parents. I've watched her with Bella and Liz and can see how selfless she is. There is more to this story, and I have a feeling Kayla rejecting love is more about others and less about herself.

Six

BENTLEY

IT'S UFC FIGHT NIGHT, AND I'M FIGHTING. EVERYBODY IS AT the fight and by everybody I'm referring to Cooper, Kaden, Caleb, Hayley, who is my medic for the fight, and Kayla. Several other guys from Cooper's Fight Club are here as well and Kayla is working with a few of them who are still coming back from an injury since she's the physical therapist for the training facility.

The last couple weeks have been calm compared to the week's prior. Kayla and I have settled into a comfortable truce. Since the night she fell asleep in my room, she has slowly come around and we actually spend time together. It's usually just working out at the gym or watching TV and Caleb is almost always with us, but it's progress, so I'll take it. Also, Cooper and Liz are officially a couple and are heading forward full force. Kayla and I even babysit Bella together while they had a romantic night away just the two of them. I'm hoping that with Liz opening her heart and giving love a chance, Kayla will see can as well.

Of course, once we got to Boulder, shit got crazy. Because what's a trip without drama? Cooper was missing Liz and saw a photo of her all over another guy at a club that she and Ashley were at—Ashley's also a mom and is a teach. His caveman ass flew back to Vegas to claim his woman and luckily it was all a misunderstanding. Now he's back and I'm about to fight against Dante Cobalt. He's an up and coming fighter in the circuit and is currently undefeated with a record of seven-and-zero. My record isn't perfect, but I have more fights under my belt with a record of nine-and-four. We're the main event for the evening so people are going nuts. A lot of people are cheering for Cobalt, but I have a decent fan base, and after I beat his ass tonight, I have no doubt it will grow even more. Regardless, it's a fucking rush being here.

Cooper and Caleb are standing in the corner of the octagon and I'm in the middle facing Cobalt. We bump fists, and then the referee goes over the rules, separates us, and say says, "Ready, ready, fight" and moves out of the way.

Cobalt immediately opens with a leg kick. I see it coming and block it. He does another leg kick and this time I'm not fast enough. He gets the meat of my leg and it hurts like a bitch.

While he's good at striking, I've practiced Brazilian-Ju-Jitsu my entire life and know that to win I need to get him on the ground because that's where my strengths are. He has obviously studied me and knows that his only way of keeping up is to keep striking. I back up a bit to give myself some room.

He comes at me with a strike to my face and grazes my temple. I attempt to strike back but he hits me again right below my eye and I can feel the blood beginning to trickle down. I quickly strike back, rocking and tagging him and he hits the ground. I've got him. It'll be over in the next thirty seconds. I immediately jump on top of him and start throwing blows to his head. He attempts to cover his face, but it's over. The ref jumps between us and calls the fight. The announcer declares me the champion and the crowd goes fucking crazy. Women are screaming my name, but I only have my eyes on one woman—Kayla.

Cooper and Caleb run out to hug me as they raise my fist in the air, and then Hayley is pulling me toward her to clean up my cuts. I've won many times, but for some reason this win feels different. It feels like everything is finally coming together. If I could just get Kayla to give us a chance, everything would be perfect.

"TO BENTLEY!" WE'RE ALL AT A LOCAL CLUB PARTYING IT UP. I don't even know what round we're on at this point and it doesn't even fucking matter. I won my fight and it feels damn good. Kayla has been eyeing me all night and I'm afraid that soon I won't be able to resist her.

Before I can think further on the subject, she's handing me a shot and sprinkling salt on my wrist. She brings my wrist up to her mouth and licks it slowly. My dick goes hard at the sight of her tongue lapping my skin. She takes the shot out of my hand and downs it, and then takes a lime and puts it into her mouth to sucking it. Jesus. She's going to be the death of me.

She closes the space between us and pulls my neck down to her mouth. After sucking briefly on my neck, she whispers into my ear, "Let's get out of here."

I pull back and assess her. Her eyes aren't dilated and she's not sweating, so I don't think she's wasted, but I ask anyway because I know I'm fucked up right now.

"Are you drunk?"

She smiles wide and says, "Not nearly enough. Let's go."

She grabs my hand and pulls me down the hallway into the ladies' room. I should probably stop this, but I want her so badly. I don't think there's anything I wouldn't give this woman. The word no doesn't seem to exist when it comes to her.

She hops onto the sink and spreads her legs. Her short dress rides up, and when I bend down, I have a clear view of her bare pink pussy. The fucking woman isn't wearing anything under her dress. I pull her to the edge of the sink and begin stroking her clit with my tongue tasting her juices. She's already wet. I don't stand a chance against her, and she knows it. I insert a finger into her core and then another. She's riding my fingers while I continue to lick and suck on her clit.

"Damn, baby, you taste like heaven."

She doesn't say anything, but moans and moves her ass, riding my face with her pussy. I insert one more finger deep inside her and hit the spot I know gets her off. It does exactly what I predict, and within seconds she's coming all over my fingers and tongue. I suck her on her clit, drinking her juices while she comes down from her orgasm.

She grabs my shirt collar and pulls me up to her face.

"Fuck me, Bentley. Please, I need you inside of me now." She hops off the sink and begins to undo the button on my jeans and then works the zipper down.

"Are you sure, Kayla?" I've warned her repeatedly that if we make this jump we're both all in.

"Yes, I'm fucking sure!"

She pulls my face toward her and our mouths collide. When she tastes herself on my lips, she moans into my mouth. *My woman likes it dirty.*

"Kayla, if we do this, you're mine."

She tugs my jeans and boxers to my knees. "Just fuck me now."

And I do. I grab her ass and lift her. She wraps her legs around me and simultaneously wraps her arms around my neck. I push her up against the wall and thrust deep inside her.

"Holy shit, woman," I groan as her warmth and tightness grips my dick.

"Move, Bentley! Fuck me."

I start off slow, fucking her up against the wall. She lowers her shirt, exposing her perfect tits, and I latch onto her nipple with my teeth, sucking hard while I continue to pump in and out of her. I can feel her pussy contracting and know that she'll soon be chasing another orgasm.

I move my body closer to hers and nuzzle my face in her neck, getting close enough to go even deeper inside her. I can feel my orgasm building, so I angle my cock to hit her deep.

"Oh, yes. Bentley, right there. Yes!"

Her pussy tightens around my cock. She's close. I thrust deeper into her tight pussy as we both find our release.

Once we've come down from our highs, I move her back to the sink and set her down. I get a paper towel, wet it, and clean her up.

She sits and watches me and when I'm done I go to give her a kiss but she pulls back.

"What's wrong?" I ask nervously

"You're always so damn sweet to me."

"That's because I love you, Kayla." I take her face in my hands and try to make her understand. This woman means so much to me.

"Bentley, I can't do this." She's shaking her head back and forth and I know I'm losing her once again.

Is she fucking kidding me right now?

"Do what?" I hope I'm wrong, but my gut is telling me I already know the answer to my question.

"I know what you said, but it was in the heat of the moment. I wasn't thinking. You can't love me. You can't say shit like that to me. I'm not capable of love. I don't want love. I'm already a fucking disappointment to my mom as it is. The last thing I need to do is give her another reason to remind me how badly I always fuck up."

Fuck, she's freaking out. I never should have used those words with her. What the hell was I thinking? I can't take it back now.

"Are you serious, Kayla? You knew how I felt. You know how I feel about you. I know we've been drinking, but I fucking asked you. You said okay. Forget your mom, please. Listen to your heart, baby." My voice bounces off the walls, getting louder with every word I speak. I'm fucking hurt and desperate and beyond pissed that I can't make her see what we can have. I should have known she would pull this shit.

She looks at me with remorse in her eyes and says, "I'm sorry but I can't give you anything more."

I see red. I'm drunk and angry and so fucking upset that all I can see is red. If she were a guy, I would fucking deck her. I don't even know how to handle this. I punch the closest thing to me—a paper towel holder. It falls to the ground, making a loud clanking noise. Kayla jumps in fear. I need to walk away.

"Fuck this!" I shout in her face. "Fuck this and fuck you. I don't need this bullshit. You're right. You said you didn't want this and I ignored it thinking you would eventually come around to wanting more. I was wrong. Enjoy your lonely fucking life because I'm done." I slam my fist into the mirror behind her, shattering it to pieces and then storm out.

It's time for me to let go. It is clear she's never going to give us a chance.

IT'S BEEN ABOUT TWO MONTHS SINCE KAYLA AND I HOOKED up and a lot has changed, some good and some not so good. It's Christmas morning and we're standing in Cooper and Liz's new home, although it's more like a damn mansion, as he kisses her like nobody else is in the room. He just proposed and she said yes. On top of that, she announced that she's pregnant with their second child. I'm happy for them. I'm happy they found their forever. Their daughter Bella doesn't even know what's going on as she chases around her new puppy, Elsa, which she named after the movie *Frozen*. Don't look at me like that…I know Frozen. It may be because the adorable almost five-year-old made me watch it and nobody in their right mind says no to her, but the point is, I know the damn movie.

I look across the room and lock eyes with Kayla. She looks so sad. I would do anything to make her smile, but she doesn't want me to be the man for that job. I look to my left at the arm hooked with my own. The owner of that arm is my girlfriend Sophia. We've been dating for about a month now and it's going okay. She's not Kayla, but she's nice and attentive and wants a future with me. Now, I know what you're thinking. Why did I move on so quickly? Don't judge until you know the whole story…

It was a couple days before Thanksgiving and I had gotten off work and decided to meet Caleb at the local pub for a drink. I was walking through the door with my head down, staring at my phone. Kayla sent me a text saying she needed to talk to me so I was texting her back to find out when and where.

Kayla: ASAP

Me: I'm at Mitch's Pub. Do you want to come here?

Kayla: No, I'll just see you at the apartment.

Me: Okay

I wasn't looking where I was going when I ran into a woman walking toward the restrooms. I almost knocked her to the ground, but luckily I grabbed her arm and caught her before she hit the floor.

"I'm so sorry. I wasn't looking where I was going. Are you okay?"

She gave me a shy smile and nodded. She had pretty green eyes unlike Kayla's light blue and red hair that flowed down her back unlike Kayla's blond hair. She wasn't skinny and toned like Kayla, but had a body shaped like an hourglass. I realized I was comparing her to Kayla and that looks-wise they were exact opposites.

"It's okay. I was in a rush to wash my hands. I spilled my martini on me and my hands are all sticky."

She raised her hands up to show me the invisible stickiness while she scrunched up her nose in disgust. I chuckled at her cuteness.

"I'm Sophia."

"I'm Bentley. Nice to meet you."

"My friend and I are just having a drink at the bar. Would you like to join us?

Now, right here is where a smart man who has feelings for another woman would have said no and walked away, but I never claimed to be smart. I've spent weeks being turned down by Kayla and to be honest it was nice to have a woman who actually wanted to spend time with me.

"Sure. I'm meeting my friend though, so let me make sure it's okay with him."

"Okay, cool! And your friend is totally welcome as well.

She showed me where she and her friend were sitting and I told her I would come over either way to let her know if we would be joining them.

I found Caleb sitting at the bar only a few seats down and told him Sophia and her friend invited us over. He reluctantly said okay and we moved down the few seats to join them.

About thirty minutes later the girls were tipsy. Apparently, they had been drinking for quite a while. I heard a throat clear behind me and when I turned around I saw none other than Kayla standing with her hands on her hips. I didn't get her anger until I realized Sophia was practically sitting on my lap at this point.

"So, I take it you've moved on to your *new* happily-ever-after."

I don't get women and I don't think I ever will. If you really think about this logically, I've pursued the woman the entire time I've known her and been around her, and of course after she has pushed me away repeatedly she decides to get mad when I'm around another woman. It just doesn't make sense.

"We were just having a drink. I thought you said you wanted to talk at home."

"Never mind. I changed my mind. We don't need to talk."

I moved Sophia off my lap and went toward Kayla. This girl has me in fucking knots. I would give anything for her to just give me a chance but she just keeps dicking me around. There's only so much a man can take and I'm sick of acting like a fucking pussy.

"Look, I don't understand why you're mad. You have said repeatedly you don't want me. I'm just trying to move forward. Have you changed your mind?"

"No, like I said, never mind."

She turned around and walked out the door. I should have gone after her, but I was just so fucking tired by the back-and-forth bullshit.

Several hours later, Caleb and I headed home. Sophia asked for my number and I gave it to her. She seemed nice enough, and since she's the opposite of Kayla, maybe it would help me get over her.

I got home to find Kayla in her room with the door shut. I knocked but of course she ignored me. I went to bed and decided it was really time to move on. I couldn't keep doing this.

The next day I received a text from Sophia and replied. We started to text throughout the day and it felt good to text with someone who wasn't annoyed by me.

Kayla, Cooper, and Liz all took off to Florida for Thanksgiving and while talking to Sophia I learned she would be alone. I invited her to join me in Boulder to visit my parents, and Caleb ended up tagging along as well.

We had a good weekend. My parents seemed to like Sophia and she seemed to enjoy herself. A few times she complained about me wanting to spend so much time with my parents and not go out, but I let it go. I've learned most kids don't have the relationship with their parents that I have with mine.

We got back Sunday, and on Monday Sophia asked if I wanted to go to dinner. After I picked her up I realized I forgot my wallet, and instead of her offering to pay, she got an attitude, so I turned around to go home and get my wallet.

"I'll be right back." I jumped out of my car and sprinted back to the apartment. We made reservations and if I didn't hurry we would be late.

I got to the apartment, opened the door, and didn't bother to close it behind me since I would only be a minute. When I came out of my room I saw Sophia and Kayla squaring off.

While glaring at Sophia, Kayla said, "Seriously? You couldn't leave the trash outside?" Whoa! I wasn't sure what her deal was, but she clearly had her claws out and ready to fight.

Before I could get between them, Sophia lunged at Kayla. I grabbed Sophia by the waist and spun her around. Then I looked at Kayla with a *what the fuck* expression on my face.

"Whatever," she hissed before retreating back to her room.

After that day, Caleb came to me and told me Kayla was moving out. As much as I wanted to stop her, I figured it was for the best. I sure as fuck couldn't make her happy, so maybe she would find happiness elsewhere.

I also decided not to bring Sophia to my apartment anymore. Since Kayla would be moving out soon there was no point in starting unnecessary drama.

Now it's Christmas and from what I've heard from Caleb, Kayla has decided to move back to Florida. I'm staring at the girl I know deep down my heart wants and it feels like it's shattering into pieces. I know I have Sophia with me and that we're dating, but I can't help feel like when Kayla leaves, she's ripping my heart out and taking it with her. I can't make her believe in love. I can't make her want a future with me. I can't make her want to give us a chance. All I can do is have faith that maybe one day our paths will cross again and she'll feel the same way I do. I know it's not fair to Sophia, so I make the decision that starting today I'm going to give her my all. The only problem is, my all is nothing more than a broken, mangled heart.

Seven

BENTLEY

Present Day

EVERYBODY IS STARING IN SILENCE, SOPHIA LOOKS LIKE SHE'S about to kill someone and is muttering a string of curse words, and Kayla still hasn't answered my question.

I completely ignore Sophia and ask again. "Is the baby mine?"

I can feel Sophia start to shake and know she's about to explode, so I turn to her and put my hand over her mouth. "Shh…I'm asking Kayla a question. Give me a damn minute." I know it's wrong to lose my patience with her, but I'm a little more concerned with the fact that the woman I was with a few months ago with no protection is standing in her doorway pregnant. I'll deal with Sophia's temper tantrum later.

I turn back to Kayla to ask her for a third time, when she answers. "Yes, I'm pregnant, and yes, you are the father." Liz gasps in the background, but nobody says anything.

"Cooper and I have decided to get married June twentieth. That's why we're here. When you wouldn't join us in Miami, we decided to come to you." Leave it to Liz to break the tension.

"Are you serious right now?" Sophia hisses. She's obviously not about to let this go.

"Soph, chill out."

"No! Are we all just going to stand here and act like this skank didn't just tell you she's pregnant with your kid when you've been with me the last three months? Who gives a shit about when those two are getting married?"

"I don't know who you think you're calling a skank, but I'll knock your ass out if you call me a skank again, and Cooper and Liz getting married is a big deal. So don't ever talk negatively about my best friend again. You need to get the hell off my property." Kayla is fuming and I need to speak to her alone. Nothing is going to get accomplished with

Kayla and Sophia anywhere near each other.

I give Liz a *please help me* look and thankfully she gets it.

"I understand this is a shock to everyone, so I'm going to ignore your comment about my wedding. Why don't we all go to the car and give Bentley and Kayla a minute?" She puts her hand on Sophia's back, but she moves out of the way.

"It's probably not even your kid, Bentley. You need to get a paternity test. All she wants you for is your money."

Kayla growls, and I quickly attempt to diffuse the situation before Kayla kicks Sophia's ass.

"Soph, please just go with Liz and everyone. I'll be there in a minute."

She huffs and stomps away with everyone except Caleb. He stays staring at Kayla for a second and she walks up to him and gives him a hug. I know they became close while she was living with us, but I hate that he gets to hug her and I can't.

"Congratulations on your contract with the UFC and on your amazing win," Kayla says.

"Thank you. Congratulations on your baby," Caleb says while continuing to hug her. I never see him touch women let alone hug them.

Kayla pulls away and wipes a tear that's falling down her cheek. "Thank you. You know, you better get prepared because you'll be this baby's Godfather."

If I'm not mistaken, I see tears pool in Caleb's eyes as well, but he just nods his head and walks back to the car.

"Wow, after the baby is born it looks like you'll have two children." Kayla smirks, her eyes lighting up with silent laughter as she refers to Sophia as my child. This is her defense mechanism. I've seen it a hundred times and decide to ignore her comment.

I move closer to her without even thinking about it. When she's near me, it's like we're two magnets and I can't help but gravitate toward her.

She swallows hard at my closeness as she tries to look away. I put my thumb and forefinger on her chin and turn her face toward mine. I look into her eyes and see a mixture of emotions. Fear and nervousness, mixed with a little bit of sadness, but my strong girl doesn't let those cling to her for long. Her final emotion is anger. It's her go-to emotion. It's what keeps her strong. If I want answers, I'm going to have to handle her with care.

"When are you due?"

"End of July."

"I thought you were on birth control." It doesn't make sense how this happened.

"Yeah, I was. But then Liz decided not to get her shot and she always scheduled the appointments for us to go together, so I forgot to go, and then when I went to go, they said I was pregnant. I'm sorry."

"Were you going to tell me?" I keep my tone neutral, not letting my frustration show.

"The baby isn't due for several months. We can figure out visitation once the baby comes. I plan to breastfeed so it will be awhile until you can take the baby anyway. I wasn't keeping the baby from you. I just figured until she comes I wouldn't bother you."

She's rambling on, so I know she's nervous. Her face is close to mine, but her eyes are darting everywhere but at me. I turn my face a little to catch her eyes and lock them in place.

"Kayla, you could never bother me. Do you really think I would be okay not knowing about the baby until after she's born?"

"No, I just needed time to figure it out. I went to…" And before she can finish, I hear Sophia coming up the walkway talking some more shit.

"Bentley, I hope you aren't believing a word she's saying. She's conning you. Why can't you see that?" She turns to Kayla. "Once you have a paternity test then we can talk about all this."

She grabs my hand to go, and before I can shake her off me, Kayla glares and slams the door in our faces.

"What the fuck?" I stare at Sophia, shocked at the person I'm seeing. I know this must be a shock to her as well, but I don't get why she's acting so nasty toward Kayla.

The plane ride home is long. Sophia is cuddled into my lap, and even though I'm seriously pissed at the way she acted, I don't bother to push her away. Liz keeps shooting glances my way and I keep looking elsewhere. I know she wants answers, but the truth is I have more questions than answers at this point. All I can think about is that Kayla is carrying my baby. I know Sophia thinks I should get a paternity test, but I know deep down this baby is mine. Kayla isn't like that. She wouldn't say a baby is mine if it wasn't.

I just don't understand why she would move to Florida to be with her parents instead of staying in Vegas with Liz. Her parents are not the nurturing kind and, while I'm sure they would support her, Kayla is independent. She doesn't need anyone. Well, actually, she does, but she would never admit that. Why would she think it's okay to hide a pregnancy from me until the baby is here? I get I can't do anything about it while the baby is in her belly, but I still deserved to know. The more I think, the madder I get. I have a feeling Kayla ran from Vegas to get away from me.

One thing is for sure is when I get off this plane, I'll be giving Kayla a call so we can talk.

Eight

KAYLA

HOLY SHIT! MY HEART IS STILL BEATING A MILLION MILES AN hour and it's been hours since everybody left. I was not expecting nor was I prepared for any of this. When Bentley stood inches away from me and touched my chin, I almost lost it. It felt so good to be touched by someone, especially him. I almost gave in. I almost admitted that I wanted to tell him but chickened out when I saw him with Sophia that day at the bar. I know it's my fault. I had my chance, but this just proves my mom's theory. One shouldn't base decisions off love. Both times I went to tell Bentley about the baby, Sophia was there and I didn't want to mess things up for Bentley. I might not be able to stand her, but I can't blame her for being pissed. She got into a relationship thinking it was just Bentley and her, only to find out it's her and Bentley plus baby and baby mama.

After I finish making my sandwich—I have now changed my mind to bananas and mayo—don't knock it until you've tried it—I go back to lying by the pool under the umbrella. I must fall asleep because I wake up to my phone ringing. The caller ID says it's Liz and I internally groan.

Might as well get this over with.

"Hello."

"Hello? That's what you have to say all nonchalantly like I didn't just find out a few hours ago that my best fucking friend is pregnant!"

"I'm sorry?" I say it like a question because I'm not sure what to say.

"Sorry?" I hear Liz's voice break and I know she's about to start crying.

"I'm sorry, Liz. I didn't know what to do, so I ran. I couldn't tell you because I couldn't ask you to keep that secret from Cooper."

"How far along are you?"

"I'm due July 22nd."

The phone goes silent and then I hear a loud squeal.

"Oh. My. God! Kayla! Our babies are going to be like a week apart. Please tell me you're coming home so we can raise them together."

"I'm home, Liz. Las Vegas isn't my home anymore. I'll be back for your wedding, though. You know I wouldn't miss that. However, I'm not moving back to Vegas."

She's quiet for a long beat and then I hear sniffling. "Kayla, your home is here with me and Bella and this new baby. Please don't do this. I need you. You really want to raise the baby around your parents? I can't imagine your mom is thrilled to be a grandmother. I remember all too well the way she acted when she found out I was pregnant. You belong here, in Las Vegas with me. Please."

Damn her and her guilt trips.

"And just so you know, Bentley is seriously pissed at Sophia. I wouldn't be surprised if they break up soon. He was totally scolding her, telling her to never call you names again. I don't even know why he's with her. I think he's just using her to get over you. "

My heart warms a bit at the thought of Bentley defending me, and I won't deny that the image of him dumping her makes me a little giddy inside. He can do so much better than her bitchy ass. It sucks that he still hasn't dumped her. What the hell? Why do I even care whether he's with her or not? Oh, I know why. Because I'm a stubborn bitch who is in love with Bentley but is too afraid to give him my heart because I don't want to get hurt again.

"I'll be there for your wedding. Why in the world are you having it so close to your due date anyway?"

"It's the only weekend before the baby comes that there isn't a fight or event going on. I just have to pray this little guy stays in here until after we say, 'I do'." She giggles and it makes me smile. I love to see her happy. My heart tightens because I miss her so much and wish I could see her and be pregnant with her. Liz found out a week ago the baby is a boy, and both her and Cooper are over the moon. I have an appointment next week for an ultrasound and I'm hoping to find out the sex. I think it's a girl, though. I just hate that I'll be doing it alone even if I only have myself to blame for that.

I clear my throat to compose myself. "I'll book my flight now."

"Okay! I can't wait to see you. I love you, Kayla."

"Me, too," I say with as much energy as I can muster up.

While I'm enjoying my sandwich, my phone rings again. This time it's Caleb. While I was living with Bentley and Caleb, we became close.

"Hey there, good looking," I say, hoping to keep it light.

I hear him breathe loudly into the phone and then he says, "Damn Kayla, it hurts you couldn't tell me, but I think I always knew."

My chest constricts. Liz let me off the hook, but Caleb's response makes me realize how badly I messed up running away. My actions are hurting other people.

"I'm sorry. I got scared."

"I get it. I do. But damn, you could have told me. You made it seem like you just couldn't be around Bentley anymore."

I think back to the night I told Caleb I was going to move to Florida.

I was sitting on the couch watching television with Caleb. It was a movie about a woman who is in love with a guy. She had her chance with him but blew it. She has to return years later to attend a funeral and sees that he's married with kids. She's forced to watch him happily kiss his wife and play with his kids. It made me feel sick.

I knew it was my fault that Bentley was dating Sophia. I could have been with him but allowed my fear of being wrong about love keep me away from Bentley, which gave him the opening to move forward.

"Do you believe in love, Caleb?"

He turned to me, lifting his one brow in question.

"Well, do you?"

"I don't know, Kayla. I haven't experienced it myself, so I just don't know."

"I think I'm going to move back to Florida."

He sat up and moved closer to me, looking angry. "Why? Why would you move so far away?"

"Caleb, please don't tell anybody this, but I'm in love with Bentley."

Caleb's head flew back as he laughed loudly, shaking his head back and forth.

"Kayla, we all know you're in love with Bentley. Look, Bentley told me a little about your mom and I get where you're coming from. Bentley has an amazingly close family. We all don't have that..."

He stopped like he was lost in thought and I wanted to ask him about his family but felt like if he wanted me to know he would tell me.

"I just can't bring myself to be with him. He deserves more than I can give him. I'm broken, while he's perfect."

"I understand being broken, Kayla. But I don't think Bentley cares that you're broken. I think he accepts you just the way you are."

I thought about this for a few minutes and knew he was right but didn't think I could handle if he ever decided he wanted someone who wasn't broken like me. I didn't think I could handle it if I had to listen to my mom tell me I told you so once again.

"I really appreciate our friendship, Caleb." I gave him a small smile as I felt the tears well up. I didn't know when I would see Caleb again.

He nodded. "I don't trust women, Kayla, but I trust you. I don't agree with you leaving, but I get it, and I'm going to miss you."

He moved his hand to mine and patted it softly. Caleb never gave hugs or got close with women, so him patting my hand was kind of a big deal and I knew it. He left his hand there while we watched the woman continue to have her heart broken over and over again. The truth is she only had herself to blame and I could completely relate. I knew I was probably making the wrong choice, but I didn't know how else to protect my heart.

"Are you mad at me, Caleb?" I ask through the phone, praying he isn't. I know he doesn't trust women, and what I did doesn't help the way he would view a woman.

"Oh, Kayla, I'm not mad. I'm hurt but I get it. You ran. You were scared. I can't judge you because me and you are a lot alike. I just don't like to see Bentley hurting. He's a damn good guy."

"I left so I wouldn't hurt him,"

"No, you didn't. You left so he couldn't hurt *you*. There's a difference. Own up to your shit, Kayla."

I can't argue with him. I told myself I was leaving so Bentley could be happy and create a life with a woman who deserves him, but the truth is, I did run. I ran because if I would have stayed he would have wanted a life with me and I didn't want to take the chance of opening my heart up and getting hurt.

Nine

BENTLEY

Me: When is your next doctor's appointment?

Kayla: In two days. Why?

Me: I'm flying out to go. I'll pick you up so we can go together. What time?

Kayla: You don't have to...2 p.m.

Me: I'll be there.

Kayla: Okay

IT'S BEEN ALMOST A WEEK SINCE I FOUND OUT KAYLA IS pregnant, and to say shit has been rocky is an understatement. Things between Sophia and I have gone from okay, to bad, to downright awful. She's currently sitting in my living room watching some stupid reality television show. I know I have to tell her I'm flying out to join Kayla for her doctor's appointment but I also know it's going to lead to an argument and I'm so sick of arguing with her. The past week, every time I text Kayla to see how she's doing, Sophia turns it into an argument.

"Bentley, who are you texting with?" Sophia asks without looking away from the show.

"Kayla. I'm flying out tomorrow to meet her for her doctor's appointment. I should be back in a few days."

She whips her head around and glares at me. "What? You don't even know if the baby is yours! And if you're going, so am I."

"Sophia, I'm not having this argument with you again. I believe Kayla when she says the baby is mine and I'm going to be in his or her life until proven otherwise. I don't think you going would be a good idea. I can't imagine stress is good for the baby."

At this moment, Caleb walks in from the gym, throwing his gear to the side next to the door.

"What's up?" He looks at me, completely ignoring Sophia.

"Nothing much. I'm flying out tomorrow to meet Kayla for an OB appointment. I think we're going to see the baby through ultrasound or some shit."

"Damn, I miss that girl. This place feels so empty without her. Give her a hug for me, please."

Caleb is one of my best friends, but one thing about Caleb is he doesn't talk much, so when he does, it has meaning, and right now I'm getting his meaning loud and clear.

Sophia crosses her arms over her chest and pouts like a child. "Kayla is a nasty slut and the best thing that could happen was her moving away. Why am I the only one who sees the real her?"

Ah, shit. She just had to go there. Caleb is loyal to a fault and he absolutely adores Kayla. This isn't going to be good.

He walks up to her and rakes his gaze up and down her like he's checking her out, but not in a good way, more of a who-the-fuck-do-you-think-you-are way.

"I get you're Bentley's girl, so I've made sure to be nice to you out of respect for him. I listen to you whine and bitch over everything every time you're here, but I ignore it. I listened to you talk shit about my friend in Florida and I let it go because I let Bentley handle it, but now you're in my home and talking shit about one of my best friends and I'm done listening to it. Kayla has made some shitty choices, but she's still a thousand times more of a woman than you'll ever be."

I can tell he's losing his patience with her, so I cut him off. The fact is I've had enough of all this. I need to focus on my baby and Kayla.

"Caleb, can you give Sophia and me some time alone?"

He simply nods and walks to his room, closing the door.

"He's such an asshole. You seriously have the worst friends, Bentley."

"I beg to disagree. Look, Sophia, this just isn't working. I need to focus on my baby and I just don't feel like we're clicking anymore."

She puts her hand on her hip and curls her lip in annoyance. "You mean you have to focus on Kayla?"

"At this point, the baby and Kayla are one in the same. It doesn't even matter. I just know that I can't focus on you."

"Whatever! You'll regret this. She doesn't even want you." She walks around the room and grabs her belongings. She doesn't have much here. I never let her leave anything nor have I offered her a drawer or storage of any kind. I think I always knew it wouldn't work out, but I was so hurt over Kayla I latched on to the closest woman.

She slams the door on her way out and I sit on the couch finally taking a deep, cleansing breath.

Caleb walks out and looks around for Sophia.

"Is she gone?"

"Yeah, she is."

"Good. Bro, how you went from a woman like Kayla to a spoiled little girl like Sophia is beyond me."

"I think that's why I did it. They're exact opposites. I love Kayla so damn much, and I think in the back of my head I knew whoever I was with wouldn't be permanent because Kayla is all I want."

He nods slowly. "Makes sense. Look, Kayla is fragile. She comes across as being tough, but she has a lot of shit going on inside her head. Just go easy on her."

I nod knowing he's right. I'm glad him and Kayla have developed a friendship.

"Have you spoken to her?"

"Yeah, she's a mess. So when do you leave?"

"Tomorrow morning. I think I'm going to hit the gym. How's the training coming along for the fight?"

"Good. I'm working with Kaden more since Cooper semi-retired. He's working me hard. I'm hoping this upcoming fight will help me make a name for myself. Every single person I've fought and beaten has been minor compared to this guy."

"You got this shit, bro." We fist bump and I take off to the gym.

Ten

KAYLA

I'M NERVOUSLY RUNNING AROUND GETTING READY FOR MY doctor's appointment. I've been to every appointment by myself and today Bentley will be joining me. We'll also be seeing the baby through ultrasound and hopefully finding out the sex. He sent me a text this morning to let me know he has arrived and is staying at the Jupiter Beach Resort right down the street from my house, which means he isn't planning to fly back tonight.

I didn't have the guts to ask him if he's still with his girlfriend and if so, if she's with him. I know if my man were flying across the country to go hang out with his baby mama I would be right there by his side. Of course that's just one more reason why I'm single.

There's a knock on the door and I'm so thankful everybody in my house is gone. When I told my mom that Bentley was coming she gave me a huge lecture on not allowing him to steer my emotions. She knows now that I'm definitely not giving the baby up for adoption, but she has made it clear how bad of an idea she thinks it would be for Bentley and me to get together.

When I open it up, Bentley's standing there. He's dressed in a white collared polo shirt that's tight enough to see the definition of his biceps and muscles but still loose enough that you can only imagine what's underneath. Of course I'm one of the lucky ones that have gotten to see what's underneath and it is pure. Fucking. Perfection. He's wearing dark blue jeans and Nikes. He's the epitome of sex. His hair is grown out just enough that I could pull on it while his face is buried deep between my legs. What the heck am I thinking? It's got to be the pregnancy hormones. I've been turned on like crazy lately. I swear I'm going to have to buy batteries for my vibrator in bulk at this point.

I look into his beautiful dark blue eyes and see laughter. Shaking my head, I try to snap out of my mini-lust daydream but it's too late. It's like he can read my mind.

"You can have this any time you want."

Laughing at his insinuation, I play it cool. "I don't think your girlfriend will be too keen on that idea. Or are you thinking a threesome? She's got quite a temper; I bet she likes it rough in bed."

He closes the space between us and pushes me gently against the door. "One, I don't have a girlfriend. Two, the only person I want to discuss being in bed with me is you. And three, I have no desire to share you with anybody else, man or woman. Got it?"

Well, hot damn. Maybe I won't need my vibrator after all…

"Have you been with anybody since you left?"

For a second I consider lying to him. I hate that Bentley has been with another woman since me, but I go with the truth because I always tell it like it is, and I'm not going to change who I am now.

"No, unlike you, I've only been with one person in the last year and that person is you."

He sighs and shakes his head. "I can't take back being with Sophia. I was hurt by your rejection. You have to know that she'll never compare to you. Nobody will, but fuck, what am I supposed to do when you won't give us a real chance?"

Whoa! Shit is getting way too deep. Time to change the subject.

"Oh, stop. We weren't even together. You can sleep with anybody you want. Yeah, we have crazy chemistry, but it's just sex, Bentley."

He smiles when I mention our chemistry, but it quickly morphs into a frown when I add that last tidbit in, and I immediately want to take it back. I hate to see him sad. It feels like my cold, icy heart thaws just a little bit every time he's around being so sweet to me.

He wraps his arms around my waist. "We're having a baby together, Kayla. You're stuck with me for life. That means I have the rest of our lives to convince you that it's okay to love me. It's okay to have feelings. What that guy did to you was wrong. I don't know what happened, but whatever he did, he was an immature little boy who didn't deserve your heart. And what your mom said was way the fuck wrong. Parents should encourage love not discourage it. One day you'll give me your heart, baby, and it will be nothing short of amazing because love is a beautiful thing."

He gives me a soft kiss on my cheek and then moves me from the door, closing it so we can leave to my appointment. He doesn't even wait for a reply, and that's probably a good thing because what the heck would I say to that? Everything he says is true, but it doesn't stop me from still being afraid.

We arrive at the doctor's office at two on the dot. I sign in and we have a seat in the waiting room. A very pregnant woman with two little kids is sitting just to the left of us. Her kids are playing with blocks and she's rubbing her huge belly.

"Do you want more kids?" I don't know what comes over me when

I blurt out this question. I swear I'm blaming all my craziness on my pregnancy hormones.

Bentley grins at me. "Damn, woman, you're still pregnant with our first kid and you're already thinking about having more?"

I smack him on his shoulder and he just laughs. "No! I was just curious how many you plan to have. You are an only child."

"Well, I guess that depends on you. How many do you want?"

I roll my eyes but answer. "I have one brother, but we aren't close. I kind of wish we were. I think it would be nice to have a couple kids. "

He nods and then leans in to me. "Once you admit that you love me, I'll give you as many kids as you want."

I chuckle at that and then smirk. "I'm pretty sure all I need to do is get you drunk and find a bathroom like the last time."

"Kayla, that shit isn't cool." His features are no longer carefree but brooding. I was only joking, but it's clear he doesn't think it's funny.

Once my name is called, we go to the ultrasound room and I get undressed below my waist, lie down on the bed, and leave my stomach bare. The ultrasound tech comes in and says hello while squirting the blue gunk on my belly to do the ultrasound.

Within seconds I hear the *Whoosh. Whoosh. Whoosh*, making me smile. Bentley looks confused, so I explain to him what he's hearing. "That's her heartbeat."

His gaze becomes mesmerized and in awe as he glances from my belly and back to the screen several times.

"So amazing." His lips curl into the biggest grin like he's already in love with her, and I feel like such a piece of shit for attempting to keep all this from him. He deserves to watch our baby grow. She's as much his as she is mine.

"You said baby girl. Did you already find out the sex?" the ultrasound tech asks.

"No, it's just a mother's intuition."

"Well, do you want to know if your intuition is correct?"

I glance at Bentley and he gives me a small smile letting me know he's okay with finding out the sex.

"Yes, please!"

She moves the doppler around my stomach, then stops and presses some buttons to zoom in and get a clearer picture.

"See those three lines right there? You're having a little girl and she's growing right on track with your due date. You were right about your mother's intuition. I'll take a couple screen shots for the doctor to look over more thoroughly and print some up for you to take home."

"Thank you."

"Um, miss," Bentley says to the tech. "Can you print some up for both of us, please? I would like to have some." Bentley looks so uncomfortable asking because it means we aren't going to the same home. I doubt she knows that, but I know that's why he's asking, and I feel horrible. But how do I change the way I feel? How do I open my heart up and risk getting hurt again? I know what happened to me was when I was younger, but the concept doesn't change once you're an adult. If I give me heart to Bentley, I risk being hurt, only this time the stakes are higher because now we have a daughter on the way.

"Sure thing," the tech says brightly.

After I get dressed and she gives us the photos, we head out. I'm thinking Bentley will take me straight home but instead he stops at an Italian restaurant down the street from the OB's office.

"Is this okay? I figured you might be hungry and it's almost dinner time."

"Yeah, sounds good." I feel so guilty I'd probably agree to anything the man wants right now.

We walk into the restaurant and my eyes go straight to the boy—well technically now he's a man—that broke my heart. What are the freaking odds of seeing him here?

Eleven

BENTLEY

THIS AFTERNOON HAS BEEN AMAZING. GETTING TO SEE OUR precious little girl on the ultrasound screen and hearing her heartbeat is nothing short of a miracle. When Kayla threw it in my face that it was just drunken sex that created our baby, I wanted to punch something, but I let it go. Sometimes when I look at Kayla I think she might be coming around, but then she closes up, and it feels like I have to start again from square one.

We walk into the restaurant for an early dinner at a local Italian restaurant I looked up and read good things about. Kayla is in front of me, and when she stops short before making it to the hostess stand, I run right into her, then grab her from behind to make sure she doesn't fall over.

"Kayla Peterson, is that you?"

A sleazy-looking guy walks up to us, never taking his eyes off Kayla.

"It is you! How are you? What's it been like, ten years?"

I'm still holding onto her and can feel her entire body tense when he speaks to her. I wait for her to say something and when she doesn't, I take over.

"I'm Bentley, and you are?" I hold my hand out to shake his and he shakes mine in return.

"Oh, shit! Aren't you the UFC Fighter? I watched your fight a few months back. My name is Jake."

Kayla is still standing there frozen in place so I continue talking to this guy. "Yeah, that's me. So how do you know Kayla?"

Yeah, I'm talking like she isn't even here, but I don't know what else to do. She isn't saying shit,

"We hung out for a little bit back in high school. Fun times."

"Fun times?" Kayla practically shrieks.

Okay. I guess she's found her voice and it doesn't sound like she would agree with the term fun.

"Fun times?" she repeats. "I wouldn't call you pretending to like me just so you could have sex with me and then dump me right afterward fun times! I wouldn't call you spreading it all over social media fun times, either! Or how about when I told you I loved you and in return you laughed at me and left? Was that fun for you? Because it sure as hell wasn't fun for me! Oh! And how about afterward, when I had to spend the next three years going to school with guys that just wanted me for sex since you told everybody how easy I was before you left for the summer and then ended up moving away? Nope, definitely wouldn't call any of those *fun times.*"

Suddenly it's all making sense—Kayla not believing in love, the guy who broke her heart who she refuses to speak of, her listening to her mom when she told her love doesn't belong in a relationship. The guy who helped make her who she is today is standing right in front of me, with his eyes wide open like the scared little pussy he is, and it's taking everything in me not to deck him straight in his face for everything he's done to Kayla.

"Look, Kayla..." he begins, but I've had enough, so I cut in. I'm not about to sit here and listen to his excuses.

"No, you don't have shit to say to her. I think you did enough. Take your punk ass out of this restaurant and don't even think about this woman again. As a matter of fact, if you ever even see her again you walk the other way. Got me?" I don't bother waiting for his answer. I take Kayla by the hand and lead her to the podium to request a table.

When we sit down, she's visibly shaking. I could ask her to tell me about what happened, but based on what she said to him, I can piece it together enough to know that piece of shit used her for sex and then dumped her. I do have one thing I need to say, though.

"Look, I know you probably don't want to talk about what just happened or what happened all those years ago, but I just need to say one thing."

I wait for her to agree then I continue. "It sucks that I didn't meet you before him because if I would've met you before that asshole, I would have had your heart, and my guess is, it would still be intact and perfect because I would've handled it with care. You may not admit it, but what we have is more than just sex and it didn't just start recently. It started six damn years ago and if I had had you before he tore your heart to shreds and you let your mom get under your skin, I wouldn't have taken it for granted. I'll never take you for granted.

"Every day you live a lie trying to convince yourself love isn't real, you're letting him win. I'm not going to give up on you. Until you're ready to give us a real chance I'll have enough faith for the both of us. I'm here, Kayla, and I'm not going anywhere." I give her a second to let it all sink in and then say, "Now let's eat some food. I'm starving."

She smiles and nods, and I know she gets it.

Twelve

BENTLEY

"SWEETIE, I'M SO GLAD YOU BROKE UP WITH THAT SOPHIA girl."

My mom and dad are in town for the wedding. They're staying at a hotel for the weekend, so I met them at the restaurant attached to the hotel for dinner.

"If you didn't like her why didn't you say something?"

"We just want you happy, Bentley. It isn't our place to judge. How are Kayla and the baby?"

After I found out Kayla was pregnant, I immediately called my parents to let them know. As an only child, my mom has been waiting for the day she'll get a grandchild. Since I told her Kayla is having a girl she has sent me packages of girl shit every day. I hope Kayla allows my mom to be a part of this baby's life. I can't imagine why she wouldn't, though. While Kayla and I still aren't together, we have reached a new understanding. I've flown to Florida for every doctor's appointment and we've reached a level of comfort where we actually laugh and talk and joke around. I can feel her opening up, but she just isn't quite there yet.

I've brought up our living arrangements, but she's hell-bent on living in Florida. I think the lack of affection in her childhood home makes her feel safe because she doesn't have to deal with emotions with her family. Caleb has told me I'm welcome to use the third bedroom as a nursery until I figure out what I'm going to do, so I currently have a crib, bassinet, rocking chair, and other essentials in the room that I'll need for the baby. I know it's wishful thinking that I'll convince Kayla to move here with the baby, but even if she's willing to visit, I want to have everything she needs for her here.

"I think she's good. She flew in today for the wedding as well. Her parents are busy so they won't be going. Work always comes first for them. She flew with Liz's family so at least she wasn't alone on the flight."

"Isn't that her?" I look over to see a very pregnant Kayla walking past the restaurant by herself toward the lobby. While my mom has never met Kayla in person, I've shown her numerous pictures of her.

I jump out of my seat and run over to her.

"Hey!" She looks at me for a moment, confused as to why I'm here.

"My mom and dad are staying here. We just sat down for dinner. Want to join us?"

She looks nervous, and I can tell she's about to say no when my mom walks over to introduce herself. She gives Kayla a hug like she's known her for years. At first Kayla stiffens, but then she relaxes.

"I'm sorry! You don't even know who I am and I'm over here hugging you! I just feel like I know you already from all the pictures Bentley has shown me of you, and I swear the boy never stops talking about you or the baby. My name is Kathleen. I'm Bentley's mom. The man over there is Ryan, his dad. Do you mind?"

She looks down at Kayla's very pregnant belly wanting to touch it.

"Mom..." I begin, but Kayla cuts me off, giving me a small smile.

"No, it's okay. Go ahead. It's rock hard. She's definitely outgrowing her space in here." She giggles a little and it makes my heart beat faster. She's so damn beautiful.

"Oh, how precious! I can't wait to meet her. Have you seen all the stuff we've sent to Bentley for the baby? If there's anything you don't like, just let me know. Everything is returnable. I just couldn't help myself. Our first grandchild! This is so exciting."

Kayla looks at me with a questioning glance. I've told my mom Kayla is living in Florida, and she knows we aren't together, but I haven't told Kayla about all the stuff I have for the baby.

Kayla gives her another small smile. "Thank you. I'm sure everything is lovely."

My mom gives me a questioning look but doesn't say anything in return. Instead she says, "We are just about to eat. Please say you'll join us. I would love to get to know you better."

Leave it to my mom to ask without actually asking. Kayla obviously can't say no to my mom because she nods and we head back to the table.

My mom introduces Kayla to my dad and then we all order.

"So, Kayla. Have you thought of any names yet?" my mom asks, attempting to keep the conversation light.

"Not really. I'm hoping it will come to me once I see her."

"I'm sure it will. I wasn't sure what we were going to name Bentley until I saw him. Will your parents be there for the delivery?"

"No, I don't think so. They're really busy at work. I'm living with them and they've offered to hire a nanny to help me in the beginning. I found a job near me, but I won't be starting until six weeks after the baby is born. There was no point in starting now and then have to take off once I have her."

"I know we just met, but would it be okay if I was there? I would be honored to be a part of the delivery, and maybe we could stay for a couple weeks?"

"You would fly all the way to Florida just to see the delivery?" Kayla asks with a mixture of shock and awe in her voice.

"Of course we would! I know Bentley will be there and I don't want to intrude, but this is our first grandbaby. I want to see her as much as possible." And this is why I love my mom. She doesn't judge. She just opens her arms for anybody.

"What the hell? I should have guessed this is how it would end." We all turn our heads to see Sophia standing there with her friends. Her hands are on her hips and she looks like she just smelled something rotten. Now that I'm thinking about it, maybe that's just her permanent facial expression. Knowing this is one of Sophia's favorite places to eat, it doesn't surprise me that she's here.

I can see Kayla clam up, not wanting any issues in front of my parents.

"Hello there, Sophia," my mom says. "I'm sorry but we're having dinner. If you need to speak to Bentley, can you please do it another time? I'm getting to know Kayla and the stress isn't good for the baby." *Go Mom!*

Sophia glares at my mom and then around the table, and luckily, deciding this isn't a battle she's going to win, walks away.

"Now where were we?" She gives Kayla a wink and continues talking about the baby. Kayla visibly relaxes and actually starts to speak comfortably with everyone.

After dinner my parents not so subtly retreat back to their room, leaving Kayla and me alone at the table.

"Your parents are really nice, and I swear the entire meal they couldn't keep their hands off each other. It was so adorable." Kayla laughs and I join in. I know I should be embarrassed at my parents' public displays of affection, but I'm not.

"Yeah, I wasn't kidding when I said they still act like teenagers."

There is a short pause and I decide to just say what is on my mind. "I want us to be together."

She gasps and then quickly collects herself. "Bentley, you just got out of a relationship a few months ago, and we're getting along great as friends. Why mess with something that is working?"

"Just because it's working doesn't mean it's for the best. Sure, a Kia will get you from point A to point B but have you ever driven in a Ferrari?"

"Yeah, well I don't think either of us can afford the Ferrari. At least the Kia won't break my bank account."

I move my seat toward her and put my hand on her thigh. She shivers, and I can feel her skin goose bump. I love that I can do that to her. I know she feels what I feel, but she's just so damn stubborn.

"Is there more than what you're telling me?"

She looks a bit taken back at my question, but after a few seconds she answers softly. "Look, Bentley. My mom warned me all those years ago I would get hurt if I lived my life through my heart, and she was right. I had to listen to her tell me how right she was and what an embarrassment I was to the family. I told myself I would never put myself in that position again. Now I'm pregnant and living with my mom listening to her once again tell me how right she was. I can't handle it. You just don't get it."

So it's not just about getting hurt. It's also seeking the approval of her mom. A mom that wouldn't know what love was if it smacked her in the head. I know how it feels to want the approval of your parents. The problem is her mom is only hurting her with her negative notions about love.

"Please. Just have a little faith in us. I can afford the Ferrari and it won't break your bank account. I promise. I know you were hurt, but isn't what we could have together worth the risk? Your mom is wrong about love and you don't need her approval. We can have what my parents have. We can be happy."

She bites her bottom lip so hard it begins to turn white, so I take my thumb and pull it out from her teeth.

"Can I think about it?"

"That's what you said all those years ago on the beach before you ran for your life."

She throws her head back and laughs. "That's true. I did say that and then ran. But I'm not running this time. I promise."

"Okay, will you go to the wedding with me? I know you'll be there with Liz as her maid-of-honor, but will you be my date as well?"

"Okay."

After we finish eating dessert I walk her up to her hotel room. When we get to the door I can tell she's torn as to whether or not to invite me inside. She has her eyes nervously darting everywhere besides at me. After a few seconds, she mumbles something that I can't hear.

"What?" I ask, refusing to give her an out.

This time she speaks loud enough for me to hear but still at a whisper. "Um, do you want to come in and watch a movie or something?"

"Sure, sounds good."

We head into the living room area and have a seat while she excuses herself to go change into something more comfortable. When she comes back she's in a cute matching two-piece pajama set. The tank top rides up and shows a small piece of her belly.

She looks down at herself shyly. "I swear it fit better the other day.

It feels like I'm getting bigger by the minute."

"Pregnancy suits you."

"Oh, she's kicking!" She comes over and sits right up against me then takes my hand and places it on her belly. I immediately feel the baby kick, and my heart constricts in my chest.

"Isn't that so cool? There's a baby in here."

I laugh at her comment. "I would hope so! Otherwise you would have some serious explaining to do as to why your stomach is growing outward like that."

"Shut up! You know what I mean. When Liz was pregnant we would sit for hours and feel Bella kicking. It's just so crazy to have a baby kicking in my own belly."

"She's a miracle. Our miracle."

Kayla looks at me with a soft smile. "Yeah, she is."

We spend a few more minutes with our hands on Kayla's stomach feeling our little girl move around. When my fingers touch Kayla's, a jolt of something hits my heart and when I look up I can see it affected her as well. I reluctantly move my hands off her stomach, but not before leaning down and giving my baby a kiss through her mother's belly.

"I love you, baby girl. I can't wait to meet you."

Kayla gives me a small watery smile before looking away toward the television.

We both get comfortable and I flip through the channels until I come across a movie she wants to watch. She yawns and snuggles closer to me and I know it won't be long until she's asleep.

"Thank you, Bentley," she says, sounding half asleep.

"For what?"

"For always being here."

"I'll always be here, Kayla."

I give her a kiss on her forehead and she doesn't even stir. She's already fast asleep.

Thirteen

KAYLA

THE WEDDING DÉCOR IS ABSOLUTELY BEAUTIFUL. LIZ AND Cooper decided to have a small, intimate wedding with just their friends and family and everything is perfect. Because of her being pregnant, she didn't want any type of bachelorette party and of course Cooper didn't want a bachelor party either. The wedding is being held at their house in the backyard, but you wouldn't even be able to tell it's a backyard. The entire area has been transformed into what appears to be an upscale picnic. On the outside of the aisles are bright yellow daisies and pink dahlias. In the center of the reception tables are gorgeous planters with the same flowers, but instead of just water filling each vase, there are sliced lemons, strawberries, and kiwis inside each one to look like pitchers of lemonade.

The linens are light pink and cover country style wooden picnic tables. Next to everyone's plates are designer sunglasses for the sun. There are also little umbrellas sticking out of everybody's cups. On the back of every wooden chair are cute handmade fans that have Cooper and Liz's name on them with the date of the wedding. The reception area is covered with large white tents and on the back where the food will be is the three-tier light pink cake that's filled with different colored summer flowers.

Liz got this idea from their first family outing. Cooper took Bella and her to the park where they had a family picnic. While it is stifling hot here in Las Vegas, the tents all have fans blowing from the top corners so it doesn't feel hot.

Since Bentley and I fell asleep on the couch together last night watching a movie, we decided to go by his place so he could get ready and then head over to the wedding together. After checking out all the beautiful décor, I head back inside Liz's house to find her. Instead I find Bella playing in her dress.

"Hey, pretty girl, you ready?"

"Yup!"

"Where's your mom?"

"She's in her room with Grandma and all the other ladies."

I give her a kiss on her forehead and head to Liz's room. When I walk in I'm immediately choked up. She looks absolutely stunning in her wedding dress. I spent the day with her yesterday, but I wanted to wait to see her dress until today.

She gives me a large smile and hugs me. Our bellies bump and we laugh together. Hayley, Ashley, and Liz's mom laugh at us as well.

I take her aside for a private moment.

"You ready to become Mrs. Cooper?"

"As I'll ever be. Doesn't it seem like so much has changed so quickly?"

I start tearing up and nod. "Yeah, it does, but for the better. I'll never forget all the nights we shared in that tiny apartment studying and playing with Bella. It felt like it was you and me against the world."

A tear runs down her cheek and she wipes it away. "It still is us against the world. The only difference is now we have more people on our side. You just have to let him in, Kay."

"I know. It's just hard. Between not wanting to get hurt and not wanting to hear my mom tell me *I told you so* once again…But hey! This isn't about me. Today is about you. You are about to be married with two kids!"

We both laugh through our tears and give each other one more hug.

"I love you, Liz. You are my best friend. I'm so happy for you."

"I love you, too. I'll always be your best friend. Please just let Bentley in. Stop worrying about your mom and come home. I miss you."

I don't respond because I don't think I can come back here. I've never lied to Liz and I'm not about to start now.

We fix our makeup and then head downstairs to meet the guys. Cooper is already outside at the alter waiting. Bella is the flower girl and running all over holding onto her basket with flowers. The music begins to play and Bella heads down the aisle dropping flowers on to the ground. Since I'm the maid-of-honor and Bentley is the best man, we head down the aisle next. I wrap my arm around Bentley's and let him take the lead.

"You look gorgeous."

I turn my head slightly and laugh softly. "Yeah, right. I look like a damn cow."

He chuckles but then says, "No, you don't. You're glowing. You were sexy before, but seeing you carrying my baby makes you even sexier."

I nearly choke at his honesty. Luckily we make it down the aisle quickly and have to separate so I don't have time to respond. Hayley and Caleb walk down next, and then Ashley and Kaden.

The music changes to the wedding march and Liz walks down the aisle with her father. She's walking so fast people start to chuckle. She realizes what she's doing and blushes. She's so adorable.

The priest begins the ceremony and both Liz and Cooper opt to say their own vows.

"Liz, the moment I met you I knew you were the one. Unfortunately it took us quite a few years to get here, but here we are, six years later, and I don't want to ever imagine my life without you or Bella, or the little guy in your belly waiting to come out..."

I look over at Bentley and he's staring at me with unshed tears in his eyes. I want to believe he's emotional from the words that are being spoken, but the way he's looking at me leads me to believe his emotions are for me. I get a lump in my throat as I listen to Cooper continue.

"...And I promise to always laugh with you and to never go to bed angry. I promise to be patient when you say you'll be ready in fifteen minutes and aren't ready for an hour. I promise to fight for both of us when one of us isn't strong enough to fight, and I promise to remind you every day why giving us a second chance was the best decision you ever made. But most of all, I promise to love you through the storms and the sunshine for the rest of my days. I'm the luckiest fucking guy in the world to get to grow old with you."

Everybody laughs and Cooper apologizes to the priest for his foul language.

"Coop, first of all, I would just like it on record that I never agree to be ready in fifteen minutes."

Bella yells out in agreement. "That's true, Daddy. Mommy keeps saying you're crazy!"

Everybody laughs and then Liz continues. "I promise to try to get ready quicker. Okay, probably not. I don't want to lie in my vows. But I do promise to trust you and respect you. I promise to support you and encourage you. I promise to give you at least one more baby..."

"You said two!"

Everybody laughs again and Bentley smiles at me and then glances down at my belly. Listening to their vows makes me think about my parents' vows. What they must have promised each other, if they made any promises at all. Then my mind goes to Jake and how he didn't want any promises. I was so willing to give him my heart and all he wanted was my body and to make a fool out of me. I look at Bentley and see the emotions in his eyes. Could I have what Liz and Cooper have together? Could I be with Bentley for more than just to raise a baby with? Could we love each other and make promises and keep them without destroying each other, or will we end up with divorce attorneys fighting over assets?

The priest announces Liz and Cooper husband and wife and they kiss. Everybody cheers and claps, and Bella runs up to join her parents. They walk back down the aisle together as a family and we follow after them.

The reception is lovely. Everybody eats and mingles and then the music starts as Liz and Cooper are called onto the makeshift dance floor to have their first dance. They dance closely to *All My Life* by K.C. and Jo Jo. Once their song ends another begins and other couples make their way to the dance floor to dance as well.

Finally it is time to cut the cake. Pieces are passed out and I enjoy the sugary goodness while watching everybody continue to dance.

Bentley comes over, and putting his hand out, says, "May I have this dance?"

I smile and nod and then stand as he takes my hand in his. He walks us to the middle of the dance floor and takes my arms and places them around his neck and then puts his arms around me as much as he can with my protruding belly in the way. We sway to the music without saying a word. For these few minutes it feels like we are in a bubble, just the two of us, and I think about how easy it could be if I would just give in and let this amazing man love me the way he wants to. The song ends and Bentley leans down and whispers in my ear, "Thank you for the dance."

As we're walking away from the dance floor I begin to feel lightheaded. Bentley takes my arm to hold on to me when he feels me stumble. A sudden pain hits my abdomen and I double over grabbing my stomach. Something feels wrong, very wrong. I look up at Bentley and he kneels down next to me. That's when I feel something running down the inside of my leg, and when I swipe my fingers along it, I see blood.

"The baby…" I begin to say, but suddenly everything goes black.

Fourteen

BENTLEY

I'M WALKING KAYLA AWAY FROM THE DANCE FLOOR THINKING of ways to convince her to be with me. I saw the look in her eyes while Cooper and Liz were saying their vows and then again while we danced together. Whether she wants to admit it or not, she wants to be loved. She was hurt and is afraid of disappointing her mom, but nonetheless she wants it. Now I just need to convince her to have faith in us.

She begins to stumble a little and I hold onto her. When she bends over I realize something isn't right. I see her wipe blood off her inner thigh and the next thing I know she passes out in my arms.

"Fuck! Somebody call nine-one-one!" I yell while laying her down gently in the grass. As much as I want to pick her up, throw her in my vehicle, and rush her to the hospital, I'm afraid to move her.

Everybody circles around and somebody says that the ambulance is on the way.

"Kayla, wake up. Please baby, just open your eyes." I send up a prayer to the man above that he keeps her close to protect her and our baby.

"Is there a pulse?" I hear Liz ask.

I place my fingers on her neck and feel it faintly. She's sweaty and all clammy, but there's a pulse.

A few minutes later the paramedics arrive and transfer Kayla onto a gurney. I explain what happened and they tell us which hospital they're taking her to.

"I'm going with you. I'm the father." The paramedic nods and I hear my mom and Cooper telling me in the background they will meet us there.

When we get to the hospital, everything happens in fast forward. Kayla is wheeled into a room, still unconscious, and the doctor says that Kayla is experiencing placental abruption and needs a C-section immediately. Because of the blood loss, I'm not allowed in the surgical room and I'm asked to wait in the waiting room.

I walk out to the waiting room to find my parents and all of our friends there. They look at me, waiting for me to say something, and I lose it. The tears are coming down as my mom's arms wrap around me. I feel so fucking helpless.

"Bentley," Liz says. I know she's worried and the stress can't be good for her baby.

My mom lets go of me so I can tell them the little bit that I know. "I don't really know much. The doctor said the bleeding is from placental abruption and because of the loss of blood they're doing an emergency C-section. She was still unconscious when they took her into surgery. They wouldn't let me go because of her condition. All we can do is wait to hear from the doctor."

I look around to make sure the sweet little girl can't hear all of this. "Where's Bella?"

"Ashley is watching her."

"I'm so sorry about your wedding…"

"Stop it! Our wedding was amazing. What is important right now are Kayla and the baby."

Liz gives me a hug, and I hold on to her like a lifeline, telling her it will all be okay. I keep repeating it over and over again trying to convince myself.

After about an hour, the doctor walks out. "Family of Kayla Peterson?"

We all stand and he comes over to us.

"First off, I want to say that the baby is okay. We performed an emergency cesarean on the mother and she's doing just fine. The nurses are getting her cleaned up and checking her vitals. Even though she was taken a few weeks before her due date her lungs are fully developed and she's doing well. You'll be able to go back and hold her in a few minutes.

"We didn't know what we were working with until we opened up Kayla. Not only did she suffer a placental abruption but she began to hemorrhage which caused her body to go into shock. I tried to stop the bleeding, but when her heart stopped and we had to resuscitate her, I had to make a decision. I performed a partial hysterectomy on Kayla. She's in the labor and delivery ward now in recovery and is in a medically induced coma. Because of the severe bleeding and her going into shock, I felt it was best to allow her body to heal. In the next twenty-four hours we will take her off the medication so she can slowly begin to wake up. Do you have any questions?"

"Is she going to be okay?" Thank God my mom thinks to ask the first question because I'm in shock right now.

"At this point, I believe she's going to make a complete recovery. Because of the partial hysterectomy she won't be able to carry any more children. However, I don't believe she will suffer any long term effects."

"Can we see her?" This time it's Liz who asks the question.

"Once she's situated we can allow two at a time back there to sit with her. She isn't awake and won't start waking up for at least twenty-four hours."

"Thank you, Doctor," my mom says. At least these women are on top of this because I feel lost as hell right now.

The doctor walks back through the sliding glass doors as a nurse walks out. "Father of baby Peterson."

Peterson? My baby girl is a fucking Cruz! But I let it go for now. If have my way, the baby as well as Kayla will be taking my last name sooner rather than later.

"That's me," I speak up, finally finding my voice.

"If you can follow me back, I can introduce you to your little girl, and once we get situated you can bring your family and friends back to see the baby as well."

"Umm…I don't have any idea what I'm doing. Kayla was supposed to be here. I mean, she was supposed to be awake. She said she was going to breastfeed. Can I have my mom come back with me?"

The nurse gives me a small smile. "Sure and don't worry, just because we give the baby formula now doesn't mean the mom can't nurse later."

I look at everyone and see Liz with unshed tears in her eyes. I walk over to her. "I didn't mean to leave you out. I just need my mom. As soon as we get situated, I'll have her come out and get you. I promise."

She nods in understanding and then I follow the nurse back.

When we get to the room, it's quiet. I spot the tiny portable crib and go straight for it. I've never even held a baby before. The nurse stops me before I can pick her up, though.

"Wash your hands first. Newborns have low immune systems so we try to keep germs away as much as possible."

I quickly wash my hands and then walk over to the crib and pick her up like I've held her a million times. I bring her face close to mine and inhale deeply. I can feel the tears welling up as I send a thank you to the man above. This all could have turned out differently, and not for the better.

"Oh, Bentley! She's beautiful!" my mom whispers with excitement. "Let me take a couple of pictures."

I pose with my sweet baby girl for a few pictures before she begins to stir in my arms. I should probably set her down to sleep, but I can't bring myself to let go of her. I find a recliner and sit down with her wrapped in my arms.

She has a small patch of light blonde hair like Kayla's but naturally tanned skin like me. She has Kayla's cute button nose and perfect little lips.

"Hey there sweet girl. I'm your daddy. Your mom can't be here yet but I promise you, you won't be stuck with just me." I laugh through my tears, trying to make light of this situation.

My mom comes over and puts her hand on my leg. "Hey, even if it was just you, she wouldn't be stuck. You are going to be a great dad. Thankfully, Kayla is going to be okay and you both are going to be amazing parents to…oh boy, I guess we don't have a name."

"Kayla said she would name her once she's born. She said she would just know. I can't name the baby for her."

"I understand. For now, we will just call her sweet girl."

"Can you go and get Liz? I'm sure she's going nuts not being able to see the baby."

"Sure, sweetie." She gives me a kiss on my forehead and then bends down to kiss my sweet girl on hers.

A few minutes later Liz walks in and starts to cry. "Oh my goodness, Bentley! She's beautiful and she looks just like the both of you! Can I hold her?"

I hold my daughter tighter in my arms but then give in. I know I'm going to have to share her. My mom laughs and says, "Well, I guess I should have just asked."

Liz takes my sweet girl in her arms and rocks her gently talking to her like all women talk to babies, with that weird goo-goo gaga voice. She continues to sleep soundly through it and I decide now would be a good time to go check on Kayla.

"Would you guys mind staying here with her while I go check on Kayla?"

"Absolutely!"

"Of course!"

Before I leave, I think of something. "Hey Liz, did you call Kayla's parents?"

She gives me a small frown and an eye roll. "Yeah, they said they have court and since she wasn't supposed to give birth for another few weeks they won't be able to make it until then."

I hear a growl and realize it just came from me. "They are both so selfish. I don't get why Kayla would even care about their opinion. They have no idea what love is. I'm going to show Kayla what love is, if it's the last thing I do."

I walk out of the room in search of my woman. She may not know it yet but she's mine, and I'll be damned if her stubborn ass is going back to Florida.

I get to her room, which is on the same floor as our baby's. Because she's in a medically induced coma they put her in her own room instead of her sharing one with our baby. When I walk in, there's a nurse taking her vitals. "How is she doing?"

She looks up and smiles at me. "She's doing good. Her blood pressure is steady. If she continues this way, we can start weaning her from the drugs soon so she can start to wake up.

"Would it be okay if I brought our daughter in here to visit her? I know it's probably not normal protocol, but I want them to be close."

"I think we can have that arranged." She gives me a wink and then walks out.

I have a seat next to her bed, taking her hand in mine. Seeing her so quiet and still breaks my heart. Kayla isn't quiet. She's loud and the life of the party.

"Jeez, woman. You definitely gave us all a scare. You can't be doing shit like that. I haven't even convinced you that you love me yet. You can't be trying to leave me. I got to hold our baby and she's absolutely beautiful. She's a perfect mix of the two of us. We need you to get better so you can give her a name, okay? I can't do this without you, Kayla." I sit with her for a little while just watching her chest rise and fall. She's so damn strong, but lying here in this bed hooked up to these monitors she has never looked so fragile. I give her a kiss on her cheek and go to get our sweet girl.

IT'S BEEN TWENTY-FOUR HOURS SINCE OUR LITTLE GIRL WAS brought into this world and I'm exhausted. I've brought her in to see Kayla several times hoping Kayla knows she's here. I hate that they can't sleep in the same room.

I've spent the night feeding and changing and burping our daughter. I'm in love with this sweet little angel. I don't think I'll ever be able to leave her side. I know Kayla mentioned going back to work. I wonder if she'll mind if I stay home with the baby. I can picture it all: mornings at the park, afternoons visiting Kayla at work. I really think it can work. I just need to convince her. We're currently sitting in Kayla's room when the nurse lets me know they have reduced the medication and Kayla should begin the process of waking up.

"All right, sweet girl. Soon you'll be able to meet your mom and she can give you a name."

Our baby girl looks up at me with the most beautiful midnight blue eyes that match Kayla's. I never thought I could love somebody so quickly, but I swear the moment they set her into my arms, my heart leaped out of my chest, into her palm. There's nothing that compares to the love a parent feels when holding their baby in their arms.

Out of nowhere a loud beeping noises goes off and the monitors start going crazy. The baby is startled and starts crying. Two nurses and a doctor rush in. "Sir, you need to leave."

"What's happening?"

"Sir, we need you to leave now. Once we know more, we will let you know."

I'm removed from the room without even having a chance to put our baby in her rolling crib as the door shuts behind me. I can hear them speaking through the door and I feel so damn helpless as I hold our daughter in my arms, trying to calm her cries and praying that her mother is okay.

"Patient is coding. Grab the defibrillators."

"Clear!"

"There's no response."

"Let's go again."

"And clear!"

Silence

"Okay, we have a pulse."

I let out a breath once I hear Kayla has a heartbeat. After several minutes the door opens and I almost fall backward holding my daughter close to me. Shuffling up the best I can with her in my arms, I say, "Sorry, I didn't even realize I was sitting against the door. Is she okay?"

The nurse nods and leads me back into the room. I put our little girl in her crib and go straight to Kayla to hold her hand, needing to be close to her.

"The patient is okay for now. It seems she went into shock again once we reduced the meds. It's not common but it can happen. We had to resuscitate her once again. Because of the damage it's doing to her heart and body we're going to keep her in a medically induced coma for at least the next seventy-two hours as well as move her to the ICU. Her body needs to rest.

"Okay, thank you."

After they move her to the ICU, I have my mom watch the baby in her room. I hold on to Kayla's hand and pray once again that she's okay. I don't think I've ever prayed so much in my life. I can't do this without her. Our baby girl and I need her in our lives. I don't know how long I sit and pray, but eventually a nurse comes in and puts her hand on my shoulder to get my attention.

"Sir, can you come with us to fill out some paper work? Your daughter will be released from the hospital today."

"Yeah, no problem."

I call my mom and Liz on the way back to the labor and delivery ward and fill them in on what happened with Kayla. Liz tells me she'll come and stay with Kayla while my mom meets me to fill out the paperwork with the baby.

I'VE FINISHED FILLING OUT THE PAPERWORK AND AM WAITING

to see what happens next. A woman dressed in business attire comes over and introduces herself.

"Hello, I'm Darla, I'm from the data department. I was processing your paperwork but you left out the spot for the baby's name."

"Yeah, her mother is in a coma. She hasn't picked out her name yet."

"I see. Well, unfortunately we can't let the baby leave without a name. You can pick the name now and, if you decide to change it later, you can always fill out a legal name change form."

I look at my precious little girl in my mother's arms and know the name I want for her.

"Faith. Faith Lizbeth Cruz."

"Great. I'll get it filled out and bring the forms out for you to double check and sign and then you can take your little one home."

The woman walks away and I look over to my mom who has tears in her eyes.

"That's a beautiful name, Bentley. I love it."

"Yeah, now I just have to pray that Kayla will be joining us at home sooner rather than later."

"It will all work out, honey. You just have to have Faith."

Fifteen

KAYLA

EVERYTHING FEELS WEIRD. GROGGY. LIKE I'VE BEEN SLEEPING for a long time yet not long enough. There's a faint ringing noise in my ears and I have no idea where I am. My eyes are closed and I want to open them to figure it out, but they won't open. It's as if they're fastened shut. I feel drained, yet I can't remember doing anything that would cause me to feel this way.

"Kayla, baby? Can you hear me?"

I hear Bentley calling my name and want to wake up to find out why, but I'm so tired. I take a deep breath and it feels funny, like there's something in my nose. If I could just open my eyes…

"C'mon woman, please wake up. Faith wants to meet her mommy."

Mommy? Holy shit, I'm pregnant! Well, I was pregnant…Does that mean I gave birth to her? Faith? Is that her name? That's a pretty name. Okay, I just need to open my eyes. On the count of three I'm going to force my eyes to open. One…Two…Three…

I will my eyes to open and they do! Everything is blurry at first, but then it all starts to come into focus. I see Bentley next to me holding a baby. That must be our baby. Oh, thank God, she's okay. I look around and see I'm in a hospital room. Caleb is standing in the corner. Hayley is next to him. Liz is still pregnant, and she's standing next to Cooper, who has his arms wrapped around her. On the other side of me are Kathleen and Ryan, Bentley's parents.

I look back to Bentley and attempt to say something, but I end up choking and coughing. I reach up and feel something in my nostrils. It must be oxygen. I pull it out, so I can breathe the fresh air. Kathleen hands me a cup of water. I take a sip and attempt to speak again.

"What happened?"

Nobody says anything at first and I start to get nervous. The faint beeping starts to go off faster and Bentley looks worried.

"Whoa, sweetheart. Calm down. Everything is okay. You need to remain calm. The doctor should be here soon."

"Please tell me what happened. The last thing I remember is feeling a pain in my stomach at the wedding. I saw blood and then everything went black."

"You suffered from placental abruption and they had to do emergency surgery to take Faith out of you."

"Faith?"

Bentley looks at me sheepishly.

"Yeah, you've been out of it for a while. They had to keep you in a medically induced coma so your body could heal. I had to name her so I could bring her home. I named her Faith Lizbeth Cruz. If you don't like it we can change it."

Faith Lizbeth Cruz. "It's beautiful, Bentley, and you named her after Liz. Thank you. How is she?" I try to sit up, but my stomach muscles throb and I wince from the pain.

"Here, let me help you." The nurse who must have been in the corner where I couldn't see, comes over and presses a button to raise my headrest.

"Thank you." I look over at Bentley and see the beautiful little girl in his arms.

"Can I hold her?"

He smiles and nods. "Absolutely. She's been waiting patiently to meet you."

I take Faith in my arms while Bentley hovers over me. He must be nervous about whatever condition I've been in.

"Hey, sweet girl. I'm your mom." She squirms a little in my arms and I'm immediately in love. She has my blue eyes and nose with Bentley's mouth and skin tone. She's the most beautiful human being I've ever seen. I can't believe Bentley and I created this perfect little person together. She's such a miracle.

I glance up at Bentley and see tears in his eyes. "Why was I in a coma?"

I hear a throat clear and look to Liz. She gives me a sad smile and I know something is off. She walks over and sits next to me, putting my right hand into hers since my left one is holding Faith.

"Your body went into shock and you almost died a few times. You gave us quite the scare. They had to bring you back. Because of the bleeding, they had to do a partial hysterectomy. We are just so thankful you're alive. Bentley has been taking care of Faith and has been at the hospital almost every waking minute checking on you."

I take a second to process everything she just said. I had to have a partial hysterectomy. That means I'll never have another baby. I can feel the tears welling up behind my lids. I know I should feel thankful to be alive and for the fact that my baby is okay, but I also feel broken inside. A piece of me was removed and I won't be able to fix it.

I glance over at Bentley and he's assessing me closely. I go to look away and he grabs my chin. "Don't even fucking think it. You aren't broken." Holy shit! It's like he can read my mind.

"We have Faith and she's perfect, and if you ever want another baby we'll figure it out. We can find a surrogate or adopt. We'll figure it out when the time comes. Don't you even start to think of reasons to push me away."

I look down at my baby girl and he's right. She's perfect, but Bentley and I aren't together. One day he'll meet someone who can love him and give him lots of babies, unlike me, who's broken emotionally and now physically.

"There is no 'we'."

He just glares at me and lets it go.

I bring my nose to Faith's forehead and breathe in her baby scent.

"She smells good. She doesn't smell like a hospital."

Everybody laughs and Bentley says, "Yeah, well, I gave her her first bath. I think she's like her mother. She loves the water. Every time she's fussy, I put her in the water and she calms right down."

"Yeah, our sink has been transformed into a baby bathtub," Caleb adds with a chuckle.

Kathleen comes over and gives me a kiss on my forehead. "I'm so glad you're okay. Ryan and I have decided to stay here for a while. We're renting a place close by so we can help out until you're on your feet."

"Thank you, but I'm living in Florida. I'm planning to hire a nanny for when I go back to work."

Bentley growls and everybody looks like they're nervous to say anything.

"Why don't we give Bentley and Kayla some time alone to talk?" Cooper speaks up and everybody agrees as they hurry out the door. As they are walking out it, a doctor comes walking in.

"How's my patient doing?" He takes a mini flashlight and points it into my eyes nearly blinding me.

"I'm okay, I think."

"Good." He checks my blood pressure, then pokes and prods my abdomen, while still allowing me to continue to hold my little girl. She really is the most beautiful baby I've ever seen, aside from Bella.

"Everything looks good. You might experience a headache for the next few days from the severe blood loss. That's perfectly normal. Because of the surgery, there's no lifting anything over five pounds for six weeks. If you are taking the pain medications, there's no driving. You'll follow up with your OB in six weeks as well. Also, no intercourse until your six-week checkup. You suffered severe hemorrhaging and I had no choice but to do a partial hysterectomy. I'm sorry. Not all women go into menopause, but if you do, you'll have to be placed on hormone treatments. We can cross that bridge if it comes to that.

Unfortunately you won't be able to conceive in the future because I wasn't able to save a fallopian tube, but your body will heal completely. Do you have any questions for me?"

"When can I go home?"

He chuckles softly. "You should be able to get out of here tomorrow sometime. I just want you to stay the night to make sure you continue to remain stable."

"Okay, thank you."

"Congratulations on your little girl."

And with that, he shakes Bentley's hand and walks out the door.

Faith begins to fuss and Bentley reaches over to take her from me. He grabs a bottle and shakes it up, and begins to expertly feed her.

"I know you wanted to breastfeed, but I had to feed her. The doctor said if you would like to start, you can try whenever you're ready."

He seems so hesitant, like he's afraid I'm going to lose it on him, and I suddenly feel so bad for the way I've acted. I was going to have this baby and then let him know about her. Jeez, I'm such a bitch. It's only been a few days, but it's clear he's going to be an amazing dad.

"No, it's okay. It's probably for the best she's bottle-fed. I can see how much you love her and we'll have to figure out a custody agreement. It won't work if I'm breastfeeding her. You deserve to see her. You're her dad."

Bentley's jaw clenches and he glares at me for a second before he speaks. "I know you plan to go back to Florida, but it's not happening. First of all, you can't go anywhere for six weeks. Second of all, you'll be living with me. We are a family and I'm not letting Faith or you leave this state. If you want to go to Florida so damn bad, then I guess I'll have to go with you. Did you notice the people in the room? Did you notice who wasn't in the room? Your parents didn't even bother to show up."

"I wasn't supposed to give birth yet."

"What the fuck does that matter? They are your parents and they should have been here. I'm done sitting back and giving you your space. I love you and I love our daughter. Just give me a damn chance, please."

I know he's right, but it is so hard to open my heart. At least with my parents I know what I'm getting, and it doesn't include my heart broken. I look at him holding our daughter in his arms like she belongs there. She's eating and is so content with him. That's exactly how I feel when I let Bentley in. Content. But I can't let Bentley in like that because he'll eventually break my heart, and when he does, I'll be stuck in his life because of our daughter.

"Look, I'll stay in Las Vegas for the next six weeks, but that's all I can give you. We take care of Faith together as equals, but I can't do a relationship."

Bentley's jaw goes tight and he looks like he's about to explode. He closes his eyes for a few seconds and then opens them. "Okay, I'll take what I can get, but just know that I'm not going to hold my feelings back, and once you see your heart is safe with me, we *will* be a real family."

"I don't want to argue with you. Are we staying in the apartment?"

"Yeah, we are. At least for now. I already have Faith's room done and you can sleep in my room."

"You are expecting me to sleep in the bed with you? You do know I can't have sex for six weeks, right?"

He looks at me like I've just lost my mind and then says, "I don't give a shit about having sex with you. I love you, Kayla. In the next six weeks you're going to see what a real man does when a woman gives her heart over to him, and by the time the six weeks are up, you'll be begging me to make love to you."

I can't help but laugh at his cockiness. "Whatever you say, Bent. Hand me over our daughter. I need to smell her some more."

He laughs and hands her over to me so I can burp her. As I hold her close I glance from my precious little girl to Bentley and back again. Is it possible to really have it all? I guess only time will tell.

There's a knock on the door and Bentley calls whoever it is in. Liz, Cooper, and the rest of the gang all pile back in. They say congratulations and give me hugs and kisses.

Liz comes over and whispers, "Bentley really handled it all while you were out. He could be named father of the year."

I smile and glance at him talking to his parents. "He's an amazing man."

Liz's eyes open wide. "Are you two together?"

"I'm staying at least for the next six weeks and we're going to be living together to take care of Faith, but no, we aren't together. Bentley deserves to be with someone capable of love. I'm not the person for him. Maybe once we're living together and raising Faith together, he'll realize it and move on."

She gives me a big hug and kiss on my cheek. "I'm so glad you are staying and I know you two will work it out. You're meant to be together. You'll see. "

Caleb walks over and gives me a peck on my cheek. "I'm glad you're okay."

"Thanks. Are you ready for us to take over the apartment?"

"I wouldn't have it any other way. I've missed you, Kayla. I'm glad you're back."

I look over at Hayley and see her watching Caleb closely. I know she has a crush on him, but he doesn't really show any interest in her. She sees me eying her and gives me a small smile and wink. I smile back. Caleb would be lucky to snag a woman like Hayley.

Everybody stays for a while and chats while Faith is passed around and doted on. Eventually the nurse comes in and kicks everybody out saying I need rest. As much as I love the company, she's right, I do need the rest. I'm exhausted.

Bentley tells me he's going to go home for a little bit to give Faith a nap and will be back up later after I've rested. I give her a kiss and then close my eyes as I let sleep overtake me.

Sixteen

BENTLEY

IT'S FINALLY TIME TO BRING KAYLA HOME FROM THE HOSPITAL. Liz and my mom both offer to watch Faith for me, but there's no way my little girl is leaving my side yet. I'll consider it when she's a little older…Maybe. Caleb and I had all of Kayla's stuff overnighted to our place. Her parents weren't too thrilled, but I didn't really give them much choice when I told them Kayla can't fly anywhere for at least six weeks. They said to let Kayla know they will be down in a few weeks to visit, and thanked me for dealing with the situation. I wanted to yell at them and tell them Kayla almost dying isn't a fucking situation, but kept my mouth shut. They're both a waste of my time and energy.

Kayla's brother, Zach, on the other hand actually seemed genuinely concerned and said he's almost finished with a couple of his summer classes and plans to visit as soon as he takes his finals. I know they aren't close, but I have to wonder if it's more because of their parents and less because of how they feel about each other.

I finish arranging all of Kayla's stuff in my drawers and closet. The woman has a lot of damn clothes. I've just finished organizing her toiletries in our bathroom when I hear the muffled sound of Faith crying through the baby monitor. I grab a bottle from the kitchen on my way to get her. I've learned quickly that my daughter demands to be fed as soon as she wakes up, so I might as well have the bottle in hand.

"Hey there, pretty girl, you ready to go get your mom?"

She wiggles her little arms and legs and I'm pretty sure it's more of the sight of her bottle dangling in my hand and less about picking up her mom, but we can pretend. I change her diaper quickly while she fusses, wanting to be fed, and then sit on the couch to feed her. She tries to suck it all down as fast as possible and cries when I stop her from eating to burp her. She finishes her bottle and I burp her one last time and then buckle her into her car seat.

"Hey there, Mr. Mom." Caleb comes out of his room laughing.

"Ha ha, funny. I'm going to get Kayla from the hospital."

"Nice. I'll probably be at the gym when you get back, but I'll see you guys later I'm sure." He walks over to Faith and gives her a kiss on her forehead before heading out the door. The guy never shows any emotion, but since Kayla and now Faith are around, he's slowly coming out of his shell.

We get to the hospital and Kayla is ready to go. The nurse insists she has to be taken by wheelchair to the car, and once we're there, she opts to sit in the backseat with Faith. I smile as I glance in the rearview mirror at my two favorite girls in the world. They are my life.

"What are you cheesing about?" Kayla asks, when she catches me staring.

"I'm just happy. You both are healthy and okay and you're back living under the same roof as me."

She blushes and scrunches her nose up, making my heart open even more. Vulnerable Kayla doesn't show very often, but when she does, it makes my heart melt.

We get home and get situated. I have Kayla lie on the couch and put Faith in her bassinet next to her so they're close to each other. My phone goes off with texts from our friends and family, asking if we're home and if they can come by. I don't want her to feel too overwhelmed and, if I'm honest, I kind of just want my ladies to myself.

I get Kayla a glass of water and then sit on the other end of the couch, pulling her feet onto my lap. I begin to softly massage her feet as she stares at me with confusion. I ignore her and bring up something I've been thinking a lot about since Faith was born.

"So I've been thinking…"

"Oh boy, that's never good," Kayla says with a laugh. "Is that why you're giving me a foot massage? To butter me up?"

I smile wide and shake my head. "I know you want to go back to work in six weeks. I've been thinking I could stay home with Faith."

Her brows sink together in confusion. "Like a stay-at-home dad?"

"Yeah, like that. I love fighting and I plan to keep working out, but I don't have a contract with the UFC. I'm sure moms who stay home still have hobbies and such, but I want to quit training fulltime and stay home with her. Fighting would just become a hobby."

"But don't you love fighting? And can you afford that? I mean, I make a decent living, and if I decided to stay here. Cooper has already told me I have a job waiting for me, but it's not enough to live comfortably on."

I know right now I should tell her that I'm an extremely wealthy man. I come from old money passed down from generation to generation. I have more money in the bank than I'll ever spend in a lifetime, but for some reason I'm scared to tell Kayla. I don't think she's a gold-digger by any means. As a matter of fact, I think the opposite. I think me having money might scare her and make her run. She's one of the most independent women I've ever met, and if she knew the amount of money I have, and the amount of money our daughter will one day have, I honestly think she would bolt. The truth is, the only people who know about my money are Kaden, Caleb, and Cooper, and they know I don't like for it to be mentioned.

"I do love fighting, but these last few days with Faith…well, I love being home with her more. Plus, I've saved up. It will actually save money since we won't have to pay a nanny. I just can't imagine leaving her with anyone. I want to be the one to be there for her first words, steps…I just love her so damn much. I don't want to leave her with a stranger when I can be here with her."

Kayla's face falls and I think maybe I said something wrong.

"Does it make me a bad mom for wanting to go back to work?" She bites her bottom lip like she's about to cry.

I get up and move to kneel in front of her. "Hey, there is nothing wrong with you going back to work. You love your career and you'll be an amazing mom and still be able to work. We are fortunate that I'm able to stay home with our daughter. If you ever decide you don't want to work and want to stay home please know you always have that option. We can always reassess the situation. "

She laughs softly, but not in a *that's funny* way, but more of a *are you insane?* "So we'll both be without an income and stay home all day with Faith? You do realize babies need things like diapers and formula, which cost money?"

"Woman, when I tell you we are fine, I mean it. Work or don't work. I don't care. You want to move from here into a bigger house? Just pick the place. Whatever you want, I'll handle it. Faith will never want for anything."

"So are we splitting the bills down the middle or what? When I lived here before it was temporary because of the fire, so I didn't pay anything. I don't want to take advantage, especially since you won't be working."

"Kayla, you aren't paying a dime here. Caleb and I have it all covered. For the next six weeks just focus on Faith and getting better, okay?"

When her body visibly relaxes, I realize just how uncomfortable this conversation was for her. "What did you think I was going to say?"

"Well, my parents split everything down the middle, even to this day. Even when we were little, they split the nanny payment because neither of them wanted to stay home, even though they could afford for one of them to. I thought maybe you would want to do the same, and I'm not sure how much this apartment is, but I know it's not in my price range."

"Nothing about us will ever be like your parents. I know they mean well, but this isn't a business arrangement. I love you."

"Bentley…" I know what she's going to say, so I cut her off by giving her a small kiss on her lips to shut her up. Her lips are soft and gentle and they make me want so much more. She pulls away from me with a glare, but when she tries to sit up, she's quickly reminded she just had major surgery.

"Ow!" she cries out.

"Be careful."

"Well, I wouldn't have to be careful if you wouldn't attack me with your mouth!"

"Don't your parents ever kiss?"

"I'm sure they do…They do have needs, but I think right now we need to keep the line clear. I don't want it getting all blurry. Let's just focus on Faith."

I steal another kiss from her and stand, and she looks at me like I'm crazy.

"What? You can do things your way and I'll do things mine," I say as I head to the bathroom, trying discreetly to adjust the hard-on I have going on.

Seventeen

KAYLA

BENTLEY HEADS TO THE BATHROOM WHILE TRYING TO HIDE his erection…like I wouldn't notice the man's large, hard dick sticking straight out while he tries to adjust himself as he walks away. I bring my fingers up to my lips where his just were. Chemistry between Bentley and I has never been the problem. The problem is the fact that Bentley wants more and more leads to heartbreak and embarrassment.

I decide to check out the nursery while Bentley is in the bathroom. The doctor said it's important to walk around as much as possible to work the muscles that had to be cut open for the C-section. I walk past Caleb's room and then Bentley's room and into my old room. It feels like a lifetime ago, but in reality it's only been six months since I moved out.

The room has been transformed into a surfer's oasis. The entire room is painted a beautiful sky blue with a darker blue toward the bottom that makeup the waves. The trim is a tan color, which I'm assuming is to represent the sand. Faith's crib bedding is different shades of pink with multicolored surfboards all over it, and over her crib is a huge adorable umbrella-looking mobile. There's a surfboard hanging over the changing table that has her name written out across it. The rug is a large surfboard, and on the wall are pictures of surfers. When I look closer, I see they aren't just any surfers…they're of me!

"Do you like the room?"

I jump at the sound of Bentley's voice, which is insane because I'm standing in my own daughter's room. It's not like I'm sneaking through his stuff.

"How did you get these pictures of me?" I ask, pointing to them.

He smiles wide clearly proud of himself. "Google. I remembered that guy said a while back you were in various competitions and such, so I searched your name and found some photos from your surfing days."

"When did you have time to do all this? I was only out of it for like a week."

His lips tip into a frown. "Actually, most of this was all done in advance. I wanted Faith to know she always has a place here, and if we were sharing custody I wanted her to have a piece of you when she was away from you and with me."

Damn it, this man definitely does *not* fight fair.

I HAVEN'T LEFT THE HOUSE SINCE I'VE BEEN HOME FROM THE hospital and I'm about to crawl out of my skin with aggravation. I need to get out of this house and off this couch! Bentley doesn't leave often, but he leaves at least once a day, usually to get groceries or go to the gym. Sometimes he'll take Faith to visit his parents. Because I can't lift, he takes Faith with him everywhere. Apparently all the guys at the gym absolutely adore her and take turns holding her. I'm not complaining because he has been the perfect partner and father. He takes care of everything and all I have to do is lie here and cuddle with our precious little girl all day, but if I don't get out of here soon I might kill somebody. Okay, yes, I'm being a bit dramatic but you get my point.

Bentley comes walking into the living room freshly showered and looking hot as hell. "My mom wants to host a Fourth of July barbecue at the place they're renting. It has a pool and big backyard, but I told her we aren't up for it…"

"Are you out of your damn mind? Call her back now! Tell her we will be there! I need to get out of this house right now! Right. Freaking. Now!"

He looks at me like I've lost my mind and puts his hands up in surrender, and in his defense I just may have.

"Okay, okay. I didn't know you were feeling this way. We can go. You sure you're up to it? You've only been out of the hospital for a short time."

"I'm definitely good to go. Get me a chair under an umbrella, a nice cold alcoholic beverage, and I'll be perfect."

He smiles and says, "Okay, done."

After we confirmed we were going, I called Liz to invite her family, and then she called everybody else to invite them.

Now I'm lounging out on the amazing back patio of a huge ass house Bentley's parents are renting, listening to music, drinking a Mike's Hard Lemonade, and holding my baby girl while I watch everyone play in the water. Cooper and Bentley are teaching Bella how to chicken fight. Cooper has Bella on his shoulders and Bentley has

Ashley's son, Tristan, on his, as they explain the object of the game. The problem is Tristan is refusing to push Bella, saying it's not nice.

"You're raising him right." I say to Ashley, who's lounging in the chair next to me.

"God, I hope so. With me as his primary role model I worry every day."

"Where's his dad?"

"Kayla! Don't be so rude," Liz chirps in.

"Sorry."

"No, it's okay. Umm…Tristan's dad isn't in the picture. He left when Tristan was born. Trust me it's a good thing. It's been hard raising Tristan on my own, but it's better this way. I don't make a lot teaching, but it's enough to support us, and my parents help out when they can."

Her comment makes me think about Bentley and me. I know I could raise Faith on my own, but these last couple weeks watching Bentley with our daughter has changed the way I see things. He's so loving and protective, and after she goes to bed every night he lies on the couch and watches television with me. It feels nice to not feel so alone. I'm just so afraid that if it turns bad I'll have to call my mom to draw up the custody papers.

Nobody says anything and luckily Hayley breaks the awkward silence. "So, I totally have a crush on Caleb and he won't give me the time of day. I think he's gay."

We all burst out laughing at her comment.

"Just because somebody doesn't want you doesn't mean he's gay!" I say through my laughter. Faith stirs in my arms but quickly goes back to sleep.

"Umm…hello? Have you seen me? I'm hot and a doctor. What's not to want?"

We all laugh harder.

"Honestly, I've never seen Caleb with anyone," Liz says. I think back to all the months I've lived here and the truth is, I don't think he has ever brought someone home.

"Just keep trying. Bentley hasn't given up yet and he's starting to wear me down, although I would never tell him that."

Laughing ensues, until Kathleen walks over.

"Am I interrupting?"

"Oh, no! Just boy talk," I say with a wink.

She sits at the end of the lounge chair and reaches out to grab Faith. I hand her over and then pull my phone out to snap a picture of her cradling her in her arms. I wish my mom were loving and supportive like this.

When I called my parents they told me it would be weeks before they could come and visit and practically blamed me because I had the baby early.

"Kayla, I don't know why you left during your third trimester to go to that wedding. Now you're stuck over there for six weeks."

"It was my best friend's wedding. I wasn't just going to miss it."

"Yeah, well, now you're shacking up with Bentley and I wouldn't be surprised if you two are back together soon, which would be a huge mistake. He's going to break your heart and then when you come crawling back home once again, I'll be the one helping you to figure out the custody arrangements of your daughter. I understood you not going to law school because, let's face it, you didn't have the drive, but to keep making these same mistakes with men is just ridiculous."

Ryan, Bentley's dad, announces the food is ready, bringing me back to the now. Everyone scurries over to the buffet they put together to grab their food. As I go to get up to get mine as well, Bentley stops me.

"I got it. Just stay here." He grabs the back of my face and, before I can stop him, he gives me a big, wet kiss soaking me…from his wet bathing suit! Get your mind out of the gutter.

Bentley's mom looks at me with a smile, not only on her face but in her eyes. "He loves you, you know."

"I know. Has he told you anything about my parents or our arrangement?"

"Yes, we're close. I hope that's okay. He's given me the shortened version I'm sure."

"I just don't know how to love like you guys do."

"Sure you do, sweetie. You just have to open your heart and let him in. He told me you were once hurt. I understand. Ever think maybe everything happens for a reason? Sure, you were hurt, but everything from that point on led you to where you are right now, with a beautiful baby girl and a man who adores you both."

"And what happens when it doesn't work out? What happens when we're just another statistic? Did you know that seventy percent of all marriages fail?"

She laughs softly and then pats my leg. "Oh, sweetie. You can't think like that. All you can do is open your heart and let the ones you love in. Nothing is ever certain, but if you don't even try you won't ever know."

Jeez! Where was she when I was a teenager and needed advice on love?

When I don't say anything, she reaches over and touches my cheek, and for some weird reason it makes me want to cry. I can't even remember the last time my parents actually showed me affection.

"Just think about it. No matter what, you have me. I'll always be here for you, even if it's just as the grandma to Faith and a friend to you."

"How long are you guys staying for?"

"We've decided to buy this place. As much as I love Colorado, I love being near you guys more."

The tears that have been threatening behind my lids, spill over, and she looks at me with concern. But before I can explain, Bentley comes over with our food and sees my tears.

"What the hell happened?" His voice carries, and Faith startles at the loudness and begins to cry.

I take her from Kathleen and put her over my shoulder patting her bottom to calm her down while glaring at Bentley.

"Sorry. I saw you crying. Is everything okay?" I think he's directing the question to me, but he's looking at his mom.

"Hey! Chill out. Your mom told me she's buying this place and it made me happy to know she'll be close by."

"And that caused you to cry?" he asks incredulously.

"Yes! Okay, I guess it's the new mom hormones but when she told me she's staying here, it made me think about the fact that my mom hasn't even made time to meet my daughter yet and your mom is moving here like it's nothing."

The tears start flowing faster and I try to wipe them off my face, but it's no use, they're falling faster than I can catch them.

Kathleen reaches over and wraps her motherly arms around Faith and me and holds me tight while whispering in my ear that it's okay, and for the first time in a long time I feel like it actually is. It also makes me realize that in my twenty-five years my mother has never held me or hugged me like this. If I had to pick a kind of mom to be like, it would definitely be a mom like Liz or Kathleen. It also makes me wonder why the hell I care what my mom thinks. Why do I keep trying to live up to her expectations? Yeah, I was hurt once, but I was young. What if this time around it works out and we live happily ever after?

Faith begins to squirm, letting us know she's ready to eat. Kathleen lets go of me and wipes my tears. I look around and see everybody staring at us and suddenly feel self-conscious. She takes the baby from me and offers to feed her while Bentley and I eat.

The rest of the day is enjoyable. It feels like I've reached a turning point and I'm seeing things in a different light. I want to be more like Kathleen and less like my mom. I want to fall in love, and I want to be happy.

Bentley announces that it's time to go. I don't want to leave, but it's nearing dusk and Bentley is hell bent on keeping Faith on a schedule, and since he's so adorable about it, I can't say no.

We get home and I jump in the shower while Bentley gives Faith a quick bath and then lays her down in her crib. I get out to find him lying in bed watching Sports Center in nothing but his boxers over the comforter. In my towel, I walk over to the dresser to get my pajamas out of the drawers before I head into the closet to get dressed.

Up until now I've been sleeping on the couch. I've said it's because it's easier to get to the kitchen and bathroom at night, but the truth is I'm afraid to sleep with Bentley. I know his ass isn't going to play fair.

After getting dressed I lie down on the opposite side of the bed.

He rolls toward me and laughs. "Finally decided to join me in bed? Any closer to the edge and you might fall off."

"Yeah, well, my back is starting to get stiff, and since I can walk around now better, and I'm less sore, I don't need to be close to the kitchen and guest bathroom. As for sleeping on the edge...any closer to you and you might try to have your way with me."

"Kayla, I already told you this before. I don't want you for sex, and when we do have sex, it will be you begging me. Now get over here and I'll play with your hair until you fall asleep."

Well, I'm sure as hell not going to argue with that. I scoot closer to Bentley, grab a pillow to put against his hard stomach, and lay my head down on it. He runs his fingers through my hair until I pass out.

Eighteen

KAYLA

TONIGHT, BENTLEY, FAITH, AND I GOING OUT TO DINNER WITH our friends and family. Liz has officially reached her due date and wants to have one last dinner before they become a family of four. On top of that my parents and brother all came in this morning and are meeting us as well. While Bentley's parents have been completely hands-on and have both been a huge help, my family hasn't even met Faith yet.

I'm getting out of the shower, and about to get dressed, when I hear Bentley talking to someone, which is weird since nobody is here. I listen closer, and I can tell by the sound of his tone, he's talking to Faith. He always makes it a point to soften his tone when he talks to her. Being nosey, I sneak over to the nursery in my towel and see my man sitting in the rocking chair holding our daughter in his arms while he reads to her.

Oh shit! Did I just say *my man*? What I meant to say was that man. He's not mine! Since the first night after the barbeque when I started to sleep in his bed he hasn't tried anything. Don't get me wrong, he sneaks in an occasional kiss here and there, but he hasn't tried anything major. He has been a complete gentleman. I'm actually starting to wonder if he wants me anymore.

I watch Bentley and Faith for a few minutes as he reads to her, and they're so precious together. She has no idea what he's reading, but she stares at him like he's hung the moon. He stops every so often and smiles at her like she's his entire world. When I watch him like this, doting on our daughter, I can't help but fall more and more for him. He was already damn near perfect, now add in doting father, and I don't stand a freaking chance.

I get dressed and then feed my precious angel while Bentley gets ready. I could hold her forever. I'm definitely going to miss her when I go back to work soon, but luckily Cooper is letting me work the hours I want so I won't have to be away from her for too long. And knowing that she'll be here with Bentley makes me feel even better.

Oh that's right, I forgot to mention I'm staying here in Vegas. Bentley and I sat down one night and talked and decided it's for the best if I stay. I haven't told him I'm seriously considering giving us a real chance yet, but I know that regardless of what happens, my home is here with Liz and Bentley and our friends. Faith deserves to see her daddy every day and I loved my job at the gym. I can't wait to watch Faith and Liz's son grow up together. I also love being close to Kathleen and Ryan. I didn't realize how unfulfilled I felt until everybody around helped fill in the emptiness.

We arrive to the restaurant and are shown to our seats. Everybody is already seated. My mom and dad stand to give me a barely-there hug and an air kiss. It brings me back to the barbeque when Kathleen held me tight and hugged me, showing me what a real mother's hug should be like. I offer to let my mom hold Faith but she declines.

"That's okay. Babies are rarely good in restaurants. We don't want to mess with her. It will be quite embarrassing if she starts crying and ruins everybody's meal. Honestly, I'm surprised you brought her. Have you not found a nanny yet?

"Um, no, not yet."

Bentley tenses up but keeps quiet. I haven't really spoken to my mom about our plans. I just don't want to listen to her tell me how wrong I am.

I walk around the table and say hello to everyone. Liz gives me a look of sympathy and I walk over and hug her extra tight. We all have a seat and, after the waiter takes our drink orders, the conversation begins. Of course my mom is the one to start it.

"So, Bentley. Kayla tells me you have been home with her since she had the baby. Are you planning to go back to work or just apply for unemployment?" She chuckles at her joke but her tone suggests the question is one meant to be answered.

"Actually, Nancy. I'm not going back to work. At least not any time soon."

I hear her gasp as she asks, "What do you mean by that?"

Bentley clenches his jaw, so I cut in. "Bentley has decided to stay home with Faith. I'm going back to work part-time in a couple of weeks. I've decided to stay living in Las Vegas and go back to work at the gym, and instead of getting a nanny, Bentley wants to stay home with her." I smile big hoping this answer will suffice.

The entire table sits in silence, darting their eyes back and forth like one would do at a tennis match.

"So, your plan is to just live off my daughter?" She aims the question at Bentley but continues to glare at me.

Bentley's mom cuts in with an "Excuse me, but Bentley does *not* need to live off of anyone."

I'm not sure what she means by that, but Bentley shakes his head and asks her to please stay out of it. She nods once and takes a sip of her water.

Bella, in all her innocence, says, "Bentley, you can be a stay-at-home mom like my mom! Daddy said she isn't allowed to go back to work after my baby brother comes. He said he wants her in the kitchen…with no shoes on…cooking…and pregnant again."

Everybody laughs and the awkwardness has been lifted.

"Yeah, well, I might be staying home, but won't be cooking or getting pregnant again anytime soon," Liz chimes in.

I feel a lump in my throat when Liz says this. She will at least have the option. I'll never be pregnant again. Don't get me wrong, I'm not jealous of Liz, just sad I won't ever have that experience again.

Bentley puts his hand on my thigh and leans in close. "Stop thinking like that. We have a beautiful little girl, and whenever you want another baby I'll make it happen."

It's when he says shit like this I just want to go all in. My mom glares at me pointedly and I know she heard his comment.

The rest of the meal goes smoothly and soon everyone is saying goodbye. I give Liz a hug and remind her to call me when she goes into labor. She laughs and says she will. Bentley offers to take Faith home so I can spend some time with my family and I say okay.

We head to the bar and I order a Jack and Coke, knowing I'll need alcohol to get through this.

"Honey, have you thought about all this?" my dad begins.

"Thought about what?"

"Bentley seems like a great dad, but him choosing to stay home and not work doesn't bode well with me. Men don't stay home. They work. Are you on his lease? What if he loses his apartment? Please tell me you at least have your own bank account."

Then my mom jumps in. "And what is with his comment about giving you another baby? I thought you told me your relationship is strictly a mutual arrangement."

Before I can answer either of them, Zach speaks up. "Jesus Christ! Do you guys ever stop? Kayla isn't an idiot and everything in life isn't about money. Damn, this family is so fucked up. Everything isn't a business deal. Just let her be. The guy isn't going to steal her money and take off. Maybe if we were raised by parents instead of nannies Kayla and I would be able to be in an actual relationship instead of pushing everyone away."

We're all frozen in place. All this time I thought Zach felt the same way as my parents, and I'm stunned to learn he doesn't at all. It gives me the assurance I need to allow myself to be open to the possibility of being in a relationship based on feelings. I thought maybe it was just me who was having these ill feelings to toward our parents but clearly he feels the same way.

"To answer your questions, Bentley doesn't let me pay a dime for anything. My income goes to whatever I want. He won't even let me split any of the bills. We're not together in any way other than raising Faith together, but he does want more, and I'm definitely considering it."

My mom nods. "Okay, well, that's good he's somehow paying his way. Just take things slow, please. I really think you should consider writing up a custody agreement and child support arrangement in case things go awry."

I don't even bother to respond because I don't feel like arguing. We move the conversation to the weather and my parents talk about their practice and how busy they are.

We all finally say goodnight and my parents take off to their hotel. They're flying back out in the morning because they have court.

Zach and I stay sitting at the bar after they leave.

"So, were you speaking from experience?" I ask my brother who is currently nursing his Budweiser.

He shakes his head a little and then says, "Yes…No…I don't know. It's just been drilled into us for so long not to get into a relationship with feelings that I feel like I second-guess every move I make."

"Same here. After Jake fucked me up, I never let another guy in. Mom made me feel like I was so stupid and I didn't want her to throw it in my face again. Bentley wants in so badly, but I'm scared. Partly, I'm scared to get hurt…"

Zach finishes my sentence for me. "And partly you're scared that Mom and Dad will say I told you so if things don't work out."

"Yeah." We sit for a few minutes in comfortable silence drinking. It feels like something between us has changed. A wall that was between us has been dropped.

"Will you come and visit more often?" I ask.

He gets off his stool and encloses me in his arms for a bear hug. "I miss you, sis. I'll definitely visit more often. I'm sorry I stayed away. I was afraid you turned out like Mom and Dad, but I think there's still hope for us yet."

He drops me off at the apartment and comes up for a few minutes to dote on Faith before he leaves to go back to his hotel room. Since he only made plans to come for the weekend we make additional plans for him to fly out for a week soon. I can't wait to spend some real time with my brother.

Once he's gone, I lay Faith down in her crib, turn the monitor on, and snuggle up next to Bentley in bed in our usual position. I lay my head down on his chest and he plays with the strands of my hair.

"How did it go with your parents?"

"Okay. They're just all about business. But surprisingly Zach let them have it."

"Good for him."

He moves me from his chest and lies on his side facing me. He traces my shoulder and down my arm with his fingers, giving me goose bumps. His fingers continue down to my thigh and his touch causes my the apex of my thighs to clench. He sees my legs tighten and his eyes dance with laughter at what he's doing to me.

"You know I can't have sex for at least two more weeks."

His face turns serious and then to lust. "There's plenty we can do without having sex."

"I'm pretty sure anything you're talking about isn't part of our arrangement," I say jokingly. I've already made up my mind that I'm going to give Bentley and I a real chance. I just want to tell him in a more romantic way.

"I'm not asking you to marry me, Kayla, but I imagine you have needs that aren't being met. Just let me help you meet them."

He scoots closer, bridging the small gap between us, and brings his lips down to mine. He's definitely right. I do have needs and those needs haven't been met since the night I got pregnant with Faith.

I roll onto my back and Bentley climbs on top of me with his forearms on either side of my head, not letting any of his weight touch me. His lips brush against mine, first softly, but then things start to get more heated.

His tongue slides into my mouth and I suck on it, causing him to moan. I grab him by his short hair and hold his face to mine as we kiss passionately, our lips making love to each other.

Bringing my knee slightly up, I rub against his hard erection while continuing to kiss him. He stops my assault by taking one hand and separating my legs, bringing his knee down to my pussy. He begins to rub my sensitive area through my cotton shorts causing me to become wet.

God! I'm so damn turned on right now. All I want is for this man to touch me and caress me, and never fucking stop.

"Bentley, touch me please. I need you to touch me." I stop our kiss just long enough to get the words out of my mouth.

"My pleasure," he growls, and suddenly he's off my body and his face is down near my pussy. He grips my shorts and panties and pulls them off in one fell swoop while I remove my shirt and bra so I'm completely naked in front of him. I should probably feel self-conscious because I did recently have a baby, but the way he touches me and looks at me like he wants nothing more than to devour me gives me all the confidence I need to be okay with my body.

He starts at my foot, kissing the inside of my sole, and slowly works his way up, placing small, wet kisses up my calf and then my thigh before moving to my inner thigh. I think he's finally going to give me what I so badly need when he bypasses my pussy altogether and goes for my breasts. He first starts off kissing each one then takes one of my nipples in his mouth and closes his lips around it. He alternates between sucking and licking. He sucks so hard it hurts, but then he licks it to soothe away the pain. He moves to my other nipple and gives it the same attention.

My thighs are squeezing so tight, trying to release the pent up tension, I swear I'm going to combust. It doesn't do any good though because Bentley's body is between my legs, so I'm just squeezing his thighs with mine. I know he can feel me pressing into him because he chuckles softly.

"Bentley, please!" I say, fully aware I'm now begging. But holy hell, it's been over nine months. I can't be held accountable for my actions at this point.

He gives me a chaste kiss and then moves his way back down to the area that is in dire need of attention. Separating my pussy lips, he puts his tongue right onto my clit and leaves it there for a second. I'm staring at him and watch him inhale deeply. I go to close my legs, but it's pointless because he's still lying between them.

"What are you doing?" I whisper-yell. I need to make sure our daughter doesn't get woken up before I get attended to.

"I'm smelling your pussy, and woman, I've missed this smell. Fuck, I'm addicted to this smell."

He doesn't give me a chance to respond before his tongue is back on my clit, licking from bottom to top, causing me to squirm and moan. My head falls onto the pillow and I let go, enjoying his mouth pleasuring me. He lifts my butt a little bit and then shocks the hell out of me when he licks my *other* hole, causing me to jump.

"Kayla…Has anybody ever fucked you here?" Him referring to anal sex so nonchalantly has my cheeks heating up. If I barely do feelings, I definitely don't do anal. I would never let a man see me that exposed and vulnerable.

My head pops back up to look at him. "No," I say softly with a shake of my head. His face lights up, and he says, "We don't have time right now, but I'll take you here…and soon." And then he goes back to licking me. He stops at my hole and pokes his tongue in quickly. I want to say it feels like he's violating me, but the truth is it feels good. That shouldn't surprise me, though, because everything this man does to me feels so damn good.

He brings his mouth back up to my clit and focuses his attention there, bringing me close to the edge and then pulling back just enough that I'm ready to lose it. He brings his fingers near my entrance, and just when I think he's forgotten I can't have intercourse and is going to stick them in me, he gathers my juices and brings them to my tight-rimmed hole, getting it all wet.

Has he changed his mind? Is he going to take me right now in the ass? His dick remains in his pants, so I don't think he is. He takes one finger and slowly inserts it into my puckered hole. At first, it feels odd…but as he pushes it in and then slowly pulls it out, it feels like he's massaging my insides. I had no idea anal play could feel this good. While fingerfucking me in my ass, he goes back to my clit. He licks and sucks and slurps up my juices, bringing me closer and closer to the precipice. He must know I'm about to fall because he inserts his finger a little farther into me and licks faster…and I lose it. My body shakes and my pussy convulses as I come harder than I've ever come before, all over his mouth. I bite down on my lip so hard to stay quiet I can taste blood.

I glance down at him as he removes his finger and then sits up on his knees. He then proceeds to make a show of licking my juices from his lips, making it clear how much he wants me in every way.

Without needing to think about it for more than a second, I sit up and grab the button of his pants, so I can return the favor, when the baby monitor goes off with the sounds of Faith crying. Bentley laughs and shakes his head, not an ounce of angry or disappointment showing in his features. He's so selfless, it's scary.

"Go wash your face and hands and I'll grab her," I say as I get up and throw on my shorts.

I walk into her room and Caleb is already standing over the crib holding her.

"Hey there."

He turns around and smiles sheepishly. "Sorry, I heard her crying and couldn't help myself. Plus, based off the noises that were coming from the room I wasn't sure if you would be physically capable of making it out here." He laughs at his own joke, and I playfully swat at him.

"Oh, my God, I thought I was being quiet! And I didn't even know you were home." I'm so mortified that I can't even look Caleb in the eyes. I go to the kitchen and grab a bottle and he hands Faith over to me so I can feed her.

"Hey," he says, his tone now serious. "You have nothing to be embarrassed about. I'm glad you and Bentley are finally together."

"We aren't together," I say. I want to tell Caleb that I plan to change that but feel like I should tell Bentley first. "I feel bad. It's like we're taking up your whole apartment. We should probably look for a place to live so you don't have a baby cramping your style. I just don't know what we can afford with neither of us working right now."

"No way, you aren't cramping anything. You know I love you guys here," he says before he goes back to giving Faith his attention.

Nineteen

BENTLEY

I COME OUT FROM THE BATHROOM AND OVERHEAR KAYLA telling Caleb we aren't together. It's a punch to my gut that she needs to remind everyone around us that she doesn't want me for anything more than to help raise our child. Every time I think I'm making progress she reminds me that she doesn't feel the same way. Maybe it is time to take a step back. A guy can only take so much rejection.

BECAUSE LIZ IS NOW OVERDUE, THEY'RE INDUCING HER TODAY and Kayla has offered to watch Bella for them so their parents can join them at the hospital. I'm giving Faith a bottle when Bella comes barreling into the apartment and jumps on the couch to join me.

"Hey, Uncle Bentley! I'm going to get a baby brother just like Faith but with boy parts!"

She's honestly the most adorable kid I've ever met, and every time she calls me Uncle Bentley I just want to hand over my wallet and tell her to go buy anything her little heart desires.

"I know, sweetie. Are you excited?"

"I'm so excited! And I get to stay with Auntie Kay and you while they have the baby. Will you help me train for the UFC while I'm here?"

Bella is determined to follow in her father's footsteps and one day be a part of the UFC. She's only five years old but swears one day she's going to be the next Ronda Rousey. It drives Liz nuts with worry every time Bella wants to practice her fighting moves, so she put her into mixed-martial-arts classes at the gym Cooper just started up for kids and teens. When he asked me if I would be interested in funding the program I didn't think twice. It's a great program and gets kids off the streets since they're offering it at a discounted and free rate if the family's income qualifies. I'm glad my money can go toward something to help kids.

I lift Faith over my shoulder to burp her. "I'm sure that can be arranged."

"What can be arranged?" Kayla asks, walking through the door from saying bye to Liz and Cooper, so they can head to the hospital. She takes Faith from me so she can lay her down.

"Bella wants to practice some MMA while she's with us."

Kayla smiles wide. She loves how tough Bella is. "That sounds like fun. Why don't you two go to the gym and I'll stay here with Faith. I can order a pizza for when you get back and we can watch a movie. What are you into these days?"

Bella looks like she's just been told she's going to Disney Land. "Yes! Yes! Let's go! I brought a movie with me. I'll show it to you later."

She runs to the door ready to head to the gym. I grab my gym bag and head out with her. We get to the gym and Bella tells me she's going to warm up on the punching bag before we get started. I see Caleb in the ring and join him.

"Yo, Caleb!" I call out. He turns around and nods a quick hello. I jump in the ring and ask if he wants a sparring partner.

"Bring it new daddy." He chuckles.

"Where's Kayla and Faith?" he asks as we circle each other, getting into a rhythm. I punch, he blocks; he punches, I block.

"They're home. I brought Bella here to practice her MMA. She's at the bag warming up." I nod my head toward the bags where the cute little girl is throwing kicks and punches to the bag with all her might, yet the bag doesn't even look like it's being touched.

Caleb looks over and laughs. "That girl is serious about fighting. I took over for Cooper this week, running the kids MMA program, and you should see her. The boys don't want to touch her and it's just making her even madder. I can't imagine being a little girl in a boy's world."

I throw a sweeping kick to the back of Caleb's knee hoping to knock him off balance, but he sees it coming and grapples me to the ground, pinning me down for the fake win.

"Damn, I'm so out of shape," I say through a laugh. "You're getting good, fucker."

Caleb smiles. "Damn right, I am. I'm going to win this upcoming fight. I want it so fucking bad."

He stands first and gives me a hand to pull me up.

"I'm ready!" Bella comes over all cute and sweaty.

"Okay, fighter. Who do you want to fight? Caleb or me?"

She thinks for a second, but before she answers, a boy says, "I'll fight her."

I raise one brow up wondering why the hell this kid wants to fight

Bella. He looks older than her but not yet a teenager. I turn to Caleb and he answers my unspoken thoughts.

"Hey, Marco! This is Bentley. Bentley, this is Marco. He's part of the kids MMA program."

"What's up, kid? Why you wanna fight Bella?" I ask out of curiosity.

"Because she's good," Marco says with a shrug. "And she has a better chance of beating me than you two. Plus nobody else wants to fight her because she's a girl."

I look over at Bella and she nods. "If she's okay with it, I am. How old are you?"

Marco puffs out his chest, and I hold back my laughter. "I'm eleven, almost twelve.

"Where are your parents?" I ask, looking around and not seeing anyone but the usual guys working out.

"Umm…well…" Marco looks suddenly nervous and Caleb jumps in.

"Marco's mom works a lot, so Marco comes by after school to practice on days we don't have class. His mom hasn't been by to sign him up yet, but we're letting it slide for now. My only rule is he has to head home before six, so he isn't walking home in the dark. Right, Marco?"

The kid nods, and I look him up and down with this new knowledge. He's wearing old as fuck shoes that look a size too small. His shirt is definitely old, and based on the brand, it's definitely a hand-me down. His hair looks like it hasn't been cut in a while. He's skinny, like he eats but definitely not more than necessary. This kid isn't taken care of and my heart breaks for him.

Until I had a kid of my own I never even thought about other kids. I can't imagine Faith not being taken care of. Her having to walk home by herself, or me not even knowing where she is. I need to remember to talk to Caleb later about this kid. Maybe there's something more I can do to help.

For the first time, I see how amazing Cooper and Liz are for starting this program. If it weren't for them where would Marco be right now? Out running the streets? Fuck, how many kids are out on the streets because they have nowhere else to go?

I notice a couple other kids and teenagers make their way over to watch the fight. Everybody knows Bella since she practically lives at the gym with her parents.

"All right, looks like we have ourselves a match up," I say, shaking all the thoughts from my head. I'll talk to Caleb later, but I don't want to embarrass the kid by talking about him in front of other people.

Bella puts on her headgear and Caleb gives Marco one to borrow. I stand in the middle of the ring and give them the rules.

"Okay, guys…" Bella clears her throat and glares at me. "And girls,"

I add, holding back from laughing.

She nods her head once, and I force my laughter down.

"No groin attacks, no knees to the head on a grounded opponent, no head butts, no eye gouging, and no biting. Keep it clean. Got it?"

Both of them say okay and I move out of the way so they can begin. Bella goes straight for Marco and throws a punch to his stomach. He's taller than her so she goes for the area where she can reach. It isn't a hard punch, but he doesn't see it coming and stumbles back with laughter in his eyes.

We all have to respect the girl. She might be the youngest and tiniest one here, but she isn't playing. She knows what she wants and she's going for it. She's determined to earn the respect.

Marco nods in a way that says, *okay, game on,* and I'm suddenly nervous. The kid isn't big, but he's bigger than Bella and could definitely hurt her if he tried.

He throws a punch straight to her face and she ducks and then kicks him. All the guys are now chanting Bella's name and it spurs her on. I pull out my phone and record her to send to her dad. I know he'll get a kick out of this.

After a few minutes of sparring, Marco gets inside and grabs Bella by her shoulders. I can see he's going to bring her down, but instead of just dropping her, he holds on to her, does a foot sweep, and almost helps her fall so she doesn't get hurt. I definitely have respect for this kid. Bella is huffing and puffing, but I know she isn't hurt. It's obvious Marco is a good kid.

Bella wrestles under him and then picks her lower body off the floor to try to push him off her. It's a damn good move, and if she was his size it would probably work, but her tiny body isn't strong enough and he closes her in, grabbing her arm to make her tap out.

They both get up and I expect Bella to cry. She's five years old. I wouldn't blame her. But she surprises me when she throws her headgear off pissed as shit.

"Damn it. I'm never going to be big enough to beat anyone." *Did my sweet innocent little Bella just curse?*

I lock eyes with Caleb and he barks out a laugh. "Clearly she's been hanging out at the gym too long," he says, shaking his head.

"Hey, bite size!" I call out. She looks over at me and glares. "Get your little behind over here and shake hands. You can be pissed, but you don't get to be a poor sport." Yeah, I know. I didn't say shit about the cursing, but c'mon…She's in a gym filled with guys. I can discuss the cursing with her later, away from everyone.

She sighs and walks over to Marco, putting her hand out. "Good fight," she says under her breath.

"You did good, Bella. Don't worry, one day you'll be bigger and you'll definitely kick ass," Marco says to her.

"Thanks," Bella says back, smiling a little.

Everybody congratulates them both on a good fight and then Bella and I gather our stuff to head out. As we're driving out of the parking lot I see Marco walking down the street. I pull up next to him and slow down.

"Need a ride, kid?"

He shakes his head. "Nah, I'm good, but thanks."

I should probably force it, but something tells me this kid is used to being on his own, and I don't want to make him uncomfortable.

"All right, see you later." I drive away and send up a small prayer that he makes it home safe, and another one saying thanks for keeping Faith and Bella safe.

Bella and I get back to the apartment, and shortly after, the pizza arrives. Bella tells Kayla all about her fight and then we all lounge out on the couches to watch a movie. Only Bella would go from trying to beat the shit out of a kid, to watching Beauty and the Beast. I hope Faith is just like her.

Twenty

KAYLA

I'M CURRENTLY SITTING IN LIZ AND COOPER'S LIVING ROOM giving baby Nathan kisses all over his face. They named him Nathan Liam Cooper. Nathan is Liz's favorite character from One Tree Hill and Liam is Cooper's real name. How she convinced him to name his child after a guy she used to crush on I'll never know. Actually, I do. Cooper is the same way with Liz as Bentley is with me. They would give us the world if they could.

Speaking of Bentley, we still aren't together. Remember when I said I wanted to tell him I want to give us a real chance in a romantic way? Well, apparently finding time for romance with an infant is easier said than done, and I still haven't told him. Also, since the night he went down on me and didn't get anything in return, he has been acting super weird. Every night when I try to return the favor he makes up some excuse as to why we can't do anything.

Hayley comes walking in the door to join us.

"I'm bored." She pouts and plops onto the couch, taking Nathan from me.

"Don't look at me," Liz says. "I just had a baby. I'm not moving from this couch."

"Kayla, come out with me, please," Hayley begs while cooing at Nathan.

"Where to?" I ask.

"We could go to the club Caleb works at," Hayley says slyly, and I know where she's going with this. I'll totally go along with this. I don't really want to go out, but I'm happy to be Hayley's wing woman.

"Okay, I'm down. Text Ashley to see if she wants to join."

"Join who, where?" Bentley asks, walking in holding a sleeping Faith in his arms.

"We're going to go to a club tonight. Want to go?"

"Are you sure you are up for that?" Cooper chimes in, looking at

Liz.

"Oh no, we aren't going. Those two crazies are going. I'm staying right here in my comfy pajamas," Liz says with a laugh.

"I'll go," Bentley says. "My parents would love to watch Faith."

"Okay, Ashley is good to go and Kaden is joining as well," Hayley adds, looking up from her phone.

We spend the rest of the afternoon sipping coffee and cuddling with our babies while the guys go to the gym to work out. Once it starts getting late Hayley heads home to get changed, as do Bentley and I.

After we drop Faith off with Bentley's parents, we head to the club on the strip Caleb works at. He's actually off tonight but is still joining us. Since he works there, he's able to get us in as VIP. I have to admit that I'm looking and feeling good. For just having a baby not too long ago I'm rocking this dress. Sure, it's a couple sizes bigger than my pre-pregnancy ones, but I'm still rocking the shit out of it. Of course Ashley and Hayley look hot as hell.

Bentley invited a few of the other guys aside from our usual group so there's a bunch of women I don't know and some I don't really care to know. We're hanging out in the VIP area chatting with everyone, and every so often a woman approaches Bentley asking him to dance, but so far he has said no.

"Let's play a game!" Hayley's drunken ass shouts over the music.

"A game? What are we, five?" Kaden asks, laughing.

Ashley smacks him in the chest. I'll have to ask Ashley later if anything has happened with them yet.

"What game?" I ask.

"Hmm…Let's play truth or dare." Clearly the alcohol has gotten to her head but what the hell.

Ashley chimes in, "I want to play!"

A bunch of other people chilling with us say they're down to play as well. Give a bunch of grown adults alcohol and it's like we're teenagers all over again.

"I'll go first," I say because if you can't beat 'em you might as well join 'em.

"Caleb, truth or dare?" He glares at me and I laugh. I mean, c'mon, the guy holds his secrets in like Fort Knox.

"Dare." Dammit, I was hoping to ask him something. I look over at Hayley and it hits me.

"I dare you to kiss Hayley." She's now glaring at me and I take a shot and crack up. I think I'm going to like this game.

"You don't have to…" she begins to say, but before she can get the sentence out, Caleb has his mouth on hers, and holy shit! The guy looks like he can kiss. There is some definite tongue action going on there while his fingers are in her hair holding her face to his. He's clearly into this kiss, and he's most definitely. Not. Gay. Everybody hoots and hollers and cheers them on.

The kiss ends and Hayley looks like she's going to pass out. I give her a small wink and she winks back. Girls have to have each other's backs.

"Okay, Caleb. Since you did the dare, it's your turn," Ashley says.

Caleb looks around and then says to one of the groupie girls I don't know, "Samantha, truth or dare?"

She giggles and says, "Truth."

"Okay. What's the craziest thing you've ever done?

She, of course, giggles as she says, "Umm…probably the time I had a threesome in the bathroom at the club."

Her friends all laugh and I throw up a little in my mouth. Please tell me I never acted like that, at least not that bad.

After they're done laughing, she looks to her friend sitting next to her and asks, "Truth or dare?"

"Dare," her ditzy friend says.

"I dare you to kiss Bentley." *Is this bitch for real?*

Hayley jumps in, "No daring couples to do sexual stuff with other people. That shit isn't cool."

The ditzy bitch says, "Yeah, but Bentley is single, right?" Fuckin' A, I'm about to cut a bitch! But I'm not about to let my anger show. I'm too mature to play these silly games.

Everybody turns to me. "Bentley can kiss whoever he wants," I say flatly. "Anyway, I'm going downstairs to dance." I walk away without looking back. I might be great at hiding my feelings, but I'm not about to watch him make out with someone else. Why did I put off telling him how I feel? Will I ever get this shit right?

I get downstairs and go to the center of the dance floor. I'm dancing for a few minutes when hands grip my waist. I swivel around to tell the person to back the fuck off when I see it's Bentley.

"Enjoy your kiss?" I sneer. Okay, I guess I'm not as mature as I thought.

"I don't know. I'll tell you in a minute." And then his mouth devours mine—tasting me, coaxing my tongue to duel with his. He tastes sweet like the liquor he was drinking mixed with something all his own. I wrap my arms around his neck and his hands move to my ass, grabbing it and pulling me closer. All too soon the kiss ends, leaving me breathless.

"I would say I enjoyed it very much." He winks and then walks off the dance floor.

Damn that man! I seriously need to tell him I want more.

We go back up to the booths where everyone is sitting and I notice the girls from earlier are all gone. When I glance over at Hayley, she laughs and walks over to me. Whispering into my ear, she says, "After you walked away, Bentley made it clear to anybody in hearing range that he's taken, and ended the game before he walked away to find you. The girls all got bored and left."

Twenty-One

BENTLEY

I'M WATCHING HAYLEY AND KAYLA WHISPER OVER IN THE booth and all I can think about is the kiss we shared. I seriously walk around with a hard-on ninety percent of the time I'm around Kayla. She looks amazing tonight in that navy blue off the shoulder dress she's wearing. You wouldn't even be able to tell she recently gave birth. Her body isn't the same as it was before she got pregnant. She definitely has curves, but every curve on this woman is sexy. Her thicker body reminds me every day that she carried our baby in her.

I can feel her giving in soon. I just need to hold out a little while longer and I'll have her.

Kaden orders a bottle of tequila and has the waitress bring over salt and limes to go with it. Before we know it, we're all downing shots.

"Remember the last time I took a shot off you?" Kayla whispers into my ear right before licking the salt off my neck she just placed there.

"Yeah, I think so," I say slowly. It's hard to concentrate with her mouth on my body.

"Mmm…it's the night we created Faith. If you want, I can give you a repeat performance." She waggles her eyebrows then tips her head back to take the shot.

I laugh at her brazen remarks. "As much as I enjoyed that night, you aren't cleared to do anything of that nature yet." I give her a kiss on the tip of her nose and wink, and then walk away once again. Damn, I love having the last word.

Twenty-Two

KAYLA

I'VE BEEN BACK TO WORK FOR A FEW DAYS AND I WOULD BE lying if I said all is well. First of all, I'm missing my little girl like crazy. I know she's safe with Bentley, but it doesn't change the fact that I'm wishing it was me home with her. I love my job, but I also love being home with Faith.

Second of all, Bentley is still totally playing hard to get. I need to get him alone so I can make sure he still wants to be with me and tell him I want more than what our current arrangement is.

I call Hayley to see if she would be willing to watch Faith. Normally I would call Liz, but after I saw Caleb kiss Hayley I think maybe forcing them into a room together might be a good idea.

I hit the Bluetooth button to call Hayley and she answers on the first ring.

"Hey, chica! How's it going?" Her voice fills my vehicle.

"What the hell are you so chipper about?"

She cracks up laughing and says, "Nothing really. Just got in and I'm watching Caleb without a shirt on working out."

"Jeez, you have it so bad. I just left work. I must have just missed you. I have a favor to ask you."

"Okay?" she says, drawing out the word.

"Can you and Caleb watch Faith for us for the night? Bentley's birthday is coming up and I was thinking I could take him out for the night."

I hear Hayley's laughter coming through the speaker. " You mean you are going to try to seduce his ass."

"No!" I yell way too loudly.

"Oh my God, Kayla. You know he isn't going to sleep with you until you agree to really be with him." I want to tell her I'm planning to be with him but again, I want to tell Bentley first. The guy has spent months begging me to be with him. He deserves to be the first one I have this conversation with.

"Can you just watch her please? It will give you an entire night with Caleb." The line goes quiet, and I know I have her.

"Okay, I'll be there tomorrow night. But you need to let Caleb know we're babysitting together. I swear he doesn't even know I exist. Other than that one kiss from the dare he hasn't even acknowledged me."

"He does know you exist. I think he's just weird about women. I couldn't believe he even kissed you. I've never seen him kiss any woman, but damn, it was hot. Don't worry. I'll let him know. Come over tomorrow at four o'clock. Caleb doesn't work at the club on Wednesdays."

She says okay and we hang up. I call up the Mirage Las Vegas and make reservations for tomorrow night. I should tell Bentley what we're doing but decide it'll be a birthday surprise since his birthday is this week. Then I stop by *Agent Provocateur* to pick up some much needed lingerie. I want the night to be amazing.

I get home to find dinner on the table and the apartment quiet.

"Hello? Anybody home?"

Bentley walks down the hall in nothing but sweatpants, which are hanging low, showing off his sexy as hell body. My insides tighten, and if it were possible, I would totally have a lady boner. He just smirks and puts a finger to his lips to shush me.

"Faith is asleep. I made dinner. I thought you would be home sooner, but I can heat it back up real quick."

I look at the table and there are two plates of delicious-looking lasagna, two bowls filled with salad, and Italian bread.

"Did you make all this?"

"He grins and nods. "Yeah, I looked up the recipe online and made it earlier while Faith was having her morning nap. I just had to throw it in the oven once it was time to bake it. I should have asked if you were going to be late." He grabs the two plates and brings them over to the microwave to reheat them.

"I'm sorry," I tell him. "Next time I'll call when I'm going to be late. I stopped at the store to pick something up." And then I hurry and change the subject before he can ask what I bought. I don't want to give anything away. "This smells so good. Thank you."

"No problem."

We sit at the table with our plates of food and begin to eat. I look around and see the place is spotless and smells freshly cleaned. The clothes on the table are folded and ready to be put away.

"You were busy today," I comment, nodding toward the clothes.

"Yeah, it's just about finding a schedule. Faith is a really good baby. My mom also came over for a little bit and played with her while I got some stuff done."

I don't know what comes over me, but tears start pouring out of my eyes and I'm ugly crying. Bentley gets out of his seat and comes over and hugs me.

"Woman, what is the matter with you? It's just folded laundry. I promise I didn't ruin anything," he jokes.

"I-I think it's my hormones. I just feel so emotional. I miss Faith so much. I love my job, but I miss her. You get to spend all day with her and you don't even need help. My parents never did any of this themselves."

"Shh…it's okay," Bentley says, continuing to hold me. He backs away a little bit and gives me a small smile.

"You just started back to work. You're on new medications that are most likely affecting your emotions. You are a wonderful mom and there is nothing wrong with you working. Once things get situated, Faith and I will even come to visit you at work, okay? It's all good."

I sniffle loudly. "Okay, I'm sorry. It's just going to take some getting used to, I guess."

He gives me a kiss on my forehead, and I wish he were kissing my lips. Hopefully starting tomorrow night things will change between us.

"You have nothing to be sorry for. Now let's eat."

EVERYTHING IS PACKED. I HAVE THE LINGERIE, BATHING SUITS for the hot tub, change of clothes, and toiletries for both of us in a suitcase by the door waiting for Bentley to get home. When I spoke with Kathleen and told her my plans, we decided to do a dinner for Bentley this weekend with everyone. Since she wanted to see him on his actual birthday, he went over there with Faith this afternoon to visit and should be back anytime now.

Caleb comes out of the guest bathroom in his towel, and before I can ask why he's showering in there, he says, "Sorry, my bathroom has a small leak. Maintenance is coming to fix it, but I figured it would be best to shower in the guest bathroom until they do."

As he's explaining himself, there's a knock at the door and without thinking about it, I open it up to let Hayley in. She spots Caleb immediately and her entire face turns beet red. Caleb looks uncomfortable and hurries to his room.

"Oh my God! You get to see that fine specimen of a man like that every day? Did you see his tattoos? Holy shit!" Hayley whispers rather loudly.

"I guess his shower is broken. He doesn't usually walk around like that." I glance back to Caleb's door wondering why he's so uncomfortable around women. I really need to corner him and ask him what's up.

Caleb comes back out dressed in a Henley and jeans and sits on the couch. Hayley sits as well, on the other side of the couch. It's beyond awkward and after a few minutes I feel the need to speak up.

"Soooo…thank you guys for watching Faith tonight. I know either of you could have probably done it alone, but I just thought two people are better than one. I wrote down all the instructions and if you need anything please call me."

Caleb nods and then glances at Hayley real quick. She looks at him and he turns away. Jeez, I hope it isn't this awkward all night.

Luckily, Bentley walks in the door with Faith. Go time!

"Are we having a party over here I didn't know about?" he asks, looking around the room.

"Actually," I say as I take Faith from him, give her a big kiss, and then hand her to Caleb. "We're going out. Caleb and Hayley are going to watch Faith for us."

Bentley's lips curl into a frown as he opens his mouth to argue. I cover his lips with my fingers. "Nope. No arguing. It's your birthday and we're going to celebrate. They know what to do and Faith will be fine."

I grab the suitcase, give Faith one more kiss, and take Bentley's hand to drag him out the door.

Once we are in my SUV, he starts his complaining. "I don't want to leave her, Kayla. What if she thinks we aren't coming back? We just left her the other night to go to that club. What if they don't know what to do if there's an emergency? I don't like this. Maybe my parents should have watched her."

"Stop! You have been super dad and partner since we brought Faith home. We've only left her once for a couple hours to go out. One night away will be good for you. Plus, leaving her with your parents would mean Hayley and Caleb wouldn't be stuck in the house together all night."

"Wait! What do you mean 'one night'? Like all night? As in we aren't coming home tonight? And woman, leave my boy alone! Don't try to play matchmaker."

I let out a sigh. "Yes, all night. Just chill out. It will be fun. Trust me. And I'm not playing matchmaker. I'm just giving them a little nudge in the right direction."

He mumbles something under his breath, but I ignore it.

We pull up to the Mirage and I have the vehicle valet parked. I grab the suitcase and head to guest services to check in. Bentley is busy on his phone, probably texting Caleb to get an update on Faith.

I order room service for dinner and dessert and have a bottle of liquor sent up as well. I'm given the keys and we head up to our room.

Twenty-Three

BENTLEY

THE ENTIRE DRIVE MY THOUGHTS HAVE BEEN ON FAITH AND worrying if she will be okay without us all night, but the moment the hotel comes into view my thoughts shift. It's been six months since I've gotten laid so you can't blame me for what enters my mind when I picture Kayla and me alone in a hotel.

The problem is I'm not budging on how I feel. The last time I gave in, she fucked me and left me, and while I don't regret it because it's how Faith was brought into the world, that shit isn't happening again.

I don't bother to ask her where she's going with this. I know what she's hoping for, but if she thinks I'm just going to give in, she has another thing coming. That doesn't mean I can't enjoy a night away with Kayla, though. I thoroughly enjoy and welcome her company in any way I can get it.

After Kayla checks in and orders food for us, we head to our room. She unlocks the door with the key and goes straight to the bedroom without saying a word. I sit down on the couch and wait for her to make her move. I know it's coming. While I'm waiting I text Caleb for the second…okay, maybe the fifth time to check on Faith

Me: How is Faith?

Caleb: See above for the same damn answer I gave you three minutes ago.

Me: Send me a picture.

Caleb: (Insert picture of his ugly mug)

Me: Fucker! Send me a picture of my daughter!

Caleb: (insert picture of the most beautiful baby in the world)

While I'm staring at the picture of Faith chewing on her hand,

Kayla comes out wearing a blood red string bikini. She walks past me and her bottoms are those sexy as fuck cheeky things that are barely bottoms at all. She looks fucking beautiful. Her hips are thick, her breasts are voluptuous, and her ass and thighs are perfect. Her stomach is soft from recently giving birth. Everything about Kayla post-baby turns me the fuck on.

She grabs a towel from the bathroom and throws my board shorts at me.

"Go get changed, birthday boy. There's a private Jacuzzi calling our names," she says with a wink.

I get changed and we head out to the Jacuzzi. She switches on her iPhone to some slow song I've never heard of and heads over to the Jacuzzi. I stand still, taking her in, as she enters the water slowly. Her nipples peak slightly from the change in the temperature and then are covered from the bubbles in the water. She looks absolutely exquisite without even trying.

"Are you going to stand there or join me?" she asks with a devilish grin on her face.

I get in on the other side and sink down into the water. It's warm and the jets feel good against my back. She sits across from me just staring at me with a sly smirk on her face.

"What?"

"Nothing," she says coyly.

I feel something hit my dick, springing it to life. I reach under the water and feel Kayla's foot trying to rub on me. I grab it and pull her toward me, her body hitting the water. Her hair is drenched and water is dripping down her face, but instead of being mad, she cracks up laughing. I love to hear her laughter. It's probably one of the most beautiful sounds in the world.

She stands, and with her hands on her hips, mock glares at me. I know what's coming next, so I beat her to it. Cupping both hands, I splash her with water right in her face. It's dripping all over her and she's spluttering the water out of her mouth while trying to wipe the water off her face.

I stand and walk toward her. Taking her face in my hands, I give her a soft kiss on her wet lips and tuck her wet hair behind her ear so I can see her face. "That's better," I say, admiring how beautiful she looks when she's happy.

She stands there for a moment, staring at me, and when I think she's plotting her revenge, instead she says, "I want this." There's so much she can mean by that, so I raise an eyebrow silently asking her for clarification.

She suddenly looks shy as she whispers, "Us. I mean, if you still want us that is."

Her eyes are half-lidded and she's never looked so vulnerable than she does in this moment. I grip the curves of her hips and yank her toward me as I sit back down. She lets out an audible gasp that quickly morphs into a nervous giggle. I pull her up into my lap, so she's straddling me. "Say it again."

She chews her bottom lip for a second. "I want us. I want to give us a real shot."

"You sure." I need to be sure this is what she really wants.

She nods slowly. "Woman, if you're doing this to get me to have sex with you, we're going to have major problems. Once I'm inside you, you're mine. Do you understand me? No going back."

Her eyes go wide and she nods faster.

"No, I need to hear the words."

"I'm yours. No going back. I've wanted to tell you for a while but wanted it to be romantic." That's all I need to hear. I bring my mouth to hers and my need for her consumes any other rational thoughts I might have. My tongue plunges into her mouth as she wraps herself around me. The water shifts from our bodies grinding up against each other. Her warm pussy is rubbing against my hard erection, and while I would definitely enjoy Jacuzzi sex, I need more.

I grab ahold of her ass and pick her up as I stand in the water. I step out of the Jacuzzi and lay her down on the balcony floor. I take a second to look at the beautiful woman in front of me and then kneel between her legs to remove her bikini bottoms. Her pussy is perfection. It's clean cut but not completely bald. Trimmed neatly. I spread her legs wide and slowly stick one finger into her.

She isn't quite wet enough yet, so I move up her body to her perfect tits. Moving the tiny triangles out of the way, I put my mouth around her nipple while pinching her other nipple with my thumb and forefinger.

"Oh, God, Bentley. Please," Kayla moans.

I continue to suck, lick, and pinch her nipples causing her to squirm. I move one hand back down to her pussy and stick one digit in again. It's definitely wetter. Now we're getting somewhere. One finger, then two fingers deep, and her back is arched as she continues to thrash her hips down onto my fingers so I'll go deeper inside her.

And what my woman wants, my woman gets. I remove my fingers from her, and she sighs from the absence of me. I trail kisses along her jaw down her neck as I remove my swim trunks with one hand, then I guide my hard shaft into her warm, wet pussy. Dropping my forehead on her shoulder, I stop halfway in and pray I don't blow my load before this even begins.

She buries her hands in my hair holding me close, and I begin to slowly thrust in and out. She feels so good, so tight. Her pussy is gripping my cock like a goddamn vice. I bring my mouth down to her tits and latch on to her nipple, sucking on it and pulling it the way I know she likes. I angle my cock to go a bit deeper, grinding against her clit.

"Oh…Oh…Bentley…Fuck!" she groans. Her wall tighten and she comes all over my dick.

I pump into her several more times, releasing myself completely into her. I drop my face to the dip between her tits and hold my breath, waiting for the excuses to come. Only they don't. I know she's awake because her hands are in my hair, gently massaging my scalp, but she isn't saying a word.

I finally decide to stop acting like a pussy and look up at her. "Do you still want us?"

Twenty-Four

KAYLA

"DO YOU STILL WANT US?"

I look into Bentley's beautiful blue eyes that are open like a window to his soul. He has always been this way with me. Every step along the way he's left his heart open and vulnerable, welcoming me with open arms, while I've pushed him away at every turn. I've had sex plenty of times in my life, but what we just did wasn't sex. It was making love. This man loves me. He wants me and only me, and I vow to show him every day how much he means to me.

He must take my lack of response as a no because his face morphs into anger as he shakes his head and attempts to get up. I tighten my hold on his hair and pull him down to me.

"Yes, I still want us. I'm sorry it's taken me this long to get on the same page as you, but yes, I want us. I need you, Bentley. Just please don't break my heart. I don't think my heart could take it," I plead. I don't know where the words come from, but I feel like I need him to understand that this isn't easy and I'm so damn scared.

He gets off me without saying a word and then scoops me up bridal style and heads back inside to our room. He lays me on the bed and then hovers above me. We're both still wet and naked soaking the sheets. He peppers kisses all over my bod, on my forehead, to each of my cheeks, and to the tip of my nose. He moves to my ear and sucks lightly on my lobe, then brushes his lips across my neck and moves downward to my collarbone. He lays wet kisses on each of my breasts and then descends to my belly, trailing kisses to my mound.

He doesn't stop there, though. His body moves downward, and he nips on my thigh, making me laugh.

"Bentley! That tickles! I bark out a laugh. "What are you doing?"

He looks up at me and his lips curve into a gorgeous grin. "I'm making sure you're real."

I laugh harder at his antics. He continues to kiss down my leg and when he gets to my foot, he nibbles on my toes, throwing me into a fit of laughter.

His grin widens. "Is this real? Are you really mine?"

My cheeks hurt from smiling so hard and my stomach aches from laughing. He's so adorable. I nod.

He comes back up my body, until we're face to face, and kisses me softly. His lips linger on mine, sucking my bottom lip out as he releases it and pulls back.

"I promise you, Kayla. I'll never break your heart, baby." He moves his lips down to the skin right above my left breast and kisses my chest right over my heart.

"Thank you for having faith in us. You won't ever regret it." He gives my *heart* another kiss and then comes up to lie with me.

The food arrives and, after we change the bed to dry sheets, we eat in a comfortable silence with me sitting on Bentley's lap as he feeds both of us. I have my arms around his neck and I've never felt closer to someone than I do to him right now. There's a new vibe between us and it feels good. Once we're done eating, Bentley plugs his iPhone into the speaker and says, "Dance with me."

The tears well up in my eyes at the flashbacks to the dinner in our apartment when he asked me to dance for the first time and then again at Liz and Cooper's wedding just before I gave birth to Faith. This time the song playing is faster paced. Sam Smith is singing the lyrics to *Stay With Me* through the speakers as Bentley holds me close and once again whispers the words of the song to me like he did the first time we danced together. Our bodies sway back and forth as he holds me tightly to him, almost as if he's afraid I might change my mind and leave him. What he doesn't realize is that I'm not going anywhere. I know it's going to take time to prove it to him, but I will. This man is all I want.

The song ends and he whispers into my ear, "Baby, stay with me."

"For as long as you want me," I vow.

He lets out a sigh of relief and then picks me up and carries me to the couch, where we make love for the second time tonight.

I WAKE UP TO THE SUN SHINING THROUGH THE WINDOWS AND the feel of Bentley holding me close. I feel him move slightly and know he's waking up as well.

"Want to order breakfast?"

"No, baby. To be honest I just want to go home to our little girl and spend the first day of the rest of our lives together as a family."

As we drive home to our little girl, holding hands, my heart is so full of love. It feels like the switch has been turned back on, like I've been stuck in the dark alone all this time, and now I'm no longer alone. Only I didn't have to stumble and find the light myself. Bentley was here this whole time ready to switch it on for me. All I had to do was have faith in us.

Twenty-Five

BENTLEY

THE CRAZY THING ABOUT BABIES IS THAT THEY GROW LIKE damn weeds! It's the end of November, Thanksgiving just passed, and Faith is officially five months old. She's sitting up, eating solids, and when she's on the floor she does this cute rocking thing on her knees, which confirms what all the moms say is true from *Mommy and Me*—she's getting ready to crawl. Yes, that's right. I belong to a mommy and me group I found online. I still think it's ridiculous that it isn't called *Parent and Me,* but I'll pick my battles since I'm the only dad actually in the group.

Faith and I have a great schedule going on. We usually start off our morning with some oatmeal or rice with fruit, we join the other moms at the park later in the morning until it's time for Faith's nap, and then I head to the gym to visit Kayla while she's at work. Some days she'll take Faith home while I work out with the guys and other days I'll go home to make dinner for when she gets home.

Right now I'm heading to the park to meet the other moms. My phone rings over Bluetooth and Faith makes a bunch of sounds in the backseat.

"Hello?"

"Hey there, Mr. Mom! What are you up to?" It's Liz, and I would bet she's home and bored. We haven't hung out with the babies yet other than when we all hang out together as a group. She's mentioned it several times, but I figured I would let her and Kayla hang out. They can get their baby and best friend time in at once.

"I'm heading to the park with Faith. What's up?"

"Really? Would you mind if Nathan and I join you? Bella's at school until later and Cooper's at the gym."

"I'm meeting my mom's group there, but I guess you can join."

"Mom's group? Why don't I know about this? Am I not cool enough to be part of your group?"

Oh, Jeez. Here we go…

"If you want to meet us, then meet us. It's not that big of a deal."

"Okay, text me the address of the park you're going to. Be there soon! Bye!"

We get to the park and I spot Monica and Sara right away. They both have daughters that are just a little older than Faith. They wave to me and I head over to them, putting the diaper bag down on the bench along the way. There are four swings and two are empty, so I put Faith into the swing and push her lightly. Her giggles start up immediately and I snap a picture to send to Kayla.

"Hey Bentley!" both women say in unison and laugh.

"Hello, Ladies. And hello to you precious little girls," I say to their daughters, tickling each of their tummies. They both give me a baby giggle.

I go back to pushing Faith as we discuss our babies' recent milestones.

"Tori is finally crawling!" Monica announces excitedly.

"Amy is almost there, but she's standing up for a few seconds against the couch before she falls back down on her butt. Maybe she'll just go straight to walking and skip crawling," Sara chimes in.

"Nice! Faith is still doing the whole rocking on her knees thing. I've baby proofed the entire apartment though just in case."

"Just in case what?" I hear from behind me. I turn around and see Liz standing with Nathan on her hip, her eyes darting between the two women and me. Damn, she got here fast.

"Hey Liz. This is Monica and Sara." I point to the two women. "I was just telling them how Faith is almost crawling, so I baby proofed the house this weekend. Ladies, this is Liz. She's my friend Cooper's wife, and this little guy is Nathan."

"And I'm also his girlfriend's best friend," she adds with a tone that sounds off.

Both women say hello and we continue the play date. A few of the other women in the mom's group show up and soon there's almost a dozen babies crawling, walking, and running all over the park. Liz is sitting on the bench while Nathan sits in front of her as she looks intently at her phone.

I sit next to her and place Faith on the ground to play with the sand toys.

"Cooper?" I ask, nodding toward her phone. She looks up and glares at me for a second, but quickly relaxes her face into more of a grimace.

"No, actually it's Kayla. You remember your girlfriend, right?"

I ignore the dig. "Cool. Tell her I said hi."

"That's it? You said hi?"

I think about it for a second not sure what answer she's looking for here.

"Um, hi and I'll see her later at the gym?"

She huffs out a "Whatever" and goes back to texting.

A couple of the moms come over and let us know they're going to head out since it's almost nap time and invite Liz to join us the day after tomorrow at the local pool.

"I'm not sure what I have going on, but thank you for the invite."

"Okay, well, it's an open invitation, and I'll send you an invite to our online group. I'll get your email from Bentley later. Let me know if Faith starts crawling, Bentley! See you at the pool," Sara says before leaving.

Everybody else says goodbye and then it's just Liz and me left.

"Seriously?" she barks out.

"What?" I'm confused as fuck as to why this woman is acting so damn weird.

"While the girlfriend-slash-mother of your child is at work, you're hanging out at the park with a bunch of hot women who are all having Daddy Bentley fantasies?"

What in the actual fuck?

"Please don't tell me you texted that bullshit to Kayla. You already know how insecure she is about being in a relationship. Would you be saying this shit if I was a woman at the park with other women? No, you wouldn't. I can't help there are no other dads that stay home or join the mom's group."

"Whatever, Bentley. I didn't say anything to Kayla, but you should."

Faith starts to whine and I know it's time to get her home for a nap. I scoop her up and wipe the sand off her body and turn to face Liz. "I'm not doing anything wrong. Don't make this something it's not, please."

She sighs loudly but nods okay.

I get home, lay Faith down for her afternoon nap and begin to work on the laundry. I start to think about what Liz said. Does she have a point? Should I tell Kayla about the mom's group I'm in? I haven't purposely kept it from her. I tell her all about Faith's day and mine, but if I'm honest I don't include the other women I hang out with in our conversations.

Every day I hope and pray Kayla won't wake up and change her mind about us. Sometimes I feel like I walk on eggshells afraid that if I do or say the wrong thing she'll walk away from me. So maybe subconsciously I kept that tidbit of info out of our conversations to keep everything stable.

My phone rings in my pocket and I see it's my mom.

"Hey, Mom, how are you?"

"Oh, I'm good, sweetie. How are Faith and Kayla?"

"Both good. Faith is sleeping and Kayla is at work. What's up?"

"Well I was wondering if we could take Faith for the weekend. I was thinking Kayla and you can do a weekend getaway and we could watch Faith. I would love some time with my granddaughter."

I laugh at her comment. The woman spends time with her granddaughter several times a week, but I'm not going to turn down a chance to take Kayla away.

"That actually sounds really good, Mom. We haven't been away since my birthday when Kayla surprised me. Now I can surprise her. Thanks."

"No problem. Why don't you guys join us for an early dinner Friday and then take off afterward? You can pick Faith up Sunday night or Monday morning."

"Perfect. I'm going to make reservations now."

I text the guys to see if they want to make it a group thing. Cooper replies a little while later saying his mom would love to take Nathan and Bella for the weekend. Caleb says he's down, and Kaden is down as well. I tell Cooper to let Liz know I'm surprising Kayla and to invite Hayley and Ashley as well.

He texts me later letting me know Ashley's parents are good to watch her son and Hayley will be joining as well. I send out a group text letting them all know to pack warm clothes because we're flying to Breckenridge, a ski resort in Colorado. My family has a cabin up there and now seems like the perfect time to take advantage of it.

I shoot my mom a text letting her know and she replies with a smiley face. Next, I make reservations to charter a private plane from McCarran international to Eagle County Regional, which is only about an hour from the ski resort.

While I'm booking the flight I get a text from Monica confirming our play date for the pool on Thursday. I send her a *thumbs up* emoticon and continue making plans for this weekend, writing down all the shit I need to pack for us and Faith. Luckily my parents keep a lot of stuff at their house since we visit often. I also jot down to remember my favorite red bathing suit of Kayla's. We will definitely be taking advantage of the hot tub at night.

Twenty-Six

KAYLA

IT'S THURSDAY MORNING AND MY ONLY APPOINTMENT OF THE day was canceled because the fighter has to go out of town for a last minute photo shoot. I decide to surprise Bentley and meet him at the pool at the local Y. Liz told me she's joining him as well. I go by the house, grab my bathing suit, and head to the swimming center.

I pay for my swimming pass and head to the locker room to change. There are a few moms changing their babies in there while conversing.

"My God, he's like sex on a stick," one woman says, fanning herself.

"Seriously, and the way he is with his daughter…If I weren't married, I would be all over that," another woman says.

"Yeah, well, I'm not married, so maybe I should be all over that," another woman says.

I hear them leave as I finish changing, and then go in search for my sex-on-a-stick. When I get to the pool I spot Bentley and Faith. Damn, he looks sexy. He's holding our daughter in the air and then brings her back down, making it look like he's plunging her into the water, but in reality he does it so gently the water barely parts. I can see her beautiful grin from here. I look for Liz and see her talking to the women I just saw in the locker room.

I walk over to join Bentley in the water, but before I can make it over, the women who were just talking to Liz join him in the pool with a baby on each of their hips.

I watch for a few minutes and it's clear he knows them. Holy shit! It hits me. *My* sex-on-a-stick is the same sex-on-a-stick they were talking about! *Oh, hell no! That shit ain't gonna fly.*

I pick up my pace and walk quickly over to the edge of the pool and walk down the steps on a mission to claim my damn man. When Bentley first sees me, he looks…shocked…or is it guilt? But then his face morphs into a huge smile.

He must tell Liz I'm here because she looks over at me and her face definitely looks guilty. One thing about my best friend is she can't hide shit from me and something tells me she knew all about this. I give her an eyebrow up silently saying *what the fuck* and her eyes bulge out knowing exactly what I mean.

I swim to Bentley and, without saying hello to anybody else around him, wrap my arms around his neck and give him a kiss that screams *mine*. He's still holding Faith and when she spots me kissing her daddy she begins to squeal in his arms wanting me to grab her.

"Surprise," I whisper to Bentley, so only he can hear.

He stares at me for a brief moment, gauging my tone, then says, "It definitely is."

He grabs the back of my neck with his available hand and kisses me once more. Faith's squeals get louder and we both separate and laugh. I take her from him and give her chubby little cheek a big wet kiss.

"I didn't know you would be joining us," Liz says nervously.

"My appointment canceled so I thought I would surprise you guys."

"Hey Bent, do you want to get out to give the babies a snack? It was my turn to bring snacks and I brought yogurts."

I look over at the woman who, not even five minutes ago, stood in the locker room and said she would be all over *that* if she wasn't married, clearly referring to my boyfriend.

"Bent?" I ask Bentley.

He at least has the decency to look sheepishly at me. "Kayla, this is Monica, Sara, and Roxy. They're in the Mommy and Me group Liz and I belong to."

I turn to glare at my best friend who has never mentioned this before.

"Um, well, actually I'm not exactly in the group. I just met them the other day. My membership is still pending upon approval from the admin."

I shoot her another death glare and she looks down at Nathan, pretending to pick imaginary lint off him. Yeah, my best friend and I will definitely be having a conversation later. But for right now, I do what any respectable woman does when she's caught off guard but can't let those catty bitches know. I fake it!

"Oh, that group! I remember you mentioning them," I first say to Liz. Then turning to the bitches that want my man, I say, "Nice to meet you. I've heard so much about you guys." I put my hand out to shake each of their hands.

Bentley looks scared as hell at this point, knowing I haven't really heard shit about the hot moms he's been chilling with.

"Sooo…yogurt?" I ask nobody in particular. Everybody nods and says yes and we all get out to get the yogurts.

Bentley tries to stop me by putting his arm on mine, but when I turn around and growl out "Not now," he stops and takes the hint.

I lay Faith on the lounge chair that Bentley has everything sprawled out on and change her wet diaper. Liz comes up to me and, like the best friends we are, apologizes with only her eyes. I nod slightly, letting her know we're good, and sit on the chair with Faith between my legs. Bentley sits on the edge of the chair and begins to feed Faith a yogurt. She gets so excited, batting at the spoon, wanting to grab it herself. This little girl is our entire world. I get choked up when I think about some other woman spending time with my daughter. Is that what Bentley needs? Does he need a woman who stays home instead of works? What if after all we've gone through to get here, I'm not the woman he needs? And then I think about the deceit. Not once has he mentioned he's hanging out with all of these hot moms during the day while I'm at work. He has to know this is wrong or else he would have mentioned it.

I close my eyes to hold back the tears that are threatening to spill over. When I open my eyes, Bentley is looking at me with a pained expression. He opens his mouth, attempting to speak, but with those women around I'm not doing this here. I shake my head, and he sighs, but nods.

We spend the rest of the afternoon at the pool, and while we have a blast as a family with our daughter, it's tainted by all the secrets that have been kept, and all the questions I want answers to. Is this where it all ends? Is this where my mom gets to say the *I told you so* I've always feared?

Twenty-Seven

BENTLEY

FUCK! I KNOW I TECHNICALLY HAVE NOTHING TO FEEL GUILTY over, but at the same time, I know I do. When Kayla closed her eyes, I could see it in her face, the insecurity that I might want these other moms over her. I could see the fear in her that I'm going to break her heart and that her mom was right and she was once again wrong. I wanted so badly to explain, to hold her and tell her she's all I'll ever want, but she wouldn't even let me talk.

The day comes to a close, we say our goodbyes, and since we took separate vehicles, Kayla and I part ways and agree to meet at home. Kayla takes Faith home with her, so I stop by the florist and pick up a dozen roses. I know it's totally cliché, but at this point I'll try anything.

I walk into the apartment and Kayla spots the flowers immediately. Tears start flowing down her face and I have a feeling flowers weren't the right move. I set them on the end table and go over to her. Picking her up, I carry her over to the couch. Faith is playing in her exerciser, twisting and turning, while banging the keys that make noise and light up.

I turn Kayla so her legs are straddling my thighs and let her cry into my shirt for a couple of minutes before I speak. "Baby, please stop crying. I'll throw the fucking flowers away. I'm sorry."

She looks up at me with wide, vulnerable eyes and quietly asks, "Do you still want to be with me?"

"What are you talking about, woman? Of course I still want to be with you. You are my forever." I give her a soft kiss on her lips. They taste salty from her crying, and it's officially my least favorite taste in the world.

"When I went into the locker room to change I didn't know it at the time but those women were talking about how hot you were and saying if they weren't married they would want to be with you. One woman even said she's not married and wants you! And then when

I saw you with them, having fun with Faith and their kids…Is that what you want? A woman who will stay home with the baby? And why didn't you tell me about this group? Do you know how crappy it feels to be kept in the dark about what you do numerous times a week?"

Jesus…women and their big mouths. I know these women have occasionally flirted, but I've ignored it. I figured it was just innocent and since most of them are married I let it go. They have never approached me or said anything remotely inappropriate. The truth is them gossiping is the equivalent to what guys do when they see a hot woman. However, pointing that out to Kayla is not going to help the situation. I might be a guy, but I'm not a complete idiot.

"Those women can say whatever they want. You are the only woman for me. I joined that group so Faith and I could socialize with other parents, that's it. I love being home with Faith. I love that you enjoy your job. I told you this before and I'll say it as many times as you need to hear it. I'm okay with you working. If you ever want to stay home, then you can do that. You choosing to work instead of staying home doesn't change how I feel about you. You are a great girlfriend and mother. Okay?"

She sniffles and nods. "Just promise me if you no longer want me you'll tell me. Please don't ever cheat on me, Bentley. I couldn't handle the humiliation."

"Stop! Don't say stupid shit like that. I'm not that Jackass from when you were a teenager. Nobody is cheating, leaving, or using anybody." I grab Kayla's chin and give her a quick kiss. "I love you. I love you just the way you are. I would never cheat on you. Just let me love you, baby. I'm sorry for not telling you about the mom's group. It was wrong of me. I'll never hide anything from you again."

I don't wait for a response because I know I won't get one. While she doesn't freak out when I tell her constantly that I love her, she doesn't say it back…yet. I set her down next to me on the couch, pick up Faith, and hand her to her. I reach down putting my arms on either side of Kayla's head, and give first Kayla a kiss, and then Faith one, breathing them both in. It's the best smell. I wish I could bottle it up and keep it forever. These two girls are my world. "Now, we have some packing to do!"

Kayla's eyes dart to me in confusion. "For what?"

"Surprise. My parents are taking Faith for the weekend. We leave tomorrow night after dinner with my parents. You need to pack warm clothes with plenty of layers…Oh! And that sexy-as-hell red bikini is a must. That's all I'm telling you."

"OH. MY. GOD. ARE YOU FREAKING SERIOUS?" LIZ YELLS, CAUSING people to stop eating and look at us.

"Shh…chill the heck out," I say while feeding Faith another bite of mashed potatoes.

"This is so exciting!" Ashley chimes in.

Once I knew we were heading out to Breckenridge on an impromptu mini-vacation with all of our friends for the weekend, I decided it would be the perfect time and place to pop the question to Kayla. I already purchased the ring awhile back, now I just need to figure out the best way to do it.

I'm currently having an early lunch with Liz, Ashley, and our kids, hoping they can help me plan something romantic before we head out of town tonight.

"Do you have a ring?" Liz asks with tears in her eyes. I've never been around women as much as I have since I've started staying home with Faith, and one thing I've learned from these women is that they are full of emotions. I've always known they have emotions, but after spending so much time with all these moms, I could write a book on how crazy their emotions really are. Happy, sad, mad, I can't ever keep up. Men have one emotion. Chill.

"Of course I do, and no you aren't seeing it before Kayla does. Now help me out here. How should I propose? Alone? In front of everyone?"

Liz frowns. "Hm, I think you should do it alone. We can all celebrate afterward, but what if she says no?"

Ashley's eyebrows shoot up. "Do you think she would say no?"

"She's going to say yes. We've come a long way. We're together and we have Faith. Her biggest fear is being heartbroken. I just need to convince her that forever is the opposite of breaking her heart."

"I agree with Liz. Do it alone. That way she doesn't feel overwhelmed or pressured."

"All right. Alone it is." I attempt to give Faith another bite of potatoes, but she isn't having it. She closes her mouth tight and shakes her head. Fucking cute kid. Just as stubborn as her mother.

We continue to discuss the different ways I can propose while Bella and Tristan play with Faith and Nathan. They're making crazy faces at them, which causes them to squeal and clap in response. Faith loves all the attention.

"Has Kayla mentioned anything about not being able to have more kids?" Liz asks quietly.

"No, but if she ever wanted to, I'll make sure it happens. For now, Faith is all we need."

"You're a good guy, Bentley. Thank you for taking care of our girl."

I give Liz a wink. Nothing more needs to be said. I'll always take care of Kayla.

I pay for lunch, then we grab our kids and all head home. Everybody will be meeting at the plane tonight to fly out together.

Twenty-Eight

BENTLEY

DINNER AT MY PARENTS WENT WELL. WE SAID OUR GOODBYES to Faith and thanked my parents for watching her. I decided it would be best to take a cab to the airport and leave my car at my parents so we don't have to deal with parking. Kayla's Volvo SUV has been having some issues so I need to look into getting her a new vehicle. I love my BMW so maybe I'll get her one as well.

When we get there and pull up to the private hanger, Kayla looks shocked that we aren't arriving in the regular terminal.

"Umm…Bentley? Are we flying on a private plane?" She darts her eyes from me to the plane several times making me laugh.

"Yeah, I figured it would be easier with all of us flying on such short notice."

"Who's all of us?"

We step onto the plane and her question is answered. Already on the plane are all of our friends chatting and waiting for us.

"Oh my God! Everybody is going away?" she screeches as she runs over to Liz, Hayley, and Ashley and gives them a group hug.

Cooper walks over and gives me a bro hug. "Finally using some of that dough on yourself, bro?"

I shake my head and chuckle. The truth is I couldn't spend the amount of money I have in my lifetime, especially not the way I live. Because of my father being financially savvy, I have money all over the place in various ventures, and the money I do spend is just from the interest and my earnings alone.

I walk over and bump fists with Caleb and Kaden, and then the pilot requests we fasten our seatbelts so we can take off.

Once we're seated and buckled in, Kayla asks, "Who is paying for all this?"

The guys all look at me quickly and then try to look around to not give anything away. It's not that I'm keeping my money situation from her. It's like I've said before, I don't want to scare her off. She has this crazy notion that people need to be equal in a relationship. I've finally gotten her to give us a real chance, and if she knew money-wise, it's like ninety-nine to one she might freak out on me. I'm just not ready to chance it yet.

However, I'm not going to flat out lie to her. "I did. I have money saved up and I wanted to do this for us. Please don't be upset. We're fine for money and I just want to have a good weekend with you and our friends, okay?"

She looks at me skeptically but luckily lets it go. If all goes well this weekend, we'll be one step closer to being married and then I'll tell her about my inheritance. I just need to take it one small step at a time with her.

We arrive in Colorado and have a van take us straight to the cabin to get settled in. It's cold as shit here, but I love it. We arrive at the cabin and Kaden is the first one to comment.

"Holy shit, dude! Is this your place?"

I try to look at it from their perspective. It's a large two-story cabin made of brick and stone. There's a wraparound porch on both the first and second story. There's a large chimney that goes up the entire side of the cabin, where smoke is rising out of the top. I had the housekeeper stock up and start the fire before we got here. In the background are the mountains.

To some, I guess the cabin would look over the top like something you would see in a photo, but to me it looks like home away from home. I spent my entire life coming here with my parents during many holidays including Christmas break.

"It's not my place, technically. It's my parents' place. We've been coming here every year since I was little. Actually Cooper has been here a few times with me when his parents would let him go."

Everybody walks inside and stops to take it all in. The inside is just as beautiful as the outside. All wood from floor to ceiling, comfy country chic furniture and décor my mom has decorated the place with over the years. Kayla walks up to the stone fireplace and picks up the family picture on the mantel and smiles at me.

"You look so happy in this picture. I hope one day we have pictures like this of Faith."

I wrap my arms around her waist and kiss her forehead. "We will and she'll be just as happy. She already is happy. Maybe if you like it here we can make coming here a family tradition."

"Really? I've never skied or snowboarded before. Can you teach me?" She beams with childlike excitement.

"Absolutely. And when Faith gets older, she'll learn to as well. You'll teach her to surf and I'll teach her to ski and fight," I say with a wink.

She laughs and it makes my heart pump a little faster. I love that fucking sound.

"All right, so where is everybody sleeping?" Caleb cuts in.

"Liz and I get our own room," Cooper adds.

"I can share a room with Ashley," Kaden says.

"Yeah? On the floor?" Ashley barks out with laughter.

"Shut up, crazy." Kaden laughs back.

"There are four rooms. Kayla and I are taking the master so you all can figure the rest out." I grab Kayla's hand and pull her down the hall to the bedroom. Let them figure out the sleeping arrangements. I have forty-eight hours alone with my woman. I don't have time to play camp counselor.

We get to the master bedroom, and as soon as we walk in, I close the door and push her up against it, plunging my tongue into her mouth. Her hands come up to my hair and she tugs lightly, trying to push me away. I try to ignore her and continue to swirl my tongue around when she laughs into my mouth causing me to laugh as well.

I back away and she laughs harder. "Bentley! I haven't even seen the bedroom yet!"

"It has four walls and a bed. You don't need to see anything else. Trust me. Now where were we?"

I push my erection up against her and go back to kissing her. This time she moans softly and instead of her fingers tugging my hair to push me away she pulls my face closer causing our kiss to deepen.

I reach down and grab her ass, squeezing tightly, Just as I'm about to pick her up to bring her to the bed there's a knock on the door.

I pause our kissing just long enough to yell, "Go away!" and then bring my lips back to hers to continue tasting her.

There's a knock again.

"What the fuck! Go away!" I yell again.

"Maybe they need something." Kayla laughs, while trying to give me her best glare.

I move us from the door and swing it open, about to kill whoever is on the other side.

"Umm…I'm sorry. I just wanted to see if there's any way to get to the resort. I was thinking I could maybe stay up there," Hayley says softly, clearly embarrassed to have interrupted us.

"What? Why would you do that?" Kayla says, pushing me away and walking out the door with Hayley.

"Well, there's only one room left and Caleb doesn't want to share."

I walk behind them down the hall, planning all the ways I can get even with Caleb for being the reason my dick is still hard as fuck and not balls deep inside my woman right now.

"You aren't staying anywhere else. Right, Bentley? We'll figure it out."

I nod then head to find Caleb to get this shit figured out. He's sitting on the living couch with his head hanging down.

"What's up man? Is it that big of a deal to share a room with Hayley?"

He sighs and shakes his head. All these years and I've never seen him with a woman except that night when he kissed Hayley on a dare.

"I'm sorry, man. I'm just not comfortable sharing a room with her. It's nothing against her. I just don't know her. I can stay somewhere else."

"No, man. It's fine. We'll figure it out. Can I ask you why though?

He looks at me and cringes. "I just don't trust women."

"All right, would you be okay with sleeping on the couch? I would feel like a dick if I ask her to and she's trying to leave to stay somewhere else."

Caleb sighs loudly and shakes his head. "Fuck, I know she likes me. I try to ignore it, but I see the looks and shit. I shouldn't have kissed her at the club. I don't know what the hell came over me. I don't want to be a dick. Let her sleep in the room and I'll crash on the couch as long as you're okay with that. She kept insisting I sleep in the room and she would sleep elsewhere. I didn't know what to do."

"Okay, cool. And it's only for two nights, so it's not a big deal. If you ever want to talk, I'm here."

We bump fists and head into the kitchen to let Hayley know the room is all hers.

"Are you sure, Caleb? I don't mind sharing a room with you…or I can stay on the couch." The poor girl looks so defeated. I never paid attention, but I think she really does like him.

"It's cool. Please take the room. I don't mind sleeping on the couch." He gives her a small smile and she smiles back accepting his answer.

We all decide to call it a night. It's late and we are going to get up early in the morning to go check out the skiing resort. We walk back to our room and the first thing I do is call my parents to check on Faith while Kayla gets ready for bed.

I'm finishing up the call when Kayla walks out of the bathroom in a sheer black nightgown. It shows everything yet covers it all up at the same time. Underneath is a small piece of material some would call underwear that is supposed to be covering her pussy but isn't really covering much at all. Her hair is down and it's just long enough that it covers her nipples so I can't see them, but I would bet my life they're budding out ready for me to suck on them.

She's leaning against the doorframe with a devilish grin on her face knowing exactly what she's doing to me. She looks fucking perfect. She *is* fucking perfect. And she's all mine. I don't know what the hell comes over me but all my planning flies out the window when I blurt out, "Marry me."

Her head tilts to the side unsure she heard me right. I know this isn't how it was supposed to happen, but fuck it. It's happening now.

I stand up as she walks slowly toward me waiting for me to say something. I meet her in front of the bed and turn her to sit her on the edge.

"This isn't at all how I planned this. I was going to do it tomorrow night. I reserved a private room at the restaurant at the resort, and I was going to get down on one knee after dessert. But then you come out here looking like you do, beautiful and sexy, and I couldn't wait another second to ask you to be my wife. I love you so damn much. I love our daughter and our life. I want to marry you and make you happy for the rest of our life."

I pull the ring out of the pocket of my luggage to show it to her. "Kayla Peterson, will you make me even happier than I already am and marry me?"

Twenty-Nine

KAYLA

I DON'T EVEN NEED TO LOOK AT THE RING TO KNOW MY answer. It could have been a freaking ring pop and I would still say yes to this man. He has become everything to me. He's an amazing father and partner, and has become my best friend. He's been saying *I love you* to me for so long and while I haven't once said it back, he has never commented or gotten upset. He has loved me unconditionally every step of the way. He accepts me just the way I am.

I realize that while I'm listing off every reason in my head as to why I'm going to marry Bentley, I haven't yet verbally said a word. And of course he continues to have patience, just waiting for me to sift through and process my thoughts and feelings.

When I finally speak, what comes out first is, "I love you."

His face brightens instantly and I want to freeze-frame the way he looks when he hears those words.

"I love you too, baby."

We stare at each other for a moment and then it hits me…I still didn't give him a damn answer! Jesus, I seriously suck at this. That thought makes me laugh and his smile morphs to confusion.

"Yes! Yes, I'll marry you." I jump straight into his arms and of course he catches me. My legs wrap around his back as my mouth crashes against his. We go from zero to sixty. We're all teeth and tongues. His hands are kneading my ass and my hands are gripping his hair pulling him closer to me as my pussy grinds up against his hard stomach seeking relief.

He walks us around to the side of the bed and lays me down, crawling on top of me and parting my legs with his knees. He takes my left hand and slides the ring onto my ring finger. I don't even have a chance to check it out and admire it before he growls out, "mine" and his mouth is back on mine once again.

We kiss for a long time—to the point that my lips feel numb and bruised—before Bentley moves to my neck. He licks and then bites and sucks and then licks once again. He works his way down to my breasts and after kissing each nipple over the sheer teddy, he loses his patience and rips it down the center. He kisses my nipples a second time, but this time without the material he's able to grab each one and suck on them, sending a bolt of pleasure straight to my pussy.

I buck my hips against his hardness through his pants, but it does absolutely nothing to alleviate the pent up tension my body is building from his touch. He continues to suck on each nipple and I swear I'm close to having an orgasm from this act alone.

"Bentley, please. I want you inside me."

He releases my nipple from his mouth and sits up to remove his shirt and then removes his boxers and jeans. Every time I get a chance to see him like this, I can't believe this man is all mine. The man hasn't trained for a fight in months yet is still hard everywhere. Toned stomach and chiseled chest, and I don't even need to count anymore to know he has an eight-pack of abs. It's no wonder every mom in that stupid mom's group wants my fiancé. Holy shit! He's my fiancé! I'm engaged to Bentley Cruz. The thought suddenly has me kind of freaking out. Will I be a good wife? Will we last forever or will we become a statistic my parents always talk about?

Bentley must sense my freak out because he leans forward and whispers into my ear, "Don't overthink this, woman. You are mine and I'm yours and that ring is never coming off your finger."

My entire body visibly relaxes at his words. His ability to calm me is almost unnerving. He gives me soft kisses on my lips, my cheeks, my chin, and then works his way down. I think he's going to kiss me between my legs, but instead he grabs my waist and flips me over onto my stomach so I'm lying face down.

Before I can even question his motives, Bentley gives my ass a hard slap causing me to moan loudly as my pussy muscles clench together. I can't see what he's doing but I feel his teeth on my ass cheeks as he bites down and then licks the bite mark to soothe away the pain. Bentley is an expert at finding the perfect balance between pain and pleasure.

His one hand begins to massage the area he bit while his other hand goes under me and begins to play with my pussy, swiping up the juices that are already flowing, grazing my clit and then moving away from it.

"Bentley…Oh God…Please…"

He chuckles at my incoherent words and then I feel it. His finger, that was just in my pussy, moves into my puckered hole. He's using my juices as a lubricant, and while I should be worried, my thoughts drift back to the last time his finger was in there and how good it felt. Remembering the pleasure his finger brought me, my ass automatically raises up in an attempt to push against it seeking that same pleasure once again.

"Patience, baby," he whispers in response.

With my ass in the air, he reaches back under me and sticks his fingers back into my pussy, gathering up more of my juices, moving them to my ass. He does this a few more times, until I can feel his finger slide right in. I can't help the groan that comes out of me.

With one finger in my ass, he moves his other hand back to my pussy and begins to rub the sensitive nub.

"Play with your nipples, baby."

Leaning onto my elbows, I grab ahold of my nipples playing with them. My body is completely over stimulated and my orgasm is building at an almost alarming rate. Bentley adds another finger to my ass while simultaneously rubbing harder against my clit.

I'm just about to explode, when I feel his cock enter my pussy in one swift motion. It's all too much and I completely lose it. My pussy contracts, my clit throbs, and as if that isn't enough he pushes his fingers deeper into my ass massaging my insides. My body begins to tremble as I explode, coating him with my release.

Bentley picks up the pace going deeper and harder and then he's coming with me.

"Fuuuckkk, Kayla, you feel so fucking good." We both come down from our high and he pulls out.

"Holy shit, woman. You soaked my cock."

Neither of us makes any move to get up. Bentley drops to the side of me and rolls me to the side with him. With my back to his front, he spoons me close, and we both quickly drift to sleep.

I WAKE UP IN THE MORNING, LOOKING AROUND, AND QUICKLY remember where we are. I glance down and laugh that we're both still naked, and then look at my left hand to see the beautiful engagement ring.

I go to get up to take a shower, but Bentley pulls me back in to his body.

"Uh-uh. Stay here."

"I need to shower and then we need to get dressed to meet everyone for breakfast."

"Only if we can shower together."

I laugh at his cuteness. "Always."

I turn the water on and let it heat up. Bentley comes in with a couple of towels and opens the door for us to go in. Grabbing the soap, I wash his body and remember back to all those years ago in the shower when he wouldn't have sex with me because he didn't have a condom.

I take the washcloth and stroke his dick, watching it get harder the more attention I give it. When it gets hard enough, I let the water rinse it off before I bend down and stick it in my mouth.

"Damn, woman," Bentley grunts.

His dick is throbbing in my mouth as I suck it root to tip. I know if I can keep going I can make him come, but that's not what I want.

I stand and Bentley looks at me confused. After pushing him lightly to sit on the bench, I turn around to face away from him and then guide my pussy right onto his hard shaft.

"Holy shit!" he growls when I'm seated all the way on his hard length.

After a few seconds of adjusting to him being inside of me, I start to move up and down, fucking him while his hand goes to my clit to help me along. Our wet bodies slap against each other as I continue to ride him. Neither of us lasts long, both of us our finding our release within minutes.

I get off of him and turn around to see a huge smile cr his face. He grabs my ass and pulls me onto his lap, so I'm straddling him. He kisses me deeply, until the shower turns cold and we're forced to get out.

We're all sitting down to breakfast at a little restaurant at the base of the mountain. The closer you get the crazier the mountain looks. I've never skied before, but how much harder can it be than surfing?

We haven't even gotten comfortable when Liz is the first to notice the beautiful multi-carat princess cut ring on my finger.

"Bentley! What happened to the plan?" She lets out a frustrated huff that makes me giggle.

Yep! I freaking giggle. That's what Bentley does to me. Turns me into a giggling, lovesick, emotional, woman, and I wouldn't have it any other way.

"She happened." Bentley nods toward me like that's the answer to all of life's questions.

"We had a plan!"

"Well she walked out of the bathroom in this black see-through nightgown and the plan was shot to hell. It's not my fault It's hers."

The guys all laugh, but the girls still look mad.

"Hey, it's okay. It was romantic and sweet," Kayla says.

Everybody congratulates us and then we order breakfast before heading to the slopes.

I WOULD LIKE IT TO BE KNOWN ON RECORD THAT SKIING AND snowboarding are nothing like surfing. While the snow here is absolutely gorgeous, I've given up on trying to do anything on that damn mountain that's full of it—it's much better to look at than try to ride on. I'll stick to the water, thank you very much. After a couple hours of falling on my ass over and over again, I gave up and told Bentley to have a blast. We can still make this a family tradition, but I'll be spending my time indoors by the fireplace with a hot cup of coffee.

Which is exactly what Liz, Hayley, and I are all doing right now—sitting in the resort's lobby drinking a hot coffee by the fireplace and gossiping like the girls we are.

"I can't believe Ashley is still out there trying to snowboard. Maybe Kaden is a better teacher," Liz says.

"I'm glad she has Kaden. They have become good friends. She needs someone like him. I don't know what her ex did to her, but she deserves to be happy."

"What about you? Are you happy?" Liz questions.

"I am." And for the first time in a long time it's the truth.

"Before Bentley, it felt like I was just going through the motions, but with him it's so much more."

"I'm so happy for you. I never imagined we would both be with amazing guys, have kids, and soon both of us will be married."

"Yeah, we've come a long way from the scared eighteen-year-old's taking care of Bella on our own."

"That's for damn sure."

I look over at Hayley and she's kind of checked out staring at the fireplace. "Hayley, what about you? Are you happy?"

She ponders the question for a few seconds before shrugging her shoulders. "I think I am. I have a nice home, a good job, parents that are loving and supportive. I just feel like I'm missing something. I want a guy to come home to, a baby to kiss and love on. I'm thirty-two years old and I'm scared it's not going to happen. I gave up all my younger years to focus on school, and then medical school. I just wonder if it was worth it."

I move closer to Hayley to give her a hug and then Liz joins in. "It's going to happen, Hayley. If it could happen for me, it can happen for you."

"Yes! Seriously! If the queen of anti-love can fall in love, it can happen for anybody!" Liz says.

We all laugh and once we end our group hug we continue our gossiping until the guys and Ashley return ready for dinner.

The rest of the weekend flies by and before I know it, we're back home and are picking up Faith from Bentley's parents. We announce our engagement and they're both overjoyed.

Kathleen gives me a hug and, through happy tears, says, "Welcome to the family...*officially.*"

Bentley's dad is next, and when he hugs me, he whispers, "I've always wanted a daughter. Thank you."

I'm choked up and overwhelmed with the amount of love this small family holds within them. I'm almost positive the conversation with my parents won't be this heartfelt.

"When are you guys thinking of getting married?" Kathleen asks as we walk to the door to say our goodbyes.

"I don't know. I don't want to wait too long. I was thinking maybe a February wedding? Something small for sure."

Bentley, of course, says, "You can have any wedding you want. If you want small we can have small, but if you want a big wedding we can do that."

I'm starting to realize Bentley isn't worried about money at all. I can tell his parents have money, and based on our trip and the fact that he can stay home with Faith on his savings, shows me he's good with money, but he must realize it will run out eventually.

"We'll see. There's no reason to waste money. Especially with us only having one income."

Bentley's mom looks a bit confused but simply says, "Sweetie, you'll only get married once. Do it the way you want to."

We say goodbye and head home. If I'm honest, I don't really care about the wedding. I just want to be married to Bentley and share a last name with him and our daughter.

Thirty

KAYLA

THE NEXT COUPLE WEEKS QUICKLY PASS BY. WORK IS GOING great, Faith is almost six months old, and Christmas is right around the corner. Of course with all the good there must be bad to balance it out, which is why I'm not surprised when I get a call from my mom a few days before Christmas.

"Why did I have to hear it from your brother you're getting married?"

"I'm sorry, Mom. I've just been busy with work and Faith and Bentley."

"Well I would imagine so when you are the only person working in the family."

I let out a small sigh knowing exactly where this is going. "Mom, Bentley might not be working, but he's still paying all the bills. He also has refused to let me pay for any of the Christmas presents, and last week when my car was acting up, we went out and bought me a brand new BMW SUV. He's refusing to let me make the payment, even though it's in my name."

"Kayla, I understand you think you're in love so your blinders are on, but what happens if it doesn't work out? Can you afford the car payment to the vehicle that is in your name? Can you afford a place if he kicks you out of his apartment? You even work at the gym his best friend owns. After all the years of hearing your father and I tell you our stories you would think you'd be smarter than this. Please don't act stupid."

I want to argue with her, but my insecurity begins to creep in. *Am I putting all my metaphorical eggs into Bentley's basket and simply hoping he doesn't drop it?*

"I'm going to marry him, Mom. So what do you suggest I do?"

"Why don't I draw up a prenuptial agreement for you?"

"Mom…I don't think that's necessary."

"Just hear me out. It will detail that if your marriage doesn't work how the custody arrangement and child support will go. It will cover you so that if you split up he can't go after you for money because you've been working and he hasn't been. This is what I do for a living, Kayla."

I don't like the thought of starting a marriage with a paper stating what will happen if it ends, but it won't hurt to check it out. "Okay, mail it to me and I'll read through it. I'm not saying I'm going to use It, but I'll check it out."

"Thank you, Kayla."

"Are you and Dad coming up for Christmas?"

"No, we have some major cases to handle. Holidays are a busy time for divorce. Once the Christmas spirit has worn off and people are left with the debt their true colors shine through and, more often than not, it tends to end with divorce."

"Okay, well, I'll send you some pictures of Faith."

"Okay, Kayla."

And without even a *goodbye* or *I love you* she's gone.

Thirty-One

BENTLEY

IT'S CHRISTMAS MORNING AND EVEN THOUGH FAITH IS ONLY six months old that didn't stop us from buying her every gift possible in her age range plus several others she won't be ready for for several months. Last night we had Christmas Eve dinner with everybody at Liz and Cooper's place. They have the large dining room, so naturally it's where we all go for each holiday—either there or my parents' place.

What nobody knows is soon we'll have one more place to go. As an engagement gift, I've purchased a home for us. What's awesome is it's right down the street from Cooper and Liz. When we were driving by it a few weeks ago, Kayla pointed out how pretty it was and I knew I had to check it out. It turned out the inside was recently completely renovated and move-in ready. I signed on the dotted lines and have the keys wrapped up as one of her gifts to surprise her.

I plan to add Kayla's name to the deed, but I have to wait because I don't want to give away the surprise.

"Babe, can you go grab my camera from my pajama drawer? I threw it in there the other day," Kayla asks while holding onto Faith as she swipes at the wrapping paper laughing at the ripping sound it makes.

"Sure." I run to our room and open the drawer that holds all her pajamas, but I don't see the camera. Maybe she meant her lingerie drawer? I open that drawer and sure enough find the camera. I'm about to close it when I see a large manila envelope addressed to her from her parents' law firm.

Opening it up, I see a contract between Kayla and me. The only thing missing are our signatures. As I skim through the attorney bullshit lingo, I see shit like custody arrangements, child support, alimony depending on the length of the marriage, and then a clause stating I give up the right to request money because I'm choosing to be unemployed. What the fuck? She had her mother draw up a fucking prenuptial agreement?

I grab the stack of papers and bring them over to the dresser, find a pen, and begin writing. Once I'm done I grab a suitcase and pack it then walk across the hall over to Faith's room to pack some stuff for her as well. I'm so fucking pissed I can't be here with this woman another fucking second.

I zip up the luggage and head to the living room. Caleb is sitting on the couch laughing as Faith crawls across the floor to get to the new toys we've already opened. He looks up and smiles at me. He doesn't smile often, but Faith tends to bring out the softie in him. I don't even have it in me to smile back.

I walk over to Faith and pick her up. She squeals from the shock of flying through the air into my arms. I hold her close and inhale her perfect baby scent. "I love you, baby girl. I'll see you soon." I give her a kiss on her cheek and set her back down.

"Hey, did you find the camera?" Kayla asks, looking back at me while picking up some of the trash. There is so much I want to say to her, but I won't do it in front of our daughter. She may be too young to understand, but I'll never put her in the middle of our fights.

"Yeah, here you go. I gotta go." I throw the camera to her and her brows dip in confusion.

"Wait, go where? It's Christmas morning." She stands to come closer to me, but I can't handle this right now.

I back up toward the door. "I'm going to stay at my parents' house for a couple days while I get my place ready. I'll let you know where to drop Faith off when you go back to work."

Caleb doesn't say a word. He just sits and watches the conversation.

Kayla looks scared, although I don't know why. She was so scared of getting her heart broken every step of the way. Meanwhile she had no problem breaking mine over and over again.

"What's going on?" she asks, her voice thick with emotion.

I glance back down at our daughter who is oblivious to what's happening. "I don't want to argue with you in front of Faith. We're done. *I'm* done."

I walk out the door and it takes everything in me not to slam it shut and then beat the shit out of everything within my reach.

As I drive over to my parents' house, my phone buzzes next to me, but I can't answer it. Not yet, anyway. Regardless of what happens, Kayla and I'll be in each other's lives until the day we die in some way or another. We have a child together. There are going to be birthdays, holidays, graduations, hopefully Faith's wedding one day down the road (far down the road), maybe grandkids. I'm going to have to get along with Kayla, but right now I'm too fucking hurt.

What I don't get is why she didn't mention anything to me about a prenup. Doesn't she see that by drawing up a contract for if or when we divorce she's already setting us up for failure? And how ironic is it, that if anybody should be requesting a damn prenup, it should be me, yet the thought never even crossed my mind. I would give that woman anything she wants.

I arrive at my parents' house and after knocking a couple times, go in.

My mom comes out of the kitchen in her apron. "Hey, sweetie! Merry Christmas! I wasn't expecting everybody until later. This is a pleasant surprise. Where's Faith and Kayla?"

Shit! I forgot we're supposed to be coming here for dinner.

I rub the back of my neck out of stress and my mom's eyes go wide from my action.

"Bentley, what happened?"

"I think it's really over, Mom."

She bridges the gap between us and, like the mom I know and love, hugs me tight. I feel so damn defeated. There's not a single fight I've been in that makes me feel as weak and vulnerable as Kayla does without even trying.

We separate and there's a knock on the door. There's no fucking way it could be Kayla. Surely she would know not to show up here after I left.

My mom goes to the door and opens it, and sure enough Kayla is at the door holding Faith in her arms. Faith is giggling and squirming wanting my mom to take her.

They both look at me. I have no idea how to handle this. My mom must sense my frustration because she takes Faith from Kayla and walks out of the room to give us some privacy.

"Bentley, what the hell happened?" Kayla walks over to me with the intent to put her arms around me, but before she can, I back out of her reach. The look of hurt she gives me almost brings me to my knees.

"What happened? What happened was the prenup you had in your drawer, all filled out, just waiting for me to sign."

She at least has the decency to look embarrassed at the fact that I know.

"Please let me explain. My mom…"

"No, I don't need or want an explanation. The fact that you even have it is enough for me. Did you hide this to get back at me for hiding being in that stupid mom's group? You had your mom draw up papers for when we divorce one day. You never thought we would last, did you? I honestly don't even know why I ever bothered."

She cringes like she's been slapped, and I know I've probably stepped over the line.

"Wow…Okay…It's clear you have it all figured out so I'll just go."

The way she doesn't move makes it clear she's waiting for me to stop her, but it's not going to happen. When she knows this as well, she nods. I can see the tears in her eyes, but she's strong so they don't release before she heads to the kitchen to go get Faith.

I walk out back and find the closest thing to me to take my anger out on. I punch the aluminum storage cabinet over and over again until I hear my dad's voice.

"It's a good thing I was planning on replacing that thing with a new wooden one. Once you're all done we can talk."

I stop punching the storage cabinet that is now completely mutilated and grab a towel to wipe my bloodied hand on. I take a seat across from my dad at the patio table and drop my head onto the table.

"Wanna tell me why Kayla is in the kitchen with your mom bawling her eyes out?"

I look up at him and shake my head slightly out of frustration. "How do you make someone believe that love is enough?"

He gives me a sad smile. "You can't. All you can do is love that person and show her every day that you love her. Nobody said love was easy."

"It's easy for you and Mom."

He chuckles softly and shakes his head. "No, it's not. We just chose to never give up. I try to live by the five rules my dad once gave me to have a successful marriage: don't be angry with each other at the same time, never go to bed without resolving the issue, never yell at each other unless the house is on fire, never bring up the past, and most importantly, always listen to understand, don't listen to simply respond."

I can't help but laugh at the one about the house on fire.

He gets up and pats me on the shoulder, but before he goes back inside, he says, "You always knew she was a little broken. I'm not saying that's a bad thing. Nobody is perfect. Now it's up to you to love her broken or let her go so somebody else can. You have to accept people the way they are, cracks and all."

Damn him for always being right.

Thirty-Two

KAYLA

AS SOON AS BENTLEY LEFT, I GRABBED MY KEYS, THE DIAPER bag, and Faith, and chased after him. It didn't surprise me that he ended up at his mom's house. I would be damned if I was going to lose him now. I didn't know what I did wrong, but I was going to find out.

I knocked on the door and was faced with his mom and then him. After she left and he said the word prenup, I wanted to throw up. Why the hell didn't I just throw those papers away? I know why. Because I'm so messed up when it comes to relationships that I'll always end up sabotaging anything good that comes my way including having an amazing man like Bentley.

I can't blame Bentley for being mad. The papers look bad, especially since I didn't even mention them. He was completely blindsided by them, and I know I would be upset if I found something like that without being told. I know how I felt when I found out about the mom's group and that's not half as bad as finding a prenup in your fiancée's drawer. The truth is I haven't even had a chance to look at them. I threw them in the drawer and completely forgot about them.

It feels like all I ever do is hurt Bentley. He loves so hard and so deep and I'm always fucking it up.

After Bentley made it a point to hurt me with his words, I headed to the kitchen to get Faith.

I'm now sitting in the kitchen, watching Kathleen feed Faith a crumbs from a sugar cookies and suddenly feel like I just need to get out of here and be by myself. I don't belong here. I don't belong in this sweet, loving, selfless home. I'm damaged and I can't blame Bentley for no longer wanting damaged goods. He deserves perfection.

I stand up, ready to go, when Kathleen pops her head up and directs her attention away from Faith to me.

"He just needs time, sweetie. Don't overthink this. He's just hurt. He might be a fighter and look tough on the outside, but he's always had a sensitive soul."

I nod in agreement. She's right. You watch him in a fight and you would think he's nothing more than a heartless asshole, but the moment the fight is over he's back to himself. He deserves more than this shit. He deserves more than I can ever give him. I give Faith a kiss on her forehead and gather up my belongings.

"I'm going to go. I have to work tomorrow, even though it's Saturday. One of the fighters at the gym just got done with surgery on his knee and I agreed to start physical therapy with him. I'm going to leave Faith here with you guys. Bentley should be with her on Christmas."

I start to walk out the door and she stops me. "Please don't go. You shouldn't be alone on Christmas."

I choke down the sobs that are threatening and shake my head. "It's okay. It's for the best."

When I get home I find Caleb sitting on the couch watching TV.

"Everything okay?" he asks.

I shake my head and he opens his arm up and nods his head to join him. Sitting on the couch, wrapped up in Caleb's arms, I cry for everything that could have been and everything that will most likely never happen.

THE NEXT DAY AFTER WORK I GO TO LIZ'S HOUSE TO SPEND time with her and the babies. When I get there I see Faith crawling all over the ground in the living room. I immediately scoop her up and give her big kisses on her cheeks.

"Where's Bentley?" I ask, looking around.

"He and Cooper had some stuff to do so he asked me to watch her."

"He could have told me. I'm capable of watching our daughter," I snap. Liz looks at me with a frown unsure of what to say.

"I'm sorry. It's not your fault. I shouldn't have snapped at you."

She gives me a hug. "I think he just figured you would be working."

"No, he's mad and doesn't want to contact me."

"Want to talk about it?"

We sit on the couch and watch the babies play while I explain to her about the prenup and how Bentley found it before I could throw it away.

"I know I should have thrown it away, but..."

"No, you should have told your mom you didn't want it to begin with," Liz says, cutting me off.

She's right, but I just can't help but get caught in my mom's web of negativity.

"I think I was afraid that if I didn't take it, and he screwed me over, she would once again let me know how stupid I am for making the wrong choices."

"At some point, Kayla, you're going to have to realize your mom is pretty damn jaded. She isn't happy and you know it. Sure, she's successful by her standards but not by most other people's. Do you really want to live your life by her standards?"

"No, I don't. I love Bentley and my life with him."

"Just give him a few days to cool off and then go talk to him."

IT'S BEEN THREE DAYS SINCE CHRISTMAS AND I HAVEN'T HEARD a word from Bentley. After I left Liz's on Saturday, I went home to sulk in bed. I found the prenup on the dresser with a note.

Kayla,

I would have given you the world and you didn't need a contract to get any of this from me. Money doesn't buy happiness. I hope you find your happiness one day. I'm sorry it couldn't be with me.

-Bentley

I ripped up the stupid contract and threw it in the garbage and stayed in bed for the next twenty-four hours crying. I did what Liz suggested and gave Bentley a few days to cool down, but I've reached my breaking point. I'm off work for the next couple days since the club shuts down for New Year's, and I want to see my daughter. I decide to text him instead of calling in case he doesn't want to talk to me.

Me: Hey, I'm sorry to bother you. I just got off work and I have tomorrow off. Can I take Faith?

After a few minutes my phone dings.

Bentley: Yeah, you can pick her up at this address. It's where I'm living now.

I copy and paste the address into Google Maps and see it's in the same neighborhood as Liz and Cooper. Hmm…that's weird. How did he find a place so fast?

Me: Okay, is now good?

Bentley: Sure, see you in a few.

I'm heading out of the gym, when I see Marco and Caleb fighting in the ring. Marco practically lives at the gym these days and totally looks up to Caleb. As a mother I can't imagine my child being away from home so often, and Caleb has made several comments that Marco's mom doesn't ever drop him off or pick him up.

"Go Marco! Kick his butt!" I yell, rooting for him. They both smile and wave at me.

Caleb has been my saving grace the last few days. He has really turned out to be an amazing friend and he never judges me, which is something I really need right now. After I finished crying on his shoulder he told me I'm welcome to stay as long as I need to. It means a lot since he's Bentley's friend and could easily write me off. I know he doesn't really seem to trust many women, so it means even more to me that he trusts me.

I follow my GPS and pull up to the beautiful house I've passed a million times on my way to Liz and Cooper's place. It is two stories tall and made of mostly tan brick except the front archway, which is made of gorgeous cobblestone. It has a three-car garage and a huge U-shaped driveway. The best part is it's completely fenced in. I can see Faith riding her bike one day in the driveway or playing with chalk on there, and being completely safe. I haven't been in the house, but I know it has a fireplace because the cobblestone from the front archway also covers the outside of the chimney on the side of the house.

I pull up and there's a keypad and call button, so I press the button, and within seconds it buzzes and the electric gate opens and then closes behind me.

I park my vehicle and then knock on the front door.

Bentley opens the door with Faith in his arms and as soon as she spots me she starts making all sorts of noises putting her arms out for me to grab her. I take her and wrap her in a huge hug never wanting to let her go. I don't even realize I'm crying until I feel Bentley wipe the traitor tears that are trailing down my cheeks.

I walk into the home, and it's just how I pictured it, if not even more beautiful, and what's crazy is that it's furnished.

"Did you move in here this weekend?" I ask in shock.

"Yeah, I didn't completely furnish it yet. I just bought the basics."

"Well, it looks great. You did all that quickly. Were you planning to leave me?"

He glares at me like I've lost my mind, but what else am I supposed to think? Who buys a house and moves in completely within two days of moving out?

"No, Kayla. This house was supposed to be our engagement present. The house key is under the tree. Did you even bother to open the presents I got you?"

"I haven't touched anything under the tree since you left. You bought this house for us? This must have cost you a fortune."

He sighs and closes his eyes briefly—I think to calm himself down. Faith is squirming in my arms to get down, so I set her down on the blanket in the room and she immediately crawls over to her toys to bang on them.

"'I don't know what to do, Kayla. I've tried to show you how much you mean to me, but it's never enough. It doesn't matter how much I love you, I don't think you'll ever truly feel the same way. You'll always view love negatively. I can love you with all my heart, but I can't make you love me back. I can't make you have faith in what we have. That fact is I haven't done anything to support your bullshit negative theories about love."

His words break my heart. How can he think I don't love him? He's not done talking, though, so I let him continue.

"The truth is I'm a very wealthy man. I come from old money that's been passed down from generation to generation. On top of that, I've made quite a few good investments that have worked out in my favor. I have more money than I can ever spend, and one day Faith will have it all passed down to her."

"Why didn't you tell me?"

He brides the gap between us and it takes everything in me not to grab ahold of him and never let go. "Maybe I should have told you from the beginning, I don't know. If you had known, maybe this whole thing wouldn't have happened. I thought if you knew it would scare you off, so I kept it to myself. The only people that know are the guys. Even when I funded the youth program at Cooper's gym I kept it anonymous. I don't want my money to define me and I don't want to be judged for having it.

"I wanted you to love me for me and to be comfortable with us. And then to see a fucking prenup is a punch to my face. It sucks so bad. I wanted you forever. What's mine was supposed to be yours. I don't give a fuck about my money. All I wanted was you and Faith. I just wanted your love. One side of me is saying I need to move on, but the other side is telling me not to give up on us because I can't imagine living a life without you by my side. I just can't do this alone."

I should probably be mad that he kept his money situation from me but at the same time I can see where he's coming from. I've been hot and cold with him from day one. I can't blame him for overthinking his choices.

We're now so close I could kiss him and it's such a tease because being this close to Bentley and not being able to touch him is torture.

I open my mouth to respond, but my throat feels dry so I clear it and then begin. "I never thought love could ever be a part of me. I was just going through the motions and thought I was smart. No love meant never being hurt. But then you came along and showed me over and over again how amazing unconditional real love can feel. Please don't take that away, Bentley. Please don't give up on me. I'm sorry it's taking me so long to get on the same page as you, but I really am trying. I promise. We can sign a different prenup. One that protects you and shows you I just want you and not your money."

"Woman, you aren't getting it." He looks into my eyes and then gives me a soft kiss on my lips.

"I don't care about the money, Kayla. I don't need or want any contract that states what will happen if we divorce. When I marry you, it's forever. And if you leave me, you can take it all. A life without you and Faith isn't a life at all. It's my job to protect you and our daughter. We shouldn't need a piece of paper to protect either of us from the other."

This man could have any woman in the world, anything in the world, and all he wants is to live a life with me and our daughter. I may not deserve him, but I'm going to spend every day earning his love.

I don't know what to say, so I do the only thing I can think of and wrap my arms around his neck and kiss him with all the love I have built up inside me. His body stills in shock at first, but after a second he relaxes and kisses me back. When we separate I feel like a piece of me is missing. I want to be tied to this man in every way.

"Let's get married."

He looks at me like I'm crazy and then laughs. "Umm…I'm pretty sure that was the plan."

"No, I mean today. Well not today because it's already too late in the day, but tomorrow. Let's get married tomorrow. I don't want to wait. I don't want a wedding or any of that craziness. I just want you, me, Faith, your parents, and our friends at a Chapel on the strip."

He grins wide and it melts my heart to see him smile. I vow in that moment to make him smile like that every chance I get.

"Are you sure?"

"Yes, I'm sure. This is what I want…I mean, if you still want to marry me that is."

"Woman, stop. You want to elope that's what we'll do. The sooner I can make you officially mine the better. Let's call my parents and our friends, and then find a chapel we can reserve for tomorrow."

He wraps his hand around my neck and pulls me close to him again. "Wanna a tour of our new home?"

"Yeah, I do. But what I would really like is the special hands-on tour after Faith goes to bed."

He barks out a laugh. "Oh, that can definitely be arranged."

He grabs Faith and we go from room to room as he shows me our new home.

364

Epilogue

BENTLEY

"DO YOU, BENTLEY CRUZ, TAKE KAYLA PETERSON TO BE YOUR lawfully wedded wife, to have and to hold, in sickness and in health, for richer or poorer, to love and cherish, from this day forward until death do you part?"

"I do."

It's New Year's Eve and I'm looking at the most beautiful woman in the world who is about to become my wife. I tried to get her to do it right by having the wedding at the Bellagio or even the Wynn but she wasn't having it. According to Kayla, if we're going to elope we're going to do it Vegas style. Which is why I'm currently standing in front of the ordained minister in the Little Church of The West with our family and friends, and by our family I mean Kayla's brother, Zach, and my parents. While she wanted to get married the very next day, once her brother said he would like to attend, we decided to hold off a couple days so he could fly over and give her away since her parents don't approve of the marriage and refused to be a part of it.

After I showed her around our new home, Kayla explained that her mom insisted on sending the prenup over to her in case things didn't work out. She said she planned to rip them up but felt guilty about not listening to her mom's advice. We agreed there would be no more listening to her mom's advice. When Kayla called to let her mom know we were eloping she flipped out. I took the phone from Kayla and made it clear to her mother that her negativity toward love and toward her daughter was no longer welcome.

We decided to have the ceremony at the Church and then hold the reception-slash-New Year's Eve party at our new place. There is no other way I would rather bring in the New Year than with Kayla as my wife and surrounded by the people who love us.

"Do you, Kayla Peterson, take Bentley Cruz to be your lawfully wedded husband, to have and to hold, in sickness and in health, for richer or poorer, to love and cherish, from this day forward until death do you part?"

"I do," she states excitedly with the most beautiful smile on her face.

I slide the wedding band on her finger that matches the engagement ring and then she slides my wedding band onto my finger. The ordained minister announces us husband and wife and tells me I can kiss my bride.

He doesn't have to tell me twice. I take my wife in my arms and kiss her, hoping to pass along every emotion I feel in this moment through our kiss. Everybody claps and Faith and Nathan both squeal and clap as well copying off of everybody else. We grab Faith from my mom and give her a kiss.

Liz takes a few pictures of the three of us and then some with my parents and Kayla's brother before we all head back to our house to celebrate.

We arrive at the house and a few minutes later everybody else is pulling up to join us. I notice Caleb isn't here yet. "Hey, has anybody seen Caleb?"

Nobody has heard from him since we left the church so I shoot him a text.

Me: Yo! Where are you? We're all at the house?

I wait a few minutes and, when I don't hear back from him, send him another text.

Me: Caleb! Everything okay?

I still don't hear back from him and I start to worry. I ring his cell but it goes to voicemail.

Kayla comes over and puts her arms around me from behind. "What's wrong?"

"I can't get a hold of Caleb."

"He probably just stopped off at home."

"Yeah, you're probably right."

Just as I'm about to call him again he comes walking in the door looking stressed.

"Hey, man! What happened? Did you get lost?"

"No, sorry, I had to stop at the gym on my way here. Marco didn't realize the gym was closed because of the holiday and wedding so I gave him a ride home."

Over the last several months Marco and Caleb have definitely grown closer. When he isn't attending the MMA classes, he's helping out around the gym cleaning windows and washing towels. Cooper doesn't really need the help, but if it means Marco is safe and off the streets he'll continue to find stuff for the kid to do.

"It's a good thing you do for that kid." And that's the truth. Caleb makes sure the kid is home safe every day even if it means he follows him home without the kid knowing.

"Yeah, I just wish there was more I could do."

"Like what? What are you thinking?"

"I don't know...I just don't know." He shakes his head, looking defeated, and I know the conversation is over for now.

We head to the backyard to join everyone in celebrating our wedding as well as New Year's. The radio counts down and when it hits midnight I give my wife a kiss. Everybody is cheering and hollering, but I can't stop kissing her. She moans into my mouth and I grab her by the ass and lift her into my arms, her legs wrapping around my waist.

"Bentley, stop." She giggles but continues to grind her pussy into my stomach clearly wanting me to continue.

Everybody is laughing at us and Cooper says, "We get it. We get it. You're newlyweds and need some alone time."

My parents take Faith back to their place for the night and after everybody leaves I grab my wife and bring her up to our bedroom to make love for the first time as a married couple.

KAYLA

BENTLEY AND I ARE FINALLY ALONE. WE MAKE OUR WAY UP TO our bedroom and when we're near the bed he grabs my hand and pulls me to him.

"I love you, Mrs. Cruz. You have made me a very happy man today."

I can't help but laugh when he says my new name. I can't believe we're married. I really am Mrs. Bentley Cruz.

"I love you, too, Mr. Cruz. Now, are you going to make love to your wife or stare at her all night?"

"I'm definitely going to make love to you."

He turns me around and unzips my white dress I wore for our wedding. It's not a traditional wedding dress, but it flowed to my knees and hugged all the right places making me feel pretty.

Once the dress is unzipped, Bentley grabs the straps and pushes them over my shoulders, letting the dress fall to the floor.

"Damn, Mrs. Cruz, you look exquisite." Of course I'm wearing white bridal style lingerie under my dress. It's silky and sheer and barely there, just the way Bentley likes it.

Still standing behind me, he takes his hands and glides them down my arms and over my ass. He continues around to my sex, pulling my body to his. Once our bodies are flush against each other he takes my face and tilts it to the side, laying open mouth kisses along my neck and then across collarbone, heading to my shoulder.

He continues to work his way down my body, kissing every square inch of my skin until he's kneeling behind me, giving my ass cheeks kisses. He turns me around and I see that at some point he took off his clothes as well because he's only in his boxers. His face is parallel to my pussy and when I look down, he's smiling.

He reaches forward and gives my pussy a light kiss and then looks up at me giving me a sexy smirk. I back up to the bed and sit down. He spreads my legs, opens up my pussy, and begins to lick.

My head goes back in pleasure, but then he stops and says, "I want you to watch. Watch me lick your pussy, baby," and my head snaps back up.

I watch his tongue dart out to my clit and lick me up and down slowly, getting me wet with desire. He inserts a finger and then two into my core while he continues to devour me. I'm mesmerized by how erotic it is watching my husband make love to my pussy with his mouth.

When my body can't take it anymore I come all over his fingers and mouth. Before I'm even come down from my high, he's up, grabbing my legs and parting them enough so he's standing between them. He lifts one of my legs over his shoulder and my other one locks around his waist. He guides his dick into me at an angle and begins to thrust deep into me, hitting my G-spot. My already sensitive pussy begins to convulse again as he pumps into me over and over again sending my body into a complete frenzy.

Bentley picks up his speed, his eyes closed, and I know he's about to find his own release. He opens them up at the last second and stares into my eyes as he comes in me. I've never felt closer to anybody than I feel to Bentley right now.

He bends down and gives me a kiss. "I love you, baby."

We clean up in the bathroom and then lie down in bed.

He wraps his arms around me holding me close.

"We did it," I whisper.

He chuckles and says, "Yeah, we did. Now you're mine for life, woman."

"I wouldn't have it any other way. Thank you for always having faith in us, Bentley."

"I'll always have faith in us, baby."

He gives me a kiss on my neck and we fall asleep.

BENTLEY

About four hours later

I HEAR THE PHONE RINGING AND JUMP UP TO GRAB IT. IT'S still dark out and my first thought is something must have happened to Faith.

I answer the phone without even looking at the caller ID but see the clock reads four in the morning.

"Hello?"

"Yes, hello. My name is Jillian. I'm a nurse at Sunrise Hospital. Is this Bentley Cruz?"

"Yes, it is," I say in a panic, praying my parents and Faith are okay.

"Baby, who is it?" Kayla groggily asks, barely awake.

"I have a Caleb Michaels here in the ICU. You're his emergency contact."

My body sags in relief that the call isn't pertaining to my daughter, but then immediately goes into distress learning my best friend is hurt.

"What happened?"

"He was brought in by ambulance. Somebody called nine-one-one and reported finding him. When they brought him in he was unconscious and beaten severely. I can't discuss the details over the phone, but his injuries are life threatening. Can you come down here?"

I jump up out of bed and grab whatever clothes I can find to throw on. "Yeah, I'm on my way."

Kayla is now sitting up looking scared shitless.

"It's Caleb. Somebody found him beaten almost to death. He's at the hospital in the ICU."

Kayla immediately gets out of bed and gets dressed as well. Once we are in the car, she texts our friends to let them know what we know. We ride to the hospital in silence, praying our friend will be okay.

FIGHTING *for your* TOUCH

Prologue

CALEB

Seven Years Ago

"WHAT THE FUCK IS GOING ON?" MY DAD YELLS AT ME, RED faced, fists tight at his side like it's taking everything in him not to punch me in my face. He's not even questioning *her*. He's already made up his mind I'm to blame. Of course I'm to blame. There's no way his precious wife could be.

I'm standing face to face with him in my bedroom with my pants and boxers around my ankles. My dick is flaccid, but let's be honest, it usually is when I'm around *her*. Don't get me wrong, there's nothing wrong with my dick. I know it works properly since I've spent most of my teenage years fucking women I wish I could forget about. You don't know how many times I've jacked off hoping it wouldn't get back up again for them. If it can't get up what good am I to her, or any of them for that matter? Maybe if it stopped working she and all those other fucking women would leave me the hell alone. Unfortunately my dick doesn't work that way—it doesn't just shut off. After a while it goes hard again whether I want it to or not, and trust me, I definitely don't want it to.

Before attempting to answer his clearly rhetorical question, I reach down and pull my pants up so my dick is no longer hanging out. The conversation is already awkward as fuck as it is, no need to add to the awkwardness of my father coming home early from a business trip to find his slutty wife with her mouth wrapped around my cock. I shoot a glare at the woman who is the reason behind all this, hoping she'll for once do the right thing and admit the truth. I know it's not going to happen, but I can hope. I have learned two things about women, they're gold digging bitches and they can't be fucking trusted. Every time I think I can trust a woman she proves me wrong.

She raises her eyebrows in defiance at me and I know I'm on my own here. I wouldn't expect anything less from that cunt.

Closing my eyes, I take a deep breath in and then exhale slowly, attempting to calm myself before I try to persuade my dad of something I already know he isn't going to believe. My hands are shaking, and I have a horrible feeling this is going to end badly for me. It's just the way my life goes.

"Dad, please listen to me. It's not what it looks like. This is all *her*." There is so much more I want to say. So much more to this whole fucked up ordeal. But my dad is under enough stress as it is. I don't want to add to it. Sure, he has made mistakes. He's definitely not perfect, but he's been through a lot these past few years and I don't want to be the reason he goes through even more.

Tears of anger and frustration are clogging my tear ducts, and the lump in my throat is making it hard to breathe. The most frustrating thing is trying to prove to someone you aren't lying without having any proof, especially without being able to explain the entire story. Because of the secrets I've been forced to keep, my dad's caught me in too many lies to count that I couldn't explain. I don't blame him for not believing me now. Trust is hard to earn and easy to lose. Shit, if I were him, I wouldn't believe me.

Even if I was a complete saint, the evidence stacked up against me looks bad, and judging by the look on my dad's face, he doesn't believe a damn word I'm saying. I want to tell him the truth. I don't want to keep these secrets from him, but once the truth is out there, I can never take it back, and I don't know how *she* will react. What if she makes good on her threats? Then every nasty, fucked up thing I have endured from all these women will be for nothing. My dad has lost so much. He deserves more than to have his entire life destroyed.

"He's lying, Adam. He came on to me. I was scared," she says with crocodile tears streaming down her face. Her cheeks are stained black from the overdone mascara her fake-ass wears. The truth is, her cheeks aren't stained from crying, it's from her taking my cock so deep down her fucking throat it choked her to the point of tears. Just thinking about her mouth on my dick makes me want to throw up.

When he turns to me, she shoots me a glare making it clear to keep my mouth shut. If he only knew the truth about his precious wife, he would run the other way and never look back. The problem is, she's a smart, manipulative bitch and he has no idea the person she really is—not like I do.

He looks at me with longing in his eyes then looks back at her with what looks like disappointment, and for a second I think maybe he's going to believe me over her, that he can see through all her bullshit and lies. Out of the corner of my eye, I see Gloria tense up. She's thinking the same thing I am.

"I didn't want this," I blurt out as a last chance, praying he believes me. Praying he chooses me. Maybe he will kick her out and she'll be out of our lives for good. I'm not sure if she'll make good on her threats if he kicks her out, but we can deal with it all together. I'll do whatever it takes to help my dad, which is precisely how I got in this fucked up position to begin with.

My dad looks back at Gloria one more time and her face goes stoic. She gives nothing away at first, but then with a small lift of her one eyebrow, she silently tells him something causing him to visibly stiffen. They appear to be having a silent conversation of some sort. I wish I knew what the fuck they were saying.

Instantly my dad's demeanor changes from sad to pissed. He cocks his fist and punches the wall I'm standing in front of, his fist going through it.

Dry wall crumbles everywhere.

Gloria screeches like she's afraid.

Give me a fucking break. That woman eats up and spits out grown men on a daily basis.

He walks up to me until we're only inches apart, his face right in mine. I'm tall at six-foot-two. He isn't quite as tall as me, but he's still a big guy. He looks slightly up into my eyes and with an eerily calm voice says, "I don't know why you would do this, but I am not going to have you destroying this family with your lies. I'm going to give you one chance to change your story or you're out of here."

My shoulders sag in defeat and my head drops down shaking back and forth knowing this was coming but still shocked. I look back up into his eyes and see a glimpse of something…it's almost as if he's begging me to change my story, but I can't do that. I might not be able to tell him the entire truth, but I'm not going to take responsibility for choosing to fuck that money-hungry, lying, blackmailing cunt. He thinks I'm trying to destroy this family with my lies…If he only knew I'm actually trying to save this family…No, fuck that. I'm trying to save him. We don't have a family; they're all dead.

I swallow back the hurt and stand straight up. I lift my chin and, with the little bit of respect I have left for myself, say the only thing I can say. "I'm out of here."

Turning my back on him, I grab a backpack to pack my shit. I can feel his eyes on me, watching me, but I can't look at him. The only family I have left just chose that piece-of-shit woman over his own son. I hear the door close behind them and a few seconds later my phone dings indicating a text.

Nasty Bitch: Don't fuck with me.

I don't bother to reply. I completely understand her text. If I try to tell my dad the entire truth she will destroy everything he's worked for.

I open the drawer of my nightstand and grab the two pictures that are tucked away under my boxers. The first is of my older sister and me. It was taken the same day Colette went missing, a few days before she died. Running my fingers over her smiling face, I remember how happy she was that day. It was my twelfth birthday and our parents took us skiing. Colette loved to ski and she was damn good. She would drag me up and down those slopes for hours.

I choke up remembering how amazing the day was until we got home. Colette was four years older than me. The entire ride home she was texting with someone. I saw her smiling and asked if it was a guy. She lied to me. When we got home she asked to go to her friend's house. She lied to our parents. Three days later she was found in the woods with no clothes on, bruises covering her body. The autopsy said she was raped and then strangled to death. After investigating, the police said she was chatting with an older guy in an online chat room. She met up with him when she said she was going with her friends. The cops were able to locate him. He was tried for her murder and found guilty, sentenced to life in prison. But that doesn't change the fact that she lied, and because of her lies, she's dead.

The day my parents found out Colette died I lost a piece of them as well. They began arguing all the time blaming each other. Nothing tears a family apart quicker than the death of a child. My mom cried for months after, saying a parent should never have to bury her own child. My dad turned to work. He went from working the standard forty hours a week to barely ever coming home. Instead of being on my best behavior, I lashed out, getting into fights, skipping school, and causing trouble. That was until I found out about the next lie. This one told by my mother.

I bring the second picture to the front. It's of my mom and me a few weeks before she died from cancer. We are both smiling, but my smile isn't real. I was thirteen at the time—almost a year after Colette died, and we knew my mom only had a short time left. I was homeschooled those last couple months so I could spend my days with her. As much as she tried to keep me away, not wanting me to see her body quickly deteriorating, I refused to stay away. I didn't want to miss a moment with my mom, with the little time she had left. She knew she was sick for a long time but didn't tell me. Another lie…More lies.

Pointing fingers at my sister and mom won't change anything, but it still hurts knowing they both lied to me. I trusted them completely and yet they didn't trust me with the truth.

I try hard not to let those be the last memories I have of them. I try to remember the good times. The times my sister would let me tag along to the local ice cream shop or hang out with her and her friends at the mall or the movies. I try to remember all the times my mom would take me to breakfast, just the two of us, or when she and

I would play cards until late at night talking about nothing, yet it felt like everything. My mom and my sister were good people, they were my entire world, and I get they aren't anything like my stepmom, but a lie is a lie, right? Lies destroy and hurt people, and I'm so sick of all the damn lies.

The pictures used to be on top of my nightstand for me to see, to try to remember all the good times over the bad, but Gloria made me put them away. I guess she didn't want to see my mom and sister's smiling faces while she was forcing herself on me.

I shove the pictures into my bag and finish packing some clothes, money I have stashed away, my toothbrush, deodorant, and an extra pair of shoes. I take one last look at my bedroom and head out knowing I'll never be back.

I throw my bag into the backseat of my car and head to Cooper's Fight Club. It's a UFC training facility I work out at as much as I can. I came across the place a few years ago while walking home from school. In exchange for cleaning the gym a few nights a week after it closes, the gym owner, Marc Cooper, agreed to let me workout here for free. I hear he's an asshole, but luckily he lives in Las Vegas and runs the gym there. The gym manager here, Diego, is really cool and lets me train after hours.

While my dream is to be a UFC fighter one day, I'm also going to college full-time. After I graduated from high school last year, I agreed to go to college because my mom left me a college fund when she passed away. She wanted to make sure no matter what happened I would have the money to go. I don't want to let her down so I'm majoring in business and finance. My dad is an investment banker so it made him happy to see me major in something similar. While I can't see myself ever using my degree to do anything like what he does, I'm determined to finish it.

I'm pounding away on the bag for God knows how long when Diego walks over to me.

"What's going on, kid? It looks like you're trying to kill the bag. You know it's an inanimate object, right?"

I can't help but laugh. He's such a smartass.

"Just a bad day. I'm apparently homeless as of a couple hours ago."

I'm not sure why I let that slip out. I usually keep to myself. Nobody knows the shit I've endured the last few years and it needs to stay that way, especially if I want to make sure my dad stays out of prison.

My phone vibrates, letting me know I have a text, so I check it quickly.

Nasty Bitch: You have an appointment at 8 p.m. Don't be late.

She can't be fucking serious right now. Does she really think I'm still going to be her fuck boy? Diego goes to say something and I put up one finger, signaling for him to give me a minute, and text her back.

Me: I'm done.

Her response is almost immediate.

Nasty Bitch: What are you going to do for money? Did you forget our deal?

Me: I would rather live on the streets broke. I'm done.

I'm hoping she won't turn my dad in if I walk away quietly. I'm not her only source of income, and if she turns him in, she'll lose her main source of income as well. She might be a poor excuse for a human, but she isn't stupid.

Nasty Bitch: You need to go to your appointment tonight. You know who it's with. I will let her know it's the last time.

I do know who it's with and it's a woman I don't want to piss off. She has the power to fuck my life up. The first time I met her at the hotel I didn't know who she was. How would I? I was a seventeen-year-old senior in high school. After I started college I learned she's the dean of admissions. When I barely made it through high school and needed to get into college I was shocked to learn I actually got in. Little did I know she pulled strings and got me accepted. As much as I would like to blow her world apart by outing her ass for fucking a teenager, it would also fuck up mine for a few reasons. One, it would out my stepmom and ultimately fuck up my dad's life. And two, it would destroy the last two years I've spent in a college I don't belong in. I only have two more to go to graduate, so I can honor my mom.

Me: Fine. Last time, though.

Nasty Bitch: That's what I thought, and remember you say a word to anybody about our arrangement I will destroy you and your father. You'll be visiting him in prison.

While I don't give a shit about her threats to me, I'll never say a word to anybody. I wouldn't do that to my dad. He's lost enough. His one mistake shouldn't cost him everything.

Putting my phone back in my pocket, I look up and see Diego still staring at me. I completely forgot he was there.

"Homeless?"

"Yeah, I had to move out of my dad's place."

He thinks for a minute. "Look, I got an available room at my place…"

Before he can continue I cut him off.

"How much is the rent? I have some money, but I need to find a job. My school is paid for, but I don't have a steady income anymore."

While I despise Gloria for what she's put me through the last four years, she did pay me. I think she justified her sick actions by paying me for my services. Like if I'm receiving money, it isn't statutory rape and blackmail. If I'm accepting money from her, I must be willing, right? Fucking wrong!

"Like I was saying, I have an extra room at my place and it's empty. It is actually an old mother-in-law suite. It's separate from my house, back behind the pool. I'll start paying you to clean the gym instead of you doing it for free, and that way you can afford food, and still keep training and go to school."

I would be a fool to say no to his offer. I definitely don't have a better one, and if I want to keep training and graduate in two years, getting a full-time minimum wage job is only going to get in the way.

"All right, I'm going to take you up on your offer. Thanks, man."

"No problem. Come by later and I'll get you settled in. It's completely furnished so you don't need anything."

I shake his hand. "I appreciate it."

I glance at the clock and see it's almost seven. I've got to shower and get ready for my last appointment. Suddenly it feels like I can breathe again. Knowing I'll never have to unwillingly fuck another woman makes me feel like a hundred pounds has been lifted off my chest.

I head to the locker room to change and run into Bentley and Cooper. I met them here at the gym. It's actually Cooper's dad who owns the gym, but I guess they don't really get along too well. Bentley and Cooper are both cool, though. They're both fighters and are training to be in the UFC like I am. They've invited me to chill several times but with everything I have going on, I've found it best to keep people at arm's length. They're always going out, chasing females, and the truth is, I want nothing to do with women. Over the last few years I have been forced to fuck every kind of woman, but a few things are always the same. They're users and cheaters, and they can't be trusted. They want a man for his money and cock. I can't even tell you how many married women I have fucked. And do they care that they've been fucking a teenager? Fuck no, they don't. I hate the female population and I'm definitely not interested in chasing one.

One day I'll be in the UFC. I'll be a fighter like I've dreamed of, and with my business and finance degree I'll be able to manage my own money. There is no way I am busting my ass to have some untrustworthy, cheating woman use me for my money and then fuck me over. Fuck that shit.

Now all I need to do is get through tonight and shit will be looking up from here on out. I say what's up to the guys, shower, and get dressed. Maybe after tonight I'll actually be able to chill with them.

Norma Silverstein, the dean of admissions, is of course a married woman. She is married to a professor at the business college so we meet at a local hotel for our appointments since her home is off limits. When I pull up, I send her a text to let her know I'm here. She texts back the room number and I head up.

I knock and she lets me in. She's dressed in nothing but the hotel robe and her hair is up in some messy bun shit women always wear. She smiles at me and holds the door open while I walk through to the main room to wait for her demands. I hear the door close behind me and then feel her hands come around me moving straight to my dick. What I want to do is take her hand and shove it away from me, tell her to never fucking touch me again, but I can't. So instead I stand there and let the woman put her hands on my body.

"You aren't hard." I can't see her since she's standing behind me, but I can hear the pout in her voice.

Of course I'm not hard. Do women seriously think guys walk around hard twenty-four seven? Do they think paying someone for their services is going to make that person instantly attracted to them? Well, I can tell you from experience, it doesn't. What's worse is these women know what kind of service my stepmom provides. They know she pimps out her barely old enough teenage stepson to service them at their demand, but do they care? No, they don't. They care about one thing, themselves. My job is to do as these women say. It doesn't matter if I don't want to or if I'm not in the mood. My job is to fake it.

The first time I had sex with Norma I was almost eighteen. I was about to graduate high school and my stepmom said if I had sex with Norma she could ensure I would be accepted to the University. Not that I had a damn choice anyway. I had already been having sex with other women for a little over a year. At least having sex with Norma would mean I would get into college. Unfortunately once wasn't enough and every time we're done she reminds me she's the only reason I'm in college. I would say I should have just gone to a local state college but would it have mattered? I still would be forced to sleep with Norma. Gloria gets what she wants or my dad will end up in prison. I don't want to see my father in prison…even if he technically deserves it.

Norma stays standing behind me and rubs my cock, hoping it will magically get hard. I close my eyes and will my dick to do something. I'm not sure if I should will it to get hard to get this shit over with or will it to stay soft so I won't have to fuck this cheating whore at all. Of course my dick has a mind of its own and after a few minutes of her rubbing on it, it gets hard. It's science, really…it doesn't matter how much I beg it to stay soft, it always ends up getting hard. It's as if it's been trained to get hard against its will, and I guess in a way it has been, by Gloria. Turning around, I decide to get this shit over with.

"What would you like tonight?" I robotically ask, because that's my job—to ask what they want and then give it to them. They all want pretty much the same thing—to get off. They want orgasms that are almost impossible to give and receive. They think because they have read some porn shit in a romance book that means it's really that easy.

"I want it rough tonight," she shyly responds. If I didn't know better I would think she's some sweet, innocent woman, but I do know better and she's neither of those. I don't know why she insists on acting shy every time she makes her demands. You're paying for sex while cheating on your husband. Do you really need to act shy? But because I don't need to piss this woman off, I go along with it.

I take her by her hand and bring her to the room, straight to the bed. I push her onto the mattress roughly and begin removing my clothes. She gets excited and strips herself of her robe. Stroking my cock to keep it hard, I climb on onto the bed and flip her over onto her stomach, pulling her ass up in the air.

"Spank me!" she screeches, so I do. Kneeling behind her, I smack her ass several times with one hand while I find her pussy through her opened thighs with my other. I push two fingers straight into her cunt and begin pumping them in and out of her, getting her wet. I add a third finger and attempt to find her G-spot. The sooner I give her what her husband apparently can't, the sooner I can get the fuck out of here.

I know I've found the spot that will make her go off when her thighs begin to close shut. I give her ass another hard smack just like she likes.

"Keep your fucking legs open." Within a few seconds of my fingers hitting the spot, she's coming. *One down.*

"Ohhh…that feels so good. I want you to fuck me in the ass now," Norma moans, coming down from her orgasm.

I grab a condom from the nightstand she left there for tonight and roll it onto my dick. I stroke it a few more times to make sure it's hard again. Then I drag her to the edge of the bed so she's leaning over the edge with her ass in the air.

Taking the wetness from my fingers, I stick them into her ass getting it ready for my cock. While I would love to go in dry and tear her shit up and really show her what rough is, I don't want to piss her off. I'm so close to being done. I just need to finish this and I'll be able to walk away finally free.

Once I know she's ready, I guide my cock to her ass and push in slowly.

"Oh my God!" she yells. "Pull my hair!"

And so I do. I grab ahold of her hair and fist it around my hand while pushing my dick all the way in.

"Hard! I want it hard!" She wiggles her ass, wanting more, and once again I give her exactly what she wants.

With her mane wrapped around my fist, I pull her head back to the point that it's got to be painful and begin fucking her ass with abandon. Harder and harder I pound into her. Does it feel good? I would be lying if I said it doesn't. I am a man after all, fucking a woman in the ass. Of course it feels good. The problem is every time I come it's tainted knowing this isn't my choice. I have never had sex by choice. Thinking about Gloria taking my virginity at fifteen years old pisses me off. I keep pounding this bitch, remembering my stepmom threatening me, telling me if I didn't fuck her she would destroy my dad, and then spending the next several years dreading every time my dad went away knowing she would be showing up to my room.

Once I turned sixteen, she began forcing me to fuck other women. I thought maybe she would stop wanting me, but she didn't. She had no problem continuing to make me fuck her even though she knew all the women she was pimping me out to. The memories become too much and I try to shake the thoughts from my head. If I think too much my dick will go soft.

"Caleb, make me come." Norma's words bring me back to the now remembering this shit is about her. It's always about the woman. They don't care if I get off. They're using me. That's what women do. They use.

I bring the hand that isn't grabbing her hair down to her clit and begin rubbing it in circles while I continue to fuck her ass. I can feel my body trying to release, but I focus on something else to stop myself from coming. I can't come before her. I need to end this shit on a good note. Thankfully her second orgasm hits and she's coming once again, allowing me to come as well. I release into the condom and slow my thrusts to a standstill. I untangle my fingers from her hair and slowly pull my dick out of her ass.

She turns around and smiles. "Thank you. That was so good."

I nod and head to the bathroom to get cleaned up, grabbing my clothes from the floor so I don't have to walk out naked.

My phone goes off in my pocket and I check it.

Diego: Great opportunity for you has come up. Call me when you get this.

I flush the condom, get dressed, and say goodbye to Norma for the last time. She, of course reminds me she'll check on my grades and make sure everything is going okay—her way of reminding me she's in control. Once I'm in the lobby, I dial Diego.

"Hey man, where are you?" he asks.

"Heading to your place now. What's up?"

"Cooper and the guys are here and want to talk to you. I'll see you when you get here."

We hang up and I head straight to his place.

I knock and let myself in like I've done a million times. I'm so thankful he's giving me a place to stay. I had no idea there was a room in the back of his house. The guys are all sitting in the living room watching a basketball game, drinking beer and eating what looks like take out from a local Chinese place. Eating healthy is a huge part of training, but most fighters will give themselves cheat days to stay sane. This must be theirs.

Cooper is the first to stand to say hi. "What's up, man?"

"Nothing much." I give him a handshake.

I glance over and see Kaden—Cooper's trainer—and sitting next to him is Bentley.

"What's going on?" I ask anxiously.

"You're out of college for the summer, right?" Diego asks.

"Yeah, I'm considering taking a couple classes over the summer, but nothing major until August. Why?"

"Could you transfer to a different college?" Bentley chimes in.

"I guess I could if I had to." I'm not sure what all the questions are about my schooling, but I'm getting kind of nervous.

"Diego told us you're in the transition of moving out. We're heading to Miami to do some promo shit and then moving to Las Vegas to train at my dad's gym," Cooper says.

I nod, but I'm still not sure where he's going with this.

"Kaden and I both decided to purchase a home over there, which leaves Bentley living on his own. He found a three-bedroom place and plans to use one room for an office, but he's looking for a roommate for the third bedroom, and when I mentioned it to Diego, he thought you might be interested. What do you think about moving to Las Vegas and rooming with Bentley? You can also train at the gym there free of charge."

Are these guys fucking serious? It's like they're handing me my dreams on a silver platter.

"Umm…that sounds awesome, but I only have a few grand to my name. I don't know how much the rent is, but I would need to get a job, and even then, with training and college, I don't know how many hours I would be able to work…"

Bentley raises his hand to stop me. "Bro, chill. I'm good with paying whatever. I just want a roommate since these two pussies have decided they need to grow up and buy a house and shit. Pay or don't pay…I don't care. Just keep your space clean, if you eat my food, let me know, and if you have a female over, try to keep her quiet."

This shit is too good to be true, but I'm not about to look a gift horse in the mouth. I could tell him he won't need to worry about me bringing any females over, but I would imagine that would raise questions, so instead I just say okay and thank him.

Coopers adds, "We're leaving the day after tomorrow. A bunch of the guys from the gym are flying out as well. We'll be in Miami for a few days and then we'll head to Las Vegas. You're more than welcome to join us in Miami."

I look to Diego to make sure this is all legit and he's okay with this. I trust him to steer me in the right direction. He nods and smiles, and I silently scream *fuck yes!* I'm getting the fuck out of here.

One

CALEB

Present Day

IT'S DECEMBER IN LAS VEGAS, AND WHILE MANY WOULD THINK it would be hot because well…it's Las Vegas and Las Vegas is in the desert, it's actually not. It's freezing cold outside. I jump into my blacked out Dodge Ram, turn the key into the ignition, and put the heat on full blast. *Fuck, it's cold!*

I go through the local coffee shop drive thru to pick up a couple hot coffees before heading to the gym. The coffee serves two purposes: one, to warm me up, and two, to wake me up. I didn't get in until almost four this morning from work and I'm exhausted. I was only supposed to work until two, but between the call-outs and the private parties at the club, the owner, Matt, needed me to stay late. I'm definitely not complaining about the hours because more hours means more money in my bank account, but when you have to get up at seven in the morning to head to the gym to train for a fight, the sleep I'm lacking feels more important than the money.

I know I should quit my job. My dream has finally come true and I have a contract with the UFC, but what people don't realize is, while a contract is definitely a step in the right direction, it doesn't mean instant stardom or money. I am lucky my roommate Bentley barely lets me pay a dime to live here. I had no idea how expensive it could be to live in Las Vegas. The problem is I know it won't be long until he moves out and I'll have to find my own place and pay real rent. Luckily, I have been busting my ass and saving for the last several years since we moved out here, and I actually have a very good amount of money saved up.

Bentley and I have been roommates for the last seven years, but a lot of shit has recently changed. First off, he and his girlfriend, Kayla, who is one of my best friends, had a baby girl in June. Her name is Faith and she's the cutest baby in the world.

I'm not going to lie; it took a little while to warm up to Kayla. I don't trust women, but living with her allowed me to get to know a female who isn't trying to use a man for his money or dick, and over time a friendship developed. She has also taught me women are human and make mistakes. Not every lie is vindictive and I need to remember that about my mom and sister. They didn't lie to be vindictive, not like my stepmom did.

Bentley and Kayla are planning to get married soon which means they'll be moving out to get their own place, leaving me in this expensive ass three-bedroom place by myself. Bentley has told me several times I can stay and he will keep paying the rent. *Rich fucker!* But we both know I can't allow him to do that.

I pull up to the gym and grab my coffee and the other coffee I picked up. I swing the door open and head straight to the office, handing Liz the hot cup.

"Ooohhh! For me? You are the best!" she says, taking a long sip. She closes her eyes and moans dramatically. "This is so good! I needed this coffee fix."

Liz is the office manager here at Cooper's Fight Club, and married to Cooper. She's another female I've gotten to know and adore. Those two women are definitely proof that not all women are gold digging, untrusting bitches. Once in a while I actually wonder what it would be like to meet a woman like Kayla or Liz. Then I remember my past. I can't see myself ever trusting a woman enough to want to be intimate with her.

A while back Cooper's dad passed away and left the gyms he owns to his son. All this took place shortly after Cooper found out he had a baby with Liz he knew nothing about. Remember the mention of our trip to Miami? Yeah, well, what happened in Miami didn't stay in Miami. Without realizing it, Liz and her best friend Kayla wound up in Las Vegas as well—Liz pregnant with their daughter Bella—and a few years later they reconnected at a UFC fight, fell in love, got married, and recently had another baby. Their son's name is Nathan, and he's almost as cute as Faith.

After Cooper's dad died and left him the gyms he decided to take a step back from fighting to run the gyms and focus on his wife and kids. Bentley is doing the same thing…well, not running the gyms. He has decided to be a stay-at-home dad. Kayla is a physical therapist at the gym, so Bentley is still around a lot, but he's no longer fighting competitively. Yep! A lot of shit happens in seven years.

As for me, not much has changed since I moved here. I transferred to a local college and a few years ago graduated with my degree in business and finance. I haven't heard from my dad or Gloria since I moved and I prefer to keep it that way. While I miss my dad, I know it's for the best. I still find it hard to believe Gloria let me go so easily.

For the first few years after I left, I held my breath waiting for her blackmailing to begin again, but it never did.

In the last few years I have won several fights and received a UFC contract, which I am on cloud nine about. I work at the club at night, train during the day with Kaden—who took me and our friend Alex on, after Bentley and Cooper decided to take a break—and chill with my friends. Life is actually really good.

After giving Liz her coffee, I head to the locker room to change. As I'm turning the corner, I run straight into Hayley. My coffee slushes around inside the cup and some of it flies out of the small slit in the lid, not much but enough to stain her shirt.

"Oh, shit! I'm sorry," I say, looking around for something to help her wipe up the coffee on her shirt.

She looks at me nervously, biting down on her lower lip. It reminds me of her face after the first and only time we kissed, when she realized I couldn't give her anything more. The truth is we never even should have kissed that night.

"Let's play a game!" Hayley shouts over the music. We're at the club I work at celebrating Kayla and Bentley going out for the first time after having Faith.

"A game? What are we, five?" Kaden asks. Everybody laughs at his question, but of course all their drunk asses agree to play.

"Caleb, truth or dare?" Kayla asks me. I know I have to pick dare even though I don't want to. If I pick truth, she'll ask me a question I won't want to answer. She's always asking why I never bring females home. I can't put myself in that position to have to lie to her.

I glare at her but go along with it. "Dare."

Kayla looks over to her left, and following her line of vision, I see her glance at Hayley and then smirk. Don't do it Kayla…but she does.

"I dare you to kiss Hayley."

Hayley glares at her, clearly embarrassed. "You don't have to…" Hayley turns to me and says. But without letting her finish, for the first time ever, I let my hormones control my actions as I pull her to me for a kiss. Her lips are soft and warm and she tastes like the sweet liquor concoction she has been sipping on all night. My tongue seeks entrance and soon we are full on making out in front of everyone in the middle of a nightclub. I can almost enjoy it, but then it hits me. Once again I'm kissing a woman against my own free will.

No, I'm technically not being forced and I wouldn't compare it to what Gloria did to me, but we aren't kissing out of love or even lust. I'm kissing her because somebody dared me to, and just like that it's as if I'm being manipulated and used all over again. It's like ice water being splashed on me. I end the now tainted kiss abruptly slightly pushing Hayley away from me. She gives me a confused, embarrassed look that turns sad, probably wondering if she did something wrong…

Since then Hayley has made it clear on several occasions she likes me, but I've continued to ignore all her advances. I know it's been seven fucking years since I left Boulder and my past behind, but I can't find it in me to be with a woman of my own free will. Every time I think about it, I feel like in some way or another it's being forced on me. I don't know how to change the way I feel.

And let's say I do find a woman that I choose to touch. How do I know I can trust her? How do I know she won't want me for all the wrong reasons or that she won't cheat on me? I think about my sister and mom and stepmom, and how I trusted each one of them in a different way and what did they do? They all lied. I think about all the women I watched cheat on their husbands. I don't know how to truly trust a woman, and I can't imagine being with someone without trusting her, but then I think about Kayla and Liz, and while neither of them are perfect, I don't believe either of them would do anything to deliberately hurt Bentley or Cooper. I trust both of those women as much as I am capable of.

And even if we get past all that trust bullshit, how do I tell her that I lost my virginity at fifteen years old to my stepmom who then blackmailed me into learning how to please a woman so she could pimp me out to cheating wives? Who the fuck wants to deal with that kind of baggage?

Attempting to shake myself out of my thoughts I see Hayley still standing there, staring at me, and fuck if she isn't a naturally beautiful woman. I first look at her eyes because they're wide open. They are light brown and remind me of the Werther's caramels my mom used to buy me at the store when I was younger. Then my eyes drift to the rest of her face and notice she has cute freckles lightly spattered across her nose. She doesn't wear tons of make up like most women do in Las Vegas. She looks like she has a bit of clear lipstick on because her lips are shiny. It makes me want to taste them. Forcing myself to look away from her face, I look at her hair. It's brown with shades of lighter brown and blonde mixed in.

Her head is tilted just a little to the side, and my eyes go back to her mouth, which is curved downward. Her frowning does something to me. I want to make her smile. Is it crazy that I want to kiss that frown right off her face? Why is she just standing there staring at me? *Shit!* Remembering I just spilled coffee on her, I grab a towel off the towel rack and go to clean her shirt. My hand hits her breast and she jumps back, her face turning red with embarrassment. *What the hell am I doing?*

"I am so sorry!" I say once again, this time for touching her without permission.

She lets out a soft giggle and it's got to be the sweetest sound I've ever heard.

"It's okay," she says, taking the towel from me. She grabs her water bottle and pours some water on the towel and proceeds to dab the wet towel onto the stain. "I just wasn't expecting you to do that." Her face is bright red as she looks down at the spot to avoid looking at me. She's so adorable.

When she removes the towel, the area is soaking wet and I can see right through her white button up shirt to her white lacy bra. From the cold water, her nipple is poking through, and for the first time in God knows how long, my dick is twitching of its own free will. I bring my eyes back up to her face and try to discreetly adjust myself. I'm obviously not discreet enough, though, because Hayley looks at my face, down to my hard-on, then back to her soaked shirt.

If it's even possible, her face goes redder and I can't help but laugh at the awkwardness of this entire situation. How did I not notice how fucking adorable this chick is? She pouts at my laughter and covers her wet shirt and pointed nipple with the towel, making me laugh even harder.

"Are you laughing?" Kaden comes over and pats my shoulder trying to assess the situation.

He glances back and forth between Hayley and me. "You must be hilarious because I don't think I have ever heard Caleb laugh."

Hayley's eyes go wide and she mutters something along the lines of, "I need to go find a new shirt," as she hightails it away from us with the towel still covering her chest.

"What was that about?" Kaden asks, watching Hayley as she walks away.

"Nothing. I spilled my coffee on her by accident. Ready to go workout for a little bit?"

He studies me for a second. "Yeah. If you want to be ready for the fight in a few months we need to start training hardcore. You ready for that?"

"I was born ready."

We begin warming up and a few minutes later I notice Hayley walking out of the locker room with a new shirt on. She walks over to Stephen, another fighter, and begins feeling his fingers. He must have hurt them somehow while training. I know she's the onsite doctor here at the gym ,so it's her job to touch the fighters to see what's wrong, but something I've never felt before hits me as I watch her touch him— jealousy maybe? I'm not sure. Then he says something to her causing her to break out in a full grin. Her head goes back and she laughs. She might have been giggling with me, but it wasn't anywhere close to the reaction he's getting from her. She might be adorable with her shy giggles, but when she laughs…she's downright fucking beautiful.

Kaden catches me watching her and clears his throat. When I force my eyes off her and look at him he's got a smirk on his face looking like he's about to comment.

I ignore him and walk to the ring ready to train. I don't know what the hell is wrong with me but I need to focus on fighting. Sure, her laughter does something strange to my insides, and yeah, she looks hot as hell with her body full of curves and toned legs that go on for miles in her high heels and skirts. And on top of all that I know from experience, she can kiss. Everything about Hayley is a complete turn on, but at the end of the day she is still a woman, and like I've said before and will continue to say, women, for the most part can't be trusted, and I doubt Hayley is an exception.

We get into the ring and get our gloves and gear on, when I hear someone call out my name. I scan the area and see Marco running over to me. Marco is twelve years old and part of the Youth MMA program Cooper is running for kids who want a safe place to practice and train. As often as I can, I teach the class. Cooper and Liz's almost six-year-old daughter, Bella, is part of the program as well. She swears one day she'll become a UFC fighter. I don't doubt it. That little girl is beyond determined.

Earlier this year, Marco started coming into the gym. He wanted to be a part of the class, but his mom couldn't afford it, so Bentley opened up a scholarship program for kids whose parents don't have the money to pay. It allows them to train at a discounted rate. In Marco's case, he trains for free.

The truth is, nobody has ever seen Marco's mom except for me. After getting excuse after excuse, I followed him home one day and saw he lives in section eight housing in a shitty area. When he went to school the next day I knocked on the door and found a woman who looked like the weight of the world was on her shoulders.

She confided in me that Marco's dad was killed in a drive-by years ago. She recently had another baby by some other guy and is between jobs. I could tell she was strung out on drugs but knew better than to bring it up. The sure-fire way to piss off a drug addict is to call them out on it. She would most likely just lie anyway. I had her sign for Marco to join the program and told her if she needs anything to let me know, not because I want to help her but because I want to make sure Marco is okay. She is another example of an untrustworthy woman, choosing drugs over her own children.

Since she signed the papers, Marco has practically lived at the gym. When there aren't classes I let him clean and sweep just like Diego did for me. It keeps him off the streets and out of trouble. Before he started coming to the gym he used to hang out down at the skate park. He enjoys skateboarding but says he loves fighting.

"What's up?" I say, fist bumping him.

"Wanna join us?" Kaden asks. The guys know all about Marco's situation and treat him like he's one of us.

Marco looks conflicted for a second, but shakes his head no. "No, I can't. I have stuff I have to do today, but just wanted to let you know I won't be able to make the training camp today."

A red flag immediately goes up. Marco has never missed a class. Ever. That kid is the first one here and doesn't leave until he has no choice. For him to miss a class, something is up.

"I'm gonna miss you in class. What's going on that you can't make it?" I ask nonchalantly trying to get him to open up. He reminds me a lot of myself. He keeps to himself and doesn't speak more than necessary.

His refusal to look me in the eyes tells me whatever he is about to say will be a lie.

"I have to help take care of Chloe. I just wanted to tell you."

Chloe is Marco's little sister. She's only a few months old. I know he helps watch her, but he's never missed a class to watch her. I let it go for now. Calling him out on this won't help the situation.

"Okay, buddy. If anything changes, come back, okay?"

"Okay," he says with a frown marring his face. It breaks my heart what this kid goes through. Yeah, my situation was shitty as a teenager, but I never had to worry about when I would eat next. I had name brand clothes, the newest cellphone, and was given a new car almost every birthday. I chose to walk away from it all the day I left, but for Marco, he doesn't get a choice. He's never been given a choice.

He leaves out the door and I rip my headgear and gloves off, throwing them to the side.

"Where are you going?" Kaden asks.

"I'm following him. Something is up. That kid doesn't miss class."

Not waiting for a response from Kaden, I run to the locker room to grab my wallet and keys and run out the door to find out where Marco is really going.

HAYLEY

I'M RUNNING SO LATE THIS MORNING AND I HATE RUNNING late. The water heater in my house broke last night, so I was forced to take an ice cold shower this morning. I tried to call around to find someone to fix it, but with Christmas so close these people want to charge an arm and a leg. So much for the holiday spirit! I still need to buy a couple more presents. I have no idea what to buy my sister, Hannah. She is seriously the hardest person to shop for.

On my way to the gym I received a call from Cooper letting me know one of the fighters thinks he might have sprained or possibly broken a couple of fingers and would like me to check it out before he goes to the hospital. His text throws me off and I completely forget to go through the drive thru to grab a coffee. Oh well! I'll have to run back out later when I have time.

I make it to the gym in record time, run straight to the locker room to throw my purse and keys into a locker, fill up my water bottle with cold water, and head back out to find Stephen, the fighter with the possibly broken fingers. I barely make it out of the locker room when I run into a wall. Okay, not a wall, a solid man whose body feels like a wall. Warmth spreads across my chest and it's not from the unrequited lust I feel for this man. Nope, it's from the warm coffee that just spilled all over my blouse. Coffee, that isn't even mine. Coffee, that I almost want to lick off my blouse in hope I will get even a little bit of caffeine running through my exhausted body.

I look up from the stain covering my chest and into the most beautiful blue-grey eyes of Caleb Michaels, the man who I have a huge crush on. I know what you're thinking. What woman in her thirties has a crush? Well, most women in her thirties are married with kids, so they don't have to crush like a damn teenager. Not me, though. After spending my teenage years studying my ass off to get into a good college, I then studied my ass off to get into a good medical program.

It has always been my dream to get a degree in sports medicine. I love sports and I love healing people so it just made sense. I did make the mistake of dating once in college. I was so busy with school, the guy ended up cheating on me with my roommate. I told myself I wouldn't date again until I could devote the right amount of time to a man.

I finally graduated and was fortunate to get a job working at Cooper's training facility right away. The hours are great and I'm able to work with athletes every day doing what I love. I get to travel to fights and it's seriously amazing. I couldn't ask for a better job. The only downside is that between all my years of school and new work, I'm thirty years old and still single with no kids. And if that isn't enough, the guy I like doesn't even know I exist. Well, I think he knows I exist, but he definitely doesn't reciprocate my feelings.

Although, there was that time at the club when he was dared to kiss me…*Hol-y shit!* It had to have been the most intense kiss of my life! I thought maybe he felt something as well, but after the kiss was over, he walked away without looking back.

Caleb looks around for a moment and grabs a towel, bringing it right to my chest. He starts dabbing my boob with it and I'm shocked he's actually touching me. My memory flashes back to the time we were all over Cooper and Liz's place. The guys had stayed home to watch Bella and Tristan—our friend Ashley's son—while the women all got drunk and had a girls' night at my place. Somehow we ended up back at Liz's place, and Caleb was there, looking sexy as hell in his own brooding way, sitting on the couch watching a UFC fight. In my intoxicated state I walked over to sit down next to him and patted his leg…

"Sorry, to ruin your little fight party." I sit next to Caleb and pat him on his leg. He stiffen slightly before he jumps up from his spot on the couch like he's on fire.

"I have to get to work," he says, and without saying goodbye to anybody, he hauls ass out the door.

Then there was the ski trip where he didn't want to even sleep in the same room as me…

We had just arrived at Bentley's amazing vacation home in Breckenridge. Caleb asked where everyone was sleeping and within seconds rooms were called. Bentley and Kayla went to the master suite, Cooper and Liz went off to another room and even though Ashley and Kaden are just friends, they're really close, so they had no problem sharing a room. That left Caleb and me and unfortunately only one room left.

"I don't mind sharing if you don't," I said.

Caleb looked around the room and saw there was only one bed, which meant sharing a room also meant sharing a bed.

"Sorry, I can't do this." He grimaced.

"I promise not to attack you in my sleep." It was my attempt to make

light of the situation. He wasn't having it though.

"No, I'm not going to be forced to share a room with you. Sorry."

Geez. I get he doesn't want to share a room with me, but damn. I'm not forcing him to do anything...

Needless to say, he ended up sleeping on the couch during our stay and has pretty much avoided me since then.

I glance at him, embarrassed. One, for realizing how ridiculous I must look for hitting on him when he's made it clear he doesn't want me, and two, for being completely turned on by his touch.

He must suddenly realize he's rubbing all over my breasts, because he pulls back and begins to apologize profusely. I can't help but nervously laugh. The guy who doesn't want to touch me is not only touching me but also unintentionally feeling me up like we're back in high school.

"It's okay," I say, unable to make eye contact with him. This is so embarrassing.

"I wasn't expecting you to do that," I add, referring to him feeling me up. I grab my water bottle and try to blot the stained area, hoping to make it a little easier to get out later. The stain doesn't seem to be coming out at all so I give up and remove the towel from my chest. When I notice Caleb hasn't said a word I finally get the courage to look at him and when I do I see what looks like lust in his eyes...but it can't be. This guy has made it clear he doesn't want me.

I follow his gaze to find my traitorous nipples are poking through my soaking wet blouse! Jesus, I don't think this situation could get any more embarrassing...until I look back at Caleb and see him adjusting what now looks like an erection in his boxing shorts. I can feel my face heating up and then Caleb laughs. He. Fucking. Laughs. I don't know what he thinks is so funny, but it's definitely not any of this.

Kaden comes over just in time and asks why Caleb is laughing. He says something about me making Caleb laugh, and before Caleb can explain and further embarrass me, I mumble about needing a new shirt and get the hell out of there.

"Can I borrow a shirt?" I blurt out when I find Liz in her office.

She looks up at me with a confused expression. I shake my head not wanting to get into it, but of course she isn't having it.

"Everything okay?"

I let out a frustrated breath. "My shower almost froze me to death, Caleb spilled coffee on me and then felt me up, and then saw me turned on, and I might be wrong, but I think my getting turned on, turned him on."

She bursts out laughing, grabs a gym shirt, and throws it to me. "Well, I guess you got your wish."

"Oh, shut up! I need to go change and find Stephen to check out his hand."

I turn to leave and can hear her continuing to laugh from her office.

She is getting entirely too much pleasure out of this situation.

As I exit the locker room, I spot Stephen and check out his hand. I don't think his fingers are broken but I'll need to take an x-ray to make sure. We go back to my office, and after running the x-rays, my suspicions are confirmed. Not broken, just significantly bruised. I put a splint on his fingers and tell him to take a couple of days off to let them heal.

As I'm walking back out, I see Caleb rushing out of the locker room. Kaden is watching him with a worried look. As Caleb exits the gym, Ashley enters. Ashley and I have become good friends over the past several months. We met through Liz a couple years ago. She's a single mom, an elementary school teacher, and just an all-around good person. With Kayla and Liz both having new babies at home, and both happily taken, we've started hanging out together since her son is no longer a baby and neither of us are taken.

"Hey sexy momma," I say, waggling my eyebrows at her. She laughs and shakes her head, walking over to me with Tristan following behind. Kaden comes over to say hi as well, giving her a one armed hug and a kiss to her temple. It's completely innocent, but I see the look in Ashley's eyes. It's the look of a woman who wants more. Since Kaden is single and has become good friends with Ashley we all hang out quite often. I've asked Ashley on more than one occasion why she and Kaden aren't dating, but she always says the same thing—she doesn't want to lose him as a friend. It's rumored Kaden isn't the settling down type, and over the years I've been working here, I've seen him with various women, but since he started hanging out with Ashley, I haven't seen him around any other woman but her.

Caleb is single as well, but is more of a loner. I haven't seen him hanging around a single woman in the time I've been working at the gym. Whenever Kaden, Ashley, and I hang out, we invite Caleb to join us, but he always says no. I try not to take it too personal.

"What's up with Caleb?" Ashley asks Kaden. "He almost plowed through me on his way out."

Kaden leaves his arm dangling over Ashley's shoulder and pulls her in closer to him, not noticing—or ignoring—the blush that creeps up Ashley's face. We'll definitely be talking later. "He's worried about Marco. He told him he couldn't make it to class today, so he's following him to see where he's going."

Poor Marco. It's no secret the type of home he comes from. When he first started coming here he was so shy and quiet, but several months later and he has grown on all of us, especially Caleb. If you didn't know better you would think Marco was a mini-Caleb. He follows him around and copies everything he does. They are both so serious all the time. It really is adorable.

"Oh, well, Tristan is here for the MMA boot camp. With school out for the holidays Cooper and Caleb are doing a mini-training camp for the kids. My parents are going to take him afterward and keep him for the rest of winter break."

"Let's go see what's going on with the camp," Kaden says, leading her to the backroom where the kids classes are all held.

"Hey, Hayley," Ashley calls back to me. "Dinner tonight?"

"Sure! I'll bring dessert."

"Sounds good!"

Three

CALEB

I FIND MARCO AS SOON AS I WALK OUT THE DOOR, ONLY HE isn't walking anywhere—he's standing in the parking lot talking to some shady-looking motherfuckers. There are two of them and both are covered in ink. Now, I'm not by any means against tattoos. I have several of my own, and because of that, I know ninety percent of the time they have meaning behind them. Staring at these guys talking to Marco, I can tell right away they're in a gang. They both have the same tattoo of what looks like a local gang symbol going up their neck and, when I look closer, I can see the tear drop tattoos on their cheeks, the universal code for how many people they've killed.

A third guy approaches from an expensive Mercedes, looking out of place. He's dressed much nicer than the other two guys in a suit, but peeking out from under the collar is the same tattoo as the other guys, telling me he is some type of leader. He hands Marco a brown package, and before Marco can leave, he grabs him by his shirt and pulls him closer whispering something to him. Marco nods nervously and then walks away.

The three guys stay in the parking lot discussing something but I don't wait around to see what they are doing. I'm about to jump in my car but think it might be more discreet to follow by foot. Without letting Marco know, I follow him, staying close enough to see him but far enough back he doesn't catch on. He walks several blocks to his neighborhood looking around. I can tell by his body language he's scared. He's gripping the bag in both hands and when he looks around, it's like he wants to make sure nobody's going to steal the package from him.

It doesn't take a genius to figure out what's going on. I seriously hope my suspicions are wrong, but when he stops walking at a house a couple streets over from his and pulls a cell phone out of his pocket, one I know damn well he can't afford, I have a sinking feeling in my gut.

My suspicions are confirmed about two minutes later when a guy walks over to Marco, looks around, and then takes the package from him. He opens it up, takes something out, dabs it on his wrist, and then licks his wrist. *Fuck.* Marco just handed this guy cocaine.

The guy nods once and then hands Marco an envelope, which I'm sure contains money. He says something to him I can't hear and then walks away. Marco opens the envelope and then calls someone. He starts walking down the street and ends up in front of an old warehouse a street over from his house. A few minutes later, the two guys from earlier pull up, take the envelope from Marco and hand him some money. Marco pockets the money, takes another brown envelope from the guys, and then they part ways. I follow Marco until he's at his house and wait until he's inside before leaving. The only reason I can think of why these guys aren't dealing themselves is they are under surveillance, so instead of handling the exchange themselves, they're using Marco, a twelve-year-old fucking kids, as a middleman.

I head back to the gym in a daze. I always knew there was a possibility of something like this happening. The kid lives in a neighborhood surrounded by druggies and those who deal the drugs to them. His own mom is a fucking druggie. I just hoped him hanging out with me would keep him away from that shit as long as possible. I join Kaden and Cooper in the kids' class. The boot camp is a blast. The kids have fun and learn a lot about self-defense, but the entire time I can't take my mind off Marco. I don't know how to handle this situation. I don't even know who to talk to about any of this.

After all the kids' parents pick them up I head to the mall to pick up a couple last minute Christmas gifts. I purchase a couple new Disney movies for Bella that Liz mentioned she wanted, some light-up musical toy for Nathan since he's five months old, and a shirt that reads, "My uncle is better than yours" for Faith. Since Kayla and Bentley live in the same apartment as me I know Faith has way too many toys, and Kayla will get a kick out of the shirt.

I take them to the wrapping station in the middle of the mall and make a donation to the school's local band for them to wrap them for me. As I am heading out, my phone dings with a text from Kaden.

Kaden: Going to Ashley's for dinner. Hayley will be there... Wanna go?

My thoughts go back to her this morning—her reaction to me touching her, her nipples getting hard, her face turning red, and then her cute-as-fuck embarrassed giggle over it all. Every time he asks me to join, I always say no. I don't want to give her any reason to think there's a chance with us, but for some reason I find myself wanting to go, wanting to see her giggle some more, wanting to see if I can bring the same smile to her face Stephen did.

Me: Sure. What time? Need me to bring anything?

I get ready for his smart-ass remark, but it doesn't come.

Kaden: 5 p.m. Just bring you.

After taking a shower and getting dressed, I search the kitchen to see if we have a bottle of wine I can bring with me. I don't want to show up empty handed. I find red wine in the cabinet and then walk out to the living room. Kayla is sitting on the couch bouncing Faith on her legs and singing the ABCs to her while Faith makes noises she thinks are mimicking her mom.

"Where are you going all dressed up?" she playfully asks, still in her singing mom voice.

"I wouldn't call a shirt and jeans dressed up…I'm going to Ashley's for dinner." I glance down at my clothes. I'm in a collared shirt, which I don't usually wear, but still…Do I usually dress so crappy she's considering this dressed up?

Kayla's eyes widen out of shock. "Just you and Ashley?"

"No. Kaden will be there and so will Hayley, I guess. Mind if I take this wine?" I try to sound as chill as possible not wanting her to question my motives.

"Sure."

"Wanna go?"

Her smile widens and she shakes her head slowly. "Nope, you enjoy your double date, my friend."

"It's not a double date. Kaden and Ashley are only friends."

"Yeah, until they both get their heads out of their ass and admit they want more."

I laugh at that. "Kaden settle down? Highly unlikely."

"You never know. Cooper and Bentley both settled down."

"Yeah, but the difference is, Bentley has always wanted to settle down and Cooper was pining over Liz for years. Plus, they have a kid together. I don't think Kaden will ever settle down."

"And what about you?" She quirks a single brow. "Will you ever settle down?"

I don't like how serious this conversation is getting, so I say something to deflect. "Not a chance in hell. The only woman I trust is taken, and plus…Bentley would *try* to beat my ass." I give her a wink and Faith a kiss on her forehead, and walk out the door before she can say anything else. She laughs as I close the door behind me.

As I walk down the stairs to my car, I start to feel uneasy. Is that what this is? Was I tricked into a fucking double date? The thought pisses me off. Once again I'm being forced into something I didn't ask for. Did Hayley put Kaden up to this?

I pull out my phone and text Kaden.

Me: Hey…is this a double date?

Kaden: No…just dinner with friends.

Me: Okay, fine. I'm on my way.

Kaden: <insert middle finger emoji>

Me: You're a dick.

While I want to cancel and not take the chance that Kaden might be lying to me, I decide to go. Kaden has never lied to me before and I don't think he would start now. If he says it's just friends hanging out, I believe him.

I arrive at Ashley's house twenty minutes later, and both Kaden and Hayley's vehicles are in the driveway. I barely make it up the sidewalk when the door swings open. Kaden is standing there with his arms crossed over his chest and a knowing smirk on his face.

"After your texts, I thought for sure you were gonna bail."

"Shut up, man." I push the wine into his chest for him to grab and follow him into the house. The aroma of Italian food hits my senses and my stomach growls loudly as I walk to the living room to sit down. I can't even remember the last time I had a home-cooked meal. Hayley hears it from the couch where she's watching television and laughs, not quite like the laughter I saw Stephen bring out of her but close.

"Hungry?" she asks, keeping her eyes on the show she's watching.

"Yeah, it's been a crazy day. I forgot to eat."

"I saw you run out earlier. Everything okay?" She turns her attention from the show to me. The way she looks at me reminds me of Kayla. Like she genuinely wants to know what's wrong. No hidden agenda. It makes me want to be honest with her. I sit next to her on the couch since Kaden is sitting on the loveseat with Ashley.

"Yes…No…Shit, I don't know."

She gives me a confused look that encourages me to keep talking.

"You know Marco, right?"

She nods, smiling. I've seen her talk to him, and she's clearly fond of him and he of her.

"I followed him home today because he said he couldn't make it to class, and I think he's selling drugs for some guys."

"Holy shit!" Kaden yells, overhearing our conversation.

"Are you sure?" Ashley asks.

"Yeah, I think so. The guy looked to be trying out the product and then gave him an envelope of money. I have no idea how to handle this."

"Damn," Hayley weighs in frowning. "Marco is such a good kid, too. What are you going to do?"

"I have no clue. His mom is in a bad place. I'm afraid if I tell the authorities it will mess up things for her."

"You have to do what's best for Marco. I see kids all the time in bad situations, and as much as I don't want to report it, I have to," Ashley says sadly. It makes sense she would feel this way. She teaches at a school close to where Marco lives. It's a poverty-stricken area, so I can imagine the shit she sees and hears from the kids.

"I need to think about how to approach it." I need to handle the situation with care. Marco trusts me and I don't want to do something to lose that trust.

"Just don't think too long," she says before getting up to go to the kitchen.

Dinner is served and the food is delicious. We eat while making light conversation. We discuss what we're all doing for the holidays. Ashley is going to her parents' house for Christmas. Tristan's grandparents picked him up after MMA class today to spend some time with him, and since Kaden's parents are in Hawaii for the holidays he's joining Ashley instead of flying back to Colorado to visit them. Hayley says her family lives here in Las Vegas, so she's joining them and her sister for Christmas. When Hayley asks what I'm doing, I tell her I'll just be home hanging out with Kayla and Bentley. She doesn't need to know most of my family is dead, and the one person who is alive, I haven't talked to in over seven years.

I do notice that hanging out with Hayley today seems different than before. She hasn't once tried to come on to me—she hasn't tried to touch me, or even flirt. Thinking about it, since the day at Bentley's house in Breckenridge when I refused to share a room with her, she hasn't tried anything. Not that she was so forward before. Just a touch here, a flirtatious smile or comment there, but now…nothing, and for some reason it makes me want her. It makes me want to make her want me. I am one fucked up son-of-a-bitch.

After we eat dessert I say goodbye and wish everyone a Merry Christmas in case I don't see them beforehand. Hayley decides to leave at the same time so I walk her out.

"Have a good Christmas, Caleb." She gives me a bright smile. Fuck! That smile has my dick twitching. It makes me want to cover her lips with mine, to feel her smile against me. It makes me want to take her right here on the hood of her car. I don't know what the hell has gotten into me today.

"You too, Hayley," I say before she shuts her door, turns on the ignition, and drives away.

Four

HAYLEY

TO SAY I WAS SHOCKED CALEB WAS ACTUALLY JOINING US FOR dinner was an understatement. I had already made the decision to stop pursuing him weeks ago at the ski resort, but that doesn't mean his presence doesn't affect me. When he showed up in a navy blue collared shirt that made his stormy blue eyes pop, hair still damp and wild from the shower, and in jeans that fit his ass perfectly, I couldn't decide if I wanted to first run my fingers through his messy hair, grab his ass, or run my hands down the washboard abs I know are hidden under his shirt.

A while back Kayla decided to surprise Bentley with a trip to a resort overnight and thought she could play matchmaker by having Caleb and me babysit together. I showed up to their apartment at the same time Caleb was walking out of the bathroom in nothing but a towel. I honestly thought I was going to orgasm right there on the spot.

His body was not only covered in sexy as hell tattoos, but he was also sporting a nipple ring. *A fucking nipple ring!* It took everything in me not to run straight to him to lick the nipple ring, and while licking it, I could have run my hands down his rock hard abs. I wasn't aware of the restraint I was capable of until that moment.

Of course he nearly freaked out and hurried to his room. He could cover himself all he wanted, that visual was engrained into my brain—and vagina—and not going anywhere anytime soon. Needless to say, Caleb's sexy-as-sin body has become the focal point of most of my self-inducing orgasms these days.

So when he walked in to Ashley's house, I thought it would be best to watch the television and not him. If I stared at him too long I couldn't be held responsible for the things that would come out of my mouth. I thought I was in the clear but then he sat next to me and I could smell his cologne—not too strong, just a light, fresh, clean scent—and it took everything in me not to lean over and give him a good sniff.

After he told us about Marco, I could see how much he really cared about him. The worry on his face was heartbreaking. Dinner and dessert thankfully went smooth, and I was really proud of myself for remaining cool around Caleb. I think he was more comfortable around me today as well and that confirmed what I already knew—he isn't into me. But it also gave me hope we could be friends. Caleb is a good guy, and I would rather have him as a friend than not at all.

After getting home, I text my sister to let her know I will be over to mom and dad's house Christmas morning first thing. The guy she's dating is joining her, so she begged me to be there when they arrive. It'll be Dad's first time meeting one of our boyfriends, which is making her nervous. Hannah is a lot like me. While she is three years younger, she's my best friend. She focused on school and college and then law school. I seriously missed the hell out of her while she was away at law school and was so excited to learn she would be moving back to accept an amazing job offer here in Las Vegas as a defense attorney for a prestigious law firm. Once she was settled into her job, she started dating, and after quite a few duds, she met Gavin.

They were at a mediation meeting—he was council for the other side—and they hit it off. They waited until the case was resolved and then went out. They've been together for about four months now and are inseparable. Because our parents were vacationing with my aunt and uncle in New York, they haven't met Gavin yet and will be meeting him on Christmas. I am definitely curious to see how they act. It's like a trial run for when, or I guess I should say, *if* I ever bring someone home.

After showering and pouring myself a glass of wine, I snuggle up on my couch to get caught up on *The Bachelor*. It's one of my favorite shows. It's so hilarious watching the women get all catty with each other, fighting over one man. I also love to watch their one-on-one dates. They are always so romantic. I would give anything for a guy to take me on a date like the ones they go on.

My phone dings with a text from Cooper reminding me the gym will be closed the next few days for Christmas, and will open back up afterward. I text him back wishing him and Liz a Merry Christmas and decide to go to bed.

As I walk through the house turning the lights off and double-checking the locks I feel the loneliness that surrounds me. It seems like everyone is with someone besides me. Even Ashley and Kaden have each other. Sure, they're only friends, but they hang out so often they might as well be together. I wonder if Caleb ever feels lonely. Does he lie in bed at night and wish someone were next to him?

After brushing my teeth and washing my face, I lie down in my dark room and turn the television on, turning it down to almost mute.

The light and sound makes me feel a little less alone. Cuddling up in my down blanket, I think about how I got to this point. Back in high school when I was so hell-bent on studying and getting good grades, I told myself college was where I would meet someone. The problem was, while in college I got cheated on and so I told myself it would be best to wait until after I graduated. Medical School came and went and I was so busy studying I didn't have time to date anyway. Jeez…when was the last time I even had sex? There was that one guy I met at the party Kaden threw. How long ago was that? It must have been well over a year ago. I seriously need to get laid.

My issue is at thirty years old I want more. While a one-night stand would definitely scratch my itch, I really want my house to be less quiet. I was so excited when I purchased this home. With four bedrooms and two and a half bathrooms, I envisioned finally having a family. The backyard is perfect to set up a swing set next to the underground pool. I can see myself having play dates and barbeques.

While volunteering at a local YMCA last year, there were people from DCF encouraging us to sign up to be a foster parent. I filled out the paperwork and got approved, thinking if I don't meet Mr. Right I can always adopt. I haven't fostered anyone yet, though. I think I keep hoping I'll meet someone and we'll choose to create kids together. Now if I could just find someone. The question is, how do I meet someone if all I ever do is go to work and home? I need to get out more often. Maybe I'll ask Ashley to join me one night. Hell, maybe I should just woman up and go out by myself.

I make a promise to myself that after the holidays I'm going to try to meet a guy. I'm never going to meet anybody if I don't try. And then I remember the dating site Ashley once mentioned. Maybe I can meet a guy on there. I roll over to the middle of the bed and stretch out wrapping my body around the body pillow and wish that one day there will be a warm body next to me.

Five

HAYLEY

CHRISTMAS WAS OVERALL A GREAT HOLIDAY. MOM MADE Christmas breakfast while we watched the Disney parade on television. It's a tradition I look forward to every year. Her cinnamon buns were mouth-watering delicious like they are every year. Dad and Gavin hit it off and watched football the rest of the day while Hannah, mom, and I cooked Christmas dinner and made cookies. I love that, even though Hannah and I are older and there are no kids running around, mom still makes cookies with us every year just like she did when we were little.

After dinner, Gavin got down on one knee and proposed to Hannah. It was a sweet proposal and the ring he gave her was beautiful. She, of course said yes, and the rest of the evening was focused on when they plan to get married and where they plan to live. I'm thankful Gavin's family mostly live local so they're planning to make roots here. They even talked about looking for a house in the same neighborhood as mine.

Of course Mom and Dad had to point out several times throughout the night that I'm three years older and still single with no kids. Hannah came to my rescue, insisting I'm still young and have plenty of time, but I know they're right. It just solidifies my plan to take the initiative to meet Mr. Right.

It's been three days since Christmas and I'm back to work. I joined the dating site Ashley recommended and actually have a date tonight with a guy name Greg. He's a few years older than me and owns a construction company locally. We agreed to meet at a restaurant in the area. I don't know this guy, so I figured it would be safer to meet somewhere public instead of him picking me up.

I'm about to leave when Alex, one of the fighters, comes over and asks me to take a look at his ankle. It's been bugging him a lot recently. I tell him to head into my office and I'll meet him there. I grab my purse from the locker room so I don't have to grab it afterward and see Caleb and Marco fighting in the ring. I'm glad to see Marco here. If he's here ,he's safe. Caleb is showing him how to do a move correctly and Marco is watching with complete rapture. Caleb catches me watching and grants me a slight smile. I give him a small wave and head to check out Alex's ankle.

"Which ankle is it?" I ask Alex. He points to his right ankle, so I grab it gently and place it on the medical bed to examine it. I feel for any tension and when I hit a certain spot, he jumps in pain.

"I take it, it hurts there." I smile at Alex before touching it again, making him jump in pain.

He smiles back a boyish grin. "Hey now! What did I ever do to you?"

"Oh, don't be a baby. I just had to make sure that's where it hurts."

I've known Alex since I started working here, but never paid attention to how cute he is. While he isn't hot like Caleb, he definitely has that whole boy next door look going for him.

"It looks like you just sprained it. I don't think it's fractured and it's definitely not broken. Keep it up and alternate between cold and hot compressions. I want to see you back in a couple days to make sure it's healing okay."

"Thanks, Doc." He gives me a wink as he carefully jumps down on his good ankle.

I lock up my office and head out the door when I see Marco leaning against the outside window staring at his phone and looking around nervously.

"Hey, Marco. What are you up to?"

He looks around again and quietly says, "I'm about to go home."

Something tells me this kid shouldn't be alone right now.

"I'm going to grab a bite to eat and could use the company. Want to join me?" I know I'm supposed to be going on a date, but I'll have to call or text him to cancel. It's not exactly the first impression I wanted to make, but the look I see in Marco's eyes tell me he needs me more.

He looks conflicted, but after a few moments, nods. "Okay, yeah, sure."

As we're heading to my car, I notice a couple of guys heading toward us. They don't look like they belong to the gym and it hits me they might be the guys Caleb mentioned Marco has been associating with. I try to rush us to the vehicle, but the faster we walk, the faster they do, and before I can unlock my doors and get us in, they make it to my vehicle.

"Yo, Marco. We've been looking for you," scary guy number one says. Marco's face pales, looking more scared than any kid should ever look. I pull him behind me and raise my chin, praying I don't pee my pants when I confront these guys.

"What do you need him for? Isn't he a bit too young to be hanging out with you?"

"He wasn't too young to take what doesn't belong to him," scary guy two spits out.

I keep Marco behind me. "Well, you shouldn't be dealing with a child. Do I need to call the police?"

"Lady, this shit ain't your fucking business. I suggest you worry about yourself," scary guy number one says, getting in my face. He places his hands on my shoulders roughly, attempting to shove me out of the way to get to Marco, but I plant my feet firmly in the ground, refusing to let him get to him.

"Bitch, you need to move out of my way." He's too strong and my body begins to sway against my will. I don't want him getting to Marco, but I'm not going to be able to go up against these guys.

I consider yelling for help, but suddenly his hands are off me and he's practically flying into the side of my vehicle. When my heart slows down, I realize Caleb has scary guy number one up against the side of my car, and scary guy number two doesn't even try to help. I don't blame him. Angry Caleb looks downright frightening.

"What the fuck do you think you're doing putting your hands on her? Did she say you could put your hands on her?"

Six

CALEB

TO SAY CHRISTMAS WAS A CLUSTERFUCK OF EPIC PROPORTIONS would be an understatement. The morning started out great. Faith woke up to a million presents under the tree from Santa. Kayla, Bentley, and I watched her rip apart the paper, not even caring what was in the boxes. I swear she loved the wrapping paper more than the items inside. Unfortunately when Kayla asked Bentley to grab her camera it all went downhill fast. Bentley found a prenuptial agreement she was hiding that her shitty lawyer mom put together and shit hit the fan. He left, then she left, and after a few hours, she came back in tears and spent the rest of Christmas day crying on my shoulder.

This isn't the first time Kayla has fucked up. She hid her pregnancy from Bentley in the beginning and moved back to Florida to live with her parents. I hate that she did that, but I know she was scared and quickly owned up to it. I think the reason Kayla and I became close was because I watched how protective she was of those she loves, especially Bella and Liz. Liz and Kayla are best friends and for years she helped her raise her daughter. I guess I choose to see the good in her. I choose to trust her to an extent, probably more than I trust any woman, but I also don't have to sleep with her or marry her. I know she's been through a lot of shit and has pretty crappy parents. I don't like some of the choices she's made, but my job is to be her friend and let her and Bentley figure their shit out.

When I think about how I'm able to open up and trust Kayla, and even Liz, it makes me wonder if maybe I could one day open up to a woman who isn't engaged or married to one of my friends. I think it's definitely easier to let a woman in that you know doesn't have a chance of hurting you. Kayla and Liz can't do anything to me. They can't use me or cheat on me—I'm not vulnerable to them. I just can't imagine being in a situation where I ever feel so out of control ever again.

And if Kayla and Bentley's shit wasn't enough to fuck up Christmas,

I got a call from my father's attorney requesting to speak to me in person. While he's an old friend of my father's, I don't know what the fuck he could want from me, and after seven years, I can't imagine there is anything left to say. The fact that my father couldn't even call me himself and had to have his lawyer call me instead speaks volumes. If he wants to talk, he can call me his damn self.

It's been three days since Christmas and since Kayla has finally got it together long enough to go to work, I decide I'm going to go train for a little bit. After a couple hours of working out, Marco shows up. I ask him how his Christmas was and he just shrugs his shoulders. Something is definitely going on with this kid. Yeah, sh_t has always been rough for him, but he never used to let it get him down like this.

I offer to spar with him and show him some new moves and he lights up. While we're working out I notice Hayley observing us. She doesn't have the look of lust like she used to, though, and for some reason once again it's making me want her. I'm pretty sure a therapist would have a field day with my fucked up logic. Her smile is more friendly and less flirty and without thinking about it I smile back at her. She gives me a small wave and I can't help but watch her as she walks away. I would be blind not to notice how sexy she is. How did I seriously not notice her before?

"Do you like her?" Marco asks, taking me away from staring at her perfect ass as she enters her office.

"Huh? Like who?" I ask, confused.

He nods toward where Hayley just was and grins.

"We're just friends," I say before throwing a punch to his gut to make him block.

"Really? Cause you look like you wanna give her some cooties," he sings while waggling his eyebrows before busting out laughing. I throw another punch to his stomach and he drops to the ground laughing and singing some stupid song about kissing in a tree.

I jump on top of him and start grappling with him. He gets serious and tries to throw me off when his phone rings. He taps out and gets up to go check it.

"Hey, I gotta go," he says, frowning down at his phone.

"Where do you need to be?"

I notice he once again doesn't make eye contact. "I gotta go help my mom out. I'll see you tomorrow, okay?"

"Yeah, okay. If you need me you know my number. Right?"

"Yeah, I do," he says distractedly, gathering up his stuff quickly.

I take a quick shower to rinse off then head to the parking lot to go home. While checking my texts I see one from Kayla.

Kayla: Bentley and I made up!! We're getting married New Year's Eve!! You're a groomsman!

As I'm texting her back, I look up before crossing the street and see Marco and Hayley near her car, only they aren't alone. The two guys I saw Marco talking to the other day are also there, and one of them appears to have his hands on Hayley while Marco is hiding behind her.

I throw my phone in my pocket and run over to them. When I get closer I hear him threatening her and everything goes red. Without even thinking, I grab the fucker by the back of his shirt and throw him up against the car.

"What the fuck do you think you're doing putting your hands on her? Did she say you could put your hands on her?" I scream into his face. He looks shocked, and out of the corner of my eye, I can see his pussy friend trying to decide if he should intervene. He takes a step back. *Good choice, motherfucker.*

"I don't know what the fuck is going on here, but whatever it is, you don't ever put your hands on a woman without her permission. Got me?"

He nods like the scared pussy he is, and I release him. Now that my hands aren't on him, he gets his balls back. "Marco owes us and we will be collecting. You heard that, Marco? You can run, but you can't hide."

"What the fuck does he owe you?"

"That's between Marco and us, *loco*," he says, walking away. I don't take my eyes off either of them memorizing everything I can about them. I have a feeling this won't be the last time they come around here. Just before they get in their car, the other guy looks right at Hayley. "You are a pretty little bitch. Maybe you can help Marco give us what he owes us. I might be willing to make a deal." He winks at her and gets in the car.

Whatever she said to them, put her on their radar, and guys like that don't let shit go. That wasn't just a comment. That was a threat, one they will most likely try to make good on.

I look over at Hayley and Marco and they both look terrified. I want to find out what the guys said to her and what Marco owes them and I will soon, but I want them both to calm down first.

"Where are you guys going?" I ask.

Hayley's body visibly relaxes and Marco comes out from behind her. "We're going to get some dinner…Umm…Would you like to join us?" Hayley asks nervously, making me realize I need to work on how I act toward her. I don't want her feeling like she can't even speak to me.

"Absolutely. Let's take my truck."

She doesn't argue. After locking up her car and getting into my truck we head to a local bar and grill Hayley suggests. While we're driving there, her phone rings. She gives me an apologetic look and accepts the call. I can only hear her half of the conversation, but it's obvious she was supposed to go out with some guy and is canceling last minute.

"Hey Greg…I'm sorry. I was just about to call you…I'm going to have to cancel…Yeah, something came up…Sure, I'll call you when I know I can make it…Okay, bye."

For some crazy reason the thought of Hayley on a date with another guy forces my fists to tighten on the steering wheel. It makes me want to lock her up and keep her for myself. Only she isn't mine.

Once we are seated and the waitress takes our drink orders I reach into my pocket and take out a twenty-dollar bill, handing it to Marco.

"Why don't you go get change and play some video games?" I nod toward the game room in the corner.

His eyes widen in shock, breaking my heart. The kid has probably never played a video game. He looks down at the money and back up to me unsure.

"Go on, and don't come back until you've spent it all."

"Thank you!" he says, before he takes off running to the video arcade room.

"What did they say to you?" I ask Hayley, getting straight to the point. I need to know how bad this is.

"Nothing really. They wanted something Marco took that didn't belong to him. I told them they shouldn't hold a child accountable and they told me to mind my own business. The one guy tried to get around me to speak to Marco, and when I wouldn't let him, he called me a bitch. That's when you walked up."

"It's got to be the drugs…or money."

"I'm terrified for him, Caleb. Those guys were scary." It's definitely not what I should be thinking about right now, but my name coming from Hayley's mouth is like an instant jolt straight to my dick. I have never felt like this before, and I have no idea where it's coming from, but it's been happening more and more lately. It's like the minute she stopped outwardly wanting me, I can't stop thinking about her.

"I'll talk to Marco and see what's going on. Whatever it is we'll figure it out."

Hayley's phone dings and when she looks down at her phone she frowns.

"Everything okay?"

She looks back up and I notice a light blush spreading across her cheeks.

"Yeah, as you kind of heard in the truck, I was supposed to go out on a date tonight. I joined some stupid dating site in attempt to meet someone. Anyway, I canceled when I saw Marco outside. I know it was rude of me to cancel last minute, but he's being kind of mean about it."

Does this woman not realize how beautiful she is? Why would she think she needs a dating site? Every guy around her that's single practically drools over her, and she definitely doesn't need to put up with some asshole who doesn't understand life happens.

"Maybe it's not too late to meet him. I can stay with Marco... Then he won't be so mad." I have no idea why the hell I'm even suggesting that. The thought of her leaving us to go on her date makes me sick.

She frowns but quickly replaces it with what looks like a fake smile. "That's okay. I already told him we could reschedule."

I want to ask her why my suggestion made her sad but then Marco comes running back, out of money, and sits down, grabbing on his drink, and my mind immediately goes back to Marco and keeping him safe. There's no way I'm letting anything happen to this kid. The waitress comes over, and after we order, I figure now is as good a time as any to ask Marco what's going on.

"Marco, can you tell us who those guys were and what they were talking about?"

He instantly looks nervous, bouncing his eyes back and forth between Hayley and me.

"You can trust us, Marco," Hayley adds in a soothing voice that makes me want to see how well she can soothe my dick. *What the fuck is going on with me?*

"Umm...Well...The guy you put up against the car is Hector and the other guy is Santos. I ran an errand for them to make some money and my mom borrowed the money I owe them. She promised to pay it back. She said she just needed to buy Chloe diapers. But she hasn't given me the money back yet, and Hector and Santos want the money because their boss Antonio needs it."

Fuck. His mom took the money he owes these guys, probably to buy more drugs. This isn't good. I can easily pay them back, but this isn't just about money. Guys like them don't like to be stolen from. This is about pride, about sending a message. They will definitely be sending a message.

"Okay, how much do you owe them?"

"Two thousand dollars."

Holy shit! What the hell are these guys doing trusting a fucking twelve-year-old with that kind of money? Hayley hasn't said a word. She looks scared as shit for this kid. I don't know much about Hayley, but I know she comes from a good family, and while I do as well, I also come from a home where my stepmom runs a strip club, which is shady as fuck, and used to pimp out her teenage stepson. Oh, I didn't mention that before? Yep, my dad met Gloria at a strip club and decided to marry her and then fund her opening her own strip club. I used to see some crazy shit go down at that club when I would have to go see her.

Then working at the clubs on the strip, watching the deals go down every night, you learn real quick how fucked up life can be. I've stood in on too many deals to count at the clubs. To make extra money I've taken private bodyguard jobs to escort guys into business meetings.

You have no idea how corrupt Las Vegas truly is until you've sat in a few of those meetings.

The difference is, those meetings were with legitimate businessmen—even if they are corrupt—not fucking gang members hanging out on the streets. The men I've dealt with aren't hiring twelve year old's to deliver their drugs for them.

"We're going to go by the bank and I'm going to give you the money to give to those guys, okay? But Marco, you can't keep running errands for them. They aren't good guys."

"I know but the money they pay me helps my mom. It gives Chloe her formula and diapers. My mom doesn't have a job right now."

"We'll figure it out. Just promise me, no more running errands for them. Got it?"

"Okay," he agrees, but I can see the fear in his eyes. There's more to this than he's telling us.

After we're done eating, I run by the bank just before it closes and take out the money. I drop Hayley off at her car and take Marco to his house. I'm not stupid enough to just give the kid the money.

"I want you to call or text those guys and tell them you have their money. I'm going to wait here while you give it to them."

"Okay."

After a few minutes, the guys pull up and get out of the car. We're parked in front of Marco's house and I tell him to stay in the car while I get out to deal with the guys.

The guy Marco said was named Hector walks up to me first. "*Que pasa, loco*? Where's Marco?" *What's up?*

"Here's three grand. The two grand he owes you and one more for your trouble." I take the envelope of money and shove it into his chest. "Leave Marco alone."

"Hey now, nobody forced him to do anything. He needed money and we offered him a job."

"Yeah, well, consider his employment terminated as of now."

"Whatever you say," he says with a smarmy smirk.

I walk back to my car knowing this shit isn't over but not sure what else to do. Marco gets out and I walk him up to the door. I can hear the baby screaming inside, so I follow him in. The house is fucking gross and smells like piss. The baby is on the floor on a blanket, red-faced, screaming and crying her head off without her mom anywhere to be found.

Marco goes straight to her, picking her up with expertise as he tries to soothe her. His mom walks out looking strung out on drugs just like the last time I saw her. Before she sees I'm here, she yells at Marco.

"Where the fuck have you been? I need you to get some formula for the baby! And I'm fucking exhausted from dealing with Chloe. It's your turn to watch her…"

Before she can finish, I clear my throat indicating they aren't alone. She doesn't even have the audacity to look apologetic that I just witnessed her treat her kid like absolute shit. She walks by me to her room and slams the door shut.

Marco goes to the cabinet and pulls out a can of what I imagine is formula since he pours some into a bottle, heats it up, and feeds it to the baby.

"I bought some last night, but she was asleep when I got home and wasn't awake yet when I left this morning," he says, like it's perfectly normal for that bitch to speak to her kid like that. I'm speechless. I'm watching a twelve-year-old act like a father to a baby when he's still a fucking baby himself.

"Hey, I'm going to take care of this, Marco. I promise you."

"Please don't report my mom. If you do, they'll take away my sister. They'll put us into foster care. Some of my friends went there and told me it's really bad. Please don't do that," he begs.

I don't even know how to respond to any of this. This is all so over my head, but there has got to be an answer.

"Okay, buddy. Let me think about it for a little bit and I'll figure it out." I take some money from my pocket and hand it to him. "Don't show your mom this. It's a hundred dollars. Use it to feed your sister and you. If you need money, you come see me. Okay?"

"Okay, thank you." He burps his baby sister and then lays her down on the couch, patting her to sleep.

Seven

HAYLEY

IT'S NEW YEAR'S EVE, WHICH MEANS IT'S ALSO BENTLEY AND Kayla's wedding night. We're all standing at a local chapel on the strip listening to them say their vows to each other. Once Kayla decided she wanted to marry Bentley after almost losing him to her ridiculous insecurities she decided not to waste any more time. If she could have she would've married him the minute he said yes. Yep! You heard me right. She proposed to Bentley the second time around and of course he said yes. She wanted to get married immediately but agreed to New Year's Eve to give her brother, Zach, time to get here for the ceremony.

"You may kiss the bride," the Ordain Minister says and they kiss. Because of the small ceremony Kayla insisted on, Liz and I are her only bridesmaids and Cooper and Caleb are the groomsmen. Everybody claps and then we take off to Kayla and Bentley's new home for their reception-slash-house warming party. As an engagement present, Bentley surprised Kayla by purchasing the home of her dreams, which is also right down the street from Liz's house. I look over at Caleb and he gives me a small smile. He looks sexy as hell dressed in slacks and a button down dress shirt, but I still prefer him in nothing but a towel hanging from his hips. It's like he knows what I'm thinking when he raises a brow and gives me a cocky smirk.

I shake my head and walk over to him. "Heading over to the house?"

"Yeah. You?"

"Yep, I guess I'll see you there." I'm about to walk away when he grabs me by my elbow, forcing me to stop in my place in shock. Caleb has never willingly touched me.

"Hey, do you think maybe we could grab a bite to eat one day?"

"Like as a date?" I don't want to assume anything.

He contemplates my question for a second. "Umm…As friends."

It's a good thing I didn't assume. "Friends…Yeah, sure. Just let me know when."

His phone dings, alerting him of a text message and he frowns at whoever is texting him. He puts it back in his pocket and looks back up at me.

"That was Marco. He didn't realize the gym was closed and needs me to meet him there to give him some money. I'm trying to figure out how to help him without turning his mom into the Department of Children and Families. I'm looking into some rehab facilities that run off private donations to those with kids who can't afford it, but even then she would need someone to take care of them unless she can do outpatient or something."

"That's really sweet of you. He's lucky to have you in his life. If you need any help, please let me know."

"Thanks."

We both head out to our cars and go our separate ways, him to the gym and me to the party.

A little while later he arrives at the reception looking completely distracted.

"Hey, is everything okay with Marco?"

"I'm not sure. Marco is acting off. I think something is going on at his house. I'm going to head over there after the party and check on him."

"Do you want me to go with you?"

"No, I appreciate it, but I would rather you not be in that area. It's not a good neighborhood."

"Okay, well, if you need anything let me know."

"Thank you, I will."

I give him a smile and reach for his arm to give it a friendly squeeze before I remember he's not keen on me touching him. I pull back just in time, give him another smile, and walk away. God, he must think I am so weird.

Walking over to the kitchen to grab a drink, I spot a bunch of people dancing outside in the backyard on the makeshift dance floor. I make myself a Malibu lemonade and head out back to watch the drunken silliness.

"Get over here, Roberts!" Alex yells over the music. I shake my head. "C'mon! Now!"

I can't help but laugh. He is definitely one of *those* drunks.

After he begs some more, I give in.

After taking another sip of my drink, I put it on the table and walk over to join him on the dance floor. The music is pumping, so I sway my hips to the music. Alex stands behind me and dances up against me. I look over and see Caleb watching us. He almost looks…pissed? But that can't be right. He wouldn't care who I'm dancing with. The song changes to a slow song and the deejay tells the newlyweds to get on the dance floor to join in. Caleb's eyes still haven't left mine. He walks my way and I'm frozen in place. I hear Alex saying my name, but I tune him out, only focusing on Caleb.

"I'm cutting in," Caleb says to Alex, his eyes never leaving mine.

A second later I'm in Caleb's arms swaying to the tune of Jason Derulo's *Marry Me*. Knowing he doesn't like me to touch him, I have no idea what to do with my hands. He notices and frowns. Then, taking my hands in his, places them around his neck, as he pulls me closer to him. He wraps his arms around my waist and settles his hands at the small of my back. We dance for a few minutes in a comfortable silence staring into each other's eyes. I can't help but think how natural it feels to be in Caleb's arms, like this is exactly where I belong.

Unfortunately his phone vibrates in his pocket ending the moment too soon. He looks down at his phone and then back up at me. With what looks like a silent apology, for what I don't know, he gives me a small kiss on my cheek and whispers, "It's Marco. I have to go. Thank you for this dance."

As he walks away, my heart pounds against my ribcage from his closeness. His words do crazy things to my body, and when his lips brushed across my cheek, I wanted to grab his face and not let go. But I know he needs to be there for Marco, so without saying a word, I watch him walk away.

Eight

CALEB

SEEING KAYLA LAUGHING AND SMILING MAKES MY DAY. THAT woman deserves her happily ever after, that's for damn sure. It has taken a little while but Bentley and her are finally in a good place, and as their best friend, it makes me damn happy to see them like this. The wedding was nice and simple just like Kayla wanted. The reception at their place is a whole other story. There are decorations everywhere including a huge sign announcing their marriage. There's catered food aligning the walls inside, and outside there's a deejay playing music. The kids have all left and it's just drunk adults left celebrating their wedding as well as New Year's Eve.

Grabbing a beer after talking with Hayley, I head outside to find Kaden or Cooper when I see Alex and Hayley dancing close on the makeshift dance floor. I have never wanted to dance with a woman as much as I do right now. She has her head thrown back in a laugh at something he said and it reminds me of the other day in the gym. I want to be the guy making her laugh.

The music shifts to a slow song and throwing caution to the wind, go for it. It will be my choice to ask her to dance. She looks over at me and gives me a small smile. She is absolutely stunning and I can't even take my eyes off her.

"I'm cutting in," I let Alex know. He nods and walks away. As I try to dance with Hayley, I notice she isn't putting her arms around me. I don't blame her. Every time she's attempted to touch me, whether on purpose or on accident, I made it clear her touch wasn't welcome. I need to change that.

Taking her delicate hands in mine, I bring them up and wrap them around my neck and then wrap mine around her perfect waist. We dance to some song about getting married, but the only thing on my mind is how for once in my life the touch of a woman feels good. Her small body fits perfectly in mine. We don't talk, but it's not awkward.

Looking into her eyes is like finding water in a desert. I suddenly feel replenished.

My cell vibrates in my pocket. I want to ignore it, but the fear that it might be Marco makes me grab it out of my pocket to look. Sure enough, it is.

Marco: I need you to come to my house.

Knowing I just left there from dropping him off and giving him some money, it must be important. I look at Hayley and wish I could ignore the text and continue to dance with her, but also know Marco can be in trouble. I try to relay to her I'm sorry.

Before I can walk away I give her a kiss on her cheek. It's warm and a bit flushed and it makes me want to kiss her in other places. "It's Marco. I have to go. Thank you for this dance." Before she can respond, I walk out needing to get to Marco.

Arriving at Marco's place, I see a couple cars along the road in front of his house I don't recognize. This shit can't be good. I jump out of my car and can immediately hear screaming from inside. Without knocking, I go right in and take in the sight in front of me. Marco's mom is on the floor naked, on all fours being fucked from behind by one guy, while another guy is holding Marco back from trying to stop it from happening. I can also hear the baby crying in another room. I assess the situation and don't see any guns drawn. They probably didn't think it would be needed since Marco and his mom would be helpless against them.

I take one look at Marco's pleading eyes, the tears silently falling, and I lose it. I grab the guy fucking his mom by the neck, pulling him out of her, and push him up against the wall. I start punching him in the face repeatedly, hoping to knock him out. In my peripheral vision I see the other guy drop Marco from the wall and stalk toward me. Leaving the guy bleeding against the wall, I turn toward him to find out I was wrong about the gun. He grabs the gun from the front of his pants and shoots me in the shoulder.

The pain is unbearable, but I can't go down without a fight. I should have called the police. I should have called someone, but I didn't. So now I'm here and need to try to at least save Marco and his sister before I bleed out. I walk up to the guy with the gun and knock it out of his hand before he can shoot me again. We start rolling around on the floor grappling. Both of us are getting punches in and I just pray I can hold on long enough to beat the shit out of this guy to the point he will black out so I can call the cops.

Unfortunately before that happens the door swings open and two more guys I don't recognize walk in.

"Go shut that fucking baby up!" the guy booms and Estella, Marco's mom, runs to the room to calm the baby down. They grab me by my arms and I know I don't stand a chance. There's too many of them. They begin punching me in my ribs over and over again. When my legs give out on me, they throw me to the ground and begin kicking me, and then I hear a gunshot and everything goes black.

Nine

HAYLEY

THERE IS NO WAY I'VE BEEN ASLEEP MORE THAN A FEW MINUTES when my phone goes off. I attempt to ignore it, keeping my eyes closed so I don't get dizzy. I didn't get ridiculously drunk tonight, but I definitely drank enough to have a hangover in the morning. I ended up taking a cab home after the ball dropped, leaving my vehicle at Kayla's house. I'll have to ask someone to take me to get my car in the morning. I was hoping Caleb would return, but he never did. I hope everything is okay with Marco.

My phone rings again. Whoever is calling must really need to get ahold of me. Looking at my cell phone, I see it's four in the morning and Kayla is the person who keeps calling me. Jeez! I was actually asleep for almost three hours.

"Hey! Everything okay?" For Kayla to be calling me on her wedding night, something has to be wrong.

"No, it's not. Caleb is in the hospital. We don't know the details, but it's not good, Hayley."

This wakes me up. I grab some clothes on the dresser that I didn't get around to putting away yet and quickly get dressed. As I'm looking around for my keys, I remember I have no car. *Shit!*

"Hey can you swing by and get me? My car is at your house!"

She tells Bentley to pick me up. Luckily my house is on the way to the hospital so they don't have to go out of their way. We hang up and I go outside to wait for them so they don't have to stop for too long.

We get to the hospital and Bentley goes to the nurse to get answers on Caleb. We don't know anything about his family, but Caleb having no emergency contact listed other than Bentley is a good indication they aren't in the picture. The nurse tells us to have a seat and she'll come out to update us as soon as she can.

A few minutes later she begins explaining Caleb's condition as Cooper and Liz come running through the door out of breath along with Kaden and Ashley.

"Is he okay?" "What happened?" Liz and Cooper ask at the same time.

"The nurse is about to tell us right now," Bentley says, turning back to the nurse and indicating for her to continue.

"Mr. Michaels is currently in the ICU but stable. We're prepping him for surgery. He was brought in a couple hours ago, but we needed to stabilize him and assess his injuries. He experienced two gunshot wounds, one to the shoulder, and one to the chest. Luckily the one to the chest didn't hit any major arteries."

I gasp hearing he's been shot. Immediately my mind goes to those guys going after Marco.

"He was beaten pretty badly. We think he has several broken ribs and his leg appears to be broken. We'll know more once he's finished being prepped and taken into surgery. Please stay out here and once we know more we'll let you know."

"Thank you," Bentley says. I can't help but wonder how this happened. He left clearly worried about Marco. It had to have had something to do with those drug dealer guys from the other day.

While waiting to hear something, I decide to seek answers. I can't get this horrible feeling out of my head. If this has something to do with Marco, is he okay? Just as I make the decision to find a police officer, I see Marco come in and with him is a police officer holding his baby sister. Marco isn't crying, though. He looks numb. His baby sister is crying loudly and he's attempting to soothe her.

"Marco, what happened?"

"My mom is dead and they beat up and shot Caleb."

Oh God! I knew it! I knew this had something to do with Marco. Trying to remain calm, I put my hands out to take his sister from the police officer.

"Are you a friend of the family?" the officer asks.

"I'm a friend of Marco's. I'm a doctor at the gym he works out at and the gentleman who was at his house, Caleb, is a friend of ours," I say, pointing to everyone around me.

The officer hands me Chloe. "We need to get them both checked out to make sure they're okay."

Marco and I sit down and I rock Chloe, trying to calm her. Marco rubs her back trying to soothe her as well. The nurse comes over and hands me a bottle of formula. After thanking her, I feed the precious baby. With her belly full, I burp her, and within minutes she passes right out in my arms.

A few minutes later, the nurse calls Marco and Chloe back, and I go with the officer to have them checked out. Once the doctor confirms they're both healthy and not injured in any way, the police officer takes Marco's statement.

In a nutshell, the men came to Marco's house to get money from his mom. When she said no, one guy forced himself on her while the other guy held Marco back. Caleb tried to save them and was beaten and shot. Marco's mom went to the room to quiet Chloe down because her crying was making the men mad, but she never came back out of her room. When the police got there and Marco went in to let her know the cops were there, he found her dead. She overdosed on drugs in her bedroom.

It's absolutely heartbreaking to listen to his recount of what happened, to hear what he witnessed. Once he's done we go back out to the waiting room and I sit next to Kayla.

"Have you heard anything on Caleb yet?"

"No, not yet. Are the kids okay?"

"Yeah, the doctor said neither of them were physically hurt." I don't have to say anything for her to know what I mean. Marco is going to need to see a therapist. He's going to need a loving and supportive home and somebody to talk to. Luckily his sister is too young to remember anything.

"I'm assuming this is Marco's sister?"

"Yeah, she's a sweet thing, isn't she?"

I see the officer standing in the corner and want to ask him some questions. "Would you mind holding her for a few minutes. I want to speak to the police officer."

"Absolutely."

I carefully hand her Chloe and then look over and see Marco is sleeping. I can't even imagine the nightmares he will have. Walking over to the officer, I reintroduce myself.

"Excuse me, I was wondering if you have contacted the Department of Children and Families?"

"Yes, ma'am. Somebody is on their way."

"Did you catch the guys who did this to Caleb?"

"We have them in custody. Because the neighbor called so quickly after hearing the first gunshot we were able to catch them leaving the scene. We're compiling evidence now, but we should have enough to put them away for a long time."

"Good. I hope they rot in prison. Thank you, officer."

I head back to Marco and, putting my arm around him, hold him close. He may have had a shitty mom, but losing her can't be easy, and to be the one who found her, my heart is breaking for him.

Within an hour a sweet woman from DCF arrives. Marco moves closer to me when she says she needs to place them in an emergency foster home for the night.

"Can he please stay with me?" I beg. The kid has been through enough. "I'm actually an approved foster parent."

"What about Chloe?" Marco begins crying. I completely forgot about Chloe. My only thoughts were taking care of Marco. It doesn't surprise me that even after everything Marco has been through his number one concern is the welfare of his sister.

"I can take her as well. I just don't have a crib or diapers or anything for a baby." I begin to panic, mentally making a list of everything I would need.

"We can take her," Kayla says. "We actually have an application in to foster since it's the first step to adopt. We recently submitted it and it might even already be approved. Because of the holidays I haven't checked."

"Okay, I'll need a copy of both your driver's licenses and social security cards. I'll call my supervisor and check on your fostering statuses."

"Thank you," I say, continuing to hold Marco close, letting him know I'm not leaving his side.

I look over at Bentley and Kayla cooing over Chloe and can't help but wonder if maybe this was God's way of intervening on these children's behalf—taking a tragedy and giving them their own little miracle.

While waiting to hear back from the DCF worker, a doctor comes out and lets us know Caleb is out of surgery. Looking at the time, I see it's just after seven in the morning. Marco is asleep with his head on my shoulder and Chloe is still asleep in Kayla's arms.

"We feel everything went good. He has three broken ribs, which caused internal bleeding. We were able to stop the bleeding without any further complications. Unfortunately, broken ribs can't be fixed, they will have to heal over time, but he's wrapped up. The gunshot wounds to his shoulder and chest were clean, so we just had to stitch him up. His leg was broken in two places, so he's in a cast. He suffered a head injury as well, but other than having a concussion there is no swelling in the brain, which is a good sign. He's in recovery now and we'll continue to monitor him. Once they get him settled, you can go back two at a time. Do you have any questions?"

"Will he get back full use of his shoulder and leg?" I know in hindsight it's not important, but Caleb's world revolves around fighting. I know he's going to want to know.

"The specialist will be in to speak with Caleb once he wakes up. He'll be able to answer that question better."

"Okay, thank you."

Just as the doctor is leaving, the DCF worker returns, smiling softly.

"Okay, good news. You both are active on the fostering list, so I was able to approve both of you to take them home. We will have to do home visits in the next few days so I'll be in touch."

Marco wakes up and looks around to find Chloe, then turns to the worker. "Does that mean Chloe and I can stay together?"

"How would you feel if you stayed with me and Chloe stayed with Bentley and Kayla? You know how they have Faith, right? So they have all the baby stuff already for Chloe."

"Can I still see her?"

"Of course you can, sweetie!" Kayla chimes in. "You can see her whenever you want. Let's just take this one day at a time until we figure out what's going to happen."

"Would you rather go with Kayla and stay with Chloe?" I ask him.

"No, I know they're good with Faith. I would rather go with you. Can we stay and wait for Caleb?"

"Absolutely," I tell him, and his body visibly relaxes.

"Thank you," I tell the worker. She lets me know she will be in touch and leaves.

"Family of Caleb Michaels," a nurse announces.

"I want to go see Caleb, please!" Marco begs the nurse. He's so worried about Caleb.

"I'm sure we can make that happen," I tell him.

"I'm sorry but only family right now," the nurse says sympathetically.

"She's his fiancée," Bentley says before I can even think of a lie to get us inside.

The nurse doesn't look convinced but doesn't argue.

"Is he your son?" she asks, pointing to Marco. Without hesitation, I tell her yes.

"Okay, he can come with you guys since he's a minor and in your care."

"Thank you."

"C'mon." Bentley puts his arm around me and walks us toward the nurse. "I'll go with you, future Mrs. Michaels."

Ten

CALEB

HOLY SHIT! MY HEAD FEELS LIKE IT'S ABOUT TO EXPLODE. I hear a faint beeping sound and try to remember where I am and why I feel so hung over. The overwhelming smell of antiseptics hits my nose causing me to almost choke. Then the memories all come crashing back.

Marco…His mom being raped…Getting the shit beat out of me…Getting shot…Everything going black…FUCK!

"Well, good morning, Mr. Michaels. Welcome back. Your fiancée and son were just here. They stepped out to get a drink of water but should be back any second. How are you doing?"

Fiancée? Son? What. The. Fuck.

I rack my brain trying to think if I could have possibly missed getting engaged. I sure as fuck know I don't have a son. I look around and see Bentley sitting in a chair shaking with silent laughter. Then, when Hayley and Marco walk in, he smiles wide and laughs out loud.

"Well, how are you?"

"Umm…I think I'm okay…" I wiggle my fingers and they work. Then I start touching various parts of my body to see if I am in fact okay. When I move my arm too far over, I feel a sharp pain in my shoulder and chest. It's kind of hard to breathe now that I'm thinking about it.

"Oh fuck!" I scream louder than I realize when I attempt to move my hand to my shoulder.

"Be careful. You were shot, Mr. Michaels. The doctor will be in momentarily to explain your injuries and what he did during surgery." The first thing that comes to mind is fighting. If I'm in this much pain there is no way I'll be fighting anytime soon.

After checking my vitals, the nurse gives me more pain meds before she leaves the room.

"Fiancée and son?"

Bentley cracks up laughing, again. "Don't look so scared, bro. I had to say Hayley was your fiancée to get them in here, so Marco could see you. The kid was worried."

Am I crazy that for a second I almost thought it wouldn't be such a terrible thing to be engaged to Hayley? Yeah, I must have been hit in the head. It's the only way to explain these absurd feelings.

The doctor comes in and explains I suffered a concussion, have three broken ribs, and a broken leg that they put a cast on and will have to remain on for about six weeks before getting it checked. My shoulder is in a sling so it can heal from the gunshot wound, and I was shot in the chest. Jesus, it's a fucking miracle I'm alive.

"Do you have any questions?"

"Will I get full rotation of my shoulder back? Will my leg be healed one hundred percent? I'm a fighter."

"It's definitely going to take some time. If you were working a desk job I would say you'll be fine, but as an athlete, you will most likely need to attend physical therapy for your shoulder and leg. Unfortunately only time will tell."

"Okay, thank you."

After the doctor leaves, I let out a slew of curse words. Fighting is my fucking life. Without it, who am I?

"I'm sorry," Marco says. And that's when I remember him and Hayley have been in the room the whole time.

"Come here, Marco."

He comes forward nervously. My cursing having him scared.

"Don't ever apologize for what happened last night. Do you understand me? I would have done it all over again if it meant protecting you."

Marco's eyes well up with tears and he throws himself at me for a hug. My chest burns and my ribs ache, but I don't outwardly react. Marco needs a hug and I don't want him to see the pain I'm in.

"Hey, buddy. It's okay," I say, trying to calm him.

Then I ask Bentley, "Have you guys been here this whole time?"

He looks at me incredulously. "Of course we have Coop, Liz, Kaden, Ashley, and Kayla are out there as well."

I choke up at the realization that all these people have been here waiting to see if I'm okay. I've felt so alone for so long, but the fact is these people have been here for me for years.

"As you can see, I'm okay. Take Kayla home and tell Cooper and everyone else I'm good. Get some sleep and call me later."

"Wait! Does that mean Chloe is leaving? I have to kiss her goodbye!" Marco says, frantically turning to Bentley and Hayley. Why would Chloe be here? And why would she be leaving without Marco?

Hayley crouches down a little to soothe Marco. "Hey, it's okay. We can go say bye to them. I'm sure Chloe is tired and wants to sleep in a comfortable bed. We can go visit them later, I promise." Why the hell does Kayla have Chloe?

Marco calms down and says okay. Bentley and Hayley share a look before she says she's going to take Marco to say bye to his sister.

Marco gives me one more hug. "I'm glad you're okay, Caleb."

"Thanks, buddy."

Bentley waits for the door to close before he speaks. "Marco's mom overdosed. Marco found her dead in her room after the cops showed up."

"Holy shit." I don't even know what else to say. I know how Marco feels to an extent. When my mom died, it hurt, but we knew it was coming.

"There's more…" I wait for him to continue. "Apparently there are no living relatives so Kayla and I are fostering Chloe and Hayley is fostering Marco so they aren't sent away and completely separated. Marco was given the option to come with us but wanted to stay with Hayley."

Wow, the fact that Hayley would do that for a kid she barely knows speaks volumes about the kind of person she is. I know Kayla and Bentley have talked about adoption, but Hayley is single with no kids or significant other. That's a huge commitment on her part.

"That's really awesome of you guys. Marco is a great kid, but you know that. I'm glad he won't be alone and his sister will be taken care of."

"So what are you going to do for the next six weeks?"

"What do you mean?"

He looks down at my leg. "Once you get out of here…You can't walk up the three flights of stairs to the apartment. You know you can stay with us or Cooper and Liz, or even Kaden. We can set up the couch for you…"

Shit! I didn't even think about that. All my friends have two-story houses and none of their guest rooms are on the first floor. There's no way I'm staying on one of their couches for the next six damn weeks.

"He can stay with us," Marco says. I look over at Hayley and Marco standing back in the doorway.

Hayley looks nervous. "Umm…Yeah…You can stay with Marco and me if you want." Then she turns to Bentley. "Marco said goodbye and we're going to come by later so he can see where Chloe is staying. Kayla is getting Chloe situated in the car and will meet you outside."

"Okay, cool. Caleb, if you need a place to stay you can stay with any of us. I'll give you a call in a little bit."

We bump fists and he leaves.

"Do you want to stay with us?" Marco asks again sounding hopeful.

Hayley still looks nervous. "My house is a single story and I have two guest rooms that aren't being used. You can stay in one and Marco can stay in the other." I'm about to argue, but she must know it's coming, because she speaks before I do. "Please don't argue, Caleb."

I want to say no. I want to argue. I want to run the fuck away from this woman who is slowly making me feel shit I shouldn't be feeling. Maybe six weeks in the same house with Hayley can be a good thing. I'm starting to catch feelings for her, feelings I don't know what to do with. I can't find a single thing wrong with her, so maybe living under the same roof with her will reveal her faults and flaws and then I can drop these feelings bullshit like a bad habit. My brain goes back to a time when I trusted Gloria—reminding me where that got me.

Fifteen years old

"Is it okay if I spend the night at David's house?" I ask my dad.

"I think it would be best if you wait until I get home. I'll be back the day after tomorrow. I don't want to make Gloria stay at the house alone."

When my parents were married my dad never went out of town for business, but since my mom passed away a lot has changed. My dad recently married Gloria, who is young enough to be his daughter. He goes out of town for business several times a month, and she never goes with him. Shortly after they met, they married and he bankrolled her new business, a strip club.

Opening a strip club makes sense, since I'm pretty sure that's where he met her. He hasn't actually said that, but between the way she dresses, the friends she has over, and the conversations I've heard, I'm almost positive she was a stripper until she got ahold of my dad's money.

I have my bedroom door closed but can still hear Gloria and her friends downstairs drinking and listening to music. Recently, the more drunk she gets, the more hands-on she gets, and the last woman I want touching me is my dad's wife, even if she is closer in age to me than her husband.

When he first started going away she would let my friends come over and we would all hang out. She was actually really cool. She would convince my dad to buy me the latest video games and electronics. She would let me and my friends drink some alcohol with her and her friends. We would order food in and watch movies together. It was like having a friend. While she didn't feel like a stand-in mom, she did kind of feel like a sister in a way. After losing my sister and mom, it was nice hanging out with someone, especially with my dad gone all the time.

Then one night everything changed. She and her friends were completely wasted and came on to me after my friends went home. They asked me if I was a virgin and when I said I was they offered to help me change that. I laughed it off to their drunkenness and went to my room, but since then she's acted differently around me. When my dad isn't looking, she'll rub her ass against me or touch me as she walks by. When we watch a movie she'll get closer, putting her feet into my lap. It's just weird.

When my dad said he was going out of town this morning she made a comment about not wanting my friends over this weekend when she usually encourages me to invite them over. I don't understand why she even cares. While I've been in my room all night, I can hear her friends and her getting drunk once again. I was hoping to get out of here, but it doesn't look like it's going to happen. Putting my ear buds in my ears, I press play on my playlist, attempting to get some sleep.

I feel the bed sink and turn over taking my ear buds out. The music has stopped and when I glance at the clock, it reads two in the morning. I've been asleep for about three hours. A hand glides down my stomach inching its way toward my dick. Before it lands on it, I grab the hand, bringing it to a stop.

Squinting my eyes to adjust to the darkness I see Gloria lying in my bed.

"What are you doing?" I hope I'm misunderstanding her being in my bed, trying to feel up on my junk.

"I want you, Caleb." I should have seen this coming…

"You're married to my dad."

She scoots toward me and continues where she left off, grabbing my dick and squeezing it.

I jump up off the bed and switch the light on.

"Don't do this shit. You got it made with my dad. If I tell him what you're doing he'll throw you out on your ass."

She deviously smirks, shaking her head. "You aren't going to tell him…because if you do, I'll tell the Feds what I know, and your dad will end up spending twenty years in prison."

I know exactly what she's talking about. I have heard her and my dad talking about a shitty choice he made that made him millions but was illegal, something to do with insider trading. If she rats him out I'll either end up as an orphan or be stuck with her, and my dad will spend the majority of his life in prison. He's been through enough between losing my sister and my mom. I can't let her do this to him.

"What do you want?"

She smiles smugly knowing she's won.

"You."

And once again another woman has been added to the list of women I can't trust.

"Caleb…are you okay?" Hayley asks, concern laced in every word.

I scrub my hands over my face shaking off the memory of the day I learned how vindictive and untrustworthy a woman could be.

"Yeah, I'm sorry. What were we talking about?"

"I said my house is a single story. You and Marco can both stay with me. Don't argue with me, please."

I hate that it feels like she's telling me what to do. I wouldn't be surprised if once I am moved in, she finds a way to manipulate me. Unfortunately, I'm not really sure what other choice I have at this point. It goes against everything in me to trust this woman, but instead of saying no, I say okay and hope she shows her true colors sooner rather than later.

Or maybe she'll prove my theory wrong…And for some reason, deep down, I really hope she proves me wrong.

Eleven

HAYLEY

IT'S BEEN TWO WEEKS SINCE I BROUGHT CALEB HOME FROM the hospital. Well, not his home, my home. I have a four-bedroom house, so Caleb and Marco are each sleeping in one of the guest rooms. I enrolled Marco in school and hired a tutor to help him in case he needs to get caught up on anything. I also set it up for him to see a therapist on a weekly basis. He needs somebody to talk to after everything he has been through. I had to go through DCF to find an approved therapist and I really like the one they assigned. Marco seems to like her as well.

Cooper insisted I take a few weeks off, paid of course, to be here for Caleb. According to him it's still working since Caleb is a fighter at the gym and I'm the doctor on staff. Caleb was in a lot of pain when we first arrived home. He spent the first week pretty much sleeping, eating, and reluctantly having me help him use the bathroom. He was on some strong meds, but the last couple days he's been starting to come around. He's sitting up more, watching ESPN, refusing the pain meds, and playing games from his bed with Marco and me like Scrabble, Monopoly, and Yahtzee. It's become part of our routine, playing a game together before Marco goes to bed.

The door swings open and Marco comes barreling into the house with a big smile on his face. Is it weird that the feeling of this pseudo-family makes my heart melt?

"Hey, sweetie. How was your day?"

He pulls a piece of paper out of his new backpack I purchased for him for school. We went by his house to see what he could bring from his mom's place before they cleaned it all out, but there was nothing but a few photos that were worth taking. I took him shopping and bought him all new clothes that fit him.

"I got an A on my math test," he whisper-yells, trying to stay quiet in case Caleb is asleep, even though I've told him repeatedly this is his home and he can talk at whatever level he wants.

Tears prick my eyes at how happy he is. I didn't know Marco well before all this happened, but anybody who knew him at all saw the sadness that resided in his eyes. Looking at him right now, it's like looking at a completely different kid. I pull him into a hug and tell him congratulations. It would be so easy for him to rebel. Nobody would blame him after everything he has been through. But instead he's focusing on the positive and shining bright.

"That's amazing, buddy." We both look up and see Caleb leaning against the wall with one of his crutches under his arm, smiling at Marco. He looks a lot better. Most of his bruising is now light yellow or completely gone, his leg is in a cast, but with his ribs starting to heal, he can use crutches when he needs to. Well, right now only one crutch, the one with his good shoulder.

"Want to see it?" Marco asks.

"Absolutely!"

Marco brings the test to Caleb and Caleb makes a huge deal out of it telling him the problems look really complicated. "I think this calls for a celebration. What do you want for dinner tonight?" Caleb asks him.

Marco looks unsure, like it's a trick question. While he's now smiling and dressing nicely on the outside, inside holds too much insecurity from years of abuse from his mother. He eats every meal like it's his last, never gives his opinion unless we beg, and asks constantly what he can do to help out of guilt. The therapist told me it's going to take time for Marco to be comfortable with just being a kid. He's never been given the chance to behave like one before.

"Umm…Can we…maybe…order in Chinese and…umm… maybe invite Kayla and Bentley over so I can see Chloe?"

Caleb looks to me to confirm it's okay with me, and I nod in agreement. I'm so proud of Marco for actually answering this time.

"Sure, buddy. Why don't you go do your homework and I'll text Bentley now?"

Marco says okay and heads to his room.

"He's come a long way," Caleb says softly to me.

"Yeah, he has. Karen from DCF has asked me if I'm interested in adopting him."

Caleb's face looks shocked. "What did you say?"

"Well, I know you and Marco are close, so I wanted to make sure it's okay with you first. I don't want to overstep."

"Of course you can adopt him. You'll make a great mom to him. I can already tell. What about Chloe?"

"Okay, good," I say in relief. "I just wasn't sure if maybe you wanted to. I agreed to foster him when you were in surgery. Oh, and Kayla said she's looking into adopting Chloe. I considered adopting them both, but I know it would mean a lot to Bentley and Kayla since she can't have any more kids." When Kayla was giving birth to her daughter there were complications and the obstetrician had no choice but to perform a partial hysterectomy to save her life. Unfortunately that meant she wouldn't be able to ever get pregnant again.

"Marco needs a mom like you. I know he'll be in good hands when I'm healed and move out. I'm glad for Bentley and Kayla. They're awesome parents."

The thought of Caleb moving out makes my stomach sink. I know he's only here because he's hurt, but these last two weeks have felt like my house is finally a home. Marco is coming around, finally laughing and watching television, and the house is no longer quiet. The thought of Caleb leaving saddens me, but at least I'll still have Marco. With Caleb's leg being stuck in a cast for at least six weeks, I decide to enjoy his company while he's here and not dwell on him eventually leaving.

"Thanks," I say, forcing a smile.

"I'll go text Bentley and Kayla and invite them over for dinner."

"Sounds good."

Dinner with Kayla, Bentley, and the babies went well. Kayla and Bentley have decided to officially start the process to adopt Chloe but insisted on making sure it's okay with Marco. He said okay but then asked what would happen to him.

"How would you feel about me adopting you?" I asked him.

"Really?" he asked excitedly. Then he turned to Caleb. "Would you be adopting me, too?"

Caleb's face sunk at his question. "Unfortunately the state frowns upon people who aren't together adopting a child together, but with Hayley working at the gym, we'll still get to hang out a lot."

Marco scowled and if not for the sad situation causing these two to both be upset, I would laugh at how adorable they both looked. Hanging out so often together has caused their facial expressions to mimic one another. They might not be related, but they are very similar in their mannerisms.

"Okay," Marco whispered, not comfortable enough yet to argue with something an adult said, even though he clearly didn't agree.

After putting Marco to bed, I come out to the living room to watch some television. Caleb is sitting on the couch with his casted leg straight out in front of him texting someone with a frown once again on his face.

"What's wrong?" I ask, sitting next to him on the couch.

He looks up and gives me a shrug. "My apartment is due to renew in a couple weeks. I'm going to have the guys move my stuff to storage. Once I'm out of this cast I'll have to find a new place to live. I don't need a three-bedroom apartment for just myself."

"I have a two-car garage and it's basically empty. Just have them put it all in there so you don't have to pay for storage."

"You sure?"

"Completely."

"Okay, cool. Thanks."

Caleb sends a few more texts and then puts his phone away.

"I guess I'll just head to bed," I say, standing, unsure of what to do. Caleb is usually in his room at night, not out here, and I want to give him his space.

"Wait! Want to watch something out here with me?"

"I was just going to watch *The Bachelor*, but we can watch something else…"

"No, *The Bachelor* is fine. I'm used to all those girly shows thanks to living with Kayla."

"Okay." I sit back down and grab the remote to put on the latest episode.

Twelve

CALEB

I DON'T KNOW WHY I ASK HER TO STAY AND WATCH TV WITH me. I don't even know why I'm sitting out here on the couch. I've been able to get up for days, but I usually stay in my room to avoid her. Before I got hurt I had asked her if she wanted to grab dinner sometime as friends but quickly thought it might have been a mistake. Now, instead of grabbing dinner, we're living together. I've been here for two weeks and haven't found a single thing wrong with this woman. She has taken to parenting Marco with natural grace. She bought him new clothes, signed him up for tons of school shit, and is home every day when he gets home. She cooks every meal and every single one tastes amazing. I even look forward to our nightly routine of playing games together before Marco goes to bed. She has given me plenty of space and hasn't once tried to hit on me. She even wants to adopt Marco. When she brought it up, clearly nervous I was considering the same thing, I didn't have the heart to say I was considering it. I know he deserves a permanent place to live, so I was looking into what needs to be done. I didn't imagine she would also be considering it.

I know she'll let me and Marco hang out, so I let it go. She'll probably make a better parent than me anyway. She isn't tainted with the past I have.

We're watching some ridiculous show about a guy who has ten women all fighting over him. I look over at Hayley and see the hearts in her eyes over this shit.

"Do you really think you can meet your spouse on a show like this?" I ask, sounding as negative as my thoughts are.

She gives it some thought for a few seconds. Her cute nose scrunches up making me want to lean over and kiss it. "I'm not sure, but based on my results on the dating site Ashley had me join, it probably can't hurt. Those guys who message me are crazy! At least on this show they have to do a background check."

She cracks up laughing at herself and so many thoughts run through my head. First, I go back to my thought of wanting to kiss her nose. I decide to ignore that shit. Next, I think about the fact this beautiful woman seriously thinks she needs a dating site to meet a man. Is she crazy? Then again, she wanted me, and I turned her down. Nope, she's not the crazy one…I am. My final thought is a feeling I only recently experienced, jealousy. Like when I saw Hayley dancing with Alex—my blood boils thinking of all these jackasses messaging her wanting a date. I'm not a hundred percent sure I can trust this woman, but I'm going to figure my shit out soon before some dumbass on a dating site scoops up the woman I'm pretty sure I'm slowly falling for.

"You're still on that dating site? Haven't you ever heard of catfishing? You should stay off that shit. A beautiful woman on a dating site is just asking for trouble."

Her eyes go wide and I backtrack realizing I just went off, and on top of that, called her beautiful. Fuck it! Let the chips fall where they may…

"Umm…Well technically I haven't gone on a date yet using the site since I had to cancel my first one the night we went out to dinner with Marco. I didn't like the way he acted about the whole situation of me having to cancel, so I never messaged him again."

Good.

I just nod, trying to be cool. We go back to watching the show and the guy is going on a one-on-one date with one of the women who won the date because they had the most in common according to some quiz.

"Do you really believe these women tell the truth?"

"Of course! They can't lie on television. Everybody would know they're lying." Wow, she is so gullible. I can't help but chuckle at her seriousness.

"How would anybody know they're lying? I've seen plenty of women lie and get away with it. I bet you could lie to me right now and I wouldn't even know."

"Okay, you're on!"

"We're going to need some alcohol for this. Go grab a bottle and then we'll play a game."

She jumps up from the couch and goes to the kitchen to grab some liquor while I watch her cute behind sway in her tight tank top and tiny little cotton shorts that reads *Will squat for tacos* across the back of her ass. She always wears them around the house at night and swears Taco Tuesday is a real holiday. And so far every Tuesday she's made tacos.

"All I have is a bottle of Patron Silver. Is that okay?"

"Sure." I take the bottle and pour two shots into the glasses she brought over.

"Okay, so what's the game?"

"It's called two truths and one lie. You'll tell me three facts. Two of them will be the truth and one of them will be a lie. If I figure out which one is the lie you have to take a shot. If I can't figure it out, I have to take the shot."

"Okay," she says smiling. "Hmmm…Let me see…" She's so cute as her eyes shoot up to the ceiling and her finger taps her chin in concentration trying to think of what to say.

"Okay, I visit New York yearly, I love fuzzy socks, and I hate exercising.

"Your lie is you hate exercising."

She smiles big. "Nope! Drink up! My lie is that I visit New York yearly. Other than going to Breckenridge and to the different sports arenas for the UFC fights, I have never been anywhere, like on vacation. I would love to go to New York one day."

I down the shot of Patron and think how awesome it would be to take her to New York. I was there a while back for a photo shoot for the UFC and there's so much to do and see.

"See?" I tell her. "It's hard to tell when someone is lying."

"I guess," she says softly. "But I wouldn't want to purposely mislead someone I'm trying to be with. If those women lie on *The Bachelor* they're basing their relationship on a lie. They must know it won't work out in the end."

My heart speeds up at her words. She's too good to be true. She is so damn sweet and innocent. I grab another shot and down it, letting the alcohol numb my brain…and my heart. She's confusing the shit out of me.

"Hey! I didn't even give you any truths or lies. You aren't supposed to drink yet."

"Sorry, go ahead. Try again."

"Okay, I love to gamble at the slot machines, I love to cook, and I love to play candy crush on my phone."

"I have no clue what candy crush is, so I'm going to go with that one for your lie because we live in Las Vegas and your cooking is good as fuck."

She giggles and pours me a shot. "Drink up! My lie was that I love to gamble at the slot machines. I have never even gambled before."

I shoot the shot back welcoming the burn in my throat. "How is that possible? Haven't you lived in Vegas your whole life?"

"Yep, but I never went gambling. I also have never been to a strip club or to watch the fountains at the Bellagio. I spent so much time studying and going to school I guess I forgot to take advantage of where I live."

Before I know what I'm saying, I blurt out, "That's going to have to change. When my leg is out of this cast we are hitting up the strip clubs, a casino, and the fountains all in one night."

She laughs and pours herself a shot. "Okay, so now it's your turn. Tell me two truths and a lie."

My cellphone rings right then and my dad's attorney's name shows up on the caller ID. He called before I was put in the hospital and a couple more times, never leaving a voicemail. I might as well answer this shit and get it over with. I show her my phone is ringing and answer it.

"Hello."

"Hey, Caleb! It's Jason Caldwin, your father's attorney."

"Yeah, I know who you are. What's up?"

I see Hayley trying to act like she's not listening next to me. I want to stand up and walk away, but I can't with my gimp leg.

"Caleb, we need to speak. It's about your father."

"I haven't spoken to my father in over seven years. If he wants to talk to me he can call me himself."

"He can't do that, Caleb. He passed away last month. I have been trying to get ahold of you. Gloria handled the funeral since I couldn't get you to answer but there is the issue of the will. I need to meet with you in person so we can go over the details."

Holy shit! My dad is dead. The man who chose his pedophile pimp of a wife over his son is dead. My last words to him were *I'm out of here.* I should hate him but my heart hurts. It shouldn't hurt, but flashbacks of life before my mom died flash in front of me. Camping, sports events, concerts, him taking my sister and me to the park on Sunday mornings to let mom sleep in. I want to hate him, but knowing he's dead, all I can feel is pain.

I don't even realize I've dropped the phone or that there are tears pouring down my face, when Hayley moves toward me and grabs my phone to talk to Jason. I don't know what is said. It's all a blur. She sets the phone down and looks unsure of what to do. Can you blame her? The crazy mixed signals I have sent…Not wanting her to touch me. How do you comfort someone without touching him? And then I lose it. The lump in my throat that feels like it's going to close up and choke me to death suddenly releases and I cry.

Before I can question it I'm laying in her lap bawling for the loss of the man I once looked up to while Hayley runs her fingers through my hair massaging my scalp. She doesn't say a word, just lets me let it all out. When I finally stop crying, I don't wait for her to ask if I'm okay. I don't know what makes me do it, but I tell her everything I've kept to myself.

"My dad is dead. I haven't seen him in seven years."

"Why haven't you seen him?"

"My stepmom raped me when I was fifteen." I hear Hayley gasp at my words, but she doesn't say anything.

I can't look at her. I don't know what makes me trust her in this moment, but I don't question it.

"After she forced herself on me and took my virginity, she had sex with me for several years while my dad was away on business. Then she pimped me out to a bunch of unhappily married women. I have never had sex of my own free will. When my dad caught us together she blamed me and he chose to believe her. I left and never looked back."

I give her a few minutes to absorb everything I just gave her. When she doesn't say anything but continues to play with my hair, I know she's waiting for me to continue.

"It's why I hate being touched. It's not that I don't want to be touched. I just want it to be my choice. I spent years being forced to touch women I didn't want to touch."

Her fingers stop moving, so I turn my face toward her stomach to look at her. I keep my eyes closed, afraid of the disgust or pity I'll see. After counting to three, I look into her eyes, only I don't see disgust or pity, I see a beautiful woman smiling at me.

"Well that's good to know. I thought it was me, like maybe I smelled bad or had bad breath. I'm glad to know it's you not me…"

I burst out in laughter. I word vomit all over her and she lightens the mood by cracking a joke. I can see why she's such good friends with Kayla and Liz. She is good.

"Are you okay?"

If that ain't a loaded question…

I left out a heavy breath. "I don't know. I hate that I never had a chance to make him believe me, but at the same time, I'm mad that he chose not to believe me. Now he's dead and his attorney needs me for the will. I don't know if I can handle flying back there and being in the same room as that cunt."

"Well, how about this? Marco has a three-day weekend coming up. You'll need help getting around, so why don't we fly there together? We can stay at a resort just outside of Boulder at one the ski resorts and take Marco to see snow."

Damn this woman and her positivity, how did I not see how amazing she is before now? Oh, that's right…because I pushed away all women lumping them into the same compartment as the women who have lied to me in the past.

"You would do that for me? After I continually ignored you and pushed you away?"

"How about we start over? Let's be friends. You're going to be here for several weeks anyway. Let's start over."

Friends? Fuck that! I don't think I want to be friends with Hayley. I want to be more than friends, but I guess friends is a good place to start…

"Okay, friends."

She gives me a full-blown thousand mega-watt smile that could seriously light up a dark room and all I want to do is grab her by her neck and pull her face to me and kiss her. But I don't. Instead, I smile back.

"I think this calls for another shot," she says. I sit up and we both take a shot. Then we go back to watching *The Bachelor*. While she swoons over the guy, I point out all the lies women are telling, making her laugh.

Thirteen

HAYLEY

IT'S FRIDAY AFTERNOON AND I STOP INTO THE GYM TO SEE A few of the fighters before Caleb, Marco, and I head to Boulder to meet with his father's attorney to discuss his will. The night Caleb confided in me I wanted to find his stepmom, Gloria, and beat the shit out of her. I wanted to make her pay for what she did to Caleb, but I knew Caleb wouldn't want my pity, so I made a joke to make light of the conversation and it worked. We even became friends that night.

I'm getting all my files situated when Alex comes walking into my office without knocking and plops into a seat in front of my desk.

"Hey Alex, how's your wrist doing?" I ask, coming around my desk, and taking his hand in mine to check out his finger function.

"It's good, Doc. Thanks."

"So what brings you by?"

"I haven't seen you around lately. How's Caleb doing?"

"He's good. He's healing."

"That's good. I was wondering if maybe we can go to dinner sometime." Before Caleb and Marco moved in with me, I would have said yes, but now I feel like I need to focus on Marco and I'm not sure how I feel about dating with Caleb staying with me.

"Can I think about it?"

"Sure. How about you take my number and call or text once you decide."

"Okay," I say, handing him my cell phone to input his number in. I hear his phone ring and he laughs guiltily.

"Now I have your number as well." He winks at me as he hands me back my phone. With a kiss on my cheek, he heads out the door.

"What was that about?" Liz asks, standing in the doorway as soon as Alex leaves.

"What?" I ask, not sure what she's talking about.

She sits in the seat Alex was just sitting in.

"Alex kissing you on the cheek…"

"Alex kissed Hayley on the cheek?" Kayla asks, walking through the door without knocking and dropping into the seat next to Liz. Apparently today is drop in on Hayley day…

"He asked me out to dinner. No big deal."

"And what did you say?" Kayla asks.

"I said I would think about it."

"Uh huh," she continues.

"Uh huh, what?" I plop back down into my seat.

"How are things going with Caleb?" Kayla asks. Of course Liz leaves the interrogation to her.

"Things are fine. He's healing. His father passed away so we're going to Boulder today to take care of his dad's will. He and I have actually become friends." I'm trying so hard to sound nonchalant.

"And how many times have you ogled his fine ass body when he's come out of the shower?" Kayla asks. Both she and Liz laugh and I shake my head. They will never let me live that down.

"He makes sure to change in his bathroom. I'm sure the last thing he wants is me seeing him without clothes on. How's Chloe?" I ask, hoping to change the subject.

Kayla smiles big and pulls out her cell phone to show us pictures of Chloe and Faith. "They are so precious!" I say, looking at the cute pictures.

"Karen, with DCF says it shouldn't take long for the adoption to go through."

"I'm so happy for you guys." And I am. I'm glad she's getting the chance to be a mother to Chloe as well. She's mentioned so many times feeling broken because of her hysterectomy. Seeing her being given the opportunity to adopt Chloe and provide a good life for her makes me so happy.

"Why do you look so sad?" Liz asks. Oh, now she wants to jump in and be observant. Fabulous!

"I'm not sad. I just don't think having a baby is in the cards for me. Don't get me wrong. I love and adore Marco. He is an amazing kid. I feel absolutely blessed to have him in my life…"

"Hey," Liz says, coming around the desk to give me a hug. "You have plenty of time to have a baby and when you do, Marco will make a great brother. You'll meet an amazing guy who will want Marco in his life and you guys will have beautiful babies."

Kayla comes around my desk and we end up in a group hug.

"Hmm…Anything special I'm walking in on? I can join if needed," Alex says from the door, waggling his eyebrows. We all laugh.

"No, but I need to get going. We should all do something soon. Poor Caleb is stuck in the house with just me."

"Stuck isn't the word I would use," Alex says smiling at me.

"Weren't you just in here, lover boy?" Kayla asks, putting her hands on her hips.

"Yeah, but I just thought I would see if Hayley has thought about what I asked."

I need to give him some credit on his persistence.

"You just asked her!" Liz laughs. I love that my girls always have my back.

"Okay…Okay…" Alex puts his hands up and backs away. "Think about it, Hayley!" he yells before Kayla closes the door on him. We all crack up laughing.

"Just for the record, I am team Caleb," Kayla says. Liz laughs and agrees.

"You both are crazy! First you need to get Caleb in the game then we can pick teams. Okay, I really need to get going. Dinner soon?" Both ladies nod as we walk out to the gym floor.

I say goodbye and head out to my car. About halfway through the parking lot, I get this weird feeling like I'm being watched. I quicken my steps and once in my car press the lock button. I glance around but don't see anything that looks alarming. I chalk it up to paranoia. Caleb got a call from the detective of his case earlier this week letting him know the four men who were arrested were denied bail, which is great, but the problem is none of those men were Hector or Santos. They are still out on the streets because they weren't there when everything went down. The guys who were at Marco's house are the enforcers, sent to scare someone into paying. Apparently Marco's mom was in some major debt from buying drugs. Because Hector and Santos are both still free, Caleb insisted I put a tracker app on my phone and requested I let him know if I'm going anywhere other than to the gym.

While driving I think about what Kayla said regarding the adoption and decide to call Karen and find out the process of adopting Marco. I want to make sure nobody can take him from me. She lets me know the process is a bit longer for a single mom, but everything should go through smoothly. I hate that Caleb won't be on the paperwork, but I need to still go through the steps to ensure Marco is mine legally.

I get home in time to see Marco getting off the bus and wave to him. While he's walking toward the house I get the feeling of being watched again. I look around and don't see anyone but the few parents walking back to their houses with their children. I am definitely paranoid!

"You ready to go see some snow?" I ask Marco, handing him a bag of snacks for the trip.

"Yes!" He beams at me and then goes to his room to put his backpack away.

Caleb comes hobbling out from the room with his crutches. Luckily when the guys broke his leg it was only the lower part so it's not a full leg cast. He can use crutches instead of needing a wheelchair.

Unfortunately they also broke his ribs and shot him in the shoulder and chest so his crutches only get used for short distances. We will be taking a wheelchair with us to the airport. Thankfully Bentley offered to charter a private plane for us to Boulder so Caleb wouldn't have to deal with his broken body on a public plane.

"Ready to go?"

Before I can answer, Marco answers for me. "Yes, sir!"

Once on the plane, I give Marco a present. I picked up an iPad for him this week so he wouldn't be completely bored on the plane and at the attorney's office. As soon as I give it to him, ready to go with apps, he goes crazy with excitement.

"This is mine?"

"Yep! All yours. I downloaded some games and if there's any other games or apps you want just let me know."

He gives me a hug and thanks me. I don't think I'll ever get tired of his hugs.

The stewardess takes our drink orders and Caleb jokingly asks if I would like some Patron to finish our drinking game that got stopped from his phone call.

"Oh no, I'm good. Root beer is just fine."

We're seated on opposite sides of the plane so he tells me to come sit next to him so we can talk.

"How was work?" For a second I wonder if someone said something to him about Alex asking me out, but I doubt it.

"It was good. How was your day?"

"I spoke to the manager with the UFC. They're suspending my contract until I'm healed. I have no idea how long it's going to take to be at a hundred percent and ready to fight again."

"I'm so sorry. Kayla is going to work with you, right?'

"Yeah, once I'm ready. I just feel so restless. Fighting is all I have ever known."

"The weeks will fly by and you'll be healed before you know it."

We get to Boulder and have a rental SUV waiting for us. Caleb sits in the back letting his leg sprawl across the backseat, and Marco sits in the front with me. We arrive at the resort, have a late dinner, and get situated. We decided to meet with his father's attorney first thing in the morning to get it over with, which will give us the rest of the long weekend to enjoy our time with Marco.

Caleb obviously can't ski with his broken body and after our last group trip where I fell on my ass a hundred times before giving up, I have no desire to, but we're bringing Marco to the ski resort so he can do snowboarding lessons and go tubing while Caleb and I hang out and watch him. I'm sure Caleb will have a lot to figure out after meeting with Jason, his father's attorney.

"Time for bed, buddy," Caleb announces after Marco's show

finishes. We both get up to tuck him into bed. Somehow it has become part of our routine for both of us to say goodnight to Marco together once he's in bed. I try not to think too hard about what will happen once Caleb is healed enough to get his own place and it's just me saying goodnight to him. I think the only reason he hasn't yet is because he can't drive with the cast on, which makes it difficult to find an apartment.

After we both give Marco a kiss on his forehead, we head to the main room. The hotel suite only has two rooms. but Caleb has insisted he can sleep on the couch. I grab a bottle of water from the fridge on my way to my room.

"Hey, wanna watch something? I don't think they have *The Bachelor* here, but I'm sure we can find some chick flick of some sort."

I laugh and join him on the couch. "Sure, you pick."

"Okay, grab a bottle of liquor and two glasses. You can't make me watch a chick flick without alcohol."

After skimming through the channels he stops on *Friends With Benefits* and looks to me for approval. I smile and he presses play.

About thirty minutes into the movie we're both cracking up and I've noticed Caleb has moved closer to me. We've had quite a few shots and I'm feeling warm and fuzzy. I need a breather from his closeness so I have him pause the movie for a two-minute bathroom break. When I return, he's glaring at my phone like it just insulted him.

"What's up?"

"Nothing."

He pats his leg, indicating for me to lay my head on his lap. I do what he asks and he presses play and then runs his fingers through the strands of my hair just like I did for him that night he confided in me. He has turned this into our go-to position when watching TV at home. We watch the movie in mostly silence, laughing at certain parts, and I sniffle trying to hold back tears at other parts. I am such a sappy romantic!

At one point Caleb wipes the tear falling down my cheek. I look up at him and he is silently laughing at my tears. I don't know when it happened, but we seem so much closer than we were when he first moved in. It makes sense since we're always together. Eating together, hanging out with Marco, watching television shows after Marco goes to bed. Everything feels like it has shifted. We went from barely acquaintances to friends in such a short time.

"Do you think it's possible?" I ask when the movie ends. "To have sex without the emotions?"

I regret the question before I ever finish it, but Caleb answers before I can take it back.

"No, it's not possible." *Did he feel something for these women he was forced to have sex with?*

Almost as if he hears my silent question, he adds, "I hated every one of the women I had sex with. I felt the contempt and disgust run through my veins for years. You can't have sex without emotions. I have never had sex that I enjoyed."

While my experience is limited to a few guys, I can honestly say for the most part they were all decent in bed. Sure there wasn't huge sparks, but I can't imagine hating the person I'm intimate with.

My cell phone dings with a text, so I check it. It's Alex. When I go to check the text, I notice one I missed from earlier. Did Caleb see the text? Is that why he was glaring at my phone?

Alex: Have you thought any more about dinner?

Alex: Just one date...

I put the phone down and turn to Caleb, moving a bit closer. "Maybe if you have sex with someone by choice you might enjoy it." I give him a small smile hoping he catches my drift. The alcohol is definitely giving me liquid courage.

"Maybe…Have you ever had no-strings attached sex?"

"Once. It was okay. I didn't really know him though. I think it would be better if I at least got to know him first."

"Like Alex?" I cringe when he says his name instead of his own. That's not where I was trying to go.

When I don't say anything, he says, "We're friends…You can tell me."

Friends…Right…And it's obvious that's all we'll ever be.

"Maybe. I don't know," I say, grabbing my phone and suddenly feeling exhausted.

"I'm going to bed. I'll see you in the morning." I don't bother looking back before I close my door and climb into bed without changing my clothes. I don't know why I thought Caleb would want me to be the person he has sex with by choice. I told myself I was done trying to be more with Caleb, but it's almost impossible not to have feelings for him when we live together and I see what an amazing person he is. The more I get to know him the more I want to be with him. Maybe saying yes to Alex would be a good idea. I can get Caleb out of my head and focus on another man. I would rather have Caleb as a friend than as nothing at all.

Me: Okay. One date.

Alex: How about dinner on Tuesday at 6?

Me: Sounds good. We can leave from the gym.

After I'm done texting with Alex, I decide to sneak in a quick orgasm. Being so close to Caleb has gotten me completely turned on with no chance of a release. I move my hand down to my shorts and panties, and pull them down to my knees. Separating my pussy lips, I put a finger into my warmth and find I'm already wet. Using my juices, I add another finger and move them to my clit. With my other hand, I pull my shirt up slightly and pinch my nipple. Closing my eyes, I imagine Caleb is the one with his hands on me...

Fourteen

CALEB

JESUS! WHY DO I FEEL LIKE A TEENAGE FUCKING BOY WHEN I hang out with Hayley? Between being turned the hell on and unsure of what to say, I feel lost as fuck around this woman. She's the only person I have told about my past life and she doesn't treat me any different than she did before she knew. We've become close the last couple weeks. I thought Kayla and I were close, but hanging out with Hayley has made me realize Kayla's and my relationship was one-sided. I wasn't ready to tell her about my shit, so instead I was there for her through all of hers. For me to tell Hayley everything, I know somewhere deep down I have to trust her. Maybe it's the way she treats Marco or the way she no longer flirts with me, but I want this woman in a bad fucking way.

When she went to the bathroom and I saw Alex's text come through, I wanted to chuck the phone across the room. His text confirms what I already knew, guys aren't blind to Hayley. I can't believe she hasn't been scooped up yet.

And then when she asked me about sex without emotions, I wanted to take her and throw her down onto the couch and show her every foreign emotion I'm feeling right now. But I remembered I have ribs that aren't healed yet and a cast on my leg. I'm not in a position to throw anyone anywhere.

I took my frustrations out on her and asked about Alex. I shouldn't have brought him up…or I should have asked her not to go out with him. He's a good guy and would treat her right. I know this, but fuck if I don't want her for myself. I clearly suck at this conversational bullshit because she practically ran from me and into her room for the night.

I need to go speak to her. I hate the way we left things and I don't want it to be awkward between us. Grabbing my crutches, I make my way to her room and knock lightly. I hear a noise and assume she's telling me to come in, so I open the door.

The room is mostly dark, but from the door opening there is now light filtering through and before she realizes I am there I see the most beautiful, erotic sight of my life. She has her shirt up, shorts down, eyes closed, and she's fingerfucking herself. What makes it even better? My name graces her lips as her orgasm hits her full force.

"Mmmm…Caleb," she says, her body bowing. I quickly and quietly close the door not wanting to embarrass her. I might have been on the fence before, but I've made my decision.

I want this woman and I'm coming for her.

THE NEXT MORNING WE ARRIVE AT THE ATTORNEY'S OFFICE AT nine o'clock on the dot. It was rough sitting across from Hayley, watching her eat her muffin with the same fingers she had in her pussy last night. I wanted to make a comment, let her know I saw, ask her if I could help her out next time, but I was afraid of how she would respond.

Once we're seated in the waiting room I look over and see Gloria. Can you say instant turn-off? She's dressed to impress in her name brand clothes my father's money has paid for. She has a face full of makeup and her hair is done to perfection. She's aged over the last several years, but she's still young, and I want to throw up just looking at her. Hayley sees me stiffen but doesn't say anything.

"Hello, Caleb. It's nice to see you, again," Jason says, shaking my hand.

"Hey, man. These are my friends Hayley and Marco."

"Nice to meet you both. Why don't we get right to it? Marco, why don't you stay out here with Veronica, my secretary?"

Hayley hands him his new iPad she bought for the trip and gives him a smile, reassuring him it's okay. "Stay here and don't move. We'll be right over there if you need anything. Okay?"

"Okay."

Gloria stands as we walk toward the room eyeing me like the vulture she is. Once we all sit down. Jason begins. "Because your father insisted you are present for the reading of the will, Gloria is hearing all of this for the first time as well."

At the mention of her name, Hayley's face whips around to look at Gloria, and if looks could kill Gloria would be in hell right now courtesy of Hayley. Feeling the need to calm Hayley, I take her hand and place it on my thigh and begin rubbing my thumb over her fingers trying to calm her down. It seems to work for the most part, but now with her hand on my thigh I can feel my dick twitching, and in this room, with Gloria sitting on the other side of me, this is the last place I want to be turned on. Suddenly, flashbacks of Gloria touching me surface and I have to swallow down the bile I feel building in my throat. I want to push away Hayley's hand, but I don't want her to think it's her I don't want to touch.

"Go ahead," I choke out, trying to get this ball rolling. The sooner we get this over with, the sooner we can get the fuck out of here and take Marco to see snow.

"Okay, first of all, I have a letter here from your father. It was given to me about three years ago. He came in to make some changes to his will and also brought this letter in. He said you are to be given this letter and he asked that you read it after I go over the details of the will."

Jason hands me the envelope with my name scrawled across the front in script that I recognize as my dad's handwriting. It feels like it weighs a hundred pounds in my hand. I place it on the desk and nod for him to continue. He turns on a recorder—I'm assuming to record this is being done properly.

"I would like for it to go on record, I am Jason Caldwin, the attorney of Adam Michaels, and I am here today with Caleb Michaels and Gloria Michaels to read the living will and testament of Adam Michaels. It is sworn before me that this is the only will and will be upheld in the court of law. I would also like for it to be noted Adam Michael was in good health and sound mind when he created this will.

Adam Michaels leaves any and all assets to his son, Caleb Michaels, including but not limited to all bank accounts, stocks, bonds, houses residing at the addresses named below, all vehicles, as well as the two businesses he owns outright named *Assets*."

"What the hell are you saying?" Gloria shouts, cutting Jason off. I'm in shock—my father has left me everything, including the clubs he built for her. What the hell happened while I was gone?

"What did he say about me?" she shrieks.

Jason clears his throat and continues to read. Judging by his calmness he already knew this was coming.

"I, Adam Michaels, leave a separate bank account to my estranged wife, Gloria. In the bank account, she will find twenty thousand dollars to start her life over with. She may also keep the Porsche SUV, which is in her name. She has thirty days to move out of the house I am leaving to Caleb."

Hol-y shit. It takes everything in me not to laugh at the look on that miserable bitch's face as she realizes the jokes on her and my father didn't leave her shit. I am now dying to open the letter from my father.

"I will take this to court!" she yells at me. She's now standing and is too close for comfort. I breathe in and out slowly to calm myself.

"Gloria, you have the right to do as you wish, but maybe spending the generous sum he left you on an attorney isn't the best idea. I can assure you this will uphold in the court of law," Jason states matter-of-factly.

Gloria is so mad she's practically shaking. I stand and shake hands with Jason and thank him. I have a lot to think about. Jason hands me a large envelope telling me everything I need to know including accounts and passwords are in here and to let him know if I have any questions.

As I attempt to grab my crutches to hobble away, Gloria grabs me by my arm, but before I can say anything, her hand is ripped away.

"Listen here you nasty bitch. I know all about you. If you ever lay a hand on Caleb again I will throw your ass out a window. Do you understand?"

Hayley says the words so quietly I don't even think Jason can hear from his desk, but her tone is made clear, and I think I just fell for this woman even more.

Gloria looks shocked, clearly wondering if Hayley really knows all about her, but she recovers quickly. "You will be hearing from my attorney." And with those words, she's out the door.

Hayley runs out after her and I think it's to go for round two, but when I get to the waiting room she's sitting next to Marco smiling and asking him something about the game he is playing. She wanted to make sure Gloria didn't get anywhere near him. My heart constricts, thinking of my own mom and how protective she was over me. I miss her so damn much. Hayley is an amazing woman and Marco is lucky to have her in his corner.

"All right, you two. Ready for some snow?" I ask, tucking the letter from my dad into my back pocket.

"Yes!" Marco says, pumping his fist into the air.

"Let's go!"

We spend the rest of the weekend having fun at the ski resort. Marco takes snowboarding lessons and after a few hours is flying down the slopes. He's really good. It's obvious he's a natural athlete. Hayley and I watch from the sidelines and every so often she heads indoors to read her romance book by the fireplace. I hate that I can't join Marco on the slopes, but decide once I'm healed, I'm going to take him back here to do some snowboarding with him.

By the time we fly back to Las Vegas, it's late. Luckily Hayley left her vehicle at the airport so we can head right home. While she's getting the luggage into the trunk I see a sheet of paper sticking out of her windshield. I grab it and open it up: *DROP THE CHARGES OR ELSE...*

I look around but don't see anybody. Since the four men who attacked me weren't granted bail this has to be from someone on the outside, most likely Hector or Santos. I'll turn this into the police station tomorrow. For now, I decide not to tell Hayley. I don't need to worry her.

Fifteen

HAYLEY

IT'S BEEN A MONTH SINCE CALEB FOUND OUT HE'S RICH. NOT only is he rich, but he's also the owner of several businesses and homes. His ribs are pretty much healed and while he hasn't been able to drive himself anywhere because of his cast, he's been making phone calls like crazy, having his friends take him places as well as taking a cab when necessary. It is only a matter of time until he finds a new apartment and moves out. I haven't brought it up, but I'm sure it's coming.

During these last several weeks things have been good between us. We've established a great schedule with Marco—he's thriving in school and at home. We spend a lot of time together, the three of us, sometimes going to the movies or out to dinner. We have Kayla, Bentley, and the babies over a lot as well. Marco loves to see his sister, and Kayla is beginning to work with Caleb on rehabilitating his shoulder. Caleb's shoulder is nowhere near back to the way it was before but he hasn't lost hope. From the outside looking in, one would think we're a family, and the truth is, I have to constantly remind myself when we're together that we aren't.

Last weekend was Bella's Birthday party so the three of us attended the party at her favorite park. Marco was nervous and told us it would be the first party he's been to. Even though he's older than Bella and Tristan, he still enjoys hanging out with them. He's a good kid. He had a blast at the party, but I could see the sadness when he told me he's never had one. I shouldn't have been shocked to learn he never had a party of his own, but I still was. Even though his birthday just passed in December, I make a mental note to throw him a half-year party this summer once school is out. It will be warm outside and we can invite his friends over and have them all go swimming.

At night Caleb and I spend time together just the two of us. We usually watch a show or a movie, but rarely pay attention it. We talk about our day, what's going on with Marco, how he feels about his dad leaving him everything. He's a complete open book when we talk. The only thing it seems we don't talk about is when he plans to move out. He did mention needing the time off to get his dad's estate in order. He seems to have turned a corner—so much more upbeat than he was before.

One night I nervously asked him about the letter his dad wrote. He hadn't brought it up yet and I was curious what it entailed.

"You don't have to tell me if you don't want to. I just want you to know you can talk to me about it if you ever want."

Caleb hobbled over to the room and came back with the letter in his hand. "I read it when we got back from Boulder. He knew everything."

I was flabbergasted by his words. His dad knew but didn't say or do anything? He chose his wife over his son?

"Did he explain why he chose her over you, yet left you everything?"

"Yeah, do you want to read it?"

"Do you want me to?"

He nodded and handed me the letter.

Dear Caleb,

If you're reading this I have passed away without getting the courage to speak to you. I have written this letter because I am a selfish man who couldn't face his own son. I am currently in the middle of divorcing Gloria and I would like to say I am truly sorry for what I did to our family. The day in your bedroom when you begged me to believe you, I should have taken your side. I didn't know for sure but I had a feeling Gloria was up to no good. I just had no idea how bad it was. After you left and I confronted her she admitted everything including blackmailing you and then having sex with you. I was so scared to end up in prison, I let her get away with what she did to you. I know nothing I say will make up for what she did and what I did to you by not believing you and choosing to believe her. You were so young, still underage, and it was my job to protect you. I'm so sorry I never protected you from her. I'm sorry I couldn't be the dad you deserve.

I have left everything I own to you. I have filed for divorce but it will take time and so I made sure to change my will in case something happens to me before it's finalized. Please don't let Gloria threaten you. She can't do anything to you. Everything I am leaving you is yours. The clubs actually make real good money. If you don't want them, sell them. Just please accept everything I am giving you. Is it guilt money? Sure! But do you deserve it any less? Hell no!

In case she gives you any trouble, please feel free to use this letter as a witness testimony to what she did to you. I also have a tape recording of her admitting what she did in my safety deposit box. Jason should have given you the key.

Please know I have watched you over the years from afar. I have watched you fight your way to the top. You are pursuing your dreams and I am so damn proud of you. You walked away with nothing but your dignity and pride and created a life for yourself. Take the money I left you and use it for good.

I love you, son.

Dad

I handed it back to him and tried to wipe the tears from my eyes before he could see. He reached over and wiped them for me.
"How do you feel about all this?"
"I feel like I am ready to move forward."

And he has moved forward. He laughs more and is way more social than before. It seems like the weight has been lifted from his shoulders and he is finally free. I hope now that he's put it all behind him, he will one day be able to date a woman. Caleb is an incredible person and deserves to be happy, even if it's not with me.

During the last few weeks I have been on a few dates with Alex. I haven't spoken to Caleb about it and for some reason that makes me feel guilty. It's not like I need his permission to date, but because we're at a good place in our friendship and I don't want to rock the boat, I haven't actually told him I have gone out with Alex. He hasn't made any indication he would even care who I date. I usually leave from the gym to meet Alex and we only go out when I know Marco is with Kayla or doing something with Caleb. The truth is I don't feel a huge spark with Alex. While he is sweet and nice, he just doesn't do it for me.

Today is Valentine's Day and I'm going to dinner with Alex. I know I shouldn't lead him on, but it's been awhile since I actually had a date for this holiday. Caleb has been gone all day, so hopefully I'll leave before he gets home. Marco is at Bentley's parents' house for the night spending time with Chloe while they babysit Chloe and Faith so Bentley can take Kayla out. Alex insisted on picking me up and I couldn't say no. I've tried to muster up the courage to tell Caleb all afternoon but have chickened out.

"Hey, want to grab a bite to eat? I didn't even realize it's Valentine's Day. The restaurants seem to be all booked, but we can go to the diner you love." Caleb is sitting on the couch, looking down at his phone. He must have gotten home while I was in the shower.

He looks up from his phone taking me in from head to toe. I'm suddenly self-conscious about my outfit. I am wearing a tight red dress that shows every one of my curves and I've paired it with black peep-toe heels. I normally don't dress up, but with it being Valentine's Day, Alex insisted on making reservations. I even straightened my hair after getting my highlights redone this morning along with a fresh manicure and pedicure.

"Going somewhere?" Caleb asks, looking confused.

Of course that's when Alex knocks causing Caleb to get up to answer the door. For a guy with a broken leg, he can move quickly when he wants to. That's when I notice his cast is off. He has a walking boot instead of the cast, which means he can now walk without crutches.

"Hey, man," Alex says, walking in. He's holding roses in one hand and shakes Caleb's hand with the other, completely unaware of the now thick tension in the room.

"What's up?" Caleb asks, darting his eyes from Alex to me.

"Nothing much. Taking Hayley out for Valentine's Day," Alex says to Caleb before he turns to me. "You look beautiful, Hayley." He hands me the flowers and gives me a kiss on my cheek. I thank him and excuse myself to go put them in water.

While I'm filling the vase, I feel a warm body come up behind me. I know instantly it's Caleb. Nobody makes my body react like his does. Before I can turn around, he presses his front up against my back. His hands lay flat on the counter caging me in, and his cool breath is so close to my ear, I get the chills.

"How long have you been dating Alex?" he asks softly.

"We've just gone on a few dates." I don't know why I feel the need to downplay it.

He moves one of his hands to turn off the water since the vase is now completely filled and is overflowing. I am stuck where I am. I've never felt Caleb this close.

"Is that who you want, Hayles?" Oh, did I mention since we've been hanging out the last several weeks he has started calling me Hayles? And did I mention every time he does, my panties go wet? Well, he does…and they do!

"He's nice," I say because it's the first thing that comes to mind. His closeness is causing my mind to go blank.

"Nice," he repeats and then chuckles without humor. One of his hands comes off the counter and moves my hair to the side, and then I feel his lips touch my neck as he gives me a chaste open-mouthed kiss right on my pulse point.

His hands move to my hips and he turns me around, not backing up at all. I can feel his cock up against the thin material of my dress pushing against my stomach.

I look up and into his glaring eyes. I'm not sure why he's mad, but I wait for him to say something else since he's holding me against the counter.

His face moves closer and I think he might be about to kiss me when he keeps going, lining his lips right up to my ear.

"Enjoy your *nice* date." Then he let's go of me and saunters out of the kitchen to his room. I didn't realize the warmth his body radiates until he's no longer touching me, causing my body to suddenly shiver. I want the warmth of Caleb back.

I put the flowers into the vase and try to compose myself as I walk back to the living room.

"Ready?" Alex asks. I want to cancel this date. I want to feign illness and find Caleb and his warmth. I want to stop trying to be into a guy who doesn't turn me on at all. But I'm not that woman, so instead I plaster a smile on my face and say, "Yep," and follow Alex out the door, leaving my warmth behind.

Sixteen

CALEB

WHAT'S THAT SAYING…YOU DON'T KNOW WHAT YOU HAVE until it's gone? I'm pretty sure that's how it goes and that's exactly how I feel right now. I'm lying in my bed in my bedroom with the door shut because I couldn't watch Hayley and Alex leave for their date.

These past six weeks with Marco and Hayley have been nothing short of amazing. I haven't been this happy and content since my mom and sister were both alive. We have somehow created our own version of a family and every day I look forward to the moments we spend together. Whether it's the three of us, or just Hayley and me, I am falling hard…Fuck it! Let's be honest…I *have* fallen hard!

I know realistically I could have moved out a couple of weeks ago. I could have found an apartment on the first floor, but I made excuses to myself not wanting to leave. I have been busy getting my father's affairs in order during the day and enjoying my afternoons and evenings with Marco and Hayley. If I'm honest with myself, I don't want to leave either of them.

I've kicked Gloria out of my dad's house and put it on the market and sold all of his vehicles, donating all the profits to the charity Bentley and I started. It is another jump up from the one he started to help pay for the MMA classes Cooper runs. We're working together to build a sports complex next to the gym for kids to come to instead of going home alone. They will be able to participate in a variety of sports and have a safe place to go to instead of running the streets. We're still in the planning stage but it's going to be cool as hell once it's done.

My next step is to deal with Gloria's strip clubs since Gloria didn't take Jason's advice and has made it clear she is going to take me to court for ownership of the clubs. Turns out she owns two clubs, one of which is right here in Vegas on the strip. I've shut them both down for renovation with paid leave for all the employees while we go to court. I could have closed them down, but I felt bad leaving so many people without an income. Plus, I had Liz take a look at the books and my dad was right, they turn a nice profit. Until it gets sorted out, the court has put a freeze on all things club related. Because Jason was the attorney for the will I need to find a new attorney to represent me in court.

I have also been attending physical therapy with Kayla for my shoulder. I won't be fighting in the upcoming UFC fight anymore, which sucks, but I do plan to fight again in the future. No longer needing the money definitely changes my outlook on life. I can see myself taking a step back from fighting for a bit. I have spent so many years focusing on my dream I didn't realize how much I was missing from life. I'm enjoying my time with Marco and Hayley.

There's been so many times I have wanted to take things further with Hayley, tell her how I feel, that I want more with her, but felt it was best to wait until I'm no longer handicapped. So today when the doctor took my cast off and put me in a removable walking boot jokingly saying, "Happy Valentine's Day," it hit me that today would be the perfect day to tell Hayley how I feel.

I tried to find a restaurant to take her to, but of course they were all booked for the holiday. I definitely didn't think this through. Then as quick as this was all handed to me, it was taken away when she walked out of her room in a sexy-as-hell red dress and fuck-me heels. I almost came in my pants from just looking at her. The way the dress swoops down just low enough to show the outline of her amazing breasts, and how it's formfitting enough to show her perfect curves that I want to grab ahold of in bed as I make love to her while she's wearing nothing but those damn heels.

Then it hit me, she didn't know I planned to take her out, which means the dress wasn't for me. So who is it for? And like the devil himself heard my question, there was a knock on the door, and on the other side was my friend Alex. Shit! How the fuck did I not see this coming? I tried hard to think if Hayley had mentioned Alex before and I am pretty damn sure she hasn't. Other than the one night I saw his text, he never got brought up again.

I wanted nothing more than to slam the door on his face, but Alex is a good guy, and he didn't do anything wrong. If I'm being honest neither did Hayley, but she could have mentioned dating him during one of our nighttime conversations. *Did she purposely keep this from me?*

When she went to put the flowers in water I watched her fine ass sway to the kitchen and wanted to tie her up in my room and never let her out. Needing to know if my feelings for her were one-sided, I cornered her in the kitchen. I know she felt something for me before, but she hasn't acted on those feelings in months. Maybe she no longer wanted me. But when I pressed my body up against hers I knew damn well she wanted me just as bad as I wanted her. And when she described Alex as *nice*, I knew I had her.

I'm not going to lie. I'm new to this dating shit. I have no idea what to do. I've had sex hundreds if not thousands of times over the years, every single time not by choice. I had a girlfriend once. I was thirteen and we went to the skating rink. I asked her to be my girlfriend, she said yes, we kissed on the lips a few times, wrote a couple notes back and forth, and a few months later I was taken out of school to watch my mom die.

Now I'm in my room while Hayley is on a date and I have no clue where to go from here. I know Kayla is probably on a date with Bentley, but fuck it, she's the only person I can ask about all this.

"Hello?" she answers the phone on the second ring.

"Are you busy?"

"Caleb? What's wrong?"

"Are you busy?" I ask again.

"No, Bentley and I are picking up the kids from his parents' house. They were going to keep them overnight, but Faith is teething and is super-fussy, so we decided to call it a night after dinner. Everything okay?"

"Did you know Hayley is dating Alex?" My question comes out a lot harsher than I intended, but of course Kayla doesn't miss a beat. It's quiet and then I hear laughter over the phone.

"Yes, I know they've gone on a few dates, but I don't think she is really into him."

"I don't know how to do this, Kayla." We've had a few discussions since I opened up to Hayley. Kayla always knew something was up, but I confirmed her suspicions one day during physical therapy. She knows I haven't been with anyone since my last night in Boulder when I fucked Norma before moving to Las Vegas.

"Well, I'm assuming you aren't referring to not knowing how to have sex…" She laughs and tries to play it off with a cough successfully lightening my mood.

"I watched her leave with Alex on a date. Shit, Kayla. I didn't think it was possible to feel so jealous of another man."

"Well, you have to tell Hayley that, silly."

"That's it? Just tell her how I feel? What about the fact I'm living here still?"

"Hayley is a grown woman, Caleb. You both put Marco first. Just tell her how you feel and see where it goes. I have Marco for the night, so maybe tell her when she gets home from her date."

"Okay…"

"And Caleb? You can't hold it against her if she's slept with Alex. She doesn't know how you feel."

Oh, fuck! I didn't even think about the fact she's probably slept with Alex. Would I hold it against her? No, I wouldn't. But it still sucks thinking about the fact he has had his hands all over the body I should have claimed months ago.

"Yeah, yeah, I get it," I say before hanging up.

I consider texting Hayley there's an emergency to get her to come home but decide against it. I'll just wait until she gets home and speak to her then.

After about an hour I say *fuck it!* And shoot her a text.

Me: You should come home.

Hayley: Everything okay?

Is everything okay? Technically it is…but also technically it's not because she's out on a date with another guy. I don't want to worry her, so I go for vague.

Me: Yeah, but we need to talk.

Hayley: About what?

Me: About the fact that I saw you calling out my name while fingering yourself in Boulder, yet you're on a date with a guy who isn't me.

Straight forward much? Yeah, but if I'm going to go in, I might as well go all the way in. I stare at my phone, waiting for a response that never comes.

Seventeen

HAYLEY

ALEX AND I ARE AT DINNER, AND I SHOULD BE FOCUSING ON him, but instead my attention is on Caleb…His lips touching my neck, my earlobe, and the way his body touching mine sent shocks of pleasure straight to my core. We're finishing up our dessert when Caleb sends me a text telling me to come home because we need to talk. At first I was worried it might be something serious and then my curiosity got the best of me. When I asked him what we needed to talk about I didn't expect the text he sent.

Luckily Alex was in the bathroom because having to explain the wine that shot out of my mouth and all over the table would have been awkward. I can't believe Caleb saw me that night in the hotel room. My eyes were closed and thinking back I thought I heard something, but I was so caught up in imagining it was Caleb getting me off I didn't even think about it.

I don't even know how to respond, so I put my phone away knowing I'm going to end things with Alex. I should have ended things sooner.

"Is everything okay?" Alex asks, sitting back down.

"Yes…No…I'm not really sure. Caleb needs to talk to me. I need to go home tonight. I'm sorry." I leave out the part about him letting me know he watched me finger myself while calling out his name.

Alex's look of disappointment solidifies my decision to end things tonight. I don't want to lead him on.

"Alex, I have had a lot of fun with you, but I don't think it's going to work out."

He gives me a small smile and nods. "Yeah, I kind of figured that when I picked you up tonight."

I raise a brow in confusion.

"Hayley, I knew you had a thing for Caleb but I still took my chances. I saw the way you acted around him. It's obvious something is going on between you two. And by the daggers he was shooting at me tonight, I would say it's no longer one-sided."

"I'm so sorry. I honestly don't even know what's going on."

"It's okay. You're an amazing woman. I can't blame the guy for wanting you." He gives me a wink and it gives me a sense of relief things aren't ending on a bad note.

Alex pays the bill and drops me off at home. As he walks me to the door like the perfect gentleman he is, I notice a car sitting a few houses down. It's an expensive vehicle, and while this is a nice neighborhood, this car looks to be worth more than even the houses are worth. It clearly doesn't belong here. I look closer and notice two dark shadows inside. This horrible feeling of being watched again comes over me, but I shake it off.

Alex gives me a small kiss on my cheek and says goodnight before walking back to his car. I wait until he takes off before I go to unlock the door. As I place my key up to the lock, the door swings open and I am met with Caleb's beautiful blue-grey eyes glaring at me.

"You didn't text me back," he growls.

My eyebrows shoot up making it clear I am not okay with how he is speaking to me. He closes his eyes briefly and when he reopens them, his eyes have lightened a bit taking the grey away. He's no longer towering over me, but has slouched a bit calming down.

I look back to make sure Alex is gone and notice the expensive car still sitting down the street. Maybe I should tell Caleb—it's probably nothing but what if it's something?

We're both standing in the doorway with the door open but he moves over to let me inside the house. When I walk through and turn around to face him he's right up against me. His mouth is so close to mine, it takes all my willpower not to reach up and kiss him. Then I remember about the car.

"Hey, without being obvious open the door back up and look down the street to the right. There's a car sitting on the side of the road. I don't think it belongs there."

His eyes widen and he swings the door open. "I don't see anything."

I look outside to where the car was, only it's gone. I know I wasn't seeing things. "It was just there. It looked like two people were just sitting in the car. It gave me a bad feeling, like I was being watched."

Caleb closes the door again. Grabbing my hand, walks us to the couch, and then gripping my sides, pulls me into his lap. I'm so shocked he's not only touching me, but that he has pulled me on top of him, I'm having trouble speaking.

"Is this the first time you've felt like you were being watched?"

I think about it for a second and remember when I was at the gym recently and had the same feeling. "No, I felt it before but didn't really think much about it. Do you think someone could be following me? Who would do that?"

"I found a note the day we came back from Boulder warning me to drop the charges. You need to be careful. Please don't leave the gym by yourself. Have someone walk you out. Don't be on your phone while walking to your car. Pay attention around you. Hector and Santos, the guys who were threatening Marco, are still out there, and remember how they threatened you before…insinuating they would accept you as payment. I'd hope they aren't stupid enough to come around with the trial coming up and their friends all in the spotlight but you never know." I didn't even think about the fact that Hector and Santos weren't the ones arrested because they weren't there the night all that shit went down. Because the cops have nothing on them but Marco saying they sell drugs, they can't arrest them. They need more evidence to build a stronger case against them.

"Okay, I'll be careful," I promise.

Suddenly feeling shy sitting on Caleb's lap, I lift up to climb off him, but he grabs my hips to keep me in place. He doesn't say anything for a good minute. He just rubs circles into my flesh with his thumbs while searching for something in my face, I don't know what. I look down and notice when Caleb pulled me on top of him, my tight dress had nowhere to go but up and my panties are visible.

I try to get off Caleb once again to pull my dress down, but before I can, he glances down to see what I'm looking at and then licks his lips at the sight in front of him. This whole scene is so confusing. Caleb has never wanted me. Whether it was when we kissed once at the club or when it was just a small pat on his leg, he always made it clear I'm not who he wants. I know a lot of it has to do with what his stepmom did to him. He's told me so himself that he needs to be in control, but over the last few months if he wanted me, he would have done something about it, right? Until today I thought Caleb didn't view me as anything more than a good friend, but now his actions are telling me otherwise.

I need to just let him take the lead. If he needs to be in control I need to let him be. The thought of Caleb controlling me causes the area between my legs to clench.

He feels my thighs tighten and raises a brow. "You didn't respond to my last text."

Oh my God, he is actually going to bring that up. Okay, then. "What would you like me to say? Apparently you saw it all, so you know I was getting off while thinking about you." My neck and face warms at my admission.

Caleb studies my face for a few seconds before he whispers, "I want you." Those three words make me want to jump this man. They make me want to take his dick and put it in me and ride him, but I choose to stay silent only nodding once in case those three words are asking for permission. I need him to know he can have me.

Gripping my ass with his hands, he picks me up. My ankles link together around his waist and he walks us to my bedroom never taking his eyes off me. He lays me on the bed and steps back, bringing his hands to his face. He scrubs his hands up and down his stubble…out of confusion? Frustration? I don't know. I have no idea what's going on in his head.

"I have no clue what to do with you," he finally says. I'm not sure what he means by this. He's told me he's had sex with hundreds of women, surely he knows what to do.

"Do you like it soft or rough? How do you want it? Do you like it missionary or from behind? Fuck! I'm going to mess this up." I see the frustration in his eyes. It's never been in his control. He's always been told exactly what to do. He doesn't know what to do if someone isn't telling him, yet he needs this to be in his control. My heart breaks for this grown man who looks completely lost.

I sit up and pat the bed next to me, giving him a small smile. He crawls up the bed and lies next to me, so we're both lying on our sides facing each other. "I want it however you want to give it to me. We don't have to have sex tonight. Let's just take it slow. You lead and I'll follow."

He nods slowly and swallows loudly. Taking my face in his hands, he brings his body closer to mine so we're lined up against one another just barely touching, and then brings his lips to mine for a small kiss. He doesn't take it any further, leaving his lips on mine, and I let him figure out what happens next. This is definitely a test to my restraint.

After pulling back, he drags his thumb across my bottom lip and smiles. "That's the first kiss I have had willingly since I was thirteen." My heart cracks, but I keep myself composed. I remind myself he doesn't need my pity.

He brushes his lips against one once again, only this time his tongue pushes against my lips seeking entrance. I part my lips slightly, welcoming him. My one hand is propping my head up and my other is holding the sheet to remind myself not to jump him.

Our kiss deepens, and it feels like it goes on for hours. His tongue entwines with mine. He tastes like the mint toothpaste I always see on his bathroom sink mixed with Patron. He must have had a drink while I was out. I think back to my date. It seems like it ended days ago, yet it couldn't have been more than an hour ago. At some point Caleb's hand moves from my face to my ass, and he tugs me toward him. We're close enough that I can feel his hard length pressing up against me. I don't make any move except continue to kiss him back, and he is an amazing kisser.

Caleb's lips break apart from mine and then he rolls me to my back hovering over me. He looks lost in thought for a moment, almost like he's in pain, but then he seems to snap out of it, coming back to me. My lips feel numb from the excessive kissing we've been doing.

His hands are resting on either side of my face, as he peppers small, wet kisses all over my face, on both my cheeks, on each of my eyelids, my nose, and my chin. Then he moves to my neck, kisses the same throbbing pulse point he did earlier tonight in the kitchen.

"I love the way you taste," he whispers into my ear causing my legs to tighten. Because he's situated between my thighs, he feels them tighten and chuckles softly. He goes back to kissing my neck, and then kisses my exposed collarbone and shoulder. I'm so turned on, I'm afraid I'm going to combust.

I think he's going to go to my breasts next, but he doesn't. He bypasses them altogether and goes straight to my feet. On his way down, he sees my dress back over my waist, so he pulls it back down over my panties. He takes each of my heels off, throwing them to the ground and then kisses my big toe. I want to pull it back out of embarrassment, but I don't. I remind myself he needs to be in control.

"I love this color on you," he says, pointing to the blood red nail polish that matches my dress. He nibbles on each toe then moves his way up to my calf, giving it a small kiss before placing my leg back down on the bed. I have no idea where he's going to go next, but I've realized once I allowed him to do what he wants how nice it feels to just let him be in control. All I have to do is lie here and enjoy his touch.

He sits up on his heels and that's when I notice he's not wearing his walking boot. He peels his shirt over his head leaving his amazingly hard body on display for me. I've seen him without his shirt on briefly at Kayla's place but it wasn't long enough to enjoy it. Since he's lived here, he's always come out of his room or bathroom dressed.

Caleb's body is as close to perfection as it can get. He's in great shape from working out but not overly muscular. He has a tattoo going across his chest that reads *Mi vida loca*. Another one on his arm of a woman and surrounding her are clouds and roses. On his side, just under his left peck, says one word: *Trust*. His right nipple is pierced and I want so badly to grab it and pull on it with my teeth. He has perfect washboard abs I would love to run my tongue down. Just below his abs, his grey sweatpants hang low resting on his perfect hips. I have never wanted anybody as much as I want Caleb.

He crawls back up my body, but instead of taking things further he lies down next to me, wrapping his body around me and pulling me close to him. He grabs my leg and pulls it up and over his thigh intertwining our legs together. He gives me another soft kiss on my lips and one more on my neck before he speaks.

"I think I could make out with you forever." His comment is so innocent, I can't help but laugh. This man, who is obviously a sex god, is perfectly content with just making out.

I point to the words on his chest. "What does this mean?"

He looks down like he needs to see the words before answering. "It means 'My crazy life.' I got it when I first moved out of my dad's house. I went right from under his roof to living with Bentley in Las Vegas. I got a job as a bouncer, the same club I was working at up until I got hurt. I went out with a bunch of guys who all worked at the club one night. I listened to them talk about their problems and realized how fucked up my life was compared to theirs. I met this Hispanic woman that night. After having a few drinks I vaguely told her about what happened between my dad and me. She told me that life can be crazy and all I can do is embrace it, but don't ever let it own me. I got the tattoo the next day. The problem was, I did let my crazy life own me. I got the tattoo to remind me of what she said, but instead I looked at it and allowed it to keep me from living my life. Every time I looked at it, I was reminded of what my stepmom did to me and what I had to do to all those women."

His story is so completely heartbreaking, yet when you look at him, all you see is strength. You would never know how vulnerable he really is.

"What about the other ones?"

"I got the tattoo of the word trust to remind me to trust, but also to remind myself not to trust too easily. My mom and sister both lied to me, and then I trusted my stepmom and I shouldn't have. I'll never make that mistake again."

I want to ask him about his mom and sister but mentally put it aside for later.

"This one," he says, pointing to the one of the woman, "is of my mom. I decided I needed something positive on my body to counteract the negative shit, so I had her picture tattooed on me. She's surrounded by flowers and clouds because she's in heaven."

He brings his shoulder forward to show me another tattoo on the back of his shoulder. It's of a young girl who is surrounded by the same clouds and flowers as his mom. "This one is of my sister, Colette. This was the last picture I have of her alive."

I gasp at his words. How did she die?

It's like he hears my question because he goes on to answer it. We lie in bed for what feels like hours while he rubs circles on my arms and my waist while he tells me stories of his sister and mom from when they were alive. He tells me about his sister lying and being raped and killed, and of his mom's death and how she didn't tell him she was dying until right before she died. He tells me how everything changed after they both passed away. I can't even imagine going through half of what Caleb has been through. He's stronger than anybody I've ever met.

After he's done telling me his stories, he asks about my family. I tell him about my sister, her recent engagement, and how she's my best friend, about how my parents are still married and how close we are. We've lived in Las Vegas our entire lives. I feel guilty because even though my family isn't perfect, we have never been through anything of what he's been through. He notices my hesitancy while talking and grabs my chin for me to look at him.

"Hey, don't feel guilty for having a nice life. Never feel bad for all the good in your life." I continue to tell him how my mom would like to meet Marco. I haven't seen any of them in weeks because they went on a last minute trip to Seattle to visit friends of theirs. Since my dad retired last year, they've been spending their time traveling. I can't wait for them to return to meet Marco. Caleb tells me we should invite them all for dinner. Eventually we fall asleep in each other's arms.

Eighteen

CALEB

WHILE LAST NIGHT DIDN'T EXACTLY GO AS PLANNED, I WOULD like to think it went even better. I never felt such intimacy with a woman before, and the fact that it was all felt without even having to be sexual speaks volumes about our connection. It goes against everything Gloria tried to instill in me. I look down and see Hayley's face mashed up against my chest. Her arm is thrown over my stomach, and her tanned sexy legs are still entwined with mine. She's snoring lightly. I notice she's still in her tight red dress from last night. I almost feel bad that we fell asleep without her changing, but looking at her dress bunched up at her waist, giving me a view of her ass cheeks, makes it worth it.

She stirs awake, rolling onto her back and stretching, and wipes the sleep out of her eyes. She's absolutely beautiful inside and out, and I want her to be mine. She looks down, and when she sees her dress is bunched up, she grabs the blanket and pulls it over her, taking away my great view, which causes me to frown.

She sees my reaction and giggles. "Don't pout." She leans in to give me a kiss but hesitates and backs up, unsure. She doesn't feel comfortable being the one to initiate anything because of the times I have rejected her. I want to tell her it's okay, but the truth is I don't know if it is. I don't know how I feel about not being the one in control. Last night I almost made love to her, but then I had a flashback of a time I was with another woman and I stopped. I don't want anything Hayley and I do to be tainted with my past.

Leaning forward, I pull her in for a kiss. It quickly builds, becoming more intense, when her phone rings ruining the moment. I give her one last chaste kiss on her cheek before heading to the bathroom.

"I'm going to take a shower. Wanna grab breakfast?"

"Sure, let me just call Kayla back. It's probably about Marco since they kept him overnight."

After I get out of the shower, I grab a towel to dry off and head back out through Hayley's room to go get dressed and put my walking boot back on. She's talking to someone on the phone but stops when she sees me. In the past a woman eyeing me made me feel sick. I used to hate the thought of another woman using me for sex, but when Hayley does it, I don't get the same feeling I used to get. I want her to look at me. I want her to want me. It's a foreign concept, but one I welcome.

I give her a small smile and head back to my room. After getting dressed, I hear her shower running so I grab my cellphone to see if I have any missed calls or emails. There's an email from Jarred Harms, the prosecutor assigned to my case, letting me know we need to meet to go over my testimony before we go to court. They have scheduled a court date. He also lets me know two of the men they caught are only being tried with aggravated assault and after they filed an appeal were granted bail. The other two men are being charged with rape and attempted murder, so they'll remain in jail until their hearings. I reply that I can come by next week sometime. I also make note to get an alarm system installed in here. With Hector and Santos around, and now the other two guys out on bail, it worries me to have Hayley and Marco out of my sight.

There's a knock at the door and when I open it, it's a young man holding an envelope.

"Are you Caleb Michaels?"

"Yes."

"Sign here, please." I sign, take the envelope from him, and open it up. It's the court documents pertaining to Gloria's lawsuit. It says I have thirty days to respond or give up my rights to the clubs. I knew these would be arriving soon, but it still pisses me off. I would burn those clubs to the ground before giving her ownership of them.

"What's wrong?" Hayley comes out in tight black jeans that mold to her curves and a loose off-the-shoulder cream sweater that makes me want to kiss her exposed skin. Her hair is wet from her shower and pulled into some sort of side looking braid thing. She looks just as gorgeous as she did last night in a completely different way.

"Gloria is suing me for the clubs. I need to hire an attorney." I sit on the couch and she walks over to sit next to me.

"Do you want the clubs?"

I have given this question a lot of thought, so I already know my answer. "Yeah, I do. Liz and I looked over the books and they turn a nice profit. While Gloria has done some shady shit behind the scenes, I've met a lot of the staff and many of these women and men need this job. I can put an end to the illegal shit she has going on and can make a steady income from these clubs. I would need to hire a new manager for the club in Boulder since I don't want to have to fly out there often and don't trust Gloria, as well as find a manager for the one here once I'm healed and start training again, but I think it would be good."

"Then you should do it. I'll have to check out these strip clubs once they reopen. Why don't we have my family over for dinner and I can ask my sister what she thinks since she's an attorney. Maybe she can even represent you."

"That would be great, thanks." I grab her by her hips and pull her into my lap. Now that I've had a taste of this woman, I can't get enough.

"Was that Kayla on the phone?" I ask, situating her so she's straddling me.

"Yes, she dropped Marco off at school. He loves spending time with Chloe. I'm so glad Kayla and Bentley are getting approved to adopt her."

"They're good people. So are you. You choosing to bring Marco home and making the choice to adopt him is one of the most selfless acts I've witnessed. Providing him this home, a room to call his own, clothes, food…You are amazing."

She nuzzles her face into my shoulder, shaking her head. I pull her back up to look at her. "What's wrong?"

"Nothing, it's just…it doesn't feel selfless…Sometimes it feels like I need Marco more than he needs me."

"What do you mean?"

"Before he moved in here, I felt so alone." She shrugs. "I'm not exactly young, Caleb. I'm in my thirties. I spent so many years focusing on school I never got serious with a guy, and with my younger sister getting engaged I realized maybe having my own kids won't be possible. Adopting Marco means creating my own family. Even if I meet someone one day—taking the time to get to know him, getting married, and him wanting kids, it could be years. What if I'm too old by then and can't have my own kids?"

I think about everything she just said and a gut-wrenching feeling of jealousy consumes me. The thought of her meeting another man and getting married makes my hands tighten on her hips. I want to be that man. I want to be part of that family she just described. I don't, however, want to scare her with too much too soon. Hell, these thoughts are scaring me.

"You are amazing, and Marco is lucky to have you. I love that a family to you isn't just biology and that you already consider Marco your child, but don't give up on having your own kids. Plus…you aren't *that* old." I give her a wink and she glares at me crinkling her nose at the word old.

"I'm not *that* old huh? How old are you?"

"Still in my twenties," I say nonchalantly. I'm only a few years younger than Hayley, but it's fun to mess with her. She slaps my chest laughing and I pull her in for a kiss. Her stomach growls causing us both to laugh, so we head out to get breakfast before she goes to work.

On our way out, I notice the car Hayley was talking about parked a few houses down but don't mention it to her. I don't want to scare her. It's the same car from the day I saw Marco talking to Hector and Santos. The third guy that was there got out of that car. He was the one dressed nicer, looking out of place.

We get to the restaurant, a little hole-in-the-wall place Hayley loves, and the waiter comes over to take our order.

"Hey, Hayley, How are you?"

"I'm good. You?"

I can see the look in his eyes. He wants her. It's obvious they know each other.

"I'm good. I haven't seen you in here recently."

"Things have been crazy busy. Can I get a coffee and the breakfast special?"

"Sure thing," he says, giving her a wink. Is this guy serious? Does he not see me sitting right here with her?

"I'm going to use the restroom to wash my hands." Hayley stands from her seat and heads toward the restrooms. Instead of taking my order, the fucker watches her ass as she walks away.

I clear my throat loudly, causing him to turn to face me. Lifting one brow, I glare at him. "You ready to take my order or would you like to continue to stare at my woman's ass?" Holy fuck. Did I just call her my woman? Yes, I did, because she's mine, and she sure as fuck isn't his.

His eyes go wide, realizing I caught him and he at least has the decency to look a little embarrassed.

"I want a coffee and a water, and I'll have the breakfast special as well."

He nods then scurries off to put in our orders.

When Hayley returns, instead of sitting across from her, I move into the booth next to her.

"What are you doing?"

"I just want to sit next to you."

She giggles and it makes my heart soar. I love that fucking giggle.

The waiter sets our drinks down and lets us know our food will be out shortly.

"The waiter has the hot's for you."

"Oh, stop it!" Hayley says, backhanding my chest playfully. "I've been eating here for years. He just knows me."

"He was watching your ass while you walked away." Hayley's head flies back against the back of the booth and she full-on belly laughs. It reminds me of the day at the gym when I saw Stephen make her laugh like that. I love that I'm the one making her laugh now—even if what I'm saying it true and not meant to be funny.

"Well, I can't stop people from watching my ass," she says, sobering up.

"No, but I can. It's my ass."

"What did you say? That you are an ass?" She laughs again.

"Very funny. I said…It's. My. Ass. I don't want anybody looking at it but me."

"How very alpha of you." Hayley laughs softly and then leans in and gives me a peck on my lips, but I want more. My tongue darts out and finds hers. She tastes sweet as fuck, and I can already tell she's going to become my addiction. As we kiss, my hand lands on her thigh and I squeeze it tightly. I've never wanted a woman as much as I want her.

A clanking sound causes us both to jump, and when I glance up, the waiter is loudly setting down our food. My fist tightens on Hayley's thigh and I can feel her silently shaking with laughter.

Taking her face into my hands, I look her in the eyes. "Mine." Her laughter stops but her smile remains as she nods her head. Damn right, this woman is mine.

After we finish breakfast, Hayley heads to work and I decide to have a chat with Jarred about the car. He lets me know that unless there is any type of physical contact there isn't much he can do. Even if it is Hector and Santos, unless they are breaking a law there is nothing we can do. He also tells me he already has a restraining order out on the men who are out on bail, requiring them to stay a thousand yards from Marco and me until the court hearing. Apparently they're looking into Hector and Santos and the man they work for. His name is Antonio and he's been under surveillance for a while now, but they don't have enough evidence against him to make an arrest. At this point all we can do is keep our eyes peeled and if something more happens let him know.

While I'm there, we go over all the specifics, the questions I'll be asked and how I should answer. Because they're trying all of them separately their attorneys have requested extensions. Luckily I will only have to give my recollection of the events once during my deposition. I won't actually have to take the stand four different times unless their attorney calls me in for cross-examination.

When I leave the courthouse, I see a text from Hayley letting me know her family's coming for brunch this coming Sunday. This will be my first time meeting somebody's parents, which makes me think about the fact that I don't even really know where Hayley and I stand. That's definitely a conversation we should have soon. I realize it's almost three o'clock and head home to meet Marco at the bus stop since Hayley is working late.

"Hey bud! How was your day?"

"Really good! I wrote an essay in Language Arts and the teacher said I am a natural writer. Want to read it?"

"Sure."

He pulls the essay out of his backpack and hands it to me suddenly looking nervous. I begin reading it. The topic is asking him who he looks up to. The entire essay is about me, and how he wants to be just like me. But what tugs at my heart is the fact that there is barely anything even mentioned about me as a fighter. Every example Marco gave was regarding me as a person. He writes about how much I care and how patient I am when teaching him to fight. He writes about how protective I am, referring to me saving him and Hayley the day in the parking lot. Then he writes about when I gave him twenty dollars to play video games and let him order anything he wanted from the kid's menu. He even says it was one of the best days of his life. Damn, this kid is just so unbelievable. To most kids, twenty bucks at an arcade is a normal occurrence, but to Marco he writes about it like he was taken to Disney Land.

I can't help but get choked up, and when I look over at him to tell him how much his essay means to me, he looks unsure of himself. "Marco, this is the best essay I have ever read. The things you wrote about me..." I have to swallow the lump in my throat so I can continue. "Can I keep this, please?"

His face lights up. "You want to keep my essay? You like it that much?"

"It's the nicest thing anybody has ever written about me." I lean over and hug him hard, not wanting to let go.

"How about we go surprise Hayley at work and steal her away so we can go do something fun?"

"Really?"

"Yeah."

We get to the gym and I look for the guys to say hi to, while Marco runs over to a couple kids who are about to begin a class. I find Cooper, Bentley, and Kaden bullshitting near the locker rooms with Alex and Stephen and a couple other younger guys who train here as well. They're all laughing and making digs at Kaden.

"What's up?" I ask, fist bumping everyone.

"We're all going out tonight and Kaden is acting like a little pussy not wanting to go out," Stephen says with a laugh,

"Yeah," Alex chimes in. "I get those two not wanting to go out," he nods toward Bentley and Cooper. "They're pussy whipped with kids, but supposedly Kaden isn't even getting any from Ashley because they're just friends, yet he'd rather go sit on her couch and hang out then try to catch some tail. What happened to the playboy you used to be?"

Kaden laughs it off. Only a few people know Kaden's story and why he acts the way he does. "First of all, keep Ashley's name out of your mouth and second, I'm getting plenty of pussy, you dick. Worry about your damn self."

Just as he says this, he looks over my shoulder like a deer caught in the headlights as Tristan comes running past us toward the class, and trailing behind him is Ashley. She clearly heard his last comment.

She looks hurt but quickly smiles and laughs, playing it off. "Yeah, don't worry. Kaden hanging out with me is only slightly putting a damper on his little black book. Feel free to go out tonight. I have to work anyway."

She walks away without saying a word and Kaden runs after her not giving a shit that they're about to argue in front of half the gym.

"What do you mean you're working tonight? I thought you only worked two days a week."

"Things changed. I have…bills to pay."

"Do you need me to watch Tristan? What's going on?"

"Nothing is going on. And no, I have a babysitter watching him but thank you." She smiles softly at him and then stands on her tippy toes, giving him a kiss on his cheek before walking away from him. Kaden doesn't go after her this time. He just stands there with his jaw clenched. I'm not sure if he's mad at himself for the comment he stupidly made or mad at her for blowing him off and acting like she didn't care. But either way, it's the most emotion I've seen from him since I've known him.

I say bye to the guys and call Marco over to join me. We find Hayley in her office where she's typing away on the computer not realizing we're watching her. I clear my throat and she jumps.

"Jeez, boys! You scared me."

"We're here to steal you," Marco says.

Hayley laughs at the excitement in his voice.

"And where are you going to take me?"

"Caleb said to do something fun, but he didn't say what."

"Well, okay then. I'm all yours." She shuts down her computer and we take off. While I'm driving I hand her the essay Marco wrote. When she's done reading it, her face is wearing a matching expression to how I feel—complete love. Words don't need to be exchanged to know how much we both love that little boy.

We pull up to *GameWorks* and its clear Marco and Hayley have never been here. It's a huge state of the art arcade that also has a five star restaurant and a bowling alley. When we enter through the doors I buy the biggest package possible that includes dinner, a ridiculous amount of credits for the video games, and a game of bowling for the three of us.

Once I hand Marco and Hayley their cards with the credits on them, we walk inside. Marco stops and looks around taking it all in, and Hayley looks at me, grinning wide, knowing what I'm up to. Marco thought the tiny arcade was so amazing—well, this place blows it away. They aren't even in the same league of arcades.

"We can play any game we want?" Marco asks in shock, never

having seen anything like this before.

"Anything you want, and you earn tickets that will let you pick out prizes at the end. Now lead the way, kid."

His first stop is air hockey. He and Hayley team up against me. Within minutes I'm kicking their asses but they're both cracking up laughing. Hayley tries to put her arm across the goal to block the puck.

"Really? You're going to resort to cheating?" I taunt her.

"I don't know what you're talking about," she says, leaning over the goal and giving me a tiny peek at her ample cleavage.

"Okay, but when the puck bruises your arm I don't want to hear it." I grab the striker and line up the puck, pretending like I'm going to hit it across the table. Hayley's eyes narrow and her head tilts slightly, daring me to try it.

I hit the puck to the left, knowing Marco will hit it, and sure enough he does. He knocks the puck into my goal and they both jump up and down giving each other a high five. They lost miserably, but it doesn't stop them from cheering about Marco's goal. Hayley walks over to me and gives me a peck on my cheek.

"I knew you wouldn't hurt me."

Taking her by her waist, I say softly so only she can hear, "The only thing I ever want to do is bring you happiness, baby."

Her lips curl up into a gorgeous grin that makes my heart melt.

"C'mon, guys!" Marco yells over the noise of the arcade.

We work our way through the various arcade games. We race each other in Mario Cart, challenge each other shooting hoops in Super Shots Basketball, play the classic Skee-ball game where I know Marco distracts me so Hayley can run up and put her ball into the highest slot, and after we're done playing probably every game imaginable, we take our cards and Marco picks out several dozen crappy prizes that he believes are the best prizes ever. We take a gaming break for dinner and afterward, we take Marco bowling for the first time.

When there is nothing left to play or win, we head home and Marco thanks us no less than a dozen times before he passes out in bed.

Hayley and I cuddle on the couch and partake in a hot make out session while watching *The Bachelor.*

"Thank you, Hayles."

"For what? *GameWorks* was all because of you."

"Yeah, but this life…my newfound happiness…it's all because of you."

Nineteen

HAYLEY

IT'S FRIDAY EVENING AND EVERYBODY'S DECIDED TO MEET AT a club on the strip for drinks. While I'm at work I can't help but think about where Caleb and I stand. We haven't had sex yet, but it feels like everything we've done has been even more intimate. The late night talks that lead to the late night kisses and cuddling. If he's able to make my body feel that alive without bringing me to an orgasm, I can't even imagine what will happen when we finally do have sex. My pent up sexual needs are at an all-time high for sure. But I'm letting Caleb run this show even if I die from sexual frustration in the process.

Since I knew I had a late meeting with one of the fighters, I brought a change of clothes with me, and Caleb is dropping Marco off at Bentley's parents' house. Kayla and Ashley are both dropping their kids off there as well. Liz and Cooper are coming out, but his mom is watching their two little ones, wanting some grandma time. As I'm unlocking my car door, I text Caleb to let him know I'll meet him at the club. I'm getting ready to drive off when I notice a piece of paper on my windshield. Ugh! It's probably one of those advertisements to lose weight or for a free dental cleaning. I swing the door open and hop out to grab it from underneath the windshield wiper and shove it into my purse.

I get to the club and valet park. The guy hands me a ticket and I thank him. I spot Caleb waiting for me near the front door and walk up to him. He pulls me into his embrace, giving me a kiss that ends far too soon. We go straight to the bouncer and Caleb must know him because they shake hands and we go right in without having to wait in line.

When we get inside, I see everybody is already here. Kaden and Ashley are sitting together laughing, Bentley has Kayla on his lap, and Liz and Cooper are slow dancing next to the booth. I also notice Alex is there with a couple other guys from the gym. I invited my sister and her fiancé, Gavin, and they're both there talking to Kayla and Bentley. Kayla and Liz both know my sister from her visits over the years. I met Liz and Kayla while working at a bistro with them years ago when I was in medical school.

Caleb and I walk up and everybody's eyes turn to us. I look down nervously, wondering if maybe I have my dress on backward or inside out, but it seems fine. Then I notice Caleb's hand is still in mine, and everybody is staring at our hands. I go to pull my hand away from his, but he grabs ahold of it tighter, giving me an *I don't think so* look. Nobody is sure what to say, so they choose to ignore what is happening and greet us.

Hannah gets up to hug me, but it's a one armed hug since Caleb still won't let go of my hand.

We walk over to Gavin and make introductions. After everybody knows everybody, we find an empty seat and order drinks from the waitress. I go with my favorite, a Lemon Drop martini, and Caleb orders a beer.

"C'mon girls, let's dance!" Kayla yells over the music. She grabs my hand and Liz's with Ashley and Hannah following behind us. We get to the center of the dance floor and the song is one I love. *Somebody* by Natalie La Rose is pumping through the speakers making me want to dance that much more. I get into the song with Ashley. While I can definitely hold my own, this woman has got some serious moves. We're grinding up against each other playfully when a couple of guys come over and ask us to join in. We look at each other, laugh and politely decline, continuing to dance with each other.

After a few minutes I see some of the guys have joined. Kaden steals Ashley away, and since I don't really want to dance with a stranger, I turn to go back to the booth when I run right into Caleb smirking at me. He pulls me close, and even though the song is one people are gyrating to, he slow dances with me.

"The way your body moves is fucking sexy, Hayles," he whispers into my ear. "I want you…tonight." His words send a shudder down my spine. I back up a little to look at him and see the lust in his eyes. I nod and put my head against his chest, continuing to slow dance in the middle of the fast song, not caring about anything other than how much I want this man. His hands go to my ass and he grabs ahold of me pulling me closer into him. I can feel his hard-on rubbing against me making me want to grind on him. When his leg hits my center I can feel how turned on I am as sparks fly straight to my core. I don't just want this man. I need him, like now. He chuckles softly into my ear as if he knows exactly what I'm thinking.

When the song ends and the emcee announces some drink specials before playing the next song, we head back to the booth to get another drink. We all hang out for a few hours, but I don't drink anymore. I want to be fully sober tonight. I want to remember everything. Then I get nervous…We haven't discussed what we are to each other, but hopefully tonight won't be a one-time thing. How should I act? Do I just lie there and let him do everything? I'm probably overthinking this, but I don't want to screw it up.

"What's got you frowning?" Kayla asks nudging me. I confide in her since she knows about Caleb's past.

"You know what you have to do, right?"

"Umm…no…what?"

Her face lights up with mischief. "We need to leave early and handcuff you to the bed!"

I'm unfortunately taking a sip of my drink as she says this so my water sprays all over the place.

"Excuse me?" I whisper, looking around to make sure nobody else heard her.

"Handcuffs…If you're handcuffed, you're giving him one hundred percent control, and then you don't have to worry about what you should be doing. He'll be doing it all."

I hate to admit it but she has a point. "Where would I get handcuffs this late?"

"Oh, I have them in my glove box," Kayla says like it's perfectly normal to have handcuffs in one's glove box. I raise my eyebrows up in question, but she just tells me it's a long story.

She whispers something to Bentley causing him to laugh then she announces our departure, saying she needs me to give her a ride somewhere before I head home. She grabs my phone and texts Caleb to meet me at home in a half hour before dragging me along behind her.

We get to my house and it's pitch black. Caleb must have forgotten to leave the outside light on. I walk inside, flip the light on, and step back outside to make sure it's working when I see that same car parked down the street. I need to remember to let Caleb know. Something is definitely off, and he mentioned getting a threatening note when we got back from Boulder. What if it's the same people? Before I can think any more about it, Kayla dangles the handcuffs in front of my face making me nervous.

"C'mon! Strip down into nothing but your bra and underwear."

"WHAT??" I squeal out.

"If you're handcuffed he won't be able to take your clothes off," she says like *duh!*

I quickly rinse off in the shower and then after taking several calming breaths put on my sexiest bra and panty set and get onto the bed to be handcuffed.

Kayla takes the handcuffs and puts them around the bedpost and then locks them around my wrists loosely. I look at them and see they're made of pink feather-like material so they won't rub my wrists raw.

"I don't even want to know why you have pink feathered handcuffs."

Kayla laughs. "Looking at you all sexy on this bed, if I swung that way I would totally be having my way with you right now."

I crack up laughing. "Get out! I'm going to lose my courage."

"Sorry, girly, but it's a little too late for that. I'll leave the key on the nightstand though."

"Oh God! I can't believe I'm doing this."

Kayla laughs again, shaking her head. "Since Caleb has a key, I'll lock the door on my way out. Good luck!"

"Wait! How are you getting home? We took my car."

"Bentley is outside waiting for me." She winks and then turns off all lights, leaving only the glow of the nightlight from the bathroom. A few seconds later, I hear the door close, leaving me here by myself to do nothing but second-guess myself.

Twenty

CALEB

WHEN KAYLA SAID SHE NEEDED HAYLEY TO TAKE HER somewhere I thought maybe Hayley was trying to get out of being with me. I made it clear to her that I want her tonight, but instead of going home, she's running errands with Kayla? After they ran out, I felt my phone buzz in my pocket.

Hayley: Meet me at home in thirty minutes ;)

Okay, I'm not sure what is going on, but I will definitely be meeting her at home in thirty minutes. Bentley says he needs to get going, but not before slapping me on my back and laughing. "Good luck tonight, bro."

I hang out with everyone else for a few more minutes and then excuse myself for the night. The drive home feels like it takes forever wondering what the hell Hayley is up to.

I get home and walk into the dark, quiet house. "Hayley?" I call out but don't hear anything. I turn on the living room light, so it's not pitch black and make my way to her bedroom first. When I open the door it's dark, but there's a small light shining through, and on the bed I see the most exquisite image laid out right in front of me.

Hayley is spread out on the bed in nothing but a tiny black bra and matching panties. They are nothing more than scraps of material barely covering her, and as I get closer the faint light shows me they're see-through. Her nipples are hard and poking through the cups of her bra and her legs are closed tight together. She looks absolutely breathtaking…and nervous.

"This was Kayla's idea. We thought it would give you control, you know, so I can't touch you. You can touch me and do whatever you want to me. But while I've waiting for you, I started to think, what if me lying here isn't giving you control because I'm initiating the sex by lying here in the first place, but you did say you want me tonight, so technically you initiated it…" She's rambling on, afraid I'm going to push her away, and all I have stuck in my head is the part where she said I could do whatever I want to her. My dick twitches at the sight of this woman handcuffed and willing to make herself completely vulnerable and uncomfortable just to make me comfortable.

I step up next to the bed and lean down to kiss her, mostly to stop her from second-guessing herself, but also because I need to taste her. She tastes of toothpaste with a hint of lemon from her drink earlier. She tastes amazing, and then I wonder what her other lips taste like. My dick twitches again at the thought.

When I break the kiss, she opens her mouth to say something else, but before she can speak I put my fingers to her lips to quiet her, shaking my head.

"You are absolutely breathtaking, baby." She looks down and if the lights were on, I would bet her cheeks are shaded with a light pink tint in embarrassment.

"Don't be embarrassed, Hayles. This is the most selfless, thoughtful thing anybody has done for me."

I remove my shirt and walking boot and then my jeans, leaving myself in only my briefs, and crawl over her to sit on top of her legs.

A flashback begins to hit me…A time from my past when I was in this same position with another woman, but I shake it off immediately. I refuse to let my past ruin this moment. I take in a deep breath and focus on the beautiful woman in front of me.

"Baby, I can't wait to make you scream my name." I reach forward and tweak one of her nipples through her bra. She wiggles and I know she's turned on. I don't really know where to start. Every time I had sex somebody was telling me what to do, what she wanted, what she needed. I never had to think about how to please a woman. I just did what I was told.

Looking at Hayley, all I want is to please her. I want to explore her body and find out for myself what turns her on. I want to see what makes her scream and squirm and orgasm. I want to know every inch of this woman. I lift myself off her and spread her legs so I'm now between them. I lean over her and start with kissing her. If I could spend the rest of my life simply kissing this woman I would be a satisfied man.

While still kissing her, I take one hand and pull her bra cup down, exposing her pert nipple. I break the kiss and move my mouth to her nipple, licking around the tight pink nub. She squirms a little, releasing a soft moan that causes my dick to remind me he's still here. I push the other cup down and lick around her other nipple while pinching the one I'd just licked.

"Oh, Caleb."

Her soft sounds let me know she's enjoying this. I take the bud into my mouth and suck on it. I notice her tits fit perfectly in my hands while I massage them, switching from nipple to nipple, sucking hard on each one and then licking the pain away.

"Caleb, please…" The handcuffs clink against the bedpost as she attempts to move. She wants more. She wants to tell me what she wants, but she stops knowing I need this. I need the control.

I suck on each nipple one more time before I begin to trail kisses down her flat stomach toward her pussy. When I get to it, it's covered with the same fabric as her bra, but it is glistening wet. I touch her middle and feel the wetness covering the material. My girl is dripping for me. I pull her panties down her legs and throw them to the side.

Her pussy is trimmed neatly and all I want to do is put my nose right up to the center to smell her scent…so I do. I inhale deeply and can smell the strawberry scented body wash she uses with a bit of something else that is just her. I spread her lips, so I can lick up her slit and I'm addicted. She moans out my name and her legs try to close. I push them back apart and lick from bottom to top, lapping up her juices.

"Do you like that, Hayles?"

"Yes, please," she says, sounding out of breath.

I push a finger into her and then another. Her ass comes off the bed meeting my thrusts as I fingerfuck her. It's even more fulfilling knowing I'm causing this woman's pleasure by choice and doing as I want to. I take a third finger and push it into her warmth continuing to lick her clit. Moving my fingers inside her in a come-hither motion I feel when I hit her G-spot. She screams out and my fingers are instantly coated with her arousal. I keep moving them inside her while licking and lapping at her clit. Her pussy tightens, so I lick faster and harder until she comes all over my hand and mouth.

"Oh my God! Caleb!" Hayley screams out, but I don't stop my fingers or tongue until she completely rides out her orgasm. Once I know she's satisfied, I grab my shirt from the floor and wipe off her juices. Then I climb up the bed on top of her.

"I want…" she begins to say but stops. That's when it hits me. Everything with this woman is so different. I want to do what she wants. I want to please her. And while I want to be in control, I also want her to be in control. I don't want her to ever not be able to tell me what she wants or needs because of my past. Trying to find my control has caused her to give up her own and that doesn't sit well with me at all. We need to find a balance.

"Tell me, baby. Tell me what you want."

"I want…"

"It's okay. I want to know. Tell me, Hayles."

"I want your dick in my mouth…please."

And if that request doesn't cause my already hard cock to get harder…

I move to release the handcuffs and she stops me. "No, just move up on my chest and put it in my mouth."

Fuck! This woman is just full of surprises. I straddle her upper body and move my cock slowly toward her mouth, not wanting to force it in. She lets out a frustrated huff and a few seconds later her knees hit my ass pushing me closer. Then she lifts her head to take me in her mouth. I move close enough so she can suck me but not too close that I'm choking her. She licks the slit and then swirls her tongue around the head, causing me to almost come on the spot. In my defense, it's been over seven years since I've been with a woman, and never one I wanted as badly as I want Hayley.

She takes me in farther and I know if I let her continue I'm going to explode in her mouth.

"Baby, stop." I back away and undo the handcuffs before climbing back on top of her. I need to make love to this woman and I need her hands on me.

Her hands are freed, but she lies still, unsure of what to do.

"Thank you for tonight. For giving me the control. But I was wrong, Hayles. I want you to be in control, too. I want you to touch me. Please, baby."

I see tears glossing over her eyes and then one falls down the side of her cheek. I bring my lips to her cheek to kiss the fallen tear, as I slowly push into her.

"Wrap your arms around my neck, baby." And she does. Her arms come up around my neck tightly as her legs wrap around my back, pushing my cock into her, and for the first time in my life I make love to a woman willingly.

Twenty-One

HAYLEY

I CAN FEEL THE SUN HITTING MY FACE SO IT MUST BE MORNING. I stretch my body and can feel the soreness between my legs. After Caleb made love to me, we showered together and once back in bed made love again before falling asleep wrapped in each other's arms. Sometime early this morning my phone went off waking us up. It was Ashley letting me know she's picking up the kids and will pick up Marco as well so we can sleep in. I was so exhausted I immediately fell back asleep.

Now I'm awake and when I look over I see the bed is empty next to me. Caleb must have already woken up. I jump in the shower quickly and while I'm washing myself it hits me we didn't use protection nor am I on birth control. I highly doubt I'll get pregnant from one night of unprotected sex, but isn't that what everyone says before they find out they're having an *Oops! Baby?*

I make a mental note to pick up condoms until I can get on birth control. I inhale deeply and smell the coffee beckoning me. I throw a shirt on and grab a pair of underwear from my drawer before following the aroma of caffeine. I also remind myself I need to let Caleb know we didn't use protection. When I get to the kitchen, he's sitting at the table with a piece of paper in front of him, looking pissed off.

"What's up?" I ask, ignoring the coffee calling my name and forgetting the birth control talk we needed to have.

"Why didn't you tell me about this?" he growls, causing me to stop in my tracks.

I look at the paper that looks like the one I grabbed off my windshield last night and read what it says. I was wrong. It's not an advertisement…it's a handwritten threat.

SNITCHES GET STITCHES. TELL YOUR BOYFRIEND TO BACK OFF OR YOU'LL BOTH

REGRET IT.

I drop the note on the table and feel myself shaking. "Caleb, I didn't know it said this. I thought it was an ad, like for weight loss or something. It was on my windshield when I got into my car last night. I threw it into my purse without looking at it. Is that where you got it? My purse?"

His anger morphs into worry and he pulls me onto his lap. "I'm sorry, Hayles. I thought you saw this and kept it from me. Yes, I got it from your purse. I was moving it from the counter to the desk to make coffee and it fell over. The note fell out. We have to report this to the police. This is a threat. Just like the one I found at the airport. My guess is, this is Hector and Santos trying to scare us so I won't testify against the guys who tried to kill me. Get dressed and we'll go by the station before we pick up Marco."

After bringing the note to the station and reporting the threat, where they said they can run fingerprints but can't really do much because it could be from anyone, we go to Ashley's to pick up Marco. When she answers the door, her eyes look red and puffy like she's been crying, so I ask Caleb to go check on the boys to give us a minute alone.

"What's going on?"

She slumps in defeat and the tears start again.

"Kaden and I almost had sex last night, but he totally pulled the brakes on it when things got hot and heavy. I just don't get it. He's with women all the time, but he won't sleep with me. It just doesn't make sense. I'm so stupid. I know we aren't anything more than friends. I never should have let things get that far. Hopefully he'll act like it never happened. He has become one of my best friends.

Then we got into a fight this morning when I told him I wouldn't take money from him when he saw a couple of my bills on the counter. I can't let him pay for my mistakes. We aren't even together. I'm just so exhausted from working two jobs. I'm tired of having to have my parents and the babysitter watch Tristan so often, but it's what I need to do."

Ashley seems to purposely leave out what bills she needs to pay, so I don't press her. I wrap her up in a hug and tell her it'll be okay not really sure if that's true but not sure of what else to say. We hear the loud footsteps approaching and when we look up Caleb is standing in the doorway.

"What's wrong?" Caleb asks, clearly worried for Ashley.

"Umm…" I'm not sure what she wants him to know, so I give her a look telling her to tell him what she wants.

"Why won't Kaden sleep with me?" she blurts out.

Caleb's eyes go wide with shock and maybe even a bit of nervousness before he quickly composes himself. "Ashley, I can assure you Kaden really does care about you, however, I can't answer that question for you. That's Kaden's story to tell."

Ashley and I exchange confused glances, but Caleb walks away calling out to Marco it's time to go, making it clear he's not going to say anything else on the topic.

"That's interesting…So Kaden has a story to tell?" I whisper to Ashley.

"I have no idea," she says clearly as puzzled as I am.

"Ready to go?" Caleb asks with Marco by his side. Tristan plops onto the couch and begins to flip through the channels.

"Hey, sweetie!" I give Marco a kiss on his cheek and hug him tightly. I missed him last night. He has become a part of us and when he isn't around, it feels like a piece is missing.

I hug Ashley once more goodbye.

"Call me if you need anything," I whisper to her.

"Thank you."

After leaving Ashley's house, we decide to stop at a local restaurant for lunch and to figure out what to do the rest of the day. Grabbing a newspaper, Caleb looks at what is going on locally. While flipping through the pages the real estate section falls out causing me to ask the question I don't really want to ask but know I need to.

"Have you looked at any apartments?"

Before Caleb can answer, Marco grabs the paper. "What do you mean? Who's moving?"

Caleb takes the paper from Marco. "Nobody, buddy. We aren't moving anywhere."

"Oh, good. I like where we live. Plus you guys just painted my room. You would have to paint it again. And if we move, I would have to switch schools and I like my school."

"We aren't moving anywhere and you definitely don't have to switch schools, but Caleb…" Before I can finish my sentence, Caleb cuts me off.

"Nobody is moving anywhere." Caleb glares at me and balls the paper up. "Now let's figure out what to do today." He's shut down the conversation of moving just like he shut down the conversation regarding Kaden. While Kaden isn't my business, he must know our living situation is and it's something we need to discuss. Maybe he just wants to wait to discuss it until we are alone.

"There's indoor miniature golf, Hershey's Chocolate World, The Children's park, or the Aquarium."

Marco gives it some thought. "Can we go to the aquarium? But can we invite Bella? She loves dolphins and I know she would love it."

"Sure," Caleb says. "Let me call Liz and Cooper and see what they're up to today."

He gives them a call and since they have no plans they join us.

And that's how we spend our day, at the aquarium as a family. I wonder in this moment if life can possibly get any better.

Twenty-Two

CALEB

AFTER I PUT A STOP TO THE APARTMENT HUNTING TALK, WE enjoyed the rest of our day at the aquarium. Sure it's probably not a good idea to ignore the obvious, like the fact that I'm capable of living on my own and shouldn't be shacking up with a woman I may or may not be in a relationship with, but can you blame me? When everyone you want and need is under the same roof, who in his right mind would want to move out from under said roof? Sure as hell not me.

I'm not ignorant to believe by ignoring the facts they'll go away, but I'm hoping maybe I can come up with a plan to keep myself under the same roof as the two most important people in my life, especially with the recent threat to Hayley. It's even more important I continue to live with them…for their safety, of course.

Being at the aquarium with Marco is like experiencing everything again for the first time. He has got to be one of the most grateful, innocent kids I've ever met. He's truly thankful for everything he is given. It just sucks he's come to be this way because of the shitty life he was raised in. I would rather him be a spoiled brat than him having witnessed his druggie mom being raped and then committing suicide.

Every single time Hayley or I bought him something he would light up like he was being given the most incredible gift. It made me want to just keep buying him stuff to see his face light up. We walked around the aquarium all day with Cooper and his family and as I compared us to them I realized to the naked eye we look just like them—a family. And that is exactly what I want—a family with Hayley. Biological or not, I don't care, as long as it's with her, and Marco is a part of it.

We get home and Marco showers and passes out from exhaustion. We both fall onto the couch equally exhausted and laugh. I could listen to her laugh forever.

"Your family will be here in like twelve hours for brunch. We should probably get some sleep." But even hearing myself say these words, I don't believe them.

"Mmm…I know, but I just want to cuddle with you." And if by cuddle she means rubbing her palm on top of my dick making it jump, then cuddling is definitely what we're about to do.

"Can you be quiet?" I whisper into her ear. A slow mischievous smile creeps across her face and she nods. I stand and, taking her hand in mine, guide her to the room and close the door behind us.

We aren't even all the way in the room before she's pulling her clothes off her body while I'm doing the same to mine. She finishes quicker and before I can push my boxers down she grabs hold of them and pushes them down for me, her body going to the floor with them. Out of instinct, I almost push her off me but catch myself at the last second. My head hits the back of the door with a thump and I close my eyes for a second to calm myself down. A flashback hits of a woman giving me head and I have to open my eyes to remind myself it's Hayley and not another woman in this moment with me.

I look down at Hayley on her knees before me as she takes my cock in her hand and, after kissing the tip and swirling her tongue around the head, deep throats me like she doesn't have a gag reflex.

My hips thrust forward as the pleasure of her mouth assaults me causing me to almost come on the spot. Not wanting to come in her mouth in two seconds, I reach down and force her mouth off my dick, picking her up and tossing her onto the bed on her stomach, ass in the air. I land a playful smack to her ass cheek when another flashback assaults me of the last time I had sex in Boulder, but I shake it off willing my brain to remain in the here and now with Hayley. She deserves my full attention.

She looks back at me with a smirk and then wiggles her ass without saying a word. Lying down on the bed, I lift her pussy up into the air a little more and then attack her clit with my tongue from behind. I lick and suck and then move the juices with my tongue to her ass, sticking one finger into her tight hole. I feel her tighten up and know she hasn't been taken there. It's probably a horrible thought to have but knowing she's never been claimed in the ass makes me want to try to replace my old memories with new ones that are with Hayley.

I go back to licking her pussy and sucking on her clit until she's coming all over my mouth.

"Baby, I'm going to claim your ass." She doesn't give me anything but a moan, letting me know she is down. Knowing her juices won't be enough, I grab some KY jelly from the drawer and smear it onto my dick and into her tight hole. I start off by sticking one finger back in her ass, fingering it slowly.

"I need more," she begs, so I give her more. I add another digit and continue fingerfucking her ass. I reach over and have her sit up straight so I can massage her tits. Pinching her nipple, she shivers and begins to ride my fingers with her ass, needing a release.

Once I know she's ready, I remove my fingers from her ass and replace them with my dick, slowly lowering Hayley onto me until she's taken me all the way inside of her. I bring my hands to her breasts and massage them.

She wiggles her ass, needing me to move, but instead of me being in control, I give it to her.

"Ride my dick, Hayles. Move up and down." And she does. She begins to bounce her ass on my cock and fuck if it doesn't feel good in her tight ass. Bringing my hand down from one of her breasts, I fingerfuck her to the same rhythm she's bouncing on my dick. I add another digit and one more and within minutes she's coming all over my fingers. "Oh my God, Caleb. I feel so full." Her orgasm causes her to push down farther onto my dick and within seconds I'm releasing my seed into her.

We both come to a stop, and moving her sweaty hair off her shoulder, I give her a kiss on her neck before she pulls herself off me.

"Shower with me?"

"I wouldn't have it any other way, baby." I give her a kiss and we make our way to the shower where we end up making love against the wall.

Twenty-Three

HAYLEY

AFTER WE HAVE SEX UP AGAINST THE SHOWER WALL, CALEB washes my body from head to toe and then I gladly return the favor. Once the water goes cold, we get out and Caleb runs to his room to grab a change of clothes. While I'm drying off I feel the excess of cum in me. I can't believe we seriously forgot to use protection again. I'm a freaking doctor for God's sake. I know the risks.

When Caleb comes into my room, dressed, he can tell right away something is wrong.

"We didn't use protection," I blurt out.

"I'm clean, Hayles. I was tested after I left Boulder years ago and you're the only person I've been with since then. Wait…have you been with someone else? Alex?"

"Whoa there! Back up. I haven't been with anybody but you. My point is I'm not on birth control and we had unprotected sex several times. I know better than this."

He just shrugs "Oh."

"Oh? What do you mean 'Oh'?"

"You said it yourself, Hayles…you're getting older…"

I'm in the middle of putting on my comfy reading socks when he says this and my head whips around to glare at him. "Excuse me?"

He throws his head back with a laugh. "I'm just kidding, babe." He walks over and sits next to me, turning my head to face him. "I'm just saying if you get pregnant, would it really be that bad? You said you wanted to have a baby…"

"So I shouldn't get on birth control?" I ask, just making sure I'm hearing him correctly.

"No, and if it happens it happens."

"But we aren't even together, Caleb…"

"Yes, we are. You're mine and I'm yours, Hayles. I have already told you that before. I'm not going anywhere, ever."

"Okay," I say, trying to remain calm and not run through the streets shouting that Caleb just said he's mine. Instead, I give him a chaste kiss on his lips and say, "I like the sound of that." Then we climb into my bed and he holds me close. We lie in silence for a few minutes and I think he might be asleep when he says, "You know how you mentioned talking to your sister for me? If she agrees to help me, I'm going to have to tell her my story."

I roll over to face him and, taking his chin in my fingers, give him a soft kiss. "She isn't going to judge you."

"I know. I just don't know how I'll feel if I have to start telling everybody especially in the open, like in court."

"What's really going on, Caleb?"

"What if everybody finds out and thinks I'm a pussy? I spent years fucking women. Most guys would high five each other over it, not cry rape."

My blood boils at the way he thinks people would view what happened to him. "Anybody who would want to high five someone for being blackmailed and forced to have sex at fifteen years old needs some serious help. Nobody that matters will think any less of you, and I'll be there every step of the way."

Caleb nods and gives me one more kiss before rolling me back over to spoon me from behind. Within minutes I can hear the evenness of his breathing and know he's asleep. I vow to myself, if I ever get the chance, I will destroy Gloria for what she's done to Caleb.

I wake up to an empty bed and hear cartoons on the television out in the living room. Caleb must have let me sleep in and gotten up with Marco. After showering and getting dressed, I make my way out to join my guys.

"Morning sleepyhead," I say to Marco, fluffing his hair as I walk by him cuddled up in his blankets, barely awake, watching cartoons. I head to the kitchen to grab a pen and paper to make a list of items we need for brunch. Before I make it to the kitchen, Caleb grabs me by my waist and pulls me toward him. I bend over and give him a kiss without thinking about it.

"Are you two boyfriend and girlfriend?" Marco asks, obviously seeing the kiss.

Caleb looks at me then to Marco. "Would it be okay with you if we were?"

Marco rolls his eyes. "I told you a long time ago you wanted to give her cooties."

I'm not sure what he's talking about but I can't help but laugh.

"Yeah, yeah. Marco told me months ago I liked you."

"Smart kid." I give Caleb a wink and make my list.

Marco and I head to the store while Caleb picks up the house and waits for everyone to arrive. After walking up and down the aisles and me agreeing to get all the junk food Marco suggests, we head to the register to check out. After bagging up the groceries, Marco pushes our cart to the car. My phone dings with a text, so I check it.

Hannah: On our way! See you soon.

Me: Sounds good!

I'm hoping Hannah will be able to help Caleb get the clubs from his stepmom, so he'll be rid of her for good, but that would mean he would have to tell her everything. I'm not sure he'll be comfortable doing that.

I look up from my text and run right into the back of Marco. When I begin to ask why he's stopped, I glance around him and see words written across the side of my vehicle.

LAST WARNING BITCH!

Instinctively, my hands grab Marco's shoulders. While scanning the area for any sign of threat, I practically drag him and the cart back to the store. Once we're inside, I call Caleb.

"Hello?" he answers on the first ring.

"I need you," I say, trying to hold back my tears. I need to be strong for Marco. I don't want to scare him.

"What's wrong?" he practically shouts, hearing the fear in my voice.

"We're at the store and someone wrote on my car. I need you to come and get us. I don't know what to do."

"I will be right there. Stay in the store, in plain sight. Okay? I'm going to three-way the police, so we don't have to get off the phone." Caleb calls the police and tells them to meet him at the store.

Once Caleb and the police arrive, they take pictures and ask questions. They say they're going to ask the store about cameras to see if they can see who did it.

"Why are they threatening me?" I ask the officers on scene. I'm not even the one testifying against them. I wasn't there. Only Caleb is testifying. Marco is underage, so he gave his statement, but we agreed it's best for him not to testify.

"My guess is they're hoping the threats will force Caleb to drop the charges out of fear for you."

"Which I won't do," Caleb says, putting his arm around me and pulling Marco into his side.

"The court date has been moved up because the prosecutor found significant evidence of drug trafficking and is ready to nail several of the guys," the officer says. "I think this is their way of trying to get Caleb to back down. With his testimony to the attempted murder charges, these guys will be going away for a long time."

Caleb offers to take my car through a car wash on his way home and insists I take his truck home with Marco.

We get home just as my parents are pulling in. I don't want to worry them, so I don't bring up why we're running late. They help me bring in the groceries and then I make introductions.

"Marco, this is my mom and dad, Lori and Bill. Mom, Dad, this is Marco."

My mom grabs Marco in a hug and tears spring to her eyes. Even though she hasn't met him yet she's listened to me talk about him the last couple months and has seen all the photos I've posted and sent her. She already views him as her grandson.

"Nonsense! You call me Nana and him Pop." She continues to wrap Marco in a hug until I insist she let him go so he can breathe.

"I don't really mind," Marco says with tears shining in his eyes. The thought of a child crying because of receiving love and affection makes me want to pull his mother out of the grave and beat her, but I stop the thoughts because the truth is she was sick. She had a lot of problems and wasn't given the chance or opportunity to fix them. I can't waste my energy being mad at her. I just want to feel blessed I get to have Marco in my life.

Caleb walks in and sees all of us practically in tears and looks horrified.

"What the hell happened?"

"Nothing," I say, laughing through my tears. "My mom was just very excited to finally meet Marco. Mom, Dad, this is Caleb. Caleb, this is my mom and dad."

"Nice to finally meet you, Bill and Lori." He gives my dad a handshake and then gives my mom a kiss on her cheek.

There's a knock at the door and in walks Hannah and Gavin with presents in their hands. Hannah has met Marco several times and insisted he call her Aunt Hannah once she found out I'm adopting him.

"Hey, kiddo!" Hannah hands him the gifts and gives him a hug.

"Are these for me? But it's not my Birthday." Marco looks confused.

"I don't need a reason to buy my favorite nephew gifts. Now go open them!"

My mom says she's going to the kitchen to start brunch and insists we all hang out while she cooks. Since Marco is busy with the new stuff Hannah and Gavin brought him, I mention to Hannah about Caleb needing an attorney.

"So, it's not really my story to tell but Caleb was left some clubs his dad owned, and his stepmom is fighting him for them. Do you think it would be possible to help him?"

"I can pay you of course," Caleb says. Hannah waves him off.

Money is the last thing she needs. Gavin comes from old money and between the two of them being attorneys they're not struggling to make ends meet.

"Caleb, why don't you come and see me this week?" She hands him her card. "We can sit down and discuss your options." She looks at her phone and then says, "Actually I have a cancellation for tomorrow morning. Would that work for you?" He looks over the card and then to me. "Yes, we'll be there," I tell her.

"Thank you," Caleb adds.

"Hayley! Look what Aunt Hannah got me!" Marco waves a pad of paper and colored pencils in the air. He had mentioned he loved coloring to us one day at lunch and of course she remembered.

"Thank you so much!" He runs over and gives her a hug.

"You're very welcome, kiddo."

Hannah and I join mom in the kitchen to help her finish up brunch while the guys set the table and pour drinks. Once the food is set out and we're about to dig in, Hannah says they have an announcement to make.

"So, we were hoping to do the whole engagement, marriage, then baby thing in order but…"

"Oh my God!" Mom yells, springing from her seat to give Hannah and Gavin a hug.

"Yep! We're expecting. I'm only three months along, but we have decided to move the wedding up so we're married before the baby comes."

"Congratulations!" I say, getting up to give each of them a hug. My dad and Caleb both congratulate them as well. We all start eating, when Marco says, "So that's what it takes to have a baby? You just have to be together?"

I drop my fork on my plate and look to Caleb for help. But of course he has a shit-eating grin on his face. He's such a damn guy. I guess I'll be handling this one myself.

"It's more than that. Two people have to love each other and when they're ready, they choose to share a bed and they create a baby."

He nods and goes back to eating. I hold my breath, hoping he's done. I definitely plan to have the sex talk with him, but I'm hoping this will pacify him while we're all eating and we can discuss this in private.

"Okay, so does that mean you and Caleb are going to have a baby since you guys shared a bed and you're boyfriend and girlfriend?"

Oh my word! He just had to go there. He is lucky I love his cute little behind.

Caleb cracks up laughing until I give him a death glare. He attempts to control his smile, but I can still see it peeking through.

"You and Caleb are together?"

"When did this happen?"

"How did I not know?"

Between my mom, dad, and Hannah, I'm being bombarded with questions that I have no idea how to answer. What I would like to do is take a biscuit and chuck it at Caleb's head. I grab ahold of the biscuit in one hand and just as I'm about to take aim and fire, he takes my hand in his and smiles warmly.

First, he answers Marco's question. "Marco, there's a little bit more to creating a baby, and after Nana and Pop and everyone leave, we'll sit down and discuss it, okay? As for right now, no we're not having a baby."

Then he says, "And yes, Hayles and I are dating, and yes, we slept in the same bed last night. I care a lot about her."

Everybody seems to accept his answer and thankfully goes back to eating. I look over at him and he leans in and whispers, "And I fully plan to practice those baby making skills…Every. Single. Night."

His words cause my cheeks to heat and I quickly look around grateful nobody heard him. I squirm a little in my seat and he chuckles next to me, then reaches over and takes a bite out of the biscuit I had envisioned hitting him on the side of the head with.

Twenty-Four

CALEB

IT'S MONDAY MORNING. AFTER PUTTING MARCO ON THE BUS, Hayley and I head downtown to her sister's office to speak with her. On our way I stop at the bank to get the recording my dad left for me in the safety deposit box. I figure if Hannah is going to hopefully represent me she should be aware of all the evidence I can bring to the table in hope of Gloria dropping her lawsuit for the two clubs. And I'm hoping we can get her to drop them sooner rather than later. There are employees that need to work to make a living and if we don't figure this out soon I'm going to eventually have to dish out more money to keep them employed.

After I run in to get the recording, which was exactly where my dad said he left it, we go to Hannah's office. Once inside, she ushers us straight back to her office and closes the door.

"Okay, what do you have for me?"

How do I even begin to explain all this? Thankfully Hayley is here and takes over.

"Caleb received two clubs from his father when he passed away. Technically his stepmom ran them, but his dad owned them outright and left them to Caleb. Now his stepmom, Gloria, is fighting for them."

"Okay...what am I missing?" She's a lawyer—of course she senses there is more to the story. And she isn't asking Hayley—she's asking me.

I clear my throat and then proceed to tell her everything—starting with my stepmom forcing me to have sex with her at fifteen to her pimping me out to other women.

"And you said your dad left you a recording of her confessing?"

"Yeah." I pull the flash drive out of my pocket and hand it to her. "I haven't heard it yet. I just grabbed it out of the safety deposit box on my way over."

"Do you mind?"

"No, go ahead."

She plugs it into the side of her computer and, after clicking on the file, presses play. I hear my dad's voice come over the speakers. It's crystal clear like he knew he would be recording.

"Gloria, I want a divorce."

"I don't really think that's what you want, Adam. I would hate to have to turn you in for insider trading."

"I don't care what you do anymore. I can't be with you knowing you forced my son to have sex with you and then forced him to have sex with other women. It's disgusting. I should have divorced you sooner."

"Don't be mad because he was better in bed than you! And give me a break. I'm less than ten years older than him. You're almost twenty years older than me, Adam."

"That's true, but you had sex with him when he was fifteen years old, Gloria! You were of legal age when we got together. And then when I caught you guys, you made it sound like it was entirely his fault. None of this was his fault. I lost my son because of you."

"No, Adam. You lost your son because you are self-centered and chose to save yourself over him."

Hannah hits stop on the computer. "Well, I would say we have enough to definitely scare the shit out of her, and if she still wants to go to court, between the letter from your dad, the will, and the recording, we have a very strong case. What you need to understand, though, is if this goes to court it will become public knowledge about you being raped and used as a male escort. Are you okay with that?"

I know what she's saying. In today's society a man being raped isn't the same as a woman being raped. As a UFC fighter, the attention this will get will be ridiculous, even if I'm not extremely popular. This is exactly what I said to Hayley, but when Hayley told me she would be by my side I knew my decision. I'm not letting Gloria get away with this.

"I understand and I'm willing to deal with the shit storm that will follow. I can't let her win. Let's hope she walks away without fighting."

"Okay, I'll file a response with the court requesting mediation and hopefully when she sees the evidence laid out against her she'll be smart enough to cut her losses and walk away."

"What should I do about paying the employees? I've had to pay them all for several weeks now. It was only supposed to be one week then it turned to two. Now I've been paying them for weeks."

"I'll also put in that if she chooses to take it to trial she'll need to pay half of the employees' incomes while the clubs assets are frozen. I'll give you a call once I know anything."

Damn, she's good.

"Thank you so much. If you need anything from me please let me know. Who do I see to pay your retainer fee?"

"Don't be silly, Caleb. We're practically family. Family doesn't charge family."

"Thanks, Hannah."

Hannah comes around her desk and gives Hayley a hug and then we head out.

After we leave the office, Hayley says she's going to pick up Marco from the bus and then she needs to go to the gym to meet with a couple fighters.

"I think I'll join you guys. Kayla mentioned I'm allowed to do light workouts again."

"Okay, sounds good. Let's go home first, so you can change and grab your gym gear."

Once we get home, I run into my room to grab some workout clothes. I'm walking through the house half-dressed checking my phone when Hayley stops me.

"You can't walk around the house like that Caleb. It's not fair. You're such a tease."

"How long do we have until we need to get Marco?"

She glances at her watch. "Not long…like half an hour."

"I know a lot we can do with that time." I pick her up over my good shoulder and, giving her ass a smack, bring her into the room, where I spend the next thirty minutes proving to her I'm not a tease.

Once we get to the gym, Hayley takes off to her office to get some work done, Marco heads to the ring to check out the guys fighting, and I head to the treadmill to warm up.

"Well, look who it is." Kaden jumps on the treadmill next to me. "You ready to get back to training, yet?"

"I'm getting there. Doc said I could do a light workout, but no fighting yet. I need to strengthen my leg and shoulder first, plus my chest still hurts like a bitch."

"Well I'm ready when you are," Kaden says, staring down at his phone. Whatever he's reading must piss him off because he shoves it back into his pocket and turns up the speed so fast one would think he's trying to literally run from whatever is bothering him.

"You good?" I ask, trying not to sound like a gossiping little girl.

"Yeah, just dealing with a stubborn ass woman."

I laugh at that. "Ashley?"

"Yeah, she's working as a cocktail waitress at a shitty strip club to make extra money instead of letting me help her out with her bills. Like I said…Stubborn."

"She was crying the other day when we went to get Marco from her house. Some shit about you two almost fucking, but you stopped it…" I just let that hang there.

Kaden winces slightly at my words then lets out a strangled breath. "Fuck, man…She's my best friend. I'm not about to treat her like all the other no-named women I've hooked up with over the years. She deserves better than a drunken fuck."

"Better like more…like you want to be with her?" Yeah, we totally sound like chicks right now.

"No, like I don't do the whole wife and kids shit. She's my friend and that's the way it needs to stay. If I fuck her, it'll ruin everything and that's not going to happen."

It's common knowledge Kaden was married at some point years ago. So he definitely did the wife shit, but this was all before I met him. Whatever went down must have been bad because he doesn't discuss it and he always makes it clear he will never settle down again.

A few minutes later Bentley and Kayla walk over. She's holding Chloe, and Bentley is holding Faith. Kaden and I both stop running to say hi.

"We have some great news!" Kayla says.

"Oh yeah? What's that?" Kaden asks. We both wipe the sweat off our hands and face before grabbing the babies from their parents. I can easily imagine Hayley and I having one of these one day soon. Faith coos and giggles at me as I hold her above my head and blow raspberries on her belly.

"DCF approved for us to adopt Chloe! We go before the judge next week to make it official."

"That's amazing!" Hayley says, coming over and giving Kayla and Bentley each a hug.

Marco joins us and takes his sister from Kaden, giving her kisses on her cheeks. She smiles and coos at Marco.

"I'll still be able to see her, right?" he asks Kayla.

Her eyebrows furrow and she steps closer to Marco. "If I didn't know how much Hayley and Caleb love you and how much you love living with them, Bentley and I would be adopting you and your sister together. You are welcome to visit her any time you want, Marco, and she will *always* know you are her brother and how much you love her. I will always be grateful to you. You brought her into our life. You cared for her when your mom wasn't able to."

Her answer seems to make him happy, but it upsets Hayley. "Marco, do you want Kayla to adopt you? Do you want to be with your sister? I would never want you to be away from her if you want to be with her. I know you originally said you wanted to live with me, but I will understand if you want to live with her now." Hayley's eyes fill with tears but she wills them not to spill over, trying to stay strong for Marco.

She looks at me and my heart breaks for her. She loves him so much she would do anything to make him happy, even if that means giving him up before she even adopts him.

"Marco, sweetie. If you want to live with Kayla, I promise I won't be mad."

I walk over to Hayley and put my arm around her.

"Please don't cry," Marco says, giving her a hug.

"Hey, bud, listen. She isn't crying because she's mad. She loves you and wants you to be happy."

"It makes me happy living with you guys. I don't want to leave. I just wanted to make sure I could still see Chloe all the time like I do now." He hugs Hayley again.

She sniffles. "I'm so glad you want to live with us and you will always be able to see Chloe any time you want."

"Well, on that note, I think we should all go out to dinner and celebrate," Bentley says, breaking up the emotional tension.

"I agree!"

"But after my MMA class," Marco chimes in. We all laugh and head over to the kids' ring to watch their class. Since I got hurt, Cooper has been running most of the classes and when we get over there we see him and Bella warming up with a few other kids.

"Hey Marco!" Bella calls out, waving him over. Marco runs over to her and warms up with her.

Kaden spots Ashley dropping off Tristan and goes to speak to her. I'm not sure what is being said, but they almost look like a couple arguing. She shakes her head and then storms out of the gym.

Kaden comes back over and rubs his palms over his face clearly agitated. I can't help but laugh. The guy almost never loses his composure. Then again he's usually the one in control. Hopefully he'll realize soon how bad he has it for Ashley.

While we're watching the kids' MMA class my phone goes off with a text from Hannah.

Hannah: Mediation set for Friday at 9 a.m.

Me: That was quick.

Hannah: When I petitioned for Gloria to pay half the employees' wages her attorney agreed to speed things up. Friday was the soonest I could get. If all goes well you should have the clubs in your possession by Friday afternoon.

Me: Thanks!

Hannah: No problem!

"What has you smiling?" Hayley asks.

"Your sister got mediation set up for Friday. It might all be over by Friday afternoon."

"That's great, Caleb." She gives me a small kiss. Before she can pull away, I grab ahold of her and deepen it. I don't care where we are. I can't control myself when I'm around this woman.

The guys all call out insults and tell us to get a room.

"Leave him alone." Kayla laughs. "He has years of celibacy to make up for."

Everybody laughs and I ignore them all, grabbing my woman for another kiss. I definitely have a lot of time to make up for.

We all decide to go to a local bar and grill to celebrate the adoption of Chloe. After we're all done eating the girls decide to take the kids home and have a late night play date and gossip session. The guys end up hanging out here at the bar to watch some basketball. Since we knew we would be drinking we agreed to have the ladies take the vehicles home and we would grab a taxi once we are done.

After Kaden slams his phone down on the bar for the millionth time, Bentley says, "Man, I don't know what's going on with you and Ashley, but maybe you need to find a way to release some of that pent up tension. It's not like you to be wound so tight."

Kaden glares at him. "I didn't see you sleeping all over town when you and Kayla were having issues. Plus, Ashley and I are just friends."

Bentley puts his hands up. "Whoa, there. Nobody said anything about having sex. I was thinking you need to go a few rounds at the gym…but if sex is on your mind, I see a pretty little thing looking in our direction and out of the four of us you're the only single one."

We all look over to see who Bentley is talking about and that's when I see her…Gloria, and she's looking our way. As soon as she makes eye contact, she saunters over. I've had too many drinks to deal with this woman, but it looks like I don't have a choice. "Cooper, call a cab, now."

"Well, hello there, stranger." Gloria steps into my personal space. She grabs my bicep and squeezes. Because I'm damn near drunk, it takes me a second to get caught up, but once I see her hands on me, I push her away.

"Don't touch me. We were just leaving." I throw down enough bills to cover our drinks and get up from the stool about to walk around her, but she steps in front of me. The alcohol is definitely slowing me down.

"I just want to talk. Maybe we can work something out regarding the clubs." She trails a finger down my arm. To an outsider it looks like a pretty woman flirting with a man. To me, it's my rapist threatening me once again, and although I'm drunk, it sobers me up enough to stop this.

I move her fingers off me and grab her by her arms roughly, setting her on the bar stool I was just sitting on. The guys are all staring at the scene in front of them not saying a word. "Are you fucking serious right now? Wasn't forcing me to fuck you and then pimping me out for money enough for you? Do you have any idea the shit storm you have created in my fucked up head? I'm going to take you to court and let every fucking person know about your pedophile cunt ass."

For a second she looks shocked, but the bitch quickly composes herself. "Nobody would believe you. I'm a woman and you are a man, a man who beats people up for a living. What proof do you have?"

I almost blurt out I have a recording of her confession safely locked away but decide to keep that information to myself. I can't wait to see the look in her eyes on Friday. Looking at this nasty cunt all I want to do is get home to Hayley and Marco.

"I'll see you in court," I say and then turn and walk out of the bar with the guys following after me. Luckily the cab driver is waiting for us in front of the bar, so we're able to get right in and give him the address to Bentley's place, where all the women are.

The entire ride is silent. They obviously all heard the conversation. I'm not sure if I should bring it up or pretend it didn't happen. I thought maybe Kayla would have told Bentley after I told her. I wouldn't ask her to keep a secret from her husband, but she insisted it would stay between us. I guess she meant what she said and didn't tell him.

Cooper pays the cab driver, and as we're all walking up to Bentley's house, the three of them stop and wait for me to say something.

"I don't know what you guys want me to say."

"The truth," Kaden says.

"My dad fucked up, did some illegal insider trading, my stepmom found out and blackmailed me into having sex with her and other women for a few years. He died and left me everything. She's fighting with me over a couple of clubs."

"Damn, man. I honestly thought all those years you were gay," Bentley says with a laugh.

Cooper hits him in the stomach. "Look, what she did was shitty. I hate that you felt you had to hide it from us. We would have been there for you."

"You were. All three of you were. You barely knew me, but you took me away from that place. The day you offered me a way out was the last time I had to have sex against my will. You three saved me. You just didn't realize it. I will always be grateful to you guys."

Each one of them gives me a hug. Nothing else ever has to be said. We have each other's backs and always will.

AFTER EVERYBODY HEADS OUT AND WE SAY GOODNIGHT TO Marco, I jump in the shower to rinse off. The thought of Gloria's hands on me earlier at the bar makes me want to scrub my body until it's raw. Once I'm clean enough, I switch the water off, grab a towel, and step out of the shower.

When I look up from drying my bottom half off, Hayley is leaning against the bathroom sink wearing only a white lacy bra and matching panties, looking fucking gorgeous. I can see her dark pink nipples poking out through the thin material and I want nothing more than to put my mouth on them…So I do. Dropping my towel, I stalk over to her, pick her up and place her on top of the counter, then take one of her pert nipples into my mouth. I suck on it for a few seconds and then give the other one the same attention. Hayley moans loudly, squeezing her legs together around me.

"Baby, you have to be quiet. Marco just fell asleep." She nods in understanding.

Taking both breasts out of the cups of her bra I bring them together and put both her nipples into my mouth at the same time sucking hard. Her hands fist into my hair as she pulls my face even closer to her chest moaning softly.

"Oh my God, Caleb. That feels so good." She tries to whisper, but she sucks at staying quiet.

Keeping my hands on her perfect breasts, I massage them softly, my fingers tweaking her nipples while my mouth moves to her neck. She moves her head to the side granting me access and I waste no time trailing kisses down her neck to her collarbone. She squirms in pleasure tightening her legs once more. I back up a little bit and, moving her panties to the side, insert a finger and then two into her tight pussy.

"Damn, Hayley. You are wet as fuck." While my fingers thrust in and out of her, my thumb rubs her clit. She grabs the back of my head and brings my face to hers, kissing me like her life depends on it. The deeper my fingers go, the harder she kisses, and within minutes, her pussy is clenching around my hand as she orgasms. Her body shakes and she tries to close her legs to stop me, but I don't stop until I know she's completely ridden her orgasm out.

"Mmm…that was so good," she says.

Before I can do or say anything in response, she's pushing me backward and hopping off the counter. A second later she's on her knees in front of me, guiding my shaft right into her warm wet mouth.

"Fuuuck, Hayley."

She looks up at me and laughs. "Baby, you have to be quiet," she says, repeating my words back to me. This woman is going to be the death of me.

With one hand, she brings my dick back to her mouth while the other cups my balls massaging them gently. I stare down at her while she fucks my dick with her mouth. She stops for a second, swirls her tongue over the head and then slowly glides her mouth upward as she takes me fully inside her mouth until I can feel my head hit the back of her throat causing her to slightly gag. The action causes a flashback and before I can think too hard about it, I'm grabbing Hayley by her arms, lifting her up into a standing position, and bending her over the sink.

I rip her panties off her body, tossing them to the side. Then cupping her mound, I pull her ass toward me, pushing my dick into her pussy a little too roughly. Luckily she's soaking wet so my dick slides in easily, but that doesn't stop her body from hitting the edge of the countertop from the force of me entering her. She grabs ahold of the edge while I continue to pound into her almost violently, my hands tightly holding onto her hips while my fingers dig into her skin. My eyes meet hers in the mirror and I then remember I'm not fucking one of the women from my past—I'm fucking Hayley…no, I'm making love to Hayley. Because it doesn't matter whether it's hard or soft, every time I touch her, it's out of love.

With my eyes never leaving Hayley's, my thrusts slow down and we quickly find our rhythm—Hayley meeting me thrust for thrust. I know when my cock hits her sweet spot because she moans loudly. I keep hitting the spot over and over again until we're both finding our release at almost the same time.

Twenty-Five

HAYLEY

IT'S BEEN ABOUT A MONTH SINCE WE CELEBRATED BENTLEY and Kayla's adoption news, and it feels like our life hasn't stopped moving in full speed ever since. In the past month the threats have become more frequent and instead of them saying things like "Last chance Bitch," they now say things like "Watch your back." The police can't prove who's sending them so their hands are tied. Thank God the court date is coming up and soon we will be able to put it all behind us.

On a more positive note, Hannah convinced Gloria it would be in her best interest to walk away from the clubs without going to court. I must admit getting to see my little sister in action was awe-inspiring. She said I was her assistant to get me in, but I had to promise not to reach across the table and strangle Gloria. My sister is such a badass!

"Good morning. My name is Lyrica Goldstein. I'll be mediating today. Who would like to begin?"

Before Gloria's attorney could even speak, Hannah was all over that shit.

"Good morning, we're here for mediation in hope of not having to go to trial so we don't have to waste more time and money. My name is Hannah Roberts and I'm Caleb's attorney. I'll be presenting the evidence that will be shown to the judge should Gloria Michaels feel it is necessary to go to trial."

"Okay, Ms. Roberts. Please show your evidence and then we'll go from there."

Hannah walked around the table with her laptop and sat it right in front of Gloria. On the screen was a digital copy of the letter Adam wrote to his son. Leaning over Gloria's shoulder, Hannah read the letter out loud. When she was done everybody knew in the room what Gloria had done.

"It's his word versus mine. And he's not even alive!"

Gloria's attorney told her to close her mouth.

"I understand that completely," Hannah went on. "That's why the next piece of evidence is absolutely crucial."

She pressed play on the recording and the room filled with Gloria's voice as she confessed everything to Caleb's father, not realizing she was being recorded. I could see the look of horror streak across her face.

The entire room went quiet.

"Would you like a few minutes to speak to your client?" Hannah asked Gloria's attorney.

"No, there's no need," Gloria whispered. She said something to her attorney and then walked out the door.

"My client has decided to drop the lawsuit against your client for the clubs. She waves all rights to anything club related."

"She never had any rights," Hannah pointed out with a smug look on her face.

With Gloria's bullshit behind us, Caleb insisted on immediately flying to Boulder to get the club handled so he could come back home and handle the one closer to us, and this time when he took Marco snowboarding he was able to join him. We all flew out together and spent spring break relaxing and having a good time.

Caleb was able to weed out the people loyal to Gloria, hire new help, and even hire Jacob, a bouncer who's been there for years and has his business degree as the on-site manager.

Once we returned back home my sister and Gavin got married. They found out they're having a little girl and are so excited. They found a house right down the street from my place and their offer was accepted last week. They're having some renovations done to the house first so they won't be moving in for a couple months but I'm so excited to have my sister as a neighbor.

Now Caleb and I are sitting in the adoption agency at the DCF office. Karen called me in to let me know she has some good news.

"I'm happy to say your adoption request has been approved. You and Marco are scheduled to go before the judge next week to swear you in as his legal guardian."

"Thank you so much!" I look over to Caleb and see the sad smile he has on his face.

"I know the adoption system frowns upon two people adopting a child when they aren't together, but do you think there's any way they could make an exception?"

"Unfortunately the DCF doesn't do exceptions. If you two were married, you could file the application together, but that would mean starting the entire process over again. The other option is you adopting Marco now and once you two are married Caleb can legally adopt Marco. Since you'll be his legal guardian you won't have to go through DCF at that point."

I hate that I'll be adopting Marco and Caleb isn't but she's right. The second option would be the easiest way to go. I don't want to start the adoption process over and who knows if or when Caleb and I will be getting married.

"Thank you," Caleb says and then stands shaking the attorney's hand.

Our entire ride home is silent. I know that it's breaking Caleb's heart not being able to legally adopt Marco right now. He said it was okay before, but now it seems like he has changed his mind. Does he want to be the one to adopt Marco? But if he does and then decides to move out, that would mean he would take Marco with him. I love Marco too much to let him go.

I go to work for the rest of the day and once I get home, Caleb and Marco go to the gym while I make dinner. I take out the pork roast I put to season yesterday, but when the scent hits my nostrils my stomach roils, forcing me to run to the bathroom. I make it to the toilet just in time to throw up everything in my stomach. I seriously hope I'm not getting sick on top of everything else.

After I am done throwing up, I make dinner and then clean up the house a little bit. I can't get this whole situation off my mind and if I stop moving I know I am going to drive myself nuts.

About an hour later dinner is ready, just as Caleb and Marco walk inside. We eat dinner, take showers, and watch a movie until it's time for Marco to go to bed. And this is how our routine continues for the next several days: Work, gym, dinner, family time, and bed. Caleb and I share a bed, and every night we make love, but we don't discuss anything. I'm getting so frustrated and confused and I know it's only a matter of time until I lose it.

Twenty-Six

CALEB

EVER SINCE WE LEFT THE DCF OFFICE MY THOUGHTS HAVE been running crazy. I know I told Hayley I was okay with her adopting Marco, and I am, but at the same time I hate the fact that they will legally be a family and I won't be a part of it. What if she decides one day she doesn't want me in her life? I have no legal claim to see Marco. I would have to walk away without having a say in anything. I hate the feeling of not being in control.

It's Saturday night and Marco's just gone to bed when Hayley finally snaps. We're sitting on the couch with her feet in my lap, watching a TV show.

"Talk to me, Caleb, please." Hayley's eyes are filled with tears and I would do anything to stop her from being upset.

"I don't know what to say, Hayles. I know you adopting Marco alone is the best choice. I just feel left out." I edge closer to Hayley and, bringing my hand to her thigh, rub up and down her legs hoping to relax her. I hate seeing her so upset and I hate that it's my insecurities causing it. She jumps slightly at my touch, but then relaxes not saying anything else. I massage the tops of her legs and she moans in appreciation. Sometimes it makes me sick, knowing my expertise of what a woman wants comes from years of being with women unwillingly, but it makes me feel better knowing I can apply those skills to a woman I actually want to be with.

I'm expecting her to argue with me, to want to talk some more, so I'm shocked when she moans out, "Caleb, rub harder." Something in my brain goes fuzzy, taking me back to an older memory from my past…and this time I can't seem to shake it off.

"Caleb, I had the hardest workout at the gym today. My muscles are so tight. Rub my body, now." Gloria lies on her stomach on my bed and I want nothing more than to choke the shit out of her so she'll disappear from my life, but we both know I'm not really capable of murder. So instead I do

as she says. I sit on top of her ass and begin rubbing her shoulders like she has taught me to do.

I move my hands down her back and massage circles into the muscles and then move lower, scooting down to sit on her legs, massaging her ass. Once I get to her thighs, I think she might be asleep until she says, "Caleb, rub harder." I do as she says and rub harder into her muscles

She flips over and gives me a devious smirk. "Come back up here. I want a full body massage. Massage my breasts, Caleb." I do as she demands because what choice do I have? I could tell her no, but then my dad would end up in prison. I continue to massage her body and of course my dick betrays me and gets stiff in my pants. Gloria thinks it gets hard because I want her. I think she has to tell herself that to justify how fucking wrong this is.

Of course she wins and we end up fucking, as I pray to God that I somehow find a way out of this shitty situation.

"Caleb…are you okay?"

My mind snaps back to the present and I realize that while my girlfriend is sitting on the couch next to me wanting me to touch her, I was having a flashback of massaging my stepmom and then fucking her. I look down and see my dick is hard. Bile rises in my throat and I just make it to the bathroom before I throw everything I've recently eaten up.

I hear her come up behind me and then her hands touch my shoulders. I know it's only out of care for me, but I can't have her touching me with the memories of my stepmom in my head.

"Don't touch me," I bark. She removes her hands from me but doesn't leave the bathroom.

"What's the matter? Did I do something wrong?" Her voice is so soft and insecure and I know it's my fault. How do I explain to her that my body is a fucking traitor and gets turned on by the thought of touching my stepmom when it should be soft by the thought of it? I shouldn't have snapped at her, but I can't stand the idea of her innocent, perfect hands touching me while I'm having sick thoughts. I don't want her tainted by my shit.

"Caleb, please, talk to me." I can't even look at her. I feel gross for even having the flashback. I feel even more disgusting for having the flashback while touching Hayley.

"I'm just not feeling well. I'm going to bed." I get up from the floor of the bathroom, flush the toilet, and walk by her without making eye contact. Instead of going to the room I've been sharing with her, go to mine and shut the door. How could I have ever thought I could live a normal life with a woman? How could I have thought it would be a good idea for me to adopt Marco? My life is tainted. Hayley deserves so much more than this. Marco deserves better than me. Hayley adopting Marco on her own is the way it should be.

And for the first time in weeks I sleep alone in my bedroom without Hayley curled up next to me.

Twenty-Seven

HAYLEY

I SAW THE SAME LOOK ON CALEB'S FACE LAST NIGHT THAT I saw the first night we made out like teenagers as well as the several nights since then we've made love. I don't know what exactly was going through his head, but I would bet my life it wasn't something as simple as him not feeling well. It doesn't go unnoticed the pained look he gives me too often when we're intimate. He doesn't realize I notice, but I do. I would bet it has something to do with his past. When he told me not to touch him, I wanted to grab him and pull him closer. I wanted to beg him not to push me away, but what right do I have?

I have to remember that even though Caleb has come a long way these past couple months, and while I know what he's been through because of the little he's told me, I'll never fully understand what goes through his head. The fact that it was bad enough to make him throw up tells me I need to give him space. He doesn't need me nagging him when he's got enough of his own shit to deal with. I hated going to bed without him. I hated that once again we didn't have the necessary conversation we need to have regarding Marco's adoption.

I drag myself out of bed knowing I'm going to have to face whatever is going on with Caleb head on. After showering, I get dressed and then make my way out to the living room. Marco is watching Sunday morning cartoons as usual and Caleb is on his laptop.

"Morning," I say, grabbing a cup of coffee.

"Morning," they both say in unison. I look over Caleb's shoulder and see the rental ads pulled up. My heart sinks. He's decided to move out. I guess I know where we stand after all.

"Hey Marco, want to head to the park to go skateboarding?" I need to get out of here and get some fresh air.

"Yes!" he yells, running to his room to get his skateboard.

"Make sure you brush your teeth after you get dressed!" I yell down the hallway. I sip on my coffee and think about how to approach this conversation. I don't want to fight with Caleb. We've never fought before. I want him to open up and talk to me.

"Do you want to come with?" I ask Caleb after a few minutes of silence.

"I can't. I have some apartments I need to look at." He says it quietly, so Marco can't hear, but do you know any kids who don't have supersonic hearing?

"Why are you going to look at apartments?" Marco asks, coming around the corner dressed and with his skateboard in his hand.

"Marco, I think we should talk," Caleb says solemnly. "When I moved in here with Hayley and you it was never to be forever. I was hurt and couldn't walk up the stairs. But I'm better now so I have to find my own place."

Huh. That's ironic considering he told me he was mine and wasn't going anywhere, ever. I guess *ever* was a lot shorter than I thought.

Marco looks absolutely crushed and for the first time I understand what parents mean when they say they want to shelter their children from all possibilities of being hurt. "You don't want to live with us?"

I should probably jump in and help Caleb, but I feel the same way as Marco.

"It's not that…this isn't my home. This is your home and Hayley's home."

"But you said you were together…Plus," Marco adds without waiting for an answer, "Hayley has been really scared about the people leaving the threats. You can't leave us. Please."

Oh damn…how will Caleb react to that? I keep my mouth shut. Caleb looks at me, begging for help and I just raise my brows in defiance. He's choosing this, not me. I'm certainly not going to help him push us away and run.

He sighs. "How about I look at a couple apartments, but I'll wait to move until I know you're both safe? I'll wait to move until after the trials are over."

Marco doesn't seem satisfied by the answer but nods anyway. Caleb gives him a hug goodbye and leaves without saying a word to me. Something in me snaps and I send him a text without thinking too hard about it.

Me: If you want to be a coward and leave…fine! But you are choosing this. I don't even know what I did wrong…I deserve better than this.

A few minutes later I get a text back.

Caleb: You do deserve better. I'm sorry.

He's sorry? Seriously? That's all he has to say…well fuck him then!

I'm not going to get run all over because of his past while he doesn't even give me a chance to be there for him.

Twenty-Eight

CALEB

I LOOK AT THREE DIFFERENT APARTMENTS AND EVERY SINGLE one I compare to Hayley's home. None of them feel right. Sure, they're nice as hell—the money my dad left me means I can pretty much rent or buy anywhere I want. The apartments I looked at have enough square footage to fit Hayley's house inside the kitchen alone. They have state-of-the art appliances, and one of them even comes furnished. No, the problem isn't the apartments themselves. The problem is none of them include Hayley and Marco. There's not a single item money could buy that would compare to what it feels like being with Hayley and Marco. If only it were that easy.

Now I'm at the bar drinking away my sorrows that I've created myself.

"Another one?" the bartender asks with a wink, letting me know if I wanted to I could take her into a bathroom and fuck her right there on the sink. The thought makes me feel sick. The only woman I want touching me is Hayley.

"No, thank you. Just a water please."

"Sure thing," she says with another flirtatious wink.

I don't even know how long I sit at the bar thinking, but my mind goes to the last couple months and how happy Hayley has made me. I realize for the last seven years I've been doing nothing more than simply surviving. But the day Hayley brought me to her house I finally started living. And what do I do when shit gets rough? I push her away, when the truth is, I should've pulled her closer. I should have explained to her how I've been feeling. I'm so hell bent on trust being so important, yet I didn't even give Hayley a chance to prove I could trust her. I tell her I would love to have a baby with her, yet I haven't even told her how much I love her, how much she means to me. I want to adopt Marco and instead of asking her to marry me so we can do it together, I get upset and run away.

I look around the bar and wonder what the hell I'm doing here when every single solution to my problems lies within two people and both of them are at home.

When I arrive at the house, I notice Hayley's car isn't in the driveway. I look at my cellphone and see it's after two in the morning. Where the hell could she be at this time of the night…well, morning…

I unlock the door and walk through the entire house. Nobody is here. The lights are all off and the beds are still made from this morning. I pull out my cell phone again and pull up the tracking app I set up for Hayley months ago. It shows about an hour ago she was in Marco's old neighborhood. I hit update, but it says her phone is offline. I try again, but it doesn't update. Why the hell is she in that shitty neighborhood?

I dial her number, my hands shaking. I have the worst feeling in my gut, but I'm refusing to think it out loud. Her phone goes to voicemail and I start to freak out.

I pull back up the app and click Marco's name. It shows he's here in the house. I run to his room and see his phone sitting on the desk in his room. Fuck!

I try Hayley's number once more, but it goes to voicemail. I send a group text to all the guys, asking any of them if they've seen or heard from Hayley. I know she went to the park with Marco today, but she should have been home by now. I call the number on the card to speak to the detective in charge of my case.

"Detective Bradley, this is Caleb. Hayley and Marco are both missing. I don't think it's a coincidence she received several threats and now I can't find them. Hayley's phone last showed her in Marco's old neighborhood before it was turned off."

"Okay, Caleb. We'll head over there now to check things out."

"Thank you, sir."

I should wait for the police to see what they can find, but I can't just sit and do nothing. I grab the gun from the lock box I purchased a while back when the guys and I used to frequent the shooting range for fun. After I got approved for my concealed weapons permit, I purchased a *Smith & Wesson .40*. I keep it locked up and out of Marco's reach with the ammunition separate, but it makes me feel better knowing I'm prepared in case anything happens, especially with Hayley feeling like she's being watched and all the threats we've received. I put the gun into the front of my pants and grab my keys, jump into my truck and head to Marco's old neighborhood. If the app is correct she was somewhere around the industrial building near where I saw Marco meet Hector and Santos to exchange money that day I was following him.

I don't even want to think about the possibilities of what Marco and Hayley could be going through right now. I'm praying this is all a misunderstanding and they're safely at one of our friend's houses, but I would rather expect the worst and hope for the best. While I'm driving I get several texts from our friends and her family saying they haven't seen or heard from her. Hannah texts saying Hayley posted a picture of Marco skateboarding earlier at the skate park. I forward it to the detective remembering I didn't mention the park during our conversation. Then I text Cooper, Bentley, and Kaden telling them I think Hayley and Marco were taken.

I get to the neighborhood and drive around looking for anything suspicious. I don't see Hayley's car anywhere. I drive by Marco's old house and it's vacant. I get out and walk around the house, but it's empty. I feel my phone buzz and see a text from the detective.

Detective Bradley: Officer found her car abandoned at the skate park earlier and reported it.

Fuck! There's no way she would have just left her car there.

Me: Hector and Santos had to have taken her!

Detective Bradley: Meet me at your house. Don't do anything stupid.

I want to keep searching for Hayley, but I know driving around isn't going to get me anywhere. I need to be smart about this. If it was Hector and Santos who took Marco and her it's because they want something. I head back home and when I get there the detective is there along with his partner. I think his name is David.

We walk into the house, and as I sit down on the couch to get down to business, David is bent over in the doorway. "Did you see this?"

I get up from the couch and grab what he's holding. It's a photo of Hayley and Marco both tied up and looking scared. Hayley looks to have a large bruise on her face. I flip it over and on the back is a note.

I warned you over and over again, but you didn't listen. Maybe now you will listen. One million in cash dropped off to the park under the bench where the car is parked by 10 a.m. or they will be killed.

"What the fuck! How did I not see this shit before when I came home?" It was dark, that's why I didn't see it, and I wasn't looking on the ground for fucking clues.

"Fuck! Since I didn't drop the charges, they want money…and I am what? Supposed to sit here for eight fucking hours and wait to drop off the money and hope they're okay?"

"No, you aren't," Bradley says. He's making calls and trying to get intel on the guys. I feel so fucking useless. I don't even know where to start looking. This is entirely my fault! If I hadn't left Hayley to go look at apartments I would've been with them at the park and this never would've happened. It doesn't go over my head every time she received a threat she was alone. I should have taken the threats more seriously. I should have insisted the police do something more. I kept thinking the trial would come around and these guys would be locked up with the other two that didn't get out on bail. I shouldn't have let my guard down. Now Hayley and Marco are God knows where scared and possibly hurt.

"What do we do?"

"We're having a couple officers go to Hector's and Santos's houses to check things out. We're also having the tech department pull up the cameras at the park from earlier today. Unfortunately other than a few anonymous threats since the graffiti on her car, there hasn't been much to go off of.

"I can't just sit here. The tracker showed her near the industrial building. I need to go there and check it out."

The front door swings open and I pray it's Hayley and Marco, but it's not. It's Bentley, Cooper, and Kaden.

"What the fuck is going on?" Bentley asks.

"They were taken?" Cooper asks.

"Yeah." I show them the picture.

"So what the hell are we doing here? We need to go find them," Kaden growls.

This is why these guys are my best friends. They would do anything for me and the people I love.

"We're having forensics take the picture. We're hoping they can pinpoint a location the photo was printed at or taken from," the detective states, taking the photo from me and handing it to someone on his team.

"A million? We can give the guys that, and they must know if they hurt them, they won't get their money," Bentley says.

"Yeah, well, I'm not sitting and waiting seven more hours to find out." I grab my keys and head out to my truck.

"Wait, you aren't going without us," Kaden says.

"Do you have your guns on you?" I ask.

"Yeah, when you said you thought Hayley and Marco were taken, we grabbed them," Bentley says as we all jump into my truck.

Detective Bradley: I can't stop you, but if you find them please call for backup. Don't go in on your own.

I don't bother texting back. I don't want to have to lie to a cop, and there's no way I'm going to find my girl and kid and sit around and wait for him to get there.

We're driving around the neighborhood for about thirty minutes and I'm getting frustrated as fuck having no clue where Hayley can be when I see the same expensive vehicle I've spotted several times now.

"That's the car," I point out. "Hayley and I have seen this car parked near us several times."

I park my truck and quickly text the detective, sending him a live location of where we are.

I take my gun out and take the safety off—the guys do the same thing.

We all walk up along the side of the building. It's the same warehouse Marco met the guys at but around back. The only way to get to the door is a small alleyway. If it weren't for the car being parked here I would have completely overlooked it. We stop at the vehicle and look inside. Nobody is in there, but on the floor of the car I can see Hayley's phone. She has to be close by. When I feel the hood, it's cold telling me it's been parked here for a while.

I hear soft footsteps coming up behind us and I turn and point my gun ready to shoot anybody that's a threat. It's the detective and several other officers. The detective puts his fingers to his lips and I nod. We walk toward the door of the building, when I hear a woman scream so loud it send chills down my spine. I know I should wait for the detective to give some kind of orders, but I don't. I try to open the door, but it won't open, so I step back and shoot the lock out.

When the door flies open the scene in front of me is one I'll never forget for as long as I live.

Twenty-Nine

HAYLEY

Nine Hours Earlier

"OH MY GOODNESS! MARCO! YOU'RE LIKE A SKATEBOARDING god! Who taught you to skateboard like this?" I'm watching Marco do ridiculously cool tricks using his skateboard and I'm absolutely amazed. The kid is so talented.

"I used to skateboard here all the time before Cooper started the MMA classes, and usually after the classes I would come here to practice, plus my friends and I practice at school during gym."

I pull out my phone and switch it to live mode to record him doing his tricks and then post it to Facebook. It's a beautiful day here and getting out helped take my mind off Caleb and the fact that while I'm here with Marco, he's off looking at apartments.

A little while later Marco comes over to me and sits down.

"Umm…so I have a question," he says nervously.

"What's up?"

"Your parents said I can call them Nana and Pop—those are nicknames for grandparents, right?"

"Yes," I say, pretty sure where this is going but scared if it's not going in the direction I think it is, I'll be heartbroken.

"And if they're my grandparents, it's like you're my mom. Right?"

"Well, I would definitely be honored to be your mom if that's what you're asking. I know you already have a mom, so I think that would be up to you."

"My mom wasn't a good mom. I'm old enough to know that."

"She wasn't perfect, but she loved you the best she could." I seriously hope I'm not botching this entire conversation. I probably should have looked up the right things to say. I'm already messing up this whole parenting thing and it's not even official yet.

"What if I wanted to call you mom?"

My heart tightens in my chest at his words. "Then you would make me the happiest woman in the entire world, but only on one condition."

"What's that?" he asks, nervous again.

"I can call you my son."

"That would be awesome. Do you think Caleb would let me call him Dad?"

The heart constricts at the idea of Caleb and I being parents to Marco. He's been close to Marco for so long, I could never keep that title from him, even if he doesn't want to marry me and formally adopt Marco.

"That is something you would have to ask Caleb, but I'm pretty sure he would be honored. He loves you *almost* as much as I do," I say with a playful wink.

Marco laughs.

"Speaking of new names. I have some good news. The adoption went through and on Friday we'll be going before the judge to make it official. You're legally mine, kid."

I reach over and give him a hug and he hugs me back. "I love you, Mom."

I choke up, but compose myself quickly. "I love you too, Son."

Marco runs back to the ramps to skateboard some more. I want to text Caleb to tell him about this conversation but don't want to bother him while he's apartment hunting. He needs his space. If he needed or wanted me he would be here with us. I can't make someone try.

I look at the time and see it's almost dinnertime, and since it's a school night we need to get home to eat and get ready for tomorrow.

"C'mon, Marco, let's go."

"Coming, Mom!" he yells. He has no idea what the significance of those three little letters mean to me. All I can do is make sure I do everything in my power to earn the title that precious little boy has given me.

I hit the button to pop open my trunk. Marco takes his pads off his elbows and knees and then takes his helmet off, throwing it all into the trunk, slamming it closed when he's done. I hit the key fob to unlock the doors, and just as we are about to get in hands come around me, one hand covering my mouth. I try to scream, but it's muffled. I'm then blindfolded and handcuffed with my hands behind by back and then thrown into the back of a vehicle where I can hear Marco screaming.

"*Cállate*," I hear a man bark out. Marco immediately stops screaming. I shift my body, so I'm touching Marco's body with mine, letting him know I'm here with him.

The guys talk minimally in Spanish and a few minutes later the car comes to a stop. Since I'm blindfolded I have no idea where I am. Then I remember I have my cell phone in my back pocket. Without being able to see, I try to unlock it and dial whatever number comes up first. But before I can even get it unlocked, the phone is smacked out of my hand and I hear it crack like it's being stomped on.

"Puta cuidadosa o morirás!" a man spits out before grabbing me and dragging me out of the car. I hear Marco crying and saying something in Spanish. The man smacks me across the face hard and then throws me onto the ground. I curl up into a fetal position while I'm kicked several times in the back and a few times to my ribs. Eventually it's too much and I throw up. They finally stop and I'm picked up and brought somewhere where I'm thrown onto cold hard cement. I try to stay calm, but my body is aching. I can taste the blood coming from my mouth, but I don't want Marco to know anything is wrong.

I only know Marco is with me because I can hear him breathing loudly. The place goes quiet a few minutes later, and I take the chance and speak.

"Marco, sweetie, are you okay?"

"Yeah, Mom, I'm okay. Are you?"

"Yes, I'm okay. Do you know what the man said to me in Spanish?"

"He said to be careful or you will die. I tried to tell him to stop."

"It's going to be okay, Marco."

He doesn't say anything back.

A little while later the door opens and our blindfolds are removed. I've read enough books to know this isn't a good thing. If the kidnappers are okay with letting you see them they don't plan to let you live. Once my eyes adjust, I see we're in an empty room in a warehouse and sure enough it's Hector and Santos along with the two guys who got out on bail. There's another guy there as well, dressed nicer than the other guys, and I wonder if he's the owner of the expensive vehicle that has been parked down my street.

"You know why I took off your blindfolds? So you can see who is in charge of your life. Let's hope you and the boy are worth a million dollars," one of the men says in his heavy Spanish accent. He takes his cell phone out and snaps a picture of Marco and me.

"And then you will let us go?" I ask.

"We'll see."

"Please just let Marco go. You can keep me. He's just a child."

"Just a child? He's the reason for this shit! Him and his druggie mother!"

"He's a child!" I yell back! The man backhands me so hard tears spring from my eyes and blood coats the inside of my mouth.

"Mom!" Marco yells. He looks so scared. All I want to do is hold him and make him feel safe even if neither of us are.

"Shut up! Both of you!" They put the blindfold back on Marco and then on me.

The door slams shut, leaving us once again in the dark.

"I love you, Marco." It's all I can say. I don't know at this point if we will live or die, but I need him to know I love him. "You are the best treasure ever brought into my life. No matter what happens I need you to know I love you, Son."

"I love you too, Mom. Thank you for saving me."

There's so much more I want to say, but I can't speak without crying, and I don't want Marco to hear me crying. My body is in so much pain and it's hard to breathe. I take a slow deep breath and pray to God somebody finds us soon.

After telling Marco over and over again I will protect him he finally falls asleep with his head in my lap. It seems like hours before the men return. I'm exhausted and it's got to be well into the night or early morning, but I'm too scared to sleep. I need to protect my son.

I hear the men getting closer. They're yelling back and forth in Spanish and while I have no idea what they're saying, it doesn't sound like they're very happy. Every few words I hear one I can translate like police and money. Damn it, I wish I had paid better attention in Spanish class back in college.

The voices keep getting closer and before I know it I hear the door swing open. Before I can react, Marco is no longer sleeping on my lap and my shorts are being ripped off me. Marco is screaming out my name and I'm just so thankful he won't have to actually see me being raped. I'm pushed onto my back and because my hands are still handcuffed, I can't stop myself from falling backward, my head hitting the concrete hard. I feel dizzy but try hard not to blackout.

"Your boyfriend made a grave mistake, you little bitch. He involved the police. His mistake is your punishment." He grabs my breasts hard and then spreads my legs so wide I scream out loudly in pain. I can't just let him rape me. I need to fight, but how can I fight without my hands or sight. I attempt to kick him hard and must make contact, because when my foot hits him, he grunts out what sounds like curse words in Spanish. I take the opportunity to begin screaming again trying to get away.

I expect him to come back at me to take my underwear off, so I bring my legs up ready to kick him again, but instead I hear a loud gunshot ring through the air, what sounds like a door swinging open, and then loud voices yelling, "Police. Put your weapons down." Suddenly several gunshots go off.

I bring my shoulder up to my face as I try to move the blindfold the best I can, but it's not working. A few seconds later, hands are on me and I jump, screaming out loud. "Shh…it's okay, Hayles. I got you." The sound of Caleb's voice allows me to relax. He removes my blindfold, and that's when I see Kaden, Cooper, and Bentley, as well as several armed police officers all pointing their guns at the five men who are on the ground bleeding, having been shot. It looks like at least two of them might be dead and the others are definitely injured.

I search for Marco and see him curled up in the corner. I get up the best I can and hobble over to him. I can't hold him, but I attempt to soothe him with my words.

"It's okay, sweetie. Caleb and the police are here. They saved us." I sit close to Marco, blocking him in case anything goes bad, hoping my body will protect his.

The officers handcuff the three guys who are alive but injured and another officer calls for more ambulances saying there are several injured. One of the officers comes over to Marco and me, and using a key, unlocks our cuffs. I immediately grab Marco, taking his blindfold off, and hold him tight, vowing to never let go of him. First date? Hope he enjoys a third wheel. College? He better be prepared for me to join him. I might even have to homeschool him.

While I'm holding him and refusing to let go, I feel hands encompass us, and when I look up I see Caleb with tears in his eyes, holding both of us.

"I thought I was going to lose you both," he says through his tears. "I'm so sorry, baby. I'm so sorry for leaving you guys."

I'm not sure why Caleb is apologizing. He didn't do this. He can't control what those men did. Then it hits me. He blames himself because he left us to go find an apartment, and I know I should be grateful we're all okay and I should tell him it's not his fault or at least say it's okay, but the fear that has consumed me for so long turns into anger. As I get up to grab my shorts, I feel a sharp pain in my side hit me and I double over before blacking out.

Thirty

CALEB

I FUCKED UP. I KNOW I FUCKED UP, AND NOW I'M GOING TO have to fix this. I walked out on Hayley and Marco to find an apartment in an attempt to push her away. All she's done this entire time is fight for me, and instead of pulling her closer and leaning on her, I pushed her away. I should have just told her about the flashbacks. I should have explained what was going on in my head, but instead I walked away like a scared little bitch.

I should have been at the park with her and Marco. If I were there with them, they never would have been taken. She never would have been so close to being raped.

I grab ahold of both Marco and Hayley apologizing over and over again. I can see when her fear turns to anger and then she gets up to walk away. What I'm not prepared for is when she doubles over in pain and a loud scream rings out in the warehouse, and I realize something is very wrong.

Luckily when the police came they also dispatched ambulances. The EMTs come running in and cut her shirt open. That's when I see all the bruises. She had to have been beaten. There are bruises all over her stomach and legs. Her face has several bruises and her lip is split completely open.

"We're going to bring her to the nearest hospital. They'll be able to assess her and check for internal injuries," the EMT says, carefully placing Hayley on the gurney. As they're rolling her out, Hayley comes to and starts calling for Marco. She's hurt and her only concern is to make sure Marco is okay.

I run over to her side and tell her Marco is with me and we'll follow her to the hospital.

Marco starts crying and I grab ahold of him, holding him close. "It's okay. She's going to be okay."

"They hurt her!" he cries.

"Did they do anything to you?" I ask. "Are you hurt?" I look over his body, making sure he's okay.

"No, they didn't do anything to me. Can we please go to the hospital? I want to make sure Mom's okay."

Hearing him call Hayley Mom warms my heart. I wonder if she knows he's calling her Mom.

Cooper comes over. "Why don't we head to the hospital with you guys and stay in the waiting room with Marco until they say it's okay for him to go back and see Hayley?"

"Okay."

On our way to the hospital I give Hayley's sister a call to let her know what's happened. She lets me know they're on their way and she'll call their parents to let them know.

When we arrive, the nurse won't tell me anything. I try to play the fiancé card Hayley played to get in to see me, but this nurse isn't having it. Thankfully Hannah comes running through the door demanding answers and since they're sisters and she's on her emergency contact list, the nurse will speak to her.

"Ms. Roberts is okay. She has a couple bruised ribs and is currently receiving stitches for her lip. They're running tests because she hit her head pretty hard, and they'll keep her overnight in case of a concussion. Once the doctor gives the okay, I'll let two at a time go back and see her."

Knowing Hayley is alone back there and in pain makes me feel sick, but at this point, we're lucky she's okay. I sit with Marco and hold him like Hayley would have done until he falls asleep.

A little while later Hayley's parents arrive, then Ashley, Kayla, and Liz all come in.

"You guys didn't have to come here. She's okay."

"Are you crazy? Of course we're here. Once I can see her for myself I'll bring Marco home with me," Kayla says.

Marco tenses up, telling me he's awake and listening. "I don't want to leave my mom. Please don't make me leave her." He starts crying and shaking his head, clearly scared of losing another mom.

"Hey, it's all right. You don't have to go anywhere. As soon as they say it's okay, I'll bring you back to see her."

We all sit and wait for another couple hours and then finally the nurse comes out and calls Hayley's name. We all stand. "Hayley is ready for visitors, but she requests that Caleb Michaels not be allowed in—I'm sorry."

Everybody's eyes fly to me and I don't know even know what to say. I should have seen this coming. You can only push someone so far before they give up fighting for you.

Thirty-One

HAYLEY

ONCE I'M BROUGHT TO THE HOSPITAL AND ADMITTED, THEY draw blood to run tests, perform scans to check out my head and ribs, and hook me up to an IV. Luckily I'm just sore with bruised ribs, but nothing major that will require surgery or a cast. The worst part is them having to sew up my bottom lip with a few stitches. I think I'm finally done being checked out when another doctor comes in and shocks the ever-loving shit out of me.

"Good morning, Hayley, my name is Dr. Jones. I've been looking over your chart and it appears you're pregnant. Were you aware?"

Immediately, my hands go to my stomach, to the flashbacks of those horrible men kicking me. I had no idea I was pregnant. "I didn't know, but I can't imagine after the beating I had I'm still pregnant," I say, feeling numb.

"You would be surprised how well the womb protects the fetus, but instead of assuming one way or another, why don't we do an ultrasound." He rolls the ultrasound cart over.

"It says you're a doctor as well. What's your specialty?" I know he's only making conversation to calm me, but I'll take it.

"I specialize in sport's medicine. I work with UFC fighters at a local gym."

"Very nice. Since I don't know how far along you are, I'm going to do a vaginal ultrasound," he says, rolling a condom over the wand and then inserting it slowly into me.

The monitor is on, but I can't look at it. I wish Caleb were here with me to hold my hand. But then I remember why I'm here. He ran, instead of fighting for us, he walked away and wasn't there when Marco and I were taken. I hate feeling so consumed with anger, but I can't help it.

Caleb doesn't deserve to be here. He didn't want me. He wanted an apartment and to be away from me. He chose to let whatever was wrong, probably his past, win out over me, over us.

"…And there's the heartbeat." I completely forgot about the ultrasound. I bring my face up to look at the screen and sure enough there's a lima bean-size baby and a heartbeat. Tears spring to my eyes and spill over.

"It's a strong heartbeat, Hayley. I don't see any tears in the uterine walls. The amniotic fluid looks good. Your body did its job. It protected your little one. You look to be close to six weeks. It's still very early and while I don't want to scare you, I'm going to recommend once you're released you take it easy your first trimester. Your body needs time to heal. I'm not putting you on bed rest, but don't overdo it."

"Thank you, Dr. Jones."

The doctor prints out a couple pictures of the cute little lima bean and then says he'll let the nurse know I can receive visitors.

"Umm, wait. Can you please let her know I don't want Caleb Michaels visiting?"

He nods once and then leaves.

A few minutes later my sister walks in with Marco. He bursts into tears and I welcome him in my bed so I can hold him. He lies next to me and within minutes passes out.

"Everything is okay, right?" Hannah asks.

It won't be long until my parents and friends are fighting to all come back so I need to tell her now. "I need to tell you something, but you can't tell anyone, not yet."

"Does this have anything to do with why you wouldn't let Caleb back? He's completely torn up. A tornado couldn't rip him from that waiting room."

"He left, Hannah!" I yell, but take a calming breath before I continue. I don't want to wake Marco or do anything to put the baby at risk. As a doctor, I know it would take more than yelling to do anything to my baby, but as a mom-to-be I'm not going to take any chances by working myself up.

"What do you mean he left?"

"He was giving me a massage and I think he had a flashback of some sort. I don't know for sure, but I have seen them happen a few times, except this time, instead of fighting through it, he left. Then he said he was moving out. Marco and I were at the park alone while Caleb was looking for an apartment to rent."

"Hayley, that's not fair," Hannah says. "I know you're upset right now, but think long and hard before you place that blame on Caleb. People get upset all the time. People leave and many women take their kids to the park alone. Most just don't have psycho drug dealers stalking them, waiting to kidnap them. Caleb leaving isn't why you're upset. He came back a few hours later. He's the reason you were even found. You know this. So, what's going on?"

I sigh loudly. I know she's right and that's why I didn't want Caleb coming in here. I'm a mix of emotions and I imagine being pregnant isn't helping.

"I'm pregnant."

"Oh my goodness!" Hannah squeals. Then she sobers. "Is the baby okay?"

"Yes, the doctor did an ultrasound and I'm roughly six weeks along. He wants me to take it easy for the first trimester to be on the safe side, give my body time to heal."

"So you aren't going to tell Caleb? Was this planned?"

"That's the thing. We knew we were having unprotected sex and we knew this could happen, but I had it in my head it would be harder to get pregnant than it actually was, and while I'm so excited about this baby, I'm afraid Caleb will regret it."

"I think you need to give him a chance, Hayley. I don't know all that happened, but the guy out in the waiting room doesn't look like a guy who would ever regret having a baby with you. On the plus side, we'll have our babies months apart." We both squeal, and it wakes Marco up.

"What happened?" Marco asks.

"Nothing, sweetie. We're okay. Go back to sleep," I say, threading my fingers through his soft hair.

Hannah and I chat for a few minutes and then she goes back to get our parents. They give me hugs and kisses, thanking God I'm oaky. As much as I want to tell them about my being pregnant, I think it's best to keep it to myself for now. Anything can happen and every person I tell will be another person I have to tell if I lose the baby.

Once they leave, my friends take turns coming in and out. Finally Bentley and Kayla are last.

"He's a mess, Hayley. I know you're upset, but he's a freaking mess out there. Please don't punish him for too long. Even if you're ending it with him, just let him know," Bentley says.

After spending the evening with Marco by my side, the nurse lets Marco know he can't spend the night. He's not happy at all, but when Kayla tells him he can have a sleepover with Chloe, he reluctantly gives in.

The next morning I'm released. Since Kayla had taken Marco home with her, she picks me up and brings us home. Marco and I both take showers. When I tell him I'd like for him to stay home one more day to get some rest, he asks if he can sleep with me. I can't even imagine how traumatized he is from all of the recent events. He obviously doesn't want to be alone and the truth is I don't really want to be alone either. I thought maybe Caleb would try to come home, but I guess not. Marco cuddles into bed with me and I put on a kid movie hoping he won't have nightmares. The kid has been through way too much.

I LOOK AT THE CLOCK AND SEE IT'S TWO IN THE AFTERNOON. I go to grab my phone and remember it was smashed the day we were taken.

Marco stirs awake, and I decide I'm not going to let what happened bring us down. It will definitely be discussed at his weekly therapy session, but I'm not going to dwell on it. We're both okay. My baby is okay, and the men who are alive will be locked away for a long ass time.

"Hey sweetie, did you have a good nap?"

He nods and cuddles up next to me.

"I need to go to the mall to get a new phone. Why don't you get dressed and we'll stop on the way and get lunch?"

"Okay."

After we're both dressed, we walk out to my car to head to the mall. I stop short, seeing Caleb's truck parked in the front of my house. "What's he doing out there?" Marco asks.

"I'm not sure. Why don't you get in the car and I'll go speak to him?"

I get to the truck and see Caleb is texting on his phone. I knock lightly on the window, and when he sees it's me, he rolls it down.

"What are you doing out here?"

"I couldn't leave you guys alone. I just figured it would be better to sit out here since you didn't want me to be around you."

God, I'm such a bitch. I refused to see the man who saved us and he sat in his truck because I didn't want him near me.

"Thank you."

"There's no need to thank me. This was entirely my fault. I saw his threats but didn't take them serious enough. And then I walked out, and while I was looking at apartments, you both were kidnapped. Do you think maybe we can talk?"

"I would like that, but Marco and I are heading out to the mall. The guys who took us smashed my phone so I need a new one. I also need to get him lunch."

"Would it be okay if I went with you guys?"

I want to say no because being around him hurts, but at the same time being around him completes me. It also doesn't help that I feel guilty for hiding this pregnancy from him. This whole situation sucks.

"Sure."

He gets out of his truck and runs in the house to change quickly and is back a few minutes later. On our way to the mall he asks Marco how he's feeling and Marco says he's okay. He also says he wants to eat at the food court, so we head straight to the mall. After we park, we go straight to the wireless store. I let them know my phone was destroyed and decide to upgrade to a new phone.

Marco and Caleb are looking at the latest technology when a salesman walks over and starts talking to Marco. "You should ask your dad to buy this for you."

I hold my breath, praying Caleb doesn't deny it. It would hurt Marco's feelings. Instead, he pats Marco on the back and says, "He just got a new iPad. We can't spoil him too much. We'll have to see how his report card is this semester."

Marco laughs and points out his grades are really good.

After the gentleman sets up my new phone, we head to the courtyard to get something to eat. Marco is so hungry he wolfs down all of his food and asks for more.

"Hey, Mom, can I go grab another chicken sandwich?"

"Sure, sweetie." I hand him money and watch him walk the ten feet over to the counter to order a sandwich.

"I don't know how I'm supposed to let him go to school. I don't want him leaving my sight."

I look at Caleb and realize I said that out loud. He's staring at me weird…like with adoration maybe…I'm not sure.

"What?"

"He called you Mom again. He did it when you were brought to the hospital."

"Oh, yeah." A big smile graces my face. "He asked me if he could call me Mom at the park. I also told him I was approved to adopt him." Tears spring forward and blur my vision.

"Why are you crying?" Caleb leans over to wipe the tears falling down.

"When we were being held hostage, I thought that moment in the park would be the only time in my life somebody would call me Mom, and I was just so glad it was Marco. And then I found out…" I stutter, realizing I almost announced my pregnancy to him right here in the food court, so I try to play it off. "Umm…when I got out of the hospital and we were lying in bed watching a movie, I realized how short life is. I really want to be a good mom." I laugh, knowing my hormones are going crazy. I seriously need to stop talking. I'm barely making any sense.

"Hayles, you deserve it all. More than anybody I know. I'm glad Marco is calling you mom. You are his mom. You're amazing with him, and you will be just as amazing with any kids you have in the future." And insert guilt because I haven't told Caleb he is going to be a father.

I look over to see Marco heading back and think back to him saying he wants to call Caleb Dad. "He asked if he could call you Dad but didn't get a chance to ask you."

Caleb doesn't have a chance to respond, but his face says it all. He would like nothing more than to be a father to Marco. I know regardless of what happens between us, he'll be an amazing father to this baby as well.

The rest of the day goes by quickly. We walk around the mall and shop a little. Marco picks out a new game for his PlayStation and asks if we can go home so he can play. My body begins to feel achy and Caleb notices, insisting we go home. When we get home, Caleb heads back to his truck, but I stop him.

"Come inside, please. I know we have stuff to work out, but until you find a place you're welcome to stay here."

He says okay and then follows me inside. I can tell he wants to say more, but this isn't the time to talk.

We sit on the couch and watch Marco play his game. Caleb joins in for a little bit but excuses himself to make a few phone calls. While he is on the phone I let Marco know it's time for bed.

"Can I go to school tomorrow?"

"Are you sure you're okay to go to school? You have your therapy session in two days…Maybe you can wait to meet with her."

"I'm okay going back. I know what happened sucks, but I like going to school and I don't want to get behind. Please."

How can I possibly say no to my kid begging me to go to school. He's so much stronger than me and I won't let my parental fears scare him.

"Okay, fine. But why don't I pick you up from school and you can practice MMA while I work in the afternoon?"

"Sounds good. Can you ask Caleb to come in as soon as he gets off the phone? I want to talk to him."

"Sure thing." I give him a kiss on his forehead and say goodnight.

When I get back out to the living room Caleb is sitting on the couch with his head sagging down.

"You okay?"

He looks up and shrugs. "They have enough evidence to put the guys who survived away. They need yours and Marco's statements but they won't need us to be at the trial. They'll be held without bail. It's over."

"So why are you sad then? That's a good thing."

"I walked away. I know I messed up, Hayles. I should have been there at the park with you guys and none of this would have happened. Please tell me you'll be able to forgive me."

I can see he's beating himself up over this and I know I need to forgive him and tell him about the baby. We need to figure this all out together, but I can't find the words.

"Marco wants to talk to you. He asked for you to go say goodnight."

"Okay, thanks."

Thirty-Two

CALEB

I PRACTICALLY BEG HAYLEY FOR FORGIVENESS AND SHE CAN barely look me in the eye. How can I expect Hayley to be on the same page as me when the last thing I said to her was not to touch me and then told her I was looking for apartments to move into? She's hurt and justifiably so. I need to speak with her, but first I need to go talk to Marco.

"Hey buddy." I walk into his room to sit on the edge of his bed. "Hayl—I mean, your mom said you wanted to talk to me."

Marco's face lights up at the word mom. He might have had another mom for the first twelve years of his life, but she wasn't one percent of the mom Hayley is to him.

"Yeah…umm…before we got taken, we were talking and she said I could call her Mom…and I was wondering…I know you can't adopt me, but well, I've never had a dad before. I was wondering if maybe you would be my dad. I know I'm older than a baby, but…"

"Marco, stop. I don't care if you are two, twelve, or twenty-two. I would love to be your father. You are never too old to have a dad and I don't care what the courts say. I love you, and since the moment you walked into that gym, I have thought of you as my son."

Marco sits up and gives me a hug and I swear in that moment it feels like all is right in the world.

"Get some sleep, bud. I love you."

"Love you too, Dad."

I walk back to the living room feeling like I'm floating in the clouds and see Hayley wiping her tears.

"You were totally listening, weren't you?" I say jokingly.

She laughs. "Yes! I had to hear for myself. Is he not the sweetest kid, ever?"

"When he asked me to be his dad, I wanted to go out and buy him a car."

Hayley cracks up laughing and shakes her head. God, I love to hear that woman laugh.

"I know we need to talk, but I'm fucking exhausted, Hayles. Would it be okay if we talk tomorrow? I just want to lie in bed and hold you, please."

She nods, and after we both change into clothes to sleep in, we climb into her bed. She lies facing away from me and I pull her close so I'm spooning her from behind. I wrap my arms around her body and nuzzle my face into her hair, inhaling her scent. I'm pretty sure today was one of the best days of my life. Hayley and Marco are both safe, I'm lying in bed with the woman I love, and Marco wants me to be his dad. The only thing left to fix is Hayley and me.

I wake up to an empty bed and when I look at the clock I see it's nine in the morning. Hayley must have snuck out without waking me up. I have some serious groveling to do. I walk through the house and see both she and Marco are gone. I grab my laptop and cell phone and begin working on a plan.

Thirty-Three

HAYLEY

AFTER GETTING MARCO OFF TO SCHOOL I GO TO THE GYM TO check on my fighters. If it wasn't for me working for Cooper I imagine I would have been fired a long time ago. I need to let him know about the pregnancy so he knows I'm planning to go part-time, and once the baby comes, I would like to stay home. I don't know what things will be like for Caleb and me, but I have money put away and I'll use it if I have to. Thinking about it, it's probably best if I let Caleb know first.

I see a couple fighters and then receive a text from my sister asking if she can please take Marco this weekend for the entire weekend. He's never been away from me for that long. so I let her know I'll speak to him and get back to her. Marco and I go to court Friday to sign the papers. I plan to surprise him by having him play hooky and spend the day with him.

I consider texting Caleb so many times throughout the day, but I don't know what to say. I don't know how to deal with him walking out. I know he's sorry, but it doesn't change the fact that he wanted to move out.

When the afternoon rolls around and it's time to go get Marco I run into Ashley who's visiting Kaden.

"Hey girly," she says, giving me a hug. "How are you feeling?"

"I'm okay. What are you up to tonight?"

"Nothing much. I'm off tonight."

"Marco and I can come over and we can do dinner." I'm totally avoiding Caleb, but I also want to spend time with Ashley. She's seemed all over the place lately and nothing works better to ignore your own problems than to focus on someone else's.

"Sounds good!"

I grab Marco from the bus stop and don't stop at home. Within a few minutes, there's a text from Caleb.

Caleb: Are you coming home?

Me: Having dinner with Ashley. Don't wait up.

Caleb: If you're staying away because of me, I can leave.

That is definitely what I'm doing, but I'm not about to tell him that.

Me: That's not what I am doing...

Caleb: Okay

As Marco and I walk up to Ashley's house, I bring up the subject of Hannah wanting to spend some time with him. "Hey Marco, Hannah asked if she can take you for the weekend. What do you think?"

"Are you okay with me going?" I love that he's worried about me, but his job isn't to worry. His job is to be a kid. My job is to worry about him and me.

"Hey, I'm fine, and I'll be okay with you at Hannah's. Your job is to have fun. Got it? No worrying."

"Okay, then I would like to go. Aunt Hannah is cool."

We knock on Ashley's door and I text Hannah to let her know this weekend is a go. Ashley answers the door and lets us in.

The boys run to Tristan's room to play video games and I follow her into the kitchen where she grabs a bottle of wine. I notice a few notices on her counter. Some say first notice, one says third notice, and one says final notice. I look away, not wanting to be nosy, but Ashley sees what I was looking at and, with an embarrassed look on her face, grabs the papers and shoves them into a drawer.

She brings the wine to the couch and I follow with two glasses, setting them down on the table so she can pour.

"Kaden brought this over the other night," she says by way of explanation.

"Who's judging?"

"I know you saw the notices, Hayley. I just don't want you to think I'm behind on my bills, yet I'm buying bottles of wine."

"Trust me, I'm the last person to judge anyone. But if you want to talk, I'm here."

Ashley lets out a heavy sigh and shakes her head. "I just don't even know where to begin. Talking about it won't change anything." She begins to cry and I cross over to the side of the couch she's sitting on and just let her cry it out while holding her.

After a few minutes, she composes herself. "Jeez, I am a horrible host."

"Hey now, I pretty much invited myself over." We both laugh.

"The truth is I'm kind of hiding from Caleb. Before Marco and

I were taken, we got into a fight. Well, not really a fight...I don't even know what happened. Anyway, it ended with him saying he was moving out. At some point, we're going to have to talk, but I'm just not ready yet."

"Well, you're welcome to hide out here as long as you need to."

We decide to order pizza for dinner and after we all eat and the boys play some more video games for a couple hours, Marco and I finally takeoff so he can take a shower before bed since it's a school night.

We get home and Caleb's truck is in the driveway, but he isn't in the living room. I notice his bedroom door is shut. Marco takes a shower, and after I say goodnight, I take a quick shower as well and go to sleep.

Sometime in the middle of the night, I feel Caleb's hands on me. It feels like he's spooning me and at one point it even feels like his hand is running across my stomach, but when I wake up and the bed is empty, I chalk it up to a dream.

I get ready for work and head out just like yesterday, except today I invited Marco and myself over to Kayla's place using the excuse he would love to see Chloe. After dinner and dessert we head home and once again Caleb is in his room. I say goodnight to Marco and go to sleep, having the same dream as the previous night.

IT'S FRIDAY MORNING AND CALEB'S DOOR IS OPEN AND EMPTY. He must have already left for the day. Marco is up early and excited for two reasons: I sign the adoption papers this morning and later tonight he'll be going to Hannah's for the weekend. She's told me she'll be by right after work to get him. I offered to bring him to her, but she was adamant I meet her at my house. So much for avoiding Caleb tonight...

"You ready to do this, kid?"

"Yeah, I am."

We get to the courthouse and have a seat in front of the room number Karen let me know the judge will be in. I'm so excited to finally get to formally adopt Marco, but it breaks my heart Caleb isn't here with us. I know he wouldn't be able to adopt Marco, but I still wish he were here to share this moment with us.

Karen arrives with the paperwork and shortly after the judge calls us in.

He reads off the required legalities asking me to confirm who I am and then asks me to repeat after him promising to care for and provide for Marco. When we're done, I sign on the dotted lines and then handed copies of the adoption paperwork. I have tears in my eyes and am seconds away from crying. I can't believe this is real. I am a mother and to the most amazing, genuine, and selfless child. I feel so completely blessed. I turn around to smile at Marco, and that's when I see Caleb sitting on the bench next to him. He has his phone out like he was taking pictures, and I lose it. The tears stream down my face and I walk over to give them both a hug.

"I love you, Son."

"I love you too, Mom."

Caleb takes pictures of Marco and me and then Karen offers to take a couple pictures of the three of us. Once we're done, we head out to the parking lot. I don't want to be rude to Caleb, but I had planned to spend the day with Marco, just the two of us.

"Umm…So…"

Before I can say anything, he saves me. "I have to get going. I have a couple errands to run. I'll see you both later. Okay?" He gives Marco a hug. "Congratulations, buddy. You have the best mom there is."

"That's because I got the best kid," I add.

We say goodbye and Marco and I head to his surprise.

After we stop at the store to pick up lunch to go, we arrive at Hollywood skate park. It is known to be one of the best skate parks. We get out of the car and I walk around to my trunk to grab Marco's skateboard.

"Are you serious?" Marco fist pumps into the air and runs around to grab his skateboard from me. He gives me a huge hug. "Thank you so much. This is so awesome."

He runs over and joins the teens that are all skateboarding. We spend the rest of the day at the park. I take picture after picture of him. When he gets hungry, he takes a break and we eat lunch together. He tries to show me how to ride on the board, but I suck at it. By the end of the day, he's exhausted and ready to go home. This time I know our day won't end with either of us being taken.

This is our second chance. Our fresh start.

"Thank you for today," Marco says.

"You're welcome, sweetie."

I give him a kiss on his forehead and then we head home.

We aren't even home thirty minutes when Hannah shows up to get Marco. I give her Marco's backpack with clothes for the next two nights and kiss him goodbye. I'm not sure what I'm going to do this weekend, but I know staying home and sulking isn't it. Just as they're leaving, Caleb pulls up and blocks my car in.

"I'm leaving. Can you move your truck for me, please?"

"No, I can't. I gave you a few days, but now we're going to talk. But first we're going out. Go get changed, please. "

I don't bother arguing. The look on his face tells me he isn't playing around. I guess tonight we'll be talking.

Thirty-Four

CALEB

WATCHING HAYLEY LEGALLY ADOPT MARCO WAS ONE OF THE most beautiful moments I have witnessed. I wasn't sure how she would feel about me being there, but I couldn't imagine not being there with them. Hopefully one day it will be my turn to sign those papers, but first I need to fix Hayley and me.

I have everything planned. I purchased the engagement ring, made the reservations, wrote down the show times, and have written out an itinerary for the weekend, so I don't forget anything. I spoke to Hannah and she was more than willing to take Marco for the weekend.

Now, I just need to pack for Hayley and me. I would tell her to pack, but that would give away the surprise of where I'm taking her and what we're doing, so I'm doing it myself. I grab a luggage from the hallway closet and pack for myself first and then make my way to Hayley's room to pack for her.

After grabbing a bunch of outfits I've seen her wear, I head to her bathroom to grab her toiletries. When I open the cabinet, I see a prescription that wasn't there before. Prenatal vitamins. Why would Hayley be taking these? Unless…Holy shit! Is it possible? Is she pregnant?

Then it hits me—if she's pregnant, she's keeping it from me. She watched what happened to Kayla and Bentley when Kayla hid her pregnancy from Bentley. She listened to me tell her how hard it is for me to trust a woman. She heard my stories of my sister and mom hiding shit from me. There's no way Hayley could be pregnant and keep something this important from me.

Thinking about it…she's been emotional lately. We've been having sex for months and she hasn't gotten her period at all. Then like a punch to the gut, I remember she was beaten up when she was taken. What if she lost our baby? What if the reason she's avoiding me is because she lost our baby because I left them and they were taken. But wouldn't she be more upset?

I should be mad that Hayley hasn't told me if she is indeed pregnant or if she lost our baby, but I know Hayley and she wouldn't keep something this important from me. She went through a huge ordeal and needs time. I'm going to show her this weekend I love her and want to spend my life with her, and I have to believe if those pills mean she is or was pregnant she'll open up and talk to me. Hayley has done nothing but fight for us and I'm not going to assume she's like every other woman who has proven they can't be trusted. I'm going to trust Hayley until she proves otherwise.

I finish grabbing her stuff from the bathroom and haul the suitcase out to my truck. I drive to the jewelry store and pick up the ring. I was able to grab another ring Hayley wears on the same finger occasionally and have them size it.

When I return home, Hayley is home and Hannah is about to take Marco for the weekend. Hayley asks me to move my truck so she can run away like she's been doing the last two nights, but that shit stops now.

Once she's dressed, we jump into my truck and head to the strip. When we arrive at the Bellagio, Hayley gets excited but tries to tone it down, remembering we need to talk. I don't want our weekend to be tainted, so I decide to have us go to the room to talk first, and then hopefully we'll enjoy the weekend.

After I'm done checking us in, we make our way up to our room.

"What are we doing here?" Hayley asks, sitting on the couch.

"I thought it would be a good place to talk." I kneel in front of her and spread her legs a little so I'm face to face with her. "Baby, I cannot even begin to apologize for leaving on Sunday. Saturday night when you were upset and I was giving you a massage you said something and I had a horrible flashback. The truth is, I get them often, but this one lasted longer and it scared the shit out of me."

"A flashback from your time with Gloria and those other women?" she asks softly, putting her hands on both my cheeks.

"Yes, I'm so sorry. It feels like I'm cheating on you when I have them."

"Caleb, don't say that. You can't help where your brain goes. You aren't cheating on me. You went through a lot as a teenager. Something like that doesn't just go away. Would you consider seeing a therapist?"

I think about it for a minute and know it's the right thing to do. Maybe speaking with someone will help me work out what goes through my head.

"Yeah, I will. Will you come with me, Hayles? I need you."

She leans down and gives me a soft kiss, and it has me craving her, but right now it's more important we talk.

"I promise you I will never run again. No matter how rough it gets,

I'm in this for the long haul. There's nowhere I would rather be than with you and Marco. I looked at three apartments and in every one all I thought was that none of them are home unless you guys are with me."

"Caleb, I feel the same way. But you seriously hurt me by running. It's not fair and I won't tolerate it. You have to trust me enough to talk to me or we will never make it. I care so much about you. Aside from Marco, you have practically become my entire world. These last couple nights I even dreamed you were holding me at night. I don't want to live without you."

I laugh softly. "Oh, Hayles, I'm so sorry. I have so much to work on and I will. I promise. And baby, those weren't dreams. I was there in your bed, every night after you fell asleep, holding you. I couldn't go that long not holding you in my arms."

Hayley wraps her arms around me and I pick her up in my arms. "I need you, Hayles. Right now I just want to make love to you."

"Caleb, there's something I need to tell you." I can tell by the sound in her voice she's going to tell me about the baby, but I stop her because when I propose, I need her to know it's about us and not because she's pregnant or was pregnant...

"Whatever you need to say can wait, baby. I need you now."

"But—" she attempts to cut in, but I cut her off with a kiss.

Thirty-Five

HAYLEY

CALEB PICKS ME UP AND CARRIES ME TO THE BED. I TRY TO TELL him about the baby, but he isn't having it.

"I'm not going anywhere," he whispers into my ear. "Whatever you need to tell me can wait until after I worship your beautiful body."

He lays me down on the bed and kisses me. The kiss start off affectionately. It's slow and sweet and he tastes so good. But after a few minutes, it gets rougher and more intense, causing my sex to clench, wanting and needing more. He sits up on my legs and unbuttons my blouse one button at a time, until my shirt falls to each side, leaving my bra exposed.

"I never imagined ever wanting to willingly be with a woman. I didn't trust women. Now I can't imagine not being with you. I trust you with everything I am, Hayles. But most importantly, I trust you with my heart. "

He takes my bra cups and pulls them down, and taking both nipples in between his fingers, pinches and pulls at them just enough to send shivers straight to my core. My legs tighten at his touch, seeking relief.

"I want to spend the rest of my life touching you." He pinches my nipples again. "Kissing you." He leans down and gives each nipple a soft, wet kiss. He moves up, and kisses my lips, then trails kisses down my neck. My breathing goes erratic at his touch.

"I want to spend every day tasting you." He slides down the bed, taking my skirt and panties with him. He throws them to the side and plants a single kiss on top of my mound. Then his tongue hits my clit and he licks it with such expertise I almost come on the spot.

"Oh my God, Caleb!" I yell, grabbing his hair so I have something to hold on to. He doesn't back off, though. He licks my clit until my orgasm hits, causing my ass and pelvis to lift off the bed, as I come all over his tongue. "Fuck, baby, you taste so good."

He climbs back up my body and crashes his mouth against mine.

His tongue plunges past my parted lips, and I taste myself on him, and holy hell, if that doesn't turn me on even more.

"I want to spend the rest of my life making love to you," he whispers against my lips as he pushes himself into me, slow and deep.

I wrap my hands around his neck as he makes love to me with his mouth and cock simultaneously. Kissing me passionately, while continuing to thrust in and out of me. I have never felt so loved and cherished before. Within minutes, we both find our release and I know without a doubt I don't want to spend another day without this man. When we both come down from our orgasms, Caleb looks into my eyes and says, " Baby, I want to spend the rest of my life with you," and then kisses me one more time before pulling out. I want to believe him so badly, but I'm scared.

He must sense my fear because he takes my chin between his thumb and forefinger and kisses me softly. "I meant what I said, Hayles. I want to be with you for the rest of my life. I'm not running anywhere. I know it's going to take time for you to believe me, but I will prove it to you. I love you, baby."

Tears spring to my eyes, hearing him tell me for the first time he loves me.

"I love you too." And it's the truth. I love him more than life itself.

We both clean up, and when I think we're going to get into bed to relax, he says, "Oh, no. Tonight has just begun. Get dressed. We have somewhere to be in"—he looks down at his watch—"thirty minutes."

I want to tell him about the baby but figure it can wait until after we go wherever he's so excited to take me. After we're both dressed, we head down the elevator. He stops at the concierge desk for a couple minutes and speaks to the man in charge. He won't let me listen in, which causes me to pout.

"It will ruin the surprise."

Once they're done chatting, he takes my hand in his and walks us back to the elevator and back to our room. When we walk in, I notice the curtains are no longer covering the back doors and at the table is chocolate-covered strawberries. Rose petals are littering the floor and bed.

He walks us out to the balcony and that's when Celine Dion starts singing *My Heart Will Go On*. Not even a second later, the fountains and lights begin to dance beautifully in tune. Caleb reserved a room where we can watch the Bellagio Fountain show right from our room! I watch the entire fountain show in amazement. It's one of the most beautiful shows I've ever seen, the way the music and water dance in synchronization. I'm glad my first time seeing the show is with the man I love. It's simply magical. Caleb stands behind me holding me close while we sway to the music playing. I can't keep the smile off my face. I'm blown away that he not only remembered I've never seen the show but put forth so much effort for us to watch it.

The show ends, and Caleb's body leaves from behind me. I twirl around to tell him thank you, but he's gone. That's when I notice he's down one knee with the most exquisite pink diamond engagement ring in his hand.

"Hayles, the moment I spilled coffee all over your blouse I knew you were the one." I laugh. "I knew you before that day but didn't take the time to see you. When I felt you up on accident and heard you giggle, I was done for. And then when you offered to foster and adopt Marco I saw what a selfless person you truly are and you won my heart over. When I made the mistake of thinking you would be better off without me and went to find my own place…I looked at those places and knew no matter what house or apartment I picked it would never be a home without you and Marco in it. I love you, baby, and I don't want to spend a single day not sleeping in the same bed as you. I know we have a long way to go, but you're the only woman I want to be on this journey with. Hayley Roberts, will you marry me?"

"I'm pregnant, Caleb." I can't believe I just blurted that out. Clearly my conscience is getting the best of me. This man is down on one knee proposing and I'm the worst person in the world for keeping this from him.

Caleb stands and, taking my hand, walks us inside the room to the couch. "You're pregnant, Hayles?"

"Yes, I found out in the hospital. I'm seven weeks along. I should have told you."

I put my face in my hands and start crying. God, these damn hormones are going to be the death of me. Caleb lifts my face and wipes my tears away. "Don't cry, baby. It's okay. You were going through a lot. Is that what you were trying to tell me earlier?"

"Yeah," I sob out.

"Do you want to marry me?"

Oh my God! I forgot to answer him. I felt so guilty for hiding my pregnancy I didn't even give the man an answer to his question.

"Yes, I want to marry you."

He slides the ring onto my finger and kisses me like his life depends on it. He picks me up and moves me to the bed where for the rest of the night my fiancé makes love to me until we both fall asleep in each other's arms.

THE NEXT MORNING, AFTER EATING BREAKFAST IN BED, CALEB takes me down to the casinos to gamble. He said he planned to take me later tonight, but with me being pregnant, he doesn't want me around the cigarette smoke. He also said we would be skipping the strip club portion of the weekend as well because he's not going to bring his pregnant fiancée into a club. I laugh, remembering when he told me he would take me gambling, to a strip club, and to see the fountains in one night. Two out of three are okay with me. We spend half of the day gambling and the other half lounging by the pool at the resort while we spend the night making love to each other.

IT'S SUNDAY MORNING AND WE'RE PACKING UP OUR STUFF TO go back home. When we arrive, I see all of our friends cars parked along the road.

"Did you do this?" I ask. Caleb just shrugs. "I told them you said yes."

We spend our day hanging by the pool with our friends and family. The guys grill burgers and when we all sit down to eat we tell them our other news.

"So, it's still early but we wanted you guys to know. I'm seven weeks pregnant. We are having a baby." Everybody cheers and gives us their congratulations. Marco comes over and gives me a big hug.

"I hope it's a boy! We can't let all these girls outnumber us!" Then he jumps back into the pool to splash Bella.

My mom comes over and wraps me up in one of her motherly embraces. "I am so happy for you, Hayley. I can't believe both my daughters will be giving me two more grandchildren in the next year."

I love that she uses the word more. I love that everybody accepts that Marco is just as much mine as this baby I'm carrying. I look around and am so thankful for everybody in my life. Last year I felt so alone and now my life is so full of love.

Caleb comes over to sit next to me. "You okay?"

"Yeah, I just feel so blessed."

"Baby, I have told you this so many times. You deserve this life and so much more. I'll never be able to thank you for fighting for me when I wasn't ready to even fight for myself. I'm sorry it took me so long."

"No, Caleb. It just wasn't our time yet. I believe everything happens for a reason, you moving here, meeting Marco, bringing him into our lives. It was all meant to happen just how it did. Marco has brought us so many blessings. He brought us together. He even brought Chloe into Kayla and Bentley's lives. We owe him more than he will ever know."

He wraps me up in his arms, rubbing his hands on my belly, as we watch everyone around us laugh and smile happily. I'm not naïve to believe life will always be this perfect, but for right now it definitely feels pretty damn perfect.

Epilogue

CALEB

Three Months Later

"WOULD YOU LIKE TO KNOW THE GENDER?" THE ULTRASOUND technician asks.

"Yes!" Marco says, before Hayley and I can even answer.

"I guess so." Hayley laughs.

The technician moves the device over Hayley's belly and then hits a button to freeze the screen.

"Congratulations! You're having a baby girl!"

"Noooo!" Marco sighs in defeat.

"Hey! You're going to be an amazing big brother to this little girl. Just like you are to Chloe," Hayley says.

"I know, but do you think after you have this baby, you can try one more time to give me a brother? There needs to be more boys than girls. Girls are too powerful."

I can't help but laugh at this kid's logic. "Why don't we get through this pregnancy first and then we'll discuss trying for a boy in a couple years."

"Okay."

After the technician prints out pictures, we head out to our vehicles.

"I need to run by the club for a last minute interview and then I'll meet you guys at home," I tell Hayley, giving her a kiss.

"Okay, babe. I have a couple errands to run as well." She gives me a knowing wink. Marco has no idea what is happening tomorrow.

I head to the club thinking about everything I need to get done so I can spend the weekend with my family. I wasn't sure how Hayley would feel about me working so closely to strippers all day, but she's actually really cool about it. She was more concerned with how I would feel working with women all day. It probably helps that I've hired Liz to manage all the books so she splits her time between the gym and *Assets*.

I'm working on hiring a manager for the club soon since I was given the go ahead by the doctor to fight again.

Hayley's going to work until her eighth month and then she'll be quitting to stay home fulltime with Marco and the baby. When she told me it was her dream to be a stay-at-home mom I was absolutely thrilled.

I pull up to the rear of club and walk in through the back door.

After I took it over, I learned that Gloria actually did a good job running it—once you remove the illegal shit from the equation. It's now an upscale strip club with a no-touching policy. I renovated it completely and it now has a high-class restaurant where people can watch the dancers while dining or go to the second floor where there is a bar and tables to just watch the dancing going on. There are VIP booths that line the walls and have their own mini dance floor and pole, and in the back, there are several smaller rooms for private parties. Even those have a strict no-touching policy. I added more bouncers and have them making sure to enforce my rules. I was lucky to have found an amazing chef as well. Several people have told me they come here for the food just as much as they do the entertainment.

Once I get situated I text Liz to let me know when the girl coming in to interview arrives. Helping me definitely isn't in Liz's job description, but she is doing me a huge favor by screening through the resumes and weeding out the ones who wouldn't be a good fit here.

"Hey Caleb…Someone is here to see you." Liz pokes her head in my door, looking extremely uncomfortable. "For an interview?" I ask. I glance at my watch and see she's early.

"No. How about I just send her in."

"Okay."

A few minutes later, there's a knock on my door.

"Come in."

I look up to see Ashley standing in the doorway. I stand to greet her and ask her to have a seat.

"Is everything okay?"

She closes her eyes and swallows slowly before opening them back up again. I've never seen Ashley look so nervous.

"I need your help, Caleb. Please. I'm begging you."

I'M TRYING TO CONCENTRATE ON WHATEVER BENTLEY IS saying, but I've been watching Hayley all day and the sight of my beautiful, pregnant wife has me losing my ability to think. Walking around in her bikini with some see-through thing that ties around her waist has my cock constantly hard. Her swollen breasts are perfect, her swollen belly even more perfect. Even seeing her mingling with people, smiling and laughing and touching her belly is turning me on.

I can't take it anymore, so while she's saying goodbye to the last of Marco's school friends and parents, I excuse myself from Bentley and join her. I angle myself against her side, sliding my arm around her back and shoulder. Then I pull her close, so she feels my hard-on pressing against her. She gives me a mischievous smile as she returns my embrace and we wave goodbye to the departing guest. As we lose sight of them, I turn her into me and whisper five simple words to sum up the thoughts of how irresistible she has been today. "You look so fucking hot." I want to say more. Shit, I want to do more, but I have to remind myself this is an important day for Marco on so many levels, so my dick is just going to have to wait until later.

Now that all of Marco's friends from school have left and it's just our close friends and family, Hayley and I go inside to grab the last but definitely not the least of his birthday presents. I swear I'm just as excited if not more excited than Marco is about today. We gather everyone around the outdoor table by the pool. Kayla already knows what this last present is, so she has her camera ready. We watch in anticipation and excitement as Marco rips open the wrapping paper and briefly reads his new-framed official birth certificate and reads aloud "Marco Alejandro Michaels." His reaction of surprise and happiness has us all crying. I pull him and Hayley into a three-way hug and declare, "We are now officially the Michaels family!" and my heart swells.

While Hayley was able to adopt Marco a few months ago, I had to wait until we were married. The day our marriage certificate came in we went down to the courthouse to file the adoption and name-change paperwork. I thought being a husband and father would be scary, but it's honestly the best decision I've ever made. I can't wait to add our little princess to the mix. All in all today has been the best half-year birthday-Fourth of July-official adoption ever.

After the full day we've had I can tell Hayley is getting tired, so I tell her to go inside and relax while Marco and I clean up. He talks my ear off about the most exciting parts of his first birthday party and all the presents he received. I don't think I've ever seen a kid so grateful. After we're done cleaning, I tell him to grab a shower and then he can play one of his new videogames for thirty minutes before bed.

While he's content in his world, I head to take a shower myself. I stop as I enter the room. Hayley is napping on the bed and I contemplate backing out of the room and taking a shower down the hall so I don't disturb her. She looks so gorgeous lying there, her face slightly pink from the sun and the hint of a smile on her lips. I wonder if she's dreaming. Before I can decide whether or not to wake her up, she stirs awake on her own.

"Hey," she says sleepily.

"Hey yourself. You feel rested?"

"Yes, thank you."

"The house is clean and Marco is showered and playing a video game…I was going to take a shower. Do you want to join me?"

"You know it."

I help her up and then lead the way into the bathroom, stripping my board shorts as I go. She playfully slaps my ass in the process and picks up my shorts to throw them in the hamper. I turn on the shower to let the water heat up, while she undresses. When I turn back around, my cock grazes her protruding stomach. Framing her face, kiss her softly. Her mouth is sweet and warm, just like her pussy.

We step into the shower, and my eyes stay trained on her the entire time she soaps up her body—caressing her breasts and rubbing her hand over her mound. I don't know if she's purposely doing it, but she is so damn sexy. I ignore my desire for her and fill her in on what Marco told me about his party.

As soon as we're done drying off, I throw on my boxers and sweats, and then peek into Marco's room. "Hey bud, it's time for bed. Mom and I will be in to say goodnight in a minute."

Hayley is smiling at me as I come back into our room to get her.

"What?" I ask playfully.

"Nothing, it's just that I'm so happy."

"Ditto," I reply as we both head back out to say goodnight to our son. I don't think I will ever get tired of saying those words. *Our son.*

After we say goodnight, we both head back to the bedroom to relax. I'm just going to be real, everyone expects you to love every minute of pregnancy but honestly Hayley's first trimester kind of sucked. She constantly had morning sickness, thought she looked fat and not pregnant despite me telling her every day how beautiful she is, and she didn't want to be touched much less have sex most days.

But if the first trimester sucked, the second has been amazing. She's no longer sick, her belly has become more pronounced, so she feels better about herself, and to top it off, she is horny twenty-four seven. If the rest of her pregnancy stays like this, I can see myself knocking her up at least a couple more times.

I look over at my wife reading on her iPad and hope whatever scene she's reading will help make tonight interesting.

HAYLEY

"ANY GOOD SCENES IN THAT BOOK?"

I look over at my husband, shake my head, and laugh. I swear his brain is hardwired to think about sex at all times of the day. "Yes but not what you're thinking. The couple in the book just said their vows and everyone is clapping for them as they kiss."

"Do you regret not having a wedding like that?"

I don't even need to think about my answer before responding. "No, all I wanted was to be married to you. I didn't need or want any of the glitz or glamour. I just needed and wanted you."

After everybody left our house after celebrating our engagement we cleaned up, put Marco to bed, and then sprawled across the couch to watch some television. The movie What Happens in Vegas *was on and Caleb made a joke about it then laughed.*

"Huh?" To be honest I wasn't really paying attention to the movie or to him. I was staring at my beautiful engagement ring and on cloud nine.

"We live in Vegas. We wouldn't even have to elope. We should go to the courthouse tomorrow and just get married."

I sat up straight and assessed whether or not he was serious. I couldn't tell.

"Are you being serious or fucking with me?"

"I don't know...if I was serious would that be something you would consider? I mean, do you want the big wedding? I want you to have whatever you want."

"Let's do it."

Caleb sat up mimicking my position.

"Hayley, are you being serious or fucking with me?"

"Are we playing copy-cat?"

"What the fuck is copy-cat?" He looked confused.

"Never mind. Yes, I'm serious. Let's get married tomorrow, just you, Marco, and me. Let's go to the courthouse and get married, and then file for you to adopt Marco."

"Hayley, are you sure? I know most women want a big wedding..."

"No, I don't. I just want you."

And that's exactly what we did.

"Earth to Hayley. You there?"

I put my iPad on the nightstand and then roll over to straddle my husband. "I'm sorry. I was remembering the night we decided to elope. Do you have any regrets?"

Caleb puts his hands on my belly and gently massages my front. "Baby, my only regret is not making you mine even sooner."

He takes me by my hips and carefully lifts me off of him, laying me on my back so he's hovering over me. Then he drags his body down mine until his face is level with my protruding belly. Lifting up my shirt until it reaches just below my breasts, he gives my belly a kiss and then looks up at me. "Have I told you today how beautiful you look knocked up with my baby?"

I shake my head, laughing at his choice of words.

"Well, that's a damn shame, because you do. You look fucking gorgeous with my baby in you. I think I might have to keep you pregnant for the next several years."

He gives my belly one more kiss then moves downward toward my pussy. He pushes my pajamas bottoms and panties down my legs and throws them on the ground. Spreading my thighs, and then spreading my folds, he softly blows onto my clit, eliciting chills straight up my spine, causing my nipples to harden.

"Baby, grab your nipples for me." I do as he says and remove my shirt, adding it to the pile of clothes on the floor. With my eyes locked on Caleb's, I take both of my nipples between my thumbs and forefingers and twist them to the point it just not hurts. I can't help but let out a moan.

Caleb gives me a sexy smirk and then his face disappears between my legs. He blows one more time on me, and then his mouth is on my clit, biting and sucking on it. My hips buck, needing more. He inserts two fingers into my soaking wet pussy and I damn near come on the spot.

He continues to lick my swollen clit while fingering me. I'm wound so tight, I need to release. I can feel my orgasm right there on the edge, and I just want to fall. I twist my sensitive nipples one last time and that's all it takes to push me off the ledge, my orgasm spilling over. My eyes close from the intensity and I swear I feel light headed.

When I open my eyes, my beautiful husband is staring at me with a huge grin on his face.

"Get up here," I demand playfully. He crawls back up my body and without saying a word enters me. His hands are on either side of my face and I can feel his abs rubbing up against my belly. He leans his face down and gives me a kiss. I taste myself on him and it's such a turn on. He lifts his upper body off me, and grabbing one of my legs, hooks it on his forearm, angling himself to go deeper. With his other hand, he begins to rub my clit. I'm already sensitive from my last orgasm and within minutes I'm coming again. Once he knows I've come, he picks up his speed and seconds later is spilling his hot seed into me.

He gets up to clean himself and grabs a washcloth for me. After we're both clean, he throws the washcloth into the hamper and lies down in bed, spooning me from behind and wrapping his arms around me with his hands splayed out across my belly. Ever since he found out I was pregnant this has become his go-to position. Some nights I would seriously like to push him away and tell him I need my space, but when he told me he read the baby can feel his warmth, I knew I better get used to sleeping in this position.

"Did your interview go good today?" I ask, remembering he's in need of a new dancer since one of the girls had to quit suddenly.

His body tenses but quickly relaxes. "I filled the position."

"That's good. You know if you ever need a fill-in once I'm no longer pregnant I can totally be your girl. I bet I could bust out some serious moves on a pole."

He nuzzles his face into my hair and chuckles quietly.

"The only place I want to see you busting out any moves is in this bedroom, baby. You are mine. Mine to touch. Mine to kiss. Mine to love."

"And you are mine."

"Damn right, baby. I am yours."

FIGHTING *for your* LOVE

Prologue

ASHLEY

Six Years Ago

"SHUT THAT FUCKING KID UP! ALL HE DOES IS CRY!"

"He's a baby. Please stop yelling. You're only making it worse! Your yelling isn't helping at all. It's only scaring him."

"Then make him shut the hell up!"

"I will if you move out of my—" *Whack!* My face jerks to the side at the impact of his hand hitting me straight across my cheek. It stings like a bitch, but I don't dare show it. I'm not about to let him know he's gotten to me. I get right in his face because I've had enough of his shit.

"You don't even want to be here anymore. Why don't you just leave?"

He laughs in my face like it's the funniest thing he's ever heard. If I knew I could do any damage, I would punch him in the face.

"You wouldn't even be able to survive without me. You're nothing more than a no-good little bitch."

I want to stand up to him, tell him that I think I'll survive just fine without him, but the fear of being smacked again forces me to keep my mouth shut and silently pray he'll walk out that door. I refuse to let him bully me anymore. Tonight is the last night he'll ever touch me again. I can't have Tristan growing up with him as a role model, and if that means I have to leave then that's what I'll do. I only pray he'll leave instead.

"You want me gone? Okay…I'm gone. I never wanted this fucking life anyway."

I watch him walk to our bedroom not believing for a second he'll actually leave. He threatens to leave every other day. I head into the nursery to check on my sweet baby boy. Tristan has already stopped crying and is sleeping soundly in his crib. He's only six months old and has learned quickly how to sleep through the screaming that's been a part of his life since the day he was born. I'm hoping with him being so young he won't remember any of this. I know something needs to change, but I've been with Tyler for so long I don't remember how to *not* be with him. I pick Tristan up and cradle him to my chest, giving him small kisses on his forehead and breathing in his precious baby scent. "I love you, little man." I vow here and now that if Tyler doesn't leave, I'm going to. I'm going to get away from him and find a way to provide a safe and loving home on my own with my son.

I set him back down in his crib, cover him with his blanket, and head back out to the kitchen to make dinner. As I'm crossing through the living room, I see Tyler with a bag in each hand. While he threatens to leave quite often, he's never actually packed a bag. I stop halfway into the living room, watching him stalk through the house, and then without giving a backward glance, he's out the door and slamming it shut. The sound reverberates throughout the house and I hold my breath, hoping it doesn't wake Tristan up. After a few seconds and no sound of him crying I know it didn't. I let out a breath of relief I didn't know I was holding in. Could he really be gone for good?

I continue into the kitchen, grabbing the chicken from the fridge and the potatoes from the counter, when the phone rings.

"Hello."

"Good evening, this is Chase card services calling to speak with… Ashley Myers regarding a personal matter. Is this Ashley Myers?

"Umm…yes, it is. Can I help you?"

After confirming my name, social security number, mailing address, and the best contact number, he says, "We're calling today because you are ninety days behind on your credit card payment and we would like to help you make payment arrangements before it gets moved into collections."

What the hell?

"I'm sorry. I don't know what you're talking about."

"Your balance on your Chase credit card is eight thousand five hundred and fifty-three dollars, and according to our records, you haven't made a payment in over ninety days. Before we send it to collections, we're asking if you would like to work out a payment plan."

Holy fucking shit! The small hairs on the back of my neck rises and chills run down my spine. This can't be happening.

"I need to call you back."

"Ma'am…"

I don't even listen to what he's saying. I hang up and run into my bedroom to the desk where all the bills are kept. I pull all my credit cards and bills out of the file Tyler keeps them all in and start calling the numbers on the back of each card.

Reached its limit.

Payment overdue.

Maxed out.
Ninety days behind on the phone bill.
Thirty days behind on the electric bill.
Two payments behind on the mortgage!
WHAT. THE. FUCK!

I drop the cards and papers on top of the desk and stare at the beige wall in front of me having no idea where to go from here. I trusted him. Sure, it wasn't always rainbows and sunshine, but I fucking trusted him. While I've been busting my ass to make the money to pay the bills, he's been gambling with my money instead of paying them. I always knew he had issues with gambling, but he had promised he would stop. Not only did he not stop, he used all our money and savings to do it.

I hear a noise coming from the nursery and will myself to shake off the tears that I feel prickling in my eyes before I go to get my little man. I look down into his crib, and he's lying on his back crying, ready for some dinner.

"Come here, little man." He immediately stops crying, smiling up at me while his arms reach up and his little legs stretch out as he kicks excitedly for me to pick him up.

"I don't know how, but Mommy is going to handle this, baby boy." I look at my sweet baby and know it's up to me to make sure something changes. I can't just sit back and wait for Tyler to return.

After throwing the chicken back in the fridge, I grab my car keys and diaper bag. With Tristan in tow, I purchase new locks for the house. Once we get home, I install the locks then grab everything that belongs to Tyler and put it all by the road for the garbage men to pick up.

The only way that motherfucker is getting back inside my house again is over my dead body.

KADEN

Eleven Years Ago

"PLEASE, GABS, I'M BEGGING YOU WITH EVERYTHING IN ME not to leave me. Please! I'm so sorry!"

I'm kneeling in front of my wife, begging.

Begging her not to leave me.

Begging God not to let her leave me.

Knowing my begging will do no good.

But still begging.

"Please, Gabs! I love you. Please, baby! Don't leave me."

Placing my hand into hers, I entwine our fingers and squeeze gently, but she doesn't squeeze my hand back. I know, no matter how much I beg and plead, she won't squeeze back. She's leaving me and there's not a goddamn thing I can do to change it. The truth is, while she's right here in front of me, she's already left.

I promised to always protect her and I broke that promise.

One

KADEN

Present Day

"LEFT JAB…RIGHT JAB…BLOCK…BLOCK…BLOCK!"

"Motherfucker, I am blocking!"

I throw a punch to his face and it hits him square in the eye. I probably shouldn't have hit him so hard, but the guy isn't fucking blocking.

"How the fuck do you plan to fight in six months if you can't even block!"

"I was fucking shot! I will have this shit under control by the time the fight gets here!"

I'm standing in the middle of the octagon in Cooper's Fight Club training one of my best friends, Caleb Michaels, for an upcoming UFC fight. No, I don't really expect him to be fighting up to par only five months after being shot, but as his trainer, it's my job to push him, especially when I see how badly he wants to come back. I refuse to allow him to hold back. When the UFC called with an opportunity for him, I told him he should turn it down, not to push himself, but he insisted he would be ready. So, as his trainer, it's my job to ensure he is.

"Maybe if you're fighting at the upcoming kids' tournament…"

"Fuck you, bro."

I laugh softly knowing that even though I'm pissing him off, it's also pushing him, which is exactly what I wanted to do, so I continue to push his buttons, getting him worked up.

"Maybe that would be a good idea. We could bring Bella, Tristan, and Marco in, and have them spar with you. You'll probably be able to take the two little ones, but I'm not sure if you would beat Marco."

Caleb growls and throws a punch to my gut, hoping to catch me off guard. Of course, it doesn't work. If he hadn't been shot while saving Marco from some drug dealers last winter, he probably would have stood a chance, but with him having been shot in the chest and shoulder, he's just not fast enough.

I jump back right before his fist connects with my stomach and laugh harder.

"Let me at him," Bella yells, jumping over the ropes. We both look over at the cute three-foot nothing, brown-haired, six-year-old jumping up and down in her fighter stance ready to kick some ass. She's the perfect mixture of her parents, Liam and Lizbeth Cooper. They also have an almost one-year-old son, Nathan. Liam, who goes by Cooper, is the owner of the gym. His father, who is deceased, is the one who hired me several years ago, back in Colorado.

I spent four years working at the gym, living with Bentley and Cooper, until I couldn't handle living in Colorado anymore and decided to make the move to Las Vegas with all the guys, including Caleb, who was moving here hoping for his big break. It paid off. I spent almost ten years training Cooper and Bentley, who were both in the UFC, but the last couple years they've both taken a step back. Cooper is running the gyms with his wife, Liz, and Bentley is staying home with his daughters, Chloe and Faith. His wife, Kayla, is the physical therapist here at the gym.

With the two of them out of the UFC, I've taken on Caleb, and Alex, who is another fighter at the gym, full time, aside from the personal training sessions I do with several other up and coming fighters. Caleb was well on his way to the top until he was injured. Long story short, Marco had a druggie mom who owed some guys money and Marco was selling drugs for them. He and his mom got in over their heads and Caleb came to the rescue. He saved Marco and his little sister Chloe, but couldn't save Marco's mom who overdosed and died that night. Caleb and Hayley—who is our onsite doctor—were married a couple months ago. Hayley adopted Marco while Bentley and Kayla adopted Chloe. If all goes well Caleb will legally be Marco's father soon. Not that it makes any difference, he's already like a father to Marco, and Marco calls him Dad.

The four of us have gotten together and are currently building a sports complex for latchkey kids. It's still in the planning stages, but once it's done, it will be a place for kids to go, where they can play all types of sports, instead of going home alone.

"I said let me at him!" Bella yells again, one of the guys holding her back. I can't help laughing. She's so tiny yet so full of life. She is UFC obsessed and will definitely be a woman's division champion one day.

"Okay, but you need to go easy on Caleb. He's still not at one hundred percent yet. I don't even think he's at ten percent," I add under my breath, laughing. That comment earns me a punch to my arm.

"Not Caleb! You!" Bella glares at me.

"Me? What did I do to you?" I look at her in shock.

"You called me little!" Her hands fist at her sides, and if possible, her glare gets meaner.

"Oh, don't let him get to you, sweetie." Hayley comes walking over with Marco. "You know what they say…those who can't do, teach."

Caleb throws his head back and laughs before grabbing Hayley and giving her a kiss.

"Ha ha, funny, Hayley. At the rate your husband is going, he'll have to resort to teaching the kids' classes for the rest of his life." That earns me another punch to my arm.

"I'm sorry, Bella. I didn't mean anything by it." The guy holding her back, let's go of her.

She glares at me for a few more seconds, letting me sweat it out. She's been hanging out with these women for too damn long.

"I guess I accept your apology. Marco, want to go spar?"

"Sure." They both head over to the kid's area of the gym.

"How was your doctor's appointment?" Caleb asks Hayley, rubbing the bump on her belly.

I know it sounds bad, but I tend to tune that shit out. While I'm happy for all my friends, it's hard watching each of them get married and go through all that family shit.

My phone goes off and I walk over to check it.

Ashley: I can't hang out tonight. Gotta work.

Me: Again? I thought you were only working two nights a week…

Ashley: I took on more shifts. Don't worry about me.

I shake my head in frustration. Ashley Myers just might be the death of me. I met her a couple years ago through our friends. She's good friends with Kayla, Liz, and Hayley, and has a son, Tristan, who is the same age as Bella. We became fast friends and our friendship has grown over time. She is without a doubt my best friend. She is also the most strong-willed, independent woman I've ever met. It's funny because the characteristics I love most about her are the same ones that frustrate the fuck out of me on a daily basis.

I decide not to text her back and instead go to her house. She tends to argue less when she doesn't have a cell phone to hide behind.

"I'm out of here," I say, packing up my shit.

"See ya, man." Caleb gives me a fist bump and Hayley waves.

I get into my black on black four-door sexy-as-fuck Aston Martin Rapide S. She was given to me for my thirty-fifth birthday last month, courtesy of my parents. Yes, that's right, I'm one of those trust fund rich kids, only I'm without the trust fund. My parents firmly believe I should earn my own way in this world and I'm happy to say I'm doing a good job at it. The only money they've ever given me was a million dollars for my twenty-first birthday. Any other money I get, will be in my parents' and grandparents' will. As a trainer for the UFC full time, I make a very comfortable living, so I took that money and put it into a couple investment accounts and haven't touched any of it. Upon moving to Las Vegas, I purchased a decent sized four bedroom, three and a half bath, two-story home on the outskirts of Las Vegas on a nice piece of property. Many epic parties have been held there around the bonfire in my backyard.

My parents' gift is more of a bribe. Since I have moved to Vegas, I've only been back to visit them once and they want me to come home soon. They're hoping by buying me the car of my dreams, it'll guilt me into coming home for a visit. They know why I don't want to go home, but they feel enough time has passed. It's been almost eleven years since my wife left me, taking our son with her, and while I've moved on, the truth is even after all this time, it still hurts like hell to go home. Memories of our life together are in every nook and crevice of that town. After they left me, I lasted about four years living in that town, but the minute Cooper asked if I wanted to move, I jumped at the chance to get the fuck out of there and start a fresh life.

The guys know I was once married and that when they met me I was no longer married, but I've chosen to keep the details to myself. I don't want or need anybody's pity. I've spent the last several years having one-night stands to try to fill a void that can't be filled. Well, that is up until six months ago. It's not that I can't go out and find a woman to get into bed—I just haven't felt like it. Call it a dry spell if you wish, I'm just not feeling it.

"Incoming call from Mom," comes across my Bluetooth. I want to press ignore on the touchscreen but know better. Sandra Scott is not a person who does well with being ignored.

"Hello, Mom."

"Hello, Kaden. How are you?"

"I'm good. Just heading to Ashley's to hang out."

"Oh, Ashley. I would really love to see her and her son again."

"She's just a friend, Mom."

"I know that, Kaden. I know that because she would never behave like all those women you have non-committal sexual relations with. I could tell that about her from the one time I met her when we visited."

I can't help but groan at my mom's comment about Ashley. It reminds that she was the last person that I...Nope! I'm not going to think about that night. It will do no good to think about the night Ashley and I almost...Fuck! I'm not thinking about that shit! She's my friend. My best damn friend.

"Mom, I'm almost to Ashley's house. Is there some other reason you called?"

"Can't a mother call her son to say hello?"

Most moms, probably—my mom, no way.

"Absolutely. Hello. Love you. Gotta go."

"Wait! Kaden…your grandfather would like to talk to you about something. He has a proposition for you."

And there's the reason for her call…

"Okay, well can we talk later?"

"Hello, Kaden. It's Grandfather. How are you, son?"

She seriously put him on the phone?

"I'm good, Grandfather. How are you?"

"Not good. Your grandmother's eightieth birthday is coming up and she wants you here for her party."

Of course, she does. They have used every possible excuse to get me to come back to Colorado over the years. This excuse shouldn't surprise me.

"Look, Grandfather…"

"And she wants you to come back with a fiancée…"

Has he lost his damn mind? I can't help the laugh that escapes. Is he going senile?

"Are you out of your…"

"And once you're married we will relinquish your inheritance early and double it."

The shock of his words almost causes me to run off the road. Luckily, I'm about to pull into Ashley's driveway. I gather myself together, pull in, and put my baby in park.

"Double it?"

"Yes, if you come to Colorado, engaged, for your grandmother's birthday and get married before the year is over we will sign over your inheritance early and double it. You will receive ten million dollars as a wedding gift."

I always knew I was going to inherit a large amount of money once my grandparents passed away, but I had no idea it was that much and for them to double it? What's their end game?

"Why is my getting married so important to you guys? I was already married once. You bought us a house."

"Your grandmother wants to see you happy. She wants to see you married and settled down. You are thirty-five years old, Kaden. You're the only grandchild and you're off getting your dick wet instead of settling down and giving us a great-grandchild."

I did give you one, is on the tip of my tongue, but I don't say the words. I know he isn't trying to be insensitive. My parents and grandparents love me, and it breaks their hearts that I went from being married and having a baby to single and fucking every available woman with no chance of ever committing to a single one of them. While my family can be a bit stuffy at times, they really are good people, and surprisingly not at all stuck up even though they are worth millions.

"How do you know I won't just find a woman to marry and divorce her the minute I get my hands on the money?"

Grandfather breathes a heavy sigh into the phone. "Because I know you would never marry a woman unless you loved her. I saw you with Gabrielle all those years ago and you wouldn't say those vows again unless it was for real. And I also know you would *never* do that to your mother and grandmother."

Fuck! He's right. There's no way I could stand in front of my family and God and vow to love and cherish a woman, until death do us part, unless I meant every word I was saying. The problem is when I made those vows to Gabby, they were supposed to be the only time I would ever make them. She was supposed to be my one and only, my one true love.

"Grandfather, I appreciate your offer, but unless a woman I can magically fall in love with, falls out of the sky and right into my lap, I don't think it will be possible."

And just as I'm saying these words, out walks Ashley, looking hot as hell, staring daggers my way as she walks past my car to her mailbox to check the mail. Long, straight, caramel-colored hair that flows down her back with matching hazel eyes. On a good day, they're mixed with green, but on a bad day they're mixed with gold, which is how they look now. Her hair and eyes are what you notice first, but it doesn't end there. Because as you run your gaze over her body, you notice her perfect-sized tits that I can attest to, fit quite perfectly into the palms of my hands, only spilling out a little. Then when you go a bit farther, you see the soft but flat stomach and amazingly toned tanned legs, which seem to go on for miles from the years of exercising and pole dancing classes she has taken at the girly gym she goes to. She almost didn't renew her membership this year, so I renewed it for her as a Christmas present. She's wearing her cocktail waitress uniform, which consists of a tight, low-cut black tank top that reads Double D's across the front in bright orange lettering—the name of the sleazy strip club she waitresses at—and tiny black booty shorts. And to finish off the outfit, she struts back up the driveway in black heels that have got to be a good five inches tall, showing off her toned calf muscles.

Since my windows are tinted, when she gets near my car, I roll down the window so she can see me wink at her, and when I do, she flips me the bird. I laugh as I watch her ass sway back into the house, and then remember I'm still on the phone with my grandfather.

"Kaden, are you there?"

"Yeah, I'm here. Sorry."

"Your grandmother wants you married and I will do whatever it takes to make sure it's done. She's not getting any younger and her one wish is to see you settle down and give her some great grandkids. What will it take, fifteen million?"

Holy shit! He's dead serious about this. You would think my grandmother was on her deathbed…

"Hold up, is Grandmother sick? Is there something you aren't telling me?"

He doesn't reply for a second, and when he does, he says, "Please just think about it. It would make her happy, Kaden."

It doesn't go over my head he didn't answer my question.

"Okay, I'll think about it. Regardless, I will be there for her birthday this year."

I might not be able to give her a great granddaughter-in-law or great grandkids, but I can at least go back for a visit for her eightieth birthday. What if she's sick and I don't go? That wouldn't be good at all. I live with enough regrets—I don't need to add any more.

"Thank you, Kaden."

And with that, he hangs up.

I turn my car off and head up to Ashley's front door. It's a small two-bedroom house in a rougher neighborhood. Not as bad as some parts of Las Vegas, but it's not the kind of neighborhood you let your kids play outside by themselves in. She said she bought it when she was pregnant with Tristan when she was fresh out of college. I don't hear much about her deadbeat ex-boyfriend also known as Tristan's sperm donor, but I do know he left her in pretty bad shape financially, hence the reason why she works part-time as a cocktail waitress. I've begged her to let me help her out, but she refuses. Stubborn ass woman.

"Honey, I'm home!" I yell out as I walk into the house without knocking in search of Ashley. She doesn't respond and the only thing I hear is music blaring from somewhere in the house. I head through the living room, following the sound of the music, and then into the kitchen, where I find her.

When I get there, the sight in front of me almost knocks me on my ass. Ashley is stirring what looks like spaghetti in a pot, and while doing that, she's shaking her ass to the song *Closer* by the Chainsmokers. She has a wooden spoon in one hand, which she's using as a microphone, while her other hand holds onto the oven door handle. Then she drops her body halfway to the floor, her ass sticking out and then slowly moves her body back up like the goddamned stove is an actual person. Is it weird that I wish I was a fucking stove right now? I'm instantly hard and have to adjust my pants before I make a fool out of myself. I clear my throat and she turns around still singing the song.

She's now allowed my body to take the place of the stove as she approaches me, almost too close for comfort, and then drops to the floor like she did a minute ago, only to come back up slowly. If I was hard a minute ago, my dick is now rock fucking solid. I step back a foot and clap at her performance.

"Nice. Good to know those pole dancing lessons are being used, even if it's in the kitchen cooking pasta."

"Hey now, you never know…Maybe I'm just working on building up my confidence before I take my moves to a real club." She takes the boiling pot over to the sink and pours the pasta into the strainer.

"Aren't you just full of jokes," I say dryly while searching for some food to taste. Ashley can cook something fierce.

"You still mad at me?" I ask, looking across the counter to find something to munch on. Fresh rolls out of the oven. Score! I pop one in my mouth.

"You know I hate it when you question my work schedule." She grabs the basket of rolls and moves them to the other side of the counter thinking it'll stop me from grabbing more.

"I get it. I'm sorry. I just hate that you work so much when it isn't necessary." I move to the stove to see what's cooking over there.

"It's very necessary. Anyway, I told you I have to work tonight. What are you doing here?" she asks, pouring the pasta back into the big pot and then looking down at her phone.

"Well, I'm here anyway. Need any help?" I lift the lid to the smaller pot, which is holding her delicious meatballs. I grab a fork, but before I can snag one, she snatches the fork from my hand.

"Oh, good! You want to help? You can fold the laundry in the dryer while I try to find a sitter for Tristan." I know she's only kidding about the laundry, but I go to the dryer and grab the clothes to fold them. What kind of best friend would I be if I didn't help her out?

After grabbing the clothes, throwing them onto the couch, and turning the NBA finals on, I yell back to her in the kitchen, "Britni canceled again? I can watch Tristan." I grab a couple articles of clothing to fold and see a bright pink thong. *Fuck!* I throw that shit to the side. I'll figure out how to fold those later.

Ashley comes out of the kitchen frowning down at her phone and then looks up at me folding the clothes and smiles. I love that smile. I would do anything to keep it on her face. There isn't anyone I've ever known besides Gabrielle whose smile can light up an entire room.

"Are you sure? I put a text into Hayley and Liz. I don't want to take you away from any plans you might have."

"Tristan!" I call out. It's a small house, so it doesn't take much for someone to hear you. I hear him running down the short hallway, and a few seconds later, he throws himself on the couch next to me.

"Want to chill with me tonight while your mom goes to work?"

"Yeah!"

"There you go. We're good to go. You staying to eat first or do you need to run?"

"I really need to run. I'm hoping to meet with Don to beg for some extra days." She's now running around the house grabbing her purse and coat and keys. She really is the most unorganized woman. Most of the time it's the guys who leave shit everywhere, not the women, but Ashley is the exception. She is forever misplacing her debit card and keys. One time she found them in the washing machine!

She gives Tristan a kiss goodbye, first. Then leans over to give me a kiss on my cheek. "Thank you, Kaden."

Before she can walk away, I grab her wrist, bringing her to a halt. "I can give you some money…even a loan if it makes you feel better. Then you wouldn't need to work at night and you can just focus on Tristan and teaching."

She lets out a heavy sigh, giving me her signature glare while her hand goes to her hip. "We have already had this conversation. I don't want or need your money. Can we please not have this argument again?"

I know there isn't any use in continuing. She's right, we have had this argument, and it always ends the same way, with her telling me no. She is determined to make it on her own. And she is. She has been living on her own, taking care of Tristan and teaching full time as a kindergarten teacher since I met her. She's also been working at Double D's since I met her. It was two days a week for extra money, she said. But recently something has changed. I've seen past due bills on the counter when she's forgotten to put them away and she's been trying to work additional days. She's been doing this same routine for years and now suddenly, she isn't making ends meet? Something isn't right. Unfortunately, until Ashley is ready to talk to me there's no getting any information out of her. She's too damned stubborn for her own good.

"Have a good night at work."

"Thanks! And don't let Tristan stay up past nine, please. It's a school night, even if school is almost over!" she yells as she flies out the door.

"Who do you want to win the finals?" I ask Tristan as I go back to folding the laundry, throwing some of his clothes at him to fold.

"I guess Cleveland," he says, not really caring since his world revolves around the UFC.

"Ugh…C'mon, kid. Don't jump on that bandwagon!" I groan.

"Whatever…Can we play UFC on the PlayStation?"

I look at the game, seeing that Cleveland is destroying Atlanta. It will most likely be a complete blowout.

"Sure, why not?"

"Yes!" He fist pumps into the air before running to the PlayStation to set the game up.

Two

ASHLEY

I GET TO DOUBLE D'S AND FIND DON, ONE OF THE TWO OWNERS of the club, hence the D in his name, and ask if I can speak to him.

"Sure, honey. What's up?"

"I was wondering if there's any way I could have some more nights."

"Honey, we've talked about this. I don't have any openings. Unless a girl quits or gets fired, I'm maxed out on hours."

"What if I danced? I've taken pole dancing lessons for years."

He shakes his head. "Ashley, I would put you up as a dancer in a heartbeat, but the women who have been dancing here longer get first dibs. If you would have come to me six months ago you know I would have moved you to the stage, but right now my lineup is full."

Yeah, the problem is six months ago I didn't need the money like I do now.

Four months ago

There's a knock on my door. A quick glance at the clock on the microwave showing ten p.m. tells me it's too late for anybody to be coming over. Kaden did leave a little bit ago…he probably forgot something. I swing the door open, immediately going to slam it shut when I see who's standing there. It's definitely not Kaden. What the hell was I thinking not looking out the window to see who was there? His foot catches in the door and then his fingers wrap around the edge, pushing it open.

When he gets inside, I look closely at the man who walked out the door almost six years ago, only he doesn't quite look like the same man. He's a bit skinnier, his clothes are rattier looking, and his eyes are bloodshot like he's high on something. It looks like he has been through hell and back.

"What do you want?" I whisper-yell, not wanting to wake Tristan up.

"I want to see our son."

"He's not our son. He's my son. You gave up your rights the day you walked out."

"That's not what his birth certificate says."

"What the hell do you want, Tyler?"

"I'm broke. I need money and you're going to give it to me."

"Are you fucking serious? Do you not remember what you did to me when you left? All the debt you left me in! I have to work nights on top of teaching all day just to keep up and pay off the maxed-out credit cards you racked up when you pretended to pay the bills, only to use my hard-earned income to feed your gambling addiction!"

He grabs me by my shirt and shoves me roughly up against the wall. "Listen here, you fucking cunt, I have a right to see my son. Either you give me money or I will take him away and you will never see him again." His voice is cold and menacing. What happened to the guy I met in my senior year of college? Who took me on romantic dates and told me he loved me at the top of the Eiffel Tower experience. That guy is clearly gone and I'm starting to wonder if he ever really existed or if it was all just a front.

"Don't do this, please. I don't have any money to give you!"

"I'll sign over my rights to our son for thirty grand."

"Where the hell do you think I'm going to get that kind of money?"

"You live in Las Vegas! There are plenty of loan sharks. Figure it out. I'll be back tomorrow. If you don't have my money, I can promise you our son will disappear. I'm sure a six-year-old boy goes for much more than thirty grand on the black market."

He lets go of my shirt and stalks out the door, slamming it behind him and causing me to jump.

I pull out my phone and text Don. If anybody knows where to find someone to lend me money it would be him. I've overheard all the shady shit he's dealt with over the years.

Me: Where can I go to borrow a large amount of money?

Don: How much we talking?

Me: $30,000

Don: Damn woman! Do I even want to know?

Me: No, you don't.

Don: Go to Giovanni Valentino. He owns a Gentleman's Club about thirty minutes outside of LV. Tell him I sent you. But Ashley, be sure about this. He only takes one kind of collateral…

Me: Which is?

Don: Women

I'm not sure what the hell he means by that, but I need this money, so I'll just have to figure it out. I can't take the chance of Tyler coming back and stealing Tristan from me. I'll deal with any loan shark's demands if it means keeping my son safe.

He texts me the address and I text him back thanking him. After calling in sick for tomorrow, I double check all the locks on the doors and windows. Then grabbing my pillow and blanket, I go to sleep on the floor next to Tristan's bed. I'm not taking any chances.

The next morning after dropping Tristan off at school, I head to the address listed. The GPS says it's a half an hour away, so I use the drive to build up my courage to beg for the money. When I get to the said address I see a beautiful sign that reads "La Stella." As I drive down the long, graveled road, the most exquisite picturesque mansion comes into view. It must be three stories tall made of brick and mortar. While it looks to be generations old, with old-style Church windows throughout and chimneys peeking out in several areas, it also has a certain modern charm to it. It's absolutely breathtaking. I pull up to the large U-shape driveway and see several expensive cars parked along the side. I follow their lead and park on the edge of the drive as well, my beat-up car sticking out like a sore thumb.

Approaching the massive size wooden front door, I take a couple deep breaths, gaining the courage to knock, when the door opens. In front of me is a gentleman, who looks to be only a tad bit older than me, maybe in his thirties, dressed in a three-piece suit and not at all shocked to see me standing in front of the door.

"Good morning, how may I help you?"

"I'm here to see Giovanni Valentino. Don sent me."

"I'll let him know you are here. And your name is?"

"Ashley…Ashley Myers."

He opens the door wider, signaling for me to enter, then leaves me standing in the foyer to, I assume, let Giovanni know I'm here to see him. From what I can see, the inside is even more beautiful than the outside. To my left is a tall brick fireplace that expands from floor to ceiling. The fire is on and crackling giving it a homey vibe. Wood beams run across the ceilings, and in front of the fireplace are a couple of brown leather couches. There is a man sitting on the couch drinking what looks like a scotch and sitting on his lap is a gorgeous woman wearing nothing more than a scrap of lingerie. She must feel my eyes on her because she turns to face me, giving me a small smile, and she's even more beautiful than I originally thought. I give her a small smile back before she turns her attention back to the man she's with.

"How can I help you?" Another man walks over, dressed just as nice as the gentleman who let me in, only this guy runs his piercing blue eyes up and down my body, assessing me.

"I'm here to see Giovanni Valentino. Are you him?"

"I'm his assistant. How can I help you?"

"I need to see him."

He glares at me for a second but nods, walking away. A few minutes later he returns.

"He will see you," the man with the piercing blue eyes says, now signaling for me to follow him. I look for the gentleman who let me in and notice he's back to standing near the door. Is his entire job to open the door?

We head in the opposite direction of the man and woman who were cozying it up near the fireplace. There's a small bar to the right with a younger gentleman wiping down the counter. He gives me a curt nod and I give him a small wave. We reach a long hallway and at the end, the man knocks once and then opens the door.

"Boss, Ashley Myers."

"Thank you. You can close the door behind you."

I walk into the room and am faced with one of the most beautiful men I have ever seen. Brown hair that is gelled to the side with matching dark brown eyes. He has stubble on his face that looks like he hasn't shaved in maybe a day or two. He's dressed in a suit that fits him to perfection with no tie, the top three buttons open showing a hint of a tattoo peeking through. It makes me want to ask him what the tattoo is of.

He stands and I notice he's tall, at least six feet with wide shoulders—he definitely works out. He gestures to the chairs in front of his desk for me to have a seat, his face showing no sign of any type of emotion.

After we both sit, he asks, "How may I help you?" Okay, I guess we're going to bypass all pleasantries and get down to it.

"I need a loan for thirty thousand dollars and was told by Don you could help me." I make sure to sound sure of myself. I don't want this guy to think I am scared shitless.

"Hmm…Did he now. Did he tell you what I accept for collateral?"

"Yes, women," I choke out.

"So, you understand, if at any time, you can't pay me back the set monthly payment you will be required to work it off here at my Gentleman's Club?"

Okay, so I guess that's what he means by women. I wonder what he makes a man do if he doesn't pay him back. Something tells me I don't want to know the answer.

"Yes, I do."

"If Don is sending you to me then I'm sure you're legit, but I will still need to run a background check. Anything you need to tell me?"

"No, I'm in debt, but that's it."

"Okay, as long as your background check comes back okay, I will loan you the money. First, we'll need to sign some paperwork."

"Like a contract? What do you think I'm going to do? Take you to court?"

He chuckles softly and points at me. "You got sass to you. Would you like to work here? I have quite a few guys who would be fond of you. You could make a lot more money than thirty grand in less amount of time." His statement sends chills down my spine.

"No, thank you."

"To answer your question. No, the contract is not for court. It's for my records and for yours. When the loan is paid off, we will both sign off on it."

"Okay."

He types on his phone and a minute later the man who escorted me back here, walks back in.

"Boss."

"Johnny, run Ms. Myers's credit, and if all is clear, put together the paperwork for a loan for thirty thousand with twenty percent interest."

"Oh my God! Twenty percent? It's going to take me forever to pay that off."

"You better hope not because you only have eighteen months to pay it back."

Holy shit! I can't do that kind of math in my head, but I know that monthly payment is going to require me to get another job.

"Is that going to be a problem?"

"No." I shake my head. I'll do whatever it takes to make sure Tristan is safe and Tyler is out of our lives for good. "You'll have your money."

Johnny comes back a few minutes later with the paperwork and asks for my driver's license to make a copy of it. After we're done signing all the paperwork and Giovanni lets me know how much I owe by the end of each month, he asks me how I would like the money.

"Um, cash please."

"That's a lot of money to be walking around with. Are you sure you don't want it wired to your account?"

"No, I need it in cash, please," I insist. I need to give Tyler this money so he can be out of my life for good. He gives me a quick nod, a small frown marring his face. It's the first emotion he's shown since I walked in the door, and even upset he really is gorgeous.

"Ashley, please remember you are now dealing with the big boys. You don't pay me back my money and you will belong to me."

"I understand."

Since the day he handed me the thirty thousand dollars, which I then handed over to Tyler, I have done everything in my power to pay back the obscene amount of money every month, but the problem is, in order to pay Giovanni back it means my other bills are going on the back burner. My mortgage is behind, my credit cards I finally got under control are not being paid, and meals like spaghetti and meatballs have become a luxury. But I can't regret my decision because Tyler did in fact sign over his rights to Tristan and walked out the door, once again not looking back.

Now it's the end of May and I'm short on my payment for the month. If I could just pick up a couple extra shifts I know I could make it.

"I have some good news," Don says, pulling me out of my own head. "Charlotte called out. She had several private parties scheduled. You can pick up her shift along with your waitressing shift. You're going to have to bust ass, but you'll make good money tonight."

"Thank you! I will handle it!" I give Don a huge hug causing him to laugh. "Go get ready, Ashley."

The changing room for the dancers is utter chaos at all times. Girls are changing outfits, putting on makeup, doing their hair, and usually bickering with each other over sections and men. It also permanently smells of aerosol and burnt hair, which makes me gag every time I step foot into the room. Since I only waitress, I'm usually in and out in two minutes, simply putting my purse and keys in a locker. I'm not big on makeup and the waitresses are required to wear the standard Double D's tank top and black shorts, so I come in ready to work.

Tonight, however, I'm going to need an outfit for dancing. I'm going through the rack the owners provide and it is severely lacking. The girls who dance on a regular basis bring their own outfits since the ones the club provides are crap. If I had known I would get to work a private party tonight, I would've tried to pick something up on my way in.

I find the best possible outfit and cringe when I hold it up knowing this is my only option. It's an ugly purple body suit that buttons down the front and underneath, and has purple and silver sequins around the neckline. *Gag!*

Just as I'm about to accept I have no choice but to put this horrendous outfit on, clothing is thrown my way, hitting me in the face.

"I heard you're covering for Charlotte tonight." I look over and see Scarlett grinning my way. I met her when I first started waitressing here and we hit it off immediately. She is your cliché stripper, dancing her way through college. She's now going through her master's program, and with the money she makes, she is completely debt free. What I would give to be debt free.

"You are a life saver!" I run over and give her a hug and kiss on the cheek. "You are seriously saving me right now!"

"You're lucky I love you, bitch. Now let's get some makeup on you. We need you looking scandalous so you can bring in some dough tonight."

First, Scarlett straightened my hair, making it pin straight and putting some oil in it to make it shine. Next, she darkened around my eyes with coal, giving me the perfect smoky eyes. Then she applied a couple coats of mascara, giving my lashes extra volume, and finally, she handed me baby pink lip gloss that made my lips look wet and shiny.

Once she was all done making me over, I put on the dress she gave me. It's all white with a black strip going across the chest. It's low up top and short on the bottom and the entire dress from the chest down is completely see through. Underneath I'm wearing black mini-scrunch panties and a matching black lace bra. The bra and panties are mine. Luckily, I put my good ones on tonight.

"Damn, Ash! You look hot tonight," Desiree, another dancer, says, smacking my ass playfully. I look in the mirror and she's right, I do look hot. Between the professional looking makeup, sleeked hair, and the beautiful black and white seamless net dress, I look damn good.

"Thanks! Let's hope I look good enough to make some money."

"Ladies, club is open! Let's go," the bouncer calls into the dressing room.

All the women file out and head to their destinations. When the women who dance aren't on stage, they walk around and offer lap dances to the men sitting at the tables. Some guys will buy a dance and some will go a step further and ask for a private room. Dances and private rooms are where the money is at. This club, like most other clubs, don't allow guys to put cash on the stage like it is depicted in the movies.

We get to the floor and a Britney jam is beating through the speakers. You won't find a strip club that doesn't play her at some point or another—the woman makes music that is meant to be danced to. I go to my section and greet my assigned tables asking them what they would like to drink since I have to work my waitressing shift on top of Charlotte's shift. After bringing their orders back to the table, I head to my first private party of the night.

IT'S ELEVEN P.M., AND MY FEET ARE KILLING ME, BUT I HAVE made more money in the last couple hours than I did during my last few shifts combined. And I still have one more private party to do.

"Ashley, your private party is in room five," Dean, the other half of Double D's, says.

"Thank you."

A private party is exactly what it sounds like— a group of guys who pay extra money to have a stripper dance privately for them instead of them sitting at a table and watching on the main stage. I never thought my pole dancing lessons would come in handy but they have. People assume pole dancing is just wrapping your legs around a pole and grinding on it, and while for some that's what happens, but here, you need to know what you're doing to be hired as a dancer. Don and Dean won't hire amateurs.

Now don't get me wrong, is this place upscale and classy? Hell no. The guys are sleazy and there are no real rules other than not being allowed to touch the dancer on stage, and that's only because it would cause fights to break out. But in Las Vegas you need to know what you're doing because otherwise every girl who has seen *Showgirls* will think they can just show up here, grind on a pole, and have tons of money thrown at them. The truth is, if you can't dance properly, the men and other women will eat you alive, so you better know what the hell you're doing.

After switching on *Body Party* by Ciara, I walk into the room using the backdoor which leads to the mini stage. The lights are turned down and the low light above the stage is just bright enough to focus on the dancer and allow me to dance without seeing who is watching. It helps me pretend I'm dancing in one of my classes for fun as opposed to dancing in front of a bunch of horny men for money. The only difference is, here my clothes end up coming off, whereas in my class, they stay on.

I make my way to the pole, and after walking once around it, hook the inside of my arm around it. Then I hook the inside of my leg around the front and, with a little hop, begin my routine with a front hook spin. I slowly come down and shift into a knee bridge, which is what it sounds like—my knees are both on the ground while my back arches into a bridge. Pretending the men aren't looking at my thong covered lady parts, I push back into a shoulder bridge by lifting my ass up into the air and bringing my shoulders down. From there, I roll backward and end up back on the bar.

As I continue my choreographed moves on and around the pole, little by little my clothing is removed. First, it's my top, then my bra. Finally, the last article of clothing removed is my shorts. While many strippers choose to remove all their clothes, including their panties, I've made the choice not to. I'm sure if I did, it would earn me more money, but I just can't bring myself to do it. Only one man has seen that private area of my body and it's Tristan's father. The next man to see it will hopefully be making love to me. I just can't bring myself to let some horny strangers see me completely vulnerable like that.

When the song ends, along with the routine, I gather up my bra and put it back on, leaving the dress off. Then I walk down the steps leading to the tables situated in front of the small stage. There are several men in their thirties sitting together and clapping. I make sure to add an extra sway to my hips as I approach the men.

"And who is the man of the hour?" I ask, attempting to add an extra little bit of sexiness to my voice.

One guy raises his hand. "It's my birthday, darling."

I walk over to him, sit down on his lap sideways, and give him a wink. "Happy Birthday, handsome. What can I get you gentleman to drink, tonight?" They each give me their order one by one and when I get to the last guy, I notice he's assessing me harsher than the others, like he's confused about something.

"What can I get for you?"

"Do you teach at Old Creek Elementary?"

My pen falls out of my hand as I scramble off the gentleman's lap, so I'm standing.

"You're my son's teacher," he adds.

"Yes, I do," I say softly. He stands and, taking me gently by my arm, walks me to the corner of the room.

"I'm thinking, by the look of shock you gave me, the school district doesn't know one of their teachers is a stripper."

"I don't usually strip. I'm filling in for someone tonight, and I would appreciate it if you wouldn't tell anyone."

"Absolutely, on one condition…you give me a private show."

Is this guy serious right now? Of course, it would be my luck I would run into a father of one of my students on the one night I'm doing more than waitressing.

"Okay, let me get everybody their drinks and I'll see which private room is available."

I put my order into the bar and then seek out Eddie. He is the bouncer tonight and oversees the rooms.

"Hey Eddie, do you have a private room available? I only need it for like ten minutes."

He gives me a questioning look. He's known me for years and not once have I ever asked for a private room.

"Room four is available."

"Thanks."

After going back to the bar to grab the guys' drinks, I let the guy who asked for the private dance know he can meet me in room four in five minutes, I just need to check on my other tables.

Once I walk into the room, I spot him sitting on the couch ready for me. I put *Here I am* by Rick Ross on the speakers and begin the lap dance without saying a word. My moves are robotic and stiff, yet still sexual as I circle around the couch dancing. Once I get back in front of him, I rub against his body then sit on his lap finishing the dance. He doesn't once try to touch me, which kind of surprises me, but makes it more bearable. When the song is over, the room goes silent as I climb off him.

"My name is Eric, Chris's dad." I think for a moment and know I have met Chris's mom. I also know she is married to Chris's dad.

"Nice to meet you. I appreciate you not saying anything about my working here."

I flick the switch to the iPod dock off. "You ready to head back to your friends?"

"Who said we were done here?"

"You asked for a private show and I gave you one."

"Did you really think when I said private show I meant you dancing for me? I meant I want to fuck you."

I let out a soft gasp. "I don't do that. I'm sorry."

I walk to the door and open it, silently making it clear he needs to leave.

"You sure about that?" The question sounds more like a threat.

"Yes, I am."

He nods once, stands, and walks out the door. When he gets to the room where his friends are, he says, "I suggest you rethink your stance on my offer before the end of the night. You might regret it if you don't."

I don't rethink his offer, and as their party comes to a close, I see the silent threat Eric gives me. I have to hope it's an empty threat.

IT'S TWO IN THE MORNING AND I'M MORE THAN READY TO GO home. After changing out of Scarlett's borrowed outfit and giving it back to her, I count my money. I've made almost enough to pay Giovanni this month's payment.

My house is dark when I walk through the door, aside from the faint light glowing under the microwave. I see Kaden on the couch, sleeping with the remote in his hand. The TV is still on and it casts a light on him. He looks beautiful. But what makes him beautiful isn't just his looks. He's beautiful on the inside and out. Black hair that is just long enough you can run your fingers through it and mess it up, and his hair always looks like it's a perfect mess. His eyes are currently closed, but when they're open, they are the most amazing shade of bright green. They remind me of my birthstone—emerald. They pop against his lightly tanned skin. His body is ripped; I am talking six pack of abs, ripped. Not overly muscular, but healthy and fit. And he's my best friend. He's been there for me this last year, providing me a shoulder to cry on, as well as an ear to listen without judgement. He can be a total goof, but he can also be downright sweet and serious when he needs to be. Him and Tristan have grown close these last several months, and I'm thankful Kaden can provide a good, male role model for my son.

"Hey there." I softly touch his cheek, causing him to stir awake.

"Hey," he answers groggily, stretching out. His voice is raspy from sleep and I can imagine him saying my name in that same voice...

Abort! Abort! No thinking about how my name sounds coming out of Kaden's mouth.

"I'm home. Thank you for watching Tristan. Was he good?"

Kaden grabs my arm and pulls me into his side, giving my temple a quick kiss. "He's always good. Although, he did kick my ass in the UFC fighter game on his PlayStation. How was work?"

"It was good." I lean in closer to Kaden, enjoying for a second the safety I feel when I'm close to him.

"Are you getting the extra hours you were hoping for?"

"No, I'm not, but a girl called out, so I got to take over her tables. I made some extra money. It was a good night."

"That's good, Ash." Kaden stands, then taking my hands in his, pulls me into a standing position as well.

"You spending the night?"

He gives me a look that tells me I'm an idiot for even asking. "Of course, I am. Don't I always?"

"Well, I don't know what you had planned. Maybe you had to put off plans with one of your black book girls to babysit Tristan for me last minute."

He just shakes his head and laughs, as he guides me down my hallway. We stop at Tristan's room and I walk in to give him a quick kiss and pull up his blanket. "Love you, little man."

After changing into my pajamas, we get into bed, and within minutes, Kaden is back to sleep. I watch him for a little while, thanking God for him being in my life. He and Tristan are without a doubt the bright lights in the darkness I'm surrounded by these days. I don't know what I would do without Kaden in our life, and I don't ever want to find out.

Three

KADEN

IT'S SUNDAY AFTERNOON AND EVERYBODY IS OVER AT BENTLEY and Kayla's house hanging by the pool. While Bentley and Caleb are manning the grill, everybody else either has a drink in their hand lounging in a chair or are swimming with the kids. I'm one of the people swimming with the kids along with Cooper, Alex, and Alex's new girlfriend, Jessica. All the other women are laying out in the lounge chairs holding babies with fruity drinks within reaching distance. I look over and see Ashley in her skimpy fucking little yellow bikini, holding Kayla's daughter Chloe in her lap while she laughs at whatever Hayley is saying.

It's times like this I think about how different my life would have been if Gabby was still in my life. How much I miss her and wish she and our son were both here with me. I look around and guilt overcomes me for the happiness I feel surrounded by my friends. It feels wrong to be happy while my wife and son aren't here to experience even an ounce of the happiness I feel.

"Kaden!" Bella shouts, waving her arms in the air to get my attention. I'm on one end of the pool, while Tristan and Bella are on the opposite end trying to explain some game to me they're insisting I play with them.

"Explain this game to me again. And please tell me why the heck it's called Toothpaste."

Bella and Tristan both laugh. "I don't know why it's called Toothpaste. It just is! Focus Uncle Kaden!" Bella glares at me and Tristan shakes his head in amusement at her.

"You name a category like favorite color or favorite food. Once one of us guesses correctly, we race from one end of the pool to the other and the first person to touch the wall and yell 'Toothpaste' wins."

"Thank you, Tristan, for patiently explaining the game to me once again."

Bella huffs and rolls her eyes. "Can we play now?"

"Okay, the category is…" I tap my chin, thinking, and take an extra-long time just to aggravate Bella, who acts like she's six going on sixteen. Marco comes from inside the house and sits on the edge of the pool, laughing, knowing exactly what I'm doing.

"Can I play?" he asks.

"Sure! You can be on my team." He jumps into the pool and swims over to join me.

"Oh, my God! Can you please pick a category?" Bella screeches.

"Bella Cooper!" Cooper yells out in his dad voice, pointing the spatula in her direction. "Don't be rude."

"I'm not, but Uncle Kaden is purposely not picking a category. I need to beat these boys!"

She looks back over at me and glares once again, causing me to chuckle.

"Okay, okay! The category is favorite food."

"Pizza."

"Chicken nuggets."

"Grilled cheese."

"Spaghetti and Meatballs."

When Tristan says, "Lasagna," I confirm he's correct and the four of us take off across the pool. When I get to the middle and see Bella about to pass me, I scoop her up, causing her to shriek. With both hands, I throw her into the air, and her body hits the water with a splash.

"Throw me, too!" Tristan yells. So, I pick him up and throw him into the deep end as well.

Bella swims to the end of the pool and steps out wiping the hair out of her eyes. "I give up," she says before running and jumping into the water cannonball-style right next to me to get my face soaked.

"Kaden," Ashley calls to me. "Your phone just went off with a text from your mom asking if you booked your plane tickets yet. Do you want me to respond?"

I grab Bella and chuck her across the pool once again. "Yeah, just tell her I'll do it tonight."

"Okay... Oh, you just got another text. It's Sabrina. She said she thought she saw you last night at Club Eleven."

Tristan swims over to me, lifting his arms up, so I throw him again. Then I swim to the edge of the pool and get out. "Just text her back, 'I'm sorry I missed you.'"

"Okay."

I get over to the chairs and look over her shoulder, dripping water all over her. I watch the droplets of water run down her chest and get lost between her tits before taking a look at what my cell phone says.

Me: I'm Sorry. I missed you. <insert smiley face emoji>

"Ashley! You can't put a damn period in there! You just changed the entire sentence! And you put a smiley face emoji at the end. Jesus, woman! She is going to think I actually missed her!"

"What?" She looks down at the phone as it dings.

Sabrina: Aww <insert heart filled eyes emoji> I miss you too!

"See? That's just great!"

"Sorry! I didn't mean to…"

Suddenly my phone is ringing and, before I can stop her, Ashley hits answer to the FaceTime call.

"Hey Kaden, what are you up to?" Sabrina's annoying voice comes over the speaker.

"Nice, Kaden! You gonna hit that?" Bentley laughs, earning him a hit to the chest courtesy of his wife.

"Oh! She's live! Like on the phone right now." Ashley's eyes bug out, not realizing she was answering a video call.

"Hey, Sabrina. It's Ashley, Kaden's friend. I didn't mean to answer the call…or is this a video? Sorry! I don't have one of those techy phones."

"Excuse me, I was trying to reach Kaden. He just texted me."

"Oh! That was actually me…Sorry!" Everyone around us is laughing while Ashley looks confused as shit and Sabrina looks like she wants to reach through the phone and rip Ashley's head from her body.

"Can you just give the phone to Kaden?" Sabrina spits out.

After drying my hands, I grab the phone and quickly tell Sabrina I'll call her later before ending the video chat and putting my phone on silent. I throw it onto the table and pick Ashley up, sitting her on my lap to get her all wet.

"Kaden!" she shrieks, batting me away. I hold her to me, shaking my hair like a dog and getting her soaked.

"Let me up! I'm getting all wet!"

"You deserve it! You just made some annoying chick think I want to hook up with her. You're lucky I don't throw your ass in the pool."

She stops fighting me and turns around. "You wouldn't dare. And mistakenly telling one of your many floozies you missed her is hardly a crime bad enough to be thrown into the water."

"Oh, it's definitely enough to throw your ass in the water. And just because you told me I wouldn't, I'm going to."

I pick her up bridal style and carry her toward the deep end, hanging her over the water. Everybody starts chanting to throw her in.

"Don't freaking do it, Kaden," Ashley demands.

But I do it anyway. Only I jump in with her. We both sink to the bottom of the pool and when we come up to the surface everyone is laughing and cheering.

"I can't believe you did that!" Ashley laughs, wiping the water out of her eyes then splashing water at me. Her hair is all over her face and she looks breathtakingly gorgeous. She's bobbing in the deep end, so I swim to her and grab her sides, bringing her body to mine to hold her up. She wraps her legs around my waist, so she can use her hands to move her hair out of her face.

"Thank you," she says softly. "I must look like a drowned cat."

"You definitely don't look like a drowned cat. You look beautiful."

"Burgers are ready!" Cooper announces. I swim us to the shallow end, then reluctantly let her go.

"Just not beautiful enough for you," she says under her breath.

She walks away and I know exactly what she's talking about—the night when we almost hooked up and I put a stop to it. She thinks it's because she isn't good enough or pretty enough for me. I know I should correct her and tell her she's completely wrong, but then I would have to explain why I'm not capable of giving a woman anything more than one night. Ashley is my best friend and I can't imagine my life without her, but I can't be with anyone. If she remains my best friend, I never have to let her go. It's selfish of me, but I need her in my life, even if it's only as a friend.

Four

ASHLEY

Three Months Ago

"OH MY GOODNESS! I SWEAR EVERY SINGLE TIME I DRINK THOSE Bahama Breeze's I get drunk. They are so fruity and delicious and I always forget they are filled with alcohol. It just sneaks up on me."

I plop onto my couch and Kaden sits next to me. He takes my feet into his lap and, after throwing my heels onto the floor, begins massaging one foot and then the other.

"Ohh, that feels so good. Between working at Double D's and teaching all day, my feet are taking a beating."

I close my eyes for a second, and when I open them, Kaden is staring at me like he wants to devour me whole. The way he looks at me gives me the confidence to do what I'm about to do. Moving my feet out of his hold, I straddle him, putting my thighs on either side of him. His hands move to my hips to hold me in place as my hands run through his messy hair.

"Ashley…what are you doing?"

The truth is, I'm not sure. I know it's the alcohol talking, and if I wasn't drunk, I wouldn't have the courage to make my move. But I also know if I was sober I would still want this man. He's my best friend and I love him. I'm aware he doesn't do commitment and I don't do one-night stands, but what I feel for him is so strong maybe it would be worth it to have one night with Kaden, even if that means I would be left broken in the morning.

"I want you." Kaden slowly shakes his head. I can't handle the rejection right now. I grab his hands and bring them to my chest. "Please."

I let go of his hands, and for a second, think he's going to move them from my breasts, but he doesn't. Instead he not only keeps them there but he begins to massage them.

I let out a small moan at his touch and it gets him riled up. He grabs my shirt and throws it over my head. Then he pulls his up and over his head.

His mouth goes to my left breast as he pulls my bra cup down and takes my pebbled nipple in between his lips and sucks. Then he moves to the other one and does the same thing. His touch causes my legs to tense up and tighten around him.

And then my phone rings.

Kaden's hands go to my ass, pulling me in closer to him. I can feel his erection through his jeans.

And my damn phone rings again!

This time Kaden removes his mouth and hands from my body, setting me on the couch next to him. He gets up and grabs my phone from my purse.

"It says it's Giovanni and he's calling you *Bellissima*. Who's that and what the fuck does *Bellissima* mean?"

Fuck! How do I explain who Giovanni is without telling him I owe a loan shark thirty grand?

"He's just a friend of mine. *Bellissima* is just an Italian word."

Kaden grabs his phone. "Siri, what does *Bellissima* mean in Italian?"

Oh jeez! "Hmm...According to Siri, it means gorgeous. Why the hell is some guy texting you saying you're gorgeous?"

"You're my friend! You don't think I'm gorgeous?"

"I didn't say that..."

"It's not what you say, it's how you say it, Kaden."

"Are you trying to change the subject?"

He looks down at the phone when another text message comes through.

"He wants to know if you're coming by tomorrow?"

I snatch the phone out of his hand. "Thanks, I'll text him back later."

"Ashley, are you seeing someone?"

It's a legitimate question, but one I can't explain, so I get defensive instead. "No, I'm not. It's nothing. Don't worry about it."

He gives me a questioning look and then closes the distance between us. It's then I notice the small tattoo on his left pec. I've seen it before but not close enough to read the words.

Gabrielle y bebe

mi mundo

I don't know what it says since it's not written in English, but I do see the name Gabrielle.

"Who's Gabrielle?"

Kaden glances down at his chest, but instead of answering my question, he walks to the couch to grab his shirt.

"Who's Gabrielle?" I repeat.

"Who's Giovanni?" he counters.

"Nobody."

"Ditto."

I grab my shirt from the floor and throw it on. "I'm tired. I'm going to bed. Are you staying over or grabbing a cab?"

"It's after three in the morning. I'll stay over if that's okay."

"You know it is."

"Look, Ash…"

"You don't have to say anything. I get it."

"You're my best friend. I don't want to ever lose you. If there's a guy, I'll understand, but I just don't get why you would be meeting him somewhere and be so adamant about hiding it from me."

"Do you want to explain who Gabrielle is?"

"No."

"Then let's drop this and pretend tonight never happened."

I walk down the hall to my bedroom without waiting for his response.

Present Day

"ASH! YOUR PHONE IS GOING OFF," KADEN SAYS, HANDING ME A huge plate of food. My stomach growls in anticipation. The last few months have been rough moneywise. Tristan is always fed, but sometimes if I'm short on money, which seems to be more often than not lately, I'll skip a meal to ensure he'll get fed.

"Thanks."

I check my phone and see it's an email from work.

> From: Wilcox, Margaret
> To: Myers, Ashley
> Subject: Meeting requested
> Good evening,
> Please plan to meet me tomorrow morning before school at 7:30 a.m. I have a matter that needs to be discussed with you.
> Thank you,
> Margaret Wilcox
> Principal
> Old Creak Elementary

A lump forms in my throat and I pray this email is not about what

I think it's about. I email her back confirming I will meet her in the morning. The rest of the evening goes by like a blur. I can't remember anything anybody says. My only thoughts are on my upcoming meeting tomorrow morning.

"MORNING, LITTLE MAN," I SAY, TURNING THE LIGHT ON IN Tristan's room. "It's the last week of school. Are you excited?"

"Yeah, I can't wait to spend the summer practicing at the gym. I don't know why I even have to go to school. I'm going to be in the UFC one day anyway."

"The same reason football and basketball players stay in school. You need an education. Plus, if they get hurt, they will still be okay because they went to school."

"Yeah, yeah." He pouts, throwing his covers off him.

"Get ready for school, please. We need to leave early this morning. I have a meeting before school."

"Okay."

When we get to school I have Tristan hangout with Megan, a teacher friend of mine, while I go speak with Mrs. Wilcox.

"Ashley, please have a seat. I know we already met earlier this month for your evaluation. Unfortunately, a situation has been brought to my attention. Before I go any further, I will ask you if what I have heard is true. Do you work at a strip club?"

I could lie, but there's no point. She already knows I do, and she could easily find out if I'm lying.

"Yes, I do. I am a waitress there."

"And if that were the truth, we wouldn't be having this conversation."

"I did do a private party one time, but it won't be happening again. I was just filling in for someone."

"Ashley, as an educator you agree to uphold yourself to certain standards. I am sorry, but at this time, after this week of school is over, I will not be able to rehire you."

"Can I get a job at another school?"

"I suppose you could, but due to the notes on your record, I would suggest you wait a few years for it to blow over. I don't believe you will be hired in this county."

"Okay."

"I am sorry, Ashley."

"I understand."

After grabbing Tristan from Megan, I bring him back to my classroom while I finish grading some papers I wanted to give back before school lets out. I look around and realize after this week I'll not only no longer be a teacher, which was my dream since I was a little girl, but I will be short a huge chunk of money since I won't be teaching summer school. Everything is spiraling out of control and I have no idea how to fix any of it.

Five

KADEN

"SHIT! THAT HURT!" I LEAN OVER HOLDING ONTO MY GUT. I'M completely off my game and deserve that kick to my stomach.

"What's going on with you?" Alex grabs a couple towels from the rack and throws one at me. I catch it and lie down on my back, wiping the sweat off my face and neck in the middle of the octagon while staring at the fan whirring around.

"Just got a lot on my mind. I'm sorry. You deserve better than that."

"It's all good, bro. We all have our off days."

"You're going to be ready for this fight. You're kicking ass. You have gotten quicker and stronger these last several months."

"It would be nice to win, that's for sure. I'm hoping if I win I can use some of the money to pay for our honeymoon. I can't believe Jessica actually said yes to marrying me." He laughs at himself.

I sit up and throw my towel at him. "I can't believe it either. I can't believe you asked her to marry you!"

"Not all of us can be bachelors for life like you. Do you think I'm making a mistake?"

I look at Alex for a second. He's not much older than I was when I married Gabrielle. I can see the love clearly in his eyes. I would recognize that look anywhere because I once had the same look before I lost it all. But instead of feeling the usual hurt, my mind switches to Ashley and how much I miss her.

"No, you aren't making a mistake. Bachelorhood isn't all it's cracked up to be."

"Do you ever think about settling down?" The first images that pop into my head are of Ashley and Tristan. Ashley making dinner. Me and Tristan playing video games. Helping Tristan with his homework. Ashley and I watching television together. Kissing her goodbye before I head to the gym. Then my thoughts go to Gabrielle. Loving her. Losing her. Missing her. My heart aches, and if I'm honest, I feel guilty

I thought of Ashley and Tristan first.

"No, that ship has sailed for me." I get up and grab Alex's hand, pulling him up as well.

"Hold on to your woman. Never let her go. Don't waste time fighting over stupid shit. Love the fuck out of her and cherish every moment with her."

I can tell he wants to ask me where this is coming from, but he doesn't.

I grab my bag and pull my phone out of it while I walk up to the front counter. Not a single text from Ashley, so I send her one.

Me: Hello

Me: I miss my best friend.

Me: Tristan had class today and wasn't there.

Me: Okay...I'm coming by your house.

Me: See you soon

I slam my phone on the counter and will myself to stay calm. I don't know what is going on with Ashley, but these last few weeks she has completely checked out. She doesn't call or text and she flat out ignores me when I text or call her. She hasn't been by the gym in weeks either, not even to drop Tristan off for class. My phone dings and I quickly pick it up.

Mom: Did you get your plane ticket yet?

This is the tenth time she has asked me this since I told my grandfather I would be at the birthday party. It's not even for a couple months, but she's hoping if I book my flight now, I won't change my mind.

Me: I will.

Mom: How many tickets?

Real subtle mom...I don't even bother to respond to that.

"Hey Kaden!" Marco says as he runs by me through the gym with Hayley and Kayla coming in after him. Hayley has her hand on her belly and is absentmindedly rubbing it. It's Hayley and Caleb's first time having a baby and they're due to find out the sex in the next week or so. It reminds me of when Gabrielle and I found out the sex of our baby. We both said we just wanted a healthy baby, but secretly I was excited to have a little boy I could teach MMA to.

"Ladies."

"Are you coming to Marco's Birthday?" Hayley asks.

"Of course. Do you know if Ashley will be there by any chance?"

"Aren't you two attached at the hip?" Kayla jokes.

"She hasn't returned my phone calls in a while. She's used every excuse not to see me. First, she was cleaning up her classroom for the summer. Then she said she picked up extra shifts at the club she works at. Another excuse she gave me was she was visiting her parents for a few days. I've been busy training Alex since he has a fight coming up next month so I keep letting it go. I'm about to go by her house right now, though."

"She said she would be at the party," Hayley says. "Now that I think about it, she hasn't responded to me much at all lately."

"Who?" Liz asks, coming out of her office with her purse, most likely heading to Caleb's club *Assets*. He inherited a strip club from his father who passed away last year, and after shutting it down and remodeling it, he turned it into one of the most sought out clubs in Las Vegas. Downstairs is a restaurant with stages in both corners that lead up to a main one in the middle. Upstairs is a bar with a large stage. There are also several private and VIP rooms. It was even on the top fifty best restaurants list as well as having received a best chef award.

"Ashley," Hayley says.

Liz frowns. "I was just renewing the kids' memberships for summer and fall, and when I didn't see her renewal, I called her. She said they'll be too busy this summer so she isn't renewing Tristan's membership."

"Are you serious? What is she so busy doing that she isn't letting Tristan do MMA all summer? There's no way Tristan is okay with that. The kid lives and breathes fighting."

"I know, Kaden. I honestly think she doesn't have the money but doesn't want to say anything. Since she didn't come out and say it, I couldn't offer her the financial aid form. And I'm not sure I would have. Ashley has too much pride to ask for help. When we met years ago in the mom group we were both part of, her ex had just left her and she was so scared but would never let anybody know. She made it look so easy raising Tristan on her own, while I was barely doing it with Kayla by my side."

"Oh, stop your crap," Kayla says. "You were and are a great mother! She had already graduated college. We were just starting out. We were babies. But I agree, she is a strong woman and full of pride. She would never admit if something was wrong."

"You can go ahead and renew Tristan's membership. Just take it out of my account. I'm going to her house now. I'll deal with this shit."

I slam the gym door behind me. I have no idea what is going through Ashley's head, but I'm going to get to the bottom of this shit. I arrive at her house in half the time it usually takes me, and when I pull up, I see an electric blue Rolls-Royce Phantom sitting in her driveway leaving me no room to park as well. Instead, I have to park along the side of the grass.

In a different circumstance, I would stop and check out the beast of a car, but right now I'm more concerned with who she's associating with that can afford this car.

As I walk up the driveway, I notice Ashley, standing outside her door on her front porch, talking to a big fucker. He's got to be six-foot-four at least and probably two hundred pounds of solid muscle. He has his hand on her shoulder like he's comforting her, which pisses me off. When I get closer, I see she's crying. What the fuck!

"Everything okay here?"

Six

ASHLEY

"TRISTAN, I KNOW YOU'RE UPSET, BUT I HAVE TO WORK THIS summer and Nana and Papa will be able to watch you while I work."

"I want to stay with you and go to MMA camp with Bella and all my other friends. This sucks!"

"Hey! Don't say sucks. I promise I'll come and visit you whenever I can. One summer without MMA will not kill you."

It's taking everything in me not to cry right now. After being forced out of my job, I spent the week cleaning out my classroom knowing I wouldn't be returning. The next week I spent wallowing in self-pity. Then I got myself together and remembered I don't have time for self-pity or to wallow for that matter. I need to make money and fast. My mortgage is several months behind and they've sent me a foreclosure notice. If I don't get caught up with the payments and pay the fees they're going to force us out at the end of July.

I called my mom and asked if she had any money she could lend me to pay my mortgage. She offered to take some money from my father's retirement fund, but I couldn't allow her to do that, so I played it off like it wasn't a big deal. Then I asked her if she could take Tristan for the summer. She's a teacher like me and was more than happy to have Tristan come and visit for the summer.

I give Tristan a kiss goodbye, but he doesn't kiss me back or acknowledge me. He's mad and I get that, but it still hurts. I've tried so hard to keep him from being affected by my money problems so he doesn't understand why I'm being forced to leave him with my mom and dad. What he doesn't get is that it's killing me to leave him with them. I would love more than anything to enjoy my summer with Tristan, but sometimes life isn't fair and it doesn't work in our favor. I just hate that he's having to learn that lesson so young.

"Thank you for taking him." I give my mom a hug.

"Is everything okay, Ashley? I feel like I haven't seen you much since Christmas."

"I'm sorry I've been distant these last few months. I just have a lot going on."

"Okay, sweetie. If you need anything, your dad and I are here. I love you."

"I love you too, Mom."

When I get back to my house, I turn on the computer to find local clubs I can call around to, to see if they're hiring, but my internet is down. Shit! I didn't pay that bill.

There's a knock on my door and I look out the window to see who it is. Yeah, you didn't really think I would ever open the door without looking again, did you?

It's Giovanni standing at the door. He knocks again. "Ashley, I know you are home. I saw you look out your window."

Damn it! I open the door slowly trying to prolong this conversation. I step outside, closing the door behind me, and he hands me a piece of paper.

30-DAY

PERSONAL PROPERTY

NOTICE

Pursuant to the foreclosure sale conducted on June 22nd, 2016, Las Vegas Community Bank is now the owner of this property. You must remove all personal property, including all furniture immediately.

On July 22nd, 2016, the doors will be locked and any items still in home will be forfeited.

"You're about to get kicked out of your home."

"Yeah, I stopped paying in January."

"Why did you borrow all that money and not pay your mortgage?" He looks at me incredulously.

"I borrowed the money to pay off my ex. He was threatening to take my son and said he would hand over his rights for thirty thousand dollars. I kept putting off paying the mortgage to pay you. I just couldn't get caught up in time."

Suddenly it all is just too damn much. The tears start falling and I can't stop them.

"I lost my job teaching a few weeks ago. I've been trying to find another job, but I haven't found anything yet."

"Oh, *Bellissima*, do you have *any* of my money this month?" Giovanni takes my chin between his fingers and raises my face, forcing me to look at him.

"I have a little bit of it. If you could just give me a little more time…"

"Beautiful, if I give you more time then I have to give everyone else more time. If I let everyone pay whenever they *could,* I wouldn't be the businessman I am. Nobody would take me seriously."

He places his hand on my shoulder, and for a minute, I let him comfort me—if that's what this even is.

"How about this? You come to work for me at my club for six months and I will wipe your debt clean."

The tears flow harder. The idea of having sex for money makes me feel sick. I get that there are women who can do it, but I just can't. I don't know how to fix this, though. I have a feeling Giovanni is trying to be nice about this, but he's really letting me know I don't have a choice. I made a deal and I couldn't hold up my end of it. I figure it'll be easier to go willingly at this point. "I guess I don't..."

"Everything okay here?"

I look around Giovanni to see Kaden standing in front of my porch.

"Everything is all good," Giovanni says.

"What's going on?" Kaden asks.

Giovanni is the one to answer. "Ashley and I were just discussing a business opportunity that has arose I think she might be interested in."

"Ashley, what the hell is going on? Who is this guy?" Kaden ignores Giovanni completely, focusing on me.

"This is Giovanni. He's a friend of Don's, my boss at Double D's. I owe him some money."

Kaden's eyebrows shoot up recognizing the name from the night Giovanni texted me. He walks up and joins us on the porch. My tiny porch suddenly feels extremely claustrophobic with these two large guys both crowding me in.

"How much does she owe you?" Kaden directs this question to Giovanni, but before he can say twenty-two thousand, I say, "four thousand." Thankfully Giovanni doesn't give anything away.

"Why do you owe him so much money?"

"I borrowed it from him to pay off some bills."

"I'm assuming you aren't going to accept a check, so why don't you follow me to the bank and I'll give you the money she owes you."

Giovanni looks to me. "You good with that?"

I want to say no. The last thing I want is to owe yet another man, but I would be a fool to say no right now.

"Yeah."

Giovanni puts his hand out to shake mine and I look at him quizzically. The foreclosure notice is exchanged from his hand to mine. He holds my hand for a moment before he says, "If you change your mind, you know where to find me." And then softly so only I can hear he adds, "Please don't be late next month."

Both men take off and I go inside to stress clean. I don't even know why I bother. In thirty days, this will no longer be my home. Hell, technically right now this is no longer my home. I'm only allowed here to remove my belongings. I take a moment to walk down the hallway and look at the pictures hanging on the wall. They start off with Tristan as a baby. Then move to him in preschool. One of him in Kindergarten. Another of him at his first MMA tournament last year. There's one of us during Christmas last year. Kaden is in the picture as well. We were at my parents' house before Tyler came through like a tornado destroying everything in his wake.

I hear the door slam shut and tentatively go down the hall to see who's there. Kaden is sitting on the couch with his hands in his hair, his face down. I can tell by his actions he's trying to calm himself down.

"Hey," I say quietly. Kaden has never yelled at me or hurt me so I don't know why I'm nervous.

"Hey," he says back, patting the couch for me to join him.

"Thank you for paying him. I'll pay you back."

Kaden shakes his head. "I don't care about the money Ash. What's going on? Liz said Tristan isn't going to Cooper's Gym anymore."

"He's spending the summer at my parents."

"You know he loves MMA. Why would you do that? If it's the money, you don't need to worry about that. I paid his membership in full for the year."

"What the hell, Kaden! I didn't ask you to do that!"

"You're right, you didn't ask. You never ask for anything. You're my best friend, and I can see you're struggling, but you won't let me in. Let me in, please."

Now would be the perfect time to tell him the entire truth, but I can't make this his problem. I can't count on another man.

"I appreciate you paying for his MMA, but he's spending the summer with my parents. And as for me, I am fine. I will pay you back as soon as I can."

He assesses me for a moment and I can tell he doesn't believe a word I'm saying, but instead of calling me out on it, he simply nods.

"Okay, let's do something fun tonight. I miss my best friend." Kaden throws his arm over my shoulder and pulls me into him, giving me a kiss to my temple. To him, it's nothing more than a friend being affectionate, but unfortunately, my body and heart don't see it that way at all, and the butterflies in my belly prove that.

"What do you want to do?"

"How about we go to dinner and go watch the fountains at Bellagio. We can take a walk on the strip."

"Okay, that sounds good. Let me get dressed."

And just like that the tension between us is gone.

"MORNING." I ROLL OVER AND SEE KADEN LYING NEXT TO ME in my bed. We had a blast last night. We ate dinner at a delicious steakhouse and then walked down the strip acting like tourists going in and out of all the little shops. We stopped at the fountains and watched two of the shows before heading home to watch a few episodes of *House* on DVD. It's one of my favorite shows and months ago I insisted Kaden watch them with me. Now he's as addicted as I am to the crazy doctor. We eventually fell asleep watching one of the episodes.

"Caleb texted asking if we want to go to breakfast with everyone. I guess they were all kidless last night and are going to breakfast before going to pick them up."

"Sure, I'm going to jump in the shower."

"Sounds good. I'll take one after you."

We get to the diner that Hayley always insists we eat at and everyone is already there. Hayley and Caleb are sitting across from Liz and Cooper, and Kayla and Bentley are sitting across from Alex and his fiancée, Jessica. Toward the back there are two seats open across from Stephen and whatever girl he woke up next to this morning. We say hello to everyone and make our way to the two empty seats.

After everyone has ordered, the conversation flows and eventually moves to Alex and Jessica's upcoming wedding. "Caleb, we should do Alex's bachelor party at your club," Stephen suggests.

"Does it bother you that your husband owns a strip club?" Stephen's date asks. *Rude much?*

If her question bothers Hayley at all, she doesn't show it. "No, not at all. Plus, Liz works there several days a week, so I'm sure she keeps him in check." She winks at Caleb and he laughs, leaning over to give her a kiss.

"I'm not planning to be there as often as I have been. I'm still getting things situated, but once it's all under control, I'm planning to train someone to manage the place."

"Before you do that you need to hire a dancer," Liz says. "Shayla got married and left last week."

"Yeah, I know. Any chance you can set me up a couple interviews? Weed out the crazy chicks…"

Liz laughs. "Already done."

"So…what about the bachelor party?" Stephen asks again.

"Yeah, I don't see why not. Just let me know the date and I'll make sure I put it down so you're taken care of."

"Nice, dude!"

Kaden's phone goes off and he checks it, frowns, and puts it back in his pocket.

"Everything okay?" I ask.

He leans over and gives me a kiss on my temple like he always does, and as usual the butterflies appear.

Hayley catches my eye, waggling her eyebrows, and I roll my eyes at her. Things between Kaden and I will never be more than friends, and I have accepted that. Whatever it is he is looking for isn't me.

"My mom is asking again about my flight to Colorado. It's my grandma's eightieth birthday coming up at the end of August. Any chance you and Tristan would want to join me? I know they would love to see you guys."

"Tristan goes back to school at the end of August. As long as we're back before he starts school, we should be good to go."

"Yeah? Awesome. I'll book our tickets tonight. You and Tristan joining me will definitely make this trip better."

The waitress delivers our food and it all looks delicious. I ordered pancakes, while Kaden ordered bacon, eggs, and potatoes. He is forever eating healthy, except for when I cook for him. Then he gives in to the temptation of the delicious carbs.

I try to snatch a piece of bacon from his plate, but I'm rejected when he blocks my hand.

"Hey! I just want a small piece," I say with a pout. He laughs, knowing I'm a faker. I'll eat all his bacon if he turns away for too long.

"A small piece to you is the entire strip." He rips off a piece of the bacon and places it up to my mouth. I part my lips and snatch the piece with my teeth, biting the tips of his fingers in the process.

"Oops, sorry."

"Yeah, I bet you are." He feeds me another bite, and I take it this time without nipping at him.

"Let's go get Tristan," he says.

"Huh?"

"Let's bring him back. I paid for his membership. I don't want him missing class. If you need to work I can watch him. Please. I miss him."

His comment makes my stomach do somersaults. For so long it's just been Tristan and me. It's weird to have someone else care about him aside from my parents.

"Okay."

"Good, we can go get him together. I haven't seen your parents in a while."

He puts another piece of bacon up to my mouth, smiling when I bite his fingers, completely missing the bacon.

Seven

KADEN

TONIGHT IS THE NIGHT OF ALEX'S BACHELOR PARTY, AND while I should be excited to see some T and A, the idea of hanging out with these guys while watching some naked women shake their ass on stage does nothing for me. I would much rather be hanging out with Ashley and Tristan. Ever since she took on more hours at *Double D's* she rarely has time to hang out, and as much as I love hanging out with Tristan while she's at work, I miss hanging out with Ashley. Tonight just happens to be her night off and while she's at home, I'm stuck going out.

Instead of lounging around her house watching one of her crazy shows, I'm in a limo on my way to *Assets,* Caleb's strip club, to party with Alex and the other guys before he gets married in a couple weeks. The bachelor party was originally scheduled for next weekend, but when the promotions manager of the UFC said they need him in New York to do a photo shoot for his upcoming fight we all got a text last minute letting us know it's happening tonight.

After getting dropped off at the front, we walk up to the hostess stand. Caleb greets her and lets her know we're going to be using private room C. She marks something off on her paper and tells us to enjoy ourselves.

Once inside, I can see why this club is ridiculously popular. Scanning the room, I see the walls are all a matted black with shiny marble flooring. There's blood red accenting the dark room, making it look seductive yet romantic—it's all tastefully done. The booths and tables are high quality, black, distressed wood with plush black leather seats throughout. Everything is clean looking. If it wasn't for the women currently dancing on the stages in the back of the restaurant you wouldn't even know it's a strip club.

We walk past the bar, which has mirrored walls behind it going up two floors with black glass covering the bar tops, to the steps leading to the second floor.

"Damn, Caleb. This place looks great," I tell him. I know he's been hard at work turning this club around while he couldn't fight, and it shows.

"Thanks, you know I wasn't keen on the idea of owning a strip club. It seems like living in Vegas, the term stripper is given a bad name. But once I started working on the one in Colorado, I realized I could make them classy. I had no idea they would blow up to be this big, though. I just sold the one in Colorado for way more than I thought I would be able to get for it, and the guy is considering buying this one as well."

"You should be proud of this place."

"Thanks, man."

Upstairs, the music is a bit faster unlike downstairs where the music is slower and quieter. There are two girls dancing, one on each side of the stage, and the place is packed with guys sitting at the bar and tables that are surrounding the two circular stages.

We get to the end of the area and there's a narrow hallway filled with several doors on each side. Each door has a small letter on it. When we get to the letter C, Caleb opens the door and the club's red and black theme continues. The room is obviously smaller than the open areas, but it doesn't look any different. It's just a smaller version of the same setup. We have a seat at the tables surrounding the stage and I can hear the faint sound of music playing in the background.

There are about a dozen of us here celebrating the end of Alex's bachelorhood. Most of the guys are from the gym, but there are a few others I was introduced to but don't know. A couple of them are his brothers and one is his future brother-in-law. I think there's also a couple guys he knows from high school.

I sit at the table with Caleb, Bentley, Cooper, and Stephen. We aren't even sitting a few seconds when the stage lights turn on and *Black Widow* by Iggy Azalea comes across the surround sound.

At the same time, a woman wearing a tight red tank top that has Assets written across her tits in black appears handing us menus.

"What can I get you fellas?" She smiles seductively at me, and it should probably do something to me, turn me on in some way, but it does absolutely nothing. Not too long ago, I would have found this woman attractive and would have been figuring out where I could take her to fuck her. Now, while I'm not blind and know a beautiful woman when I see one, the only woman on my mind is Ashley.

I decide to keep it simple. "I'll take a Jack and Coke."

"Sure thing, handsome."

She moves on to the other guys and I take the opportunity to check my phone. I have a couple new texts from Ashley. They were sent a couple hours ago.

Ashley: Hey can you watch Tristan tonight? I got called into work.

Thirty minutes later.

Ashley: Okay, you must be busy. Tristan is spending the night at Hayley's. If you want to come over later I should be home around 2.

Me: Alex's bachelor party got moved to tonight. I'll come over when it's over.

She doesn't keep her phone on her while she's at work, so I stick my phone back in my pocket without waiting for a reply, then look up to see the curtain opening and a woman walking out onto the stage. It's too dark to see her at first, but once she gets to the center of the stage where the pole is located, I can see her clearly.

Caramel-colored brown hair pin straight down her back and light eye makeup making her hazel eyes pop are just the beginning. She's wearing a black lacy top that is just not see-through with her perfect-sized tits peeking out enough to tease me. My eyes trail down her toned stomach and land on black silky-looking shorts. Her legs are long and toned and she's wearing black fuck-me heels.

She walks to the pole but doesn't stop until she's standing in front of it. Raising her hands above her head she grabs the pole behind her with both hands and drops her body almost all the way to the ground, allowing her back and ass to glide down the front of the pole. She is without a doubt fucking stunning.

Lowering herself a little farther to the ground, she bends backward, causing her shorts to stretch, and giving the entire room a sneak peak of what's underneath. The sight of her body on display shakes me out of my frozen state of shock and it hits me. The stunning woman isn't just any woman—it's fucking Ashley! What in the actual fuck!

I look around at the guys gauging their reactions. The ones who know Ashley are all sitting in silence unsure of what to do. The ones who don't know her are making comments about her body and how they would love to have her beneath them. Caleb looks over at me with wide eyes, and I realize he isn't shocked to see Ashley on stage. He's shocked that I'm seeing her on stage.

Without thinking, I get out of my seat, knocking it over in the process, and jump onto the stage. With her back to the tables, she doesn't see me coming, but the instant I grab her by her torso and fling her over my shoulder, she screams, not knowing what is going on. She starts hitting and kicking me, trying to get me to let go of her and put her down, but I'm not having it.

"Don't fucking move!"

"Kaden?" She stops trying to break free when she realizes it's me carrying her.

"Yeah."

I'm not even sure where I'm going at this point, but I know I need somewhere quiet to calm down. I find a door open at the end of the hall and walk into it, slamming the door behind us. There's a couch up against the wall and a mini stage in front of it. I drop her onto the couch then back up, needing to take a minute to breathe.

"Kaden…"

I turn around and Ashley is no longer sitting on the couch. She's standing up and walking over to me. She places a hand on my arm. "I don't want to argue about this."

"Argue about what? About the fact that you aren't really a fucking cocktail waitress at *Double D's*? About the fact that you are a goddamned stripper! Or how about we *don't* argue about the fact that you would rather take your fucking clothes off for money instead of just letting me help you! What the hell, Ash! How the fuck did I not know that you were stripping at Caleb's club?"

Her hand goes to her hip and her head tilts to the side slightly—her telltale sign of her defenses going up.

"You didn't need to know! It's my business. I needed the job and Caleb gave it to me. It has nothing to do with you."

"When the fuck did you start working for Caleb anyway? How long have you been lying every time you leave for work while I watch Tristan for you?"

Eight

ASHLEY

Three Weeks Ago

I WALK INTO CALEB'S RECENTLY ACQUIRED RESTAURANT AND strip club *Assets* for the first time and it's gorgeous! What he's done to this place is nothing short of amazing. It's only four in the afternoon so the place is deserted and quiet. I'm assuming someone is here or the door wouldn't be open.

"Hey, Ashley! What are you doing here?" Liz walks down the steps to greet me, giving me a hug.

"Do you guys just let anybody walk in?" I ask, stepping back to check out the place.

"No, there's a silent bell that rings in our offices. I unlocked the door because Caleb has a couple interviews today."

"That's actually why I'm here."

"You have an interview?"

"Umm…No, I don't, but I was hoping I could apply for the dancing position."

Her eyebrows raise slightly. "Ashley, you know if you need any help with money…"

"Liz, I love you for offering, but you know I won't accept any money from you or from anyone for that matter."

Liz gives me another hug, holding me tightly. "I know, but I had to try."

"And I appreciate it."

She releases me from her embrace. "I'll let Caleb know you're here to see him."

"Thank you…and Liz…"

"Yeah?"

"Can you please not tell anybody I'm here?"

"My lips are sealed…but if you need anything.…"

"I know. You got my back. Thank you."

I follow her up the stairs and down the hallway, until we get to the last door on the left.

"Why don't you give me a minute to let him know you're here?"

"Okay."

A few minutes later she comes out, giving me a small smile.

"Are you sure you want to do this?"

"Yes, I'm sure."

She nods. "Just knock before you go in."

I walk over to his door and give it a small knock.

"Come in."

Caleb is looking down at something on his desk, but once I enter, he looks up. Then he stands and tells me to have a seat.

"Is everything okay?"

I close my eyes and swallow thickly, trying to work up the courage I need. When I open my eyes, I take a deep breath and say, "I need your help, Caleb. Please. I am begging you."

"What's going on?"

"You said you were hiring a dancer. I would like to apply for the position. I have taken pole dancing lessons for several years and I'm good. Actually, I'm more than good. I worked at *Double D's* for close to six years so I know how this business works. I can work the bar when needed, waitress, work private parties, whatever you need."

He stares at me in shock but quickly snaps out of it. "Why do you need this job so badly?"

"I was let go from my teaching job and *Double D's* doesn't have the availability to give me the hours I need. Plus, dancing means getting the lap dances and private parties, which means bringing in more money. And I need the money. Waitressing isn't enough."

"If you need money, I can…"

"No, stop, please. Liz already offered. Kaden has offered over a dozen times. I am not taking a dime of anybody else's money. I just need a job, please."

"Does Kaden know you're here?"

"Kaden has nothing to do with this and I need you to promise not to say anything. He can't know. He would be so pissed I chose to strip instead of taking money from him. Nobody can know I work here, please."

He scrubs his hands over his face. "Ashley, Kaden is going to be pissed if he finds out."

"That's between me and him. I need this job. I'm begging you. If you need to tell Hayley, I understand. I wouldn't ask you to hide it from her."

"How about this? I'm looking for a manager. I could train you to take over. You said you know the business."

"I don't want preferential treatment. I'm just asking to dance here. You wouldn't hire anyone else who came in here for the dancer position, to be a manager."

Caleb takes a deep breath. I can tell he's torn as to what to do, and I know I'm making this hard on him, but this is my last chance.

"How about you start as a dancer and slowly I'll show you the ropes so you can eventually take over as manager? You would be helping me out. I'd like to have someone managing this place before the baby comes, so I only have to be here a couple days a week."

"Okay, I can agree to that. Thank you."

"No problem. But if anything changes I can help…"

I shake my head to stop him. "No, this is perfect, thank you!"

"When can you start?"

"Would tonight work?"

"That will work."

"Thank you so much, Caleb!"

Present Day

"YOU'VE BEEN WORKING FOR HIM EVER SINCE WE ALL MET FOR breakfast? That was weeks ago! Why didn't you say something?"

"I knew you wouldn't understand why I'm dancing instead of waitressing. I need the money."

"Damn right I don't understand and you're not dancing! You're stripping! There's a big fucking difference. You should have told me. If money is that bad, I can lend it to you."

"I was embarrassed."

"Well, now that I know, you can quit." Kaden closes the distance between us, putting his hands on my hips and tugging me close to him. Then he pulls me into a hug, nuzzling his face into my hair.

"Whatever money you need, I will give it to you."

"I know you will, but I don't want you to. I need to handle this on my own. I can't depend on anybody but myself."

He backs up and raises a brow. "Ashley, you are quitting," he says slowly.

I make it a point to say it back the same way. "No, I'm not."

"Are you fucking serious right now? I'm not letting you strip at a club for other men."

"You aren't the boss of me, Kaden. You are my friend. You don't control my choices."

He nods his head slowly. "Okay, we'll see about that. You're my best friend and it's my job to look out for you." He takes me by my hand and heads to the door.

"Where are we going?"

"To speak to Caleb about this."

"No! You can't do that. He might be your friend, but he's my boss. Can we please just go to my house? I've been embarrassed enough. Just be my friend tonight and take me home, please?"

He stops in his tracks, his eyes running down my body. I can see when he gives in temporarily. His jaw goes slack and shoulders slouch a little, telling me he's finally calming down. "Okay, do you have clothes so you don't have to walk out like this?"

"Yeah, in the dressing room. It's right over there."

We go to the dressing room and I change back into the clothes I came to work in. Then we head outside through the back, so Kaden can't accidently run into Caleb. Since he didn't come in his car, we take my car back to my house.

"I'm going to wash this makeup off and change into pajamas. Want to order a pizza and watch a movie?"

"Sure."

Kaden follows me into my room, grabbing a pair of sweats and a shirt from the drawer of clothes he keeps here for the nights he ends up staying over.

After he orders the pizza, we plop onto the couch. Kaden goes to grab the remote, but I remember I don't have working cable. "Want to watch a DVD?"

"What's wrong with your cable?"

"I'm not sure," I lie. I'm not about to tell him I'm three months behind so they canceled my service until I get caught up with the overdue balance. That will just lead to another fight over money.

He scrutinizes me for a moment but lets it go. We decide on one of the Fast and Furious movies and after popping it in, we snuggle up like we always do.

"I'm assuming you didn't know who was in the room you were working in tonight," Kaden says after a few minutes.

"No, I didn't. Caleb didn't mark it down on the sheet in the back that the bachelor party got moved up a week. I wasn't even supposed to work tonight. One of the girls called out and I agreed to cover her shift. I didn't have time to ask who was there."

Kaden doesn't say anything else. He just pulls me into his side and gives me a kiss on my forehead. We watch the movie in silence...not necessarily uncomfortable, but not exactly comfortable either. I know Kaden isn't going to let this all go, but living in denial can be a great thing.

Nine

KADEN

I WAKE UP AND ROLL OVER ONLY TO FIND ASHLEY'S SIDE OF the bed is empty and the shower running. I roll back over onto my back and stare at the ceiling remembering everything that happened last night: The bachelor party. Ashley being the stripper. Hearing the guys say they wanted to fuck her. Me, throwing her over my shoulder and then demanding she quit stripping. Her, refusing to quit stripping. Me, realizing that I'm falling for my best friend.

Yep, you heard me right. I'm falling for Ashley, and I know what you're thinking, how the fuck did I not realize this sooner? It's called denial. Don't act like you've never experienced it. The problem is, I have absolutely no intention of acting on my newfound feelings. She deserves better than what I'm capable of giving her and Tristan. My heart split in half and was taken with my wife and son eleven years ago. Ashley deserves more than the broken man that's left of me.

I rub my hands repeatedly up and down my face hoping last night was a bad dream, but knowing it wasn't. I don't know how to handle this whole situation with Ashley. She is stubborn as hell and is refusing to quit stripping. Thinking about this is just pissing me off, so I get up and throw on my workout gear. I need to head to the gym to train with Alex and Caleb today. Fucking Caleb! I can't believe he hired Ashley as a goddamned stripper. I don't know what the hell he was thinking.

I go into the kitchen and open the cabinet to find something to eat and notice every cabinet is about empty. I open the fridge and it's empty as well. What the hell are she and Tristan eating? I scour through the drawers hoping to find a K cup to make myself a cup of coffee at least but only find a stack of papers. They're similar to the bills I found a few months ago which Ashley insisted were being handled. The only difference is those were first notices and these are final notices. I flip through the papers and find one that says notice of foreclosure. The date is scheduled for July twenty-second, which is a week away.

I hear her footsteps coming down the hall, so I quickly throw all the papers back in the drawer and walk out to the living room.

"Morning."

"Morning, were you looking for coffee in there? Sorry, I haven't had time to go grocery shopping."

"No problem, why don't we grab coffee and breakfast out?"

"Okay, cool. I need to go to the gym anyway to get Tristan. Hayley is meeting me there with him."

After stopping at a small diner for coffee and a bagel, we head straight to the gym. As we're walking up to the door, Hayley, Marco, and Tristan are walking up at the same time.

"I'm going to go catch up with her," Ashley says.

I walk to the locker room and throw my gym bag and phone into a locker. Then I head to the octagon to go find Alex. Before I can make it out of the locker room, I hear Stephen and a couple of other fighters talking.

"Bro, you should have seen her! She looked smoking fucking hot. I would sink my dick into her in a damn heartbeat."

"Fuck yeah, man! And that outfit…Goddamn! That shit ended too quickly when Kaden threw her over his shoulder and…"

I walk up to the group of them, and grabbing the kid who just commented on her outfit, throw him up against the wall. "Say another fucking word about Ashley and I will knock your teeth out. That goes for all of you. Got it?"

They all start apologizing, but I don't even stop to listen. There's one person responsible for this shit and he and I are about to have some words. I stalk out to the main floor and look for Caleb. I spot him laughing with Cooper on the mat next to the octagon…and I snap.

Without even thinking, I grab him by his shoulder to spin him toward me and deck him in the face, sending him flying backward. Yeah, it was a sucker punch at its finest, but I don't give a fuck.

"What the fuck!" he shouts at me, his fingers touching his bloody lip.

"What the fuck were you thinking hiring Ashley to work at your fucking strip club! And on top of that not telling me!"

"Kaden, it wasn't my place to say anything." He shakes his head.

"Caleb!" Hayley comes running over and gets in his face, and judging by the tone in her voice, I have a feeling I wasn't the only one he kept this secret from.

"Is it true? Is what Kaden saying true? Did you hire Ashley as a dancer?"

"Hayles…"

"Oh no! Don't you 'Hayles' me! What were you thinking?"

Caleb glares at me, pissed I just got him in the doghouse. Well, good! He deserves it.

"Hayles, can we not do this here, please?"

"Fine, we'll talk about this at home." She pokes him in the chest with her finger and then stomps off.

I turn my attention back to Caleb. "You're firing her."

Caleb doesn't even think about it before he says, "No, I'm not."

I see red and go to deck him again. But before I can, Cooper and Alex jump in front of me to hold me back.

"Kaden, you need to walk away right now. Go for a walk, bro. Cool the fuck down. You aren't doing this shit here. Not in my gym." Cooper signals to the front door.

I shrug their hands off me and walk out the door, slamming it behind me. Once I get outside, I keep walking. I have no idea where I am going, but Cooper was right, I need to calm down before I do something I'll regret.

"Kaden!" I hear someone calling my name, so I look behind me to see who it is and spot Tristan running after me to catch up. I slow down to wait for him.

"Everything okay?"

"Yeah, I saw you punch Caleb and yell at him. I heard what you said. You told him to fire my mom."

Oh fuck!

"You can't have my mom fired. If you have her fired then she'll have no job at all."

"Listen buddy, I shouldn't have said all that in front of you. It's not your job to worry about grownup problems. Plus, your mom does have a job. She's a teacher, remember?"

He shakes his head. "No, she's not. I heard her tell Nana she was fired from work. And she packed up all her stuff from her classroom. She never packs it all up because every summer she teaches, but this summer she isn't teaching."

What the hell is going on? Why was Ashley fired from the school she works at? So much isn't adding up. She's been making ends meet for years. Something has changed, and whatever it is, she doesn't want me to know about it. And I have a sneaking suspicion that guy Giovanni is somehow tied to all this as well.

"It's okay, bud. She's not going to get fired from her job."

"You promise?"

"Yeah, I promise. Does your mom know you followed me out here?"

He gives me a sheepish look, which tells me she has no idea.

"Let's head back before your mom freaks out."

Ten

ASHLEY

IT'S BEEN A WEEK SINCE KADEN FOUND OUT I'M A STRIPPER and walked out of the gym pissed when Caleb refused to fire me. To say I was shocked Kaden actually punched Caleb in the face is putting it mildly. I felt so bad, I offered to quit, but Caleb wasn't having it. He said he and Kaden would work it out. I just wish I wouldn't have placed him in the middle of my cluster-fuck.

The day after the fight, Kaden texted me several times asking if he could bring dinner over. When I didn't respond, he showed up with a pizza in his hand asking why I was ignoring him. I realized then my cell phone had gotten shut off because I couldn't pay the bill, but there was no way I was telling him that. Instead, I told him it was broken.

As a result, the next day he showed up after work with a new iPhone. He added it to his plan and told me he got a good deal on it. It's probably the most expensive phone I've ever touched so I seriously doubt he got a deal on it. I tried to refuse it, but he totally played the mom card on me, insisting Tristan might need to get ahold of me while at camp.

He, again, showed up with food, this time Chinese. The three of us watched a movie, and after Tristan went to bed, we caught up on more episodes of *House*. Every morning this week, he has insisted we all go to breakfast before he and Tristan head to the gym. And when he walked into the kitchen as I was packing Tristan a peanut butter and jelly for lunch, he told me the program was buying them all lunch. I didn't remember reading anything about them buying lunch, but I'm not going to look a gift horse in the mouth.

The fact is, Kaden has been a godsend this past week. I don't even know how I would have fed Tristan and me. And just like he promised he would, every night he has watched Tristan on the nights I have had to work. I'm kind of surprised he hasn't once asked me to quit my job, but I'm hoping he has realized my money issues are my problem and it's not his place to tell me where to work.

While Tristan has been at camp all week, I have spent every day in search of another job. I have filled out hundreds of applications, but I haven't gotten a single bite. When I run out of places to apply to each day, I head over to *Assets* to learn more about the club and restaurant business. Caleb has been walking me through all the specifics of running a club, getting me acquainted with the ins and outs of the business, such as scheduling, hiring, and ordering. Liz covers all the payroll, Daniel, the chef, covers the menu items, and Jevon, the bar manager covers the bar ordering, but he wants me to learn it all so I when I take over, I'll be able to know what it is I am supervising.

Now it's July twenty-first and I have less than twenty-four hours to move all mine and Tristan's stuff out, but instead I'm at work. I'm well aware my being in denial is completely irresponsible and stupid, but I don't really know what else to do at this point. This is the first time in my life I feel completely out of control and helpless. Even when Tyler walked out the door, I handled my shit.

Since I'm not sure what's going to happen with the house, or when they'll be showing up to lock me out, I told Kaden I needed to bomb the house for bugs and asked if he could please watch Tristan at his place. He agreed without questioning me.

Before going into work, I moved our clothes and photo albums into my car the best I could until I figure it all out, but I'm at a complete loss as to what choice I should make. If I move to my parents' house, I'm too far to commute to work. If I don't move there, we'll be homeless. I've already told my mom Tristan will be going back to her house for the rest of the summer. She clearly knows something is going on but has learned I need to handle it myself. Thankfully, she always agrees to take Tristan without asking questions.

I've considered asking Caleb if I can sleep on his office couch on the nights I work but decided against it. I have put the poor guy through enough.

What I do know is if all my shit isn't out of the house soon, the doors will be locked and I won't be able to get any of it. Unfortunately, I can't deal with it right now because I'm at work and need to focus on making money.

"Hey boss." I knock once and enter Caleb's office. He's rolling his neck from side to side in a circular motion.

"Everything okay?"

"Oh yeah, it's just great. My very hormonal pregnant wife has decided she's going to hold a grudge for not forcing you to become my manager and has stuck my ass out on the couch for the last week. I think my neck has a permanent kink in it."

"I'm so sorry, Caleb. I can talk to Hayley. She didn't mention it when we were hanging out the other day."

Caleb waves me off. "Don't worry about it. It's all good."

"Okay, well, I was just checking in before I go on the floor. I checked on Daniel's order and realized he forgot to place it. I added it to the calendar so it will alert him every week. He always seems to forget, so hopefully that will help him remember. I also moved some of the girls around because Kora is running late, and Annalise's daughter has the stomach bug, so she might be out for a couple days."

"Thank you, Ashley. Any more thoughts on hanging up your dancing heels and taking over full time?"

"Not yet, but I appreciate your confidence in me."

"This might be a personal question, but I have to ask. Are you going back to teaching in August?"

"No, my teaching career is over."

"Okay, I'm sorry about that, but let's keep working on you managing this place. Hayley is due in November so that only gives me four months to train you fully."

"Okay, sounds good."

"Hey Ashley!" Bianca pokes her head into the office.

I turn around to give her my attention "Yeah?"

"Your shift technically doesn't start for five more minutes, but you have a private dance request."

"Okay, thanks. I'll be out in a minute."

I turn back to Caleb. "Duty calls."

After quickly changing into my dancing costume, since I'll be dancing tonight and not waitressing, I head to find Bianca. She's the hostess and sets up all the private rooms as well as handles all the restaurant's reservations.

"What room number?"

She glances at the sheet. "Room A."

"Thanks, girly. Any requests?"

"Actually, yes. He requested a pole dance and a lap dance."

"Ay, ay, Captain."

I give her a mock salute as I head upstairs to room A, hoping whoever is in this room will be a good tipper. I'm still a little short to pay Giovanni and only have a couple more days until the end of the month. Knowing I already lost my house, I gave up trying to pay my bills and have just been focusing on paying him. The last thing I want is to be owned by a man like Giovanni. I have enough trouble taking my bra and shorts off when I'm stripping, I don't even know how I would handle being required to have sex with strangers.

After picking out the music, I turn the lights up on the stage and down on the floor and then begin my performance. Thanks to the lighting, it's almost impossible to see whoever is sitting there watching me, and to be honest, I prefer it that way. Once I've made it halfway through my performance, I remove my bustier. Then a few moves later, my shorts are removed, leaving me in only my G-string and high heels. The song, and performance, ends, but I don't bother collecting my clothes yet. Bianca said the guy requested a lap dance, so I might as well leave my clothes off and get it over with.

I'm sauntering down the steps of the stage as a new songs transitions, when I notice the guy sitting at the table in one of the chairs is Kaden and he looks delicious. He's wearing dark wash blue jeans and a powder blue button down collared shirt with his sleeves rolled up to his elbows. His hair is still wet like he recently showered and is all messy like always. He's lounging in the chair with his legs spread wide like he doesn't have a worry in the world. His beautiful green eyes are piercing into mine and it causes my breath to catch. I suddenly remember I'm standing in front of him in nothing but a scrap of fabric and heels. Feeling extremely vulnerable, my hands go up to cover my breasts.

"Why are you covering yourself? It's nothing I haven't seen before." *Ouch!*

"I didn't expect to you to be here. Where's Tristan?"

"He's at my house with Kayla."

"Okay…" I'm not sure what Kaden's intentions are, but I'm not going to question it. It's not a secret that while this man is my best friend, I would give almost anything to have one night with him. However, Kaden has made it clear he has no desire for us to be anything more than friends so why he's here is a mystery to me. One I'm sure he will reveal soon.

"Where's my dance?" Kaden places his hands on the curves of my hips and tugs me toward him. Okay…so he really wants a dance from me. The same guy who wanted me to quit stripping…I need to figure out what his end-game is here.

"Nuh-uh," I say, backing away and removing his hands from my body so we're no longer touching. He tilts his head to the side in confusion, and his bottom lip juts out, making himself look adorably sexy.

I move my pointer finger back and forth to push my point. "No touching the dancer. It's the rule."

Kaden gives me a smirk but doesn't argue. The song transitions into *Na Na* by Trey Songz and I begin teasing him. Since he's sitting in a chair, I circle around the back of it, running the tips of my nails across his chest, shoulders, and back, then up his neck. I feel him shiver under my touch, which makes me smile inside. Once I get to the back of the chair, I lean forward so my breasts rub up against his neck as I trail my fingertips up his body, starting from his hard abs that I can feel even through his shirt.

Moving to the side of the chair, but without taking my hands off him, I begin dancing next to him lightly rubbing my body up against his side as I move back around to the front. Once I'm in front of him,

I drop to my ass and kick my legs over from one side to the other. He looks down at me on the floor, his eyes widening at the sight of my pussy only being covered by a thin piece of almost completely see-through fabric. I swear I hear a growl come from deep within his chest, and I have to hold back my grin.

I stand, parting my legs just enough so his leg is nestled between mine, and continue to dance. My eyes close, and I get lost in the feel of the music, rubbing against his jean clad thigh. A soft moan escapes from my lips as an orgasm slowly builds. Before I can even open my eyes, I feel Kaden's hands on my hips once again lifting me up onto his lap so I'm straddling him.

I grind down on him, the area between my legs sensitive and wanting. His hands go to my breasts, and my back arches forward, encouraging his touch.

"Fuck, baby," he growls, taking both my breasts into his mouth, one at a time, sucking on each one as I continue my grinding. My fingers are tangled in his hair and I'm pulling his face closer, forcing him to suck harder. Between the sensation his mouth is causing and the grinding of my pussy on him, an orgasm overtakes me, and before I can stop it, my entire body shakes with pleasure.

Kaden, still sucking on my breasts, picks me up and carries me over to the couch. My back hits the cold leather and I remember where we are.

At a strip club.

In a private room.

Where I work.

Where I'm getting paid to dance.

I push him off me and sit up, covering my chest before I quickly walk to the stage to throw on my clothes.

"What's wrong?" Kaden says as I grab my bustier top, then walk to the other side of the stage to grab my shorts. I put them all back on, but I still feel completely underdressed. I walk back over to the couch and sit next to him.

"I can't do this…We can't do this. We got caught up in the moment. This is where I work. I don't do this with guests. You and me…We're friends. You are literally my best friend. I can't become your next one-night stand."

Kaden flinches at my words. "You could never be a one-night stand, Ash. You know that. But you're right, this isn't the time or place to be doing this. I only came here to see you. I was hoping if you saw me here, you wouldn't want to strip and you would agree to quit. The last time I was here at the bachelor party you said it embarrassed you for me to see you. I'm probably grasping at straws, but I just didn't know what else to do. I didn't plan on it going this far. I'm sorry."

I'm stuck on the words *you could never be a one-night stand.* Does that mean he wants more? Does he want to be with me for real? The thought gets me excited until I remember I'm a stripper and I'd never date a guy while working here. It wouldn't be fair to him. I know it's technically not cheating, but I just couldn't do it. It would feel like cheating to me and I care about Kaden too much to disrespect him in that way. Plus, I need him in my life too much to take the chance that after one time he won't dump me like he's done to all the rest of the women he's been with.

"I'm not quitting my job here, so you can leave now, if that's all you came for."

Eleven

KADEN

THE NIGHT I FOUND OUT ASHLEY WAS STRIPPING TO MAKE ends meet, we went back to her house and I started to pay close attention. First red flag, her Wi-Fi wasn't working when I went to get on the internet. Then when we went to watch TV, I noticed her cable wasn't working either. We would only watch DVDs. The next red flag was finding the foreclosure notice while looking for coffee. To solidify my suspicions, when I texted her the next day and she ignored me, only to blame it on a broken phone, I knew I had to take matters into my own hands. I'm not sure what trouble Ashley is in, but I know one thing for sure. She's in over her head.

While she doesn't have the income coming in from teaching anymore, there is no way she isn't making enough to pay her bills working at *Assets*. After I calmed down and spoke with Caleb, he told me how much the girls make on average dancing there, and it's enough to pay her bills.

Every day I made sure Tristan and Ashley were fed, whether it was ordering in, bringing food with me, or asking them to join me. I knew if I tried to give Ashley money, she wasn't going to accept it, so I had to figure a way to go around her. I was hoping sometime this week she would mention having to be out of her house by tomorrow, but she didn't mention it at all. If it wasn't for the notice stating the date and details, I wouldn't even know.

Then my grandfather texted me asking if I had found a potential wife and it was like a light bulb popped up on top of my head like it does in the cartoons. Ashley needs money, and I need a wife. What could be better than fake marrying your best friend? So, I put a plan into motion. I spoke with the guys and their wives, letting them know that Ashley needed to move out of her house and, to make it easy on her, I was going to move everything to my place. They all knew there was more to the story but also knew if I wanted them to know I would have told them.

So, once Ashley left for work, we all began moving her stuff into my garage, minus Caleb since he had to be at the club. After the place was emptied, I texted Caleb to see what time Ashley would be off, and when he said not until two a.m., I decided to go to the club. I needed to talk to Ashley and was hoping maybe if she danced for me, she would get embarrassed and it'd make her want to quit. Also, if I'm honest, I was a little curious to see her in action. Okay, maybe a lot curious. Don't get me wrong, I'm one hundred percent against her stripping, but when we went to the club for the bachelor party, I threw her over my shoulder before I could see her dance. Plus, if she's dancing for me, that means she isn't dancing for somebody else, and since she's refusing to quit, I might as well be the one to reap the benefits.

And holy fucking shit, did I! Watching her ass dance on that stage, the way her body glided with natural grace across that pole, had me painfully hard. And when she removed her clothes I thought I might come in my pants. When the girl asked me if I had any requests, I said I wanted it all hoping to have extra time with Ashley. What I didn't know was 'it all' consisted of her sexy-as-sin body grinding on my own until she fucking came right there on my leg.

The orgasming on my leg part better be a bonus only I get.

If she wouldn't have pulled the brakes, I would have been balls-deep in that woman within seconds of throwing her ass on the couch. When she accused me of simply wanting a one-night stand with her, like I do with other women, I wanted to throw up. How could she ever put herself into the same category as those other women? She's my best friend for God's sake. I love her. And if I was capable of giving my heart to someone, it would without a doubt go to her. She and her son are the two most important people in my life. I will never do anything to lose them, which is why I'm glad she stopped us before anything really happened.

I'm not stupid. I know there's no way I could go into a fake marriage with Ashley objectively after having been inside her. She only orgasmed on my thigh and I just about lost it.

This was not exactly how I planned to bring my proposition up to her. The issue is, if I don't tell her, she's going to leave work and head home to an empty house. So, it looks like I'm going to have to just bite the bullet and throw it all out there for her.

"There's something I need to talk to you about." I look at her and can't help but glance down at her pebbled nipples poking through her practically see-through top. Needing to cover her up so I can focus on what I need to say and not her perky fucking nipples, I unbutton my shirt, which leaves me in just a white undershirt. I hand her the shirt and she puts it on, covering herself without buttoning it up. She faces me on the couch and sits Indian style giving me her full attention.

I need to lay this out in a certain way to reel Ashley in, so she doesn't think I'm trying to save her or some shit. "You know how my grandmother is turning eighty next month?"

She nods.

"Well, I have a feeling she isn't doing so well. My grandfather kind of insinuated she might not live much longer."

"Oh, Kaden. I'm so sorry." *Hook.*

"He asked me for a favor…I guess she has a dying wish, but I don't think I'll be able to grant it for her."

"Is there anything I can do to help?" *Line.*

"Actually, there is…You can marry me." *And sinker.*

Her eyes bug out like marrying me is the worst thing that could happen to her. So, I quickly add, "For pretend, of course."

Her face morphs from concerned to angry in point-two seconds, and I have a feeling I'm about to lose my fish—figuratively speaking— if I don't say the right thing.

"She wants to see me get married before the year is up. And if I do, my grandfather will give me fifteen million dollars. I don't care as much about the money as I do seeing her happy, but I sure as hell won't turn it down. And I'll split it with you. I'll pay you to marry me. To make my grandmother's dying wish come true."

I hold my breath, waiting to see if she's going to take the bait…

And then she storms out of the room.

I guess I lost that one…

I take off after her, down the hallway to the stairs, down the stairs to the restaurant. Holy shit, this woman can haul ass in heels! I almost catch up to her when I see the guy from her porch the other day. *Giovanni?* He's in a three-piece suit that's tailored to fit him. He's clean shaven and his hair looks professionally cut. The guy screams money.

Ashley comes to a screeching halt right in front of him and I'm not completely sure but I think she quickly shakes her head at him. His eyes glance over her shoulder and land on me. He gives her a small nod, as he lets her continue on her way. I want to go after her, but something tells me this guy is who I need to speak with.

"Giovanni, right?"

He gives me a once over, sucking on his teeth like he's trying to decide how to respond. He's clearly sizing me up, and while he may have twenty pounds and a couple inches on me, I would knock this fool across the room in one hit, and if he sucks his teeth at me again, I just might consider it.

His manners win out and he sticks his hand out to shake mine. "Giovanni Valentino," he says with a bit of an Italian accent.

"Kaden Scott. Mind if we have a word?"

He considers it for a moment, then heads over to the hostess to let her know he's decided to sit at the bar. We have a seat and, after ordering drinks—him, a Macallan, me, a Jack and coke—he's the first one to speak.

"What can I do for you?" He takes a sip of his whiskey sounding like he's already bored of this conversation.

"You can tell me why you keep showing up where Ashley is."

"Not that it's your concern, but she and I have a deal. I couldn't get ahold of her, and since her phone wasn't working, I came by here."

"Her phone broke. I bought her a new one. What deal do you have with her?"

He gives me a side glance. "You her boyfriend?"

"She's my best friend. I'm worried about her."

"I normally wouldn't tell someone's business, but I like her, and she's in over her head. She owes me twenty-two grand."

I choke on my whisky. *What the hell, Ashley!*

"Adam," I call to the bartender. "Can you call Caleb down here for me?"

"Sure thing."

I turn back to Giovanni. "If she pays you that amount in full, your business with Ashley would be done?"

"I'm a businessman, Kaden. I just want my money."

"I don't have that kind of money on me, but I'm sure my friend does in his safe. I'm going to give you the money so your deal with Ashley will be over."

Caleb walks over, slapping his hand on my shoulder. "What the fuck happened with Ashley? She got changed and left. Did you tell her you moved all her stuff to your place?"

Fuck! I completely forgot to tell her. She's probably on her way to her empty house.

"I'm assuming you keep money in your safe here for emergencies."

"Yeah, a little bit. What's up?"

"I need you to give Giovanni twenty-two thousand. I'll give it back to you tomorrow after I go to the bank."

Caleb's eyes ask a million questions, but he doesn't voice any of them.

"Right this way."

We follow him to his office and after he gives Giovanni the money, we shake hands.

"It's too bad…I was looking forward to her coming to work for me. She's lucky to have you in her life."

"What do you do for a living?" I ask out of curiosity.

"I own a gentleman's club…El Stella's Bordello."

"A brothel?" Caleb asks.

Giovanni nods. "Yes." He pulls out his business card. "If you gentleman are ever in the need of female companionship, let me know. My club offers different levels of memberships. It was nice doing business with you."

He walks out, leaving Caleb and I stunned stupid.

"I need to go find Ashley."

Caleb just nods slowly having no clue what to even say. *Yeah, man…I know exactly what you mean.*

I text Kayla, Hayley, and Liz asking if they've seen or heard from Ashley. They all respond with a no. She must have gone straight to her house.

I pull up in the driveway next to her car, and my headlights shine on the porch, lighting up Ashely, who is sitting with her head down.

"You okay?" I ask, sitting next to her. She doesn't say anything, but her shoulders silently shake up in down—she's crying.

"Hey, now. Don't cry." I put my arm around her shoulders and pull her into my side.

"Everything is so messed up, Kaden. I've lost everything."

"What? Your house? It's just a house, Ash. I know that's not what you want to hear. but it's all going to be okay."

She looks up at me, her sad eyes connecting with mine, and I use my thumb to wipe away the tears that are falling down her cheeks.

"You know about my house?"

"I know bits and pieces. It's time you tell me the entire story. Why did I just have Caleb give a guy who owns a brothel twenty-two thousand dollars?"

Twelve

ASHLEY

I AM SURPRISINGLY RELIEVED THAT KADEN KNOWS ABOUT ME losing my house. It's one less secret I have to tell him, but what shocks me is when he tells me he had Caleb pay Giovanni the twenty-two thousand I still owe him.

"Kaden…" He shakes his head at me, not giving me the chance to argue. "Why, Ashley?"

I let out a long breath and start from the beginning. I tell him about Tyler and how we met in college, how he was sweet and wooed me. How everything was great until he started gambling, and then it was far from great.

"So, you were working full time and he was paying all the bills?" He only asks to understand, and it reminds me why this man is my best friend.

"I was so busy with Tristan and going back to work, I just let him take it all over. When he told me to buy a house when I was pregnant, I thought it was a great idea. I wanted nothing more than to provide my baby with a home like the one my parents gave me growing up. I didn't think about why he didn't want it in his name. I didn't ask questions… I trusted him." The tears come back when I think what my naivety has cost me.

"But this was years ago. Did something happen recently?"

"Yeah, Tyler came back in January, threatening to take Tristan away from me. He said with him having rights he was going to disappear with him before I could even take him to court."

"Motherfucker. Why the hell didn't you come to me?"

"It all happened so fast. He wanted thirty thousand dollars in exchange for signing over his rights and he only gave me less than twenty-four hours to come up with it. I asked Don for a number to a loan shark and he sent me to Giovanni."

"What the fuck… The guy owns a whorehouse."

"I know…"

"You know?"

"I didn't have anything to give him to ensure I would pay back the loan…so…I used myself as collateral."

I close my eyes knowing Kaden is about to freak the hell out, and I'm right. He does. He stands and punches the window behind us. Glass shatters everywhere, and when I rush over to him, I can see his hand is bleeding from the shards of glass. I rush inside my house to grab a towel and remember there's nothing in the house. I have no idea why the door isn't locked, like the bank said it would be, but they emptied out my entire house.

Remembering I have some clothes in my car, I run out to it and grab an old shirt. Taking Kaden's hand in mine, I blot his hand with the shirt. "You shouldn't have done that. We need to run it under cold water to see if there's glass under your skin."

He pulls his hand away. "I don't give a fuck about my hand! You sold yourself to a man who sells women to rich men so they can fuck them?"

"No! I agreed if I didn't pay him back I would go to work for him, but so far I've paid him back…"

Kaden gives me a look. "Well, except when you paid him the four grand I was behind…" He gives me another look. "I almost had enough to pay him this month!"

He lets out a groan and shakes his head, having a seat on the porch swing and patting it for me to join. "I'm assuming Tyler signed over his rights?"

"Yeah. Then he disappeared. Thank God."

"What about your job?"

"How did you know about my job?"

"Tristan overheard you talking to your mom. He was worried."

Talk about failing as a mom.

"A dad from the school I worked at blackmailed me, and when I refused to take him up on his offer, he reported me to the school. The principal pretty much forced me to resign."

"What's his name?"

"Oh no, you aren't going after him. It's over with. Caleb is working on teaching me the insides of the club. I am really loving it. I never imagined running a strip club and restaurant, but I'm finding it to be fun, and I'm good at it."

Kaden and I sit for a few minutes in silence before I speak up. "All my stuff is gone. I thought I had until tomorrow night, but it's all gone. The bank must have taken it all."

"It's all in my garage."

I whip my head around to look at him. "Your garage?"

"I saw the notice the other day. So when you left for work earlier,

Cooper, Bentley, and I moved all your stuff to my garage. You and Tristan are moving in with me."

"I'm not even going to argue because I know I have nowhere else to go, but I promise you I will work all the hours Caleb will give me and I'll not only pay you back for you paying off Giovanni, but we will be out of your hair as soon as possible."

"About that…If you marry me, for pretend of course, not only will it make my grandmother happy, but I'll split the fifteen million with you." It doesn't go over my head that he once again makes it clear this marriage isn't real. Of course it's not real. Kaden is sexy and wealthy with a nice job. He has a beautiful house and an expensive car, and that's just the exterior. He is sweet and selfless. He could have anyone he wants, so why would he ever settle for a poor stripper single mom?

Then it hits me what he said.

"Kaden!" I screech. I don't even know what else to say. "I can't take…like…seven million dollars from you! I owe you money, not the other way around."

"Technically after taxes it would only be around four million. The IRS is a bitch like that. But if you don't marry me, I don't get any money and my grandmother will die without ever seeing her only grandson marry and have his happily-ever-after."

Damn, guilt-trip much.

"Okay, I'm going to agree to marry you…for fake." I add it in there just like he did so he knows I'm not going to try to rope him into a real marriage or something. "But I can't accept seven million dollars from you."

"It's non-negotiable." I decide not to argue knowing he's going to just keep at it until I agree with him. When the time comes, I will just refuse the money. Kaden has done so much for Tristan and me, there's no way I am taking his family's money.

"C'mon, Ash. Let's get you home so you can change out of my shirt and those tiny shorts."

I follow Kaden back to his house trying not to think too hard about the fact that Tristan, Kaden, and I will all be living under one roof. Instead I focus on taking in my surroundings. Kaden lives on the outskirts of Las Vegas in one of the wealthier areas like his friends all do. But while his friends, Cooper and Bentley, live in a neighborhood filled with cookie cutter houses with zero land, Kaden is in a gated community where every home is on a nice piece of property. Each home is on a minimum of five acres, so the houses are far apart. A lot of people who live in this community even have horses with barns and such.

We pull up to Kaden's country-style home and the front porch light is on. I'm always blown away by the beauty of his home. He bought it years ago but has renovated it little by little. It's a multi-story home with several bedrooms and bathrooms. The outside has been redone and has the cutest wraparound porch with a blood red front door. The red door was my idea. With the different color bricks and the white windows with black shutters, he had to have a red door.

The inside has a spacious, open floor plan. There's a fireplace in the center of the house that can be seen in the living room as well as the dining room. The master bedroom is on the first floor along with a guest bedroom and his office, and on the second floor are two more bedrooms. The kitchen is completely stainless steel and is gorgeous.

We're usually at my house because of convenience. Tristan has all his stuff at my place and I worked right down the street at the elementary school. But occasionally Kaden will throw a party here and I swear I spend the entire time just admiring the house.

"Hey girly!" Kayla comes walking out of the guest room to give me a hug, thankfully ignoring my outfit. "I see Kaden got his way." She gives me a wink and giggles.

I look down in embarrassment. I know she's joking to lighten the mood, but it reminds me I've lost my house. I've lost everything.

"Hey," Kayla says. "Don't do that. Shit happens. I don't know the details as to what's going on with you, but you will work it out, and you have all of us. Please don't shut us out."

Tears well up in my eyes and I lose it. Kayla pulls me into her arms and rocks me softly, not letting go of me until I feel hands on my waist pulling me out of her arms. Kaden puts his arms around me and holds me tight. His warmth makes me feel safe, something I haven't felt in a long time. I breathe in his fresh scent and it feels like home.

There's a knock on the door, but Kaden doesn't let me go. The door closes and he still doesn't let me go. We stand in the middle of his foyer for I don't know how long with him just holding me, letting me cry until I run out of tears.

Thirteen

KADEN

I HOLD HER UNTIL SHE FINALLY STOPS CRYING. THEN AFTER going upstairs to check on Tristan, we go to bed. I know she's physically exhausted from working all night and emotionally exhausted from all this shit. She just needs a good night's sleep and tomorrow will be a fresh start. Lying down in my California King, we have more than enough room, but instead of lying on our own sides, Ashley lays her head on my chest while I play with her hair until she finally passes out.

"ASHLEY," I WHISPER. SHE ROLLS OVER AND GRUNTS FOR ME TO shut up. It's five in the morning and I need to get going to the gym. "I'm leaving for work." Another grunt.

I walk out to the kitchen to grab a cup of coffee and see Tristan at the table eating a bowl of sugary cereal for breakfast. I never carry food like that in my home, but knowing Tristan would be living with me, I had Kayla help me out by taking Tristan to the grocery store last night to buy food he likes. Watching him makes me think of my son and everything I'm missing out on not getting to watch him grow up. It pisses me off knowing Tristan's dad signed away his rights for a measly thirty grand. If it were in my control, no amount of money could ever keep me away from my child. Too many people take the important things in life for granted like family and loved ones.

The past couple years Tristan and I have gotten closer. I'm aware he isn't a replacement of my son and I'm not a replacement of the father he's never known, but I love that kid like he's my own. I find myself looking forward to spending time with him, and now with him living with me, I hope our relationship will grow even more. Tristan means a lot to me just like his mom does.

"Morning."

Tristan looks up from the iPad in front of him, the one I bought him for his last birthday. "Morning, are you going to the gym?"

"That I am, want to go?"

His face perks up out of excitement. "Can I?"

"Sure, go get dressed. We'll let your mom sleep in. She's probably exhausted from working late."

I write Ashley a note letting her know I took Tristan with me and leave it on the nightstand, so she doesn't freak out once she wakes up, then take off with Tristan to the gym.

He spends the first hour working out with me, but once Bella and a couple of his friends arrive, he takes off to the kids' area. Cooper decided last year to split the gym into two areas: the smaller part is the kids' area and the larger main area is for the fighters. That way the kids won't hear the cursing and bashing that goes on when you stick a bunch of amped up fighters into the room together. The kids who belong to the fighters always venture into the adult area, but for the most part it works out well, especially for the kids who are only here for the kids' MMA classes.

Alex arrives shortly after seven and we begin training immediately. After an hour of warming up, we start working on some takedown defense moves. His opponent, Gavin 'Stunner' Fitzgerald's strength is submission, while Alex's strength is stand-up—his area of expertise boxing. Most fights, Alex will win with a knockout, but if his opponent gets him to the ground, he'll be in trouble, and that's what we need to prepare for.

"I can't believe you're planning a wedding the month before your big fight. Talk about adding more stress."

"Well, if it helps we're holding off on the honeymoon until after the fight so I won't miss any training other than the day of the wedding… and the day after." He waggles his eyebrows up and down giving me a wink. I use him being distracted to take him down, and before he can even think about his next move, I pull him into a quick arm bar forcing him to tap out.

"Fuck!" he says, standing up, pissed.

"Just don't think about fucking your wife during the fight," I say, patting him on his shoulder. "Oh, by the way, right after the wedding, I have to go visit my family for a few days. My grandmother is turning eighty and is demanding I'm present. I've asked Bentley to train with you. You'll learn some good moves from him. Make sure you work his stay-at-home daddy ass hard."

"Thanks, man! Will do."

I see Ashley walking into the gym out of the corner of my eye, so grabbing a towel, I wipe the sweat off me while heading over to see her.

"What are you doing here?" I ask, giving her a sweaty side hug. She scrunches her nose up in disgust, so I go all in, giving her a bear hug.

"Ewww! Kaden, stop! You are so gross." She laughs, grabbing my towel to dramatically wipe her face and neck off.

"Better get used to it, soon-to-be-Mrs. Scott."

Her smile spreads across her face, but she quickly straightens it out. "Thank you for letting me sleep in. I definitely needed it."

"No worries. I'm working with Alex right now and Caleb this afternoon. but I'll be home later. Want to order in for dinner?"

"Hey, Kaden!" Stephen comes over. "The guys and I are all going to *The Hideout* tonight, it's ladies' night. You in?"

Before I can answer, Ashley answers for me. "You should go. I'm actually here to pick up Tristan." Then she walks away without even giving me a chance to answer.

"Nah, man. I'm going home after work," I say, my eyes never leaving Ashley's ass as she sashays to the kids' area to get Tristan.

I pull up to my house with Thai takeout and don't see Ashley's piece-of-crap car in the driveway, only the oil stain it left behind. It really does need to get replaced, but she would probably skin me alive if I tried to buy her a vehicle. I got so busy at the gym I didn't have time to text her all day. Hopefully she and Tristan haven't eaten yet.

"Honey, I'm home," I yell out like I do most of the times I enter her house.

"Hey Kaden!" Tristan yells out from the living room, playing my PlayStation.

"You hungry? Where's your mom?" I bring the bag of food into the kitchen.

"She's at work." It's not Tristan who answers this time, but Britni, his babysitter.

"Uhh, hey. What are you doing here?"

She looks at me confused. "I'm babysitting Tristan. Ashley went to work about thirty minutes ago."

Oh. Hell. No.

"You can take off. Do you need a ride home?"

"No, I can have my boyfriend pick me up."

I pull out some money from my wallet to pay her her full amount since it's not her fault I'm sending her home early. Then I shoot a text to Caleb.

Me: Is Ashley working tonight?

Caleb: Yeah...

Then a thought strikes me.

"You know what, Britni? Would you mind watching Tristan? I'll give you some extra money for the mix-up. I need to run an errand."

"No problem, Kaden. I'll let my boyfriend know to pick me up later."

"Thanks! And there's Thai food in the kitchen for you and Tristan."

I take quick shower and get dressed in a pair of nice jeans and a button-down dress shirt. I throw on my shoes and quickly dry off my hair before heading out. On the way, I give Caleb a call.

"Hey man, I need a favor."

"I'm going to assume it has something to do with Ashley working tonight. You know I'm not getting in the middle of that shit. It was bad enough I was stuck on the couch for over a week for not telling Hayley before. I'm finally back in my bed and getting laid again."

"I just need you to book her for a private party for tonight. If she has any other parties, give them to someone else."

"Fuck, Kaden," Caleb groans.

"I'll pay."

"You know damn well it's not about the money. It's about fucking with Ashley. She's good for my business and I'm hoping she'll eventually manage this place. Pissing her off isn't going to help with that."

"Just do it."

He groans louder but agrees.

I arrive at *Assets* a few minutes later and am let in right away. Caleb has us all on his VIP list so we never have to wait to get in. When I walk through the restaurant I don't see her so I head upstairs to the bar area. She's up on the main stage in only a thong barely covering her pussy, as she moves her body up and down the pole. She is breathtakingly beautiful and every man watching her is entranced by the way she dances so gracefully on the stage. Unlike in some of the trashier clubs, *Assets* doesn't allow men to stick bills in the girl's underwear or throw it up on stage. Girls take turns dancing a couple times a night, but it's mostly to advertise themselves. Seeing them on stage is what makes a man want her to perform for him up close. I can't even imagine the amount of men that request Ashley.

Waitresses aren't allowed to give private dances, which is why, according to Caleb, Ashley left Double D's to work here for him. As a dancer, she can make money from the private dances and parties.

Once she's done dancing, the curtains close around her so she can grab her clothes as she heads out back. Caleb sends me a text letting me know which room to go into, so I go straight there to wait for her.

I get comfortable on the couch this time and wait for the music to start for my private performance. A few minutes later, the music begins and she's back to climbing and grinding that pole, only she's in a different outfit this time. A light blue dress with a matching bra and panties. When she's done, I make it a point to clap loud and slow. She looks past the bright lights and sees me sitting there. Throwing her sexy see-through dress back on along the way, she walks toward me until she's standing in front of me.

"What are you doing here? When Caleb said VIP, he didn't mention you."

"The real question is what are you doing here?"

She looks around dramatically mocking my question like I'm an idiot for even asking. "I. Work. Here," she says, slowly enunciating every word.

Grabbing her by her waist I bring her into my lap so she's straddling me. "You're my fiancée. You aren't working as a stripper."

"I'm your *fake* fiancée." She makes sure to emphasize the word fake. "And I have to work so I can pay you back and get a place for Tristan and me."

"We'll discuss that in a moment. Why didn't you have Tristan stay with me?"

"I thought you were going out tonight. I didn't want to cock-block you."

"One, you said I was going out, not me. And two, there's nothing to cock-block, unless you want to deny me yourself."

I don't know what comes over me, maybe it's her accusation that I would rather be out trying to find an easy lay than home with her when the truth is I haven't fucked a single woman in God knows how long, but I bring my hands up to her head and pull her into me, smashing her mouth to mine almost violently. She tenses up at first, but I can feel it when she gives in and starts kissing me back. Her hands slide around my neck as her hot pussy begins to grind against my already hard dick through my jeans causing me to groan into her mouth.

She grinds against me harder and seconds later I'm lifting her dress up and over her head throwing it to the floor. Next, her bra is removed, and then I'm grabbing her ass and changing our positions so her back is on the couch and I'm hovering over her. My lips curl around her taut nipple, sucking it roughly. She grabs my hair, moaning loudly at my assault, spurring me on. I continue to suck her on her tits for several beats before I head farther south.

I place an open-mouthed kiss through her thin panties, and her ass jerks upward, bringing her pussy closer to me. Ripping the thin strip of material, I dive right in to taste her. My tongue hits her clit as my fingers enter her to see if she's ready. She is. She's dripping fucking wet. Sticking one digit in, then another, I fingerfuck her while my tongue continues to lick her clit.

"Kaden…Oh, shit. Kaden!" Ashley's pussy walls tighten around my fingers like a vice. Taking her clit between my teeth, I bite down softly then suck on it. Her back arches up and her hands fist my hair as she grinds her warmth against my mouth trying to fuck my mouth with her pussy. My tongue strokes up and down her clit as she face-fucks me. Her moans get louder and her hands fist my hair tighter. Then her entire body tenses, her thighs clenching around my head. "Oh. My. God!" she screams in pure ecstasy as her orgasm rips through her.

"Holy shit," is all she says when she's finally catches her breath. Moving my fingers out of her pussy, I unbutton my pants and pull them down to my knees, taking my briefs along with them. I line my dick up at her entrance but stop when I look at her wide eyes.

"What's wrong?" She shakes her head, but her pained expression tells me otherwise. "What's wrong?" I repeat.

"We shouldn't be doing this. I keep putting myself in this position with you when I know there's only one way this is all going to end. Badly. This engagement isn't even real. The marriage will be fake. I'm a stripper for God's sake. Men see me naked almost every day. I know we aren't together for real, but it would feel like I was cheating on you if we get together and I continue to work…and I will be continuing to work. I promised myself I would never be with a guy while I'm stripping."

Ashley covers her eyes with her hands. "Jeez, I'm such a freaking tease. This is the third time I've stopped us from having sex. I'm so sorry. If you want to be with someone else, I'll understand. You have needs."

I remove her hands from her face. "What are you talking about?"

"I can't have sex with you. I don't want to lose you."

I pull my jeans and briefs back up, tucking my dick back inside, pissed. Not pissed we didn't have sex, but pissed she would insinuate I would ever be with another woman while being engaged and married to her—real or fake.

I stand from the couch, feeling my blood boiling. I need to walk away. I shouldn't be this hurt by such a simple comment, but I am.

"I can't believe you would think I could ever think so little of you that I would cheat on you. I gotta go."

"Kaden, wait." Ashley jumps up from the couch still completely naked. "Have you ever had sex with a woman more than once."

I want to say yes. I had sex with my wife exclusively for many years, but I don't say that. I can't say that. That would raise too many questions I don't want to answer.

"No." I give her the half-truth. Since my wife left me, I have never spent more than one night with a woman.

"Don't you see? If we have sex, it will change everything. Sure, we're attracted to each other, but you don't do commitment, and even if you stay faithful to me during our fake engagement and marriage, once it's over, you will move on, and where will that leave us? Where will that leave me?"

"I could never just drop you, Ash."

"Kaden, right now I'm your best friend, and our friendship works because sex isn't part of it. There's no commitment. If we step over that imaginary line, there's no going back. I couldn't take it if you stopped talking to me. You can say you would never do that, but your actions speak for themselves. You have never been with a woman more than once. I can't take that chance."

I don't know what to say. She's right to an extent, but it's different with Ashley.

"I'm pretty sure my tongue and fingers in your pussy was us crossing over the line."

"And I don't think we should do that anymore, but if we had sex, it would definitely be crossing the line. We could never come back from that."

Not wanting to continue this argument, I say, "Okay, but can you at least quit dancing? Once we're married, you're going to be rich. You don't need to strip."

"I'm not taking your money, Kaden. I'm going to keep my job and pay you off. I'm not ever going to owe anybody again. I can't take your money. The last time I depended on a man, he nearly destroyed me."

She'll be taking this money, but there's no point in going back and forth with her.

"I'm going to go home and relieve Britni from babysitting."

"Okay."

I start walking out as Ashley calls my name. "Kaden…are we okay?"

I turn around to face her. Her eyes are hooded and her lips are curled down into a frown. Her hands are covering her chest because she never had a chance to put her clothes back on. I ignore her nakedness, closing the distance between us, and wrap my arms around her tight. "We will always be okay." I pull back enough to give her a chaste kiss on her forehead, then I head home to relieve the sitter.

Fourteen

ASHLEY

IT'S BEEN TWO WEEKS SINCE KADEN GAVE ME A MIND-BLOWING orgasm only to have me stop him once again before we had sex. I still can't believe I stopped him, but I knew it was for the best, especially after these past couple weeks. Kaden is what women call *husband material*. He is selfless in every decision he makes. He picks up dinner on the nights I don't cook, and he doesn't let me spend a dime of my own money on anything. He takes Tristan to the gym with him on the mornings after I work late, and he never complains about the house now being *lived* in. Last weekend, we all took the kids to *Cowabunga Bay*, a waterpark about thirty minutes away, and had a blast. The entire time he focused on Tristan and me, acting like we're really a family.

When everybody looked at us like we're crazy, and Liz got excited thinking we were really a couple, I felt it was best to tell our close friends the engagement and wedding are fake for his grandmother so they wouldn't be confused once we get divorced. Kaden wasn't thrilled about it but reluctantly agreed. That hasn't stopped him; however, from acting like we're together. He holds my hand and kisses me like it's a natural thing. I should probably ask if we can get this marriage over with sooner rather than later because I can already feel it…once our marriage is over, I'm going to be left heartbroken. And the longer we wait, the longer I fall even deeper in love with this perfect specimen of a man who isn't mine for the taking.

It's Saturday night and I have the night off. I can't even remember the last time I was off on a weekend night, but I'm not complaining. Kaden and I are watching a UFC fight in the living room, and Tristan is in bed for the night—he watched a few fights but passed out before the main event. Kaden promised to record it for him so he can watch it tomorrow.

"We need to get you a ring," Kaden says out of nowhere, glancing at his cellphone.

"What made you think of that?" I'm lying on the floor on my stomach, looking at the Cosmo magazine on my phone.

He shows me his screen. It's a picture of Jessica and Alex's engagement pictures on social media. It's a beautiful picture of them smiling into the camera with her hand sticking straight out showing off her engagement ring.

"We can just get wedding bands. I don't want you to waste money on a fake engagement ring." I scroll down and come across an online quiz: *HOW WELL DO YOU KNOW YOUR GIRLFRIEND?*

"We'll see," Kaden says. "Did you get a sitter for their wedding next weekend?"

"My parents asked if they can take him for the week. We leave the following day for your grandmother's birthday party so they wanted to see him before we go." I click on the quiz and the first question pops up. I read through it.

"Ashley? Are you listening?"

He was saying something? "Yeah, sorry. I'm looking at this quiz. It determines how well you know your girlfriend. Want to take it?"

Kaden laughs. "Those quizzes are crap."

I pout. "Please."

Kaden rolls his eyes. "Fine. Hit me with it."

"Yay! Okay, what color are my eyes?" I quickly close my eyes so Kaden can't cheat, and he laughs.

"Seriously? Your eyes are hazel. Sometimes with a hint of green when you're happy or excited. When you're sad, they have more of a gold to them." Well, all right then…I open my eyes.

"That one was easy. Do you know my favorite movie?"

"*Save The Last Dance*. And you cry every time they fight and he walks away." *Damn…*

"Okay, here's a hard one. What are one of my dreams?" There's no way he can answer this question. I don't even know the answer myself.

Kaden gives me a small smile. "To provide a safe and loving home for Tristan. That's the only dream I can think of. Since I met you, you haven't focused on anything else but doing that." His answer makes me choke up, and tears prickle behind my lids. I shake them off and laugh.

"I'll give you credit for that one." I look down at my phone and click yes, bringing up the next question.

"Do you have any other dreams?"

I think about his question for a minute. Growing up I always wanted to be a teacher. I guess it wasn't so much teaching but working with kids.

"I would love to work with kids. Spend my days making a difference in their lives, even if it's not as a teacher. Okay, next question. Do you know who my friends are?"

Kaden looks at me like I have three heads. "Are you serious? We have all the same friends."

I laugh. That's true. "Okay, next. Do you remember how we met?"

"At Cooper's house." Wrong!

"Nope! We met at the gym when I brought Tristan in for a trial class."

"Wrong. We met at Cooper's house. You and the girls showed up drunk and I volunteered to give you a ride home. You passed out halfway to your house and I had to go through your purse to find your address. I carried you both inside and put you to bed."

"Oh, my God! How do I not remember that? Is that how you got my number? I thought you got it off my paperwork at the gym!"

Kaden throws his head back with a laugh. "You gave me your number in the car and told me you weren't against me sending you naked selfies."

I cover my eyes laughing. How do I not remember any of that? I must have been seriously drunk that night.

You know…if you still want a naked selfie of me, I'll gladly send you some." Kaden winks, making me blush.

"Let's move on to the next question, shall we?"

We go from question to question. Kaden's not only able to answer every single one, but on many, he takes it a step further and explains. I hit finish on the quiz, so it can give me his score.

"You did good," I say nonchalantly, trying to play off how well he did. "So, what is it we were talking about before? Alex and Jessica's wedding?"

"Oh no! Give me that phone." Kaden grabs the phone out of my hand and swipes up to pull the screen up with the quiz results.

"One hundred percent. It says 'Boyfriend of the year. Don't let this man go. Chance of you finding someone who knows you that well are slim. Hold on to him and don't let go.'"

Kaden is grinning from ear-to-ear and waggling his eyebrows. "I normally would disagree with anything from the internet, but in this case, I definitely agree." Yeah, if only he meant it the same way the quiz means it.

"Yeah, yeah…give me back my phone." I snatch the phone back from Kaden. "So, what is it you were talking about?"

"I was telling you that I went ahead and booked a room at the hotel the wedding is being held at so we can drink and have fun. Just don't get too drunk. If you ask me for naked selfies again while you're drunk, again, I might just have to give in and send you some."

"Sounds good," I say, refusing to acknowledge his comment about the naked selfies. "You know if you want to get separate rooms so you can…"

"Don't even finish that sentence." Kaden pounces on me, making me fall onto my back on the floor. My phone flies out of my hand,

and he pins my hands above my head. His face is holding a mock glare with his beautiful green eyes only being shown through small slits. It makes me laugh before I bring my knee up to his stomach to playfully push him off me. I don't know why I even bother, though. I'm like a hundred and twenty pounds at most, dripping wet, while Kaden is probably double that and all muscle.

He lets me knee him and falls to the floor onto his back dramatically, allowing me to switch our positions so I have his hands pinned down. Because he's so wide, my thighs barely make it around his waist. My knees are barely touching the ground, and my hands are up so high because his arms are so long, it puts my chest right in his face nearly suffocating him.

"Nice view." His voice is muffled, but I can still hear his smile. When I try to move backward out of his reach, he grabs my hands in his, holding me in this position. My sex is grinding against his stomach, and when his knees come up, his dick hits my ass…and it's hard. Heat pools between my legs. I try to move my hands to get off him, but he isn't letting it happen. He starts laughing, knowing he's outmuscling me. I'm on top of him and I can't even get up!

It's clear my hands aren't moving, so I do the first thing I can think of and bite him. Yep! I bite him right on the neck. He jumps in shock, letting go of my hands. I use this opportunity to roll off him, but he's too quick and seconds later he has me pinned under him, his legs pinning me down with both my hands in one of his. His other hand comes down and…he starts tickling me. *Tickling me!*

"Kaden! Stop!" I'm yelling at the top of my lungs, but the tickling is so bad I'm barely getting any words out at all. I can't stop laughing, and if he doesn't stop, I'm going to pee my pants.

"You think you were slick, huh? Biting my neck?"

He continues his tickling assault. His fingers dig into my ribs and I lose it. "Kaden, I'm going to pee in my pants!" I shriek, still laughing because it's completely out of my control.

He laughs but stops tickling me. With his one hand still holding both of mine, the hand that was just tickling me comes up and runs along my cheek. I lean into it, making eye contact with Kaden. I can see it on his face. He is filled with the same lust I feel being in this close of proximity to him.

"Kade…" And then his mouth is on mine. His hand that was just on my cheek comes down to my breast and massages it while his tongue seeks entrance.

"Mom?" Tristan calls out from his room causing us both to part. Kaden quickly adjusts himself and I run up the stairs to see what Tristan needs.

"I had a bad dream," he says, rubbing his eyes. I hear footsteps coming up the stairs. Then Kaden is entering the room, handing

Tristan a glass of water.

"Thank you." I give him a small smile of appreciation. "It was just a dream, sweetie. I'll leave your bathroom light on, though. Okay?"

"Okay, Mom."

"I love you." I give him a hug and a kiss on his forehead before pulling his covers back up.

"Love you, too, Mom."

"Goodnight, buddy," Kaden says, leaning over Tristan and ruffling his hair up.

"Goodnight, Kaden. Love you."

Kaden stops and stills. I can hear him swallow, but then he visibly relaxes and gives Tristan a smile. "I love you, too."

I want to ask him why the words *I love you* coming from my son's mouth looked like it caused him physical pain, but I'm afraid of the answer I might get, so I don't.

Fifteen

KADEN

WHEN TRISTAN SAID *I LOVE YOU* TO ME, IT FELT LIKE MY HEART, which was buried six feet under, was put back into my chest. Not completely pieced back together, but enough that I could feel it beating again. It warmed me up and scared the shit out of me all at the same time. I realized in that moment, I want more. I want to be somebody's dad. I want to be somebody's husband. But not just anybody—no, a certain somebody. I want to be Tristan's dad and Ashley's husband. But the guilt that came with my sudden realization of feelings made me feel sick to my stomach. The thought of replacing Gabrielle and our son made me feel like the biggest piece-of-shit.

I know Ashley felt something was wrong, but she didn't call me out on it, for which I appreciate. She asked if I wanted to go with her to drop Tristan off at her parents' house, but I said no. She looked disappointed and it broke my heart, but I needed some space. She was right. At the rate we're going, when this is all over, hearts are going to be broken. And we'll be over because I can't marry anyone else. I just can't do it. It doesn't matter how much I love Ashley and Tristan, I can't just replace my wife and son.

Without Tristan around, Ashley and I don't have to put on a happy front—not that we're usually fake, because we aren't. Our friendship has always been an open book. Hasn't it? Well, except for her hiding her violent ex-boyfriend…and the fact that she used herself as collateral to pay him off…and the fact that she has no idea I was ever married with a baby.

Now, that I'm thinking about it, we've kept quite a lot from each other. And now that it's all starting to come to the surface, we aren't handling it very well at all. The tension between us is palpable, and I don't know what to do about it. Well, actually, I do know what to do about it—tell her the truth, which is something I'm not ready to do yet.

Ashley and I have successfully avoided each other all week. It's Saturday, the day of Alex and Jessica's wedding, and the day before we leave for Colorado. Ashley even made it a point to sleep in the downstairs guest room instead of in my bedroom with me. I'm showered and dressed in my suit for the wedding. My luggage is up against the front door, and I'm waiting on Ashley to finish getting ready. We figured since we're going to be spending the night at the JW Marriott, where the wedding and reception are both being held, we might as well bring the luggage for our trip and leave from there to get Tristan and go to the airport.

"You ready to go, Ash?" I call out.

"Ugh! Yes, I think so," she says, huffing and puffing. I turn around and am nearly knocked back by how amazing she looks. Her hair is in waves over her shoulders, her makeup is done lightly, and her thin, light pink, strapless dress is tight in all the right places and loose in others. She's wearing black heels that are delicate and feminine, and her toes and fingers match her dress.

"You look beautiful." Grabbing the two suitcases she's attempting to wheel behind her, I bring them out to the car.

"Thank you," she says shyly. "You look good too."

After hauling the luggage into my car, we head to the wedding. After valet parking, we head straight back to the large gazebo where the ceremony is being held. We find our seats only minutes before the wedding march starts. Once everyone has made it down the aisle, Jessica and Alex begin to say their vows. I try to stay in the present, but my mind goes back to the day Gabby and I said ours…

"Gabrielle, you are my everything. You are my past, my present, and my future. I promise to love and cherish you through good times and bad, in sickness and in health. I promise to always protect you and be by your side. I promise to love you and only you for the rest of our lives."

I slide the wedding band onto Gabby's ring finger. Her eyes are smiling as small tears fall down her cheeks. I reach over to gently wipe them away, trying not to ruin her makeup.

"Kaden, thank you for loving me. This is just beginning for us, and I can't wait to see what is in store for our future. If it's half as amazing as these last five years have been, I will be a very happy woman. I promise to love and cherish you through good times and bad, in sickness and in health. I promise to be a good wife to you and stand by your side. I promise to love you and only you for the rest of our lives."

She takes my hand in hers and she slides the ring we picked out for me onto my finger.

"I now pronounce you husband and wife. You may kiss the bride."

"Kaden?" I look down at my empty ring finger and feel for a second for the indent that has long disappeared.

"Kaden? Are you okay?" Ashley is looking at me worriedly. I glance around and notice the wedding is over and everybody is filing out.

"Yeah, I'm okay." Her brows scrunch together, and a frown mars her face, but she doesn't call me out.

Once at the reception, we find the table we're assigned to. It was obviously done with thought because we're sitting with all our friends. After the newlywed couple is announced and have their first dance, I take my jacket off and ask Ashley if she would like a drink from the bar.

"Sure, a Bahama Breeze please."

After grabbing myself a Jack and Coke and her Bahama Breeze, I have a seat. Ashley isn't sitting where I left her, instead she's out on the dance floor dancing away with all the women. I don't bother sitting down. I just stand there like a lovesick fool watching the woman I can never have, laugh and smile, and wish it were me putting that smile on her face.

"Dude, you have it so bad," Caleb says, slapping my shoulder.

"Yeah, but we both know nothing can come of it." I have no idea why I say that and immediately wish I could take it back.

"Why? Because you were married once before? Fuck that. It obviously didn't last for a reason. Maybe Ashley was the reason."

It's not his fault because I've never told him what happened with my wife, and I know he wouldn't be saying what he's saying if he knew the truth, but I don't think about that when I shove him up against the wall. "Don't you ever talk about my wife that way. It's my fault she's gone! Mine! I'm the one who deserves to be alone for the rest of my life."

Caleb's eyes go wide. "Bro, I'm sorry. I don't know what happened, but nobody deserves to be alone. I, of all people, know that shit firsthand."

"I need a drink."

Grabbing my shoulder as I walk away, Caleb turns me around to face him. "I'm sorry. I get you don't want to talk about whatever happened between you and your wife, but regardless, you deserve to be loved, Kaden, and so does Ashley. And if you can't love her, you need to let her go. I've gotten to know her these last couple months and she's a damn good woman. A woman who's been through a lot of shit and deserves to have some good."

"I know."

Picking my drink up, I down it like a shot. Then I head to the bar to order a double. And I spend the rest of the evening drinking my confusion away.

Sixteen

ASHLEY

THE WEDDING IS SO ROMANTIC AND THE RECEPTION IS A blast. I can't even remember how many Bahama Breezes I've had, but it's enough that I'm drunk. Kaden spent the reception moping over God knows what and I'm so over his shit. I'm in too good of a mood to let him bring me down. A wedding should be a joyous occasion, not a reason to brood in a corner alone. Although, now that I'm thinking about it, last year when we were part of Liz and Cooper's wedding, Kaden kind of acted the same way.

The party comes to an end, and after congratulating Jessica and Alex, we all part ways, going to our own rooms. When we get to our room, Kaden goes straight to the mini fridge and pulls out a few mini bottles of liquor, downing two of them after he drops to the couch. I grab the last one out of his hand and down that one.

Putting his head back against the couch, he closes his eyes. We're both trashed and we know it. Only I'm hyper and not ready to pass out quite yet. I notice an iPod dock in the corner of the room, and grabbing my awesome iPhone Kaden got me, plug it in and switch on iTunes, clicking shuffle.

I'm n Luv (wit a stripper) by T-Pain blasts through the small portable speakers, and I crack up laughing at the irony of this song. Kaden's head tilts forward as he glares at me, clearly not finding the humor in it, which makes me laugh even harder. *Well, fuck him!*

Kicking off my heels first, so I don't break my neck (I'm drunk, not stupid), I climb up onto the coffee table and start to dance to the rhythm of the music. I'm staring straight at Kaden, and he's staring back, watching me with the undeniable lust in his eyes. I sway my hips seductively, just like I do on stage, singing the words to the song.

I laugh as my words come out with a slur and definitely not to the beat of the song. Then I drop my ass to the table, spreading my legs, and give Kaden a complete visual of my pussy, since I didn't wear panties to the wedding—can't have panty lines ruining the dress.

His eyes widen at the visual.

"You better be a good tipper. I don't show just anyone my goods."

That gets me a smirk from him. He reaches into his back pocket and pulls out a crisp one-hundred dollar bill from his wallet. I laugh but keep dancing. I roll onto my stomach and then pop back up onto my feet, peeling my dress off me and throwing it at him.

He chuckles lightly and stands, wobbling his drunk ass up to the table. I don't stop dancing, though. I turn around, backing my ass right up to him and shake it. I feel a hand land right on my ass cheek with a smack, causing me to crack up. Once I turn back around, he places the bill in the cup of my bra, letting his hands linger on my body. He moves them slowly down my sides until they land back on my ass cheeks.

"No no, you know the rules. You don't get to touch the stripper."

Kaden growls…*fucking growls*. Then grabbing my ass with both his hands, lifts me off the couch, and throws me onto the bed.

"You are my fiancée. I can touch you whenever the fuck I want. Got it? This pussy is mine…Mine."

Seventeen

KADEN

FUCK! WHO THE HELL IS BANGING ON THE DOOR? OR IS IT THE wall? I open my eyes and realize the banging isn't coming from anywhere. It's my head pulsing so strongly it feels like a constant banging is taking place right behind my eyes, in my head. Scanning my surroundings, I remember I'm in the hotel where Alex got married, and next to me is a naked woman. The blanket is wrapped around her shoulders and head, but from the waist down is nothing but silky smooth skin. I know right away it's Ashley. I would recognize her sexy legs from a mile away. But why is she naked? I try to remember what happened but can't. My head is pounding and the more I try to think about last night, the harder it pounds.

Needing to take a piss, I get out of bed and head to the bathroom. When I go to pull my briefs down, I notice I'm naked too. Fuck! It all comes back to me in flashes.

Her: dancing on the table.

Me: Hauling her over my shoulder.

Then…nothing. I can't remember shit after that! Fuck! Did I have sex with Ashley and was too drunk to even enjoy it? I mean, I'm sure I enjoyed it. But I can't remember how her pussy felt wrapped around my cock. How it felt to be fully inside of her. Damn it! I'm such a fucking idiot.

I shower and get dressed, when I'm done, Ashley is up and floating around the room getting things together to leave.

"I'm going to get in the shower since you're out."

"Ash, wait." I gently grab her wrist. I need to apologize for taking advantage of our inebriated states last night. "I'm sorry…"

She flinches, pulling her arm from me. "There's nothing to apologize for. Let's just pretend last night didn't happen."

Now it's my turn to flinch at her harsh words. I wasn't thinking it was a mistake at all. I was thinking the opposite. But if that's how she feels…"Got it."

We forgo meeting everyone for breakfast, going through a drive-thru instead. The drive to her parents is silent. Ashley is reading a book on her phone. She's so funny when she reads, letting all her emotions show. At a good part, she'll smile or laugh. At a sad part, she'll frown. It's so adorable, especially since she has no idea she's doing it.

After grabbing Tristan, we drive to the airport. My grandma's birthday party isn't until Saturday, but we're staying the week and flying back after the party is over. Tristan starts back at school Tuesday with open house Monday, so Ashley asked if we could be home Sunday so she can get him situated. Ashley's decided to sign him up at the school in my school zone so she filled out all the necessary paperwork. She said it's a lot nicer and closer and Bella goes there as well, so it makes sense. I like the idea of him going to school here, maybe that'll keep her living here that much longer.

After bringing our bags through security, we make our way to the first class lounge to wait to be called. "Do you want something to drink, bud?" Tristan has been acting weird since we picked him up.

"No," he says, quickly shaking his head.

"Are you okay?" He looks at his mom and then back to me. "What's going on?"

"He's never flown before," Ashley admits, nervously.

"Never?" I ask incredulously.

"Nope," Tristan answers softly.

"Oh, Tristan. We need to get you out more, buddy! This is going to be great. First class is awesome. This trip is short, only around two hours, so no dinner served, but the flight attendant will bring you whatever you want to drink and tons of snacks. There's Wi-Fi available and there are TVs in all the seats to watch movies. Plus, they give you a pillow and blanket and your seat reclines."

Tristan's eyes go wide in excitement, and Ashley smiles at his excitement. They both make my heart melt and I'm already planning where to take them next.

After the short flight to Denver International, we grab our bags and head to the car rental area. I get an Audi SUV so we're comfortable, then we make the thirty-minute drive to my parents' place.

"Welcome to Cherry Hills Village," Ashley says, reading the sign as we enter the community my parents and grandparents live in.

"Is this where you grew up?" Tristan asks in amazement, looking out the window as we pass by the huge homes. Cherry Hills Village is a community within itself just outside of Denver. It gives people country living without having to drive an hour to get to the main city.

"I was born and raised here." Ashley looks at me like I have two heads. The truth is, I once even owned my own home here, until I sold it to have a fresh start away from here. When my parents visited me in

Las Vegas they stayed with me but asked numerous times if I'm okay on money and if I need them to buy me a house. I could fit about five of my houses into the house my grandparents purchased for Gabrielle and me for our wedding present.

"There's a golf course! Can we play golf, Kaden?" Tristan shouts enthusiastically.

"Sure, buddy. There's also a community pool and tennis courts, and if you want, my mom can take you for a ride on her horses."

"Wow! I want to ride a horse!"

"Your parents have horses?" Ashley asks.

"Yeah, not in their backyard or anything. They board them at the club."

She nods softly, a frown marring her beautiful face.

"Is something wrong?"

"I just didn't picture her like this when she came to visit with your dad."

"Just because we have money, doesn't mean we're snobs."

"No! I wasn't thinking that…"

I laugh. "Yes, you were, but I get it. I'm a UFC trainer. I make a good living, but nothing like this. I'm lucky. My parents encouraged me to follow my passion. Sure, my father and grandfather would have loved for me to join them in their businesses, but mixed-martial-arts was always my passion."

"That's great, Kaden. I can't imagine you doing anything else."

We pull up to my parents' house and, before the doors are opened, Sandra Scott is running outside waving her arms in excitement with her husband, Stewart, walking slowly behind her shaking his head, laughing.

"Oh, Kaden! You're here!" She gives me a hug not letting go for several seconds. Then she moves on to her next victim, Ashley. "Oh, sweetie! I'm so excited to see you and that precious son of yours." She looks Tristan up and down. "I swear you have grown a foot since the last time I saw you."

"It's wonderful to see you, too, Mrs. Scott," Ashley says.

"Mom, you saw him like seven months ago."

"Oh, hush! And Ashley, if I can't get you to call me Mom, at least call me Sandra, please. Let's go inside. I made cookies. Your grandparents should be over shortly. We're going to go to the club for dinner tonight so we don't have to deal with cooking. Tomorrow, your father has scheduled for you guys to go golfing."

Tristan looks over at me and I give him a wink. "Cool, I'm going to bring Tristan with me, and sometime this week, can you take him to meet Shorty and Copper?"

My mom beams at someone wanting to meet her horses. "Of course! We can go for a ride! Ashley, would you like to join?"

"Sure."

"And I was thinking tomorrow while the boys are golfing, we can go to the club and have a spa day."

Ashley suddenly looks nervous. "Umm…that's okay. I thought I could just hang out by the pool…"

"Nonsense, it's my treat! I'm so excited to spend time with you."

Eighteen

ASHLEY

WE'RE ALL SITTING IN THE BEAUTIFUL FAMILY ROOM. TRISTAN is eating cookies and playing on his iPad while Kaden's parents play twenty questions with Kaden, trying to catch up on what's going on in his life. He tells them about Alex's fight coming up and about Tristan and me moving in with him. I'm thankful he doesn't tell them the reason why.

"Kaden, honey?" We all look to the door where we see a beautifully-aged woman waving her cane in the air toward Kaden. He gets up, smiling ear-to-ear, and hugs her.

"Grandmother, I've missed you so much!"

"Oh, dear boy. You have grown into such a handsome man. Please don't ever leave for this long again."

Kaden nods, giving her a kiss on her cheek. He hugs his grandfather next, and they exchange a few words as well. It's clear Kaden is loved and wanted here in his hometown. What I don't understand is why he ever left, and why he hasn't wanted to come home. The love surrounding him is so strong. His grandparents are still married and clearly in love, and so are his parents. So why doesn't he want to get married? I remember the name Gabby written on his chest and wonder if maybe he had his heart broken.

"And who do we have here?" His grandmother turns to face Tristan and me.

"This is Ashley Myers and her son, Tristan." Kaden puts his hand in mine, putting on a show for his family.

"Ashley, Tristan, these are my grandparents, Rose and Victor."

"Oh, sweetie. You are gorgeous. And hello there, Tristan. It's wonderful to meet you both. Let's go to dinner and get to know each other. Shall we?" Kaden's grandmother says, heading back toward the foyer.

"Sounds good, my love," his grandfather says, following his wife.

Their love is adorable.

"Ready?" Kaden asks.

"Yep, let's do this." Then it hits me. Kaden is going to announce we're engaged and we haven't told Tristan! He's going to be so confused. I didn't even think about him in all this. What kind of mother am I?

"We need to explain this to Tristan!" I say, whisper-yelling after Tristan jumps in to the Audi. "We didn't think about him at all in this. He's going to think we're getting married for real. I can't have him get hurt."

"No, you're right," Kaden says. We get into the car and Kaden turns around to face Tristan. "Hey, bud. When you're in school, do you ever play make believe?"

"Yeah," Tristan says.

"While we're here, your mom and I are going to play make believe. We're going to pretend to be engaged to be married. So, if you hear the grownups talking about it, it's just pretend. Okay?"

Tristan looks at us both skeptically. "Okay, but why can't you get married for real?"

His question stumps us both. Kaden says, "Umm…well…the thing is…"

I jump in to help him out. "Kaden is my best friend."

"So, you can't marry your best friend?" Tristan asks. *Damn kid!*

"Well, I guess you could," Kaden says slowly. "But your mom and I aren't that kind of friends. She's my friend like how you and Bella are friends. My grandmother is really old and she wants to see me get married, so we're going to play pretend to make her happy."

"Well, when I get older, if Bella is still my best friend I would want to marry her for real and not for pretend."

"You would?" I ask.

"Yeah, she's really nice and always spars with me in class. She always shares her Oreos with me and plays UFC with me. She's good at fighting, too. And she's not all girly like the other girls in my class. And if I marry her, I could play with her whenever I want."

Kaden looks at me with a smile in his eyes, clearly trying to hold back his laughter. What I would give to be able to live my life through the eyes of an innocent six-year-old.

"That's very nice of Bella," I say. "But Kaden and I are just going to be friends."

We both hold our breath, waiting to hear what Tristan has to say. "Okay, but if you do want to get married for real, that's okay too," he says, grabbing his iPad ending the conversation.

We both turn around in our seats ,knowing my six-year old is probably the most logical one in the car.

WE'VE BEEN IN COLORADO FOR THE LAST FIVE DAYS AND HAVE all had a blast. Sandra and I had our spa day, one I will never forget. I'm considering taking some of Kaden's inheritance just so I can go to the spa on a weekly basis, after I pay off all my debt of course. The Swedish massage was so relaxing, and the spa pedicure…holy moly! I almost passed out from feeling so stress-free. We had lunch in the club afterward and she introduced me to all her friends.

The next day, Tristan, Kaden, and I went horseback riding through the trails with Sandra. I rode behind Kaden and Tristan rode in front of Sandra. Tristan started begging me to buy him a horse, but Kaden promised him we would come back and visit. Sandra then recommended to Kaden that he should build a barn on his property and purchase a horse. He laughed her off, but it reminded me how different we really are. I'm stripping to make a living while Kaden comes from a wealthy home with horses that are worth more than I make in a year.

Kaden's parents and grandparents are beyond sweet and have welcomed Tristan and me with open arms. There hasn't been any talk about us being engaged, for that I'm thankful, but I know it will come out before we leave.

"Hey," Kaden says, walking into our room. Tristan has his own room next to us with his own bathroom. I tried to insist on separate rooms, but Kaden said they only have two guestrooms right now because the third is filled with stuff they're donating.

"Yeah?" I ask, putting my iPad down. I'm not even concentrating on the book I'm reading anyway.

"I'm going to go meet my grandmother for brunch. When I get back, want to head into town? Go do something fun with Tristan?"

"Sure."

Kaden leans down and gives me a kiss on my nose, and then one to my forehead. "I'm really glad you and Tristan came with me."

"Me, too. We've had a lot of fun."

"I'll text you when I'm on my way back."

"Okay."

After Kaden leaves, I go in search of Tristan and find him in the back of the house throwing stones into the pond. Kaden taught him how to skip rocks last night after dinner and he's become obsessed with seeing how many times he can get his rock to skip.

"Hey sweetie. Want to go to the pool with me after I make us breakfast?"

"Yes!" he yells, throwing one last rock. It skips along the pond three times before disappearing into the water.

"Good job!"

"Kaden can make it skip like six times."

"It takes practice."

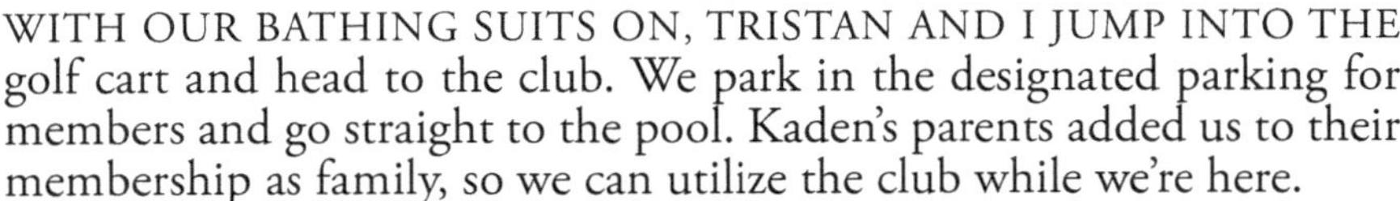

WITH OUR BATHING SUITS ON, TRISTAN AND I JUMP INTO THE golf cart and head to the club. We park in the designated parking for members and go straight to the pool. Kaden's parents added us to their membership as family, so we can utilize the club while we're here.

As we are walking to the back, I spot Kaden and his grandmother and decide to stop and say hello—I didn't realize they were having brunch at the club. Before I get to them, though, a beautiful Hispanic woman, who looks to be accompanied by her parents, taps Kaden on the shoulder. He stands with a smile, and gives her a hug, then a kiss on her cheek. My heart stills. It's probably just an old friend, but then I think, what if it's Gabby, the name he has inked on him? His grandmother stands up next, hugging each of them. I watch them all for a moment before thinking it would be best not to intrude.

"Mom, there's Kaden," Tristan says a little too loud before I can get us out of the room. Kaden looks over his shoulder hearing his name. His beautiful happy face morphs into…shock? Or is it guilt? I turn to go to the pool, suddenly feeling like an intruder. Only Rose isn't having it.

"Ashley, Tristan, come here you two. I would like for you to meet Juan and Margarita Nievez and their daughter, Danielle. This is Kaden's fiancée, Ashley, and her son, Tristan."

I guess Kaden told her the news.

Mr. and Mrs. Nievez both look shocked and if I'm not mistaken, sad, at the mention of me being his fiancée but both quickly smile. Danielle, on the other hand, doesn't even try to hide how upset this makes her. Tears well up in her eyes, and she quickly excuses herself.

"I should go find my daughter, but it was nice to meet you. I'm glad Kaden has found someone and was able to move on. He deserves to be happy," Mrs. Nievez says before excusing herself to go after her daughter.

Mr. Nievez watches her walk away, then says, "I agree. I'm glad you have moved on, Kaden." Then he turns to me. "It was lovely to meet you."

After he walks away, we all stand there in silence until Rose speaks up. "Kaden…Please tell me Ashley knows about Gabrielle and Gab…"

"No, she doesn't," Kaden says, cutting her off.

"Oh, sweetheart. Why wouldn't you tell her?"

Kaden doesn't say anything, just shakes his head.

"Why are you guys here?" Kaden asks me, his tone cold enough to freeze hell. This shocks me, because no matter how mad he gets, he's never cold with me.

"We were going to the pool. I'm sorry. I didn't mean to intrude."

There's so many questions I have, but now is not the time to ask them, and I'm a bit pissed at the way Kaden just spoke to me. I don't know what is going on, but I didn't ask to be brought here nor did I ask for this fake engagement. This was all him, so he better figure his shit out.

"That's okay, dear," Rose says. "Kaden and I were just finishing up our brunch. I'm going to have my driver take me home. I'm feeling a bit tired. Kaden, you should join them in the pool."

"Yeah, Kaden! Will you come swimming with us, please? You know my mom never gets in unless you throw her in." Tristan bounces up and down, completely oblivious to the adult tension in the air.

"Sure, bud. Let me walk my grandmother out, and then I'll meet you guys at the pool."

"Okay, bye, Grannie," Tristan says. She smiles at his name for her. The first time he called her that I tried to correct him, but she just chuckled and said she loved it.

Nineteen

KADEN

MY PAST AND MY PRESENT ARE COLLIDING AND THE GUILT that's eating away at me is causing bile to rise into my throat. I never imagined in a million years that Ashley and Tristan would be meeting Gabrielle's parents and twin sister, which is stupid seeing as we're all members at the same damn club. I clearly didn't think any of this out properly.

When my grandmother introduced Ashley as my fiancée to Danielle and her parents I felt like a piece-of-shit. I wanted to warn them, but I didn't have time. As I watched Danielle run away, I wanted to chase after her so I could explain it's not real. I didn't want her thinking I would ever hurt her sister like that.

The look Ashley gave me was one that said she knew something was up. I've managed to keep my past separate from my life, but I'm going to have to explain it to her. I owe her that much.

"Why wouldn't you tell that sweet girl about your wife?" my grandmother asks while we wait for her driver to pull up.

"I haven't told anyone."

"Oh, dear! Does she know about your son?"

"No, nobody knows anything."

"They're not your dirty secret, Kaden. What happened was horrible. A horrific tragedy. But that doesn't mean you pretend it didn't happen."

"I'm not pretending it didn't happen. I live with the guilt of what happened every damn day, Grandmother."

"Kaden…" my grandmother takes my hand in hers, giving me a look of sympathy. "It's okay to move on. It's okay to remember your past and still embrace your present, as well as look forward to the future."

When I don't say anything, she takes a box out of her purse. "This is my engagement ring your grandfather bought me. I want you to have it to give to Ashley."

Taking the box from her, I open it up to find a beautiful vintage diamond ring in a simple platinum band. In the center is a large circle diamond and accented on each side are several single cut round diamonds. There are six in total, three on each side. I remember my grandmother wearing this ring years ago. I look down on her hand and see a simple platinum band.

"Why are you giving me this?"

"I'm getting older, Kaden. I haven't worn the ring in many years. I can see the way you love Ashley and her son, and it makes me so happy. I would be honored for her to wear the ring your grandfather gave me sixty-two years ago on my eighteenth birthday."

"The way I love her?" I ask. I know I love Ashley, but she can see it as well?

"The way you look at her, like she's the only person in the room. And the way you treat her son, like he's your own. It's beautiful to watch. I can't wait for the wedding. I hope you will consider having it here, so I can attend. I'm not sure I'll be able to handle flying. I'm not the young woman I once was."

"Of course we'll have the wedding here." I give her a kiss on her cheek, helping her into the car. Then I jump into my rental and head to the first place that comes into mind. My brain is foggy and my heart is pounding. I love Ashley. I've always known it, but I've refused to accept or acknowledge it, because loving Ashley would mean replacing my wife with her and I can't do that.

"She's not here," Margarita says when she opens the door. "Why don't you come in?"

"Thanks, I just wanted to apologize. There's something you guys need to know. I should have warned you. I didn't think my visit through and how it would affect you and your husband…and Danielle."

We sit on the couch, Juan joining us. "Kaden, you don't have to feel bad for moving on."

"That's just it, I didn't. I wouldn't do that to Gabrielle. My grandmother is getting older and my grandfather asked for me to marry to make her happy. It's all fake. I would never marry again, I swear."

I hear a gasp come from the side and turn to see Danielle standing in the doorway. "What do you mean it's fake? What is wrong with you?"

I'm taken back by the tone of her voice. I thought this would make them all feel better. "Of course it's fake. I would never disrespect your sister by marrying again. I promised her forever. I promised to protect her. I messed it all up."

"Oh no, Kaden." Danielle sits next to me on the couch and takes my hands in hers. "Sure, it hurts to see you move forward knowing my sister never will, but don't you ever for a second think anything that happened was your fault. You deserve to fall in love again. To be happy. You loved my sister with everything in you, but she's not here. It's okay to still love her and move on. It's okay to love someone else."

"But...I promised," I say, choked up with tears. "I promised to love her for my entire life." I stand, not sure how to deal with the emotions squeezing in my chest.

With a hand on my shoulder, Margarita turns me around and wraps me into a motherly embrace. "But your life isn't over, Kaden, and you're still so young. Please, don't you ever push love away. My daughter would never want you to live alone."

"Do you love her, Kaden?" Juan asks. "Do you love Ashley?"

I don't even have to think about it for a second. "Yes, I do. I love her so damn much. It's just..."

"No," he cuts me off. "Don't make up reasons why not to be with her, especially if you're going to place the blame on my daughter. It's okay to love, and I know my daughter would never want you to live alone and miserable."

Danielle and Margarita both pull me into a hug. "You will always be family," Danielle murmurs.

"We hope you will invite us to the wedding, Kaden. We would love to be there," Margarita says.

"Thank you, guys. Thank you for everything."

Once I'm in my car I remember I was supposed to meet Ashely and Tristan at the pool. Fuck! I call Ashley and thankfully she answers on the first ring. "Everything okay?"

I take a calming breath, finally feeling free from the guilt I've carried over these last several years.

"Yeah, it is. I'm so sorry. Are you and Tristan still at the pool?"

"We're about to head back to your parents' house now."

"Okay, please tell him I'm sorry. Can you get dressed when you get back? I need to take you somewhere. I'll have my parents watch Tristan."

THE CAR RIDE IS QUIET. ASHLEY DOESN'T TRY TO INITIATE A conversation and neither do I. I pull up to Fairmont Cemetery and can feel Ashley's eyes on mine while I drive down the dirt road. I've only been here once, eleven years ago, but I could never forget my way to where we need to go.

I park on the side, then taking Ashley's hand, we walk to our destination. When we stop in front of the two headstones, Ashley reads aloud, "Gabrielle Scott." She gasps, her hand going to her mouth.

"Your tattoo. This is Gabby." She looks at the headstone to the left. "Gabriel Scott," she reads aloud. When she doesn't say anything, I know she's trying to put it all together. The birth and death date on

Gabriel's plot are both the same. I can feel my heart squeezing in my chest. It hurts so fucking bad. I thought I could keep it all together, but being here for the first time in years is harder than I thought it would be.

Ashley's hand squeezes mine when she finally puts it altogether. Then she releases my hand to hug me. "I'm so sorry for your loss." When she pulls back, she has tears in her eyes, but they aren't the pity look I always pictured. They are full of sadness and love. My eyes burn with unshed tears, and my throat feels like I've swallowed a baseball. I pull Ashley back into a tight hug and hold her for a few minutes while I try to get myself together.

"Let's have a seat. I need to tell you what happened. Why I am the way I am."

We sit in the grass in front of the two most important people of my past.

KADEN

Eleven Years Ago

"LEFT JAB…RIGHT JAB…BLOCK…BLOCK…BLOCK!"

"I am blocking!"

"You aren't blocking and if you keep blocking like that you're going to get your ribs smashed in at the tournament this weekend."

I hear my phone ring and run over to it. I don't normally keep my phone on me while I'm teaching an MMA class but these days I have a good reason to keep it on me and everyone understands. I look at the screen and grin at the picture staring back at me of the most beautiful woman in the world.

"Hey Gabby, is everything okay?"

"Yes, but it's time."

"It's time for…?"

"Kaden! It's time to have this baby!" She giggles into the phone, making me grin harder. I know what she means, but I like to mess with her.

"I'm on my way home to get you."

"Maybe we should meet at the hospital…"

"No way, Gabs, you're not driving while in labor. I'll be right there."

"Okay, *mi amor*. I'll see you soon."

I hang up and grab my gym bag from the side of mat.

"Gotta go! Gabby is in labor."

Everybody cheers, wishing us luck, as I run to the car to go get my wife. I get to the house in less than ten minutes and she's sitting on our porch swing staring down at her belly, probably talking to the baby. She's always talking to him.

"You ready?"

She looks up and smiles. "I am! I can't wait to meet this little guy."

Grabbing her bag from next to her, I hold her arm while she adorably waddles to the car and gets into the passenger seat. I reach over her and buckle her in.

"I can buckle myself in, silly!" She giggles.

I give her a kiss on her cheek and laugh. "I know you can, but you're in labor. I'm going to make sure you don't have to do anything but bring this little guy into the world."

"You spoil me, Kaden. *Te amo*, baby."

"I don't spoil you enough. I love you too, Gabby."

I back out of the driveway and begin heading to Foothills Hospital. It's only about fifteen minutes from our house and the hospital her obstetrician delivers at.

"Ohh…Wow!" Gabby holds her stomach.

"Are you okay?" I glance over at her, concerned.

"Yeah, the contractions are just getting stronger. Distract me."

"Are you rethinking the no-drugs decision yet?"

"Very funny. I'll let you know once we get there."

"Okay." I chuckle, wondering how long it will take for her to start begging for the drugs. Her pain tolerance is probably a three.

"Do you think he will look like me or you?" Gabby asks.

"I hope he looks like you. I hope he has your dark curly hair and your black chocolate chip eyes."

"No way! My hair is a mess! I hope he has your green eyes with my tanned skin."

"What are you saying? I'm pale?" I joke.

"No!" She laughs out loud. "Well, yeah…but you know you're pale!"

"Yeah, but only against your beautiful Venezuelan skin."

The light turns red and I take a moment to glance over at my wife. She's smiling at me, excited to finally get to meet our son.

"I bet he's a beautiful mixture of the both of us," she says, looking down at her belly once again.

The light switches to green and I press the gas, moving forward slowly into the intersection. There must be some sort of accident because the road in front of us appears to be backed up.

It happens in slow motion yet so fast. In the corner of my eye, I see the tractor-trailer, and he's coming right at us. He must have run the red light. He's already too close, and I know it's too late.

Instinctively, my hand goes over Gabby's chest to protect her as the tractor-trailer hits the passenger side of the vehicle taking us with him.

And then our vehicle starts rolling.

There are screams.

A crushing sound.

More screams.

And then silence.

The vehicle has stopped rolling and we're back to being in an upright position. I frantically start shouting to call nine-one-one. With shaky hands, I unbuckle my seatbelt and reach over to Gabby.

"Gabs, are you okay?" I'm shaking her shoulder, trying to wake her up.

She doesn't say anything. I search her face, but her eyes don't open. I jump out of the car and run to her side of the vehicle.

"Sir, don't move her. The ambulance is on its way."

"She's in labor!" I yell.

I open her door and reach over to unbuckle her seatbelt. There's blood everywhere: a huge gash on her forehead, cuts from glass all over her arms and legs, and then I look down and see blood all over the seat.

"Gabby, baby. Hang in there. Help is on the way." I rub her belly just like she always does and tell our little guy everything will be okay.

The EMTs arrive and within minutes they have Gabby in the ambulance. They ask to check me out, but I refuse treatment. My wife and unborn son are the only things on my mind.

We get to the hospital and they take her back, not allowing me to follow. I take the time to use the nurse's station's phone to call our families to let them know what's happened. They all let me know they're on their way.

After about an hour of waiting and pacing back and forth, a doctor walks out. "Family of Gabrielle Scott."

"Yes, I am her husband."

"I am so sorry but Gabrielle and the baby didn't make it. The internal bleeding was too severe and she lost too much blood. Her heart stopped and we couldn't save her."

"What about our son? Couldn't you take him out?"

"We attempted to deliver him via cesarean but the impact from the crash was too much. He didn't survive. I am so sorry."

I hear our family around me crying. My mom tries to hug me and I let her. I feel numb. This all feels so surreal. Like it's a bad fucking nightmare. One I will wake up from. Only it's not. It's reality, and in this moment, I wish I could go to sleep and never wake up.

"Can I see her?" I ask.

"Yes, you can see her, if you wish to."

I follow him back to the hospital room, but before the doctor opens the door, he says, "I must warn you. The accident left her banged up. She might not look like the same woman. She's covered with a sheet. Many don't wish to remove it, they would rather have the memory of them alive than of them after they have passed away."

I simply nod then open the door. Gabrielle is lying on the bed with a white sheet covering her body.

I grab a chair from the corner and sit down next to the bed. I don't know what to say so I do the only thing I can think of. I beg her to come back to me.

"Please Gabs, I'm begging you with everything in me not to leave me. Please! I'm so sorry for not protecting you."

I push the chair away, so I'm kneeling in front of my wife.

Begging her not to leave me.

Begging God not to let her leave me.

Knowing my begging will do no good.

But still begging.

"We promised each other forever. Dammit, Gabs! Remember our vows. I love you. Please, baby!"

Lifting the side of the sheet up, I place my hand into hers, entwining our fingers and squeeze gently, but she doesn't squeeze my hand back. I know, no matter how much I beg and plead, she will not squeeze back. She's leaving me and there's not a goddamn thing I can do to change it. The truth is, even though she's right here in front of me, she's already left.

I promised to protect her and I broke that promise.

Twenty

ASHLEY

"YOU DIDN'T BREAK YOUR PROMISE. YOU COULDN'T HAVE possibly done anything different, Kaden. You are not to blame."

Kaden looks at me with sadness in his eyes, hot tears flowing down his cheeks. All these years, he's been blaming himself for his wife and son's death. I want to grab ahold of him and shake him until he realizes there was nothing he could have done.

"I know that on some level. I know it was the truck's fault for running the red light. I know it was bad circumstance, the accident in front of us leaving us in the middle of the intersection. I know all of this, but it doesn't ease my guilt. I was the one driving. I promised to protect her, and in the car with me driving, she and our son died. The most fucked up part is that the day my son was supposed to be born, he died. He never even got a chance to live."

"Tell me about her. How you two met, how you fell in love."

Kaden gives me a small smile. "We met when we were sixteen. We were sophomores. I was at the gym working out, and she decided to try out the gym. I recommended the boxing class to her while she was checking out the calendar. She showed up to the class the next day and asked if I wanted to be her partner.

"We found out we both lived in the same community and went to the same school. I couldn't believe I never noticed her before. We didn't really hang out in the same crowds, though. She was a cheerleader and I spent my time at the gym. School wasn't really my thing. I went there, did what I was supposed to do, then spent my afternoons and weekends at the gym.

"We started dating and became inseparable. After graduation, we got engaged. Gabby went to college here in Denver to get her business degree. She wanted to work with her dad. I got a job training and teaching classes locally. A couple years later, we got married, and then she got pregnant…

"After she died, I tried to live here, but it was hard. I ended up taking a job with Cooper's dad's gym. We owned a home in the same neighborhood as our families, but I couldn't live there anymore. I sold the house and moved in with Coop and Bentley for about four years.

"But even working somewhere else and living somewhere else wasn't enough. Friends of ours would see me and look at me with pity. I just couldn't take it anymore. When they decided to move to Las Vegas, I made the choice to move with them. I decided to get my own place, though. I needed to somehow move forward, so I purchased the home I live in now. Caleb was going through his own shit, so Coop asked him to join so he could room with Bentley since Cooper was buying his own place as well. This is my first time coming back to their graves since we buried them."

"So, this is why you've been single and only do one-night stands." Knowing this is the reason why my best friend doesn't want to settle down, breaks my heart.

"What if the love I have left to give isn't enough? What if I go to give my heart to someone and the pieces that are left aren't enough. If you're putting together a puzzle and only have half the pieces, can someone really feel satisfied only seeing half the picture?"

"When you find someone who loves you without limitations, she will accept any pieces you give, and her pieces will fit into that same puzzle creating a picture, it may not be perfect, but it will be beautiful nonetheless because it will be your picture. Who needs a corner piece anyway? Tristan always loses them," I say, rolling my eyes, trying to lighten the mood.

Kaden cracks the smallest, saddest smile, and my heart shatters all over for him. He's been through the worst thing anybody could ever go through, losing not only his wife, but his unborn son. He's the most beautiful man on the inside and out, and he deserves the world. Which is why I only have one choice…

"I can't marry you."

Kaden turns his head to look at me, his eyes widening. Before he can ask why, I explain.

"I want what you two had. I want a love like that. I met Tyler when I was in college and knew he wasn't good for me, but I was too young to fully get it. Listening to you tell me about Gabrielle and you, what you had was real love. I want real love. And you deserve real love. You're an amazing man, Kaden. The fact that you thought you had to stay single for the rest of your life to stay true to your deceased wife speaks volumes about the person you are. One day you're going to meet a woman who will knock you off your feet, and she is going to come with all the pieces to the puzzle you're missing. You'll fall in love, and while it won't be the same as what you and Gabby had, it won't be any less. It'll just be different. You're older and wiser, and you're capable of love."

I wipe the tears that are falling down my face. I would give anything to experience, even for a short time, the love Kaden and Gabrielle experienced.

"I can't fake marry you. I can't let you stand in front of your family and say fake vows. I'm sorry. I have never been married before, and I hope one day, when I get married, I'll have a love like the one you and your wife had. It sounds like a truly amazing kind of love."

I get up and head back to the car, not being able to sit here any longer. Kaden never says a word. He drives us back to the house in silence. While he's driving, I think about everything he told me and everything I said in return. I love Kaden. I love him with all my heart, but I know that if I married him for fake, it would leave me heartbroken in the end. And knowing he's capable of loving a woman so strongly, I can't accept just a piece of him. He deserves to meet a woman he can fully give his heart to. I know with all my heart, he would fill all the pieces to my puzzle, but it can't be one-sided. I can't put the puzzle together myself. I need his pieces to intertwine with mine.

The rest of the day flies by. Kaden tries to get me alone to speak with me, but I don't allow it. I'm already too emotional as it is and I don't want to talk with him under his parents' roof. I excuse myself to bed early after Tristan is asleep, and Kaden tells me he'll be in later. He wants to hang out with his parents since it's our last night here. Tomorrow, after his grandmother's birthday party, we'll be taking a late flight home.

THE BIRTHDAY PARTY IS BEING HELD IN A PRIVATE ROOM AT the country club. The tables are filled with various beautiful flowers, and there must be over a hundred people in attendance. Rose sits in her seat at the head of one of the tables like a queen at her throne while everybody comes over to wish her a happy birthday. She seems more tired today, reminding me why she wants Kaden to marry soon. She wants to be present. I feel bad that I can't go through with marrying him, but I don't think deceiving her with a fake marriage would be what she would want for her grandson.

"Having a good time?" Sandra asks, sitting next to me.

"I am. Tristan has made some new friends." I point to my son in the corner, playing a board game with a couple other kids.

"He's a sweet little boy. You are a wonderful mother."

"Thank you."

"So, Kaden told me he went by Gabrielle's and Gabe's graves yesterday. I take it he finally told you about them?"

"He did."

"And how do you feel about all that?" I'm not sure what she's asking me. Am I able to love a man who already gave his heart to another woman? How do I feel about the fact that he already had a child with another woman? Some women might feel threatened by the ghost of a wife and son, but if Kaden was really mine, I wouldn't be. I have learned from experience, there's different kinds of love. One isn't better or more than another.

"I hate what he went through, but I'm glad I met Kaden. He came into my life at a time when I needed a friend, and while I hate he moved to Las Vegas because of what he went through, I feel blessed to have met him. He's a strong man. He's held me up so many times when I wasn't able to stand on my own two feet, and I know one day he'll make an amazing husband." I make sure to leave anything out about being friends and not really a couple. I'm not sure if Kaden has told his family we won't be getting married after all.

"I'm so glad my son met you as well, Ashley." Sandra gives me a soft kiss on my forehead before heading to sit next to her mother-in-law.

Twenty-One

KADEN

BRINGING ASHLEY TO THE GRAVES WHERE MY WIFE AND SON were buried was probably the hardest thing I've ever had to do, aside from actually burying them. I feared what she would think or say, but she handled it with such grace. I shouldn't have expected anything less from Ashley. What I didn't expect was that she would fully understand the young love Gabby and I shared. And not only did she understand it, but she accepted it.

When she told me she couldn't marry me because she wanted to find that kind of love and that she wanted me to find it again, the image of me and Ashley popped into my head because I've already found that love again. And she's right, it's not the same kind of love, but it's just as meaningful. The only difference is, with Gabby, I went in head first, but with Ashley, I've kept her at arm's length.

I felt the ring burning a hole in my pocket, but knew no matter how understanding Ashley is, asking her to marry me for real at a cemetery is a no-no. I tried several times to tell her how I felt once we left, but she avoided me the rest of our time at my parents' house. She put Tristan between us on the plane and slept the entire drive back home.

She left early Sunday morning with Tristan, leaving me a note that said she needed to buy him school supplies. I used the quiet time to get myself together. I need to make it clear to Ashley that I want more with her. I have lived so long with the guilt, blaming myself for my wife's death, that I don't even know what it feels like anymore to just focus on my own happiness. Speaking with Gabby's family was a huge turning point. When they told me they wanted me to be happy, I felt like I was finally set free. Danielle is Gabby's identical twin sister, part of why I had to move. I couldn't handle seeing her around, the same face as my wife, but still living and breathing. Her telling me it's okay to love again meant a lot to me.

"Kaden! Look what Auntie Hayley got me." Tristan comes running into the house holding a backpack with the letters UFC sewn onto the back.

"That's awesome!" Tristan runs back outside, so I follow him to see where he's going. I walk outside to see Ashley's hood popped open and the sweetest ass bent over the front of the car. She's in tiny white jean shorts, and as she reaches onto her tippy toes to look farther inside, a bit of her ass cheeks peak out, causing my dick to twitch.

"Ahem." I make a noise in my throat, and she pops up, turning around to look at me. I'm not sure what happened, but Ashley is covered in what looks like grease. She puts her hands on her hips, letting out a loud huff as she frowns.

"What happened?" I attempt to wipe some of the grease off her nose, but it's pointless. It just spreads worse, leaving her looking cute as hell.

"I don't know. The oil light came on, so I thought I would check the oil, but I can't find where it's located."

I chuckle at her obvious frustration. "Let me have a look." I open the cap to the oil, pulling the dipstick out to check how much is in there, and see it's extremely low, which makes sense since it all seems to be on my driveway.

"You definitely need more oil. When was the last time you got an oil change?"

Her nose scrunches up in confusion. "I'm not sure. One time I needed a new tire and they were running some special on oil changes, so I got it done…Maybe like a year ago?"

I break out in laughter at that. I mean, it's not funny, but it really is. "Ash, you're supposed to get your oil changed like every three to six thousand miles."

Her face grows even more confused. "Really? I read once it said recommended, but I didn't know it was actually required."

I laugh even harder, shaking my head at how clueless she is. "Why don't you bring it by my mechanic this week? I'll let him know you're coming by. He can do a tune-up, oil change, and make sure everything is running okay. There might be a leak in your oil pan."

She shrugs her shoulders. "Okay, but I'm paying for it myself."

"Whatever you say." I'll be calling him ahead of time to make sure he charges the services she gets done to my card.

When we get inside, Tristan is in the living room with school materials, spread out all around him. Pens, pencils, notebooks, crayons, markers, it looks like my living room shit out the Target back-to-school section.

"Damn, kid. You got enough stuff there? I hope you plan to get straight A's with all those school supplies."

He just laughs while filling his backpack.

"I guess I went a little overboard," Ashley says, sounding nervous.

"I've never been able to buy him everything he needed. I promise I'm going to pay you back the money you gave to Giovanni. I've already figured out a budget and payment plan. Now that I bought him his school supplies, I'm going to focus on saving for a place for us and the money to pay you back."

"Hey, stop. I don't give a shit about what you bought him or about you paying me back. Did you get everything he needs?"

"Yeah, he's fine," she says quickly.

"Mom, you said you would buy me clothes and shoes once you get paid. Don't forget!"

"So, you didn't get him everything he needs?"

"He has his clothes from last year. They'll be fine until I get paid."

I remember when I was in school and every kid would show up to school on the first day sporting new threads. There's no way I'm letting Tristan go to school in last year's clothes when I can help.

"Let's go."

"Go where?" Ashley asks.

"To the mall. We need to get Tristan clothes and shoes. Let's go."

"Kaden, I'll handle it. He's fine."

"I know he's fine, but I want to do this. So, stop arguing and get your ass in the car, please. Tristan! Let's go, bud."

The mall is fucking crazy! Everybody is doing last minute school shopping. Moms are yelling at their kids to try on clothes, kids are arguing they hate collared shirts. A dad is arguing with his daughter that the skirt is too short, while the daughter pouts. A little boy, no older than Tristan, is begging for two hundred dollar shoes because they're made by his favorite basketball player. It's great!

After we pick up all the clothing necessities and Tristan picks out the shoes he wants (and no, they aren't the two-hundred-dollar basketball shoes), we head to the food court to eat dinner, where we run into Hayley and Liz.

"Oh, my God, is Kaden shopping at the mall willingly?" Liz and Hayley both laugh at Liz's dumb joke.

"Don't hate because I'm here while your husbands are…where exactly?" I look around dramatically.

"Very funny, but they actually are here. Thank you very much. They're getting our food with Bella and Marco. I made Caleb come to hold all the bags. I'm freaking exhausted. I can't believe I still have like two months to go." Hayley rubs her round stomach.

"Bella showed him the new dress she wanted out of the Victoria Secret catalogue I left on the counter and he nearly blew a gasket, insisting he join us to ensure she doesn't buy the dress." Liz rolls her eyes. I laugh at the image of Bella showing him a piece of lingerie and him almost having a heart attack.

"Why did you get dragged here?" Hayley asks.

"He didn't." Ashley huffs. "He made us come here."

I smile wide, knowing I got my way. The looks on Tristan's face when he got to pick out all the clothes he wanted was worth it. Ashley and Tristan are mine to take care of, and once we get time to ourselves to talk, Ashley will understand it's no longer her against the world. It's now me and her against the world.

"Tristan, let's go get food. Ash, pull a table over and we'll join them for lunch." I give her a quick kiss on her lips and walk away with Tristan before she can argue.

Twenty-Two

ASHLEY

"FOR A GUY WHO IS ONLY MARRYING YOU FOR PRETEND, HE seems really into you," Liz says when Kaden and Tristan walk away. When Kaden kissed me, it left me stunned. I told him I no longer wanted to marry him, so I don't know why he's still acting like we're a fake couple. We'll need to have a talk about boundaries. He keeps acting like this and I'm going to have my heart even more broken than it already will be.

"Are you guys going to Alex's fight this weekend?" I ask, ignoring Liz's comment.

"Of course," Hayley says. "I've been dying to go to New York! Caleb, Marco, and I are going to make a weekend out of it."

"We're going as well. Bella will miss school Monday, but it's fine. Cooper is going up Tuesday with Alex and Kaden, and the kids and I will meet him there on Saturday. We're flying out early Saturday morning." Liz pulls out some baby food and, after placing a bib on Nathan, starts feeding him.

"Are you going?" Hayley asks.

"Going where?" Caleb chimes in, setting their food down. Cooper and Kaden set their trays down as well, and the kids grab their happy meals from Chick-fil-A, taking them to a table next to us, apparently starting their own kids' table.

"New York," I say, then turn to Kaden, who's taking a bite of his grilled chicken sandwich. "I didn't know you were leaving to New York on Tuesday."

Kaden finishes chewing. "Yeah, we leave early as hell Tuesday morning. You and Tristan should join me. You guys can fly over with the other women for the weekend. Saturday will be crazy busy, but we can spend the day together Sunday and Monday before we all fly back."

"I'm not sure I can take off work. Caleb already let me off for the week to visit your family. It would be rude to ask for time off again.

Plus, I need the money," I whisper to Kaden, hoping nobody else hears.

"You can have off." Caleb winks at me and Kaden laughs.

"And we're taking the private plane so it won't cost you a dime," Liz chimes in.

"Are you working tonight?" Kaden asks.

"Yeah."

"We need to talk."

"Okay, but it's going to have to wait. I actually need to get going soon, so I'm not late to work."

Kaden glares but doesn't say a word.

"Mom, when is the *Newbreed* tournament?" Bella asks Liz.

"Next month, sweetie."

"Can Tristan go?"

"That's up to his mommy, Bella."

The Newbreed tournament is a fighting tournament for amateur fighters and focuses on the fighter's techniques they've learned in class such as Brazilian Jujitsu. The classes Kaden and Bentley teach are mostly BJJ and grappling. Bella goes to most of the tournaments in the area and some in other states, but Tristan and Marco have never been. They're expensive to enter, and if they aren't local, you have to pay for travel and the hotel.

"Marco and I are going," Bella says. "Can Tristan go too? We're going to visit Mickey at Disney too!"

"That sounds like a lot of fun, but..."

"That does sound like fun," Kaden cuts me off. "Tristan, would you want to go? Do you feel confident enough to enter the tournament?"

Tristan's face lights up, and I want to punch Kaden in his face.

"Yes! I know I'm ready. Can I go, Mom?"

"We'll talk about it at home. I really need to get to work. Say goodbye to your friends."

I get up quickly, throwing my food away, then say bye to everyone. I start walking quickly to the car, ignoring Kaden calling my name. Once I'm at the car, I have no choice but to wait outside the passenger door for him. I obviously didn't think this through.

"What's your deal?" Kaden asks when he catches up to me.

"Can we talk about this later?" I glance Tristan's way hoping Kaden will get my hint of not wanting to discuss this in front of Tristan. I'm embarrassed enough that Kaden brought it up in front of our friends. He knows damn well I can't afford to just fly to Orlando, and there's no way I'm taking more money from him. I owe him enough as it is.

We never get a chance to talk, though. I rush off to work, and then get home late. When I get up in the morning, Kaden is already gone to the gym. Tristan and I head to visit his new teacher and new school at open house. Then we go to lunch with Hayley. I hate spending unnecessary money, but Hayley pretty much threatened our friendship if I didn't join her.

"Hey girly!" Hayley adorably waddles into the restaurant. "Did you meet your teacher, Tristan?"

"Yeah. Her name is Mrs. Luongo and she's nice."

"I can't believe Marco is starting middle school this year! I had to drop him off for his open house. They spend the day showing the sixth graders around so they aren't lost and confused tomorrow."

After the waitress comes over and takes our order, Hayley says, "Soo…Caleb said he's hoping you'll take over managing soon."

"I hope so, too."

"Why are you still…" She leaves out dancing since Tristan is sitting at the table with us. He's coloring a picture on the kid's menu, but you never know what he's listening to. "…if he offered to let you train without…"

"I'm not letting him just give me the job. I'll lose the respect of all the other employees there. I need their respect to run the club. I'm learning a lot and I plan to switch to management before the baby comes."

Hayley rolls her eyes but doesn't argue. "Okay."

"Have you thought of any names for the little girl in your belly?"

"Yes, but Caleb, Marco, and I aren't in agreement. I should get the final say. I'm the one incubating this little princess for nine months, after all. Do you think you will ever have another baby?"

"I hope so, but the next time I have a baby I'd like to be in a relationship that's more stable. I would rather not have to do it on my own again. But right now, I need to focus on finding a place to live."

"Did Kaden kick you out?" Hayley's eyes turn sinister, switching into best friend mode. We've become extremely close over the last year or so.

I want to tell her about Kaden and what I now know about him, but it's not my place to say anything.

"No! No, he would never do that. But I've told him I can't marry him for pretend anymore. I want to marry a guy that I love. A guy that loves me back, and not just as a best friend."

"Well, I know you love Kaden…as more than a best friend."

"Yeah, but he doesn't feel the same way. He doesn't want to get married for real, and even though I respect his choices, I can't be the one to do it."

"Have you told him this?"

"Yeah, and he wasn't too thrilled. He's said we need to talk, but we haven't had time. We've both been crazy busy since we got home."

My cell phone dings.

Kaden: We had to leave for New York today instead of tomorrow. The photoshoot needed a couple more shots before

the fight. Can Britni babysit tonight? Or you just quit?

"Oh, shoot. Kaden let me know they had to leave earlier than planned. He was supposed to babysit tonight. I forgot to tell him Britni left for college. He's been home with Tristan lately, so I forgot to mention it."

Ignoring his comment about me quitting, I type back: **I'll handle it. Have a safe flight!**

"Why don't you just have him spend the night with me?"

"Okay, thanks. Damn, it's his first day of school. I wanted him to get a full night of sleep at home."

"It will be fine."

After lunch, Hayley takes Tristan with her, so I can head to work. The night isn't too busy, and I'm able to close the club down on time right at two with the help of Scarlett. After I started working at *Assets*, Scarlett applied for a job and was hired as well. I love getting to work with her again. Thursday through Saturday the upstairs is open, but Sunday through Wednesday only the first floor with the restaurant are open.

"How's the training going?" she asks as the bouncer on duty escorts us to our vehicles.

"It's going good. I just always thought my career would be geared toward children, not managing a club. You know, with your business degree and experience, I bet he would train you as well. He is going to need someone else once he's back to fighting full time."

"That would be awesome. I'd love to learn more about the club business. I'm getting my master's in business management. I'd love to manage a club. I'm actually hoping to open one myself one day."

"I'll talk to him and see what he says."

"Thanks, Ashley. Have a good night."

After I get home from work, I'm shocked to find Hayley and Caleb both sleeping in the guest bed and Marco and Tristan asleep in Tristan's bed. I'm so thankful to have the friends that I have.

Twenty-Three

KADEN

I NEVER GOT A CHANCE TO SPEAK WITH ASHLEY BEFORE I HAD to leave for New York, but I'm going to speak to her once she and Tristan arrive Saturday. I just need to make arrangements for Tristan so we can speak alone.

Me: How would you like to do me a favor?

Hayley: What kind of favor?

Me: Watch Tristan for Ashley and me Saturday night. I need to talk to her alone.

Hayley: Does it involve you breaking her heart?

Me: I'm hoping the opposite.

Hayley: Don't fuck it up or I'll beat your ass!

Damn! When did Hayley get so violent?

Hayley: That wasn't me! That was Caleb! But I agree with him! <insert red faced mad emoji>

Every day I've been gone, Ashley and I have texted but it's been very formal.
How are you?
What are you up to?
How was Tristan's first day at school?
Now it's Saturday and I'm excited to finally see her and Tristan. It's crazy how much I've missed them.
I wanted to be there at the airport to pick them up, but I need to focus on Alex and his fight. Caleb flew in with all the girls, so he's driving them to the hotel to get situated before they meet us here at

Madison Square Garden for the fight. I insisted Ashley and Tristan stay with me in my room so she can't say anything about spending money on a hotel room.

THE NIGHT IS LONG BUT FUCKING AMAZING. ALEX IS THE MAIN event and kicks ass. He wins with a knockout in the third round and the crowd goes crazy for him. I'm damn proud of the kid. We all decide to meet up at the local club to have a drink to celebrate. Hayley didn't want to go to the club in her pregnant state so she and Caleb brought Tristan and Marco back to the hotel with them. I'm planning to have one celebratory drink then taking off with Ashley so we can finally talk.

Since the arena was crazy, and Ashley was sitting with Cooper, we agreed to meet up at the club. Somehow, I got here first, right after Alex and his wife. We order a round of double shots of Johnny Walker Black, toasting to his win. Because of the fight being on pay-per-view, Alex is VIP and we have an entire area to ourselves.

I feel small hands come around my waist, but when I look down they're fake and painted red. Ashley's nails are real and she paints hers herself. Grabbing the woman's hand, I remove them from my body and turn around to move her away as well. When I turn, she quickly moves her body up against mine, attempting to grind up against me.

"Hey there, handsome, want to buy me a drink?" She reaches past me to grab one of the shots, and downs it.

"Umm, no, I don't. So, take that shot as a parting gift and walk your ass away now." Unfortunately, she isn't taking no for an answer and tries again by running her hand down my chest. This time, I take her hands in mine and, holding them tight, push them off my body, forcing her body away from mine. She pouts but gets the message.

I grab another shot and sit in one of the booths to look for Ashley. Through the crowd, I spot a glaring Liz, but don't see Ashley or Cooper. She walks toward me, her eyes shooting daggers.

"Where's Ashley and Cooper?"

"I'm pretty sure she went back to the hotel room."

"What? We said we were meeting here."

"She saw that skanky woman all over you and took off. Cooper chased her outside."

"Fuck! I need to go find her."

I run out of the club to see if I can find Cooper and Ashley, hoping she hasn't left yet. I spot Cooper walking back with no Ashley in sight.

"She took off. I made sure she got safely into a cab."

"Damn it! All right, I'm going to go find her."

A cab pulls up and I jump in. "Four Seasons."

"Sure thing."

After swiping my card to pay, and adding a tip, I head through the lobby to the elevator to the room Ashley and I are sharing, praying she's in the room. She's never traveled anywhere and New York is not the place to go exploring on your own.

"Ash? You here?" I call out.

She's sitting on the couch, crying. "Go away."

"I'm not going anywhere until we talk about us."

"I have nothing to say to you."

"There's plenty to say."

"What? Like you are a manwhore, who would rather be with random women than with one who actually cares about you." She sniffles, refusing to make eye contact with me. The manwhore comment rubs me the wrong way, and before I can think about what I'm doing, I lash out at her.

"Seriously? I'm a manwhore? That's rich coming from a stripper." I regret the words the minute they leave my mouth.

"Wow, Kaden…real nice. I'm stripping to make a living. You're whoring around by choice."

"I'm sorry, but I'm not whoring around, Ash. The only woman I want is you." I raise my voice, getting pissed off. This is not how I wanted this conversation to go.

"Yeah, for fake."

"No, for real. I want you for real, Ash."

"What about all the women?" she spits out.

My arms open wide to make my point. I'm so fucking annoyed right now. "What fucking women, Ashley? What. Fucking. Women?"

"What about the woman at the bar tonight? Huh?"

"Oh, give me a damn break! You saw some skank come on to me and didn't even stay long enough to see the outcome. You saw what you wanted to see. You have it in your head I'm off sleeping around with all these women, when the truth is, I haven't had sex with anyone but you in the last nine fucking months! And sadly, I don't even remember us having sex."

"You haven't?" Her eyes finally meet mine, and I take a deep breath.

"No one, baby. You're all I want." I bend in front of her, taking her hands in mine. "The day we talked at the cemetery, I knew you were it for me. No, that's a lie. I've always known it was you. I just chose to be in denial out of guilt. The day in the cemetery, when I told you about Gabby, and you didn't get jealous, but instead said you wanted what we had, I finally accepted it. I love you, Ashley, and I don't want to live in guilt anymore. I want to love you and Tristan. I want to marry you for real."

Ashley gives me a watery smile, wiping her eyes. "I love you too, Kaden."

That's all I need to hear. I grab Ashley's ass, pick her up and carry her to the bedroom, tossing her onto the bed. "The last time we had sex doesn't count. I was drunk and didn't remember it, and I'm sure I fucking sucked. But I promise you, tonight, when I make love to you, not only will I remember it, but I will make up for the first time, and you will never forget it."

Ashley laughs loudly. "We didn't have sex, Kaden. Yeah, we made out some, but then you felt sick and ran to the bathroom to throw up. I brought you some water and you threw up on me as well. We both got naked and showered, and when I tried to get dressed, you grabbed my clothes and hid them. You were so adamant we sleep naked, I didn't want to argue with your drunk ass."

"Oh, thank God." I remove my shirt and shorts, leaving only my boxers on. She sits up, lifts her shirt over her head, then lifts her ass up, pushing her pants down. Getting onto the bed, I go to hover above her, but instead she pushes me down so I'm lying on my back. Then she crawls onto my lap, placing one leg on either side of me. Her ass is grinding against my stomach as she leans down to kiss me. Her lips are soft, and her tongue moves in perfect sync with mine.

Grabbing her ass, I sit up, moving her body down, so it's rubbing against my cock. We continue to kiss, our tongues moving frantically against each other as she grinds against me, creating perfect friction with our bodies through our clothes. Reaching behind her, I unclasp her bra then bring the straps down her arms, exposing her perfect, luscious tits. Just as I'm about to take one of her perky pink nipples into my mouth, she pushes me back down again.

Starting at my chest, she trails wet kisses down my torso slowly, too damn slowly, until she gets to my cock. My fingers are entwined in her hair, letting her know it feels good, but not forcing her to do anything she doesn't want to do. She clearly wants to be in control and I'm man enough to give that to her.

She gives my cock an open-mouthed kiss over my boxers, then looks up at me smiling shyly. Her smile is infectious. She moves my boxers down just enough, that my hard cock springs out ready for her. She wastes no time grabbing the shaft, jerking it slowly as she swirls her tongue over the head. She brings her mouth down the entire length until I feel the head of my cock hit the back of her throat. "Holy fuck, Ashley."

She moans around my dick, then continues to suck and pump my shaft. For several minutes, she fucks my me with her mouth and tongue…fucking her mouth isn't even the right word, though. It's like she's making love to it, worshiping it. The slurping and sucking sounds cause my dick to grow even harder, to the point I feel like I'm going to come. I refuse for this to come to an end this soon, though.

As I gently pull her head up by her hair, her mouth comes off my dick, making a popping sound. She looks up at me frowning like I just took away her favorite toy. "Baby, I need your pussy."

Grabbing her ass, I flip us over so I'm once again on top. Her lips are plump and swollen from being wrapped around my dick, begging to be kissed. Leaning down, my mouth connects with hers. Our tongues move frantically against each other. I can't get enough of her.

She grips my dick cock and strokes it. "I need you," she murmurs against my mouth.

Needing to feel her lips once again, I give her a chaste kiss then nibble on her bottom lip. Then I lick it once, needing to taste her before I move to her tits, sucking on each one until her nipples harden into perfect rosy peaks.

"Kaden..." She moans out my name with need.

"I got you, baby."

Grabbing her hands, I place them on her tits so she can continue to play with her nipples herself, as I lick a trail down her middle.

My eyes never leave her hands as they twist and pull at her nipples, causing her to moan softly. Once I'm at her pussy, I pull her panties down, then give her bare pussy lips a soft kiss. Spreading them open, I run my tongue over her clit then bite down softly.

"Kaden, please..." Ashley's moans get louder, needier, more desperate.

Placing two fingers into her, I fingerfuck her while I suck on her clit. I look up and see she's still massaging her tits, her eyes are closed and her head is tilted back in pure ecstasy. I stick another digit in, pushing in deep to hit her G-spot. Her back arches, telling me she's close. I could make her come like this, but something in me needs to be in her when she comes.

I pull my fingers out, then crawl up her body until my dick is lined up with her warm center. I move her hands from her tits, replacing them with my own as guide myself into her tight pussy. Slowly thrusting in and out, I tease her pussy while tweaking her nipples.

"Kaden! Harder! Please..."

Grabbing her hands and placing them in mine, I pin them over her head then start to pump my cock in and out of her, faster and deeper.

"Yes, fuck yes," she groans.

Grabbing her leg, I lift it up and over my shoulder so I can go deeper. Ashley's groans turn to screams, her voice now hoarse. A few deep thrusts more and she's coming all over my cock. When she comes down from the orgasm, she sits up and, pushing me back, grabs my shaft in her hand, guiding my hard length back into her warmth. Up and down, she rides me as I watch, entranced by her perky fucking tits bouncing up and down. I grab one in my hand and pull it to me to suck on it hard, causing Ashley to pick up the pace. Her inner walls grip my cock like a vice, letting me know she's ready to come again.

To help her along, I push my thumb into her wetness. I can feel her pussy wrapped around my dick, gliding up and down. Using her juices, I massage her clit. "Fuuuck…Kaden! I'm going to come again," she screams. Her pussy contracts as she finds her orgasm, only this time I'm right there with her, spilling my seed into her as she milks my dick of every last drop.

Twenty-Four

ASHLEY

AFTER WE BOTH FIND OUR RELEASE, I ATTEMPT TO MOVE OFF Kaden, but he isn't having it. "Not yet. I just need to hold you for a minute." Leaning down, I put my head on his chest, feeling his flaccid cock still in me, our mixed juices running down the insides of my thighs.

"I'm on birth control," I whisper. I don't want him to think I'm going to trap him into anything.

"Well, you need to get off that shit immediately. What are you on? The pill?"

"Yeah…"

"Throw that shit away. I don't want to waste any more time with you. I'm thirty-five years old and I'm sure as shit not getting any younger. I was a fucking idiot, Ash. I want to marry you and I want us to have mini versions of us running around." He gives me a kiss on my forehead as I turn my head to look at him. I'm shocked at what I'm hearing. Not even a week ago he was sharing with me stories about his deceased wife and baby, and now he's telling me he wants me to mother his future children. I sit up and try to get off him again, needing some space. This time, he lets me.

Taking the blanket from the bed, I wrap myself up and go straight to the bathroom to get cleaned up. I turn the shower on and wait for it to heat up.

"What's wrong?" Kaden asks. coming up behind me. I didn't realize he followed me into the bathroom.

"It just seems too good to be true. I've learned the hard way that if it seems good, there's probably a catch." I'm still facing the shower, my back to his front, not wanting to look him in the eyes, not wanting him to see the insecurity I feel.

Kaden bridges the gap between us, dropping the blanket to the floor and wrapping his arms around me. He places soft kisses along my neck. "What we have is real, baby. We've always had this. I was just too consumed with guilt to open my eyes and see what I have right in front of me. I love you and Tristan." Kaden turns me around, then drops to one knee, and right there in the bathroom, with both of us naked and vulnerable, he opens a small black box showing me the most beautiful diamond engagement ring. "Marry me, Ashley. Not for pretend or for an inheritance. Marry me because you love me and I love you, and we belong together. I can't change the past, baby, but I can create a future, and I want to create one with you and Tristan as a family."

His words choke me up. My throat feels like it is clogged with a large lump in it, not allowing me to speak. So, I nod. I nod repeatedly as tears spill down my cheeks. Then I wrap my arms around Kaden and kiss him like he is everything to me. Because he is.

He throws the ring box onto the counter and picks me up, my legs wrapping around him, and opens the shower door, taking us both inside without breaking our kiss. The hot water rains down on us as he pushes me against the wall devouring me. His hard length pushes against my ass, so I wiggle a little to let him know what I want. Kaden chuckles softly, stopping our kiss.

"You want me in you, baby?"

"Yes."

"Oh? So, you will say yes to my dick, but not to my marriage proposal?" He moves my wet hair from my face, then starts to suck on my neck until it tingles.

"Yes! Yes to marrying you. Yes to having babies with you. Please, just fuck me."

"No."

"No?" I snap my head up, rejecting him access to my neck.

"What do you mean no?"

"I'm not fucking you, Ash. I'm making love to you. It might be dirty as fuck, but I'm making love to you."

Tightening his grip on my ass, he pushes me farther against the wall, then with one hand, guides his dick into me. He starts off slow, thrusting in and out of me, but once his dick is completely hard and deep inside me, he grips my ass and begins pounding into me, the sound of wet flesh slapping echoing in the bathroom. The angle at which he hits, ignites a spark deep within me, and a few thrusts later, my pussy spasms around his dick as Kaden grunts out his orgasm.

"Jesus, I can't get enough of you." Kaden sets me down on shaky legs and I use the wall to hold myself up. Three orgasms in one night is a record for me. Tyler was the only guy I slept with, and he was way too selfish in bed to try to make me come once let alone three times.

Kaden and I wash up in silence, then he turns the water off, grabbing us both towels. Once we're both dried off, we grab clothes from our luggage. He looks sexy as hell in his basketball shorts and white shirt, while I'm in my long cotton pajamas. I probably should have packed something sexier.

"My relationship status is Netflix, pajamas, and wine," Kaden says, reading the front of my shirt. "I will gladly Netflix and chill with you, baby, but your relationship status is taken." Kaden laughs at his own joke, giving me a wink.

"You're such a cheeseball!" I slap his chest, laughing at his cheesiness. I grab a bottle of water from the mini fridge then climb into bed, pulling the covers over me. Kaden runs back into the bathroom then joins me, lying on his side and pulling me close to him. He grabs my leg and hooks it over his own, cuddling close to me, then holds out the black box from earlier.

"We didn't make it to the part where you put the ring on. This is my grandmother's ring. She gave it to me while we were in Colorado to give to you. She knew I was too in denial to admit how much I love you. Will you wear this ring and become my wife?"

This time, I voice the words I couldn't earlier. "Yes, Kaden. I will marry you."

He plucks the ring out of the cushion and places it onto my finger. It fits perfectly.

"It's beautiful."

"You're beautiful. The ring simply complements your beauty." He brings his lips to mine, making love to my mouth before he makes love to me for the third time tonight.

Twenty-Five

ASHLEY

"I WANT TO GO TO SEE LADY LIBERTY!" BELLA SQUEALS.

"Yeah! Me, too!" Tristan agrees.

"Oh! And I want to go to American Girl!"

"No! I don't want to go there. I want to go to the big Toys 'R' Us." Tristan shakes his head in disagreement.

When we told Cooper and Liz we were going to spend the day checking out New York, they decided to join us. Hayley, Caleb, and Marco flew back this morning with Alex and his wife, Jessica. We're all going to fly back tomorrow afternoon.

"How about we take the ferry around the statue of liberty, then while Bella goes to American girl, we can take you to the toy store?"

"Yes!" Tristan and Bella both yell in unison, jumping up and down.

"You and I are going to come back here, just the two of us, one day," Kaden says into my ear. "I want to show you central park, take you shopping, and spoil you with fancy eating."

"You already spoil me. I don't need any of that. I just need you." I give him a quick peck on the lips. He pouts when I pull away, pulling me toward him and deepening our kiss.

"Eww! Mom! Kaden! I thought you were just playing pretend for Grannie. That's not pretend!" We both stop kissing, and see Tristan's cute little face all scrunched up in disgust.

"Yeah, guys. Thought it was pretend…" Cooper adds with a laugh.

"Oh. My. God!" Liz shrieks, grabbing my left hand and narrowing in on my engagement ring. "This ring is most definitely not pretend!"

"Yeah, about that…" I begin to think of a way to explain to my almost seven-year-old about our engagement, but Kaden beats me to it.

"Remember you said it would be okay if I married your mom for real?"

"Yeah."

"You still cool with that, bud?"

"Yes!" Tristan runs to Kaden and throws his arms around him. Kaden picks him up and hugs him back, before setting him back down.

"So, when's the wedding?" Liz asks.

"We haven't picked a day…" I say, but Kaden cuts me off. "As soon as possible."

"I guess as soon as possible," I repeat, laughing.

We spend the entire day experiencing New York. After we take the ferry around the statue of liberty, we go to the nine-eleven memorial site. Then, while Bella goes with her parents to American Girl, we take Tristan to the toy store. Kaden buys him tons of toys that Tristan swears are only available in New York. Afterward, we all meet up to eat dinner before heading back to the hotel for the night. It was a great day, one I won't ever forget.

IT'S MONDAY NIGHT AND WE'RE BACK HOME AND JETLAGGED, lying on the couch watching TV. Tristan passed out the minute we walked through the door. Kaden's phone rings alerting him of a Facetime call. "It's my grandmother." He swipes accept, then her face comes onto the screen. "Hello, Grandmother. How are you?"

"I'm good, sweetie. I just wanted to check in…any news?"

Kaden chuckles. "Real subtle, Grandmother." Taking my hand, he puts it up to the camera for her to see. "Oh! Yay! I am so glad you are wearing my ring."

"It is gorgeous, Rose. Thank you for passing it down to us. I will always cherish it."

"And when is the wedding?"

"We haven't picked a date yet."

"How about a spring wedding?" she suggests.

Kaden looks to me for my approval. A spring wedding in his hometown sounds beautiful.

"I think that would be wonderful."

"Victor! Did you hear that?" Rose calls out, moving out of the line of the camera.

"Yes, Rose, honey. I heard. A spring wedding. Congratulations, you two."

"Thank you, Victor."

"Thank you, Grandfather."

"I'm going to call Sandra and let her know we need to start planning a wedding. Ashley, dear, would it be possible for you to visit soon so we can go dress shopping?"

"I'll have to look at my work schedule, but I should be able to make it work." Kaden glares at me, and then it hits me, my work schedule. I'm engaged to be married to Kaden and I'm still a stripper.

After we say goodbye, I address the elephant in the room. "I'll speak to Caleb about only managing the club. I'm still going to pay you back, though."

"No, you aren't. You're my fiancée, soon to be my wife, and hopefully soon to be the mother of my children. You aren't paying me back a damn dime. Part of being in a relationship means everything separate comes together as one."

"Kaden, I can't just take thousands from you and not pay you back."

"It's *ours*, everything is ours. And once we're married, you will be an extremely wealthy woman so you better get used to it. I'm not going to stop you from managing the club, but once you're pregnant, I hope you'll consider taking some time off. You said before you had to work while Tristan was little. You don't have to work, baby." Kaden takes my hand in his, squeezing it lightly. "Just think about it, okay?"

"Okay, I will. Do you think we should wait until after we're married for me to get off birth control?"

"Hell no. I researched it on the plane and it can take months for the hormones to leave your body. Tristan is already almost seven years old. No more pills, and if you get pregnant, great. We'll be married soon anyway." Kaden leans toward me, our lips meeting for a moment before he pulls back. "Let's go to bed. I think we need to practice making a baby. Practice makes perfect, you know." He shoots me a flirty wink before he stands up and, taking my hand in his, guides us to the bedroom where we practice making a baby…three times.

"NO. NO. NO. NO!" MY FOOT PRESSES THE BRAKE WHILE MY hands hold tightly onto the steering wheel. Cars are honking and flying around me as I try to steer my car to the side of the road. I finally get it out of traffic and turn it off. Stepping out of the car, I smell something burning, and before I can pop the hood, a loud booming sound goes off and my hood is in flames.

My phone, purse, and keys are all in the car, so calling nine-one-one is out of the question. It's a busy street and luckily someone pulls over. A gentleman who looks to be in his mid-thirties gets out of his sports car and comes jogging over to me. I recognize him from somewhere, but I can't put my finger on it.

"Your car is going to explode, you need to get back," the gentleman screams at me. Grabbing my body, he drags me away from the car and, a few seconds later, my car does indeed explode. The entire car is in flames. Black smoke is rising from the hood, and the windows are shattering from the force of the heat.

The man who saved my life calls the fire department and gives them our location, then after he hangs up, hands me the phone. "I'm thinking you might need to call someone to let them know."

"Thank you. How did you know my car was going to blow up like that?"

"My name is Benjamin Fields. Racing is a hobby of mine. Cars are my life. I saw the color of the smoke coming out of your hood and knew immediately it would blow. I'm just glad I got to you in time."

"Thank you for saving me. My name is Ashley Myers. Do I know you from somewhere? You look so familiar."

He gives me a sheepish smile before he says, "Yeah, I'm friends with Caleb, your boss. I've been to *Assets* a few times. I bought the one from him in Colorado and I'm interested in buying this one as well. I've seen you dance."

Okay…and now it's officially awkward.

We both stand at a distance from the car in silence, watching the fire engines and police pull up and work together to put the fire out.

"I'm going to call my fiancé." I hold up the phone he handed me a few minutes ago. He's probably at the gym and doesn't have his phone on him, but I try anyway.

After the third ring, Kaden answers. "Kaden Scott."

"Hey…Kaden, it's Ashley."

"Ashley? What number are you calling from?"

"Umm…Well, it's a long story, but I'm using Benjamin Fields's phone…"

"Who the hell is Benjamin Fields?"

"A man." I mean, really, how the heck else do I answer that?

"Ashley, why the *fuck* are you using another man's phone to call me?"

"Kaden! If you would stop cutting me off, I can explain," I whisper-yell, not wanting Benjamin to think Kaden is crazy.

When Kaden doesn't say anything, I continue. "My car kind of had an issue, and I need you to come get me." Benjamin chuckles next to me at my downplaying of the vehicle blowing up.

"What kind of issue, Ash? You were supposed to bring it to my mechanic."

"I know, but we got busy with going to New York. I might have forgot…and umm…well…it may have caughtonfireandblewup."

"It what?"

"It caught on fire and blew up."

"What. The. Fuck. Woman! Where are you?"

I give Kaden the location of where I am, and he tells me he's on his way before hanging up.

"Thank you," I say softly, handing him back his phone. "You don't have to stay. My fiancé will be here shortly."

"That's okay. I think I'll wait here with you. He sounded kind of pissed on the phone," Benjamin says worriedly.

"Okay, if you want."

We both have a seat in the grass and watch the firemen continue to work on containing the flames that are still rising from my burnt hunk-of-junk.

"So, you want to buy Assets?" I ask, trying to make conversation.

"Yeah. I own several clubs. At the time when I bought Assets in Colorado, he told me he wasn't interested in selling the one here, but he's apparently changed his mind. I love the concept he's created and would love to buy this one from him so I can trademark the name."

Before I can respond, Kaden pulls up. "Oh, my fiancé is here." I point to his car stopping right in front of Benjamin's car.

"Your fiancé drives a fucking Aston Martin while you drive that piece of shit?" Benjamin looks from me to Kaden's car incredulously.

"Yeah, well, I am a stripper, remember?" My hand goes to my mouth to stop the word vomit.

Benjamin shoots daggers at Kaden as he comes running over to us.

"Baby, are you okay?" Kaden pulls me into his arms, planting kisses all over my face and neck.

"She would've been killed by fire in that death trap if I hadn't pulled up and gotten her away from the vehicle," Benjamin barks.

Kaden stops kissing me and turns to Benjamin. "Thank you for saving my girl's life. I owe you one for sure." Kaden assesses Benjamin for a moment before extending his hand to offer a shake.

Benjamin glares at his hand. "Why the fuck is *your girl* driving around in that death trap while you're driving that." He points from the scraps of my burnt-to-crisp car to Kaden's vehicle that I'm sure is worth more than most people's homes.

"Trust me when I tell you she won't be driving around in a piece of shit like that again."

"She shouldn't have been driving around in it in the first place, let alone working at a strip club."

"I thanked you for saving my girl, but now I'm going to ask that you mind your own damn business."

The guys stare each other down and I swear I can smell the metaphorical piss running down my leg as Kaden takes me into his arms.

"Okay, well, Benjamin, I appreciate you caring about my well-being, but since you don't know us, you wouldn't know that I chose to drive this car. I don't accept help very well. So, let's all calm down."

"It looks like the fire is close to being put out. I'll let them know I was here when it happened in case they have any questions. I'm sure I'll see you around, Ashley."

Benjamin gives Kaden a curt nod before walking toward the police officer.

"How the fuck does he know you work at a strip club?"

"He's been in there before. He owns the club in Colorado and is looking to buy the one here from Caleb as well."

"First, we're going to go get Tristan from school, then we're going to buy you a new car, and I don't want to hear a single complaint out of your mouth." Kaden grabs my hips and gives me a kiss that makes me want more.

"Okay."

"And Ashley…"

"Yes?"

Kaden looks me in the eyes. "Please, baby. No. more. Stripping."

"Okay."

Twenty-Six

KADEN

WHEN ASHLEY TOLD ME HER CAR HAD ISSUES, I WAS PISSED. AT myself, for not forcing her to get a new car sooner. At her, for being so damn stubborn. Then, once I got there and saw her piece-of-shit car looked like a marshmallow placed over the bonfire for about ten hours too long, I just about flipped my lid. Ashley could have been killed. The car could have exploded with her in it.

The visual of the car on fire caused my anger to dissipate, fear taking its place. Visions of Gabrielle dying in my car all those years ago invaded my thoughts. Then to have that motherfucker insinuate I'm letting Ashley strip while putting her in danger by making her drive that shitty car while I'm driving a two hundred thousand dollar car made my blood boil. I don't give a fuck what Ashley wants, she's getting a new, expensive, top of the line, safe vehicle and she better not argue with me. I've let her run this show every step of the way, but I'm done.

After we pick Tristan up from school and go by the wireless store to get Ashley a new cell phone, we head to the Land Rover dealership.

"Oh, c'mon, Kaden. A Range Rover? Everybody always gets one of those. Don't make me be a cliché, please."

"Okay, so what do you want?"

"I don't know…like a Toyota, maybe."

"Ashley, you can be reasonable or I will get you whatever I want."

She huffs loudly, annoyed with me. I don't give a shit. She's my queen. She should be driving something equivalent to me. I know it's fucking petty, but that Benjamin guy pissed me off.

Using her phone, she searches through images of vehicles until she stops at one, showing it to me. "This one is cute."

"A Maserati Levante? It's more than cute, babe. That car is badass." She has no idea she just picked out a car almost worth half of mine.

I pull up the directions to the Maserati dealership in our area and see it's not too far from us.

With Tristan in tow, we park and enter the dealership. Without letting her see any prices, I ask the salesman if Ashley can test drive the car she wants. After giving them her proof of insurance and driver's license, we all get into the SUV to check it out.

"I love this car!" Ashley is bouncing around in her seat like a little kid on a sugar high as she runs her fingers across the leather and messes with all the knobs. When she puts the vehicle into reverse, the view behind her pops up. "Oh, my God! It has a camera! Like Liz's car!"

We pull out onto the main road and go for a quick test drive. The car drives smoothly and Ashley is in car heaven. Once we get back, we park and head back inside so we can purchase the car.

While I'm talking to the salesman, I hear Ashley screech. "Kaden! That SUV is like a hundred grand! I can't get that!"

I laugh at her freak out. She test-drove the SUV and fell in love immediately. She's getting the vehicle. I figured she had no idea of the kind of vehicle she showed me and her freak out right now confirms it, but it's neither here nor there.

"What color?"

"Kaden! How can you afford this car?"

"It's just a payment, babe. It's fine."

"Yeah, a goddamned mortgage payment."

"What color, Ash?"

Tristan is running around the dealership checking out all the cars, picking out his future car based on how many televisions are in the seats. Priorities.

"White, I guess."

"White, really?"

"Well, I heard once white is cheaper than other colors."

I laugh at that. "I'm pretty sure that's not true. Paint is paint. They just usually have white in stock. Now, what color do you want?"

"Umm…well…I like the blue your car is."

"Aww, babe, you want to have matching colored cars?" I throw my arm over her shoulder and give her cheek a kiss. "That's such a couple thing to do." I shoot her a wink.

After we have her car ordered and paid for, they send us off in a loaner so Ashley will have a car to drive until her new one comes in. The color and style she wants needs to be shipped from another location.

"I have to work tonight. Can you take Tristan, so I can go straight to work?"

"Sure," I say, giving her a kiss tenderly. I'm so thankful today didn't end up with her hurt or worse…dead.

"No stripping, Ash," I whisper into her ear.

"I didn't think about it, but I'm already on the schedule tonight."

"I already texted with Caleb and he said it's fine."

"Kaden!"

"Love you, babe." I smack her ass and walk to my car where Tristan is already in the back seat, Facetiming with my mother. They've grown close since our trip to visit them almost a month ago and she likes to Facetime him a few days a week.

"Hey, Kaden," Ashley calls my name.

"Yeah?"

"Thank you. I love you." She runs over to me and, throwing her arms around my neck, jumps up knowing I'll catch her. I kiss her hard for a good minute before we need to break for air.

"You're welcome."

I watch her walk away, swaying her hips without even meaning to, and smile to myself. This woman and her son have fast become my entire world.

Tristan and I get home and take showers. I cook us dinner, and we watch some television until it's nine o'clock, which his bedtime.

When I walk into his room to tuck him in, I notice his room is plain. It doesn't look like a kid's room. It still looks like a guest room.

"Hey, bud. What do you say after we get back from the tournament we have your room decorated how you want?"

"Really? Can I have UFC stuff?"

"Sure."

"Wait! Does that mean I can go to the tournament with everyone?"

"I signed you up today. You're good to go!"

"And we can go to Disney with everyone, too?"

"Of course." I ruffle his hair, then kiss his forehead. "Night, buddy."

After doing the dishes and rotating a load of laundry, I sit down to go over some bills, when I see a recent transfer of fifteen million into my account. I immediately call my grandfather.

"Kaden, how are you, my boy?"

"I'm good, Grandfather. Really good."

"And how is Ashley?"

"She's good. She's the reason for my call."

"Okay, talk to me."

"I saw the money you transferred to me. I don't want the money you offered me to marry someone. I'm marrying Ashley because I love her and I don't want it tainted with a bribe from you."

"There's my grandson. Welcome back, son. We missed you."

I chuckle softly. "I must admit, your bribe did give me a reason to pursue her and get her to come with me to Colorado. I have a feeling if it wasn't for you twisting my arm, we'd still be here, dancing around our feelings for each other."

"I am very happy for you, Kaden. The truth is, we always planned to give you your trust fund. I was just hoping it would push you to find love again. The money was wired a few days ago, and if you recall, I originally said once you're married. You aren't married yet."

"Why didn't you ever tell me? I always assumed I would just get some money in your will."

"We wanted to make sure you earned your way in this world first. We always planned to give it to you once you turned thirty-five but held off when you appeared to still be lost."

"Damn, Grandfather, that's a lot of money. Are you sure?"

"Your grandmother and I have had that set aside for you for many years. You're our only grandson. We love the man you've become. Now continue to be that man for Ashley and Tristan."

"I will. I love you."

"I love you, too, my boy. Goodnight."

"Night. Tell Grandmother I said hello and I love her."

"Will do. You've made her very happy finding Ashley and bringing her to Colorado with you. She loves Facetiming with Tristan. Goodbye."

"Bye."

I make note to call my accountant in the morning. While I plan to spend my life with Ashley, I know first-hand anything can happen, and I need to make sure she and Tristan are taken care of. I also need to get ahold of her account info so I can transfer some money over to her. I hate the idea of her only having the money she makes at *Assets* to spend.

Twenty-Seven

ASHLEY

IT'S BEEN FOUR MONTHS SINCE KADEN AND I OFFICIALLY became engaged for real, and everything has been going great. I've been managing the club full time, which makes Kaden happy, even though he's let me know several times I'm welcome to stay home. I know the money I make is nothing compared to the money he makes and has, but it's important to me to work and be independent in some way. I look at the employment ads daily, hoping maybe I can find something else I might enjoy, but nothing jumps out at me.

Hayley gave birth to a beautiful little girl the day before Thanksgiving. 7lbs 4 oz., 21 inches. They named her Mackenzie Colette Michaels. Mackenzie was Caleb's mom's name, who died years ago from cancer. Colette was his sister's name, who was tragically killed. Caleb and Hayley wanted their names to live on through love. She is a perfect mix of the two of them.

For Christmas, everyone decided to go to Bentley's cabin in Breckenridge. Since his parents' place only has four bedrooms, when the home next to theirs went on the market, he snagged it up. Six bedrooms and four bathrooms, the place is stunning. Kaden and I spent the week skiing with Tristan. Kaden insisted on him taking lessons, and after a couple days, he was skiing like a pro. Kaden also had us check out a couple places in the area. We would love to make coming here for Christmas a yearly tradition.

For New Year's, we visited my parents. They have an annual New Year's party and we missed it last year for Kayla and Bentley's wedding. At the end of the night, Tristan ended up staying with my parents and Kaden surprised me with a romantic night at a resort. I smile at the memory of us on the balcony…

"Close your eyes."

"Why?"

"Just do it, woman."

Squeezing my eyes shut, I rely on Kaden to walk me to wherever we're going. I already know we're at the Palms, a luxurious resort in the area.

I hear a door click open and we walk a little farther. Another door opens…or maybe a slider?

"Okay, open."

"Oh, my God! Kaden! This is amazing." We're standing out on a balcony on the top floor. It must be the penthouse of some sort. There's a beautiful mini-pool that's just ours to use. The balcony railing is see-through glass, creating an illusion of the pool water flowing down over the balcony. There are candles spread out around the perimeter of the pool, and in the corner is a bottle of champagne in a bucket of ice with two glasses.

"It's beautiful. What is this all for?"

"Well, aside from it being New Year's, it's also our four-month anniversary. You agreed to marry me four months ago, today."

Reaching up onto my tippy toes, I give Kaden a kiss. "Thank you."

"There are bathing suits in the bathroom. I had our stuff sent up while I was checking in."

"Can anybody see us in the pool?" I look to both sides and there's a concrete wall. I glance down and see the beautiful city of Las Vegas.

"No."

"Then I'm pretty sure we don't need bathing suits." Giving Kaden a flirty wink, I remove my dress, bra, and panties, then walk into the heated pool. "Are you joining me?"

"Hell, yes." He throws his shirt over his head, then pushes his jeans and briefs down. He saunters toward me with a mischievous smirk, and before I can consider why, he walks right into the pool and picks me up, wrapping my legs around his body.

"I love you, Ash," he murmurs, pressing his lips to mine. Suddenly, his soft kisses aren't enough. What was tender between us becomes more ravenous and soon we're both all hands and mouths and tongues and teeth. Kaden sits me on the edge of the pool, then leaves me to grab the champagne from the bucket. After popping the cork, he spreads my thighs.

"You know what would taste even better than your pussy?"

"Hmmm?" I ask, distracted by the fact that he's about to eat me out.

"Ashley with a side of champagne. Lie back."

I do as he says and a few seconds later, cold champagne is running down my breasts. Kaden is hovering above me, sucking the champagne off my nipples. Then he pours some into my belly button, eliciting a shiver out of me from the coldness.

"Damn…This is some good champagne. Want some?" he taunts.

"Yes," I moan. He's sucks the champagne out of my belly button and the feeling of his tongue on my body sends sparks straight to my core.

"Sorry, you'll have to wait. I'm not done drinking yet."

I lift my body up a little bit so I can see him. He's back on the steps of the pool and his face is parallel to my pussy. He spreads my lips, then lifts the champagne above my mound, pouring the cold liquid over me. Keeping the bottle in one hand, while holding my lips open with the other hand, his face disappears between my thighs, slurping the champagne off my clit.

My body ignites from the pleasure.

"So. Fucking. Delicious, baby." He pours some more over my clit. He sets the bottle down then disappears again, eating my pussy like he's a starved man.

Just as I'm about to come, Kaden lifts my ass up slightly and pushes a finger into my tight hole, causing my body to detonate. My eyes close as my climax hits and fireworks go off in the back of my eyelids, my body shaking from the intense orgasm.

When I no longer feel Kaden's mouth and hands on me, I open my eyes and see him smiling at me.

"What?"

"It's a beautiful sight watching you come."

Taking my hand, he guides us over to the lounge chair. "Come ride me, baby."

I admire him for a few seconds. His cocky smile. The couple days of scruff on his face that, without a doubt, left red marks between my thighs. His toned pectoral muscles and tight six pack of abs that I love to run my tongue down. His throbbing dick that's standing at attention waiting for me.

"It's my turn," I say.

Kaden looks at me quizzically, lifting one eyebrow.

I grab the champagne from the ground where he left it. Then, sitting on top of his legs, I pour a small amount of champagne over his dick and watch it trickle down his thick shaft and balls. Leaning down to take his balls into my mouth, my hard nipples brush up against his thighs causing me to shutter.

I suck the champagne off each of his balls, then lick my way up his shaft to the head. Pouring a little more champagne over the top of his dick, I swirl my tongue around the hole before taking him all the way into my mouth.

"Fuck, Ash. I need to be inside you."

I continue to fuck him with my mouth, until he pulls my head up by my hair, his tell-tale sign he's about to come. Lifting onto my knees, I hover above his dick then impale myself right onto him.

"Fuck, baby!" Kaden growls, throwing his head back. I rise up until only the tip of his dick is touching me, then sit back down again, his dick hitting my cervix.

I lift up once more, but this time when I come down I keep moving up and down riding Kaden. His dick hits that spot deep within me over and over and over again, and it feels so good. Kaden's hands hold my hips tightly as his lips close on one of my nipples. My eyes shut and seconds later I'm climaxing.

Before I can open my eyes, Kaden has me flipped over so I'm underneath him, my back flat on the lounger. His hands are on either side of my face and he's gazing into my eyes as he enters me. Slowly but deeply he thrusts inside me, his eyes never leaving mine.

His dick is rubbing my clit just right and I can feel an orgasm already starting again. "C'mon, baby. Give me one more." His thrusts are done with purpose, rubbing my sensitive clit repeatedly. His mouth comes down, sucking on my bottom lip. Then he moves to my neck, sucking on my sensitive flesh right below my ear. The friction between his dick and my clit is too much and my body spasms around him once more, this time bringing Kaden over the edge with me.

He thrusts still and presses his lips to mine, giving me a soft kiss. "Maybe this is the time we created a mini us." He smiles wide and I laugh.

"And if it's this time, which sex will it be, oh wise one?"

"A girl, of course. Missionary is a girl."

Bringing my thoughts to the present, I shake my head with a laugh. It's been four months since I stopped taking birth control and I haven't gotten pregnant yet. The doctor said it can take several months so we aren't worried, but Kaden always jokes, wondering which time it'll be when we create a baby.

His silly behind researched baby-making and found some ridiculous site that showed statistics on which positions will create which gender. He swears he's keeping track to see if they're correct, but I don't see how. As often as we have sex, I don't think he'll know which position was the one that made the baby.

"What are you smiling about?" Kaden asks. I didn't hear him come into the room.

"I was remembering New Year's Eve. The champagne."

"Oh, you were, huh? Does my dirty girl want a repeat of that night?" Kaden wraps his arms around me and suckles my neck.

"Mmhmm."

"We can definitely make that happen, but not right now." He smacks my ass and laughs, walking over to the luggage.

"Not cool." I pout.

"If we don't leave here in the next fifteen minutes, we're going to miss our flight to Orlando."

"I seriously doubt Bentley is going to let the plane leave without us."

The Newbreed tournament is this weekend, so we're all flying to Orlando. The tournament will be all day Saturday, then Sunday and Monday will be spent at the Disney parks. Kaden and Tristan will be flying home Tuesday, but I'll be flying to Colorado to go dress shopping with Sandra and Rose.

We've decided to get married the weekend before spring break, so we're planning to stay the week in Colorado to take Tristan skiing again. The kid is obsessed!

Twenty-Eight

KADEN

THESE LAST FEW MONTHS WITH ASHLEY AND TRISTAN HAVE been nothing short of amazing. The moment I pushed the guilt of my past away and accepted what I already knew, that I'm in love with Ashley, everything seemed to just click into place. Not a day goes by that I don't think about Gabrielle and our son, but I've learned I can love and remember them and still be happy. I've also learned my girl has the biggest heart I've ever seen.

I came home one day to find Ashley cleaning out the room I use for storage. We discussed turning it into a playroom for Tristan, and using the guestroom for a future nursery. She was staring down at something in her hands and crying softly…

"Ash, you okay?"

She swivels around, her eyes growing wide.

"Yes, I'm sorry."

"What are you sorry for? What's wrong?"

She holds out a picture frame for me to take. I take it from her and study it for a minute, the memory of the day it was taken. It was at the baby shower Gabby's sister threw for us. We were holding up a onesie that read, "Daddy's little fighter." We're both smiling happily in the picture. I place the photo back into the box Ashley took it out of.

"I feel so guilty," Ashley says. She blinks a couple times to let the tears spill out. Reaching over to her cheeks, I wipe them away. She swallows thickly and continues.

"I feel like I was meant to meet you, like you were supposed to be in my life, be my husband. But then I see these pictures and remember that in order for you to have met me, you had to lose your wife and son, and I hate that. I hate that you had to go through that.

"Thinking that if she and your son were alive, we would never have met and fallen in love makes me so sad, but if I could snap my fingers and bring them back to life for you, I would." Tears stream down her face and I just want to kiss them all away. So, I do.

Taking her by her waist, I kiss each of her cheeks, tasting the saltiness of her tears. "And I love you for that, baby. I love your heart. But we can't think like that. You're the one that reminded me that we can't live in the past."

Taking a different photo out, one of a 4D sonogram of Gabe, she says, "I think we should frame it and put it in your office. You shouldn't keep it hidden. You may not have gotten to raise him, but he was your son, Kaden."

I get choked up by her words, so I just nod. Then after swallowing the lump in my throat, I say, "That would be nice."

The next day when I got home from work, when I sat at my desk in my office to go over my schedule for the following week, right there on my desk was a simple silver picture frame and inside it was the 4D ultrasound picture. Ashley will never understand what that simple gesture means to me, or maybe she does, and that's why she did it. I'm definitely one lucky man to have her in my life.

"Hello…Kaden are you spacing out?" I look at Ashley waving her hands in front of my face. She's the most captivating woman in the world, and I can't wait to make her my wife.

"Sorry, just thinking about how much I love you." I give her a chaste kiss before getting up to grab the bags we brought on board.

"You ready for this tournament, bud?" I ask Tristan.

"Yeah, but do you think we could go to the gym at the hotel and practice? I'm kind of nervous."

"Can I go, too?" Bella chimes in.

"Yeah, I want to practice, too," Marco adds.

"Absolutely. And tomorrow we can get there early so you can warm up and practice."

After we all file out of the plane, we pick up our rental cars and head to the hotel.

"Kaden," Tristan says on our way to find the hotel gym.

"Yeah, buddy?"

"Tomorrow, at the tournament, will you stand ringside when I'm fighting."

"Of course! Just call me your personal trainer." I give him a wink.

"Umm…do you think when you and my mom get married you could be my dad *and* my trainer?"

My breath feels like it's been knocked out of me. "You want me to be your dad?"

"Yeah."

"I would be honored to be your dad, Tristan."

He runs the short distance to me and gives me a hug around my waist. Bending down, I give him a kiss on top of his head. I would never wish Gabrielle or Gabe harm, and I know without a doubt if they were alive, I never would've met Ashley or Tristan, but in this moment, I feel like the tragedy that was out of my control brought the blessing in front of me. Tristan may have a shitty father, but I vow to do everything in my power to make sure he never lacks the dad he deserves.

IT'S SATURDAY MORNING AND WE'RE AT THE NEWBREED tournament. The place is filled with hundreds of people. The competitors ages range from six years old to adult, and there are gi and no-gi competitions. Boys and girls under twelve fight each other. Because of the age range, even though Tristan recently celebrated his seventh birthday, there's a good chance he and Bella will still be fighting each other. Marco will be competing in the teen competition with the twelve and thirteen-year-olds. All three of them are signed up for the gi and no-gi tournaments, so it will be a long day if any of them win their fights.

"Check out the schedule." Cooper hands me the lineup. Sure enough, if Tristan and Bella both win their first fight, they'll be fighting each other in the following round.

"You know Bella is going to kick Tristan's ass, right?"

"Hey, now. Tristan and I were sparring last night and he's gotten good."

"No, not because he isn't good. Because there's no way he'll hurt Bella."

I chuckle at that. Cooper has a point. While Tristan loves fighting, if it's possible for a seven-year-old to be in love, then Tristan is most definitely in love with Bella. They might be young but their friendship goes deep.

"You never know. He takes fighting seriously."

"We'll see."

I find Tristan waiting outside the makeshift ring he's going to be fighting in. He's watching the two kids go at it with complete rapture, pointing out the strengths and weaknesses he observes in each fighter knowing whoever wins could eventually be his opponent. The kid in the red shorts grapples the other kid to the ground and quickly moves him into a position, forcing him to submit. The kid taps out.

"You ready?" I ask him. Unlike in class, where we focus on all types of MMA skills, Newbreed Tournaments focus on skills and submission. It's a grappling only competition, which means there's no striking of any kind allowed.

Tristan puts his mouth guard in and nods.

"You got this, buddy."

He walks to the middle of the mat, and after the referee quickly reminds them of the rules, Tristan and his opponent shake hands to begin the fight. I see Ashley on the other side, gnawing on her bottom lip and clapping nervously.

Immediately, the other kid dives down and grabs Tristan's legs, bringing them both to the mat. Tristan uses this opportunity to wrap his legs around his opponent's waist, and his arms go into a head lock. His opponent pushes up several times and breaks free.

Before he can get on top, though, Tristan moves back on top of him and forces him into an arm bar triangle. The kid taps out. The entire fight couldn't have lasted more than a minute.

"Yeah, Tristan!" I yell, clapping. He smiles at me, then at his mom. The referee holds both their hands, then raises Tristan's hand up in the air, announcing him the winner.

"Good job, Tristan!"

"Way to go!"

Everyone in our group mauls him, quickly congratulating him. Tristan thanks everyone then goes in search for someone. "Where's Bella?" Tristan asks. "Did she see?"

"I saw you, Tristan! You did so good!" Bella gives him a hug. "I won, too! My dad said that means we'll be fighting each other!" Bella looks ecstatic while Tristan looks like someone just broke his PlayStation.

"I'm fighting you?"

"Yep! After Marco's fight!"

"Great." Tristan sounds like it's anything other than great, though. Cooper catches my gaze, and smirking, gives me a knowing wink.

"Tristan, come here, bud. We need to talk." Cooper hears me and starts laughing.

"Yeah?"

"Let's talk while we walk over to where Marco is about to compete." Ashley eyes me warily so I give her a quick wink. She walks over to Hayley, taking Mackenzie out of her arms to hold her. The baby looks like she belongs in Ashley's arms. I can't wait until my fiancée is knocked up.

Slinging my arm around Tristan's shoulder, I ask him how he feels about fighting Bella.

"I want to win, but…"

"But?"

"I hate hurting her. Whenever we're in class, I always let her win. I don't want her to be sad if I beat her."

"Tristan, I can't tell you what to do, but if I were Bella, I would want to win fair, not because you let me win."

"But what if she stops talking to me?"

"If Bella is your friend, she won't stop talking to you for winning."

"What if I hurt her?"

"Did you hurt the kid you just fought?"

"No, but Bella is a girl."

"Tristan, my man, don't let a woman hear you say that…especially Bella. When you're fighting here and in class, there are no boys and girls. It's just fighters, and you and Bella are both the same color belt. You're both equal."

"Okay."

We stop in front of the ring just in time to see Marco's fight begin. This past year the kid has grown a few inches and is starting to gain a little bit of muscle. After about three minutes and a close fight, Marco's opponent forces him into submission. After the referee announces the winner, Marco stalks off pissed.

"I'll go talk to him," Caleb says, running after Marco.

The rest of us stay here waiting for the next fight to be announced, which will be Bella and Tristan. I see Cooper talking to Bella but can't hear what he's saying. Her hands are on her hips and her head is tilted in defiance. Whatever he's saying, little Bella isn't liking.

The referee stands in the middle of the ring and Bella and Tristan's numbers are called. They both go to the center and wait for the ref to finish replaying the rules before they shake hands. Cooper is standing on one side and I'm standing on the other, both watching to see what will happen.

After a couple minutes of grappling, it's clear Tristan is giving it his all. He's on top until Bella pushes him off. Bella then gets the upper hand, her legs locking around Tristan's upper body with his arm locked above her legs. Tristan tries to buck her off and successfully gets her on her back, but she twists her body so his arm gets pulled back farther and he has no choice but to tap out.

The referee announces Bella the winner, raising her hand into the air, and once he let's go she runs to Tristan, giving him a hug. "You almost beat me!"

"You did good, Bella."

"Thank you."

The day goes by quickly. Bella fights three more rounds and wins them all, making her the no-gi champion. The gi-on tournament goes by quickly. All three of them win their first and second round, but only Bella wins the third, so she and Tristan won't be fighting each other. She wins the fourth and fifth round, and she's officially the gi and no-gi champion for the kid's six and seven-year-old division.

"How does it feel to be a two-time champion?" I ask Bella at dinner. We're all eating out at a local Hibachi restaurant. I hold the spring roll I'm about to eat up to her mouth, making it a fake microphone.

"It feels good! I think I'm going to one day become a UFC women's division champion, and then I will start a petition to change the rules so I can beat all the boys too." Everyone laughs.

"How do you know what a petition is?"

"Mommy told me what it is."

"So, I have to ask. Before your fight with Tristan, your dad was talking to you, and you looked mad. What did he say?"

"He told me not to be mad at Tristan if he beat me. I told him he's crazy! Tristan is my best friend. I could never be mad at him. That's just stupid."

Cooper looks over at me and smiles, knowingly nodding. We have some damn good kids.

"Hey, Dad!" Tristan calls across the table. "Tomorrow at Disney, can we go on all the rides?"

Ashley gasps. "He called you Dad?"

"He asked me last night if I would be his dad. You were in the bath when we got back to the room and then it completely slipped my mind."

She looks at me with unshed tears in her eyes, then rubs her nose trying to stop herself from crying. "I love you."

"I love you, too, babe." I give her a kiss on her cheek.

"We can go on all the rides," I tell him. "We may have to stand in line for hours at a time, but we can go on anything you want."

"Yes!" Tristan fist pumps. "You hear that, Bella? All the rides!"

Twenty-Nine

ASHLEY

"OH, DEAR, THAT DRESS LOOKS GORGEOUS ON YOU. HOW DO you like it?"

I glance at the price tag and almost have a heart attack. It's a beautifully simple sweetheart A-line dress with a beaded sash. It has a strapless bodice and the back is crisscross strapped like a corset holding everything up top in place. The dress is fitted up top but gently flares out at the bottom. It's floor-length with no train, which I love. It fits me perfectly, and if I'm honest, it makes me feel like a princess. However, I could live off the cost of this dress for like three years.

"Umm…well, it's beautiful, but…"

"But what? What's wrong?" Sandra gets out of the leather seat she's been sitting in and puts down the complimentary champagne the sales associate gave us when we walked in. When she walks up to me and puts her hand on my shoulder, I choke up. I don't know why but I've been so emotional over the little things lately.

"Talk to me. Why are you crying?" She wraps her arms around me in a hug.

"What's wrong?" My mom comes out from the bathroom and rushes to me. I didn't know it, but when I showed up in Colorado, my mom was getting off her flight as well. Kaden surprised me, knowing I would want my mom to be here when picking out the details for our wedding. It was one of the best surprises I could ask for.

"Sandra, give the girl some space," Rose speaks up from her chair. When I look at her, she gives me a wink.

"I'm sorry. I love the dress. It's just a lot of money. I don't feel right spending this kind of money on a dress. Kaden and I are supposed to become equals, partners in a marriage, right? Isn't that what Dad and you always said?" I direct my question toward my mom. "I just feel like I have nothing to contribute."

"Oh, sweetie, you contribute plenty," Sandra says. "You make

Kaden so happy. There was a time when we thought he would never find love again, but he did, and he found it with you and your sweet son. Partnership isn't about money. It's about trust and friendship. It's about supporting and respecting one another."

Rose stands and places her hands in mine. "Don't allow money to come between you and my grandson. Whether you are rich or poor, money can destroy a relationship. Don't ever feel like you are inferior. No amount of money can buy the friendship and love you and Kaden have created. Let him love you. He wants you to have the perfect wedding. Don't look at prices. Enjoy yourself, so when you look back you remember the beautiful moments. Don't allow them to be tainted with who has more money." She pulls me into a loving embrace and kisses me on my cheek. "Welcome to our family, my sweet girl."

I turn to look in the three-way full length mirror and without thinking about the price, fall in love with the dress. "This is the one I want."

After picking out the dress and sending pictures of the bridesmaids' dresses to the girls, who let me know they appreciate me not sticking them in crazy ugly-colored dresses, we go to meet the wedding planner, Julie, for lunch.

"Is there a venue you're thinking of for the wedding?" Julie asks.

"We can just do it at the club…Wouldn't that be the easiest?"

Rose and Sandra exchange a look.

"What?"

"Well, it's just that Kaden and Gabrielle got married there."

"Oh no, I didn't even think about that. I'm so sorry." I bury my face in my hands. How could I not have thought about the fact that Kaden has already been married? What if I choose the same colors they had or the same style dresses? Will he remember her instead of thinking of me? Tears quickly form and I have no choice but to release them so everything isn't blurry.

"I'm sorry, Julie. I know you came here to discuss the wedding, but I don't think this is a good idea."

I drop my napkin onto the table and rush outside, needing some fresh air to collect myself. I'm walking down the sidewalk, not paying attention to where I'm going, when I run into a woman walking in the opposite direction.

"Excuse me." I look up and see a ghost. It's the woman in the pictures. Gasping, I look around to see if someone is playing a joke on me. "Gabrielle?"

The woman's eyes widen before smiling sadly. "No, she was my sister. You're Kaden's fiancée, right? I saw you that day in the club when we ran into Kaden, but you probably weren't thinking about that at the time."

"Oh, right. You were hugging him. I didn't see your face clearly.

You're Gabrielle's twin?"

I palm my forehead at the stupid question. Why else would this woman be a spitting image of Kaden's dead wife? "I'm an idiot. Please ignore me."

The woman laughs. "That's okay. My name is Danielle. It's nice to meet you. You looked like you were in a rush, and you're crying. Are you running to or from something?"

"From…I was at a lunch with the wedding planner and I kind of got overwhelmed. But you don't need to be bored with the details of my crap." I wave my hand.

"I don't mind. Kaden and I have been friends for years. I'm happy he found you. When he came to visit my family a few months ago he seemed to be turning a corner. Congratulations on the engagement."

"Thank you. And I'm sorry for your loss."

"Thank you. So, what had you feeling overwhelmed?"

"It's going to sound stupid, but I was supposed to pick the venue, so I picked the country club, which was the same location where Kaden and your sister were married. Now I'm second guessing everything. It's my first wedding, but he's already done all this."

"Ahh…and you're afraid you'll either be repeating what they did or he won't like what you chose and compare it to their wedding."

"Yeah. Stupid, right?"

She laughs softly. She has a pretty smile just like her sister did in all the photos I looked through. "No, it's not stupid. Talk to Kaden. Tell him how you feel. Otherwise you'll drive yourself crazy with worry."

"You're right, I will. Thank you. It was very nice to meet you."

"You, too. I look forward to the wedding." Danielle gives me a quick hug, then walks off. The wedding? I never would have thought her family would want to attend our wedding…

My phone goes off.

Kaden: Ash….

Me: Yes?

Kaden: Talk to me, babe. My mom said you ran out of lunch crying.

Me: Can we just elope like Caleb and Hayley did?

Kaden: We can do whatever you want, baby.

I think about how selfless he is. I know if I really wanted to, Kaden would go to the strip, find a little church, and marry me tomorrow. But then I remember our family, especially his grandmother, who wants to see us get married. It would be selfish to deprive them from being there to witness us getting married. I feel so lost and confused. I sit on the bench and start crying again.

Kaden: You there?

Before I can reply, my phone rings.

"Hello?"

"Baby, are you still crying? What's going on?" The sound of his voice makes me cry harder.

"I-I don't know what's wrong with me." My cries turn into sobs. "We were deciding on a location and I pick the wrong one. I picked the one where you married Gabrielle." I'm now crying so hard I'm hiccupping, and I can't stop.

"Ashley, baby, please calm down."

"I-I can't. What if our wedding is horrible? What if you liked your first one better? What if I say the wrong things? Or pick the cake you already had? You didn't want to get married again because you were only supposed to get married once. You already had your perfect wedding."

"Oh, baby. I wish I were there so I could wrap my arms around you and hold you. I miss you."

"I miss you, too." I sniffle and it sounds horribly unladylike, "Ugh! I'm all snotty. I sound like a vacuum sucking up snot."

Kaden chuckles softly.

"I don't think I can do this, Kaden."

"Do what? Marry me or plan the wedding?"

"Plan the wedding. Of course I want to be your wife."

Kaden sighs into the phone.

"I'm sorry."

"You have nothing to be sorry about. How about we do something a little untraditional? How about I plan the wedding? You already picked out your dress, right?"

"Yeah."

"So, everything else is just details. I don't like you sounding like this. It's not worth the stress. Our wedding will be one-of-a-kind because it'll be ours. Everything could be the same: the colors, the venue, the food…It wouldn't matter because the only important detail, the only thing I care about, is you and me and Tristan. It will be perfect and original because I'll be marrying you."

"Everything you say is always so damn perfect." My cries that slightly subsided start back up again in full force and Kaden chuckles into the phone.

"They weren't meant to make you cry, Ash. Go back to the restaurant and eat lunch. Enjoy your time with our moms and my grandmother. Go to the spa, get a massage, and then come home. I'll handle the details. Okay?"

"Okay."

"And baby…"
"Yeah?"
"I love you and your cute snotty sniffles."
"I love you, too."

Thirty

KADEN

"WHAT THE HELL WAS THAT ABOUT?" BENTLEY ASKS. THE GUYS are all over my house to watch the Super bowl. With Ashley being out of town, we all figured my place would be best to drink beer, eat shitty food, and watch the game. No women are allowed. Cooper, Bentley, Alex, and Stephen are already here and Caleb is on his way over with Marco.

Just as I'm about to answer, Caleb and Marco walk through the door. "What's up!" Caleb says hi to everyone then grabs a beer from the fridge before plopping onto my couch, Marco joining Tristan to play video games in his room.

"That was Ashley. I guess there's something I should tell you guys."

Everyone looks at me waiting for me to continue. "So, you know I was married before, but you assumed she left me, and I let you believe that without correcting you. The truth is I was married before, but she didn't leave me. Her name was Gabrielle and she was killed in a car accident on our way to the hospital for her to give birth to our son."

I give the guys a minute to soak in what I just said before I continue. "Ashley's upset because she went to pick out the venue and it was the same venue where Gabrielle and I were married."

"Fuck, bro. That's why you got upset when I mentioned your wife at the wedding. I'm sorry." Cooper comes over and gives me a bro hug.

"Nah, it's all good. My mom just said Ashley is extremely emotional and feels bad. I told her I'm going to plan the wedding. I don't want her to think anything she plans won't be good enough or will upset me because I already experienced it with Gabby."

Bentley smirks. "Your ass is going to plan the wedding?"

"How difficult can it be? Pick out some colors and shit, a cake… good to go…right?"

All the guys bust out laughing. "You're fucking nuts," Alex stops laughing long enough to say.

"The gesture is sweet as fuck," Cooper adds. "But you better make sure it's the wedding of Ashley's dreams. Sure, she's upset and willing to let you take over the planning right now, but when the day gets here she'll be expecting a goddamned fairy tale."

All the guys nod repeatedly in agreement. I pull out my phone to text my mom, realizing I'm going to need back up. I have a feeling I'm in over my head, here.

"Who are you texting?" Caleb asks.

"Who else? My mom."

The guys all laugh.

"Hey, I spoke with the contractor for the Rec Room and he said they should be able to break ground next month." Even though the four of us have gone in equally to build the sports complex for kids to go to, Bentley's taken on the brunt of the work. We purchased the property next to the gym and had the old building demolished. Bentley has been dealing with the architects, the city, and now the contractors to get this place built.

"If all goes well we should have this place up and running by the end of the year," Bentley says. "We're going to have to start thinking about staff. We don't want to wait until the last minute."

"With that Benjamin fucker buying Caleb's club, maybe Ashley would be interested in running the place. She loves working with kids."

Caleb laughs. "Benjamin fucker? The guy saves your fiancée's life and you're still pissed at him for calling you out?"

"Fuck him. Anyway, what do you think?"

"I think It would be a great idea. Liz has already agreed to handle all the accounting shit," Cooper says.

"Ashley is great at managing the club, and with her experience as a teacher, I think she'll be great," Caleb adds. "Talk to her and let us know."

"Sounds good."

THE GUYS HAVE ALL LEFT, TRISTAN'S SLEEPING, AND I'M WIPING down the counters after putting away all the food and drinks, when my phone rings. Pulling it out of my pocket, I see it's Ashley video calling me. I hit accept and her beautiful face appears on the screen.

"Hi," Ashley says softly. I can see a bit of the background and know she's in my old room at my parents' house. She and her mom both fly home tomorrow.

"Hey baby. I miss you."

"I miss you, too. I forgot what it's like to sleep by myself. I would take your snoring over the quiet any day." She laughs at her own joke, making me smile. Earlier, when she was sad, my heart was broken. I don't like to see her sad, ever.

"So, what are you wearing?"

"Ashley," I say admonishingly. "Are you trying to start phone sex with me while sleeping in my old bed in my parents' house?"

"Maybe." Her cheeks turn a light pink and it makes my cock stir. I go to our bedroom, pull my basketball shorts off, and lie on the bed. "I just laid in bed and I'm in nothing but my briefs. You?"

She looks down and her cheeks turn brighter. "Can I pretend I'm in something sexier? I'm in a shirt that says, 'I'm crabby in the morning' and there's a crab on it."

I laugh. She has tons of shirts like that. They all say weird and funny shit. I wouldn't expect her in anything else.

"How about you take it off, then tell me what you're wearing?"

The phone gets put down and when she comes back I have a view of her shy face and a little bit of her tits at the bottom of the screen.

"Okay, now I'm naked." My cock swells.

"Ash, put your fingers in your pussy, baby. Is it wet for me?" She does what I tell her to, and I know when her fingers are in because her eyelids flutter in pleasure.

"That's it, baby, finger yourself good."

"Kaden..."

"Yeah, baby?"

"Will you...do it, too?"

I look down at my hard cock that's already getting stroked. "Oh, I am, baby."

"Tell me something you want to do to me. Something we've never done before."

This woman is going to be the death of me.

"If you were here right now, I'd start by fingering that perfect pussy of yours. Then after making you come, I would put you on your hands and knees, and taking that baby oil you put on your body every night, I'd squirt some right onto your ass."

"Mmm...Kaden. Are you about to fuck me in the ass?" Ashley's eyes are closed and I can hear the noise her pussy's making as she fingers herself. She's soaking fucking wet.

"Baby, I am about to *devour* your ass."

"Keep going."

"I'd rub the baby oil all over your ass cheeks, then opening your ass up, I'd apply it to your tight hole, sticking one finger, then two in there, getting it ready for my dick."

"Stick it in my ass, Kaden."

"You want me to fuck your ass, baby?"

"Yes!"

"You got it, baby. Lining my cock up, I would slowly push in until you're completely full of me. Then I would reach forward, and wrapping your hair in my hand, I would fuck your ass. I would make you rub on your clit so we would come at the same time. Are you rubbing on your clit, Ash?"

"Yes, yes, Kaden! I'm about to come."

"Me, too, babe. Where do I come? In that sweet ass of yours or all over your ass and back?"

"In my ass. Holy shit! I'm coming, Kaden." Watching her throw her head back in ecstasy, pushes me over the edge, and my hot seed spurts out all over my hand and stomach as she moans into the phone coming as well. After a few seconds of quiet, I ask, "You still there?"

Ashley's eyes open and she looks at me shyly. "Yeah, I'm here. Umm…Kaden…"

"Yeah, baby?"

"Can we do that for real when I get home?"

"Hell, yes, we can. You don't have to ask me twice."

Ashley giggles into the phone. "I'm going to get cleaned up. I'll see you tomorrow. Love you."

"I love you, too."

Thirty-One

ASHLEY

IT'S BEEN ALMOST A MONTH SINCE I GOT UPSET WHILE TRYING to plan the wedding. Since then I've noticed my emotions are all out of whack. My mood swings are getting worse and I'm crying over the littlest things. Physically, I have sore boobs, I'm feeling sick all the time, and I missed my period, again. I would say all signs point to my being pregnant, but I haven't picked up a test yet.

Work has been crazy busy. Caleb went through with the sale of *Assets*. Luckily, for at least right now, Benjamin's keeping things the way they are. I'm still managing the club while Benjamin assesses everything. It's Friday night and Benjamin's out of town dealing with another one of his clubs.

After confirming the schedule and lineup for the night, I meet with Bianca to discuss the private parties for the evening. I can already tell it's going to be a busy night. I check on the tables, the bar, then work my way upstairs. When I get to the dressing room to check on the girls, there is utter chaos.

"What's going on?"

Michelle, a newer dancer, is packing her stuff up while Veronica is screaming profanities at her back. I'm confused because not only are they best friends but they're roommates.

"Whoa! Calm down. Veronica, what are you upset about?"

"This bitch slept with my boyfriend."

"You said you were broken up!"

"It doesn't matter!"

They're about to start a cat fight when Steve, the bouncer on duty, breaks it up. "Both of you, let's go." They both yell and scream, but he's not having it, forcing them to leave with him.

"We're now short three dancers," Scarlett says.

"Three?"

"Yeah, Stephanie called out. She wasn't feeling well."

"Okay, let me go down and check the schedule."

I get over to the hostess stand and take a look at the reservations for the night.

"We're going to have to cancel the party. I don't have a dancer."

"These men are VIP who do dealings with Benjamin. Are you sure it's a good idea to cancel them?"

"No, but I don't know what else to do."

I've tried to reach Benjamin several times, but his phone just keeps going to voicemail. I know the logical thing to do would be for me to cancel their party, but I'm afraid Benjamin will fire me for incompetence. He leaves and one girl calls out, and two get into a fight, leaving me short staffed.

"Ashley, they're here." The gentleman all walk in and you can tell they scream of money. They're going to be pissed if I have to tell them I don't have anyone to entertain them. Without thinking, I tell her to send them to the room, and then I go to the dressing room to get changed. I'll just have to handle this one party myself. Deep down, I know Kaden is going to be pissed when he finds out, but I'll explain to him it was a one-time thing and figure out from Benjamin what he wants me to do in this situation in the future, since there's no way I'll be making this a regular occurrence.

I borrow one of Scarlett's outfits, a sexy see-through top with leather booty shorts. I won't strip down completely naked. I'll just dance and get them some drinks. Maybe they won't even want lap dances. Who am I kidding? Of course they're going to want lap dances. I will just have to figure it out.

"You're stripping tonight?" Scarlett asks, walking into the dressing room.

"I don't know what else to do. We're short several girls and the party I was going to cancel are apparently associates of Benjamin's."

"Okay, how about you do the dance, and by the time you're done, I should have my tables under control, and I can take over and do the rest?"

"Oh, my God! Thank you!"

I quickly apply some makeup, doing a quick smoky eye, then throw on a pair of my shiny black fuck-me heels.

I take the back hall to the room then slip in the back to turn on the music and start my dance. The dance goes well. It reminds me I need to find time to take my pole dancing lessons again. I really enjoy them when my clothes are *all* on…and stay on.

After the song ends, I don't see Scarlett yet, so I do one more dance, hoping to buy some time. About half way through the song, I'm about to remove my bra when I see Scarlett walk in to take drink orders. I'm so thankful she's got my back. Dancing is bad enough, at least I don't have to explain giving lap dances to Kaden.

As I'm walking to the dressing room to get changed back into my work clothes, I am pushed against the wall from behind.

"Well, well, well. What do we have here?" I recognize the voice but can't place it right away. Before I can twist back to get a view of the guy's face, he grabs my hair and pulls my head up violently. The hairs on my head feeling like they're being ripped from my skull.

"Please don't hurt me." I try to push against the man, but he's stronger than I am.

"Hurt you? I'm about to make you feel so good." His breath is hot, and I choke on the smell of the alcohol dripping off him.

"Please don't do this," I beg, still unsure who this is. Regardless, this can't end well. We're in a dark hallway and nobody but management comes back here. Taking my sharp heel, I stomp on his feet, which only pisses him off further.

"You think you can walk around here dressed like a slut and not get fucked? You're nothing more than a cock-tease. It's time you act on it."

Keeping my hair firmly in his hand, he pushes me toward Benjamin's office. I start to yell for help, but he covers my mouth with his hand. I try to open my mouth to bite his hand, but I can't get a firm grasp on his skin. We get to the door and I pray Benjamin's in there but know he won't be. Once he's closed the door behind us, he throws me onto the couch and I finally get a look at him.

"Eric?" It's the gentleman from *Double D's*, the man whose son I used to teach. The same man who turned me in and got me fired.

"We never finished what we started. I saw you a couple weeks ago when I came here and knew one day I would get my chance, and then while looking for the bathroom I stumbled down the wrong hallway only to see you once again dressed like the fucking tramp you are. I knew it was meant to be."

"Look, Eric. I'm sorry. I never tried to tease you. Please don't do this. I'm engaged to be married."

"I don't give a shit! You ruined my life. After I reported you to the board, the principal told my wife! She left me and I've lost everything. It's all your fault! And for what? I didn't even get to fuck you."

Eric undoes his belt and drops his pants. I look around to see if there's a weapon to use on him, but there's nothing more than a tissue box. Then I remember I still have my heels on. Pulling my legs back, I kick at him as hard as I can, trying to delay him from entering me as I scream at the top of my lungs for help.

Eric jumps on top of me, covering my mouth with his hand. I bite down on his palm, hard enough that I can taste blood and scream again.

"Bitch! Shut the fuck up!" Eric slaps me across my face and grabs my shorts, pulling them down. I kick my legs, trying to stop him, but it does no good.

I feel sick to my stomach, like I'm going to throw up, but I don't give up. I keep kicking and screaming until there's a punch to my face. My head feels fuzzy and everything goes black.

"ASHLEY…ASHLEY, OPEN YOUR EYES."

My eyes open at the sound of Benjamin's voice. "Everything is going to be okay, Ashley. I've called Kaden, and the police just arrived. That fucker is being detained as we speak. He didn't get a chance to rape you. I walked in, in time. Fuck! Are you okay?"

"He didn't rape me?" I feel sick as I recall Eric on top of me. I jump from the couch and make it to the trash can just in time, throwing up everything in me.

"No, he didn't. Here, put your shorts back on." He hands me the tiny leather shorts Eric pulled off me. "My schedule got all messed up and my flight was delayed. I came straight here to meet with my business associates. I walked in and Eric was hovering over you but nothing happened. I called Kaden."

After wiping my mouth with the tissues, it hits me. He called Kaden. "Why would you call Kaden?"

"Why the fuck wouldn't he call me?" Kaden storms into the office and takes me into his arms. "You were attacked! Why the hell wouldn't your boss call your fiancé?"

"I'm sorry." Hot tears spill down my cheeks, and Kaden steps back to assess me.

"Why are you in a stripper costume?" His eyes sear into mine before he jerks his vision to Benjamin. Kaden grabs him by the collar, pushing him against the desk. "Why the fuck is my girl in a stripper costume?"

"Kaden! Stop! Don't hurt him, please. He didn't know."

"Didn't know what?" Kaden still has Benjamin pinned. Benjamin could easily fight back or push him away, but he doesn't.

"Three girls called out, and I didn't know what to do. I just danced on stage. I didn't do any lap dances or take off my undergarments, I swear."

Benjamin shakes his head. "Ashley, you shouldn't have done that. I appreciate you going above and beyond, but you should have just cancelled the party."

Kaden lets go of Benjamin and comes toward me. "You promised to never strip again." He says the words slow and so low I barely hear them.

"I know. I'm sorry." I look at Benjamin. "It was some associates of yours and I didn't want to cancel on them."

"Ashley, you are a manager. If you weren't here, do you think I would've stripped down and danced?" I appreciate the humor, but Kaden isn't having it.

There's a knock on the door. It's a police officer and he asks if I can please recall what happened. I start from the beginning, replaying the events that led to the assault, and when I get to the part where Eric slapped me, Kaden growls, "That fucker is dead."

I continue to recount what happened until I blacked out from the punch to my temple. Once Kaden hears I'm okay and wasn't raped, he stands. "Let's go home."

"Who's watching Tristan?"

"Liz is with him."

The drive home is silent and once we get inside, I thank Liz for coming over last minute.

"Anytime. Is everything okay?" She looks at Kaden warily.

"I was kind of assaulted at work." I try to whisper so Kaden won't hear me and freak out, again.

"Oh no! Are you okay?"

"Yeah." My eyes shift to Kaden, who is looking at his phone. Liz, thankfully gets the message.

"I'm going to go." She gives me a hug. "If you need anything, please let me know." She closes the door behind her, and I wait a few minutes for Kaden to say something.

When it's obvious he's not going to say a word, I do. "I know you're mad, but can we talk about this?"

He looks up from his phone then walks away from me.

I follow him into our room where he packs a bag. "Where are you going?"

"I'm going to stay at a hotel."

"Are you leaving me?" My words come out broken. The last time I watched a man pack a bag, it was Tyler, and my reaction to him leaving was relief. Right now, I feel the opposite of relief. I begin to panic.

"Kaden, please talk to me. I'm sorry. I'm sorry for dancing. I'm sorry for leading that guy on."

"What the fuck did you just say?" Kaden stops packing and glares at me, and I repeat what I said.

"I don't give a fuck if you were walking around buck-naked. You didn't lead anyone on. That fucker was wrong! He had no right to put his hands on you without your permission."

"Then why are you leaving me?"

"I just need some time, Ash. I get you want independence, but you chose to take your clothes off and willingly dance for other men tonight. We have more money than we will ever need, but you insist on working, and I've accepted that. But what you did tonight, I'm not okay with. And you promised. I don't blame you for being assaulted. That guy is a piece-of-shit. But you promised not to strip anymore and you lied."

He zips up his bag and then walks out the door, causing me to jump as it slams behind him.

I listen for the revving of his car engine, then I sink down the back of the door and, with my face in my hands, I cry, until there are no tears left. Then I grab a blanket from the hall closet and fall asleep on the couch. There's no way I'm sleeping in our bed without Kaden.

I get up in the morning and feel hungover. I guess ugly crying for hours will do that to a person. I check my phone for any missed calls or texts, but there aren't any. I remember from when Tyler left all those years ago, keeping busy is the best way to live in denial, so I make Tristan pancakes and eggs for breakfast, then wake him up to come eat. It's Saturday morning so technically he could sleep in, but I need the distraction. While he's scarfing down his food, he reminds me of Bella's upcoming birthday party.

"Next weekend is Bella's birthday party! Can we go pick out her gift today?"

"Sure, sweetie. Finish your pancakes and get dressed. Do you have anything in mind?"

"I'm not sure. I need to think about it."

"Okay, I'm going to jump in the shower."

After we're both dressed and I put on some cover up to cover the faint black and blue marks on my face, we head to the mall to pick out Bella's gift. Kaden is on my mind the entire time, though. Which hotel did he go to? Will he come back? Are we over for good? I fucked up and broke his trust in me. What should I do or say to make it better?

And that's how the entire week goes. I try to text him a few times but he only responds letting me know he's okay. I go by the gym to see if he's there but he's not. Nobody mentions anything so I don't bring it up. His mom calls me a couple times, but I'm afraid she'll ask for Kaden and then I'll have to admit he left me, so I don't answer. When Tristan asks about Kaden, I tell him he's out of town. It's technically not a lie, right?

By the end of the week I'm sick to my stomach with worry. I called in sick to the club and Benjamin was more than understanding. Not knowing where Kaden and I stand, now is not the best time to take off work and risk the chance of losing my job, but between the crying and throwing up, I can't get myself to function properly let alone go to work.

If I wasn't sure before, I'm positive now, that I'm either pregnant or have a horrible case of the flu, and the way I'm throwing up and sick to my stomach I'm considering the latter. I don't remember ever throwing up this badly with Tristan. I make a note to make an appointment with my doctor to confirm one way or the other.

I decide to go over my bills, figuring out which ones to pay first.

I log into my account and notice there's way too many freaking zeros in the balance. Clicking on the account overview, I see a deposit was electronically made four months ago! How the hell did I not bother to check my account for that long? Thinking back, I haven't gotten any debt collection calls in a long time. My paycheck is direct deposit and the only money Kaden lets me spend of my own is when I go to the grocery store. I've been so busy with my new life with Kaden, I haven't bothered to deal with everything else.

Sadly, after I borrowed the money from Giovanni, I stopped paying the credit card debts and just let them all go to collections. I'm going to need to get them up to date. With the ridiculous amount of money sitting in my account, I will finally be able to pay off all my debt and have a fresh start. I sign in to the various debt collectors I owe money to, but every single one shows a zero balance. I log on to check my credit score, to see what's still outstanding and it shows everything is current! The previous delinquencies are still on there, bringing down my score, but I don't owe anything. Every single one says satisfied in green. Kaden must have taken care of everything.

After logging out, I join Tristan on the couch to watch his movie with him. My phone goes off and I check it hoping it will be Kaden.

It's a group text with Liz, Hayley, Kayla, and me.

Hayley: Let's all do something fun with the kids. Caleb is busy at the gym training.

Liz: I'm down.

Kayla: Parrrttyyyyy!

Hayley: Ashley??

I go to type I'm not feeling well but that would raise questions I'm not ready to answer yet, so instead I type back: **Okay.**

We all agree to meet at Wet and Wild, a huge waterpark. The little ones will enjoy it and so will Marco. We meet in the front, pay, and once in the park, find a shaded spot to lay our towels down on a couple of lounge chairs.

"Mom, can we go in the lazy river?" Tristan asks.

"Sure."

We spend the next several hours relaxing in the water, the kids going on almost every water ride and slide known to man. When they start complaining they're hungry, we make our way to the food pavilion to order lunch. The kids grab a table next to the adults and immediately start talking about the upcoming UFC fight.

"How's the wedding planning coming along?" Kayla asks. Not wanting to mention Kaden and I are on the outs, I keep my answers simple.

"It's going. Kaden is handling it all."

"I should have made Cooper handle it all. As much as I loved my wedding, planning it was stressful, and it was over in a few hours."

"That's why Caleb and I eloped." Hayley shakes her head, laughing.

We enjoy our lunch, gossiping about nothing of importance, and it's nice to take my mind off my problems on the home front, even if it's just for a little while.

IT'S SATURDAY AND BELLA'S BIRTHDAY PARTY IS BEING HELD AT their house. There are bounce houses and water slides all over the backyard, a cotton candy machine is set up, and there are kids running around everywhere. I look around for Kaden and am shocked when I spot him sitting in a chair under a large tent they put up for shade. I'm not sure whether to go say hi to him, but the decision is made for me when the smell of the barbeque sends my stomach rolling and I have to sprint to the bathroom to upchuck my small breakfast.

I'm sitting on the floor of the bathroom with my head down, praying Liz recently cleaned this toilet, when there's a rap on the door.

"I'll be out in a minute."

"We're coming in."

The door opens and in walk Hayley, Liz, and Kayla.

"You okay?" Liz asks.

"Yeah, just not feeling well," I say, getting off the floor.

Hayley gives me a knowing look. "Or are you pregnant?"

"That could be it. Although the timing would suck..."

"Because you and Kaden are fighting?" Kayla asks.

My eyes shoot over to hers. "He told you?"

"He told Bentley when he got here. My nosy ass overheard. You should have told us when we were all at the water park."

"I messed up."

"How?" Hayley asks.

"Long story short. I promised Kaden I wouldn't strip ever again and then the club was busy and we were short girls..."

"And you stripped," Kayla says, finishing my sentence for me.

"Yeah, only that wasn't all. This douchebag, Eric, the one who turned me in for stripping when I wouldn't screw him, was there and assaulted me."

"What the fuck!" Kayla yells.

"Are you okay?" Liz asks.

Hayley wraps me up in a hug.

"Yeah, I'm okay. Luckily, Benjamin, the guy who bought the club from Caleb, walked in and stopped him. Then he called Kaden."

"Oh boy," Kayla says.

"Oh boy is right," I say.

"Let me guess. Kaden found out you stripped and that you were assaulted. He was scared and pissed. So of course, he acted on being pissed because he's a man. Easier to focus on being mad than on being scared," Liz adds.

"Yeah, well, he's been gone for a week now. And I'm pretty sure I'm pregnant."

"Does he know?"

"No, I don't even know for sure. And I'm not going to tell him. I don't want him coming back just because I'm pregnant."

"I understand that completely, but Kaden loves you. This is just a fight," Hayley says.

"Let's do a test to find out. I'm sure I have one somewhere," Liz says.

The four of us go to her bathroom and sure enough, she has a box of them. "Damn, girl. You trying to get knocked up again?"

"No way. They're from Nathan. Bella and Nathan are enough for me. If Cooper had it his way, he would keep knocking me up, but I think I'm done."

"Same here. Marco and Mackenzie are all I need," Hayley says.

"Bentley wants to adopt one more time. Chloe and Faith are definitely enough, but I wouldn't be against having another little one in the house one day."

I pee on a stick and of course the girls all stay. Apparently once you have kids you no longer care who's in the room while you're peeing.

The stick reads *PREGNANT* and the tears start falls.

The girls all gather me in a group hug.

"Don't cry, sweetie."

"I'm just sad Kaden isn't here with me right now. He's like a hundred feet from me, yet it feels like he's hundreds of miles away. I don't know how to fix this."

"You can start by putting on a super skimpy bikini and we all go play on the water slides!" Kayla laughs.

"And how will that help?"

"Umm…duh! He's a man…One look at your sexy ass in a bikini and he'll be salivating for you."

"I didn't bring one. Liz doesn't have a pool."

"Which will be changing soon. Cooper agreed to build one! But I have a couple extra suits I bought on sale and haven't used yet. We're almost the same size."

After we all change into our swimsuits, Kayla says, "Don't take this the wrong way, Ashley, but how far along are you?"

"Why? Do I look fat?"

"No, you look great, but your belly is definitely showing a bump."

"I'm not sure…I haven't gotten my period in two months, so maybe like six to eight weeks."

"Make an appointment to see a doctor soon."

"I will."

We all walk out to join the kids for fun and Kayla whispers to me, "Don't look at him. It'll make him want you even more."

It takes everything in me, but I don't look at Kaden. I can feel his eyes on me, though. I want nothing more than to run to him, sit on his lap and kiss him, while apologizing for messing up. But I don't. I walk by pretending the love of my life doesn't exist, praying I'm still his.

Thirty-Two

KADEN

"FUCKIN' A, I'VE GOT THE HOTTEST WOMAN HERE." BENTLEY waggles his eyebrows.

"Bullshit, my wife is the hottest." Cooper hits Bentley on the chest.

"Both of you guys are a bunch of dumbasses. Hayley's perfect ass blows them all away."

I just chuckle at the three man-children arguing over who's woman is the hottest. Then I look to the left and see the four women all walking toward the water area, and my eyes land on the sexiest fucking woman at this party. Fuck that! In this goddamned universe. Ashley is swaying her hips in a bathing suit I've never seen. It's pink and white striped and looks to be just a smidge too small on her, fitting her curves like a glove. I don't even bother arguing with the other guys. Hands down, my woman is the sexiest, most beautiful one here.

My woman? Is she still mine? She's texted me several times this week, apologizing, but I've only texted back if she asks me if I'm okay. I would never want her to think something's happened to me, but I'm not ready to talk to her about us yet.

When the call came in, saying she had been assaulted at the club, I freaked the hell out. I was beyond pissed. But when I learned the entire story, I became a mix of emotions. Sure, I was still pissed. But I was also hurt and scared. I was pissed she lied and stripped for a bunch of men. I know she didn't let them touch her, but I was still pissed, nonetheless. I was hurt she put her job above our relationship. She never should have let those men see her like that. But more than that, I was scared because she was assaulted and almost raped by some crazy fucker.

Looking at her right now, I just want to grab ahold of her and kiss the fuck out of her. I want to love her and protect her and worship her.

"You still not talking to her?" Bentley nudges me.

"Benjamin told me what happened," Caleb says. "Is she okay?"

"Yeah, I think so. I was so pissed she stripped after promising she wouldn't, I left."

"Your girl gets assaulted and you left?" Cooper exclaims.

"It wasn't like that. I was pissed she fucking stripped after she promised she wouldn't. I made sure she was okay before I left."

Cooper looks at me like I'm stupid. Fuck! He's right. I left her after she was assaulted and almost raped all because I was pissed she stripped. I'm a fucking asshole.

"Kaden! Cooper! Someone come here!" I look over to the waterslides to see Liz sitting on the ground holding Ashley in her arms. I shoot out of my chair straight for Ashley.

"What happened?" I ask, taking Ashley out of Liz's arms and pulling her into mine. Her eyes are droopy and her skin is pale.

"We were running around chasing the kids and she said she felt lightheaded. She hasn't been feeling well. I think she's dehydrated."

Cooper brings over a bottle of water and hands it to me. I open it up and put it up to Ashley's mouth. She guzzles it too quickly before I can tell her to slow down and then bends over to throw up.

"Shit, baby. You can't drink that fast when you're dehydrated. We need to take you to the hospital. If you're throwing up over a small drink, you can be severely dehydrated."

"I'm okay," Ashley says softly before she bends over to dry heave.

"All right, up you go. I'm taking you to the hospital."

"We can watch Tristan for you," Liz says.

I pick Ashley up and carry her bridal style to my car.

"Kaden, wait!" Liz comes running out, waving something in her hand. "Clothes for Ashley."

I look over and see she's still in her bikini. "Thanks."

Once we get to the hospital, I sign her into the ER and begin filling out the forms.

"Umm…actually, I'm pregnant," Ashley says when she sees me checkmark *not pregnant*. My pen stops writing and my eyes go straight to her stomach. She's wearing a hoodie and sweatpants Liz ran and grabbed her to throw on over her swim suit.

"Why didn't you tell me?"

"I just confirmed it today with one of Liz's tests. I haven't been to the OB yet." And fuck if I don't feel like the biggest asshole for walking away. At least now her mood swings these past several weeks make sense. And now that I'm thinking about it, we haven't had to stop having sex due to her period in quite some time.

"Baby, have you been sick all week?"

"Yeah, I haven't been to work all week. I'm pretty sure Benjamin is going to fire me."

"You don't even need that job. You're pregnant with our baby. And you're sick and now possibly dehydrated. You need to take care of yourself. Please don't worry about working." Ashley's eyes fill with tears.

I finish filling out the form and give it back to the nurse. Once I'm sitting back on the bench, I pull her to me so her head is in my lap. I play with her hair until I can hear her soft snores, telling me she's asleep. My mind goes to when I found out Gabby was pregnant. We were so excited the day she missed her period, we ran to the store together and picked up the test. She took it, and when it showed two lines, we called everyone in our family and then went to dinner to celebrate.

Ashley has been sick all week, worrying over whether I was going to leave her. She took a test with her friends instead of with me, and instead of telling me, she pretended like she wasn't pregnant or hurting because she didn't know where we stood.

"Ashley Myers," the nurse calls out.

"Ashley, wake up, baby. They're calling your name." She stirs awake and stands. Her legs wobble and I catch her.

"Can we get a wheel chair, please?"

"Yes, sir." The nurse grabs one and Ashley sits in it.

Once we get to the room, the nurse asks her a bunch of questions and takes her blood. She has her give her a urine sample and tells us once the tests have been run, the doctor will be in to speak with us.

"How are you feeling?" I sit next to her and take her hand in mine.

"My stomach feels sore."

"From throwing up nothing. You were dry heaving earlier. They'll more than likely give you fluids through an IV to prevent you from throwing it up."

Ashley nods and closes her eyes. The nurse comes in a few minutes later and sets up the IV. "This is to help you hydrate. Your urine came back and shows signs of dehydration and with you saying you can't keep anything down, we want to make sure you're hydrated."

She inserts the needle into Ashley's vein, and after setting up the fluids, leaves. Ashley goes back to sleep and I continue to hold her hand praying everything is okay with her and the baby.

Thirty-Three

ASHLEY

"MY NAME IS TONI AND I'M THE ULTRASOUND TECH. I'M JUST going to wheel you down the hall to do an ultrasound and then the doctor will come in and speak to you once he reads the chart."

Toni wheels my bed to the room and once she sets up the ultrasound machine, lifts my shirt up. "I'm going to try to see from here, but since we don't know how far along you are, I might have to switch to a vaginal ultrasound."

She squirts the warm gooey gel onto my stomach and starts clicking buttons on the monitor. "Okay, I'm able to see like this." She presses hard into my stomach and I want to tell her to chill the fuck out before I puke on her, but I keep my mouth shut.

"Let's see here." She continues to click. A whooshing sound hits the speakers, and I know it's the heartbeat. The breath I didn't know I was holding releases. Kaden squeezes my hand, giving me a knowing look. I forgot that even though he doesn't have any children, he and his wife went through this so he must recognize the sound of a heartbeat.

"Okay, that's the heartbeat." She types *baby A* on the monitor and screen shots it. "And…. there's the other heartbeat." She types *baby B* and screenshots it again. It takes a second for me to put two and two together, but it takes Kaden less than a second because he blurts out, "Holy fuck! There's two…like two babies in there?"

"Yep! Two babies, and it looks like you're about ten weeks. Your due date is estimated to be September seventeenth, but it can change once you see your OB."

"Huh…Well, Kaden, which position do you think it was we created twins in?"

The ultrasound tech looks at us in confusion, but Kaden throws his head back with a laugh.

"It could have been any number of them. Maybe it was the time in the bathroom…"

"Okay!" I cut him off. "I'm pretty sure Toni here doesn't want a play-by-play of our sex positions."

"Hey now! You asked."

Thankfully, the tech speaks up. "I'm just going to take a couple more shots of the uterus for the doctor and then I can print a couple pictures of your little kumquats."

"Excuse me?" I manage to find my words. "What did you call my babies?"

Toni laughs. "Kumquats. It's a small fruit. I always use fruits to determine the size of the babies. Week eleven they'll be the size of Brussel sprouts and at twelve weeks they'll be the size of a passion fruit! My favorite week though is week twenty-nine, butternut squash. I love butternut squash! Oh, and week thirty-three! Pineapples! You'll have two pineapples in you!"

Pineapples? The heavy green fruit with hard pointy things sticking out of it? I must give Kaden a look of horror because he stops her from continuing. "That's great. Can we get those pictures you mentioned?"

"Sure thing." She prints them and wheels me back to the room. My eyes don't leave the pictures of my two Kumquats. Jesus! I'm going to need to find another way to describe them. I can't spend the next seven months calling my babies fruits! Holy shit! I'm having two babies!

"Yes, we are." Kaden smiles at me.

"Huh?"

"You said you're having two babies."

"I said that out loud?"

Kaden laughs and nods.

After the doctor comes in and confirms what the ultrasound tech already told us, he lets me know he's going to keep me on fluids for a few hours to make sure I'm hydrated. Apparently being pregnant with twins ups your HCG count and can cause you to have even worse morning sickness. He prescribes me nausea medication and prenatal vitamins.

After I'm released from the hospital, Kaden goes through the pharmacy drive-thru to pick up my prescriptions then takes me to get something to eat. After we're seated, Kaden orders us both waters.

"Anything look good?" He looks up from his menu to me.

"Everything…nothing…I don't know. I'm afraid whatever I eat will make me sick."

He hands me a pill for nausea. "You have to eat. Even if it's something small."

I take the pill with the water the waitress delivers. When she returns to take our orders, I order chicken noodle soup and a piece of chocolate banana cake, then change my mind when I wonder if a banana is on the list of baby sizes. "Actually, I'll take the cheesecake."

"With strawberries?"

"No, no fruit. Thank you."

Kaden laughs, then orders a grilled chicken sandwich with a side of vegetables.

"I'm sorry I haven't texted you all week."

"Where have you been?"

"At a hotel. Working out at the gym there. With Alex taking his honeymoon this week, I took the week off."

"I don't want you to forgive me and marry me because I am pregnant."

He reaches into his pocket and pulls out a rectangular box. "Open this."

Lifting the lid, I see two silver puzzle pieces. They're put together and have an engraving across them. One reads: *YOU ARE MY MISSING PIECE.* The other reads: *YOU FIT ME PERFECTLY.*

"I saw them in the storefront yesterday and had them engraved. You're my missing piece, baby."

"You bought these yesterday?"

"Yes, obviously before I knew you were pregnant. I planned to talk to you today after the party. I just couldn't figure out how I felt about all of it. But I knew I loved you. I love you so much, baby. No matter what. And I'm sorry for leaving."

Kaden gets out of the booth and comes around to my side of the table, scooting in close to me. "You were assaulted and I put my anger above your feelings and wellbeing. Can you forgive me?"

"Yes, I missed you so much. And I'm quitting the club. I just want to focus on our babies and on us and Tristan."

Kaden grins and gives me a kiss. "I would really love that, but only if that's what you want to do."

"It is."

He takes my keys out of my purse and slides the keychain onto my keys. "So, you always have a piece of my heart with you."

"I love it."

"There's actually something I have been meaning to talk to you about. You know the recreational center will be breaking ground hopefully next month."

"Yeah, I can't wait to see it all done. It's going to be amazing."

"The guys and I were talking and we thought you would be the perfect person to run the place. You'll have help of course. Liz will be handling the accounting side, and we'll have to hire people and reach out to those who wish to volunteer, but you mentioned you would like to work with kids so I thought maybe you would want to work there."

"Kaden, I would love to manage the rec center. I have so many ideas. The different sports and programs we can offer. While I was teaching, I saw so many kids wish for after school activities that weren't offered because of budgeting. I'm so excited."

"Perfect. The place won't be up and running until the beginning of next year, but we want to make sure we're doing it right along the way. We can sit down and go over the plans, see if there's anything we need to add or change. Sound good?"

"Sounds amazing."

After we finish eating, we go to Liz's to pick up Tristan. The party has ended and Tristan and Bella are in the living room watching Ultimate Fighter on the television.

"How'd it go?" Liz whispers.

"Kaden knows."

"Okay, good. I wasn't sure whether to say anything outside. I'm so glad you're okay!" Liz pulls me into a hug. "How did he take it?"

"How did who take what?" Kaden comes over and puts his arms around me absently rubbing my belly as he nuzzles his face into my hair, giving me a kiss under my ear. I sink back into his arms welcoming the feel of his body against mine after a week of being without it.

"How did you take me being pregnant."

"You're pregnant?" Tristan comes into the kitchen with Bella following him.

"I am. What do you think about that?"

"I think that's awesome. I hope it's a boy, so I can have a brother."

"You can borrow my brother if you want," Bella offers.

"You don't like your brother?" Cooper asks.

"Of course I do! I love him. But if Tristan needs to practice, I don't mind lending Nathan to him."

We all laugh. "That's very sweet of you."

"Well, it might be a boy and girl," Kaden says, snuggling his face back into my neck.

Tristan looks at us confused.

Liz gasps.

Cooper laughs.

"You're having twins?" Liz looks down at my stomach.

"Apparently so."

"Well, that makes sense. Why you're so sick and your tiny belly is already protruding!"

"Yeah, I'm only like ten weeks. We aren't going to tell everyone until I'm out of the first trimester, but there are definitely two little ones in there."

"Aww…If I remember correctly isn't ten weeks a lemon?"

"Oh no! Not you, too!"

Kaden cracks up. "Nope, it's a kumquat."

Cooper laughs.

"What's a kumquat?" Tristan asks.

"Okay, I don't know what's up with you all and measuring the size of a fetus by fruits, but my babies are not freaking kumquats!"

Everybody laughs.

Thirty-Four

KADEN

"UM, WHAT ARE THESE?" ASHLEY IS STANDING IN THE BACKYARD, staring at my four-wheelers like they're personally offending her.

"Baby, you've never seen a four-wheeler before?"

"Oh, I've seen them. I'm just wondering what so many of them are doing back here and why my son is sitting on a mini-one."

It's a three-day weekend and the entire gang is over for a barbeque. I'm assuming by the look on Ashley's face, she hasn't been to the detached garage in the back to see all my toys, four of which are four-wheelers. Since Tristan is too small to ride a regular one, I had a Honda 90 delivered for him, along with a chest guard and helmet. He took one look at that machine and jumped on it ready to go. But now looking at the death glare Ashley is giving me, I'm thinking that maybe I should have mentioned it to mama bear first.

"Can I ride on the back of Tristan's?" Bella squeals.

"You should ride on the back of mine, Bella," Marco cuts in. "I'm older and can drive better. You'll be safer with me."

"Since when can you drive?" Caleb grills Marco.

"Well, I haven't yet, but I'm older and almost thirteen."

"There's no way Marco is riding that death-trap by himself." Hayley is standing next to Ashley and if I don't do something quick the women are going to overpower us.

"The guys will each take one, and Marco and Bella can ride behind one of us. Tristan's got his own, though. He has to learn how to ride." When Ashley's eyebrows go up in defiance, I jog over to her to defuse the situation. "Baby, I'm going to be with him the entire time. It's an automatic so he doesn't even have to shift. He has head and chest gear. I wouldn't let anything happen to him."

I give her a small kiss on her lips, but it doesn't work. The tears well up in her eyes just begging to be released. "B-but he's m-my baby."

"Yes, he is, but the babies in there"—I point to her stomach—"are making you a tad emotional."

If looks could kill, I would be a dead man.

"Are you saying my concerns for my child aren't real? That I'm only worried about the well-being of my only son because you knocked me up and I'm carrying two babies in here?"

I hold my hands up, palms out, silently waving the white flag, but it's too late. She's revved and ready to ride.

"And even if I am a tad emotional, don't you think it's a bit rude to point it out? It's not my fault my hormones are all over the place. Maybe you should have thought about this when you insisted I get rid of my birth control. Now my son is sitting on a death contraption about to go riding through the millions of acres of woods where he can get lost or hurt."

Damn, I love this woman. I feel a smile grace my lips and quickly try to reign it in before she catches it.

"So….does that mean we can't go riding?" Bentley whines. Kayla smacks him.

Ashley huffs and storms off, but I chase after her. Yeah, yeah, I'm pussy whipped. I'll be the first to admit it. "Wait, Ash." She stops and turns glaring at me. "If you don't want him to ride on his own, he can ride on the back of mine. I'm sorry, baby. I don't want you stressed."

I'm granted a small smile, warming my heart. "Ugh! He can ride. Just be careful, please. I'm going to go start on the side dishes for lunch. I can't be out here and watch this. It's going to give me a heart attack."

I look back and forth between Tristan and Ashley trying to decipher the code of what she just said knowing if I make the wrong choice, my ass will be in the dog house tonight.

"Tristan, we'll practice with your new four-wheeler later. You're on the back of mine, bud."

I hear a soft giggle behind me, then tiny hands come up behind me. "Good decision. You'll definitely be rewarded tonight."

"HOLY SHIT, BRO! THOSE TRAILS ARE SOMETHING ELSE."

"Yeah, we need to go again, and soon."

"I can't believe after all these years, we've never gone mudding after a good rain."

We spent the good portion of the morning and early afternoon riding the trails that line up to my backyard. Once we returned and got cleaned up, the ladies had lunch ready to go. Ashley can make a mean homemade cornbread casserole.

I look around and take a moment to thank God for everyone at this table. Everybody is chowing down and talking. The kids are laughing.

We're all healthy and happy.

"You okay?" Ashley looks at me quizzically.

"Yeah, I am. Thank you." I bring my lips to hers, and what starts off as a quick kiss quickly turns into something more. Suddenly there's a piece of food hitting me in the side of my head.

"Hey!"

"Quit making out like teenagers at the lunch table." Cooper laughs.

Ashley leans over and whispers into my ear, "Later."

That one word has my dick twitching.

Thirty-Five

ASHLEY

"MOM, YOU LANDED ON PARK PLACE, AND DAD HAS A HOTEL on it. You owe him…"

"Fifteen hundred." Kaden waves his monopoly card in the air excitedly. I would like to smack that smirk right off his damn face.

Let's have a family game night, they said…

It'll be fun, they said…

Fun, my ass! While Tristan and Kaden are holding all the damn deeds to everything that matters, I have like two hundred bucks left and own Oriental freaking avenue!

"I need to go to the bathroom real quick! Don't let Mom steal my money." Tristan runs out of the room to the bathroom.

"Hey Ash…"

"What?" I glare at Kaden, knowing I'm about to lose. I hate losing. And for the record, I am so done with family game nights.

Kaden moves closer to me, giving me a kiss on my cheek, then bites down softly on my ear lobe. The act sends sparks right to my core. This pregnant woman is horny twenty-four-seven these days.

"If you give me a blow job behind the hotel I own, I might consider your debt paid."

I laugh out loud, throwing my money onto the board. "I'm out."

"Oh, c'mon, baby. I'm sure we can work something out."

"How about you put Tristan to bed while I take a shower and then we can meet in bed to negotiate?" I squeeze his semi through his jeans.

"Tristan!" he yells. "Time for bed." Then he turns to me. "I'll meet you in bed, and you better be naked."

"FUCK. YES!" KADEN IS LYING IN BED WEARING NOTHING BUT A pair of briefs watching TV when I walk out of our bathroom naked, as he requested.

I wave the Park Place deed in the air. "So, I apparently owe you fifteen hundred dollars. I'm here to work off my balance."

When I get close enough, Kaden moves to the edge of the bed, then grasping my hips, pulls me toward him, so his face is level with my protruding belly. I'm now fourteen weeks pregnant, and while you would think a month wouldn't make a difference, when you're carrying twins, it does.

After placing several small kisses on my belly, Kaden looks up and smiles at me. "I love you."

I entwine my fingers into his hair, then lean down to give him a kiss. "I love you, too."

Squatting in front of him, I quickly pull his briefs down so his beautiful dick pops out.

"Get up here." I look up in confusion.

"I don't want my fiancée sucking my dick tonight. I want to make love to you." Grabbing me under my arms, he lifts and places me on the bed.

"Do you know what today is?" Kaden starts raining kisses all over my face: my cheeks, my forehead, my lips. Then he moves downward to my neck and collarbone.

"Sunday?"

He laughs as he moves lower to kiss each of my nipples, causing me to stir.

"Yes, it's Sunday. But it's also three weeks until we get married."

Holy moly! I can't believe it! In three weeks, Kaden Scott will be my husband.

"I need to make love to you as many times as possible before then," he says with urgency.

"Why? What will happen once we're married?"

Kaden looks at me like I'm stupid before he breaks out into a huge grin. "I'll never be able to make love to you as my fiancée, again."

"You're so silly!"

He gives me a kiss on my belly. "Hey there, little ones. Hopefully you have no idea what is going on because I am about to make sweet, sweet love to your mama."

He looks up at me and winks, soaking my non-existent panties in the process. Then he does just as he promised, and makes sweet, sweet love to me for hours.

Thirty-Six

ASHLEY

like it's the first time she has ever seen my wedding dress.

"I'm just so glad Sandra was able to get the seamstress to bring it out more. I need to hurry up and get married before my belly grows again!"

We're sitting in one of the rooms at the amazing wedding venue Kaden and his mom picked out. Parkside Mansion is gorgeous on the inside and outside. The ceremony will be held out back under a huge white tent, which will shield the blazing Colorado sun, and the reception will be held in their ballroom.

Most of our guests flew in yesterday, some early this morning. Since it's a tradition for the bride and groom to not see each other the night before the wedding, the girls planned a spa day for us yesterday with lunch. It was the perfect bachelorette luncheon. The guys all stayed at Bentley's cabin and spent the day skiing, returning this morning.

Earlier this morning, Kaden's mom brought me by the venue so I could see everything before the wedding. She told me that it will all feel like a blur once the wedding gets started so she wanted me to take it all in now. The outside is simple. White wooden back chairs that lead up to the front where we will say our vows. Light pink petals are littered along the walkway and upfront.

The ballroom is filled with large circular tables with light pink linens all covered with sterling silver vases that are filled with fresh gardenias. It's all simple and elegant and I love it. The linens even match the bridesmaids' dresses.

"Oh, Ashley, you look beautiful!" Hayley comes over and gives me a one-handed hug since she's holding something in the other. "This is for you, from Kaden."

I take the wrapped box from her hand and unwrap it. Inside is a puzzle box with the image of what the puzzle will be when it's completed. It's a picture of Kaden, Tristan, and me holding up the sonogram we got last week at my appointment where we found out the sex of the babies.

"A thousand-piece puzzle?" Kayla laughs. "That's more like work than a gift."

"No, it's perfect."

Inside the box, there's a note on top of all the pieces.

Ashley,

Love is like a puzzle, hard to piece together, but beautiful when all the right pieces are put together. I can't wait to spend my life putting all our puzzle pieces together, baby. I love you.

Love always,

Kaden

"Don't you cry! You can't go messing up your makeup until he at least sees you!" Rose pulls me into a hug. "Thank you, my darling girl. You took my broken grandson and pieced him back together."

"What did you get him?" Hayley asks. I feel the blush hit my cheeks.

"I did a boudoir photo shoot…"

"Nice!" Kayla exclaims, and all the women giggle. I look over at Rose, embarrassed that I just admitted to doing a sexy photo shoot for her grandson, but she just smiles and winks.

"You ready?" My dad opens the door, extending his hand to me. "Yes, I am more than ready."

Once we get to the backdoors of the mansion, Bella and Tristan walk down the walkway first. Bella is the flower girl and Tristan is the ring bearer. Next, Hayley, Liz, and Kayla all walk down the aisles escorted by their husbands. Once they get to the end, the wedding march begins and my dad walks me down the aisle.

As my dad kisses my cheek giving me away, Kaden takes my hand in his. "There are no words, Ash. You look gorgeous."

"Thank you. You look handsome yourself. Thank you for the puzzle."

"Do you know what it took to make my dick go down after seeing those pictures of you right before having to come out here?" Kaden whispers, making me smile.

We stand in front of the Ordained minister and say our vows to one another. We've created our own vows but decided to keep them simple—beginning and ending them the same. I couldn't memorize mine to save my life, so I pull the paper out of my dress. Kaden chuckles.

"I, Ashley, choose you, Kaden. To stand by your side and sleep in your arms. To be the joy to your heart and the food for your soul. To learn with you and grow with you. I promise to respect you and cherish you as an individual, a partner, and an equal. I vow to support you, push you, and inspire you, and above all love you, for better or worse, in sickness and health, for richer or poorer, as long as we both shall live."

I take the ring Tristan hands me and put it on Kaden's finger. He looks down at it for a moment then back up at me with unshed tears in his eyes.

"I, Kaden, choose you, Ashley. I promise to choose you every day, to do the hard work of making now into always. To laugh with you, cry with you, grow with you, and create with you. I promise to protect you and above all love you, for better or worse, in sickness and health, for richer or poorer, as long as we both shall live."

Kaden takes the ring from Tristan and slides it onto my finger.

"Kaden and Ashley Scott, I now pronounce you husband and wife. You may kiss the bride."

Kaden bridges the gap between us and kisses me. Everybody claps and cheers.

After we take way too many pictures, we make our way to the reception where the deejay announces us as Husband and Wife.

After we enter, we're called to the dancefloor for our first dance. Kaden insisted since he was planning the wedding he would also plan the song for our first dance. *Then* by Brad Paisley comes across the speakers and tears hit my cheeks.

"May I have this dance, Mrs. Scott?" Kaden puts his hand out for me to take and I nod because words can't be spoken.

He pulls me into his arms and my face goes to his chest as he softly sings the lyrics of the song to me. When the song ends, Kaden stops moving and lifts my chin so I'm looking him in the eyes. "You're my whole world, baby. My missing puzzle piece. Thank you for making me the happiest man in the world."

We spend the rest of the night celebrating our wedding with our family and friends. I dance with my father and father-in-law several times, as well as with all the girls. The night is amazing and I couldn't ask for anything more.

As the night comes to a close, Kaden lets me know the valet has pulled our vehicle up. He has a surprise for Tristan and me and is driving us to it tonight. We decided since Tristan was off school for a week, we would bring him along with us, and honeymoon family style.

"Thank you everyone for joining us." Kaden, Tristan, and I wave to everyone then get in the car to head to the secret destination.

"The wedding was amazing. Thank you." We're driving down the dark highway to wherever it is Kaden insists we will love.

"I'm glad you enjoyed it, baby. It was fun planning it with my mom, but I'm glad I don't ever have to plan another one." He squeezes my hand. I turn in my seatbelt to check on Tristan and Kaden stops me. "I can see him in the rearview mirror. He's fine. Don't even think about taking your seatbelt off."

I turn back around and reach down to grab my iPad to read, since I don't know how long we'll be driving for. When my head pops up, I see a set of bright lights coming toward us as Kaden's hand hits my chest to protect me.

There's a flash of something, I don't know what, but it looks like beautiful angel wings, and then everything goes black.

Epilogue

KADEN

Nine Months Later

"I MISS YOU SO DAMN MUCH. HELL, WE ALL MISS YOU. BUT I know you're up there with Gabe and Gabby looking down on us, watching and protecting us all."

"Of course she is, Kaden."

I turn to see my beautiful wife standing next to me.

"I'm just glad my grandmother got to meet the twins before she passed away."

"Me, too. Thank you for giving me a few minutes at Gabrielle's grave alone."

"Of course. You ready to get back to my parents and the kids?"

"I sure am."

We get back to my parents' house, and after searching the house, find them on the back porch. Morgan and Emma, our twin girls are both in portable swings and Tristan is sitting in front of them, just watching them. My mother and father are sitting at the table, drinking iced tea and eating lunch.

"Tristan? What are you doing, bud? The twins are only three months old. You know they sleep a lot."

"You told me to watch them. This is the first time you both left them. I had to make sure to watch them good."

"He hasn't left that spot since you both left. He takes being a big brother very seriously," my mother says.

"You're the best big brother," I point out to Tristan, making his face light up. I sit next to him, looking at my beautiful little girls, remembering the night I thought for sure I would never get to meet them.

The bright lights.
The crunching sound.

The screaming.
The silence.
For the briefest moment, I thought for sure fate was fucking with me and presenting me with the most sick, twisted form of déjà vu. The ambulance was called, and when we got to the hospital, I wasn't allowed in the back with Tristan because legally, I wasn't his father. The nurse broke the rules and let me know Tristan had a couple bruises on his head but was otherwise perfect.

Ashley was rushed back to be assessed, and after a thorough check, had nothing more than a broken arm. The babies both had perfect heartbeats and the doctor said everything looked good. It was a close call, but for whatever reason, we were all protected. Ashley swears Gabby and Gabe were our guardian angels, looking down and protecting us.

The next day, since the hospital insisted on keeping the two of them over night to be monitored, we made it to our destination. I purchased a cabin near Bentley and Kayla's so we could continue our tradition of skiing during the holidays. We spent the rest of the week at the resort taking it easy, and once we returned home I doted on Ashley the entire rest of her pregnancy.

After the accident at the hospital, and the doctors refusing to talk to me about Tristan since I wasn't his legal guardian, Ashley and I filed the papers with the court for me to legally adopt Tristan, only to find out the papers that asshole Tyler gave her were fake. I hired a PI to locate him, and we found out he was killed shortly after taking the money from Ashley—a fight gone bad. Since he was no longer living, it made it easy for me to adopt Tristan, officially making him my son four months later.

Two months after me legally becoming Tristan's father, Morgan and Emma made me a father of three. They graced us with their presence on September second via Caesarean.

Once the twins were six weeks old, we brought them to Denver to meet my grandparents and I'm glad we did because a few days later, my grandmother passed away in her sleep. We stayed for the funeral and flew home a few days afterward. Now we're back for Thanksgiving, since we're planning to go to Breckenridge for Christmas.

Morgan stretches her tiny arms and Tristan jumps up to make sure she's okay. He is not a fan of them crying at all.

"She's okay, bud."

"Mom, I think she's hungry. Grab her a bottle."

Emma starts wiggling as well. "Mom, wait!" Ashley looks back at him from the doorway. "Emma needs one, too. Hurry before they cry."

I look over at my wife and smile, and she holds back her laugh. "Sure thing."

Both babies start to whine, waking up more, ready to be fed. "Dad, grab Emma, and I'll pat Morgan."

When I don't pick her up quick enough, Tristan says, "Dad, now!"

"Tristan, you know it's okay for them to cry, right?"

He looks at me like I just told him he would never be allowed to fight again. "Okay, okay. Got it."

I pick up my sweet princess, talking softly to her as she continues to stretch. Before the crying starts, Ashley hands me a bottle and I pop it right into Emma's mouth.

Ashley picks up Morgan, and once Tristan is situated sitting Indian style with a nursing pillow in his lap—we bought it just for him to hold the babies so he could feed them—Ashley sets Morgan down and hands Tristan the bottle. Morgan starts to whimper, but Tristan puts the nipple into her mouth before it gets loud. "Whew, that was close," he says, dead serious.

We all look at each other, holding in our laughter.

ASHLEY

I LOOK AROUND AT THE PEOPLE IN FRONT OF ME. TRISTAN IS feeding Morgan, softly patting her head, and Kaden is feeding Emma. The night of our wedding, when we got into that car accident, I knew we would all be okay. Many people don't believe in ghosts and angels, but after that night I'm not one of them.

When the car hit us, I know what I saw, two pairs of angel wings flying above. I believe Gabrielle and Gabe were watching us from above that night and protected us, and nobody will ever tell me any different.

When we came to Denver to visit Kaden's family, I insisted on needing a few minutes alone with Gabrielle and Gabe at the cemetery. I needed to thank them for shielding us and protecting us from harm's way. Kaden doesn't really believe it or understand. I don't blame him. Unless you saw the wings the way I saw them, it's hard to convince someone to believe.

I sit down in front of the two headstones and place a single rose on the top of Gabrielle's. "Hey there, I'm Ashley. Although you probably know that, since you're up in heaven looking down on us. I just wanted to say thank you for protecting us. I want you to know that I'm going to make sure Kaden is always happy. I've seen the pictures of you two and know how much you loved each other. Your love is one people wish for their entire lives and I promise to live every day loving him the way you would have. Thank you for being our guardian angel that night."

Turning to Gabe's headstone, I place a set of boxing gloves. "Thank you for protecting us. Your daddy misses you every day. Soon you'll have a couple of siblings. I'll make sure they know you saved them that night."

"Hey Ash, you ready to go home?" I shake myself out of my memory and see both babies are fed and smiling. Tristan is staring at Morgan in awe and Kaden's parents are both smiling at us.

"Yep, I sure am."

Kaden and I both stand. He hands me Emma, but before releasing her, pulls me close to him, giving me a kiss. "I love you, baby."

"I love you, more."

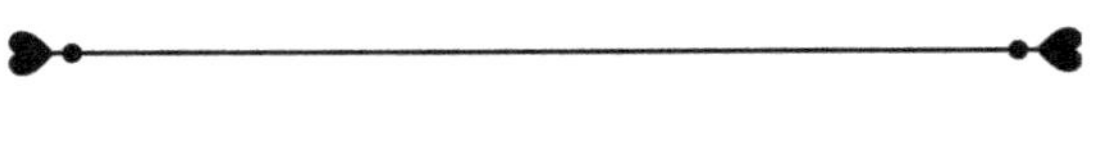

KADEN

Eight Years Later

I'M SITTING ON TOP OF THE PICNIC TABLE IN THE BACKYARD staring at my wife's ass while she lays out on her towel in the grass next to Hayley, Kayla, and Liz. They're all talking quietly and every now and then I hear my wife giggle. I love that fucking giggle. They all stand at the same time. Hayley walks with Ashley toward the table where Caleb and I are sitting, while Kayla and Liz walk toward Bentley and Cooper who are dicking around on the four wheelers.

"Hey Dad." Tristan throws the wet towel at me from the four wheeler he's cleaning. "After dinner, can you drop me off at Bella's to study for our finals."

"Yeah, sure, but why didn't she come over for dinner."

"She needed to study…just like I do."

Caleb is sitting next to me texting on his phone, looking frustrated, but I can't think about what has him annoyed when my wife is getting closer to me in her tiny bikini. Even after having three kids, my wife's body is banging.

"I'm going to go start dinner." She gives me a chaste kiss before walking inside.

Hayley sits next to Caleb. "Everything okay?"

"Yeah, just texting with Marco. I don't think we're going to win this battle, Hayles."

"I'm going to miss him like crazy, but Caleb, we have to let him go and spread his wings. He'll be twenty-one in six months."

Giving them a few minutes to talk in private, I follow my sexy wife inside the house.

"Ash," I call out.

"In here."

I find her in our room changing out of her bathing suit, but before she can put her feet into her shorts to put them on, I grab her by her hips and pick her up placing her on top of our dresser.

"Hey."

"Hey." She giggles. "I need to start dinner."

"How about I just eat you instead?"

"Hmm…that would be great, but what would everyone else eat?"

"Fuck them." I spread my wife's legs and pull her to the edge of the dresser, my tongue darting out straight to her clit.

"Kaden, we have company!" The last word comes out in a long moan and I know I've got her.

"Fuck them," I repeat. I start to tongue fuck her, circling her hard nub, then gliding my tongue up and down her slit. She moans louder.

"Shh…Ash. We have company," I mock her words.

"Fuck them," she growls as I bite down on her clit. Her hands go to my hair and she pushes my face into her pussy needing more. As she moans my name, I bring my hand up to her inner thigh, fingertips brushing her pussy lips. Inserting one, then two fingers deep in her, my wife begins to buck in pleasure. "Play with your nipples, baby," I say before I continue to devour her pussy with my fingers and tongue. A few minutes later and Ashley is praying to the gods as she comes all over my face.

Not even waiting for her to come down from her high, I stand, grab her off the dresser, and turn her around, bending her over the edge of the dresser. My cock slides right into her slick pussy and I still for a second, willing my dick to cooperate so I don't come in seconds.

"Kaden, what are you waiting for? Fuck me." And I do. Grabbing the curves of Ashley's hips, I pound into her pussy from behind. The edge of the dresser keeps her in place as I fuck her hard. With the mirror in front of us, my eyes find hers, which are filled with lust and love—the same way I feel. Reaching around the front of her, I massage circles on her hard nub. Already sensitive from her just orgasming, she squirms and moans, her eyes never leaving mine.

When her moans get louder and her pussy clenches tight around my cock, I know she's close. I pick up the pace, pounding deeper and harder. Seconds later, Ashley's eyes roll back and her lids close briefly. The vision alone has me coming right behind her.

We both stand there for a minute, me still inside her, both of us catching our breath. Then I lean down and give her a kiss on her shoulder. She gives me a small smile that always makes my heart rate pick up.

This woman is my missing puzzle piece and I'm so damn blessed to get to spend the rest of our lives, putting our puzzle together.

"KADEN, CAN YOU GO OUT BACK AND TELL ALL THE KIDS TO wash up for dinner. And please tell Tristan not to walk through the house with mud all over his boots again." Ashley's in the kitchen cooking dinner and Hayley is sitting on the counter talking to her while she cooks. Kayla and Bentley are bringing dishes out to the picnic tables, and Cooper and Liz are somewhere around here.

"Sure thing." I walk out back to see Emma and Tristan washing down their four wheelers with the help of Nathan, Liz and Cooper's son, and Chloe and Faith, Bentley and Kayla's two little girls. The rain came through yesterday, which means today was the perfect day to go mudding.

I look for Morgan and see her, Lilly, and Mackenzie sitting in the grass gossiping just like mini versions of their moms.

Lilly is Liz and Coopers seven-year-old daughter. Liz found out shortly after Ashley gave birth to the twins that she was pregnant. After cussing Cooper out for knocking her up once again, she got excited that she and Ashley would have kids less than a year apart. Lilly, Morgan, and Mackenzie are all inseparable.

"Hey dad, can you bring us to Lilly's house when you drop off Tristan?"

"No way! We aren't babysitting you guys. You can hang out here with the rest of the circus. We have actual studying to do."

"Your brother needs to study for his finals. He only has three years left before he goes off to college. He needs to keep his grades up."

"Dad, can we go to the gym tomorrow?" Emma yells.

"Sure."

"Ugh! I don't want to go to the gym. You know I hate it there, and so does Lilly and Mackenzie. It's smelly and gross." Morgan crosses her arms over her chest pouting adorably like a mini-version of Ashley.

"You don't have to go. So, stop pouting and go wash up for dinner."

"Damn, I'm hungry," Caleb says, looking up from his phone.

"Everything okay?" I ask him, sitting down.

"Yeah, I'm just worried about Marco. I get he needs to find his place in the world, but can't he find it while training at Cooper's gym?"

"The training facility in San Diego is a good one, and he'll be staying with people he knows. He'll be fine," Cooper says, sitting next to his wife.

"After his last win, he thinks he's rolling in the dough. He doesn't understand how quickly that paycheck will run out," Caleb says.

"Then he'll learn," I point out.

We all sit at the table and start scooping up the food. Ashley is an amazing cook.

"Mom, Dad said I can go to the gym with him tomorrow." Emma shovels piles of food onto her plate then starts digging in. While both girls look like mini-versions of Ashley, Emma without a doubt has my personality and love of fighting. She is always begging to go to the gym with Tristan and me.

"Okay, sweetie." I give my wife a wink and she rewards me with a smile in return.

I look around the table at my wife, our three kids, and our friends that are more like family, and thank God once again for the people in my life. I will never understand how, that horrible night, Ashley, Tristan, and our babies weren't taken from me, but I stopped questioning how this world works a long time ago. I've learned to count each and every blessing and to be thankful for each day we're given. To love those around you like it's your last day, and never take a single moment for granted. To this day, Ashley swears it was Gabrielle and Gabe who saved us and, although, I sometimes give her a hard time about it, I would love to believe that was the case.

The End!

About the Author

Reading is like breathing in, writing is like breathing out.— Pam Allyn

Nikki Ash resides in South Florida where she is an English teacher by day and a writer by night. When she's not writing, you can find her with a book in her hand. From the Boxcar Children, to Wuthering Heights, to the latest single parent romance, she has lived and breathed every type of book. While reading and writing are her passions, her two children are her entire world. You can probably find them at a Disney park before you would find them at home on the weekends!

www.ingramcontent.com/pod-product-compliance
Lightning Source LLC
Chambersburg PA
CBHW070257310726
48976CB00005B/1467